REDEEM THE TIME

REDEEM THE TIME

SUE FROST

HUTCHINSON
LONDON

© Sue Frost 1996
The right of Sue Frost to be identified as the
Author of this work has been asserted by Sue Frost
in accordance with the Copyright, Designs and Patents Act 1988

All rights reserved

1 3 5 7 9 10 8 6 4 2

This edition first published in 1996 by Hutchinson

Random House (UK) Limited
20 Vauxhall Bridge Road, London SW1V 2SA

Random House Australia (Pty) Limited
20 Alfred Street, Milsons Point, Sydney,
New South Wales 2061, Australia

Random House New Zealand Limited
18 Poland Road, Glenfield, Auckland 10, New Zealand

Random House South Africa (Pty) Limited
Box 2263, Rosebank 2121, South Africa

Quotation from 'Ash Wednesday' by T. S. Eliot
from *Collected Poems 1909 –1962* reproduced
by kind permission of Faber and Faber Limited.

A CiP record for this book is available from the British Library

Papers used by Random House UK Limited are natural,
recyclable products made from wood grown in sustainable forests.
The manufacturing processes conform to the environmental
regulations of the country of origin.

ISBN 0 09 1801877

Typeset in Ehrhardt
by Pure Tech India Limited, Pondicherry,
Printed and bound in Great Britain by
Mackays of Chatham plc, Chatham, Kent.

For Pete

The greatest revolution of our times is the discovery that human beings, by changing the inner attitudes of their minds, can change the outer aspects of their lives.

William James

Prologue

Eva Delamere

She was 'pert as a pixie' with 'eyes as deep as the Grand Canyon', but it is not for the blurb-writers' epithets, apt though they might have been, that a generation of cinema-goers remember the French actress Eva Delamere, who died this week. A tilt of the chin and a toss of the silver mane only served to render Delamere virtually indistinguishable from the scores of velvet-lipped lovelies who made Hollywood their holy grail in the Thirties, those ever-hopefuls who drifted back to the ice-cream parlours, the dime stores and the brothels when the luck, or the gall, finally ran out.

It was one film, *Casey's War*, that made Eva Delamere famous. One film, and the tragedy that accompanied its première. A whiff of scandal, a hint of murder, and Worldwide Pictures lost not only its leading male star, but with Delamere's subsequent disappearance, a promising career that had only just begun. If this were a plot for the movies, her story might have had a happy ending. But reality is rarely so kind, and it seems she never recovered from the tragic events surrounding *Casey's War*. Whatever the truth, she was never seen in Hollywood again.

There is a certain poignancy in the fact that when she died, comfortably into her eighties, at a convent hospital in Paris, Eva Delamere had just completed a cameo role in a new film. Rediscovered by cult movie-maker Daniel Duval, she had been persuaded to appear in his newest production, a metaphysical thriller entitled *The Rose Garden*.

One of the last people to talk to Eva Delamere before her death was television journalist Beth Carlisle, in Paris for the filming of a new TV series.

'She was an extraordinary personality, powerful and prepossessing,' says Carlisle. 'But very private. I learned precious little about what happened after she left Hollywood, and virtually nothing about the time she spent there.'

Carlisle is unwilling to speculate on what might have prompted Delamere's sudden flight from stardom in the Thirties, or whether she mourned the loss of her film career at its greatest moment.

'Eva Delamere was an enigma,' she says. 'Content to remain a mystery to the end.'

(Obituary by Candice Carter, *Sunday Chronicle*)

Book I: Beth

Chapter One

Get This, Dear Reader. Romance is Dead. Discredited, Doomed, Dispatched. And romantic novels, should you ever wish to read one, are Trash. Who says? Why, none other than Our Heroine, the slender, blonde, and eminently successful Beth Carlisle, soon to grace our television screens with a new six-part series, *Moonlight and Roses*, which, she tells us gravely, is all about The Cult of Romance in Western Society.

'Romantic fiction with its overt agenda helps keep women in thrall,' she declares, flashing the famous emerald eyes. 'All those feisty heroines with dark secrets in their past. All those tough guys with eyes like ice and hearts of fire. All that steamy sex with never so much as a condom in sight . . . The purpose of these tawdry tales is clear. As long as women afford romance a central role in their lives, the rules governing society's sexual behaviour go largely unchallenged.'

Okay Ladies? So now you know.

'Public Persona: Beth Carlisle' (the Candice Carter Interview, *Sunday Chronicle*)

I've always hated Paris. Thought it a showy, overblown sort of place, full of itself and full of rude Frenchmen.

I've never understood its amorous reputation either, reckoning that few things work so soundly against romance as garlic, large amounts of *vin ordinaire* and rip-offs in the Champs-Elysées. The hotels are dingy and faded with unfathomable plumbing and precarious balconies, and the lifts creak and moan until dawn. One night in Paris, declared an old pop song, is like a year in any other place. Indeed.

And yet that day, Paris glowed. The gardens bristled with new green buds, the river sparkled clear silver in the thin, crisp air, and the spires yearned up into the blue with measureless grace.

Perhaps it was the wine. I'd skipped the endless flutes of free champagne at the spring shows, and with a few hours to spare, settled instead for a half-bottle of Rhône which I drank alone at Duval's favourite eating place, a grubby bar somewhat grandly titled the Café des Arbres. The trees were puny but the terrace was edged with brilliant daffodils, and the food was surprisingly good. I was convinced nobody knew nor cared who the hell I was, and everything felt right. The wine was fruity, the sun was hot, all was well with my world. But then a shadow fell over my table.

'It's Beth Carlisle,' said the shadow, taking unwelcome substance. 'Beth, sweetie, you look divine. But what on earth are you doing in this godforsaken place? Let me take you away from all this . . . Or at least buy another bottle so you can't see it clearly.'

Clive Fisher, one-time colleague on some long-forgotten radio station, now a scandalmonger for the *Sun*, grinned benignly down and waved a jug of wine under my nose.

'My dear Clive!' I said jovially, fighting a fleeting stab of panic. 'You can buy me whatever you like. But it's hardly worth your while. I'm not doing anything remotely newsworthy. I'm not even drunk. Not yet, anyway.'

'What are you doing here?' he repeated, sitting down beside me and splashing new wine into my empty glass. 'I always thought you hated Paris . . .'

'Did I say that? Well, a girl can change her mind, can't she? I've been filming here, as it happens . . . My new series. *Moonlight and Roses* . . . Taking the rise out of romance in the lovers' city . . . You can give me a plug, if you like.'

I'd beaten the panic. I was bold. I was brave. No tabloid hack was going to make me sweat, nor even gently perspire. I picked up my Raybans and flashed him an enigmatic smile.

'Ah yes.' Clive Fisher looked down into his glass, seeming to consider his words. 'I read about it in the *Sunday Chron*. The Candice Carter interview . . .'

'That sarky bitch,' I said, momentarily ruffled. 'She made me sound like Germaine Greer on a bad day.'

'Germaine who?'

We both laughed and I poured us two very large glasses of wine.

'There, there, Clive,' I soothed. 'Don't trouble yourself about the social and intellectual implications of that crazy thing called Love . . . Tell me instead, what are you up to in Paris? You're obviously here on dirty business. Whose naughty weekend have you got in your sights?'

He amused me with tales of the minor glitterati, Georges Camou and Princess Marika, about to marry, Zelda Carlton and Franco Cabaretti, about to divorce. Lou Mason, Amanda Harrington and Chérie de Sykes, simply about. But then it got personal.

'Not to mention Daniel Duval . . .'

'What about him?'

'Isn't he still married to the lovely Genevieve?'

'As far as I know.'

'Shouldn't you know? I mean, haven't you two been working together? That's what Candice Carter said . . .'

'I simply borrowed Duval's editing suite . . .'

Clive Fisher leaned forward, and the wine in his glass tilted alarmingly.

'Genny Duval's mother is second cousin to the Queen,' he said mysteriously.

'So what?'

'So the bust-up's bound to make a juicy tale . . .' He smiled and waited expectantly.

'I wonder who's been screwing Daniel Duval?' he enquired at last.

I took a long deep draught of the wine and thought this over carefully. Nothing was impossible, of course. But if Fisher had me in mind for his juicy tale, why would he tip me off?

'I don't know who's been screwing Daniel Duval,' I said lightly, swilling the dregs around my glass and glancing at my watch. 'But it must be someone with no sense of style. Duval's a little short on chic, wouldn't you say?'

'Well, maybe someone's been slumming,' he said slowly.

I knocked back the last of the wine and stood up. Oh God. Was it really worth it? All that huffing and panting and careful containing of bodily fluids, and for what? So a no-good worm like Fisher could fix me with his bleary eye? Maybe it was time to move on. I was fond of Duval, but it was true about the chic. Yes. I'd ring home just as soon as I got the chance. Take the morning plane back to London. Jamie could meet me, and we'd lunch at that new Vietnamese place on the Brompton Road.

'What's this movie Duval's making?' my dogged companion persisted, rising to his feet and making to follow me out of the Café des Arbres. 'Cult viewing, is it?'

'It's called *The Rose Garden*,' I said carelessly. 'Lots of moody shots and meaningful lines, I expect.'

'Who's in it?'

'Susannah Lamont,' I replied, more cautiously this time, an unworthy idea beginning to form. 'You know her, of course. A pretty young thing.'

'Isn't she a pal of Jamie's? Doesn't she play Shakespeare?'

'Well, that's a matter of opinion. But yes, she was Bianca opposite Alex Chapman in *Taming of the Shrew* when Jamie played Petruchio . . . Come to think of it, Clive, she has been seeing a lot of Duval lately . . .'

He raised a quizzical eyebrow.

'Susannah Lamont and Daniel Duval?' he enquired archly. He was watching me carefully, and suddenly I faltered beneath his gaze, the voice of conscience muttering, if not exactly shrieking, in my ear.

'Well, maybe not,' I mumbled. 'It doesn't seem all that likely.'

'Still,' said Fisher. 'Worth a shot, eh?'

I stared at him blankly, not knowing in that moment who had aimed the shot, nor who stood in the firing line. I was mildly drunk, considerably confused, and just a little ashamed.

'Poor Duval,' I said at last with a forced little laugh. 'He can't even make a bad movie in peace.'

'Peace?' echoed Clive Fisher in mock amazement, taking my arm and steering me out into the silvery Paris air, 'Oh come, Beth. There's no such thing as peace for the rich and famous. You know that . . .'

I kissed Clive Fisher goodbye, found a cab and sailed away from the crumbling alleys of the shabby *arrondissement* that was home to Duval's apartment, towards the shimmering boulevards and the glitzy cafés, along the riverbank to Notre Dame, not caring where I went. When I fancied Fisher was following me, I leapt out and dived into the cool of the cathedral, the sudden chill shocking me into awareness, like icy water knifing through bare skin.

I sat down and tried to quell my paranoia. After all, I reasoned, I'd been my usual scrupulous self. It would have taken Maigret himself to catch me sneaking into Duval's apartment.

Yet Clive Fisher's behaviour had been odd, to say the least. How had he found the Café des Arbres? Why had he mentioned Duval? I didn't need the marriage-breaker label on the front page of the *Sun*, that much was certain, not just as my musings on romantic love were about to hit the TV screens of Britain.

'Please, God,' I said, to myself and any deity that might happen to be listening, 'get me out of this one.'

As though the prayer had already been answered, I felt calmer at once, and when I walked into the spring sunshine again, there was no sign of Clive Fisher.

I grabbed another cab, certain now I had nothing to worry about, and by the time I made the ramshackle studio Duval liked to call his editing suite, I was only an hour late. I resolved to be tactful and encouraging whatever I thought of his film, reckoning I'd make up for any perceived lack of enthusiasm with one final virtuoso display of the horizontal arts later that night. Duval was an appreciative lover, a quality that rendered him unusually deserving.

'Where have you been?' he asked anxiously, inspecting me closely as I sank into the battered velvet of the editing room. 'I was starting to worry . . .'

I squeezed his hand, smiled sweetly at his assistant, the invaluable Louise, accepted another glass of wine, and raised it boldly to the room's only other occupant.

'Hi, Beth,' said Susannah Lamont, forcing a weak grin. 'How are you?' She looked ill at ease, her pale face set, the lips compressed in a thin, startling slash of crimson, and she seemed reluctant to meet my eye. For a moment I wondered if, by perverse chance, I'd hit the nail with my suggestion to Clive Fisher.

I shot a covert glance at Duval, realising with faint unease that I wouldn't be at all happy to find I'd been sharing with Susannah. He caught the look, smiled, and I was reassured at once. Duval might cheat on his wife, but I couldn't believe he'd cheat on me.

I nodded curtly to Susannah, and then we all settled back to watch the first rough-cut of *The Rose Garden*.

I wasn't optimistic. Duval was the movie-maker who never broke even. In a Duval film there was usually no plot, and even, on one disastrous shoot, no script. I often wondered how he raised the cash for his esoteric meanderings through the twentieth-century psyche, and could only guess that his wife's wealthy family kept the credits rolling. But we had never discussed his wife, so I didn't really know.

The Rose Garden passed in a blur of mystical landscapes, bizarre images, obtuse points about the decline of European culture and melancholic evocations of a golden age. The wine had gone to my head, and I missed most of Susannah's performance, but through the alcoholic haze I saw enough to get the gist. Bare-breasted nymphets clutched olive branches and an aged parody of the Madonna, swathed in blue, sprinkled the dying land with blood. This was, I deduced, the Eternal Feminine, denied, tortured and reviled, finally to be resurrected for Civilisation's last gasp. New Age crap, typical of Duval.

'A fascinating concept,' I declared with only the slightest hint of irony when it was finally over, slipping my arm through Duval's, and smiling guardedly at Susannah. 'I particularly liked that old dame, the warrior-goddess type. Who is she?'

There was a moment's silence, then Louise spoke.

'That's Eva Delamere,' she gushed. 'Wasn't it a wonderful

performance!' She turned to Duval. 'I hoped she'd make the viewing today, but I called the convent, and they said she wasn't too well . . .'

Then the detail suddenly stopped, as though a warning glance had intervened.

'Eva Delamere,' I repeated, and the name seemed to hang upon the dusty air of the viewing room like a charm, mysterious and magical. Eva Delamere. Familiar, and yet elusive. Eva Delamere . . .

'Who is she?' I asked again. 'How do I know that name?'

'She's no one,' replied Louise shortly. 'Not any more. All through, Dan? Then I'll see you tomorrow. Are you coming, Susannah?'

We were alone, and Duval reached forward to caress the nape of my neck. 'You liked it,' he murmured happily, and I didn't demur.

'Let's make love,' I said, eyeing the faded *chaise-longue* that so often played host to our energetic embraces. 'You be the great Hollywood producer, and I'll be the shy little virgin who wants a part. Half-way through I change my mind, so you have to tie me up.'

He laughed and glanced nervously towards the door.

'Come on,' I said, kicking off my shoes. 'Remember why I'm here? Strictly for the ride, my dearest Duval . . .'

I undid the button on his pants and slipped my hand inside.

'I'll just lock the door,' he said, 'and check that Susannah has gone.'

'Well, if she hasn't, bring her in. She can be the chaperone who bursts in at the end and gets so excited she jumps on too.'

He faced me across the *chaise-longue*, a lean, untidy man with a mass of dark curls and unnervingly brilliant navy-blue eyes. For a moment I thought I'd shocked him, but then he laughed again and raised my fingers to his lips.

'I love you,' he said, 'but I don't believe you.'

The great Hollywood producer had just got the shy little virgin's knickers to her knees when I remembered Eva Delamere. Yes, of course. The making of *Casey's War*. There'd been a scandal. A death. And then Eva had disappeared, never to be heard of again . . .

'Beth, you're not concentrating,' Duval laughed. 'Shy little virgins don't do that.'

'Sorry,' I said absently. 'Let's take it once more from the top . . .'

But my head was full of Eva Delamere. How had she arrived on the set of Duval's movie? Why did she quit Hollywood all those years ago? Where had she been since? What story did she have to tell, and most important of all, would she tell it to me?

I didn't hurry to the convent next day, but took a cab to the Jardin des Plantes and wandered through its leafy calm, idly kicking the smooth

gravel and inhaling the fragrant air. The blossoms nestled in the branches like tiny seed pearls, partly hidden by sheaths of brown but sufficiently matured to give the appearance of pale pink frost dusting the
trees. The weak sun touched my bare arms gently, like a lover returned
after too long away, and my spirits opened up in wanton gratitude.

It had taken no great ingenuity to track down Eva Delamere. I simply
went through Duval's pocket book when he was asleep. There was only
one possible address: The Sisters of the Divine Faith convent, rue Poli-
veau.

The previous night, which I'd decreed should be our last, began well
enough over a bottle of Dom Perignon in an out-of-town restaurant.

'Why don't we eat at the Café des Arbres?' he'd asked.

'Because I want to go somewhere special,' I said, determining I
wouldn't give Clive Fisher a second thought, and certainly not a second
chance.

I paid for the wine and took pains to be the amusing, risqué personality Duval had met on the very first day I'd arrived in Paris with my
crew and hired his editing suite.

I'd rehearsed a civilised farewell speech, but I never got to make it
for we suddenly found ourselves in the middle of a squabble. The
bourguignon was tough, the *crème brûlée* was burnt, and Eva Delamere
was declared out of bounds.

'I could write about her,' I said irritably, 'and you could use the
publicity.'

'She won't give an interview,' he said mildly. 'She never talks about
the past. And she doesn't like journalists.'

'I can persuade anyone to do anything. I'm famous for it.'

'You don't have to tell me that. But not Eva.'

'Why not? Because you say so?'

'If you like.'

'Then fuck you.'

'Okay,' he said amiably, 'but not here.'

And not, I decided in a fit of pique, anywhere else either. We drove
back to his apartment in angry silence, our first row in six months on
this, our last night.

When he finally retired to bed alone, I called Candice Carter at the
Sunday Chronicle in London. She owed me a favour after that bitchy
piece she wrote, so please, could she check out *Casey's War* in the
cuttings files?

A few minutes later I had the whole Delamere story, the Worldwide
Pictures intrigue between Carlotta du Bois and Saul Bernstein, the Will
Sutton tragedy, the suicide of Sutton's wife, a long-forgotten minor
starlet called Christine Romaine . . . The tale resounded with double-

dealing and mystery, and many questions about the making of *Casey's War*, it seemed to me, had gone unanswered.

Why did David Klein, among the most successful and astute Hollywood directors of his day, hire a failed scriptwriter, one Toby Truman, who also happened to be Eva's husband? How did Delamere, who'd never made a film in her life, and who, unlike Carlotta du Bois, seemed a reluctant starlet, land the leading role? What lay behind Klein's abrupt departure for Europe so soon after Sutton's death? Why did Eva Delamere quit Hollywood at the height of her fame, and why had she never gone back?

'What's it all about?' Candice Carter asked curiously.

'I don't know yet,' I snapped. 'But if there's a story, I'm first.'

I was excited and hopeful. What, I wondered, would Eva Delamere say about it all? Would she reveal whether Christine Romaine really planned to kill her husband, as the police seemed to think? Had Eva been in love with Will, as the gossip writers later inferred? Why did she quit Hollywood in such grand style, and where had she been this past half-century? The story had to be worth telling, if I could persuade her do it.

Now I walked on through the Jardin des Plantes, out of the green and into the frantic streets, absorbed by the hectic showcase that was Paris, determined to go my own way. Then in a quiet and dusty sidestreet, I opened a rickety timber gate and came suddenly upon the Divine Faith convent, a stolid sandstone château languishing behind a high, turreted wall and a glen of glossy leaves.

It shimmered before me on a sea of glittering grass like a magic castle beckoning on some questing knight, strange and beautiful in its improbability, but also forbidding, its long windows shuttered against the brilliant morning. Did demons await the unwary traveller? I shivered suddenly in the sheltered green of the glen, and then quelling an unlikely faintness of heart, set out upon the primrose-bordered path for the door.

Eva might not see me, it was true. But in that case I'd lost nothing. Duval need never know. And if she did? Why then I'd have proved him wrong.

'Madame Eva is not receiving visitors, Mademoiselle. She has been unwell.'

A pretty young Parisienne guarded the castle entrance with all the deterring power of a gorgon.

'I'm so sorry,' I said politely, 'I was merely wishing to pay my respects. My name is Beth Carlisle. I'm a friend of Monsieur Duval . . .'

'Duval?' She repeated the name with a transforming smile as though I had proffered the password. 'In that case, wait one moment, please.'

She picked up a phone, gabbled in rapid French, and then turned to confuse all my plans.

'Monsieur Duval is with her right now,' she said. 'I've told them you're here.'

I gaped. Duval had told me he was going back to his editing suite.

'It's all right,' I said quickly. 'If Miss Delamere is unwell, then . . .'

But my retreat was cut short by the appearance of a smart middle-aged woman with shoulder-length silver hair who looked me up and down and then faced me squarely.

'Ah, Dr Blanche,' cried the gorgon. 'This is Miss Carlisle, a friend of Daniel's. She's come to see Madame Eva! Perhaps you'll show her the way?'

The doctor nodded curtly, and without enquiring what my business might be, led me protesting along endless polished corridors, past open doors through which I glimpsed sunny rooms and high metal beds. Silent nuns glided in and out, laden with trays of gleaming green food. The convent was clearly a hospital, and I began to fear what I might find. Was Eva Delamere in some terminal state? Perhaps this explained Duval's prohibition.

'I'm afraid I'm intruding,' I said anxiously. 'Maybe I could call again some other time?'

'It's not for me to say,' she replied in flat, faultless English. 'Wait here a moment, please.'

She stopped in a bay overlooking another sweep of brilliant turf and I was left briefly alone with the view. I saw then that I'd approached the Divine Faith convent from the rear. This lawn was dotted with wheelchairs and shaded daybeds on which reclined a number of indistinct figures. I peered towards them, thinking there could hardly be a more idyllic spot in which to convalesce.

'What the hell are you doing here, Beth? I thought I'd made myself quite plain.'

Duval appeared from a doorway along the corridor, his face dark with displeasure, the blue eyes fixed in manifest wrath. He grabbed my arm roughly and I cried out in surprise.

'Go back to London,' he ordered. 'Go back to Jamie where you belong, and stay away from here.'

'What on earth is all this about?' I demanded angrily, shaking free from his grip. 'You can't tell me what to do . . .'

Behind us there came a sharp emission of breath, a small and carefully controlled expression of anger. I turned to see the silver-haired doctor watching us closely.

'Excuse me,' she said coldly, addressing us both with a steely incline of the neatly coiffured head. Then she turned to me. 'Please come this way,' she said.

Eva was waiting in a whitewashed sitting room crammed with icons and crucifixes, a delicate, ancient creature with iron-coloured hair cropped close to her head, deep, clear eyes and pale, translucent skin. She was sipping weak tea and reading *Le Monde* through a giant magnifying glass, and as we entered, she signalled to a perky little nun, hardly younger than her charge, who then darted to a tall oak bureau by the fireplace and produced a dusty bottle of cognac.

'My name is Beth Carlisle,' I began unhappily, aware that Duval, who'd followed me into the room, intended no introduction. 'I'm a journalist —'

'Oh come,' he interrupted, his voice tight and strained. 'Miss Carlisle belittles herself. She's a famous personality. She makes TV documentaries and interviews important people. She writes books and reviews films. She does all manner of exceedingly useful things.'

I had rarely seen him angry, never glimpsed belligerence or sarcasm in the time I had known him, and I was lost for a response. I shot Eva an anxious glance.

She laughed and extended a thin hand to Duval. He raised her gently to her feet, and then as she moved towards me, a slight figure draped in pearly silk, the reflected light from the window fronting the luminous gardens wrapped her in a sudden cloak of fire, transforming the iron of her hair into palest gold. Her skin shone white and fair and her eyes were lit with a shaft of brilliant violet. Her figure was slender as a sapling, her back erect. She was at the very end of her life, and yet I seemed to gaze upon a woman in her prime, the beautiful Hollywood actress whose presence had suddenly been mystically restored.

It was a trick of the light, but I was bewitched. A transfiguration had occurred before my very eyes, and I turned uncertainly towards Duval.

He was staring out of the window on to the sparkling green, shoulders hunched, hands deep in the pockets of his raggy black jacket. Then suddenly, without a glance at me or a farewell to Eva, he walked swiftly from the room and slammed the door.

'Now then, Beth,' Eva said, unperturbed, motioning me towards a wooden settle by the fire, 'how can I help?' And she raised the violet eyes to stare into my soul.

I was distracted and confused, and unaccountably upset by Duval's behaviour. Why hadn't I heeded his warning about journalists? Why was I there, and what was I going to say? The long-ago Hollywood scandals were not only irrelevant in this hallowed setting, but the very

name of Will Sutton now seemed positively blasphemous. I trembled to
think that I might have asked her about an affair.

'Cognac?' she enquired softly, and poured me a hefty glass. I'd eaten
little since the burnt *brûlée*, and the alcohol hit my gut like a blow, but
it failed to produce its usual loquacious effects.

'I was very impressed by your performance in *The Rose Garden*,' I
mumbled, urgently seeking some convincing rationale for my presence,
'but I confess the film as a whole left me somewhat perplexed . . .'

'It's a romance!' Eva chided with a little smile. 'You know all about
Romance, don't you, Beth? Isn't that the subject of your new television
series? *Moonlight and Roses*, I believe it's called?'

I was taken aback, and I stared at her foolishly. She smiled again,
fingering a tiny silver filigree cross which nestled at her throat, nodding,
waiting.

'Is that what he told you?' I muttered, embarrassed, wondering what
else Duval had said about me, seeing in that moment that the tables had
been neatly turned. Now I was the one with something to hide, not Eva
Delamere.

She leaned forward, and the silver cross danced before my eyes. 'Romance is a most fascinating subject,' she said with evident mirth. 'And
what, I wonder, will you tell us about it?'

I didn't intend to deliver a speech, but I seemed suddenly to have lost
my bearings, like the novice presenter in front of a faulty autocue.

'Romantic love is a powerful myth,' I mumbled. 'It has shaped and
restricted women's lives throughout the ages, and ironically, never more
so than in the twentieth century . . .'

Still she nodded and smiled, eyes glowing distantly in the light from
a meagre fire which the old nun had beaten into reluctant flame.

'I think the movies are partly to blame,' I said, emboldened by her
silence. 'You know, all those handsome heroes carrying off besotted
maidens and living happily ever after . . . But it was a different story
off-screen . . . Wasn't it?'

The words were no sooner out than regretted, but to my immense
relief, she laughed.

'Now you're fishing, my dear. You want to know about Will Sutton?
Yes, of course you do. What shall I tell you? Will Sutton was no hero,
it's true. He drank too much.'

My hand was on the cognac bottle, and it faltered briefly as another
peal of merriment rang round the room. Then I slurped a new measure
of liquor into my glass.

'So you weren't in love with Will?' I ventured, thinking for one heady
moment that I might really get the story.

She laughed again.

'No, my dear . . . I fell in love long before I met Will Sutton. Once and only once! Very romantic . . .'

I was fascinated, but unsure of my ground and strangely unwilling to pry. Was this Toby Truman, the Hollywood screenwriter who'd been her husband? Or was she thinking of someone else?

'Did you marry him?' I asked cautiously.

Another laugh, strange and silvery, like angels giggling.

'What else do you do when you love a man?' she demanded jauntily.

I was ruffled by this reply, feeling in some obscure way that it reflected upon me.

'The great deception is the unquestioned belief that romantic love and marriage belong together,' I said huffily, as though some hidden director had suddenly flicked a switch. 'In truth, romantic love is necessarily short-lived. The famous lovers of literature and history are all thwarted, or else they die young . . .'

I listened to myself in growing embarrassment, unable to halt the flow, no longer the TV presenter spouting a script, but a schoolgirl delivering her lines to a long-suffering teacher.

'The movies overturned all that,' I burbled. 'I mean, I'm a fan of David Klein like everyone else, but nevertheless, his vision was deeply suspect. Happy Ever After is a dangerous myth. It's a con.'

'You think so?'

'Yes, I do. And the facts bear me out. By all accounts Klein was a very tough operator. But to watch *Casey's War*, you'd think he was a hopeless romantic . . .'

This seemed to amuse her greatly, and as I threw back a second glass of the liquor, she wiped her eyes, still nodding and smiling, fingering the silver cross at her throat, waiting. When I said nothing more she leaned forward, taking my hand between hers, gently stroking my naked ring finger.

'So you've no time for hopeless romantics?' she asked me softly.

'Certainly not,' I said primly.

'And you never wanted to marry?'

'I've never been able to see the point.'

A straightforward answer, neat and perfectly sound.

'And children?' said Eva. 'You've never wanted children?'

Then I felt my lungs contract, as though I'd dived into a clear, still pool to find a wicked undercurrent pulling me down. Breathe deep, Beth. One, two, three, four . . . the way they tell pregnant women to breathe . . .

'No,' I said unsteadily. 'No, I haven't.'

'And now, Beth, I suppose you're going to tell me you've never been in love?'

The hidden director flipped me into overdrive, one final, beleaguered attempt at extolling the correct line.

'Love is the illusion that keeps women from being themselves,' I declared in a curious monotone I barely recognised. 'The means by which we're encouraged to keep reality at bay . . .'

Eva gave me a long careful look, and I looked back to see disappointment and reproach. She wanted the truth. She had no time for anything else.

I took a long, deep draught of the cognac.

'I was in love once,' I gulped. 'A very long time ago . . . His name was Michael,' and mortified, I burst into loud sobs.

The golden light died on the lawn outside, and the nuns moved noiselessly in the whitewashed room, lighting slender, scented candles and smoothing the tapestry cushions on the great oak settle, pouring tiny bowls of thick dark coffee and proffering trays of diced meats and cheese.

The candles flickered and fumed, and a plaster Messiah, his twisted body slashed with scarlet paint, his silver halo glittering in the glow of the flames, craned down from a gilded crucifix on the mantel wall.

It seemed I sat in a heavenly court, called to account before the assembled statuettes. Their pale forbearance encouraged my tears, their silent pity magnified my woe. Poised upon the edge of eternity, weighing hope against hell, I awaited the judgement.

Eva murmured, her voice unreal, unearthly, like the music of distant choirs:

> 'Redeem
> The Time. Redeem
> The unread vision in the higher dream.'

The words spun in my befuddled brain, familiar, and yet tantalisingly elusive.

'It's a quotation,' Eva said softly, 'from a poem. They're also the opening lines of Daniel's film . . . I thought you might remember them.'

I wanted to ask why she'd agreed to appear in *The Rose Garden*. I wanted to know how she'd met Duval, and what he'd done to secure her approval. I wanted to hear about her life, her childhood, her husband.

But I asked none of this; instead I allowed her own cross-examination, delicate but discerning, a subtle and seamless reversal of roles that brought my tawdry history spilling into the charged air between us. I trembled with unaccustomed effort as the halting tale unfolded, an impassioned, ramshackle resurrection of long-buried emotions and events.

'After my mother's death, the world became a different place,' I wept. 'I had to go on living in it, so I became different too . . .'

I heard my words in disbelief, shattered by the power of long-ago pain to erupt without warning. I was drunk and I knew it, but even so, confession was foreign to my nature. Something in Eva Delamere had summoned it forth.

'My poor dear,' she whispered softly. 'But your family? Don't you have a sister?'

I swallowed hard and Sarah's face swam before me, pale and composed, so like my mother with her swath of chocolate-brown hair.

'Yes, I do . . . We don't see too much of each other these days. I'm very busy, and she lives out of London. With her husband and two little boys . . .'

She listened, and a strange quiet descended upon the room, not the stillness of exorcism nor the peace of absolution, but something altogether more tangible, a kind of presence. I turned and looked towards the door, convinced for a moment that someone else had entered. But there was no one, nothing.

'As for Michael,' I whispered at last, my head bent, my voice low, 'I never saw him again. Although I do know that he married someone else . . .'

When I looked up again at Eva, I saw a change in her face, a perceptible fading of the violet eyes, a pallid tinge upon the frail cheekbones.

'Well, my dear, maybe you'll meet him again some day,' she said faintly. 'And on that day, perhaps, you'll understand that no parting is ever permanent, no infinitesimal measure of love ever lost from the universe . . .'

I jumped to my feet and yanked on a bellrope at the side of the mantel, fearful that I'd wearied her, angry that I'd missed the signs of fatigue.

At once the nuns were at her side, fussing and soothing, leading her gently from the room and into the long dark corridors beyond. I picked up my jacket and stumbled after them, careering into a porter's trolley as I went, scattering plastic medicine bottles across the wooden floor. My progress was stopped by the steely-faced Dr Blanche.

'I trust you're not thinking of leaving, Miss Carlisle,' she said brusquely, taking my arm and pushing the trolley back against the corridor wall. 'It's late and if you'll pardon my saying, you are looking a little unwell. It would be altogether better, I think, if you spent the night with us.'

Next morning I woke to the unbearable stab of sunshine through gauze drapes, the aroma of bitter black coffee, and the pale, composed face of a young nun.

'I hope you're feeling better, Mademoiselle.'

I struggled upright on the narrow iron bed, my temples swelling in the effort. I looked at my watch and saw that it was past noon. I had missed my flight home.

'Miss Delamere?' I croaked feebly, anxious to make my apologies. 'Is she awake yet?'

'Mademoiselle, I'm afraid I have distressing news,' said the young nun gently, handing me a cup of the pungent coffee. 'Miss Delamere is dead. She passed away in the night.'

I was unaccountably dismayed. I fumbled among inept condolences and inarticulate regret, feeling a rush of shaming tears to my throat. I'd earned no right to mourn Eva Delamere, and I fought against an inappropriate show of emotion.

'I wanted to see her again,' I muttered distractedly; 'I wanted to talk some more . . .'

'I'm very sorry, Mademoiselle.'

'Can you tell me anything about her?' I asked suddenly, seeing my chance. 'Is there family, for instance?'

The young nun hesitated, and I rushed on, not wanting to embarrass her.

'She mentioned Mr Truman,' I said, not altogether truthfully, 'Mr Toby Truman . . . I wondered if . . .'

The young nun brightened.

'Mr Truman is here now,' she confided. 'But, naturally, he is very upset . . .'

So there it was, the mystery of Eva's life solved. She had ended her days with the man she married so many years ago. I felt oddly relieved, and smiled my gratitude at the young nun.

'You may see her in the chapel, Mademoiselle,' she said shyly, moving away from my bed; 'if you so wish, that is.'

She left me, and I dressed quickly, my mouth dry, my mind numb. I wasn't at all sure I wanted to view Eva's corpse, but outside my bare hospital room I found the inscrutable Dr Blanche waiting, and so we walked together along the polished corridors, just as we had done the day before. At the bay where Duval had found me, I paused briefly. The daybeds were back on the shimmering grass, and in the distance a young man bent down to the hidden occupant of a wheelchair, turning it swiftly so the patient might catch the sun. The silver spokes glinted in the light.

'What is this place?' I asked suddenly. 'What kind of people are treated here?'

'This is a hospice for the incurably ill,' replied the doctor coolly. 'And now, Miss Carlisle, if you're certain this is what you want, perhaps you would care to come this way . . .'

At the chapel door, I faltered. I hadn't gazed on the dead since the day I'd been summoned to view my mother's broken body, and for a moment the force of that memory undermined my calm. But then I strode into the room and stood by Eva's plain white coffin, looking down upon the still, spent form.

The violet eyes were closed, the parchment skin softened and relaxed. The hands were clasped across her breast, and in the fingers lay a printed prayer card. I bent closer to read the words: '*All shall be well, and all shall be well, and all manner of thing shall be well* . . .'

For a moment I felt my throat constrict, but as I looked down at the empty human shell before me, my unsentimental self settled upon me like a comfortable old coat. I smiled at the stern-faced doctor, the reassuring smile of one who is back in control.

Then I turned and walked out of the Divine Faith convent, away across the sparkling grass, down the primrose-bordered path, past the cool of the dense green shrubs, through the rickety timber gate and out into the dazzling Paris day. The night before was no more than a dream, a phantasm, an aberration.

This was the end of Eva Delamere.

Chapter Two

Beth Carlisle is not inclined to talk about her own True Romance. But Handsome Shakespearian Actor, soon to be playing Hamlet, and Glamorous Television Personality, soon to be holding forth on the mysteries of Love, is a beguiling combination, particularly as they co-exist in seeming idyllic harmony, not to say luxury, on the banks of the Thames.

'You met Jamie MacLennon when he was playing Romeo,' I remind her. 'That sounds like something straight out of a romantic novel.'

She will not be drawn, commenting only that her nine-year relationship with MacLennon 'works to the mutual satisfaction of us both'.

'What's it like living with Hamlet?' I persist, determined to glean something of her private life, no matter how trite.

'Very dangerous,' she says, without the trace of a smile. 'All those swords lying around the place. You never know what might happen.'

'Public Persona: Beth Carlisle' (the Candice Carter Interview, *Sunday Chronicle*)

'So what's new?'

I stared around at my home, the Liberty drapes and the Chinese rugs, the black ash and the rattan, the rag-rolled walls and the Hockney limited edition above the inglenook fire.

'The cat's gone missing,' Jamie said. 'I put down the Whiskas and she never touched it.'

'Is that all?'

'No. I left a dish of tinned sardines as well. The tom from Number Six got that.'

The great actor was lying on the white leather sofa in a coffee-coloured linen suit, belligerent and beautiful, the glossy black hair waving into his neck, an invitation for fingers to rumple it.

'Anything important?' I muttered peevishly, knowing that I was hoping for a message from Duval. 'Anyone been in touch?'

'Oh, everyone, darling.' He poured me a drink and motioned me down to the sofa beside him. 'Your director and your publisher. Your agent and your researcher. Your hairdresser and, let me see . . . one ex-lover. You know, that awfully nice sergeant from the CID, the one who couldn't find the fucking burglars so he fucked the victim instead . . .'

I smiled sweetly and sat down on the sofa.

'Unfortunately,' Jamie intoned, 'he hasn't found our video or our microwave, but he wants to know if you're feeling secure or if you could do with another . . . um . . . consultation, I think, was the word he used . . .'

The pause was perfectly timed for dramatic effect, and I smiled again.

'Sam Lutz says to call him at the Studios right away,' Jamie continued. 'And that bum Clive Fisher from the *Sun* wants you to call. How come he's ringing you up, darling? I hope you haven't been keeping bad company.'

'Anyone else?' I asked absently, determining not to panic at the mention of Fisher, frowning down at a statement from Abbey National. Our mortgage was ludicrous.

'Your sister came to tea,' Jamie said. 'A surprise trip.'

I stood up suddenly, splashing my gin on to his sleeve.

'Sarah was here?'

'Do be careful, darling! You're not drunk already, are you?' He peered at me archly, an exaggerated gesture designed to annoy. 'I do hope you haven't been over-indulging. Alcohol shows in the face, you know. Gives you lots of nasty little furrows. Unlike sex, which plumps up the tissues . . .'

'Sarah was here?' I repeated, unable to imagine what might bring my sister to my home.

'Don't worry, darling. I entertained her magnificently. Earl Grey tea in the conservatory. Apple strudel from Fortnum and Mason's. Cream served in your mother's silver milk jug . . . I told her you were off on a dirty weekend, but she didn't seem to believe me.'

I took a long draught of the gin. I hadn't seen my sister in months, hadn't spoken her name in as long, until, that is, it spilled so indecorously into the holy air surrounding Eva Delamere.

Jamie refilled my glass.

'And now, darling, I know I'm not supposed to ask, but I find myself wondering what the fuck you've been doing. Or, should I say, who the fuck you've been fucking . . . I hope, most sincerely, that it isn't Clive Fisher. I think I'd find that terribly hard to forgive.'

'Luckily I'm not seeking forgiveness,' I said airily, fighting the memory of Clive Fisher and our peculiar exchange. 'What did he want anyway?'

'Something to do with Paris, I believe.'

I laughed, a little too heartily, and sat down again on the white sofa, sliding my free arm into his and fingering the stained sleeve, caressing the fine black hairs on his wrist.

'Let's go out,' I said, seeking to divert him. 'Or let's stay in. What do you fancy?'

'Sorry, darling. I'm busy tonight. Life doesn't stop the moment you walk out the door. It all throbs on without you, I'm afraid.'

'A date? Who with? Anyone interesting? I could tip off my old pal Clive Fisher. Make a nice splash in the *Sun*.'

'Don't joke, darling,' Jamie said severely. 'One morning we'll wake up to the news that Somebody Up There doesn't like us any more. Then they'll really go for us. Don't hasten the day.'

I followed him into the bedroom and watched while he changed, eyeing the lean dark body as it emerged from the coffee-coloured suit, the broad glossy shoulders with their tufts of silky black hair, the firm, strong legs.

'Do you really have to go? We could play actors and actresses . . . You be Hamlet and I'll be Ophelia's mad twin sister. I'm waiting just behind the curtain, and when Ophelia exits stage left, I leap out and rip off your tights . . .'

He twisted the diamanté stud in his ear, peering approvingly into the dressing-table mirror.

'You're incorrigible, darling. But you know that, don't you? That's what it's all about. However, I'd advise you not to be too clever. Incorrigible you may be. But you're not invincible. One day someone will get your measure. And mine too, I expect.'

'You mean Candice Carter?' I snapped, my good humour suddenly gone. 'Well, I don't give a shit about her.'

'I'm delighted to hear it, darling. But take a look at this . . .' He delved by the side of the bedside cabinet and produced a pristine copy of *Mews and Mansions*, spilling its gaudy centre spread across the duvet. I sank down on to the bed and read with unease.

AT HOME: Jamie MacLennon and Beth Carlisle, the celebrated actor and the television star. He's rehearsing Hamlet for the Royal. She's making a series about Romance for Metro TV. They go together like powder and paint or spit and polish, as vital to each other as Martinis and Maraschino cherries . . .

They're pictured here with Thomasina the Tabby in the main

bedroom of their 18th Century converted warehouse, a haven of muted olive and jade . . . 'We like to entertain in the boudoir,' says Beth with a giggle. 'After all, why restrict your socialising to the dining room? Share and share alike, that's our motto.'

I threw the magazine back on to the bed.

'That was meant to be a send-up,' I said hotly. 'Who was that nosy bitch anyway? Some bimbo designer pretending to be a reporter?'

He gave a final twist to the earring and adjusted a mauve silk tie.

'It doesn't matter who wrote it, darling. They printed it. That's the point.'

I got up off the bed and moved towards him.

'Don't go out,' I said suddenly. 'I want to talk. I want to eat. Cook something nice for me, Jamie. Please . . .'

'Sorry, darling. Somebody else needs me tonight.'

'Who needs you?' I demanded. 'Who needs you more than me?'

He blew me a kiss and opened the bedroom door.

'None of your business, darling,' he said softly. 'You know that. But seeing as you ask, it's Susannah Lamont . . . She just flew in from Paris and I'm taking her out to dinner.'

I stared at him unhappily, discomfited by this unexpected disclosure, hoping Susannah would keep her mouth shut about me and Duval. Jamie didn't approve of married men, and nor, in truth, did I. But with Duval, somehow, it had all seemed different.

'You could take me out to dinner,' I muttered hopefully.

He shook his head, and then leaned forward to kiss me swiftly on the mouth.

'Sorry, darling . . . Not this time. Night-night, now . . . Sweet dreams.'

I dreamed, not of Jamie, nor Duval, nor even Eva Delamere, but of Michael. Michael Cameron, nineteen years old, tall and strong with bright gold hair and wide grey eyes, bound for the service of God and Mankind, full of passion and power and all the pity of youth.

'I've been looking for you, Beth,' I heard him say.

'Here I am,' I cried, but when I turned to face him, I found myself alone, the tears wet on my face.

'Michael,' I whispered, but the voice that replied belonged to my mother.

'For heaven's sake, Beth! What on earth are you doing? Get up at once and get on with it.'

I woke in a mild sweat and threw off the duvet. I sat up on the bed and snapped on the bedside light, then lay down again, reassured. Breathe deep, Beth . . . One, two, three, four . . . I am a mature, responsible person in charge of my own destiny. I live as I choose. I live as I choose. I live as . . .

The room descended into blackness once more and I seemed to hear Eva Delamere's soft, angelic voice, whispering from the shadows.

>   *Redeem*
> *The Time. Redeem*
> *The unread vision in the higher dream.*

I closed my eyes, but the pitiless power of memory stabbed deep into the vanished years, prodding into life with merciless fingers all the half-remembered scenes and whispered dialogues of distant dramas.

I was back in my mother's crumbling cottage on the day I first saw it, regarding its flaking walls and spongy woodwork with a jaundiced eye. The conservatory door swung limply before me and I stared out on the riot of buttercups beyond, heart heavy at the prospect of life amid a rural wilderness.

'This is it, girls!' my mother declared, propelling us up the trembling stairs. 'I hope you're going to like it, but if you don't, that's just too bad!'

She opened the bathroom door with a defiant flourish and ordered us in. 'Explore!' she commanded, as though a tarnished iron bath and a pair of Victorian taps might excite us to acceptance. 'Imagine how it's going to look when we're finished.' She swept out to inspect the bedrooms.

'It's got wet rot,' I said darkly to Sarah, 'and that bloody conservatory is about to fall down.'

My little sister, ever keen to preserve the peace, frowned and said nothing.

'There is no wet rot!' shouted my mother from the landing. 'And just wait till I get to grips with that conservatory.'

I turned on the taps and a stream of rusty liquid shot into the bath.

'Stone cold,' I scowled. 'You've probably got to stoke the boiler for a week before you can take a shower.'

My mother threw open the bathroom door and glared at us both. 'There is unlimited hot water,' she announced. 'And if there isn't, Leo will fix it.'

Sarah threw me a warning glance.

'Bugger Leo,' I said fervently as soon as we were alone again. 'This is all his fault.'

And it was. Dr Leo Frankish and his summer school on 'The Death of the English Novel' had turned my mother's head. She was persuaded, after years of playing the merry divorcee, that she needed a career. She was clever, she was well read, she was ex-Cambridge, and it scarcely mattered that she hadn't actually taken her degree. Leo, genius that he was, could arrange a little part-time tutoring in his department . . .

So now my mother had a new lover, a new job, a new home in the country and one deeply dismayed daughter whose heart was still in London.

'It's not so bad,' Sarah tried to console me. 'It's quite pretty, really . . . At least you'll be away to college in the autumn. Think of me!'

We sat down on the conservatory step, staring moodily out upon the gaudy buttercups. A cloud of flies buzzed around a neat little pile of rabbit droppings on the path. A solitary swallow swooped and dived in the dusky blue above, prompting dire predictions about the summer to come. A large, overfed magpie perched briefly on the rotting gate which led out of the garden, calling forth yet more dire predictions.

And then suddenly, carried on the stillness of the scented evening air, came the unmistakable sound of a chamber orchestra, amplified across the empty fields, sweet and elegiac, unlikely and unreal.

My mother heard it at once and joined us on the step.

'What is it?' she asked in wonder, as though there might truly be fairies at the bottom of her garden. 'Someone's playing Vivaldi!'

We hadn't heard Leo's arrival, but now he stood behind us, his hand resting upon my mother's brilliant brown hair in a peculiarly compulsive gesture of possession.

'It's the Camerons,' he said knowingly. 'One of their charity nights, I guess. They must be having an open-air concert.'

'The Camerons . . .' My mother repeated the words as if they were a magic incantation, the charm that might summon the music of the spheres.

Leo laughed and raised her to her feet, tightening his arm around her waist.

'It won't take you long to discover the Camerons,' he said carelessly. 'There's no escaping them.'

My mother kissed Leo lightly on the cheek, squeezed his hand and led him back into the cottage. My sister followed, but I stayed outside in the deepening gloom, morose and malcontent, plucking buttercup heads from the tangled garden and weaving them into chains while over the distant fields the band played on and on.

Next morning I opened my eyes on the jade and olive boudoir to find Jamie's silk-pyjamaed body beside me. I was glad he'd come home, and ran a teasing finger across his buttocks.

'Now, now, darling, don't be tiresome,' he murmured. 'Make the tea,' so I got up and meandered into the kitchen, selecting Earl Grey and the best Doulton cups, preparing the tray with an embroidered Victorian teacloth that we'd picked up for a song in the Portobello Road.

When I went back he was asleep again.

'How does my good Lord Hamlet,' I enquired, 'and what were you doing last night, forsooth? Country matters, I'll be bound . . .'

'What's the time?' he demanded suddenly, rolling away. He looked at his watch and then shot from the bed into the shower.

'Where is the beauteous Majesty of Denmark?' I began, but he bellowed angrily through the deluge.

'Beth, I'm late! And knock off the Hamlet stuff, will you? It's wearing ever so slightly thin.'

'Sorry,' I said, genuinely contrite. I'd had great fun with Jamie's prissy Orlando and his dimwitted Antonio. Even more with his sex-mad Romeo. I'd raised plenty of laughs from his psychotic Macbeth, and even a few, so help me God, from his insufferable Petruchio. But Hamlet, it seemed, was no joke.

'Will you be home tonight?' I demanded, following as he flew to the front door, trailing sheaves of notes and assorted bottles of deodorant. 'There's steak in the fridge. I could tart it up with a few bits of lemon and a pot of that fat-reduced cream . . .'

'Good grief, what a dreadful prospect. Keep your hands off that steak . . . Anyway, I'm out tonight.'

'Out again? Where?'

'Bye-bye, darling.' He kissed me gingerly on the cheek and then cursed as his car keys fell to the floor. 'Now don't sulk. You've plenty to do. You could even shift your pretty little arse and go look for the cat.'

Left alone, I felt uneasy and unsettled. I'd tried to shake off a lingering melancholy, convinced that my fevered remembrances of the night before were no more than the inevitable residue of my strange experience with Eva Delamere. And yet, something remained. The feel of Michael Cameron's dark gold hair, silky against my fingers. The sound of my mother's voice, consoling, and yet oddly provocative.

I was also, I had to admit, still perturbed by my farewell scene with Duval and hoping he'd call. I always tried to avoid unfinished business. I liked to stay friends with ex-lovers, although sometimes, as with the CID sergeant who'd investigated our burglary, it proved a mistake.

I needed comfort and support, that was it. I needed the wise words of my best friend, Vicky Lutz . . . But Vicky's marriage had seemed a little rocky of late and I wasn't sure I could face it. Maybe I'd call my sister instead.

I scoured the house for my address book. I couldn't remember
Sarah's number and when I finally found it, I got the unobtainable tone.
I must have written it down wrongly. I hung up and tried Vicky.

'Hallo. You've reached the home of Sam and Victoria Lutz. I'm sorry
we can't take your call right now . . . Don't forget to speak after the
squeak.'

Dammit, why wasn't Vicky home? Where could she be? Should I
try Sam at Metro TV? Maybe not. He'd want to know where the hell
I'd been. That was the worst of working with your friends, and with
Sam it sometimes got particularly tough. Quick to promote me, he was
also quick to knock me down, and he was unduly critical of my private
life.

I replaced the phone, stood up and wandered uncertainly around the
room. Was everything okay *chez* Lutz? I cared about Vicky and Sam,
truly I did. I hadn't forgotten how far back we all went. But sometimes,
just sometimes, I didn't want to be involved.

I looked at the list of calls I still had to make and when the phone
rang before I could make a start, I picked it up eagerly, sure that it had
to be Duval.

'Beth, sweetie, hallo! *Encore une fois*! Clive Fisher here.'

I'd chosen to ignore this particular message, having no idea why
Fisher should wish to speak to me again, and not particularly wanting
to know.

'I've had the most marvellous idea, Beth . . . Now get this! Why don't
I plug your new series in the *Sun* with a nice little snappette? You and
Jamie staring into each other's eyes over a bottle of wine? Hamlet and
his true lady love. Very sexy . . . very romantic . . . What do you say?'

I said nothing, simply stared uneasily into the phone. What was going
on? I had no reason to refuse a newspaper plug for my show. Fisher
knew that. He scarcely needed to ask.

'I don't see why not,' I said at last. 'Although Jamie's pretty tied up
with rehearsals at the moment . . . I'd have to ask him.'

'Do you know an actor who doesn't want his picture in the papers?'
asked Fisher. 'He'll make time . . . Eight o'clock on Friday all right?
How about Francine's? That's one of your haunts, isn't it? We'll provide the booze . . .'

I replaced the receiver and began to stride restlessly around the room.
What was Clive Fisher up to? Anything or nothing? Jamie and I were
always good for a picture, it was true. The tabloids, on a dull day, could
make a downpage headline out of our supposed marriage plans. But
nevertheless, Clive Fisher's interest niggled.

It was too early for a drink, so I made myself more tea and resolved
to put it from me. There was nothing I could do about Fisher or the

Sun. And suppose he was setting me up? Suppose he did have something on me and Duval? I could brazen it out. I could lie, just the way I'd done a dozen times before. I began to feel better.

I was starting out on my calls once more when the wretched phone rang again.

'Hallo, Beth. It's Candice Carter from the *Sunday Chronicle*.'

'Candice who?'

There was a short pause, followed by a low laugh.

'Okay, Beth. I know you didn't like my piece. But it was quite witty in parts, wasn't it? Sam Lutz actually called me up to say thanks. It was a pretty good plug for *Moonlight and Roses*, after all.'

'And what can I do for you now?' I asked stiffly

This time there was no discernible pause.

'I'll come clean, Beth. After you called me from Paris, I checked up on Eva Delamere. I found out where she was living, but by the time I followed it up, she'd died. However, I was told that you'd met her, and as I'm writing a short obituary for the *Chron*, I thought you might give me a quote . . .'

I tried to breathe slowly. One, two, three, four . . .

'Who told you I'd met her?' I whispered.

'One of the nuns.' Carter was clearly surprised at my tone. 'Is anything wrong, Beth? Were you planning to do something on Eva yourself?'

'Nothing's wrong,' I said quickly, anxious to conceal the details of my encounter with Eva. 'I'm not doing anything about her, and I'm happy to give you a quote . . . But there's very little I can say. She didn't want to talk about her past . . .'

'I'm not surprised,' said Candice Carter. 'Murder, suicide, adultery. It was all in there. Do you think Daniel Duval got anything out of her?'

I didn't intend to be drawn on the subject of Duval, so I rushed on into my quote.

'Eva Delamere was an extraordinary personality, powerful and prepossessing,' I heard myself declare. 'But very private . . .' I rambled for a few moments more, dredged up the meagre details the young nun at the Paris convent had offered, and then produced what I hoped was a good, usable line.

'Eva Delamere was an enigma,' I concluded grandly; 'content to remain a mystery to the end.'

'It'll do,' Carter said somewhat grudgingly. 'But I could use something more. Do you have a home number for Daniel Duval?'

'No, I don't,' I snapped, and slammed down the phone.

Afterwards, I paced ever more anxiously around the house, unable to concentrate on anything. I'd left Paris believing myself finished with

Eva Delamere. I neither wanted, nor expected, to find myself recalling
our extraordinary meeting, but now my head was full of the little room
at the Divine Faith convent, the fuming candles, the grotesque body of
the plaster Messiah above the fireplace, the sea of luminous grass outside the window, the mysterious tinkle of angelic laughter . . .

And so I found myself drawn back once more, resistant and regretful,
into the past Eva had forced me to confront.

My mother was sitting on the cane settee in the conservatory, sewing
rhinestones on a velvet bolero she meant to wear for dinner at the
English Department, her face fixed in a familiar frown that was part
effort at the tiny stitches, part displeasure with her elder daughter.

Outside in the garden Leo Frankish hacked away at the buttercups,
swinging a fearsome scythe through the undergrowth, pausing every
few strokes to wipe the sweat from his neck with one of my mother's
fluffy pink bath towels. I couldn't think what Leo would wear for dinner
with the department, and imagined him dressed in his usual scruffy
cords and black polo neck, showing off the elegant Eleanor Carlisle,
tutor extraordinary.

'Beth, I simply won't have you moping around like this until September,' my mother said sharply. 'You'll have to try a little harder. Why
don't you go for a walk with Sarah? There are some marvellous walks
on the edge of the village. She's met lots of people already.'

My heart was in London with the life I had left and I wasn't about
to go for country walks. I picked up the book that lay on the cane settee.

'I'm working,' I said primly, wondering if I dare suggest she ought
to be working too. 'I've got to finish this essay.' I looked down at my
notes.

'The hope for time restored resonates throughout the Eliot canon,' I
had written; 'as though Humanity, by its intense yearning for what
might have been, could yet redeem the dream . . .'

'Oh come on, Beth. There's a cricket match at the Camerons' place,'
said Sarah, sticking her head through the conservatory window. 'We
could walk up there and take a look.'

Leo paused from his labours at the bottom of the garden and turned
to give my mother a wave. He raised the scythe across his shoulder and
its silver blade flashed cruelly in the sun.

'Who are these feudal Camerons?' I enquired petulantly. 'Does anything else go on around here, or are we dependent on the third baronet
for all our entertainment? The third baronet! What a joke. Lloyd
George has a lot to answer for . . .'

Sarah had quickly discovered that such diversions as the village could

offer all centred on the big house behind the church, and in the week
since our arrival had spoken of little but the Camerons and their social
munificence. Midsummer barbecues, autumn fêtes and Christmas parties. As Leo had predicted, there was no escaping the Camerons, though
I was determined to do my best.

'Jack Cameron seems very charming,' my mother said lightly. 'And
he doesn't make a big thing of the title – although I gather his wife likes
to be properly addressed. I'd guess she came down in the world when
she married . . . Anyway, they're keen to be neighbourly. Lady Cameron has asked me to a coffee morning, and we're all invited to the June
barbecue. I hope, Beth, there'll be no silly cracks about squires and so
forth.'

I finally walked out with Sarah because I couldn't spend all summer
with the good and the great of English Lit., and because I owed my
mother a minimal effort to settle. It was true, after all, that I wouldn't
be living there much longer. I was merely required to endure the next
few months.

'I bet you'll fancy the Cameron boys when you meet them,' Sarah
giggled, anxious that some mitigating prospect should snap me from my
woe. 'They're very good-looking.'

I said nothing, but kicked savagely at a bobbing dandelion head in the
hedgerow.

'Jonathan's the elder. He's doing PPE, and the whole village is invited to his twenty-first at Christmas. He'll be the next baronet . . .'

She pulled at a dog rose that wound its way around the churchyard
gate, and nipping off the thorns, stuck it into my hair.

'Michael's nineteen. He's reading law, but he wants to give it up and
do theology . . .' She hesitated, trying to weigh up my likely response.
'He's just finished his first year at Cambridge,' she said at last.

It had been my mother's hope that I would follow her to Cambridge,
but I'd flunked the interview and was now set for an undistinguished
redbrick instead. The failure still rankled with us both, though I determined that I'd have the final advantage. I would finish my degree.

'Theology!' I exclaimed to Sarah, dislodging the dog rose and tossing
it to the ground. 'What on earth's the point of doing that?'

'Well, I don't know. If you believe in God, I suppose there's a point,'
Sarah said crossly. 'Look, Beth, I hope you're going to make an effort
to be civil.'

We walked on. The village was an appealing place, even to my jaundiced eye, not yet taken over by wealthy commuters and prettified into
postcard England, but retaining a faintly melancholic rural charm. It
was the charm of a wild churchyard, overrun with briars and hemlock,
of a tangled spinney with a curious if unremarkable ruin at its heart, of

rose-hips and blackberry bushes in hidden lanes, and rows of cabbages
in back gardens. The church, a squat medieval structure with square
bell tower and erratic gilded clock, brooded above a meandering main
street, and behind it, veiled from the road by a grassy bank and a rank
of ancient elms, rose a vast Georgian mansion, unreal in its golden
beauty, long sash windows winking in the summer glare, terraces
studded with blood-red geraniums in marble urns. A long gravel drive
swept up to a flight of steps, the pillars of which sported two unrecognisable stone beasts, heads bent and teeth bared. Outside the stable
block, set back from the east wing, four vehicles were parked on that
day, a muddy Range Rover, a tattered MG sports, a smart new Escort
and a pristine black Bentley, long, low and ostentatiously luxurious.

'The Cameron place!' Sarah announced.

Even I was impressed. Although I knew the Camerons owned much
of the agricultural land around the village, I hadn't anticipated this
aristocratic splendour, imagining a generous farmhouse or, at best, a
minor country residence. But the Camerons were clearly grade-one
listed, with all the privilege and power, connections and cash that such
a house implied.

'Oh, it looks as though we have to pay,' said Sarah, stopping suddenly. 'I haven't brought any money, have you?'

We'd walked round to the rear of the house, and among the sculpted
lawns and formal rose gardens came upon a quivering marquee. At the
opening sat a plump, sweating woman whom I recognised from the
village grocery store.

'Two pounds each,' she said, smiling at Sarah. 'And that gets you a
free glass of champagne.'

'How is it free when you have to pay two quid?'

'Shut up, Beth.' My sister smiled apologetically at the grocery pro-
prietress: 'We thought we could just watch the cricket.'

'Sorry,' said Mrs Village Store firmly. 'It's for Christian Aid.'

'Couldn't you chalk up our names in the shop window?' I asked
cheekily. 'We'll come in tomorrow and pay.'

'Allow me,' said a voice from behind, and a five-pound note fluttered
over my shoulder into the cash box.

I turned to confront a tall, flaxen-haired figure dressed in white flannels
and pullover, his wide grey eyes meeting mine in evident amusement.

I stared back, taking in this vision of well-bred youth, the bright gold
hair worn slightly long, the strong forehead, the refined nose, the white,
even teeth. The smile was open and encouraging, engagingly frank, the
grey eyes appraising and interested. I returned the smile.

'Oh, hallo Michael,' said Sarah, flustered. 'This is my elder sister,
Beth.'

'Hallo, Beth. Come and drink champagne for Ethiopia.'

'Your change, sir,' cried the keeper of the village store with deferential propriety, but already he'd taken my arm and was leading me into the dim interior of the tent, across the springy turf towards the champagne. My feet were light and my heart lighter. Onward, onward I glided, with never a backward glance. Towards the champagne, and towards the unbridled indulgence of first love, with all its passion and its preposterous promises, its torment and its tumultuous tears. Onward, onward, dance as you go. Towards the defeat of desire and the death of hope. Onward, onward, blithely step. Towards a broken heart.

Eventually I called all the people I was supposed to call, then went shopping at Harvey Nicks. I tried Vicky Lutz from the restaurant, got the answerphone again, lunched alone, and then went back home.

There was a message waiting from Vicky: 'Beth . . . I'm taking Chloe to my mother's place in Spain next week. I'll call you as soon as I'm back . . . P. S. How's Paris?'

There was no sign of Jamie, and no message from him. I'd thought that if he couldn't make dinner, he might come home for tea, but it wasn't to be, and I idled around the sitting room disconsolately, suddenly missing Thomasina.

Where had the wretched creature gone? Just like a cat, of course, to bugger off when the going got tough. So the tom from Number Six had been scoffing her grub? Well, that was life. The rest of us just had to get on with it.

I gazed at myself in the gilt-edged mirror above the fireplace. How did I look? Not too bad. The hair was a touch brassy, perhaps. Maybe I'd get Carlos to take it down a shade. But the thirtysomething wrinkles were still at bay, and my weight remained the half-stone below normal demanded by the television screen. Well, almost. Maybe I shouldn't have had the avocado at lunch. I peered closely at the eyes so engagingly described as 'seawater green' by a writer on *TV Times*. Did they still sparkle? Or was the booze showing? I decided to give up gin for a month, and poured myself a farewell glass.

I was still restless. I poured a second gin, and then another. I called Vicky once more. Maybe I could catch her before she left for Spain. No reply. So where the hell was Sam? Why wasn't he home from work? Metro TV's ace producer was a busy man, but surely he had to touch base sometimes?

Then I tried Jamie at the rehearsal room and was told he'd left, destination unknown. A few more calls to assorted friends, a bit of desultory chat, and still I was on my own. I even dialled the operator to check on my sister's telephone number, having nothing much else to do, thinking I'd get the correct number and write it down somewhere like a proper sister should.

'Discontinued line,' the operator said.

They must have changed their number. Oh well, at least I wouldn't have to speak to Sarah's husband, the odious Charles, nor receive his studiously guarded and cool replies. Charles was a pain in the neck. If it weren't for Charles, I frequently told myself, I might actually visit my sister a bit more often.

When the doorbell rang I couldn't imagine who it might be, and in a sudden flash of rage, deduced that it must be the man from CID checking on my window locks and trying out his luck. If so, I was just drunk enough to assault a police officer.

'It's me, Beth. I take it you're alone?'

Duval was standing in the shadow of the porch, raincoat collar turned up like some renegade from an old movie. I was inordinately pleased to see him, and desperate to bury our disagreement, but for one dangerous moment I nearly laughed.

'Are you alone?' he repeated tersely. 'I won't come in if you're not . . .'

'It's okay,' I reassured him, pulling him gently inside. 'How good of you to call. What on earth are you doing in London?'

It was odd to see him standing in my hallway, for I'd somehow imagined him confined to Paris, as though he had no existence beyond the gloomy alleys and the blustery boulevards. He certainly didn't belong in my house, a fact that his manner instantly conveyed.

'I won't stay long,' he muttered. 'I have something for you, that's all. I had to come to England, so I thought I might as well deliver it myself . . .'

I tried to part him from his raincoat, ushering him into the living room and inviting him to sit down on the white sofa, but he was determined not to linger. He gazed around for a moment in frank admiration, and then fumbled in his raincoat pocket for a small, grubby envelope, which he handed over carefully.

'Eva wanted you to have this,' he said. 'Please don't ask me why.'

'Eva? But I don't understand . . .'

I opened the package warily, and a relic from the grave spilled into my hand – Eva's tiny filigree cross on its bright silver chain.

'What is this?' I demanded, bewildered. 'What's going on?'

'I really don't know, Beth,' he said awkwardly. 'I guess she just took a shine to you. That's the kind of woman she was.'

I blinked down at the cross. I was perilously close to tears, though I could not trace their source, and there was an uncomfortable silence as I struggled for control, and lost.

'You're holding out on me,' I accused him suddenly. 'You must have seen Eva before she died. What did you tell her about me? And what did she tell you? I must know!'

He moved towards the door, unnerved by this unlikely show of emotion.

'She just gave me the cross, Beth. She asked me to bring it to you . . . That's all.'

'But why? Why should she do that? What does it mean?'

We'd reached the hall and I put out my hand to stop him opening the front door when it suddenly swung inwards to reveal Jamie, dishevelled and dirty, his hands caked with dark mud.

For a moment we all stared at each other.

'I don't think you've met,' I said at last, regaining my wits. 'Jamie, this is . . .'

'Duval,' mumbled my former lover unhappily, as though he truly believed I might have forgotten his name. 'Daniel Duval.'

Jamie showed no interest in this information.

'The cat is dead,' he announced in ringing tones. 'Flattened by a delivery truck. I've buried her in the back garden.'

I turned, a muffled sob escaping my throat, and Duval, his raincoat collar up once more, vanished into the night behind me, closing the door as he left.

'No mourning, Beth,' Jamie said severely, making for the bathroom. 'You didn't give a fuck about that cat. I bought all her food. The bloody thing would have starved if she'd been relying on you. You never even turned a hair when I told you she was missing.'

I followed him into the bathroom, weeping profusely, clutching Eva's silver cross in my hand.

'It's an omen,' I said, not knowing what I meant.

Jamie lathered the burial remains from his fingers.

'If there's any omen,' he said tightly, 'it's bloody Daniel Duval. I must say I'm surprised, darling. Your moral standards are slipping, to say nothing of your common sense.' He slammed out of the bathroom and I was left staring down into the muddy basin.

That night it seemed that Eva came to me, sweet and fresh as a spring flower, her face shining with youth and hope, her eyes deep and mysterious, like violet pools in an Alpine valley. I saw her dancing through wide streets, silvery hair swaying in the wind, arms open to embrace the life that teemed all around. I saw her stoop to touch the sparkling pavements and then stretch high to release a tiny white bird into the vast skies above.

'All shall be well,' she murmured, reaching out to caress my cheek with a gentle hand. 'All manner of thing shall be well.'

Chapter Three

If Beth Carlisle has a romantic past, then she's not letting on. A sequence in her new TV series shows her interviewing young lovers in Paris. She's not afraid to ask highly personal questions, but it seems she won't answer them herself. Does she, for example, remember her first love? The first time she had sex?

'Of course I remember,' she says brusquely. 'But there was nothing special about him, or it. That, I suspect, is most people's experience.'

Well, maybe. But the young lovers in *Moonlight and Roses* tell a different tale. It is surely disingenuous of Carlisle to refuse us the benefits of her own experience, particularly as she's setting herself up as a commentator on everyone else's . . .

'Public Persona: Beth Carlisle' (the Candice Carter Interview, *Sunday Chronicle*)

───────────

Sunday morning, the rashers sweating in the Le Creuset pan and the croissants luxuriating in the Lurpak . . .

Sunday morning, made in heaven for colour supplements, saturated fat, and, if you can get it, sex.

Jamie, of course, had his own plans.

'You're going to church?' I moaned incredulously. 'What the hell for? Don't tell me. The curate's in love with you, and you're trying to let him down lightly.'

He'd made some unspeakable hangover remedy involving raw eggs and orange juice. Now he looked set to throw it over me.

'You have a very coarse streak, darling. Did you know that?'

'It must be the company I keep.'

He dressed quickly and carefully, one eye always on the mirror, flick-

ing the lovely hair away from his face, replacing the diamanté stud in
his ear with something smaller, discreetly gold.

'Drink up your juice, darling,' he said, opening the wardrobe door,
'and don't forget your bacon's frying. Maybe you'd better save it.'

I crawled from the bed and reached for my wrap.

'I thought we'd get a new cat,' I said. 'We could go to the shelter and
play God. Choose the scruffiest moggie they've got and feed it on lemon
sole.'

'I'm going to church.'

'When did you ever go to church, for God's sake?'

He fastened a cream wool jacket over his best navy silk tie and abandoned the earring altogether, peering critically at the tiny pink blemish
it left behind. The tie was respectful, even funereal, but when the jacket
was undone it revealed a tiny Mickey Mouse at the point. I'd bought it
in LA for a hundred dollars.

'As it happens, I'm not going for God's sake. You remember Alex
Chapman, don't you? Well, it's for his sake. A celebration of his life.
Right after morning communion.'

'Alex Chapman . . . Is he dead?'

He turned towards me, irritated.

'Don't you read the bloody papers unless you're in them? He killed
himself last week. The *Sun* loved it. Your friend Clive Fisher got a
wonderfully heartrending interview with his old Mum . . .'

I was silent, trying to recall when I'd last seen Alex Chapman. It must
have been *The Taming of the Shrew* when he'd played Lucentio. I'd
known he'd got it, of course. Everyone did. But there was nothing to
be done, no conclusions to be drawn. So he'd killed himself instead of
waiting for the long, slow death, and now the Terrence Higgins Trust
would be a few quid richer. I might even give something myself.

'Is there a collection?' I looked vaguely round the room for my bag.

'There's no collection. It's a celebration.'

I shivered and got back into bed, willing the world to rewind to a time
when bodily fluids were something you controlled with Mum Rollette.

'I suppose I should come,' I said unconvincingly as Jamie opened the
bedroom door. 'I rather fancied old Alex.'

'Did you really? Then maybe you should. Alex liked a little bit of
both and he wasn't too fussy. You could give thanks for your deliverance.'

I pulled the quilt tight around my shoulders, wrapping myself into
the folds like a caterpillar refusing its wings. I could smell the bacon
burning, but I didn't care.

'Fuck off,' I said to Jamie. 'And watch you don't catch it from the
communion cup. That would be a nice little turn-up, wouldn't it?'

He paused at the open door.

'You know what, darling? Underneath that delightful, lovable exterior of yours, you're really quite a nasty piece of work . . .'

I was penitent at once.

'I'm sorry. I was genuinely fond of Alex. It's terrible that he killed himself . . . This whole AIDS thing is unutterably tragic.'

'Now, now darling,' Jamie said softly. 'Don't start getting sincere. Stick to irony. It suits you so much better.'

'Have you finished that essay?' asked my mother in surprise as I tossed my Eliot book to the floor and reached for my hat. It was of palest satin straw and I'd tucked a handful of daisies into the brim. Their fat yellow middles matched the colour of my hair, their creamy petals the shade of my dress. I knew I looked good.

'Sarah's going to church,' I said idly. 'I thought I might go with her.'

'Church!'

My mother's gilt-rimmed spectacles advanced along her nose and she stared over them with evident scepticism.

'They have choral Evensong at St Botolph's,' I said defensively. 'It's reckoned to be very good.'

My mother turned back to the pile of books on the conservatory table, flicking open her own copy of Eliot and scribbling something in a margin.

'I see. So this doesn't reflect a sudden concern for the state of your soul? You're simply after the aesthetic experience?'

'She's after Michael Cameron,' Sarah said with a giggle. 'He's in the choir.'

I was too confident to be cross, too excited to be quashed. 'He happened to mention he'd be there,' I said smoothly, 'and he suggested we might walk to the spinney afterwards. There's some kind of Gothic ruin in the middle, apparently.'

Now Sarah was impressed, but my mother looked at me sharply, casting a calculating eye upon the flimsy dress and the extravagant hat. She was about to speak, but at that moment Leo rapped gaily on the conservatory window, waving a bright woolly arm, looking for all the world like Uriah Heep, never mind the author of a respected tome on the uses of caricature in literature.

'You look lovely,' he mouthed, seemingly to me, but his eyes were on my mother and the sheet of glossy chocolate-coloured hair which, just for a moment, concealed her expression.

We walked to the church through fragrant, hazy air, warmed by the gold of an English summer's eve, chased by a cloud of moaning gnats

who dipped and dived around our heads, sobered by the toll of a solitary bell from the ancient church tower.

I hadn't been to church since I was twelve when, at my grandmother's insistence, I'd been prepared for confirmation, a process both
bewildering and boring. At the last minute I'd tried to renege, balking
at giving a meaningless promise to a man in a ludicrous hat, afraid
sophisticated schoolfriends might spy me in my white pleated skirt and
angora cardigan. But as ever, my grandmother prevailed.

Not for long, however. I became as adept at foiling her morally improving schemes and deflecting her disapproval as my mother before me.

'Humour her,' my mother advised, and so I did, wondering from time
to time whatever happened to cosy, red-cheeked grannies who gave out
five-pound notes and defended their granddaughters against punitive
mothers. My grandmother didn't even want to be called Granny, insisting it made her feel old. We were to call her Rhoda, as her daughter
had always done before us, and feel grateful for the privilege.

Still, the ailing Rhoda was easily outsmarted, and when her health
finally failed and she could no longer attend morning communion with
her dutiful granddaughters at her side, I skipped to the swimming baths
instead. By my thirteenth birthday I could do twenty lengths in the
time it took to celebrate the Eucharist, and by the time Rhoda died, I
had finished with the Church for good.

Now I stepped inside the hallowed walls of St Botolph's unrepentant,
shivering in the chilly gloom, the heels of my sandals clattering on the
worn flagstones, the gauze dress floating behind me as I walked down
the aisle. I wanted a pew with a view of the choir stalls, and Sarah's
discreet efforts to steer me to the back were flatly ignored.

Dearly beloved brethren, the Scripture moveth us in sundry places . . .

Perhaps if I'd listened I might have been moved, but I could think of
nothing except Michael, resplendent in black cassock and white sur-
plice, thick gold hair curling over the edge of his collar, wide grey eyes
clearly pleased when, briefly, they held mine.

I had no idea Evensong took so long. Interminable prayers, endless
Bible passages. Outside at last I breathed deeply in the scented air,
pulling nervously at the wild roses which hung around the church gate,
anxious and uncertain, my confidence suddenly gone.

'He's probably talking to the vicar,' Sarah said, snatching the hat
which I now carried in my hand and setting it on her own head. 'He's
very into the Church, you know. Serves at communion in the mornings.
Runs the Christian debating society . . . Come to think of it, he's really
not your type at all.'

'I'll decide who's my type,' I snapped, grabbing unsuccessfully at the
hat. 'But I'm not waiting much longer.'

Then he was there, smiling and complimenting Sarah on the hat, unaffectedly receiving the greetings of exiting churchgoers who all appeared to consider him intrinsically worthy of their esteem, joking with the curate about some minor mistake the choir had made, taking my bare arm with his hand to steer me through the church gate so that my flesh contracted with an unexpected shock of desire.

'We'll drive to the spinney,' he said. 'The folly is right away from the village, across the brook . . . It's a fair walk.'

Sarah sauntered determinedly beside us, and I began to panic. The announcement had been made with perfect decorum, politely including my little sister should she choose to accept. I threw her my best scowl, but it bounced off the brim of the cream straw hat and she strolled blithely on.

Fate intervened in the shape of elder brother Jonathan, who suddenly appeared in the lane before us, swinging a tennis racquet, two leggy young ladies in neatly cut shorts trotting one on either side. The introductions were lazily made. Clare and Fiona Spencer, long-term friends, the daughters of Lady Cameron's old school chum. Top-drawer girls, I quickly concluded, with rabbit teeth, mouse hair and brains equipped to serve either species.

'We thought you'd make up a four,' Fiona said to Michael, looking up at him eagerly. 'There's time for three sets before the light goes.'

She was the younger of the two, prettier than her pale-faced sister who now hung back behind Jonathan, slashing idly at a clump of dandelions with her racquet.

'Perhaps Sarah would like to play?' Michael said slowly, at one time managing to convey an apology and solve our dilemma. 'I promised Beth I'd show her Uncle Malcolm's folly.'

It was settled in a moment, and then all six of us stood outside the Cameron stable block, surveying the assembled fleet of vehicles.

The tattered sports belonged to Jonathan, and Sarah was whisked home to change. I was led, improbably, to the capacious Bentley, handed in through its shining doors like the Queen Mother, and chauffeured out through the vast iron gates at the end of the meandering drive. The Spencer girls were left standing in the shadow of the great house, staring after the disappearing limo like a pair of cultivated orchids gazing upon wild flowers blowing in the meadows beyond.

'This is a ridiculous car,' I laughed, admiring the stout leather seats, the mahogany fascia, the tortoiseshell cigar lighter. He took the bend in the village street with a deliberate flourish, flashing the headlights at Sarah who was emerging from Jonathan's sports car outside our front door.

We drove out of the village to the wooded ridge above, looking down upon the straggle of houses and the squat-towered church. The spinney dipped back towards the brook from this point, a dense emerald tangle of saplings and spiky shrubs stretching for acres along the rim of the Cameron estate.

'Does all this belong to you?'

He'd left the road and plunged the car deep into the enveloping green, taking a narrow track he obviously knew well, slamming to a halt in a secluded glen which, I couldn't help remarking, was completely concealed from the lane above.

'Officially the spinney is on Cameron land,' he said, switching off the Bentley's engine and immersing us in a magical, whispering peace, 'but it really belongs to the village. There'd be an uproar if it were ever enclosed.'

He led me down into the woodland's heart, draping his jacket around my shoulders when branches tore at my naked arms, lifting me effortlessly across muddy channels which threatened my delicate sandals, talking easily about Great-Great-Uncle Malcolm who'd built the folly in the spinney, about the Camerons, who'd come south after the Union, about his father, who'd studied history at Cambridge and then quietly returned to the landowning life of his forebears, about his mother, the former Lady Beatrice Gilbert whose fortunes had helped restore the Camerons' own and ensure the immediate future of the great Georgian mansion . . .

'It won't go on for ever,' I said provocatively. 'You'll all end up living in the servants' quarters, showing plebs round the ballroom for fifty pence a head.'

He laughed. 'You think so?'

'Oh yes. You should hear what happened to my grandmother, the beautiful Rhoda, the Lady of Shalott . . .'

This was by far the most interesting item concerning my own family history and the only tenuous link I could claim with the aristocracy myself, so I didn't hesitate to use it.

'My grandmother's second husband was Sir Rupert Connaught, something junior at the Treasury under Harold Macmillan. He had a stately pile in Wiltshire, and he imprisoned my grandmother there. He hated her to go out, so she used to sit alone in one of the windows, sewing and dreaming of towered Camelot . . . She called herself the Lady of Shalott.'

'I don't believe a word!'

'It's true! Then Sir Rupert died of food poisoning, and Rhoda thought she'd inherit the lot. But there was some great cock-up over the death duties, and she didn't get a penny. She ended her days in a basement flat in Highbury, and now the big house is owned by the National Trust. We went round it in the summer holidays one year . . .'

He laughed again.

'What happened to your grandmother's first husband?' he enquired archly.

Now I was forced to laugh too.

'The mysterious Victor Martineau . . . She had us believe he was some great hero in the French Resistance, but my mother says that wasn't true. Apparently he died right at the beginning of the war . . . However, the other stuff is gen, I swear it! So beware! The Camerons' comeuppance may be just over the horizon.'

He looked at me seriously.

'My mother doesn't think so. She reckons the Tories will get in this time, and then the aristocracy will reign once more . . .'

I glanced up at him quickly, anxious that I'd started out on politics too soon, unwilling to risk unhindered progress to the inevitable consummation of what was clearly a strong mutual attraction. I wanted Michael Cameron with a passion that startled me by its intensity.

'Well, maybe your mother is right,' I mumbled awkwardly, concentrating on the stubble beneath my feet.

'Oh, I don't think so,' he retorted. 'I think the ruling class has had its day. And about time, too.'

What this remark suggested about Cameron household dynamics and a filial relationship in which luxurious limousines were loaned but family allegiances derided, mattered rather less than the unexpected revelation that our politics appeared to coincide. It was more than I'd dared imagine, and my fervent socialist consciousness swelled in delight.

However, there remained a niggling doubt that he might indeed be excessively religious, and as soon as we stood within the crumbling walls of Uncle Malcolm's Gothic folly, a strange, turreted erection of moss-covered stones with a small enclosed cell at one end, I determined to find out.

'What on earth was it meant to be? A chapel of some sort? Don't tell me your great-great-uncle was a religious nutcase?'

He tested a loose stone with his foot, kicking it carefully back to security.

'That's how he appeared at the time. He called this place the Hermitage . . . Used to come here to pray, and tried to get some of the villagers to do the same. This was before the Oxford movement got under way, and it all seemed very Roman. Quite wicked in fact. There was a complaint about him to the Bishop.'

I stared round at the green walls, imagining Uncle Malcolm communing with the Almighty in solitary splendour.

'How romantic,' I murmured; 'and how luxurious. I don't suppose villagers in the last century had too much time to spend praying.'

The grey eyes looked deeply into mine, summing up.

'You think prayer is a luxury?' he asked slowly. 'It doesn't seem that way to me. More like hard work, I'd say.'

A quip about the interminable quality of Evensong died on my lips, and I leaned back on a cool, mossy slab, closing my eyes for a moment against the eerie green light.

'Prayer is a nice idea,' I murmured. 'If only we knew that it worked!'

He laughed and took my hand, leading me back to the centre of the ruin.

'If you want instant results, you may well be disappointed,' he said. 'Try reading the lives of the saints. It took some of them years before they realised their prayers had been answered.'

He was close to me, so very close I was aware of the beating of his heart, the faint rise and fall of flesh beneath his shirt. His breath seemed slightly quicker than normal, and I was sure he would kiss me, but then a shaft of brilliant light from an unnoticed window in the wall high above us pierced the ground at our feet, turning the grey stones to pink and throwing the dingy green walls into dappled relief. He moved swiftly into the beam.

'Look, that's what I wanted you to see! It only happens at this time of day, and then only at certain times of the year.' He pointed up to the window where a small haloed figure could now be spied, shining down.

'St Augustine of Hippo,' he said softly, 'Uncle Malcolm's favourite saint.'

I said nothing, aware only of an irreverent petition beating through my brain as the rosy light warmed my face. *Oh God, make him want me as much as I want him. Oh please God, make it all work out . . .*

We walked back to the car in near silence, and I felt uneasy and subdued, as though Uncle Malcolm, or perhaps St Augustine, had somehow cast a shadow along with the unexpected beam of light. Perhaps Sarah had been right. Perhaps Michael Cameron wasn't really my type at all. And he hadn't kissed me. Maybe sex was against his principles.

'You're very quiet,' he said at last as he swung the Bentley from its secluded hollow and eased it back on to the road.

'I was thinking about St Augustine,' I said cautiously, fearing I might have a great deal to lose. 'Wasn't he the most frightful old lecher who repented and then tried to saddle everyone else with a mortal fear of the flesh?'

'I'm afraid he was. Makes you wonder if old Uncle Malcolm had a dark secret, doesn't it?'

We both laughed, and the doubt lifted. He took one hand from the wheel, briefly caressing my hair before the bend in the village high street drew his attention away. Outside my mother's cottage, he switched off the car lights. Then he leaned across to the passenger seat and kissed me on the mouth, an intimate, inviting, demanding kiss, conveying at once the welcome if unlikely intimation that some prayers, at least, are swiftly answered.

'I'll call you tomorrow,' he whispered.

Inside the conservatory Sarah was dancing, peering out from behind the lace curtain as I strolled up the path.

'What have you been doing?' she demanded, giggling. 'Clare Spencer was most terribly put out! She kept saying it was far too late to be in the spinney and that you'd be terribly cold in your thin dress. And Michael was due back for dinner at eight. His mother seemed rather put out too.'

I was perversely pleased at having snatched a prize from the covetous paws of the rabbit-toothed Clare, and not at all perturbed at what Michael's mother might think. But my own mother was another matter.

She looked at me keenly, taking in my rumpled hair and the cream gauze dress, stained with the moss of Uncle Malcolm's folly.

'What is it?' I demanded crossly, angry at this unnecessary scrutiny, bristling with all the virtue of one who has done nothing remotely reprehensible, but might well have done, given the chance.

She waved my sister from the room, and I flopped down beside her on the cane settee, picking up T. S. Eliot once more.

'I've had Michael's father on the telephone,' my mother said brusquely, taking off her gold-rimmed spectacles and shuffling her papers into a haphazard pile. 'He wasn't too happy. He said Michael shouldn't have taken the car, and that he wasn't to be trusted in it . . .'

'He seemed okay to me,' I said obliquely, poring over the Eliot book with exaggerated concentration, wondering whether Michael's trustworthiness was deemed to relate solely to the Bentley, or whether my mother had something else in mind.

She stood up and returned the delicate spectacles to their red leather pouch which lay on the table before us.

'I'm glad you've found a little diversion,' she murmured at last, staring over my shoulder at the famous lines which she now had difficulty deciphering. 'I really wouldn't want you cooped up with T. S. Eliot all summer.'

She bent closer, frowning at the book, and a swath of the lush brown hair cascaded across one cheek.

'Just one thing,' she said lightly, leaning forward and tracing the scribble in the margins with an elegant finger. 'Don't get pregnant, Beth, will you? Take it from me. It really does spoil things.'

Lunchtime. No roast beef, no Yorkshire pudding, no Jamie. I guessed they'd all gone straight from church into the pub. The reverent celebration of Alex Chapman's life had obviously turned rowdy.

I scanned the papers idly. FOUR HUNDRED LOST IN PHILIPPINES FERRY DISASTER. EIGHT-YEAR-OLD GIRL RAPED AND STRANGLED IN DORSET. FIFTY PER CENT OF AFRICANS MAY BE HIV POSITIVE.

Then I turned the page and found myself staring at Eva Delamere, the photograph accompanying Candice Carter's obituary.

She was young and preposterously beautiful, pictured gazing rapturously upon Will Sutton's bronzed features in a still from *Casey's War* while Carlotta du Bois, who'd played a ravishing nun, looked on. VINTAGE HOLLYWOOD STAR DIES.

I didn't want to think about Eva and I certainly didn't want to read the obituary containing my own anodyne quote. I flipped over quickly. HOMELESS FIGURES SET TO SOAR. OXFAM PREDICTS NEW CRISIS IN SUDAN. NEO-NAZI GANG FIRE MOSQUE.

I threw down the papers, and poured myself a gin and Slimline tonic. I walked into the kitchen and ate a bowl of Special K. I scrubbed the tiles at the back of the cooker and set about defrosting the fridge. But I couldn't shake off the image of Eva.

I took a paperback from the shelf by the inglenook – *Discovering the Movies* – and read a laborious and largely uninformative chapter on the art of David Klein and how he would have changed the face of cinema had he not been shot in Paris by the Nazis. Eva merited one paragraph.

'The making of *Casey's War* was a triumph of Klein's will over circumstance,' I read. 'He had little time for either Carlotta du Bois or Eva Delamere, and for their part, the actresses seemed almost to conspire against the success of the film . . .'

I picked up a copy of *Hollywood Dream Queens*, and read the section on Carlotta du Bois. There was much about her infamous affair with Saul Bernstein and the subsequent wrangles with Bernstein's daughter Rebecca after his death, but virtually nothing about Eva.

'Du Bois and Delamere had little in common,' I read. 'Off the set, they went their separate ways, and on it, they barely spoke to each other.'

Then, desperate for distraction, I picked up the papers again. PENNILESS MOTHER FED DOG MEAT TO BABY. DISABLED PENSIONER BLINDED IN ATTACK. CANCER STRIKES AT ONE IN FIVE.

But always, I was drawn back to the picture of Eva. There was something about the tilt of her chin, the lift of her shoulders, the faint smile that played around her lips, something that beguiled me. I remembered that moment in Paris, that trick of the light when she'd appeared transformed, a wizened creature changed suddenly into the lovely young woman she'd once been. Was it this that had prompted my unlikely confession in the little convent room? The intimation of other-worldliness, of approaching death?

Whatever, a chill wind from that little room had stirred the debris of my past, whipping it into my face. And now I could not think of Eva without thinking of my mother or of Michael. Michael Cameron. Thirteen years had passed since we parted. Good, productive years. The years of my fruition, from radio station hack to television star, from impoverished student to the centre spread in *Mews and Mansions*.

What had happened to Michael? I knew, of course, that he'd been ordained priest in the Church of England and that, equally predictably, he'd married one of the Spencer girls; not the prettier Fiona, but the pale, intense Clare. I knew too that Jack Cameron was dead, felled by a heart attack on a golf course in Scotland, and that Jonathan Cameron was now the fourth baronet.

These fragments had mostly been gleaned from the personal columns of *The Times*, which I read whenever I had nothing better to do. In recent years, however, I'd been busy. I had no idea if Michael Cameron had become Archbishop of Canterbury, turned Buddhist, given up God altogether, or taken to crack.

I stood up, carried my empty cereal bowl out into the kitchen, washed it up, walked back into the living room. None of it mattered, of course. Not the Camerons, not my mother, not Eva Delamere. The living only harm us if we let them, and the dead stay dead for ever.

I looked down at Eva's lovely face once more. I closed my eyes, and saw the pale mask of death as she lay in the Divine Faith chapel. I threw the newspaper aside and poured myself a new drink. I drank it. I picked up the obituary and stared at Eva's picture again. Then I walked into the bedroom, ferreted far into the dressing-table's depths, extracted the grubby envelope that Duval had given me, and in a gesture of pure melodrama, fastened Eva's silver cross around my throat.

My mother's darkened conservatory, the night of the midsummer barbecue, my face hot from too much Planter's Punch, my bare skin prickling beneath Michael's urgent hands.

'When will she be back?' he asked anxiously, snapping open the catch on my bra.

'She won't. She's going home with Leo. They're probably in bed right now.'

His lips released my nipple and he sat up abruptly, causing the cane settee on which we were sprawled to creak in alarm.

'Quiet,' I commanded. 'Sarah's still awake.'

'Your mother sleeps with Leo Frankish?'

'Well, I don't imagine they spend all night discussing Dickens . . .' I watched as he ran a hand through his thick gold hair, a now familiar gesture of concern, and I wriggled out of my remaining underwear impatiently. 'Michael . . . are we going to spend all night discussing them?'

We didn't, and the shedding of our mutual virginity proved an intense, emotional affair, charged with a passion that for all our previous fumblings, I hadn't foreseen.

'I want you,' I said, wincing with desire as his fingers found the place.

We were both naked now, gazing on each other's bodies in the glittering half-light from the night sky above.

'I want you too,' he whispered thickly, probing far inside, stroking, pressing, caressing with his thumb.

The Planter's Punch had brought us to the moment, a moment I'd been anticipating since that first night in the spinney, a moment for which, I thought, I was well prepared. I was nothing if not my mother's daughter, suitably primed and sufficiently empowered to take my fate into my own hands.

'I'll be careful,' he said doubtfully.

'Just do it, Michael. Please.'

'I might not be able to stop.'

'It's okay. I don't want you to stop.'

'Yes, but —'

'Michael! For God's sake. Just do it!'

The tone of my voice made us both jump, and then he did it, ramming into me with remorseless rhythm, pounding and shuddering, and when inept attempts at control were finally abandoned, exploding in a fury that made the flimsy settee tremble. For all I wanted it, I was shocked by the reality of invasion, and the sudden fusion of bodies seemed so ultimate and animal a thing that I could have wept in anguish for our lost restraint, an infinitely human quality which we seemed, suddenly and irrevocably, to have shed.

But I was beaten to it.

'Don't cry, Michael,' I muttered in fascinated alarm. 'What is it? Please Michael, don't cry!'

'I'm sorry,' he sobbed, 'I'm sorry,' and when at last he forced himself up from between my legs, face still wet and the bright hair plastered on his cheeks, I was sick with fright at what might follow, expecting no less than a dictate from St Paul on the evils of fornication.

'I love you, Beth,' he said shakily. 'And I swear to God I always will.'

'Oh, I love you too,' I whispered, sobered and sore but nevertheless sincere.

We both cried then, and told each other that all things were not only possible in Love, but right. And for a moment it seemed that a fragile belief called Romance had been put to physical trial, and had stood the test.

But then the vulgar bits and pieces of reality, the inescapable truths of gender and biology, conspired to make their unpalatable point.

'You might be pregnant,' he said softly, taking my hand and raising it to his lips.

'No, I'm not,' I admonished dreamily. 'I'm on the Pill.'

I saw the error at once, and tried to redeem it. 'I got it for my periods,' I said quickly. 'The doctors give it out to make you regular. Everybody takes it . . .'

There was a long pause, and the world lurched on its axis.

'Why didn't you tell me?'

'It's private,' I said lamely. 'I didn't like to.'

He sat up suddenly and reached for his jeans, scrambling into them with an urgency that I couldn't mistake.

'That's not the way it's supposed to be, Beth,' he said bitterly, buttoning his shirt as he opened the conservatory door. 'You should have told me the truth. You're nothing but a little tramp.'

The empty day gave way to empty night. Still no Jamie, and I opened a bottle of Chablis to speed me through. I'd downed most of it when the phone rang, and as I grappled for the handset, I shot the remains across our prized Persian rug.

A long pause met my terse greeting.

'Hallo . . . Is that Beth?'

The voice was male. Low, cultured and immediately familiar, though I hadn't heard it in more than a decade.

'Who is this?' I demanded, convinced that either the wine or my preoccupation with Eva, or possibly both, had driven me to delusion.

'It's Michael, Beth. Michael Cameron.'

The room began to undulate gently, a dizzying spectacle of colours and lights with the Hockney print dancing in the middle. My hand flew to Eva's silver cross at my throat.

'Is this a joke?' I snapped, summoning my wits. 'Who's speaking? And how did you get this number?'

'It's Michael Cameron,' the voice repeated cautiously. 'Sorry to call you out of the blue.'

My mind careered through unlikely possibilities and with drunken logic settled upon the most bizarre. I had conjured him up. I hadn't thought of him in years, hadn't spoken his name until that night in the

Paris convent, and now here he was, the material embodiment of my fevered remembrances, emerging like the genie from the lamp.

'I hope you don't mind me ringing you at home,' he said at last, breaking the silence in which I struggled for an appropriate response. 'I realise it must seem a little odd.'

Odd? Oh God. Was this the start of booze-induced hallucinations, or some unholy, supernatural force at work in my life?

'How did you get this number?' I repeated, desperate to establish some kind of control, vowing that if this be hallucination, then I was damned if I'd let the other guy know. There was a brief pause.

'I can't quite remember,' he offered uncertainly. 'From Sarah, I expect.'

My sister's name brought me back to the moment.

'I'm very surprised to hear that,' I said coolly, deciding now that this had to be an extraordinary coincidence unconnected with my experience in Paris. 'Sarah knows I'm very careful with my private number. I'll take it up with her next time I'm visiting . . .'

The truth was that Sarah and I never spoke of the Camerons, and I couldn't imagine under what circumstances we'd do so now.

'She probably won't remember either,' he said. 'And anyway, it's not important. I wonder, did Sarah happen to tell you where I'm living at the moment?'

The room was now rotating at alarming pace, and I grabbed at the arm of the sofa, fearing I might fall off. What in God's name was going on? Why would my sister know where Michael Cameron lived?

'A small village in rural Northumberland,' he was saying, 'set in a bay on the edge of the sea . . .'

I stared into the phone, dazed. Whatever the purpose of this unprecedented communication, real or unreal, I wanted no small talk, no polite exchange of personal history.

'Look, I don't give a damn where you live,' I retorted. 'Will you kindly tell me why the hell you're calling up?'

I was perversely pleased to hear his discomfort.

'I'm sorry,' he said quickly. 'It concerns an obituary I read in this morning's *Sunday Chronicle* about an old Hollywood actress . . .'

The spinning room gathered speed, the Hockney print began to blur. I touched the silver cross again, fingering its smooth, solid surface.

'You mean Eva Delamere?' My voice was a croak, incredulous, unearthly.

'The obituary said that you met her in Paris . . .'

'What if I did? What's it got to do with you?'

I was dimly aware that this hostility was unwarranted, but now I was losing my grip, on the white leather sofa in my sitting room, on the wall

I had so carefully erected between the present and the past, on the wavering line that separates fantasy from fact.

'Well, put like that, it has nothing to do with me . . . But I wondered how you'd met Eva Delamere, and what else you knew about her . . . Where she was born, for example.'

'She was born in Paris,' I snapped. 'It's all in the newspaper cuttings.'

'Oh, yes. The newspapers . . . Nevertheless there's something about Eva Delamere that wasn't mentioned in the *Chronicle*'s report . . .'

I took a deep breath. Perhaps I was going mad. Perhaps this was some kind of weird joke, Duval setting me up, maybe, first with the silver cross and now with a fake phone call. Or could it be that I'd simply spent too long alone and drunk too much?

'Something that wasn't mentioned?' I repeated smartly, persuaded finally that nothing could throw me if I refused to let it. 'Oh really? And what is that?'

'She's to be buried in my churchyard,' he said.

Book II: Eva

Chapter Four

I am required to begin a Journal for the Enlargement and Expression of my Personal Thoughts. (That is what Miss Lamont says!) By this method I may come to Know and Understand myself, and thereby avoid all kind of errors in my Future Life. (Miss Lamont again!) But it seems to me that a Journal should begin at the beginning, and as I have already spent twelve years of my life with no reflection upon the things that have happened, I must record The Facts. I was born upon the Eve of Easter, 1908, and my birth and early upbringing were both happy and uneventful . . .

The Journals of Eva Delamere, edited by Blanche Duval

When the east wind smacks the foam upon the jagged turrets of the offshore isles, it sometimes sounds like a great beast in pain, a creature that has lost its watery way from some legendary land and now seeks revenge upon a foreign shore.

The wind at such times, usually in spring and always when the tide is full, seems then to behave like a living thing, tearing at the bristly shrubs among the dunes as if in search of food, whipping up the waves in spiralling plumes, feverish and parched.

Indeed, on that angry April night, Easter's Eve, 1908, the stormiest of all such nights for many a spring, it was said the wind had ripped young lambs from their mothers' teats and tossed them into the air, throwing the mauled remains back into the fields as though some creature of prey had gorged itself until full.

No one at St Cuthbert's vicarage, however, secure in the warmth of a vigorous driftwood fire which crackled in the parlour grate, and equally content in the robust certainties of the Christian faith, was susceptible to such superstitions.

Blanche Brannen was busy with the teacups, pausing every now and
then to finger the white-gold filigree cross which hung at her throat,
while the vicar himself browsed among the pages of *A Singular Call to
a Devout and Holy Life*, hoping for some inspirational message to
underpin his Easter Day sermon. Edward Brannen was reading the
newspaper, and Harold was trying to outwit himself at chess, a stiff task
for one of the brightest fourteen-year-olds the Royal Grammar School
had yet been privileged to entertain.

Only young Richard Brannen felt sufficiently compelled by the
elemental uproar beyond the stout vicarage walls to leave his toasted
muffins and take a look.

He stood at the vast leaded window of his father's bedroom, gazing down upon the flying sand and the furious waters, straining his eyes
in the dying light for sight of St Cuthbert's island and its precarious tower which, local folk maintained, would surely tumble into the
sea on one such wild night. Indeed, a piece of stone had fallen in
a rogue storm only the previous month, precipitating a terrible accident.

He stared, and imagined himself the hero of some fine rescue,
launching out into the churning seas in his brothers' frail dinghy, noble
as Grace Darling herself, out to St Cuthbert's rocks where shrieking sailors clung for dear life to the shattered debris of their stricken
ship.

He stared, and then stared again. A small, hunched figure, dimly
discernible on the gloomy shore, appeared to be struggling in the towering waves. A long cloak concealed its precise proportions, but as it
faltered and threshed on the shifting shingle, he formed the impression
that the shape was female. A woman in the sea! A true drama, and a life
at stake! Richard Brannen, with a child's belief that the eye never de-
ceives, uttered a shrill cry of alarm, and clattered down the vicarage
staircase to inform his papa at once.

'Someone in the sea? On a night like this? Oh Dickie dear, do use
your loaf!'

Harold waved his bishop's pawn and laughed in the peculiarly mocking tone that some older brothers seem born with. But Edward merely
smiled and peeped benignly over the top of his newspaper.

'One April storm Tom Howard thought a whale had been washed up
on the beach,' he remarked. 'However, it was just sand, blown into a
great whale shape.'

'I didn't see a whale,' cried Richard, jumping from one foot to the
other, 'I saw a woman!'

Matthew Brannen stood up and patted his youngest son reassuringly
on the shoulder. A tall, sturdy man with unruly fair hair and dark,

weather-worn skin, he looked more like the fishermen he served than an Anglican cleric of High Church persuasion, and it might have been imagined that unorthodox appearance combined with unfashionable theology would work against him in the parish.

But an easy manner and a generous spirit had endeared him to a people denounced by John Wesley a century earlier as rude, lethargic and uninterested in the ways of the Lord. Matthew Brannen was what later generations would see as a man out of his time, and now, recognising children to be worthy of encouragement and respect, he went obediently with Richard to stand at the window overlooking the seething bay.

A great commotion quickly followed. Jed Marchbanks the gardener was summoned from his cottage, Harold was told to saddle the black mare and fetch Dr Orde at greatest speed, Blanche Brannen was instructed to make ready blankets and a warming-pan while Joan the cook was to heat her best broth. The vicar himself, pausing only to throw his greatcoat around his shoulders, set off across the treacherous sands, Edward and Jed at his side.

'Will she be drowned, do you think?'

Richard had been refused permission to join the rescue party, and now Blanche led him firmly from the bedroom window, fearing the worst.

'Your father will know what to do,' she soothed. 'He always does.'

But as the night wore on, it became plain that Matthew Brannen did not know what to do.

Drenched and shivering, he had borne a young girl back from the raging waves, wrapping her senseless form in his own coat, and when he'd seen that she was heavy with child, that one man must carry her, for she could not be slung between them, he'd swung her gently into his arms, shielding her dripping hair from the driving rain, as though the sea had not already done its worst. Then he'd laid her upon the bed in his own room, the only bed Dr Orde pronounced suitable for medical examination. He'd stood aside while Blanche and Joan rapidly removed her clothing, and he'd prayed for her deliverance, eyes open, seeking God in the primeval fury outside his bedroom window. Then he'd waited while Orde completed his prognosis.

Dr Orde, a small, neat man with a reputation for efficiency, had not hesitated to interrupt his Saturday supper to meet Harold Brannen's request. Now he surveyed his new patient with a critical eye.

'She'll die before morning,' he declared at last. 'The lungs are damaged. They will not sustain breath more than a few hours.'

'And the child?'

Dr Orde gathered together his rubber tubes and his compresses, packing them carefully into his brown leather bag, frowning at an instrument which did not seem to fit correctly.

'If I were to cut now, there's a slight chance I might save the child.'

'And is that your recommendation?' Matthew Brannen enquired.

The two men faced each other across the bed, the wiry-haired priest and the sober-suited doctor, men whose paths crossed often in the course of professional duty, men between whom trust and friendship might have proved valuable working tools. But they did not like each other; the one discerning cynicism, the other seeing only sentimentality.

'I recommend this wretched creature be allowed to die in peace,' the doctor snapped, picking up his bag.

'But if there is a chance?'

'A slight chance, Reverend. Those were the words I used. And just supposing the child were to live? What kind of destiny would await it?'

Matthew Brannen turned away. He did not need to be lectured upon moral certainties, the simple truth that those born in poverty and sin can expect only more of the same. As minister serving the Percy Orphanage in Alnwick, he knew only too well what the unborn child who lay curled in his bed, as yet secure in its watery world, might face if it ever came to birth. A life of institutional deprivation and neglect if it were lucky, the destitution of the streets if it were not. A boy might find a menial job, but would more likely fall into petty thievery. And a girl? The city brothels would claim her, exactly as, Matthew Brannen suspected, they had already claimed her mother.

'It is far more charitable, Reverend, to do nothing,' Dr Orde said heavily, adding swiftly, as though in ironic response to the question hovering above his own judgement, 'May the Lord receive her soul.'

Matthew Brannen, who had tended the dying and consoled the bereaved through twenty years of service to the Church, had never before faced such a choice. And now he faltered, unsure about what was right. Let the woman die in peace . . . Was that it?

'You must try to save the child!'

Blanche Brannen had been standing in the shadow of the bedroom door, and now she walked quickly to the bed, confronting the two men.

'Madam, I assure you, the possibility of success is negligible . . .' began Dr Orde.

But Blanche, a usually gentle-mannered woman whose unremarkable exterior concealed an occasionally fiery temperament, fixed the doctor with a baleful stare.

'There can be no delay!' she commanded. 'It is our human duty to rescue whatever possible from this tragedy! Dr Orde, commence your operation at once. We will help in any way we can.'

This time neither man argued, their doubts apparently subsumed in Blanche's awesome certainty, and in a moment the gruesome work began. Kettles were boiled, candles lit, carbolic soap sliced. At one point the young woman seemed to stiffen, as though she felt what was done, and if the doctor could have reassured his assistants, the pale-faced Joan, whose nervous disposition ill-equipped her for such a task, and the resolute vicar's wife, then he did not do so. He simply worked on, silent and grim-faced, raising his eyes from the girl's senseless form only to gaze briefly at the filigree cross that bounced upon his assistant's apron. Ridiculous that so valuable an ornament, so ancient and so prized, should be subjected to everyday wear. Suppose it were lost? He would speak to Brannen about lodging it with the bank.

Downstairs in the kitchen with Harold and Richard dispatched to bed, Matthew and his eldest son began on the task of examining the clothes.

They were of plain quality weave, such as a parlourmaid or upstairs girl might wear, but the undergarments were trimmed with French lace. Either the young woman had a rich benefactor, or she had indeed come from a city brothel.

But what was she doing fifty miles from the city? How had she arrived on this desolate shore, and why, if she were determined upon self-destruction as seemed the case, had she chosen these wild waters to take her life? The dank River Tyne flowed past the city brothels, and miserable girls regularly threw themselves into its oily stillness. When hope is gone, what does it matter where one dies?

'Papa, I've found something. Look!'

A tiny silk handkerchief, richly embroidered with violets, had been tucked into a hidden pocket in the petticoat. In one corner, palest pink stitching revealed a single name: Eva.

There was nothing more. Not a tailor's label in the cloak, not a laundry mark on the underskirts. Not an item of jewellery nor a maid's timepiece. Not a purse, not a pocket booklet, although it was possible these had been lost in the sea.

'We must make enquiries,' Matthew Brannen said, staring at the small square of silk with its enigmatic lettering, though as he spoke, he knew how fruitless this was likely to prove. The girl did not come from his parish, that much was certain. He knew every face within the boundary. Nor from a neighbouring parish, he guessed. A woman with a foreign-sounding name who took delivery of French lace petticoats could not go unremarked in the small communities of rural Northumberland. And he had never heard mention of such a person.

That meant the unfortunate woman had almost certainly travelled, in some manner, from Newcastle. And to trace such a woman, with only a single name to identify her, was virtually impossible. Her street comrades would keep her secrets. The police were unlikely to be interested. An advertisement in the *North Mail* might produce something, but such advertisements always brought a rash of informants clamouring for reward, requiring much sifting of evidence and a certain hard-heartedness in dismissing it.

Matthew Brannen sighed and bundled the sodden clothes into a laundry sack. Then bidding Edward goodnight, he went back to the parlour where only a few hours earlier he'd been sitting in comfort and peace with his family, contemplating the coming of Easter and the rebirth of Christian hope. He took up the sermon he'd been writing and began to read.

'Out of the human tragedy of the Cross was born the divine gift of salvation. Out of despair came determination. Out of tears, came joy. What then must we make of the suffering and death which surround us, if not to seize the opportunity for compassion, for tolerance, for vision and for reform?'

The parlour door opened behind him, and Blanche Brannen, her hair escaping its pins, her face flushed and eager, held out a tiny, still form, swathed in her youngest son's christening shawl.

'Alive!' she pronounced in triumph. 'A beautiful baby girl . . . Alive!'

Matthew Brannen nodded, as though in that moment all had become clear, as though the ways of God were no longer mysterious or hidden, as though what was to come was no more, no less, than what was always meant to be.

He took a deep breath and uttered a silent prayer. A prayer for the future. A prayer for this child, and for all other dispossessed children born into God's world on this wild and devilish night. Then he walked towards his wife.

For a moment he said nothing, simply stared down at the sleeping infant in her arms. Eva, he thought. Eva who came from the sea.

'What are we to call her?' Blanche asked, her pink face bowed towards the child, her voice suddenly hushed.

'We must make the necessary enquiries,' Matthew Brannen began, but as he spoke, he knew that nothing would be learned about the young woman whose fate had been placed in his hands, that nothing now could change the pattern of events he had foreseen. 'And then my dear,' he said slowly, 'if no information is forthcoming, and I rather believe that this will be the case, then I feel we have only one choice. We must call her Brannen.'

*

Six summers gone, and Eva Brannen was running through the wiry grass of the dunes, her tiny black boots kicking up the white sand, her bonnet straps streaming in the autumn breeze.

Close behind her, a sturdy youth came chasing, laughing, plunging between the dips in the towering turrets of sand, calling, calling.

'Eva, come back! It's not a game . . . We're cutting Harold's goodbye cake. Edward has gone to fetch Miss Forster. Harold and Lizzie will be there any minute! You're to come in to tea at once!'

Across the flat, empty beach, weaving between the scattered dinghies and the tangled nets, Eva ran shrieking with merriment, waving and bobbing behind the tattered sails. You won't catch me, Richard Brannen. You won't catch me!

She darted over the churchyard wall, dodging among the slanting slabs, past the nameless marble headstone with its enigmatic text, GOD WILL WIPE AWAY ALL TEARS, and past the frozen angel whose pristine arms embraced the glittering inscription: *Blanche Brannen, beloved wife of Matthew, departed this life April 12, 1914.* She paused briefly, as she always did at this reminder of her loss, but then with a child's gift for celebrating the moment, ran joyfully on and dived beneath an overhanging laurel bush, a favourite place, green and secret. He wouldn't find her here. No one ever came to this secluded corner with its mossy mausoleums and ancient, crumbling crosses.

Then Richard's cries ceased, carried away on the shifting wind blown in from the islands, and the churchyard fell still. He'd lost her. He hadn't seen her jump the wall, and now he'd run along the beach, imagining her concealed among the grassy dunes. She smiled, reckoning she'd allow him five minutes' searching before she rose from the bush to vault the sturdy wall once more. Then she'd creep through the soft sand and surprise him.

But the September sun had warmed the powdery earth beneath the laurel bush, and her hiding place was warm and comfortable. She was tired from the dash along the beach, and in moments, she fell fast asleep. Nothing stirred the sunny Sunday peace and her breathing was slight, no more than the sigh of the laurel leaves as they rose and fell in the warm air.

'Oh Harry, we shouldn't. Not here. It's sacred ground.'

'But my darling Lizzie, we've nowhere else to go. Anyway, these old buggers won't mind. They've been dead for centuries.'

At the sound of Harold Brannen's voice, Eva awoke with a start. There was room to squat beneath the laurel bush, and although she knew it was only Harold and Lizzie Howard, daughter of the landlord at the Dolphin Inn, and that Harold, Eva's favourite among her much-loved brothers, would shout with laughter were she to leap out upon

them, for some unknown reason she kept silent, crouching in the green
gloom, waiting, watching through the thick glossy curtain that hid her
from the sweethearts.

'All right then,' said Lizzie, settling herself upon the shady ground
in front of the laurel bush. 'But we must hurry up. The party will be
starting soon . . . Oh Harry, you will look after yourself, won't you?'

'It will all be over by Christmas,' he soothed, sitting down only inches
from the trembling laurel leaves to lift Lizzie's skirts, 'and it's a splen-
did lark. Half of Jesus College has volunteered. Lucas Forsythe, Marcus
Woolf, the Hon. Frankie Harrington and Paul Duval . . . We'll all be
there together.'

Lizzie began to unlace her camisole, and Eva, her face frozen in
appalled fascination, suddenly clapped her hands to her eyes, thinking
she might die, so fast and unnatural seemed the beating of her heart.
Then the sighing of the laurel gave way to Lizzie's little gasps and
Harold's eager grunts, and Eva moved her hands from her eyes to her
ears.

Afterwards, Lizzie began to cry.

'I don't want you to go,' Eva heard her say. 'I don't understand what
this war is all about . . .'

Harold said nothing, standing up to button his breeches, staring
white-faced into the thicket by the churchyard wall as though he had
suddenly glimpsed a ghost; not the aggrieved spectre of one whose
hallowed plot he had so cheerfully violated, but the ghost of history, as
yet unwritten.

'Let's get back,' he said roughly, yanking Lizzie to her feet. 'There's
not much time. God knows why they've organised this wretched party.'

Later, Eva, nibbling at her dark plum cake, pushing the chopped egg
sandwiches around her plate in the vicarage parlour, found it hard to
look her beloved Harold in the eye.

Instead she watched Edward, solicitously attending Miss Helena Forster, the squire's daughter, wondering if they, too, met beneath the
sighing laurel bush and if Miss Helena Forster unlaced her camisole
when no one but Edward was watching. Indeed, Eva wondered, could
it possibly be that all the world behaved in such a way?

'The trap is here!' Richard cried suddenly, and there was a great rush
of activity, doors slamming, dogs barking, the black mare stamping as
Harold loaded his valise into the carriage. Matthew Brannen stepped
forward, his ruddy face set in a wide smile. He clasped his son by the
hand, and if he believed it a mercy that Blanche hadn't lived to see the
day, then no hint of such pessimism clouded his brow.

Joan the cook, weeping loudly, presented a garland of flowers: lupins
and cornflowers picked from the kitchen garden. Jed Marchbanks

quieted the mare and motioned to Harold. They would miss the Newcastle train if they didn't set off at once. Lizzie sobbed silently, and
Miss Helena Forster seemed equally affected, burying her pretty pink
face in a fine silk handkerchief.

Harold kissed Lizzie, slapped his brothers on their broad shoulders,
bowed with mock gallantry to Joan and raised Helena's gloved hand to
his lips. He embraced his father and turned once more to Lizzie, lightly
brushing her cheek with his fingers.

But the last farewell was for Eva.

Kneeling on the cobbles of the vicarage driveway, Harold Brannen
folded her into his arms, stroking her long silvery hair, whispering her
name.

'My precious little sister,' he muttered. 'Remember me when I am
gone . . .'

And that night, understanding little of what had been and nothing of
what might come, Eva wept as she had never wept before, lost in the
terrible knowingness of grief which has no name, consumed by that pain
whose source rises not within ourselves and the petty details of our
individual lives, but somewhere far beyond, deep in the heart of the
perverse and petulant universe.

Christmas passed in a fog of disbelief, a fog as icy and impenetrable as
the silver mist which curled its cruel tentacles around the rim of St
Cuthbert's Bay.

'Peace on earth, and mercy mild,' sang Eva in the front pew at
church, her heart frozen as hard as her fingers. 'God and sinners reconciled . . .'

From his vantage point in the pulpit above, the vicar watched
anxiously. How long before this little girl might recover her hope, her
sense of joy, the Christmas gifts which death, for all its sombre power,
could never quite destroy? How black and enveloping was the shadow
cast by the loss of her beloved Harold? What could he do to make her
smile again?

'Some excellent news, Eva,' the vicar declared one morning the following spring, searching now, after a wearying winter, for anything that
might raise the child's spirits. 'The Forsters have taken on a tutor to
coach young Aidan. You're to have lessons too. Sir Ralph has been most
charitable.'

Matthew Brannen raised one eyebrow as if to comment upon this
hitherto unobserved phenomenon in the village squire, and provoking
no response from his daughter, who sat staring out into the vicarage
driveway as though she still expected Harold to come cantering up on

the old black mare, sighed imperceptibly, and knocked out his pipe upon the parlour grate.

'I know you're not fond of Aidan Forster, but it's a fine opportunity. Your French is already remarkably good, and there will be other lessons too. Latin, music and arithmetic.'

Still Eva said nothing, and Matthew Brannen looked keenly at his cherished little daughter, for so he regarded her, as surely as if her mysterious birth had been divinely ordained to provide him with a source of comfort his two remaining sons, for all their fortitude and love, could not quite match.

She'd known too much suffering, this wise-eyed child. She'd lost Blanche, and now she'd lost her beloved Harold. Thank God for Lizzie Howard and her little daughter, Harriet. Without a baby to delight in, Eva might truly have lost all hope.

Matthew Brannen stood up and walked to the girl's side. There was much he could still achieve. Eva's brothers had already given her more than most young women could hope for – the rudiments of a classical education. If that might continue now, and Forster had finally accepted his offer of a shilling a week for Eva to join Aidan's classes, then she might be eligible for the Church High School in four years' time.

'Come, Eva,' he said, leading her gently away from the parlour window. 'We'll walk up to the Forster house together so you can meet the new tutor. I'm told there's another little girl staying there, at the lodge. Just your own age. She, too, has lost her mother, but like you she's much cherished. She's the daughter of a very important person, the man who is rebuilding Sir Ralph's house . . .'

The Forster house, a gaunt and somewhat unlovely grey stone mansion, stood on a hill overlooking the bay, its south wall shielded from public view by the lodge which nestled amid a dense row of conifers, its sea-facing frontage a mass of glittering windows, now blinded from within by black drapes. This was the conservatory Sir Ralph had constructed for his wife so she might spend agreeable mornings looking out to the islands. But the windows had been covered for many a year, ever since the Forsters' elder son, young Ralph, dived from the rocky outlet of St Cuthbert's isle on the morning of his twenty-third birthday, smashed his head upon a submerged stone and drowned as his mother watched helplessly from above.

Now Sir Ralph was extending the house along its west façade, adding a ballroom, a library and guest bedrooms, a wing to accommodate his new friends and associates, the men who came to tour his vast munitions factory on the edge of the city fifty miles to the south.

Eva had visited the house before, mostly when Edward had been paying his respects to Helena, but she invariably felt oppressed by its interior gloom, and it was true she disliked Aidan, whose predisposition to scoff seemed to have grown along with the proportions of his home. Sir Ralph and Lady Forster were remote figures who passed at the end of long corridors, always hurrying elsewhere to supervise their building works or welcome their guests.

Eva's expectations, both of the tutor, whose efforts, certainly as far as she herself were concerned, would go largely unmonitored, and the little girl, whose important father would doubtless have imparted something of his status to his daughter, were not high.

But still, she walked dutifully along the beach with her father, digging her boot heels into the fine white sand, lifting her stinging cheeks to the keen east wind.

'Eva, look! The seals are playing. That means the storms are over and spring is truly here.'

Matthew Brannen was pointing out to sea, and Eva stopped her dilatory progress along the empty beach to stare at the shimmering rocks out in the bay. Sure enough, the emerald seas were frothing with activity, the waves boiling with a dipping and diving motion that meant only one thing. The seals had come back to St Cuthbert's isle. It seemed in that moment a speck of light to set within the long black shadow cast by Harold's death.

They walked on, past the silent churchyard with its weathered drystone wall, past the beached cobles and dinghies, through the grassy dunes and on to the stony road that led up to the Forster house.

Sir Ralph was seated in the drawing room before a vast array of plans and sketches; he looked up only briefly when the vicar and his daughter were announced, as though he knew nothing of the purpose of their visit.

'Ah yes, Aidan's tutor,' he said at last. 'He's in the schoolroom with Aidan right now . . . But first, I think, we must hear something from this new pupil,' and his eye settled upon Eva in her stiff mourning gown and her black felt cap, taking in the white of her skin against the drab material, the tilt of her chin as she rallied her spirits to meet this new challenge. Matthew Brannen administered an unexpected poke in the back, and the girl jumped.

'I can conjugate a Latin verb, sir,' she said. 'Or if you have a book of French prose, I can read you a passage. I can also recite from the works of William Shakespeare.'

'Is that so?' enquired Sir Ralph archly. 'Then, my dear child, let me hear all three . . .'

It was half an hour later when Eva, her face flushed and her heart thumping wildly, finished her recital of Portia's famous speech, and for a moment Sir Ralph seemed lost for response, his lips pursed in a peculiar, melancholy half-smile.

Then he laughed.

'She's been well taught, Brannen,' he said. 'Quite the little actress, is she not? And I do believe she might pass for a young Parisienne! Well, my dear child, I fancy you could teach Aidan a thing or two . . . And that may be all to the good.'

He smiled broadly, but Eva didn't return the smile. There was something cold and unloving at the heart of Sir Ralph, and she would not be taken in.

Helena was summoned to lead her to the schoolroom, and they walked together past the darkened conservatory and up the grand staircase, Helena subdued and unresponsive to Eva's questions about the new tutor and the important man whose little girl had not yet been mentioned. Eva guessed that Helena was missing Edward, fretting, as she was herself, upon his safe return from Flanders.

Outside the schoolroom door they both stopped dead, startled by an extraordinary commotion from within.

'You're a cheat and a liar, Aidan Forster!' a shrill voice proclaimed amid thuds and bangs. 'But you won't get away with it!'

Helena threw open the door. 'Tutor, I must protest —' she began in earnest, but there was no tutor present to receive her admonition, merely a heaving tangle of legs and arms upon the floor, a flurry of petticoats, a flash of bloomers, and then a piercing yell from Aidan, who sat up suddenly and broke into loud howls.

'She bit me!' he cried, pointing to the girl who sat on the floor grinning savagely.

'Get up!' said Helena commandingly. 'Get up, both of you! Your fathers will be informed of this behaviour. Eva, please sit down. I shall find the tutor at once . . .'

She hurried away, and Aidan Forster, throwing a fearful glance at the young tigress who was now gathering up her skirts and rising from the floor, ran blindly after her.

Eva stared at the dishevelled figure, her head a mass of wild dark curls, her pinafore awry, her smocking half undone, and the girl stared back from mischievous deep blue eyes.

'I suppose you're the vicar's daughter?' she said at last, shaking the unruly curls and smoothing down her pinafore. 'Well, I hope you're a better sport at chess than Master high-and-mighty Aidan Forster . . .'

'What did he do?' Eva enquired politely, knowing only too well that Aidan could never be relied upon to play fair, not in chess, chequers nor even tag.

'Moved his bishop the wrong way when he thought I wasn't looking.'

The girl was attempting to secure the extraordinary curls with a ribbon, frowning into the mirror on the schoolroom wall, arching and stretching behind her neck, grabbing at wiry strands which would not be contained.

'He's not just a cheat,' she said darkly. 'It's much worse than that. He's a liar. He dared to call my father a builder . . .'

'And isn't he?' Eva asked innocently.

The girl laughed.

'My father is an architect,' she said scornfully. 'Sir Ralph may have lots of grand friends and lots of money in the bank, but without my father there would be no big factory on the Tyne! He designed and built it. You might even say that without him, there'd be no guns to fight the war . . .'

Eva received this news in silence, wondering for one illogical moment whether this mightn't be a good thing.

The girl had caught nearly all her curls, but one coal-black twist still eluded her.

'Shall I tuck it in for you?'

The girl looked up. Her eyes met Eva's in the mirror, and then, in one of those rare and unexpected moments when kindred spirits recognise themselves and the bonds of class and culture slacken, never to be tied again in quite the same fashion, the two children smiled at each other.

'What's your name?' the dark girl demanded.

'Eva Brannen. What's yours?'

She pulled the ribbon tight and her smooth olive face was revealed as a perfect oval, wide and beautiful.

'I think we're going to be friends, Eva Brannen,' she declared, holding out her hand in formal greeting. 'My name is Anya. Anya Klein.'

Chapter Five

As I sit by my father's bedroom window, staring down upon the empty sands and lifting my eyes to the distant islands and St Cuthbert's ruin, I find myself thinking not so much of what has been, but of what will come. Is it true that the seeds of the future are planted without our knowledge or consent? Must we all become what the past dictates we shall be? Or is there in each of us a spark, a flutter like the first trembling movement of folded wings, a spirit which calls us to freedom? I would believe that it is so. That we are not simply the Objects of Circumstance nor the Tools of Time . . . Yet experience teaches me that history weighs heavy upon us all.

The Journals of Eva Delamere, edited by Blanche Duval

Edward looked older, thinner, with a shrapnel scar upon his cheek and a preoccupied look in his keen brown eyes. But he was still the same Edward, tall and smart in his scarlet-trimmed dress uniform, and he swung Eva into the air as she raced across the cobbled driveway to meet the trap.

'We're having a picnic tomorrow!' she cried, unable to keep the secret for a moment. 'It's your surprise! We're all rowing out to St Cuthbert's isle.'

It was the celebration she'd planned for Harold's first leave from the Front. But that leave never came, and now the world had moved on. There was Lizzie's little daughter, Harriet. There was Richard's sweetheart, Ida Charlton. And of course, there was Anya.

Two boats were required to ferry the whole party, *Lady Luck*, a smart blue-painted dinghy loaned by Tom Howard, Lizzie's brother, and the vicar's own rather tattered vessel, *Island Star*. Edward and Helena Forster, the guests of honour, sat at the prow of *Lady Luck* while Richard

and Ida took the oars. Matthew and Lizzie rowed the other little craft
with Eva and Anya minding young Harriet in the stern.

The sea was like cloudy glass, flat as a plate. The morning sun
touched the black rocks with glitter and the distant cries of the seals
drifted in on the breeze, a strange, guttural moaning which seemed to
disturb Edward. Briefly, he pressed his hand to his brow and Helena
turned to him anxiously.

'I thought I wasn't to come!' Anya whispered to Eva as they tried to
calm the fractious Harriet, trailing her little fingers in the tepid sea and
feeding her sweetmeats from the picnic basket. 'The Sabbath begins at
dusk, and your father had to promise we'd be back for tea. My father
trusts him because he's a Christian! Isn't that ridiculous?'

It was certainly amusing, but Eva couldn't believe there was anything
illogical or sacrilegious about the friendship that had grown between
Matthew Brannen, the country parson, and Emmanuel Klein, the master builder.

They were both men of learning, men whose religious heritage took
them to common ground and for whom the great divide, the birth and
destiny of the Jewish Messiah, seemed a matter not so much for conflict
as for inspired debate.

Eva had heard them talking in the vicarage parlour late into the night,
had heard her father's low sonorous voice quoting from Isaiah and
Klein's short, explosive bark as he read from the Torah. Then, always,
she heard the opening of the roll-top desk, the clink of glass and the
sound of laughter. It was as if the two men understood each other's
passion without sharing it, could allow the other his salvation without
seeking to qualify or persuade.

And yet Matthew Brannen embraced the saving grace of Jesus Christ
with passion and with hope, preaching love and repentance and justification by faith to every fisherman and scullery maid who would make
the Sunday journey to St Cuthbert's to listen. He did not waver, nor
prevaricate.

This much Eva knew, and sometimes when her dear friend Anya
stopped at the churchyard gate, refusing even to step upon the Infidel's
ground, she wondered how it was that her father and Emmanuel Klein
seemed to have overcome two thousand years of bitter history in a
decanter of ruby port.

'You'll be back for the Sabbath,' she observed to Anya. 'The tide will
be turning by afternoon.'

They landed the boats in a leeward cove and Harriet squealed in
frenzy at the sight that met her eyes. Dozens of plump rabbits scuttled
away to the green hinterland beyond the shore, their bright black eyes
winking in the sunshine.

'Should've brought my gun,' Lizzie remarked drily, sizing up the furry bodies. 'We could use a couple of those for the stewpot . . . Harriet! Get away from those rabbits!'

Helena Forster shuddered with distaste, and buried her nose in a pretty embroidered handkerchief. Matthew Brannen took her arm, leading her quickly away from the shore.

The rabbits were vermin, introduced by an unknowing hermit at some distant point in the past, and they were fair game for passing fishermen, who would often put ashore on St Cuthbert's isle to bag a pair for supper. Sometimes the bay resounded with gunfire, as though a bloody battle were being fought at sea. Eva, who was unsentimental about such things and enjoyed a hearty rabbit stew, was nevertheless glad there was to be no bloodshed today. She did not wish to hear a mention of guns, and she threw a swift glance at Edward, but already he was striding up the steep hill which led to the ruin, hurrying after Helena who now seemed quite overcome, though whether at the thought of slaughtering rabbits or the effort of the climb, Eva could not tell. The vicar stopped and gently mopped Helena's face with the embroidered handkerchief.

The island was a barren, unprepossessing ledge of rock loved of few but the terns, the puffins and the seals. Visitors came to picnic and watch the birds nesting or the seals at play, but no one had attempted residence since the seventeenth century when a virtuous monk built a tower on the spot where it was believed St Cuthbert had prayed during his long, lonely sojourn on the isle.

'Is that the monk's tower?' Anya asked suspiciously, staring at the pile of wind-pocked stones that rose into the breathless air, still sound but for the tip of the western wall which had tumbled into the sea a decade before.

'You needn't go inside,' Eva smiled. 'Oh look! They've chosen the picnic spot and Lizzie is setting out the cloth.'

They dined on salt beef sandwiches and mustard chutney, slivers of hard-boiled egg and crisp white lettuce from the kitchen garden. There was gooseberry pie and shortbread to follow, and clear, icy water from the monk's well to drink. Lizzie presided, as though this were her natural role, and Ida Charlton, who would surely become Richard's fiancée before he went away to war, made it her business to select the juiciest sandwiches, the choicest slice of pie, for the vicar. Helena and Edward sat some little way apart, gazing down into the tranquil blue sea.

The picnic was not what Eva had hoped. She remembered happier times, when the brothers had chased her among the rabbits and she'd played hide and seek with her father. Once Harold had taken her up the fragile steps to the top of the tower, pointing out the spot where divers used to plunge into the sparkling sea until the terrible accident which killed young Ralph Forster had put an end to all such escapades.

Now Harold's absence seemed to hang upon the picnic party, at least for Eva. Helena still seemed distressed, and Ida Charlton had gone to sit with her, producing lavender salts from the depths of the picnic basket, thoughtfully provided by Joan the cook in case the sea should turn rough. Edward showed little interest in the food, and though he tried to make Eva laugh with tales of railway journeys and incompetent porters, he had an odd habit of stopping mid-sentence as if some other thought had occurred and would not be dismissed. Richard, meantime, had fallen asleep, and Matthew Brannen was strangely preoccupied, walking around the old ruin and gazing down into the sea, his brow furrowed, his lips tight. Only Lizzie, who might have been expected to miss Harold most of all, was cheerful, chopping up the picnic remains and merrily marshalling the children to feed them to the puffins that waited hopefully only a few feet from the cloth.

Later Eva took Harriet and Anya to watch the seals at play, the older girls reclining lazily upon the wiry clumps of sea pinks which cushioned the shore while the baby tore at the tough green stalks in frustration, trying to collect enough for a posy. Eva made a chain from the vivid flowers and wound it through Harriet's bright gold hair, but the child was irritated and shook the blooms from her head in disgust.

'Even she's not enjoying herself,' Eva said regretfully.

Anya sat back on her heels, resting from the task of prising shells out of the hard wet sand beneath a tuft of pinks.

'Well, I'm enjoying myself,' she declared, 'but everyone else is thinking dark thoughts . . . Edward can't forget the war and Richard can't forget that he must soon be going too . . . Ida's wondering if there'll be a wedding before Richard goes, and Helena is crying because she knows she'll never marry Edward. But I confess I don't know what's the matter with your papa . . .'

Eva looked up quickly. Anya's firm opinions rarely failed to amuse her, and although her conclusions were sometimes suspect, her information was usually sound.

'Why won't Helena marry Edward?' she asked at once. 'I'm sure everyone else thinks she will.'

'Well, you see, she must do as her papa says. And I think her papa has another husband in mind.'

Eva considered this in silence. The two girls had often discussed the engaging subjects of marriage and husbands, and indeed Anya seemed something of an expert in such things, declaring it an unfortunate fact that no man would wed Lizzie Howard now that she had a bastard child, opining that Ida Charlton was far too flighty for the serious Richard, and asserting that she herself would never marry for love, seeing that love was such an uncertain commodity. But Eva had never heard mention of Helena and Edward, and now she stared at Anya in alarm, fearing a refusal would break her brother's heart.

'You're wrong,' she said staunchly. 'Helena loves Edward, and if you love a man, then, of course, you have to marry him.'

Anya had uncovered a perfect pink shell and the fate of Helena and Edward was forgotten as she seized upon it with joy. Harriet waddled to the pool demanding her own pink prize, and for the next hour the talk was all of shells.

But Eva was preoccupied. For all their intimacy, she'd never told Anya what had happened in the churchyard the day Harold Brannen left to go to war, what she, Eva, had witnessed from beneath the laurel bush, the secret act which, she now understood, had resulted in the birth of Harriet Howard. She gazed unhappily at Edward and Helena. The ways of love seemed both perplexing and dangerous.

'Harriet Howard, you're an ungrateful little wretch,' Anya said at last, having failed to persuade the child to take all the shells if she, Anya, might be allowed to keep the pink. 'Have the lot, if you must, though I declare you're terribly spoiled!'

She gazed up at the sky anxiously. 'Remember,' she said to Eva, 'I must be home before dusk!'

Home to Anya was the pretty lodge cottage at the Forster mansion where Emmanuel Klein maintained a kosher household for himself and his daughter while supervising an ever-increasing volume of building works along the Tyne.

Eva often wondered if the Kleins missed their own home in Paris, but when she'd asked, Anya declared the question irrelevant.

'The Jews have no home,' she said squarely. 'Since my mother died we've lived in Poland, in Germany, in England and in France. When the war is over we shall probably go to America. Or back to Paris.'

Meantime the lodge cottage continued to offer merriment and hospitality to Eva and her father. It was upon the steps of the lodge that Anya invariably imparted her information and her opinions after luncheon or tea, and Eva always listened intently, knowing that her friend was uniquely placed to watch the comings and goings of the world as it made its way to the Forster house.

But that Sir Ralph should wish Helena to marry someone else? That Edward, her beloved Edward, might not be fine enough for Miss Forster? Could Anya be right? Helena, surely, would never allow her feelings to be denied in such a way?

As the picnic party set out for the mainland once more, Eva stared moodily into the silky waters of the North Sea, and it seemed in that moment as though the darkening depths contained all kinds of monstrous and unknown things.

'Land ahoy!' called Ida Charlton with a great shout as the leading boat beached on the soft sand. Edward handed Helena on to the shore, the others climbed out behind them, and the day was done.

'Did you enjoy the picnic, Papa?' Eva asked her father anxiously, seized suddenly by that melancholy which sometimes grips the heart at the end of a summer's outing.

They were walking home alone across the silent sands, but for once Matthew Brannen had nothing to say to his eager little daughter. His eyes were fixed upon his feet, and as Eva grabbed his hand, she found, to her surprise, Helena Forster's embroidered handkerchief, screwed to a minute ball in the centre of his palm.

He looked down at her then, and smiled, an anxious, absent smile that she hardly recognised as his own. But still he said nothing, simply quickened his pace so that they might make St Cuthbert's in good time for Compline.

In the space of that summer, it seemed to Eva that the world grew old. The pews at St Cuthbert's were packed with bowed heads, respectfully covered in black, and Matthew Brannen's preaching grew ever more impassioned. But when the Archdeacon of Lindisfarne recommended a short holiday in the country, he refused to leave his flock. He was charged to impart God's word, and he would not shirk his holy duty.

'Life is a series of random events and our universe is ruled by chance . . .'

The words from that particular Sunday sermon seemed to pound through Eva's brain, and she heard a muted rustle of alarm from the pews. It was widely rumoured that the vicar had gone mad, his mind irreversibly freed from its tenuous hold upon orthodoxy, cut loose by tragedy.

'Ruled by chance,' Matthew Brannen declared, clasping the great carved eagle that crouched upon his pulpit and gazing down upon the faithful who faltered beneath his stare, 'but not at the mercy of chance. No, my friends. Not at the mercy of war and suffering, nor at the mercy of death which overcomes us all.'

A woman sitting near the chancel step began to sniff and then to weep openly, and the vicar bowed his head. Two telegrams had been delivered to the vicarage in the space of a week. Not one of his remaining sons taken, but two. Both. All. For a moment Matthew Brannen's knuckles on the great wooden bird gleamed white, but when he lifted his head to his flock once more, his ruddy sea-worn face was composed.

'Love is the life-beat of this cruel, unconscious universe,' he proclaimed. 'Love, only Love, the name which all must speak. And where do we experience this love, my friends? Why, in the love we bear each other. Parent for child, brother for sister, friends and neighbours for each other . . . And yes, my friends, most of all, in that intimate relationship between man and woman which is the mirror of Christ's consuming love for his Church . . .'

Eva stared at the carved pulpit, uncomprehending, her face fixed in grief. Lizzie Howard sat by her side, head tilted in graceful defiance of any who might doubt her right to occupy the vicar's family pew. Across the aisle sat Ida Charlton, swathed in black, Richard's bright ruby ring still on her finger, her sister and her ma taking one arm each lest she throw her hands into the air and begin her keening once more. In the pew behind sat Sir Ralph, Lady Forster and Aidan, comfortable upon their tapestry seats, a luxury traditionally afforded the squire and thus far immune to Matthew Brannen's reforming zeal. Helena Forster was absent, reputedly unable to rise from her bed.

'I have seen the face of God,' the vicar announced, his voice rising in dramatic crescendo. 'Not only in starry visions and dreams of Heaven. Not only between the pages of the Holy Book . . .' He fumbled for a bible which lay beneath the lectern and brandished it wildly in the air. 'Not only in the beauty of this building—' he gestured towards the great stained-glass window which depicted St Cuthbert on his island retreat, a white tern feeding from his hand.

'No, my friends. I have seen the face of God most clearly in the love shown me now, in this, the hour of my need . . .'

Here Matthew Brannen paused and stared down at his daughter who smiled bravely back, comforted momentarily by the knowledge that whatever further woe might be visited upon her father, the mud of Flanders could not claim her too.

'In the commonplace details of a myriad mundane lives, the great story of Love is told,' Matthew Brannen concluded gravely. 'There is nothing Love cannot achieve, so therefore, my friends, do not despise it. Do not make little of your husbands and wives. Do not chastise your daughters and your sons without charity or respect . . . And never give way to Despair, my friends. Despair is the greatest, the most powerful, of the enemies of Love!'

Later that day, when the autumn sun had all but disappeared behind St Cuthbert's isle and the sky was tinged with crimson, they tramped the open shore, Eva and her father, Emmanuel Klein and Anya, looking for a sheltered spot in the dunes beyond the graveyard wall, a site where the sand mingled with the black earth of the hinterland, fostering the reluctant growth of a few wild irises.

Matthew Brannen carried a great iron spade upon his back, and behind him, incongruous in black dress coat, came Emmanuel Klein, also carrying a huge spade, and with it a long, thin stick. His daughter kept pace with Eva, each of them shouldering a canvas bag.

'Here!' said Matthew Brannen, at last setting down his spade, and the two men began to dig. The girls stood and watched as the trench grew wider, shivering in the darkening air.

'For Harold, for Richard and for Edward,' Matthew pronounced in a low voice, emptying the contents of the canvas bags into the trench. 'May these flowers bloom on the shores they loved so well . . .'

He seemed to shudder, his shoulders to tighten and heave, but then he began to cover the lifeless seeds with the precision of a man possessed, pressing the thin wet earth around each one with his bare fingers, scraping away the layer of sand where it seemed too heavy, sprinkling clods of soil along the length of the trench so that every chance might be given to new growth.

'Poppies won't thrive in this earth,' Anya muttered to Eva. 'They should have been planted inside the graveyard wall!'

'They're rock poppies . . . They flourish by the sea.' Eva had no doubt that the flowers would grow.

The work done, Matthew Brannen drew a battered prayer book from his greatcoat and began to read from the Vespers of the Dead.

'Rest eternal grant to them, O Lord, and let light perpetual shine upon them . . .' His words rang out across the still sands, borne aloft on the evening breeze into the thundering seas beyond, dying into windy voicelessness.

Emmanuel Klein cleared his throat.

'There is an old Hebrew prayer,' he said softly. 'A meditation which commends the dead into Yahweh's care. Hold hands, please . . .'

The girls stood in the middle, the men at either end. Eva listened to the strange melancholy language, her heart calm, her mind blank.

'Now Eva,' said Emmanuel Klein gently when he was done, 'write your message in the sand,' and he handed her the long stick he had been carrying. 'Any message. Anything you wish to say . . .'

Eva took the stick and began to scratch at the thick damp sand. *I Miss You*, she wrote, and then, as though this might not be enough, she added: *I Love You*.

Only when she was alone in her bedroom did the tears flow freely. Only then, when the wind had obliterated her words and it seemed the poppy seeds must surely be exposed if not blown into the turbulent waters of the North Sea, did she open her heart to the horror, the waste, of it all.

And as she sobbed and twisted and pulled at her silvery hair, pummelling her hands upon her pillows and flailing her legs up and down upon her bed, the words from that morning's sermon returned:

'Never give way to Despair, my friends. Despair is the greatest, the most powerful, of the enemies of Love.'

The rock poppies bloomed feebly the following year, but then as war gave way to peace, the green shoots multiplied and Eva too began to blossom. Matthew Brannen had nurtured his hopes for his daughter along with the memory of his sons, and the time had come to bring hope to fruition.

The road to Morpeth was neither long nor arduous, passing by green meadows busy with frolicking lambs and stone-faced villages where children shrieked in the spring sun. Indeed, the pony and trap arrived in Morpeth far too quickly for Eva, who wasn't at all sure that she wanted to be there.

The Church High School, offering preferential rates for daughters of the clergy, not only claimed to produce accomplished ladies with musical skills and a true understanding of the Christian life from the raw material of pubescent girls, it also offered, somewhat surprisingly, French education and dramatic art.

'Each year there is a production of Shakespeare.' Matthew Brannen, reading from the prospectus, had tried to enthuse his daughter: 'All girls are encouraged to participate and those with particular talents may receive Voice Coaching and Training in Dramatic Expression.'

Eva had proved an avid reader of Shakespeare, and under the encouraging eye of Aidan Forster's tutor, had excelled in recitation. Her heroines were Rosalind and Miranda, and when she could persuade Anya to take the complementary role, she liked nothing better than to act out their dilemmas.

But when the war ended, Anya and her father had left the Forster lodge for Paris, where Emmanuel Klein had new commissions. Lessons had become dismal sessions with only the petulant Aidan for company, and although the two friends corresponded with intense regularity across the Channel, Eva was lacking the company of other young women. The Church High School in Morpeth, always Matthew Brannen's ambition for his daughter, was now deemed a necessity.

'I think you'll like Miss Lamont,' he said to Eva as they rounded the watchtower in Morpeth town centre. 'A most enlightened headmistress, I'm told. And of course, my dear, if you're unhappy, I shall fetch you home at once!'

His kind words brought tears to Eva's throat, and she knew she must try very hard to be happy at the Church High School. She must practise her recitation and improve her French pronunciation, which had already earned the admiration of Aidan's tutor for its purity and precision. This much she owed her father who, she knew, was making a considerable sacrifice in letting her go.

But who now would serve his hot rum at suppertime, who would fetch his outdoor boots when he went walking on the beach or pick a jug of golden poppies to stand by his bedside? Who would play with little Harriet Howard on the sands, and who would visit poor Ida Charlton, whose grief had not subsided in two years, afflicted, so Dr Orde had told the vicar, with a debilitating emotional disorder for which there was no known cure?

'I'm sure I shall like Miss Lamont,' Eva agreed in a small voice. 'And the Church High School sounds very nice.'

Her optimism was boosted as Matthew Brannen's trap pulled into the driveway of a pristine town house and a tall, equally well-groomed woman with short grey hair and a wide open smile marched down the steps to meet them. It was further rewarded when Miss Isabel Lamont escorted them into her study, served them tea from her own silver pot, and proceeded to expound the philosophy of the Church High School.

'It's not that we expect our girls to emulate Miss Sarah Bernhardt,' she smiled, 'although, of course, that would be rather good! No, it's simply that dramatic art gives girls such confidence, such poise . . .'

She leaned forward, surveying Eva closely.

'And it is most edifying, is it not, this living out of other lives within the drama? What young lady could speak the words of Rosalind without absorbing something of her wit?'

Miss Lamont could hardly have chosen a better example to promote her wares, and Eva felt her reservations slip away.

'A true understanding of the Christian life,' pursued Matthew Brannen, anxious that all doubts be banished. 'That is a very large subject. Perhaps you could give us some little idea of how you pursue it at the Church High School?'

Miss Lamont stood up and walked to the window of her study, gazing out upon a group of laughing girls who were sketching in the garden beyond. When she turned it were as though to deliver a difficult speech, a performance which might not necessarily meet with applause.

'A young Christian woman should know that she is equal in the sight of God,' she said carefully; 'that in Christ there is neither male nor female, and that the purpose of his mission upon Earth was to bring each one of us to fulfilment . . . That is a true understanding of the Christian life as I see it, Reverend Brannen.'

The vicar smiled and nodded thoughtfully.

'Quite so, Miss Lamont. I too believe that young Christian women have a duty to themselves as well as to any man they might marry. . . . But may I ask, is this a subject you presume to include as part of your Christian curriculum? The responsibilities and requirements of married life, should this be what your girls choose?'

It was a delicate question, cautiously raised, but one which a widower with no close female relatives must surely ask of his daughter's headmistress.

'We instruct our girls in matters of hygiene,' replied Miss Lamont briskly, 'and we hope they emerge from our care with a sense of what life may hold in store.'

It was understood, and this time they both smiled, turning expectantly towards the new pupil.

Eva looked round at the study, lined with volumes of Shakespeare and the Lives of the Saints. She looked at Miss Isabel Lamont, who had chosen to devote her energies to giving young women a good opinion of themselves. She looked out of the window at the girls in the garden, neat in their navy blue smocks and now quietly absorbed by their sketchpads.

'I should like to see the dormitory,' she said bravely. 'And I should like to be allowed to the gate to wave my father goodbye.'

Under Miss Lamont's careful tutelage, Eva grew up.

She learned to weigh her desires against what was practical, and yet retain her hopes in what might be possible, considering that nursing might be a more sensible career than the stage, but that the theatre would remain a part of her life.

She also learned about hygiene, and mammal reproduction, she learned how to speak impeccable French, and she learned to deliver the great speeches of William Shakespeare with ever-increasing flair and conviction. But there was much she still had to learn.

'Everything changes,' she wrote one summer's evening in the journal Miss Lamont urged all her girls to keep. 'Nothing is for ever. People fall in love, then they lose their lovers, and so they fall in love with someone else . . .'

She was sitting among the dunes, the brilliant bank of yellow poppies dipping away before her towards the milky sea, watching her father apply a new coat of varnish to the *Island Star* and contemplating the ways of the world.

This had been a difficult homecoming. Not only was there the news that Lizzie Howard, contrary to Anya's dire prediction, was to marry a fisherman from Farnworth, twenty miles up the coast, but Helena

Forster had called on Eva's first afternoon back at the vicarage with a new companion at her side.

Joan had shown them into the parlour, for there was no longer a downstairs maid.

'I want you to meet Paul Duval,' Helena had said briskly of the tall, dark-haired gentleman whose empty sleeve was tucked neatly into his pocket. 'His father is French, but his mother was English. He was educated here, and he was a friend of your brother's.'

Eva was sure she must mean Edward, and she smiled uncertainly, wondering if Helena were now reconciled to the loss of her sweetheart or if she still sorrowed at mention of his name. But it was Harold whom Paul Duval had known.

'Your brother was a fine sportsman and a soldier,' he said, sitting beside Eva on the stiff leather sofa and cleverly extracting a cigarette from a silver case with his one good hand. 'He was a wonderful joker, and a first-rate actor. He was also my very good friend. We were at Cambridge together, before the war . . .'

Eva's memories of Harold had begun to fade. She still kept his likeness upon her bedroom mantel, and lit a candle each year upon the anniversary of his death. But she had lost the sense of his fun, his endless good-natured mocking, his lightness of heart. Now his presence returned in a rush of remembrance, and she was forced to swallow hard.

'He told me all about you,' said Paul Duval with a kindly smile. 'Eva *de la mer*, he called you: Eva who came from the sea.'

Eva had smiled back. She'd no idea what this kindly man was talking about and she was concentrating hard on keeping back the tears. She did not want to upset Helena.

'It was good of you to come,' she'd said at last, and Paul Duval stood up, bowing politely. Eva extended a hand and then flushed with embarrassment, realising for the first time that it was his right arm he'd lost. But Duval merely offered his left and pumped her hand vigorously.

'You must come and see us when we settle in France,' he'd said heartily. 'We'd be delighted, wouldn't we, Nell?'

Helena had seemed flustered, and Eva had been confused. Only later did she realise that the purpose of the visit had nothing to do with Harold.

Now, sitting among the bright gold flowers, the living reminder of her lost brothers, she chewed her lead pencil in melancholy meditation.

'It seems that Ida Charlton alone has proved constant,' she thought, 'and yet everyone knows that poor Ida is mad . . .'

Matthew Brannen looked up suddenly from his labours on the prow of the *Island Star*, aware that his daughter was unusually quiet. He saw

the thick leather-bound notebook in her hand and smiled indulgently.
The journal was a weighty matter, this he knew, and he would never
interfere nor question. But Eva caught his eye and, snapping the volume shut, ran down to the flat sand where the boat rested.

'I was thinking how beautiful the poppies are this year,' she said
uncertainly, knowing this wasn't what she'd been thinking at all. She
stood back to admire the *Star*'s new coat of varnish, and Matthew
Brannen surveyed her carefully.

'There were many who said they'd never bloom in this sandy soil,'
he replied at last, 'but the ways of Nature are surprising.'

Eva said nothing, and Matthew Brannen sat down upon the dry sand,
pulling his pipe and tobacco tin from his pocket, leaning back against
the unvarnished stern of the *Star*.

'Like the ways of men and women, Eva,' he went on. 'They can be
rather surprising too, I'm sure you'll agree . . .'

He was inviting her to speak, and she did not hesitate, her pain and
confusion flowing forth in a torrent of angry questions.

'How can Helena forget Edward so soon? Is it true that Sir Ralph
prevented them marrying? Don't you despise the Forsters – all of
them?'

He listened gravely to her questions. Was Helena too grand for a
vicar's son, as Anya had said? And what of Paul Duval? Did Helena love
him the way she'd loved Edward? What, too, of poor mad Ida and her
delusion that Richard had not died at Vimy Ridge but was wandering
the Flanders plains, wounded and senseless, endeavouring to return to
her arms? Wasn't she, Ida, the one true keeper of Love's Flame?
Good heavens, even Lizzie had forsaken Harold's memory and was
about to entrust little Harriet's upbringing to a fisherman from Farnworth . . .

Matthew Brannen nodded and smiled, and did his best. It was true,
he confessed, that Sir Ralph had wished Helena to marry Paul Duval.
But Helena would never entirely forget Edward . . . although, as poor
Ida Charlton showed only too well, in the end you had to let the dead
go, to begin living again.

'As for Harriet,' he said soberly, 'a girl's place is with her mother . . .
In the normal course of events, that is . . . So Harriet will grow up in a
new family, and her mother's husband will be her father. That's as it
should be, and we, Eva, must let her go.'

And then, knowing this to touch only sparsely upon all she needed,
Matthew Brannen tried to explain what the Church High School's lessons upon hygiene and mammal reproduction, for all their noble intent,
had not begun to encompass.

'One day, Eva, you'll experience passion,' he said. 'You'll believe that nothing could ever separate you from the one you love. But alas, there are many things that may go wrong. War is only one of them . . .'

He paused, and Eva divined in that moment that he was thinking not of his sons and their sweethearts, but of his own wife, Blanche, dead of the consumption before Eva had seen her sixth birthday.

'I often think of my mother,' she said suddenly, taking his hand. 'I think I was too young to miss her at the time, and of course, I had my brothers and you . . . But now I miss her . . . Very much.'

He turned, clearly startled, searching her face with an anguished expression she did not recognise and she jumped to her feet, thinking she'd angered him in some unknown way.

'No, no,' he soothed, 'it's nothing . . . I was thinking merely that it proved an extraordinary blessing your mother died when she did.' He spoke awkwardly, in a tone she had not heard before, as if the right words would not come, although she'd never before known him stumble in his speech.

'I mean that she did not live to see the war . . . That she did not suffer the loss that I . . . that we . . .'

He turned away from her, facing the gently ebbing sea, eyes fixed upon the graceful curve of the shoreline edging the bay, white upon blue, the colours of peace. And if he thought in that moment of other times, when the sea crashed pitilessly upon the battered sands and the wind roared like a great beast in pain, when a stricken woman floundered in the waters and a child was plucked from her womb, then he did not reveal it.

'Come, Eva,' he said briskly, knocking out his pipe on the hull of the *Island Star*. 'There's apple cake and a new batch of scones for tea. Let's not keep Joan waiting!'

Chapter Six

I am forced to consider the value of talismans, for my father has left me the Brannen cross. He was quite plain about the matter himself. 'Don't be sentimental, Eva!' he warned me. 'The cross is a piece of jewellery, nothing more. It has no magical powers, and you must sell it at once if the need arises.' But he also told me that if it stayed with me, and if the moment came for me to pass it on, then I would surely know who should have it next . . .

The Journals of Eva Delamere, edited by Blanche Duval

There is a calm after a certain kind of storm that is brutal in its nonchalance, and so it was that bright spring day when the light from the east loomed hyacinth pink and the flat, open sky stretched into silver. A pale sun rose blinking and incredulous above the shadows of the offshore islands, and the North Sea shone like polished pearl.

Eva stood at the bedroom window, a diminutive figure in stiff mourning black, staring at the glittering shoreline and the great white sweep of the dunes, their sandy earth now tipped with flashes of brilliant gold. The rock poppies were in bloom once more.

She closed her eyes against the relentless brightness of the sea, and when she looked again, seemed to glimpse through the blur a boisterous fishing party. Three sturdy youths, caps tucked beneath their elbows and feet bare, were winding lobster pots from among the tangle of tattered dinghies that bobbed in the bay. By their side, a slight, fair-haired child clapped hands and waved her bonnet in the wind.

Herself. The ghost of her former gladness dancing on the empty cream sand. And running with her, always a little ahead but ever mindful of her inferior speed and her billowing aprons, those other ghosts, the laughing young men who would never dance again.

'Miss Eva . . . We're leaving for church now.'

Joan the cook stood at the bedroom door, strange in a black satin boater and cape, her brown country face crumpled by the emotion she could not hide. Eva smiled bravely back, smoothing the starched taffeta of her mourning frock, straightening the cap that perched upon her tightly coiled silver hair. And then, squeezing Joan's arm with gentle concern, she walked quickly from the room.

Down the great mahogany staircase she went and into the parlour where the sealed coffin lay. Last night she had taken leave of the still, silent form, bending to place her lips against his own one last time, undaunted by the storm that thundered in the heavens above, though when a flash of fire split the sky, briefly illuminating the pale skin of the corpse, she'd drawn back from the coffin in momentary alarm.

Now she merely gave a final rub to the bright brass handles, and shivering in the chilly air, moved quickly to the window where the morning sun had warmed a patch of threadbare carpet.

'Ah, there you are, Eva!'

The voice came from the darkness at the far side of the room, and she turned to see Dr Orde advancing towards her, an unfamiliar figure in black overcoat and top hat.

'I have something for you,' he said brusquely. 'The item your father asked me to retrieve from the bank . . . It was placed there when your mother . . . that is to say, Mrs Brannen . . . departed this world.' He thrust into her hands a small brown envelope.

'You will, of course, remember that it is very valuable . . . the only item of value your father possessed. I often sought to persuade him that it should be sold. Certainly it would have eased his finances in earlier years.' Here Dr Orde coughed vigorously and fumbled in his pocket for a handkerchief.

Eva fingered the tiny filigree cross which slid from the envelope into her hand. It was small but surprisingly heavy, fashioned not from silver as might have been assumed, but from white Celtic gold.

The Brannen cross. She'd heard the tale of its supposed origins among St Cuthbert's band of monks many times. Certainly it was ancient, and it had passed through many generations of the Brannen family. Her father had spoken of it on the day he died. His frail form had lain propped against the cushioned rails of his great brass bedstead and although he hadn't uttered a sound for several hours, the voice, when it came, was lucid and calm, betraying nothing of his earlier delirium.

'I have nothing to leave you, Eva. Except the Brannen cross. Orde persuaded me to put it in the bank. It's yours, my dear. You are the last of the Brannens . . .'

Now Dr Orde surveyed her critically as she gazed at the cross. 'I'm told it would fetch a considerable sum,' he said curtly, 'and I would advise you to think of selling, Eva. There is nothing else. No income once the household effects are disposed of, no other property of worth.'

'My mother wore it until she died,' Eva said with a modest show of defiance, remembering in that moment the warm, pink face of Blanche Brannen. 'And so shall I.'

With trembling fingers she fastened the cross around her neck. Something about Dr Orde's manner, rooted, perhaps, in the long antipathy between himself and the vicar which neither had ever sought to deny, unsettled her. Eva did not want the doctor's advice, would not become the recipient of his grudging concern. She would go her own way, and she would treasure the white-gold cross for what it offered: a slender thread of continuity in the unremitting chaos of life, a precious reminder of a family's ties throughout the ages.

The parlour door opened cautiously, and Joan's anxious face peered in.

'Miss Eva . . . Tom Howard and the men are here.'

The landlord of the Dolphin Inn, accompanied by five broad-backed fishermen, marched respectfully into the parlour and with minimal effort swung the mortal remains of Matthew Brannen on to their shoulders.

Out into the driveway they went, picking their way across the precarious cobbles, Eva behind them, poised and upright, nervous but proud, like a young pony on its first trial between the shafts.

Next came Dr Orde, Joan, Jed Marchbanks the gardener, and Rose, the downstairs maid who'd moved to the Forster house after the war, returned now to boost the meagre ranks of the Brannen retinue.

Round by the wind-blasted wall the sober party went, past the thrusting poppies, the fishermen sweating beneath their unaccustomed collars, kicking the sand from their shiny black boots.

Eva stared fixedly at the shifting ground beneath her feet, as though she could not contemplate the view she and her father had so often shared. A fresh spring breeze whipped the shoreline into white, touching the glinting waves with foam. Above the humps of the Coquet rocks the terns swooped and dived in eternal forage, their jeers carried to the shore on the wind. Out in the bay St Cuthbert's tower rose like a sentinel to heaven, as though its vanished guardians still kept eye for Viking marauders from the east.

The casket swayed on, through the yew gate, between the rows of sea-stained crosses and weatherbeaten angels, into the cavernous church, stopping at last by the eagle's breast on the great carved pulpit. Only then did Eva raise her eyes from the ground.

She saw line upon line of pews crammed with Matthew Brannen's parishioners, all of them clad in their Sunday clothes, dark, respectful bonnets trimmed with black muslin, starched shirt fronts, polished shoes and carefully pleated cravats. Everyone was there. The fisherfolk, the farmers, the gentry and their servants, the girls from Alnwick Co-operative Store where the vicar had bought his tobacco . . . The choir, the parish councillors, the churchwardens and their deputies, the verger and the reserve organists . . . The entire Howard clan with all their children and cousins, Lizzie and her fisherman husband from Farnworth, and Harriet Howard, standing a little apart from the rest, a slender, self-possessed young woman with shining, dark gold hair just like her father's . . .

Then the Charltons, minus poor Ida, and Sir Ralph and Lady Forster with Aidan, still in their padded pew, and Miss Isabel Lamont in a discreet but stylish purple two-piece . . .

'I am the Resurrection and the Life, saith the Lord,' began Matthew Brannen's curate in faltering tones. 'He that believeth in me, though he were dead, yet shall he live . . .'

The eulogy was delivered by the Archdeacon of Lindisfarne, a tall, kindly-looking man with the meditative air of the monks whose territory he'd inherited. He spoke of passion and of fire, the forging, cleansing fire of the Holy Ghost, and of trust, that Christian virtue most exquisitely displayed in the life of Matthew Brannen.

'He wept, but he did not despair. He knew that God would never leave his loved ones comfortless . . .'

There was talk, too, of the late vicar's controversial views, his belief that all people, Christian and Infidel, were equally loved of the Lord, his hope for a world in which pacifism would prevail, his assertion, often repeated from the pulpit where the archdeacon now stood, that the God of Jesus was yet the God of Jacob, urging Christian and Jew to forge ahead together towards a new Promised Land . . .

It was as she stood at the graveside, heart empty, watching the dry sandy clods showering down upon the dark oak of the coffin, that Eva spied Emmanuel Klein, standing discreetly at the back of the assembled mourners. She had not expected him, had not known him to be in England. There had been a letter of sympathy from Paris, but not a hint that he might travel to his old friend's funeral.

She tried to catch his eye but he hung back, and when she looked up from the grave once more he had vanished, returned like the outsider he was to a world beyond the consolations of Christian community.

She smiled briefly at the well-wishers, and then when stoicism would serve no more, walked quickly from the churchyard on to the open shore. There was to be a wake with cakes and tea in the parish hall, and she would be there as required, receiving the sympathies of Matthew Brannen's many friends. But for now she wanted only the pale washed sky and the whisper of the waves, eternal, unchanging elements in a world that had been rendered hostile and unknown.

She climbed into the *Island Star*, beached upon the spot where her father had last hauled it, pulling the black taffeta dress around her knees, sinking her head into her chest.

It might have been minutes later, or it might have been an hour, but when Eva looked up again, Emmanuel Klein was standing a few yards from the boat, a small leather-bound book in his hand.

Without a word of greeting or consolation, he motioned her to his side, took her hand and then began to read the old Hebrew meditation; strange, incomprehensible words that were at the same time deeply familiar.

The incantation calmed her, but above the gentle, mellow sounds it seemed another harsher note rang out, the protest of her heart. '*There is no God,*' it seemed to say. '*There is only darkness and pain and goodbye . . .*'

Afterwards they searched the beach together for a suitable piece of driftwood. *I Miss You*, Eva scrawled in the soft wet sand. *I Love You . . .*

Emmanuel Klein left her then, and when she saw him disappear behind the seaward wall of the graveyard, a great cry of anguish escaped her at last, ringing out across the empty bay, unheard by all except the calling seagulls and the distant seals.

It was later that evening, when the wake was over, when the condolences had all been received and the vicarage settled into an odd, unnatural calm, that a rapping came upon the great brass knocker on the front door.

'Miss Eva,' said Joan, 'it's Mr Klein.'

They sat, they took a pot of tea, they remembered, and Eva allowed herself to weep.

'I'm fortunate to have a number of options open to me,' she said at last, drying her eyes. 'My post at the hospital in Alnwick has been kept free and I can lodge in the village, at the Dolphin Inn. Alternatively, I'm invited to live here, should I wish, with the incoming vicar and his

family. I could even offer French lessons to his daughters . . . And then
again, Dr Orde could secure me a nursing position in Newcastle should
I like to try city life . . . At the Royal Victoria Infirmary, no less, with
accommodation provided!'

She was trying to be strong, to be practical about her future. But her
fortitude collapsed in the face of Emmanuel Klein, sitting now upon the
stiff leather sofa where he'd passed many an hour in theological debate
with his old friend. She'd offered him a glass of ruby port, thinking it
might soothe them both, but he'd declined politely, staring in melancholy rapture at the bottle which Matthew Brannen had been in the
habit of producing from his roll-top desk.

'It's most useful for women to have an occupation,' he said at length.
'I often wish that Anya . . .'

He paused and then looked at Eva reflectively.

'But she leads a very gay life at her uncle's café. It's all fun and
laughter. And there are other young people. . . . My brother's boy
David, from California, and all the rest of the café's clientele . . . Writers and musicians and painters, and a young gentleman from Boston,
a Mr Bertie Levine.'

Here he paused again, removing the spectacles from his nose and
polishing them vigorously, seeming lost in his thoughts once more.

'And, of course,' he continued briskly, the polishing accomplished,
'there is Victor Martineau . . . My sister's son . . . No doubt Anya has
told you of her cousin, Victor?'

The last question was posed hopefully, and he looked intently at Eva
again. But she shook her head absently, fighting back the tears he had
unwittingly summoned forth.

'Victor Martineau,' she repeated, for it seemed he expected some
response, though she couldn't remember Anya having mentioned this
particular cousin. 'No, I don't think I recall that name . . .' She broke
off and buried her nose in her handkerchief.

'This is merely a suggestion to add to your other options,' Emmanuel
Klein said quickly, seeing her renewed distress and making to leave.
'You'd be welcome to live in my house, Eva, for as long as you wished.
And I do believe you might enjoy Paris.'

She stared at him in surprise, not having guessed his intention until
this moment, unable to voice her gratitude at this unexpected kindness.

He mistook her silence for doubt.

'You may prefer to retain your independence, of course. But if you
wished to take up your nursing career in Paris, I could be of assistance.
There is a small convent hospital not too far from where we live . . . I'm
sure that with your excellent command of the language and your Nursing Certificate —'

'I hardly know what to say!'

'Then please, my dear, say nothing at all until you've thought it over. You may reach me in London before the end of the week if you decide . . .' He fumbled for an address card in his pocket book and handed it to her.

'You're not staying at the Forster house?'

'Ah, no . . . I regret a parting of the ways with Sir Ralph. We are no longer associates, and it was inappropriate for me to stay in the village. I came merely for your father's funeral, and now −' he looked quickly at his watch − 'I must go and catch the London train. Think about it, Eva, please. My motives are not entirely unselfish. I do believe Anya would benefit greatly from your company . . . and, may I say, your influence?'

He bowed politely and was gone, leaving Eva alone in confusion. Paris? Anya, and her Uncle Jacob's café? Eva knew something of the life Anya led, although the passionate intensity of earlier letters across the Channel had lately been replaced by more sparse communiqués. Certainly, she'd heard of Anya's American cousin, David Klein, of the writers, poets, musicians and painters who frequented the café, of the drinking and debating that seemed to take up all their waking hours, and she'd wondered what Anya made of it all.

But she'd never imagined that she might live in Paris too.

How could it happen, when her heart, her very identity, was rooted upon these northern shores? There was nothing, surely, that could prise her from her precious memories. How could she ever leave the land she had loved so well?

The following day she found the handkerchief.

Tearful and weary, but with the restless energy that marks out the newly bereaved, she had decided to clear the roll-top desk in the parlour.

Knowing that what must be done was best done quickly, she'd already sorted her father's clothes and his books. But the drawers of his desk were packed with letters and papers, and she'd been delaying the task.

It proved simpler than she'd thought. His sermons she piled into neat bundles, tying them loosely with garden string. The bills and household accounts dating back over many years she threw into a basket for Joan to burn in the kitchen furnace. He had kept them, it seemed, despite Eva having taken over the household affairs, turning, she now saw with some satisfaction, a long-term Brannen deficit into a healthy profit. Her careful management of the vicarage garden produce, the small flock of sheep which church land allowed, and the fish periodically landed in the *Island Star*, had secured them a comfortable addition to Matthew Brannen's living. As he'd warned, however, none of it could provide for her future.

The sentimental items in the roll-top desk required more sifting, but Eva determined to be ruthless.

There were the birth certificates of the three Brannen boys. There was a miniature of St Cuthbert's isle painted on parchment by Blanche and dedicated to her husband to mark a distant anniversary. There was a satirical poem written by Harold for his father's birthday, and there was her own Certificate of Nursing, awarded by the Alnwick Memorial Hospital only a year ago and still in its protective tissue wrapping.

Then there were various newspaper cuttings. A review in the *Morpeth Gazette* acclaiming Miss Eva Brannen's performance as Viola in the Church High School's end-of-year performance. Another review, this time from the *Alnwick Herald*, noting that 'Miss Eva Brannen, a cadet nurse at the Memorial Hospital, makes a most welcome addition to the Alnwick Players.' And a further item from the *Herald* concerning Isabel Lamont, who had 'scandalised the parents of pupils at the Church High School by seeming to support the cause of Women's Suffrage in her Founders' Day speech'.

She discarded everything except Blanche's painting and the nursing certificate, which she looked at now with gratitude. In the years since she'd left the Church High School, Eva had not only secured her own livelihood, she'd had the comfort of knowing herself fully qualified to care for her father in his final illness. She put the certificate carefully to one side and returned to her task.

The handkerchief was concealed in a small velvet box at the back of the bottom drawer. She opened the box carelessly, expecting a specimen shell from the seashore or an isolated cufflink, and had not been perturbed by the piece of faded silk with its embroidered name: *Eva*. She imagined her father had bought it in Alnwick years ago, and simply forgotten to present it. She fingered it fondly and tucked it into her sleeve.

'Where did you find that, Miss Eva? That handkerchief was never meant for you to see . . .'

Joan, serving supper for one in the dining room, was transfixed by the piece of silk which had dropped on to the table as Eva reached for her spoon.

'It was in the old desk . . . And whatever do you mean, Joan, not meant for me to see?'

The words were regretted at once, and Joan, flustered by the circumstance and still deeply grieved at the death of her beloved employer, suddenly burst into loud sobs.

'I can't tell you, Miss Eva,' she cried. 'You ask Dr Orde, if you must know. He always said you should have been told. But it's not for me to tell you now . . . Nor for me to say your pa should have spoken up before he died.'

With that she ran from the room, leaving Eva to stare at the crumpled handkerchief in growing anxiety. Something nagged at her memory, dipping in and out of her grasp . . .

And then she recalled a stormy evening when her father had been gripped by one of his mysterious fevers, a night so wild that yet another piece of St Cuthbert's tower had been shaken loose and plunged into the sea. Her father had struggled to the window in his bedroom, staring out across the reeling dunes, and in his delirium, had muttered something about an embroidered handkerchief . . . an embroidered handkerchief and a French lace petticoat. What was it he'd said? Try as she would, Eva could not remember. But she would ask Dr Orde. Most certainly. She would ask him just as soon as she could.

The next morning they walked along the dazzling shore together, following the ragged trail of seaweed that marked the high point of the vanishing tide, Eva listening in growing disbelief to Dr Orde's gruff words.

The catcalls of the birds and the guttural yelps of the seals seemed suddenly to mock her former assurance, as though nothing was now what it had seemed and the noises of wild creatures no longer the friendly, familiar voices she had once known.

'Extensive enquiries were made,' the doctor mumbled, striding ahead through the shifting sand, pausing every now and then so Eva might fall back into step, 'but very little was discovered. You were taken to the Alnwick orphanage for the first few weeks of your life. Your mother – that is to say, Blanche Brannen – was concerned that everything be done according to the regulations. You were formally adopted once it was certain no relatives of the unfortunate young woman could be found . . .'

Her mind was curiously vacant, emptied by the unreality of the moment. She could think only that Dr Orde must feel uncomfortably constrained by his collar and tie on so mild a morning.

The doctor cleared his throat and ran a finger under the stiff ridge of linen at his neck.

'It was established that she alighted from the Newcastle train at Alnmouth, from which point she must have walked along the coast. Impossible to imagine how she came so far in her condition on such a night . . .'

Eva stared at the sea, benignly blue to the horizon's edge, milky as bathwater at her feet.

'The sea was truly wild that evening. It had been a vicious spring, mad as March one minute, balmy as June the next. Only the week before, a piece of St Cuthbert's tower had been felled by the wind . . .'

Pitching seas and furious winds. She had known them all her life, but now it seemed there was only this insidious, becalmed ocean, flowing into eternity.

'The mystery is what she was doing at all in this part of the country. She had not been resident in Newcastle, it seemed. A porter remembered assisting her at the Central Station. She had arrived on the London train . . .'

Pitching seas, the roar of the waves. Now she could hear them inside her head, beating out their remorseless rhythm.

'The City of London police were asked to investigate. Your father – the vicar – he had some idea she might be foreign. The name, I suppose. Eva . . . And indeed, police efforts revealed that a woman answering the description had entered England some days previously . . . on the boat from France. But unfortunately her identity could not be uncovered . . .'

The boat from France. Pitching seas, the sweet, sickly odour of engine oil. Eva could smell it, drinking in the stench until it tore at her throat.

'And the handkerchief?' she managed to gasp.

'A quality item, almost certainly hand-made in Paris. It was tucked into her petticoats . . . Nothing to go on there, I'm afraid.'

A French lace handkerchief. The pitching seas closing over her head, brine in her nostrils, wet sand dragging at her ankles.

'I always assumed, of course, that Brannen would do his plain duty and tell you all this. But let us think the best and suppose that at the end he was simply too ill, too confused . . .' Here Dr Orde paused, as if to reconsider the notion of duty, and in particular the duty he now performed, that of telling a bastard child the truth about her origins, a duty which, in truth, he had always planned to fulfil had Brannen lacked the courage to do it himself.

He seemed, for a moment, to falter.

'If you will permit me to say, Eva,' he began awkwardly, 'you were the child of his heart.'

He paused again, the romantic phrase hovering oddly upon his lips, a final belated attempt to do justice to the emotions of a man he had never understood.

'The child of his heart,' he repeated more boldly. 'As much his own as any of the others. A gift from God, he used to say. Eva, who came from the sea . . .'

The pitching seas, the towering waves, the long, black tunnel that was surely death itself, stretching into nothingness.

The pitching seas . . . Eva drew breath as though fighting for life itself.

'Excuse me, Dr Orde,' she said faintly. 'This warm air is a little stifling. Perhaps you will escort me back to the vicarage?'

Once inside the house she waited for him to go, assuring him she felt no untoward emotion. It was simply the shock, the sheer unexpectedness of it all.

Then when he was gone she wrapped her black mourning cloak around her and ran to the churchyard, throwing open the yew gate, and in her haste, leaving it swinging vainly in the breeze.

She ran past the towering angel and its testament to Blanche Brannen, past Matthew Brannen's still-fresh grave and its banks of wind-blown blooms, on towards the sea wall which once she'd leaped with laughing abandon as Richard Brannen gave chase along the sands.

Then she knelt by the enigmatic headstone: GOD WILL WIPE AWAY ALL TEARS. No name, no date. Nothing to signify who lay beneath the sandy soil.

Eva pressed her fist to her mouth. Her beloved father was not her father after all. Harold, Edward, Richard: they were not her brothers. Why hadn't he told her? Had his courage failed him at the last? What did he think she might do if the truth had been spoken?

She sat back on her heels. Who, then, was this woman whose bones lay at her feet? How could she, Eva, ever find out, when Matthew Brannen and the City of London police had failed? It was impossible.

Her fingers flew to the filigree cross at her throat. Now, surely, it belonged by right to Harriet, and not to her? She was no longer the last of the Brannens; indeed, had never been. She unfastened the cross.

Above her in the bright noon sky the terns and seagulls swooped and spun. Out on the island rocks, the seals sunned themselves in the mid-day heat. Nothing had changed, and yet everything was different.

For a moment longer she stared at the headstone, and then she turned away, suddenly composed. She stooped down towards Matthew Brannen's grave and selected a small spray of lilies whose creamy white petals showed no hint of brown. She walked back to the grave by the sea wall and laid them carefully in front of the stone.

Then she cleared a few withered flowers from Matthew Brannen's grave and rearranged the rest, working quickly and efficiently, making the mound neat and good. Finally she delved into the pocket of her cloak and hung the silver cross around her neck again.

The words of her father, for so she determined in that moment to remember him always, came back to her. 'The Brannen cross . . . It's yours, my dear . . .' He had deemed her the last of the Brannens, and so she would wear the cross for him, as the child of his heart.

And if the moment seemed right to give it away, then as he'd promised, she, Eva, who came from the sea, Eva *de la mer*, would surely know.

It was raining the day she left. Not the furious squalling of dark spring days, but a steady curtain of fine water which blocked the islands from view and enveloped the shore in a dank colourless cloud. The gaudy golden poppies cowered into the dingy dunes and the sand was grey as ash. There would be no farewell on the beach today.

She'd already made her final pilgrimage to the churchyard, crouching in silence at the unmarked stone once more, dismayed that in all the years she'd skipped so blithely through the graves, she'd never thought to ask.

GOD WILL WIPE AWAY ALL TEARS. If only that might be true . . .

On this ultimate visit she'd brought a vase from the vicarage, a robust and ugly cut-glass flute which had somehow escaped the dealer's inventory. Filled with poppies picked from the shore, it perched defiantly amid the wayward tangle of grass. The vase would hardly survive another violent spring, but nevertheless it seemed a tiny piece of herself to leave behind, a belated homage to the woman who'd given her life.

Matthew Brannen's grave had now been cleared of its mass of withered blooms, and she'd placed poppies there too. And for Blanche, who'd never known the poppies, she had gathered flowers from the kitchen garden, early lupins which flourished in the shelter of the vicarage walls. Then she'd risen swiftly and walked to the memorial in the village square, placing more poppies upon its new-cut steps, fingering the bright gilt lettering of the inscriptions: BRANNEN, EDWARD; BRANNEN, HAROLD; BRANNEN, RICHARD . . .

In the past few days Matthew Brannen's parishioners had called to wish her well. All spoke gravely and kindly of the late vicar's good works. None mentioned, nor even hinted, that they knew of his greatest good work, the rescuing and raising of a foundling child snatched ignominiously from the sea. And Eva did not ask. Better that she should play her part to the end, the vicar's dutiful and devoted daughter, the sole inheritor of his flesh.

There had been other goodbyes, too. Sir Ralph Forster had paid an unexpected visit, sitting erect on the stiff sofa in the parlour, eyeing Eva with a dour, disapproving expression that seemed designed to quell any deeper thoughts.

'I trust you will deport yourself well in your future life,' he said archly as he rose to leave. 'Your father was an honourable man. His memory warrants your best effort.'

'I'm sure I shall behave as he would have wished,' replied Eva coldly.

She might not know the detail of Sir Ralph's disagreement with Emmanuel Klein, but she was quite certain whose fault it must be, and she wanted her feelings made plain.

The truth was she had never forgiven Sir Ralph for refusing to let Edward marry his daughter, and after this frosty farewell, she intended no more dealings with the Forsters. She'd sent a vague, noncommittal reply to Helena Duval's letter from France urging her to visit once she was settled in Paris. There was no need, she told herself, to feel she must be polite, to fuss over Helena's children, nor to think that Paul Duval's long-ago friendship with Harold implied any special relationship with her. It all belonged to the past.

The day before her departure brought another clutch of farewells. The Charltons called with a present of a pocket needle-case worked by poor Ida, and Tom Howard came, accompanied by Lizzie and her fisherman husband from Farnworth. Miss Isabel Lamont came too, and shook Eva warmly by the hand, pressing her not to neglect her talent for the drama, nor indeed the precision of her French pronunciation.

'I'm retiring soon,' she told Eva, 'and I intend to purchase a small cottage in St Cuthbert's village. There'll always be somewhere for you to stay, Eva, should you wish to visit to your old home.'

Eva was touched by this gesture, though it was hard to imagine returning to St Cuthbert's.

She smiled, and nodded her thanks.

'Tell me about Harriet Howard,' she urged, for although Harriet had come to say goodbye, she had proved strangely sullen and unforthcoming. 'How is she getting on at the Church High School?'

Isabel Lamont took some time to consider her reply.

'Harriet is an extraordinary girl,' she said at last. 'Most talented, most accomplished. Indeed, only rarely have I encountered such a pupil, one whose abilities seemed so thoroughly natural . . .'

She hesitated. 'Eva, never once have I come across a girl I believed good enough for the professional stage . . .'

Eva smiled, surprised. 'Are you telling me that Harriet has the necessary talent?'

'I believe so, yes . . . However, that's not to say such a step would be wise. Harriet is a difficult girl. It hasn't been easy to advise her . . . I confess I've no idea what her future may be.'

'I'll write to her,' Eva promised, feeling that Matthew Brannen, who, while providing for Harriet's education had always insisted that she be left to her new family, could hardly have objected. 'I'll tell her she ought to be guided by you.'

Miss Lamont frowned.

'I don't imagine that will make any difference at all,' she said soberly. 'And I would counsel against concerning yourself too much with Harriet. She seems to harbour a certain resentment that while she was your brother's daughter, she was nevertheless forced to grow up in a fishing family . . .'

Eva gazed at her old schoolteacher unhappily.

'You mean Harriet has borne a grudge? All these years?'

'It's nonsense, of course. Your father was most generous to Harriet. . . . But yes, I believe she considers herself hard done by. You, however, have your own future to consider, so think no more of it! May all go well with you, Eva.'

After this, it remained only to assemble the few clothes and possessions she planned to take into her new life, and say her goodbyes to Joan, the last remaining member of Matthew Brannen's staff.

'I don't see why you have to go, Miss Eva. And that's God's truth! What difference does it make? You're still the same person you always were.'

Joan had wept every day since Eva's announcement, blaming herself for the discovery of the truth about the handkerchief.

'Yes, I'm still the same.' Eva made this last goodbye with a resolution she didn't quite feel. 'But you're wrong about it making no difference. I don't belong to this place in the way I once did . . .'

In the cobbled vicarage driveway Dr Orde waited, stroking the steering wheel of his pristine Ford, its gleaming wings temporarily dulled with mud from the sodden lanes.

Eva kissed Joan and pulled her close.

'I'm not turning my back on St Cuthbert's and all it has meant to me,' she tried again, hearing her words fall strangely in the thin morning air. How could she explain to Joan that while her sense of her self held good, its centre had been subtly shifted, like a familiar tune reworked in a minor key?

'The Brannens were my family,' she said, 'but there's no one left now . . . I have to start afresh, Joan. And so do you! I'm sure the new vicar will appreciate your apple cake!'

'It was very kind of you to recommend me,' began Joan, weeping again, and Eva pushed her away gently.

'Goodbye, Joan! Goodbye . . . I'll send you a postcard from Paris!'

Dr Orde's magnificent vehicle glided off into the damp morning, Eva waving from behind the streaming windows, smiling, watching.

But she saw nothing of the rocky island with its crumbling tower, nor the golden poppies bending on the ragged dunes as she went . . . Nothing of the great white sweep of the shoreline, nor the battered flotilla of fishing smacks in the bay. Nothing of St Cuthbert's spire, nor the tangled churchyard with its weatherbeaten crosses.

Past the Dolphin Inn they went, and Tom Howard, sweeping the sand from his forecourt, raised a hand in silent salute as Dr Orde's car slid by.

Past the war memorial with its gilded list of names they went; past the great stone edifice of the Forster mansion and the little lodge house where Anya had lived with her father . . . Out of the shrouded coastal plateau they went, up above St Cuthbert's village and into the dank stillness of the hills beyond.

Her heart was composed, her mind made up.

'I shall always keep St Cuthbert's in my heart,' she whispered to herself. 'But I shall never come back. I shall never, never come back.'

Book III: Beth

Chapter Seven

The deepest psychological potence of the Romance myth lies in the notion of completion, the idea that there is one man for one woman, one special person set aside in the universe who will provide the lost half of the diminished self. And so the self seeks restlessly for its mirror image, picking over the fellow humans thrown into its voracious path, looking for the one who will provoke the right response, sound the harmonious chord, make all the dreams come true . . .

Moonlight and Roses: The Cult of Romance in Western Society, by Beth Carlisle (published by Harridan Press to accompany the Metro Television series)

I could scarcely believe what I'd been told about Eva Delamere. She was not the French-born starlet that every Hollywood history insisted. She was a North Country vicar's daughter, and she'd asked to be buried in her father's churchyard. St Cuthbert's churchyard. The Reverend Michael Cameron's churchyard.

I combed all the likely books, the most recent Carlotta du Bois biography, *The Anatomy of Cinema*, *The Making of the Stars*, the endless tomes on David Klein. There was nothing beyond what I already knew, and now knew from Michael to be wrong. I turned it over and round a thousand times, but it made no sense. All I could fix on was that I had to attend Eva's funeral, no matter how painful that decision proved to be.

I phoned Michael back after I'd recovered from the shock of his extraordinary call, heart hammering as I dialled, and when a woman's voice answered, friendly and intimate, completely unlike Clare Spencer's clipped tones, no matter how much she'd mutated into vicar's wife during the intervening years, I was thrown. My mouth was parched, my palm slippery as it clutched the receiver.

'Is that Mrs Cameron?' I asked uncertainly, knowing it wasn't but unable to form a more sensible enquiry.

'No . . . Who's this calling, please? Did you want the vicar?'

I got the impression that despite the amiable style, her task was to protect the vicar from unnecessary calls, yet when I snapped out my name and demanded to speak to him, she responded at once.

'Yes, of course. I'll get him. Hang on.'

Breathe deep, Beth . . . One, two, three, four . . .

If he were surprised to hear from me again, then it didn't register. If he were flustered at the thought of our impending meeting, then he didn't reveal it. Unlike our previous conversation when he'd been hesitant, unsure, now he was efficient and concise.

'You're coming to the funeral? Right, well take the A1 to Alnwick and turn off for Alnmouth. St Cuthbert's is signed along that road . . . You can stay at the Dolphin Inn if you don't mind roughing it. Just a minute, I'll get you the number . . .'

I wanted to prolong the talk, to get some inkling of how it might be when we met again, to know whether we might greet each other as rueful adults looking back on a failed teenage romance, or whether the past would still hang heavy upon us. But he showed no willingness to extend the conversation, and I divined nothing beyond the arch courtesy, an onerous formality which promised only vacant smiles and guarded exchanges when we met.

'How was this funeral arranged?' I barked into the phone. 'There must be somebody who knows all about Eva. Where do I go for details?'

'I can't tell you anything more,' he said quickly. 'I'm sorry.'

'Then who can?'

There followed a brief silence and I waited with barely controlled agitation, anticipating the irony of what was to come.

'There's one person you could try,' he offered at last. 'You may already know him . . . Daniel Duval?'

Now I knew that Duval had been in England, not to see me, nor to deliver Eva's gift, but to organise the burial. Now I knew there had to be more to Eva's appearance in *The Rose Garden* than he'd wanted me to think. Why wouldn't he come clean? Eva had left me the silver cross, and no doubt it was a worthless trinket, but it still meant she'd liked me, trusted me even. Why wouldn't Duval do the same?

He didn't answer his Paris phone nor respond to any of my curt messages, and when I tried Louise at the editing suite, she told me he was staying with his mother.

'His mother? What the hell for? Is she ill?'

'A family crisis,' Louise confided. 'I'll tell him you called.'

But if she did, it made no difference. Duval had disappeared from my life, and although this was precisely what I'd intended, to my confusion it not only rankled, it hurt.

Now I could focus only upon Eva's funeral, and the knowledge that at her graveside I would encounter two former lovers, each of them, I guessed, determined to conceal our relationship from the other. Well, they could do as they wished. I was going for Eva, that was all.

It suited me, in any case, to get away again. Apart from Clive Fisher's publicity picture for *Moonlight and Roses*, I had nothing much to do, although insistent messages from Sam Lutz suggested that I ought to be doing something. But I found myself suspended in that dead time between one job and the next, waiting for one show to be screened, hanging on offers being confirmed for another. There were independent producers I might have courted, lunches I might have bought. There were directors I could ring, researchers I could summon, but I wanted to see what plaudits *Moonlight and Roses* would bring.

'Going away?' queried Jamie peevishly. 'But you've only just come back! You know, you are required to spend a teeny morsel of your time at home, darling. Just occasionally I need you here with me . . .'

Hamlet himself was lying upon our white leather sofa, stroking a great costume sword, raising it slowly to dissect the air around his shoulders, then letting it fall to rest against his thigh.

'I'm going anyway,' I said.

He frowned.

'Who with this time? Not Daniel Duval, I hope. That could prove a bad mistake. Did you know his wife's mother is second cousin to the Queen?'

'I'm going to a funeral,' I said curtly. 'In Northumberland.'

'Northumberland? What fun. All those sheep . . .'

He lifted the gilded sword and fingered it meditatively, turning it in the light of the gas flame from our inglenook, so that it glittered and glowed, the Prince of Denmark contemplating his quarry. And a vision rose before me: Doctor Leo Frankish, redoubtable literary critic, scything the buttercups in my mother's unweeded garden, looking up from the blade to stare at me as I sat on the conservatory step. I shivered in the overheated room.

'Whose funeral?' Jamie asked unexpectedly.

'Nobody you know,' I said.

'And who do you know who lives in Northumberland?' he demanded, rising from the sofa and advancing towards me with the sword. 'Forgive me, darling, but I can't believe you're going to a funeral simply to grieve. There must be more to it than that. I know you too well . . .'

He folded me to his chest, the sword pressing against my back, and when I tried to break away, he held me tight, digging the plywood scabbard into my spine, his free hand cupping one breast.

'You know less than you think,' I said angrily, repressing a wince as his fingers compressed my flesh.

He released me then and we sprang apart like two pieces of warped wood nailed against their pull.

'Oh come, darling,' he reproached. 'I know everything. I'm your best friend, remember. In fact, sometimes I think I'm your only friend . . . What on earth's the matter with you, anyway? What is all this?'

'Nothing's the matter,' I snapped. 'I just don't want you or anyone else interrogating me, that's all. I am a mature responsible person in charge of my own destiny. I live as I choose.'

He looked away from me then, spinning his sword.

'You know I love you, don't you darling?' he said.

'I know,' I replied, briefly chastened. 'I love you too. But right now, it just isn't enough.'

Perhaps if my mother had never read English literature at Cambridge . . . If she hadn't given a damn about the Death of the English Novel . . . If she'd never met Leo Frankish . . . If she'd turned her back on that tutoring post . . .

Misconceptions, mistakes, accidents, lost chances, the past is made of these. There is no such thing as malevolent fate, but why did my mother happen upon that cottage, that village?

We'd spent the afternoon varnishing ancient kitchen cupboards, chipping off the caked-on paint of decades, chiselling and planing. In just a few short weeks the cottage had been transformed from picturesque wreck to bijou residence. Bath taps had been silvered, banisters stripped, floorboards polished. Sarah and I attacked the cupboards and my mother was hacking up ancient lino from the floor while Leo pressed on with his labours in the garden, shovelling trailing vines into hanging baskets and planting rows of stiff, prim border shrubs around his new lawn.

I'd begun to resent the disappearance of the wilderness, and even my mother had suggested we leave the unruly hawthorn hedge. But Leo wasn't easily dissuaded and the hacking went on while my mother patrolled her boundaries, pleading for rogue hawthorn branches and clumps of celandines which nestled in the shade.

I could see her still, sitting on the cane settee in the conservatory when the day was done, painting her fingernails a new shade of crimson, meticulously unravelling the tangles of my heart.

'So you've fallen out with Michael?' she enquired at length, twisting the minute brush in the neck of the lurid phial and wiping the tiny drips from its bristles with excessive concentration. 'That's a shame . . .'

I'd spent days waiting for the subject to be raised, and now instead of the casual response I'd so carefully planned, I had to swallow hot tears at the back of my throat.

'Michael's a prig,' I gulped. 'I never want to see him again.'

'Oh dear . . . Well, I suppose you know best. But don't let a little tiff spoil your fun.'

A little tiff! Was this what she had concluded? I'd been rejected, insulted and then ignored by Michael. My pride was shattered, my heart all but broken. I felt my hackles prickle like spines on the hawthorn hedge, and I turned away from my mother in blatant reproach.

'I hate all the Camerons,' I said over my shoulder. 'Who the hell do they think they are? Bold Sir Jack swaggering round the village as though he owns it . . . Lady Cameron dispensing coffee and cakes to the peasants . . . They go on like something from a bloody Victorian novel.'

In the bathroom above us Leo was taking a shower, running water into the recently enamelled bath. I imagined him naked, thick white legs and protruding belly covered in my mother's raspberry shower gel, or perhaps some manly concoction of his own, and I shuddered instinctively.

'Jack Cameron does own the village,' my mother said briskly, glancing up at the ceiling above as if she fully expected Leo and the bathwater to come cascading down upon us, 'but he doesn't strike me as the swaggering sort . . .'

'Like a Victorian novel,' I said darkly, ignoring this opinion of Jack Cameron. 'The young master goes slumming with the village girl and reckons he's been led astray.'

I regretted the remark at once, but my mother merely laughed.

'You're a mature responsible person in charge of your own destiny,' she said lightly. 'If you believe that, then you must accept that you live as you choose . . . And in any case, you'll find there are very few situations you can't turn to advantage one way or another.'

She stood up then and walked to the conservatory door, throwing it open to let in the warm June breeze. Leo had planted honeysuckle in a tub on the step outside and its sweet, heady scent flooded the little room like the cheap bath oil I imagined him using upstairs. I began to feel faintly sick, the result, I knew, of a week's pent-up emotion.

'That's what you do, isn't it?' I said shakily, thinking of Leo again and all his predecessors. 'Turn the situation to your advantage?'

She leaned her head against the door, staring out into the growing gloom, surveying the clipped hawthorn hedge, waving her hands in the breeze to dry the polished nails.

'I've taken opportunities as they've arisen,' she said coolly, her back still to me. 'And of course, like every other woman on God's earth, I've made mistakes. Perhaps you're thinking of one in particular?'

A little thrill of fear ran through me. Was she inviting me to talk about my father? This was dangerous territory. I hadn't mentioned Raymond Carlisle in years, not since the day I'd tracked him down only to be told by a frosty second wife that he didn't wish to meet me. The pain was acute, so much so that for a time I'd abandoned Carlisle in favour of my mother's maiden name, signing myself Elizabeth Martineau and thinking it sounded rather grand. But it didn't seem right. I felt myself to be Beth Carlisle, my father's daughter, for better or worse. My mother had married him, after all, and nothing could change that. Now, however, and not for the first time, I had to consider that her judgement of men might be seriously flawed.

'I don't know what I was thinking,' I muttered, unsure of what I could say, not wanting to hurt my mother or myself, biting my lip in a bid to stop the perilous tears that now threatened to overcome me.

She sat down beside me once more on the cane settee.

'I'm not trying to tell you what to do, Beth,' she murmured, taking my hand. 'I just don't like to see you unhappy, that's all. If you're so miserable without Michael, and he's so miserable without you, then something should be done. Why don't you ring him up?'

I seized on this golden nugget of news at once, though scarcely able to jerk out my words.

'Michael's miserable?' I whispered.

'So his father says. He's supposed to be studying, but he's not doing much. His mother's very worked up about it all. I get the impression that Michael can be rather unpredictable . . . Jack says he's quite capable of announcing that he's not going back to Cambridge and then running off to join a community of monks.'

I jumped up from the settee at this alarming suggestion, ready to race to the Camerons' at once if need be, determined that whatever the outcome of Michael's sexual initiation with me, it wouldn't be a life of celibacy.

'Don't be too eager,' my mother said quickly. 'Keep it cool.'

But my mind was made up, and now I simply wanted to hear his voice again, no matter what he said. I ran to the phone and, almost dragging the socket from the wall, took it into the under-stairs cupboard, sinking into warm, private darkness.

'Hallo? Hallo? Can I speak to Michael please?'

There was a long silence in which I imagined Michael staring at the phone in disgust, thinking up some suitably impassioned retort. But the voice when it came was female, young and decidedly cool.

'Who is this speaking?' she demanded.

'It's Beth, of course!' I snapped. 'Who's this?'

'This is Clare Spencer.'

There followed a further silence and I waited, not knowing if she'd gone to find him or if she'd simply left me dangling, a possibility that suddenly seemed likely, if not logical. For some reason Clare Spencer intended that her disdain for me be known.

But then the world came right again and my fleeting intuition about Clare was gone, lost in the overwhelming relief of reconciliation.

'Beth? Is is really you? I didn't dare hope you'd call, and I hadn't got the nerve to ring you myself . . . When can I see you? Tonight? It has to be tonight . . . I'll pick you up at eight. Oh Beth, I'm so sorry. I love you. Oh God, I love you . . .'

Unreal city. London was as damp and damned as I'd ever known it, and I drove to my photo call with Clive Fisher through choking fume-filled streets, the rain lashing from greasy pavements into gutters thick with sodden rubbish.

In a dingy alley I glimpsed a tattered form lying full-length on the ground. A couple of office girls tottered above him on high-heeled boots, glancing anxiously back towards the motionless traffic. One folded her umbrella and gazed heavenwards, as if in hope of a parachuting paramedic, and then, disappointed, unfurled the umbrella again and persuaded her companion back to the thoroughfare. A blast from a car horn behind propelled me into action and I lurched forward another few yards, losing sight of the prostrate man who still lay, presumably, in wait for his Samaritan.

I turned on the radio and caught an interview with an unknown junior minister, indistinguishable from countless other junior ministers. The trickle-down society. The get-up-and-go culture. The stand-on-your-own-two-feet philosophy . . .

Another traffic snarl-up, and I fiddled with my radio, trying to get a music station as the swelling city chaos disappeared behind a fog of condensation. I snapped on the car blower, and could no longer hear the radio. I switched off, and put an anxious hand to my throat where it met with Eva Delamere's tiny silver cross.

At once I felt a great surge of emotion; excitement and anticipation mixed with doubt and fear. What would happen when I met Michael Cameron again? How would I feel? How would he react?

'Hey, lady! Look! Look here!'

A dishevelled black youth, no more than seventeen, was peering in at my windscreen, his pinched features framed by a ragged anorak and bright green woolly hat. I stared in alarm as he gesticulated wildly, pointing towards the BMW's door. Frantically I clicked the central locking device and nudged forward a few feet towards the traffic lights. But he followed me, shouting and pointing until the lights changed and I sped off, leaving him jumping on the kerbside, still pointing. I shuddered and drove on.

When I finally arrived at Francine's café, flustered and ill at ease, I found Clive Fisher waiting with a bottle of Dom Perignon, two Waterford crystal glasses and a photographer who'd just given up smoking. There was no sign of Jamie, and half an hour later when the photographer was threatening to punch Clive Fisher and I'd suggested we call it off, we cracked the wine.

'Here's to Love,' Fisher said, raising his glass to mine. 'Anything you'd like to say on the subject, sweetie?'

'It makes the world go round,' I said jauntily, trying to raise my game along with my glass. 'But it's never been clear to me whether that's an advantage.'

He laughed, the photographer snarled, and the glasses were refilled.

'You'd think I had fuck-all else to do,' growled Jamie when he eventually arrived, matching the photographer's mood precisely.

'Oh dear, something rotten in the state of Denmark?' I enquired icily, fed up with the whole thing and anxious to be home.

'Let's have another bottle,' said Clive Fisher nervously, and so we posed with the wine, smiling and kissing and clinking our crystal flutes. It was all done in ten minutes flat.

'Did you call Metro?' I asked Fisher. 'I usually let them know about any publicity I'm doing.'

'I called the great Sam Lutz himself. Left messages at his home. Asked his secretary to call me back. But not a dicky in return. Seems he's left his wife and gone to live in a hovel in Camden Town. Never mind, I'm sure he'll approve . . . Now finish the bubbly, won't you? And have a lovely time together.'

He disappeared into the night with the roll of film, and I turned to Jamie in disbelief.

'Sam left home?' I said urgently. 'Have you seen him? What's going on? Don't just sit there . . . Say something!'

Jamie stood up.

'I wouldn't have thought there were any hovels left in Camden Town,' he said, 'but if there are, you can bet your backside Sam Lutz isn't slumming it all by himself.'

'They're supposed to be our friends,' I snapped back. 'Don't you care?'

'They're supposed to be your friends, darling. Maybe if you were around a bit more, you could offer a spot of marriage guidance . . . What do you think? Is that your thing? Consoling the broken-hearted and building bridges? Well, maybe not . . .'

I stared at him unhappily. It was true. I wasn't at my best when it came to the Lutz marriage problems.

'We could call round now,' I suggested hopefully. 'Vicky's going to Spain, but I think she'll still be there . . . She talks to you. You've always got on well.'

He swilled the remains of his champagne in the bottom of his glass.

'Sorry, darling. You know how it is. I live as I choose, and right now, I choose to do something else entirely.'

'Like what?'

'Like go back to work. See you later, darling. Don't drink all that bottle yourself, will you? Remember what I said. Alcohol shows in the face. One more furrow and you'll be out of a job.'

So I was left alone in an empty club with a three-quarter bottle of Dom Perignon. I stared at it uneasily. Should I leave it, or should I ask for the cork and take it home?

'What can I get you?' called Francine from behind the bar. 'You want some supper? Some nice *foie gras* to go with your champagne?'

'No thanks,' I said, pushing the bottle away resolutely, 'I'll get my coat.'

'Oh dear,' said Francine, helping me into my Ralph Lauren mohair. 'Whatever's this?'

We both looked down at the hem of my cream-and-honey coat, nine hundred quid in Harrods sale, which now flapped limply around my boots, thick with black grease.

'It's been hanging out of the car,' Francine commiserated. 'What a shame. Wouldn't you think some kind soul would have let you know? Tapped on the window or something?'

I said nothing, simply smiled wanly and left for my journey home, thinking of a wild West Indian face, a ragged anorak and a bright green woolly hat, of nightmare streets on which beleaguered drivers locked their doors against their fellow men, of a city where nameless individuals fell to their fate in dingy alleys . . . Of misconceptions, paranoia, and lost chances. Of a present in which no risks were taken, a future which offered only more of the same, and a past whose promise could never be retrieved.

I dressed with care. My high-heeled patent sandals, my cream calico

skirt, the jade silk shirt with the jet buttons and underneath, my black
lace front-fastening bra and a new pair of black bikini knickers.

The shirt reflected the colour of my eyes, which I plastered in green
frosted shadow. My hair was newly cut, lightened from its conventional
gold with an ash-blonde rinse. I looked at myself in the bathroom mirror, pleased.

'Michael's here,' announced Sarah, who had been infuriating me with
her excessive interest in the ritual preparations. 'Aren't you wearing
your tights? It's chilly out.'

'Mind your own business,' I snapped, and slammed from the cottage
into the waiting Bentley, noting only the twitch of a lace curtain at
the conservatory window as I went. My mother was watching my progress.

The row was furious, beginning as soon as he parked the car in the
whispering shade of the spinney, ending with us both near tears. In the
relief of finding that he still wanted me, I'd forgotten my anger and my
hurt. Now it all came flooding back.

'I don't know why you brought me here,' I raged. 'A little tramp like
me!'

'I was angry,' he pleaded. 'You have to be in charge, don't you, Beth?
It has to be what you say, what you want . . .'

'I don't want to get pregnant!' I shouted. 'That's something I really
don't want.'

'I don't want that either. I'm not stupid. We should have discussed it.
But you couldn't wait, could you? It had to be when you decided . . .'

'So you didn't really want to do it?'

'I'm not saying that . . .'

'Then what are you saying? You're a fucking hypocrite!'

I shocked us both with the unfamiliar obscenity, and when I saw him
recoil, I thought for a moment that I'd gone too far. We were both
shaking with emotion, and I'd begun to feel sick. I wound down the
window and took a deep gulp of the sweet evening air. The tears were
close, but I would not cry.

'I love you, Beth,' he said unsteadily. 'Really I do. I wouldn't make
love to you if I didn't. Maybe that makes me different from anyone else
you've met.'

The implication of this was unavoidable, and I turned on him at once.

'I've never made love to anyone else!' I stormed. 'Believe it or not, I
wanted to be in love, too. I thought I was. But how wrong can you be?'

I opened the car door and made to get out, wanting to lose myself in
the deep dark green beyond, or perhaps bring Michael tearing after me,
pursuing me to Uncle Malcolm's folly and pulling me down on to the
soft mossy stones. But he grabbed me roughly and for a moment we

wrestled in angry silence until he wrenched my arm, and in sudden awareness of his superior strength, let me go.

'I'm sorry,' he whispered, the grey eyes bright with tears. 'Please, is there some way we can forget all this and start again?'

I rubbed my arm, took another few gulps of air, and began to think. I could accept this offer and swallow my humiliation, I could tell him to get lost, or I could take a gamble.

'You're right,' I said at last, closing the car door and turning to face him, composed and in control, 'I shouldn't have gone on the Pill without telling you. I thought I was being sensible, but I've only succeeded in making you think I'm some sort of vamp who goes around seducing innocent young men. That isn't true, but I quite understand how you feel, and now of course, I'm going to stop taking those wretched pills . . .'

He lowered his head to the steering wheel and listened in silence.

'You're not supposed to quit in the middle of a month, otherwise I'd have flushed the whole lot down the loo already. But I'll stop just as soon as I can . . . We won't be making love again, so there's no point carrying on.'

Still he said nothing, but his fingers tightened on the wheel, and I guessed I'd played a winning hand.

'You'd better take me home now,' I said in quiet triumph. 'We both need time to think.'

For one anguished moment I thought he was going to start the car and in panic I stretched out my hand to touch his hair. He lifted his head, and when our eyes met, I knew I was vindicated. His arms went round me, and in seconds he'd undone the green silk shirt and the lace bra. A minute later the calico skirt was round my waist.

'Michael,' I whispered jubilantly, 'I don't want you to do anything you might regret . . .'

'Shut up,' he said, pulling down the black bikini knickers in one deft movement, 'and get on the back seat.'

The preliminaries were short and not very sweet, then he plunged into me with terrifying power, and I gasped in shock. I could think of nothing but that stabbing, merciless heat, and then, as the Bentley shook on its springs and he began to subside, I tried to move, breathless from his weight and bruised by the arm-rest digging into my side.

He sat up and took my hand, caressing the fingers and lifting them to his lips.

'You belong to me, Beth,' he said softly. 'You're mine, and you always will be. Sex is sacred. It's a gift from God. Nothing can take away what we mean to each other . . . So remember, what God has joined together, let no man put asunder . . .'

I stared at him blankly, astonished.

'That didn't feel very sacred to me,' I muttered. 'It hurt.'

'I can make you come,' he whispered, unperturbed by this rebuke, and then he lowered his mouth to my damp thighs and licked and sucked until I screamed and convulsed and yelled out that I wanted to die.

Afterwards, as he stroked my hair and lifted me into his arms, a new and terrifying thought occurred.

'Michael . . . Have you ever done that to anyone else?'

'Absolutely not. I just read the right books, that's all.'

We stared at each other through the green gloom, and then we both grinned, the sombre mood vanquished in a moment, blown away on a gale of blessed laughter and shared relief.

'Let's go,' he said, retrieving my knickers from the front seat and tossing them back to me. 'We've just got time for a drink at the Boar.'

And so we drove off into the balmy night, away from the secret green world of the spinney, back towards the village lights and the winding street, the gilded clock on St Botolph's tower which struck ten as we passed, the great façade of the Cameron house and the neat curtained windows of my mother's cottage. We laughed, we kissed, we vowed we'd quarrel no more. We planned, we promised, we pledged our faithfulness until the end of time. We swore that nothing on God's earth would part us . . .

And neither of us mentioned the Pill. Not then, nor ever again.

'What do you know about the objective correlative, darling? I told the director I'd ask . . . You're the expert on T. S. Eliot, aren't you?'

My house was luxuriating in the morning sunshine, shafts of lemon light dancing over the pale walls, french windows thrown open to the scented pots upon the balcony, everything dappled and serene. But I couldn't wait to be gone. I meant to spend the weekend in St Cuthbert's village, and now I wanted only to be on my way.

Hamlet, however, was having an existential crisis.

'Eliot reckoned the emotion was in excess of the facts,' I said briskly, pulling my Louis Vuitton bag from the back of the wardrobe. 'It didn't correlate. So Hamlet was terminally puzzled. He couldn't understand why he was so screwed up. Shakespeare couldn't either, so how the hell can we?'

I was mooching around the bedroom in my underwear, trying to decide what to pack. It was important to choose the right stuff. Something to intimidate Michael, and something to impress Duval. How did I wish to appear before two ex-lovers, possibly in the same room at once, each pretending to the other that we'd previously enjoyed only the most proper of relationships? I stared into my wardrobe. The swirling, twirling black chiffon, slashed for maximum movement, £1,800 at Chanel Boutique? My strapless gold-lace David Fielden, £987 to order? Or should I rush out and buy a twin-set?

'So Hamlet was making too much bloody fuss?'

'Something like that.'

'But if he were clinically insane,' said Jamie moodily, 'he would make a fuss, wouldn't he?'

'I suppose so. I don't know.'

'A preoccupation with death and the inevitable decay of all things to the point at which life itself becomes valueless,' Jamie droned, 'indicates a pathological state liable to express itself in violent acts upon others or in suicide . . .'

The sword suddenly scythed through the open door and he advanced towards me, resting the point at my throat.

'You're not listening, darling!'

'Yes I am. Hamlet was a nutter. Very perceptive, but I think you'll find it's been done before . . . For God's sake watch what you're doing with that thing.' The plaster sword was unnervingly sharp at its tip, and I pushed it aside impatiently.

'Hamlet was a nutter,' he repeated slowly. 'Thank you, darling. Very useful. I'll work on that, shall I?'

'I've got a better idea,' I said, deciding upon a couple of cashmere sweaters, the silk shirts I'd picked up in Harvey Nicks' sale, assorted pants and skirts that wouldn't make me look too flash, my scarlet cashmere wrap, and for the funeral itself, the black Karl Lagerfeld suit. 'Ring the Samaritans. Tell them your uncle killed your dad and started sleeping with your mother. Maybe they'll come up with some good advice.'

'Oh, very droll, darling. We are on form today, aren't we?'

He arched the sword swiftly above my head, flicked it under the left strap of my camisole, sliced the ribbon neatly in two and before I could retreat, performed the same manoeuvre with unerring precision on the other strap. The satin crumpled round my waist and I lunged for the sword.

'Hey, that was a good trick,' he said, waving the weapon out of my reach. 'I might suggest that in rehearsal . . . Ophelia in a flimsy nightie. What do you think?'

I ripped off the camisole, struggled into jeans and T-shirt, grabbed the Vuitton bag and made for the door.

'I think Hamlet was a fucking little shit,' I shrieked as I ran down the stairs. 'Why not try it that way, darling? I'm sure you can do it!'

Outside in the gaudy spring air, I stumbled into the garage, fumbled with my car keys, dropped the contents of my handbag into a patch of

oil, then fell into the soft, secluded interior of my BMW. I trembled in
its welcome darkness, my hands shaking on the driving wheel.

Around me and beyond me, the whole creation writhed and moaned.
War, genocide, murder, treachery, the massive wrongs of history, and
interwoven with them in a deadly dance of inconsequence, all those tiny
everyday acts of unthinking unkindness. Spite, jealousy, envy and indifference. Broken vows and forgotten promises . . . No wonder Hamlet
made such a fuss.

Chapter Eight

A look, a smile, a kiss may hold the key to love, and so deep is the hunger for union, so pervasive the myth of completion, that rational women are lost in its pursuit. If the purpose of our forebears was to procreate, the purpose now is to love. And not just any love. We must all seek the one True Love, the romantic experience that is mystical in its intensity.

Moonlight and Roses: The Cult of Romance in Western Society, by Beth Carlisle (published by Harridan Press to accompany the Metro Television series)

The traffic was mercifully light and I cruised along the Edgware Road, taking in the unexpected warmth of the day, indulging a curious holiday feeling which had little substance in fact.

But I told myself that though the trip would be brief, if I kept wayward emotions at bay, then it might prove pleasant enough. After all, I didn't have to see Duval. And I needn't spend more than an obligatory ten minutes with the vicar of St Cuthbert's and his wife. I could unwind in the country air, relax with a view of the sea, and although the Dolphin Inn sounded less than luxurious, I'd been assured that it was at least private.

I planned to walk along the beach where Eva played as a child, to look for her brothers' names on the village war memorial, to pay a silent tribute to what I guessed had been an extraordinary life, and so lay to rest the lingering unease that our meeting in Paris had summoned forth.

I also planned to visit my sister on the way north, and soon I found familiar signs flashing by. Peterborough, Stamford, Oakham . . . the village where my mother had dumped her reluctant daughters lay a mere twenty miles from this road, and yet I'd never once been tempted to take the turn-off, never been drawn back to view our old cottage again, nor to visit St Botolph's tangled churchyard where my mother lay.

Sarah continued to tend the grave, or so I imagined, for I hadn't been near since the day it was closed. I'd wanted cremation, arguing that my mother hadn't given a damn for religion or church services. I'd seen myself scattering her ashes in the garden she loved, throwing them high over the wiry hawthorn hedge, watching while the swallows cruised above in the summer blue until the last specks of dust were borne away on the June breeze.

But my little sister, previously so mild and accommodating, had claimed the right to decide. It was she who led the mourners to the church, she who threw pink rosebuds into the abyss as my mother's coffin disappeared beneath the dark Rutland soil, she who chose the hymns, the lesson, the headstone, the epitaph.

I could see her still as she looked on that day, like a tragic Resistance heroine, pinched face set bravely beneath black felt beret, black trench-coat belted tight around her waist, teetering on ludicrous stiletto heels, the only shoes that could be found to match. Throughout the service she'd clutched the pale roses to her breast like a nervous bride, caring nothing for the thorns. And when she'd knelt at the graveside, hands bleeding and torn, Charles had produced a clean white hanky to stem the flow. One by one she threw her flowers down, the gold and sapphire ring flashing in the sun as her fingers moved, the tears wet upon her cheeks. When the last bloom had fallen Charles raised her gently to her feet, embracing her hunched figure in his enveloping arms, leading her off to his safe new world while I laid a small bunch of buttercups picked from the garden and then walked back to the cottage in my denim dress and cowboy boots, dry-eyed and alone.

Now, as always on the rare occasions when I visited my sister, I dreaded seeing Charles. Unable to unearth any small patch of common ground, we relied on careful civilities to see us through. We never talked politics or TV, and never mentioned the Church, of which he and Sarah were stalwart members. Instead we talked gardens and children, although to my shame, I found it hard to warm to my nephews. They reminded me too much of him.

Things went much better when Jamie was there. The great actor needed only the faintest hint of acclaim to put on a first-rate show and Charles had proved quick to applaud. Indeed, love of theatre was his one redeeming trait, but even here he and I couldn't agree. He maintained that little of note had been written since the war, and a ludicrous dispute over Beckett and his trash cans had once brought us closer than we'd ever come to voicing our mutual dislike.

I tried, but I simply couldn't understand why Sarah married him. When she'd first introduced the nervous, bespectacled trainee teacher and announced their impending engagement, I'd gaped in outright surprise. But who knows the secrets of another's heart? Who can say precisely why one woman is attracted to a particular man? I'd learned not to judge when Vicky married Sam, a match which seemed so fated that I fully expected Cassandra to show up at the wedding. Yet they'd lasted ten years, and by prevailing standards, that didn't seem so bad. Sarah and Charles, meantime, had made it past their first decade and I had no doubt that they'd coast into companionable senility together. My little sister had done all right for herself. She was secure and content, a combination of life experiences that, for better or worse, had somehow contrived to pass me by.

Now I pulled into the cramped cul-de-sac where my sister and her husband had raised their two sons, a little loop of squashed semis with spare room extensions over the garages and tiny squares of lawn outside.

Sarah's garden was invariably clipped and pristine, and she ran the kind of household where pruning shears and stout gloves were always to hand, third cupboard on the right, second shelf down. So I looked in surprise at the unruly grass and straggling daffodils as I pulled up on to the pavement. Surely Charles wasn't letting standards slip?

I was leaning on the doorbell when I realised that I'd brought nothing for the boys. I managed to remember birthdays and always sent book tokens for Christmas, but now it seemed thoughtless to have arrived without so much as a bar of chocolate. I decided I'd give them a tenner apiece and resolved to do better next time.

I pressed the doorbell again. It was clear that Sarah wasn't home, and I settled down to wait in the car. I felt she couldn't be long. It was nearly lunchtime and the boys came home from school for dinner. I hoped there'd been no change to this arrangement for I wanted to be on my way before Charles himself came home. The sooner Sarah showed up, the better my chance of avoiding him.

What would my sister make of my unannounced visit? It was no more odd, of course, than the visit she'd made to London when I was in Paris, and I found myself wondering just what had taken her up to the city. She hadn't called me since, and hadn't asked that I call her, so I assumed it must just have been a shopping trip with a spare hour or two to fill in.

I couldn't pretend, however, that concern, or even curiosity, had brought me to my sister's doorstep. In truth I wanted to hear what she knew of Michael, how she'd come to give him my number, whether she'd had any other contact with the Camerons in the years since we all parted.

I clicked the car window shut, shivering suddenly at this prospect, pulling my scarlet wrap tightly round me, kicking off my shoes and curling my stockinged feet beneath me. The spectre of my sister's disloyalty rose to confront me. How could she have given my number to Michael? I began to doubt that I could even speak the name of Cameron without unleashing a torrent of long-buried bitterness. What might then be said that had lain so long unspoken? I closed my eyes and lay back on the BMW's plush upholstered seat, willing time and memory and the demons of regret to lie down together and let me be.

'You have your mother's style,' Leo Frankish remarked, observing me candidly over the top of his reading spectacles. 'Lively and pithy, but far too subjective, I'm afraid. Idiosyncrasy is for literary critics, Beth, not undergraduates. I'd advise you to tone down your ideas a little. Pay attention to the critical tradition. Don't be too quick, at this premature stage, to have your say.'

I was pleased to have finished my T. S. Eliot essay, and scarcely aware of Leo, the esteemed literary critic, sitting in the far corner of the conservatory, I'd demanded my mother's appraisal.

'Leo will help,' she'd said wryly. 'No sense having an expert around if you don't make use of him.'

I saw that she was avoiding any show of her own expertise, yet I couldn't imagine that her unexpected elevation to university tutor had proved in any way daunting. Her reticence had to do with Leo himself, as though she had chosen to play the willing subordinate, a role which, I guessed, had been crucial to their dealings in the first place.

Now I scowled at Leo, hoping to convey my contempt.

'I'm not going to university just to absorb other people's opinions,' I said icily. 'I'm going to learn how to voice my own.'

Leo removed his spectacles, folded them carefully into a little leather pouch, handed back my essay and smiled benignly, a polite little curl of the lips, intended to discourage if not entirely to dismiss.

'You can do that perfectly well already,' he said archly. 'But do your opinions count for anything, Beth? Ask yourself that . . .'

He laughed then, and my mother looked up from her own work, a new set of course notes for 'The English Novel. Amis, Barnes, Weldon, Tremain . . .'

'Received opinions are there to be challenged,' she objected mildly, raising a consolatory eyebrow in my direction. 'There's nothing worse than a student who can quote every critical view from Johnson to Leavis, but can't say why he enjoyed *David Copperfield*.'

'Quite,' said Leo crossly. 'But before you can challenge received opinions you have to show that you understand them.' He looked over at my mother's notes.

'I don't know why you've got Nick Howard on that list,' he snapped. 'He isn't in the same league.'

My mother simply smiled back, for ever calm and in control.

'You need a joker,' she said. 'Just to keep everyone on their toes.'

'Leo's on his way out,' I said later to Sarah. 'And a bloody good job too. Can you believe him? Those awful corduroy trousers and that mucky black jumper . . . Tatty clothes and tatty ideas. He ought to be wearing a sports jacket and cravat! How has he survived in the department, do you think? I suppose he's been there so long they can't get rid of him.'

'Leo's okay,' said Sarah, considering. 'He did get her the job, after all. She can't dump him before term's even begun.'

No, of course she couldn't. And yes, Leo was okay. He was more okay, for example, than the painter my mother met on holiday in Cornwall, who'd ended up pouring yellow ochre into her underwear. And he was only slightly less okay, for another example, than the Czech *émigré* poet who'd written revolutionary odes in my mother's honour, then set fire to her bed with a Gauloise.

Nevertheless, I disliked Leo in no small measure. I considered him inferior to my mother in every way: intellectually, socially and physically.

'I wish she could meet someone decent,' I confided to Michael, who by this time was privy to all my secret hopes and fears. 'I wish my mother would really fall in love . . .'

He stroked my hair and kissed me, soothing and concerned.

'She's starting out on a new phase of her life,' he said. 'She'll be meeting all sorts of different people. Anything's possible . . .'

'It's all Rhoda's fault,' I said morosely, recalling with sudden venom the tyrannical grandmother who'd blighted my childhood with her strictures and complaints about virtually everything I said or did or wore. 'The Lady of Shalott, my mother called her, and treated her like some feared despot who had to be appeased. Madame Martineau, she called herself. She was Lady Rhoda Connaught until old Sir Rupert dropped down dead and she failed to get his lolly! After that it was back to the noble Martineaus . . . I hated her, and I didn't even have to live with her! No wonder my mother rebelled.'

'Well, maybe she'll rebel again,' Michael said thoughtfully. 'Though somehow I don't imagine Leo will go without a fight.'

I shivered suddenly, chilled by the deep green heart of the spinney, wanting his arms around me, needing to know that it would all be different for me.

'I love you, Michael,' I said. 'I'll always love you, no matter what happens.'

'I know,' he whispered gently, 'I know,' and the dense whispering spinney seemed to match its sighs to our own, in sympathy, or perhaps in derision.

Oh I love you, I love you, I love you . . . Oh yes, I always will . . .

I was startled by a fervent rapping on the BMW's window, and opened my eyes upon my sister's driveway to see my elder nephew grinning and waving, jumping up and down in apparently genuine delight. Behind him stood the younger boy, also smiling and waving. Damn and blast, why hadn't I used this time to find the shopping centre and buy them something nice?

Then Sarah appeared, thinner than when I'd seen her last, the chocolate-coloured hair, so like my mother's, looking unusually long and bedraggled.

'Beth, what a nice surprise,' she said uncomfortably.

We walked into her gloomy hall, the boys racing on ahead, through to the makeshift kitchen, which Charles had extended and then failed to equip with new cabinets. Tins and jars were stacked on ancient shelves, cardboard boxes stood in corners, but there appeared to be a new stainless-steel sink unit which, in the absence of anything else, I proceeded to admire.

'Kitchen's coming along,' I remarked foolishly, delving into my bag for the money I planned to give Sarah's sons.

She looked up quickly. 'No, it's not. We ran out of cash.' She scrabbled in a sagging cupboard and produced a bag of potatoes. 'There's not much for lunch, I'm afraid. We're having sausage and chips. I don't suppose you eat chips?'

'No, never,' I said absently, discovering with alarm that I'd nothing in my purse except twenty-pound notes. She began to slice the potatoes and I made a quick decision. No good telling the boys to share a note. I handed them one apiece, and they stared in outright disbelief.

'Twenty quid each,' shrieked one. 'Whoopee!'

'Good heavens,' said my sister uneasily. 'That's very generous, Beth. You really shouldn't.'

I knew I shouldn't, and now I felt worse than if I'd given nothing at all, the big sister from the big city who couldn't help demonstrating her profligate ways.

'Well, I don't see them much,' I mumbled weakly.

She cooked fat slimy sausages that would blow my calorie count for a week while we talked of nothing much: the boys' progress at school, her so-far fruitless search for a job 'now that the children can manage without me', Jamie and Hamlet, *Moonlight and Roses*.

'We're looking forward to seeing it,' she said.

I nodded politely, not knowing whether she meant *Hamlet* or my series, recognising with faint remorse that so distant had we become, it scarcely mattered. There was nothing I could say to Sarah about my private life or my work.

I ate my sausages bravely and attempted some banter with my nephews, but they were uncommunicative once the food arrived, and as soon as the meal was done raced out into the garden, leaving me free to tell my sister just why I was there. I decided to waste no time dreaming up tactful openings.

'I got a call from Michael Cameron the other night. He said you gave him my number.'

The effect was immediate. Sarah turned from the sink where she was washing the lunch plates, knocking a mug from the drainer on to the tiled floor. It shattered into a dozen pieces and she stared down, plainly unnerved.

'Michael?' she queried, her face hidden from me as she picked up the shards of pottery. 'What did he want?'

'Nothing much. Something to do with a funeral he's conducting. I must say I thought it strange that you gave him my number . . .'

She threw the remnants of the mug into the waste bin, set the kettle on to boil, and then seeming to make a decision, came to the kitchen table and sat down beside me.

'I've never given Michael your number,' she said slowly. 'I've never given anyone your number. I know how you feel about your private number.'

She paused. 'I can't imagine how he got it. I don't think we even have your number written down . . . If we had, I suppose he could have looked it up in our address book. We usually keep it on the hall table, right next to the telephone . . .'

It took a moment for this to register and then I turned to her, astonished.

'You mean Michael was here? In your house? He came to look at your address book?' It made no sense. The greasy meal suddenly threatened my stomach, and I clutched at the edge of the kitchen table.

Sarah stood up and walked back to the sink, pouring boiling water on to a pair of limp tea-bags. She stirred the brew with long, deliberate movements while I waited, the bile rising at the back of my throat.

'No, Beth, I don't mean that,' she said quietly. 'I mean that Michael's often here. He comes to see us whenever he visits his mother. If we had written it down, he could have looked up your number on any one of a hundred occasions. He's a friend, Beth. A good friend. He always has been. Ever since . . .'

The words were left unspoken and I stared at my sister, stunned. For a moment I thought I would burst into loud howls, weeping like a woman bereaved, or worse, throw up the slimy sausage on my sister's well scrubbed kitchen floor. But instead I reached for my bag, fumbled inside for a tissue and blew my nose. Breathe deep, Beth . . . One, two, three, four . . .

'I see,' I said, standing up. 'So it's been all mates together, has it? You and Charles, Michael and Clare. A cosy foursome?'

My sister gazed at me unhappily, stirring the foul tea in the ludicrous cups.

'Clare died five years ago,' she said at last. 'It was very tragic, and Michael was left with a young child. There seemed no reason to tell you at the time.'

I said nothing, fighting a host of warring emotions that I could not disentangle. My sister's betrayal, the unexpected news of Michael's bereavement, the knowledge that he had a child . . .

'Michael has a child?' I whispered at last.

'A daughter. Catherine. She's seven.'

'I'm sorry to hear about Clare,' I mumbled shakily, not knowing what else I should say, wanting to be gone, alone with my confusion. 'How did it happen?'

'They were on holiday in Greece,' Sarah said, looking away. 'She drowned in the hotel pool . . . Very traumatic, of course. But Michael's over it now. In fact, we've got high hopes that he's about to marry again.'

I gazed at her dumbly. Now I knew the source of that warm female voice at St Cuthbert's vicarage with its intimate northern tone. But I didn't know if it would prove any easier, confronting Michael's bride-to-be, than facing the woman I'd imagined still to be his wife.

I smiled at my sister unsteadily.

'I suppose it's all part of the Christian code,' I said with effort. 'Let bygones be bygones. Love thy enemy.'

'Michael was never an enemy,' Sarah replied carefully. 'Not mine, anyway.'

At that moment the boys came tearing back into the kitchen, locked in some dispute that demanded their mother's intervention. I listened dully while she negotiated and they complained, and then when it was done and they left us alone again, I found I'd no heart for further talk of Michael. I picked up my bag and nodded briskly at my sister.

'Must be off,' I muttered, unwilling now to reveal that I was on my way to Eva's funeral, that I would soon be meeting Michael myself, in the light of all these new revelations.

'I hate to think I've upset you, Beth,' she said anxiously. 'I haven't forgotten just how painful it all was . . .'

I walked over to the kitchen window and rapped smartly on it, waving goodbye to my nephews, playing the interested aunt.

'I never think about it,' I said, retrieving a stray piece of broken pottery from beneath my foot. 'The Camerons haven't crossed my mind in years. It was a surprise to hear from Michael, that's all.'

'So you're not angry? That he and I kept in touch?'

'It's nothing to do with me. I have my own life and I'm happy with it. I don't see any point in brooding, playing out the past over and over again . . .'

My sister looked at me doubtfully, then followed me into the hall.

'I'm very relieved to hear it,' she said. 'Still, I can't think what possessed Michael to call you up after all this time. It hardly seems sensible, and it's most unlike him.'

I looked round at the hall with its little wrought-iron telephone table, imagining him standing beside it, surreptitiously rifling through the address book. The hall needed re-papering and the banisters were in urgent need of paint. Indeed, the whole place had an uncared-for feel now I thought about it, as though the man of the house had abandoned ship. I looked again at my sister's unkempt hair and thin face. 'Where's Charles?' I asked suddenly. 'Is everything all right between you, Sarah? He hasn't gone off or anything, has he?'

'No, of course he hasn't! Whatever gives you that idea?'

Now I'd offended her, and I cursed my repeated failures to make any kind of connection with the sister I'd once loved. Nothing served to bring us closer together, certainly not the past, and not, it seemed, the present either. I longed for some sign, not that we still cared for each other, for this seemed too much to expect, but simply that we each understood something of the other's life.

'I'm sorry,' I said in faint desperation. 'I'm not thinking straight. Vicky and Sam have just split up, I've had a wild few months in Paris, then there's Jamie mooning round the house with his bloody sword . . .'

She smiled, the tight little half-smile that I remembered so well upon my mother's lips, and the resemblance between them struck me like a blow in the face. For a moment my beloved mother lived again, ticking me off one minute, building me up the next.

'Give Jamie my love,' Sarah said. 'And bring him to visit soon. Charles does so enjoy seeing him! He's like a breath of fresh air.'

She smiled again and in an unexpected, welcome gesture, squeezed my hand.

'I do wish the two of you would get married,' she said. 'It's not my business, but I simply can't understand why you don't. Everyone can see how well you're suited!'

My heart, lifted for a moment, plummeted back to familiar depths at the level of our misunderstanding.

'By the way,' I enquired as I left, anxious to return the conversation to trivialities, 'what's up with your telephone? I tried to reach you and couldn't get through.'

'We got cut off,' she mumbled. 'Forgot to pay the bill . . . But it's okay now.'

Out on the road again, heading north, grey spring drizzle falling on the flat fields, spray flying from the car wheels, foot to the floor, the way I always drove, I reconsidered the prospect before me . . . Now I had to face Michael Cameron, the tragic widower, in the knowledge that he'd become my sister's friend, and that he probably knew a great deal more about me than I about him. What had Sarah told him? That I lived an idyllic existence with a famous actor? That we were perfectly matched and needed only a prod to propel us into wedded bliss? However far from the truth, Sarah's misconceptions about my life were no more startling than mine about hers. For a moment I'd seriously imagined that the dour and donnish Charles might have run away with another woman.

Poor Sarah. Poor me. No way forward, no way back. Nothing to give to each other, and nothing to receive.

'Family life!' I moaned to my sister as we climbed into bed in our shared room above the conservatory. 'Thank God we never had any.'

I'd spent the afternoon in the Camerons' silk-walled drawing room, staring fixedly at the little clusters of tea tables, sipping my orange pekoe and nibbling on a shortbread petticoat tail, trying to be civil to Clare Spencer, who seemed determined to dislike me, wishing desperately that Michael would stand up and signal our retreat.

I'd been invited for my official introduction to the family, for although Jack Cameron had called on my mother, and we had all attended the coffee morning held on the Cameron lawn in aid of St Botolph's roof repair fund, I had yet to be formally appraised by the Lady of the House.

Beatrice Cameron had welcomed me with well-practised grace, extending a jewelled hand, guiding me over pastel-hued carpets and seating me on a cream brocade sofa as far away from her younger son as seemed possible.

'Miss Carlisle . . . Elizabeth . . . Now do come and sit over here, next to Clare. You've already met Clare, haven't you?'

A tall, decorative woman with pale peach skin and fine golden hair sculpted into a painful-looking pleat, Lady Cameron managed to convey the impression of pins buried somewhere deep, torturing her scalp. For all I knew, that might well have been the case, but with inevitable egocentricity, I imagined at once that her pain had to do with Michael's passion for me.

'What a beautiful room,' I said politely, and then, as Clare Spencer offered me a biscuit. 'It must be terribly difficult to keep clean.'

'Oh, we're rather good at overcoming our difficulties,' Lady Cameron replied, and at once I divined that any minor difficulty I appeared to present to her ordered household would, if she had anything do with it, prove purely temporary.

'Do you live in a stately home as well?' I asked Clare Spencer, taking another petticoat tail.

'I live on a farm,' she said coldly. 'This is a farm too, as it happens. Perhaps you hadn't noticed?'

I noticed little that afternoon beyond what seemed to me a total absorption on Michael's part with Fiona Spencer. While Jack Cameron and Jonathan maintained a studied reserve, and the rest of us exchanged our vacant remarks with barely concealed boredom, Michael and Fiona chatted and smiled, and even, at one impulsive moment, laughed aloud.

'You might have rescued me,' I complained as he walked me home. 'I've been stuck with Clare all afternoon. I haven't had half as much fun as you and Fiona . . .'

I shot him a sly glance, not because I doubted his devotion to me, nor even because I harboured the smallest pang of jealousy towards either of the Spencer girls. No, like any young thing beloved and in love, I simply wished to hear it restated.

Instead, he dropped his arm from my shoulder and swung me round to face him.

'Clare's okay,' he said seriously. 'I'm very fond of her.'

'Are you?' I asked, piqued.

'We've been friends for years . . . Ever since we were kids. I'd like you to be friends as well, Beth, really I would.'

'Then you'd better tell her that,' I said peevishly

'I have told her,' he replied. 'The truth is she finds you rather . . . unfriendly.'

I said nothing, unwilling to acknowledge my hostility, not just to Clare, but towards the entire Cameron clan and their cronies, knowing then, as I'd known from the beginning, that no amount of polite conversation or quasi-friendship could bridge the social gap between my family and Michael's. He might love me, but his family never would. Nor did I wish it. I would survive, indeed triumph, without Cameron approval.

'I'm sorry Clare feels that way,' I said petulantly to Michael as we parted. 'She can be pretty unfriendly herself, if you ask me.'

Later that night, alone with my sister, I derided Clare Spencer for her hypocrisy, Beatrice Cameron for her prejudice, and Jack and Jonathan for their careful disinterest, denouncing the stultifying rituals of upper-class family life in general and afternoon tea in particular. But Sarah would have none of it.

'We've got our own family life,' she objected. 'We've got our own little ways, our own rituals . . . All families have them. They're important.'

Maybe they were. Maybe our little threesome, the wise and wonderful single mother and her smart, accomplished daughters, was a very model of family togetherness. Certainly I'd always thought so. I might not have called it 'family life' for there were no aunts or uncles, no cousins, indeed, after my grandmother's death, no surviving relatives at all, except my father, who didn't count. But I believed in our corporate strength, a cosy invincibility which outsiders could never touch.

That was why, of course, Leo and his predecessors never posed any real threat. We tolerated them, laughed at them, sometimes even liked them. My mother's lovers were periodic necessities, like trips to the dentist or stocking up the larder. Often they were tiresome, occasionally they were fun. We lived in hope of better, all three of us, but even so, a better man would never change our way of doing things.

'I'm not talking about us,' I said to Sarah, 'I'm talking about the Camerons. I'd hate to live like them, that's all.'

'Well, Beth, maybe you'll never have to,' said Sarah, snapping off the bedside lamp and plunging me into darkness.

The light had gone by the time I arrived in St Cuthbert's village, and I saw nothing of the moody mauve hills that towered behind me to the west, the great cream stretch of sand that curved round to the rim of the bay, the brilliant bank of lemon poppies that crowded the dunes from the wall of St Cuthbert's vicarage garden to the edge of the dark emerald sea. I saw nothing of the jet black islands that glittered in the foam far beyond St Cuthbert's rocks, of the white-winged seabirds that swooped in their hundreds on to the empty beach, of the tattered fishing boats and the jumble of lobster pots stacked on the ancient stone jetty.

Instead I saw stiff grey terraces of fishermen's cottages, the brooding spire of the church gleaming softly in the starlight, and St Cuthbert's vicarage itself, a solid Victorian manse still with its cobbled driveway. I drove quickly past, intent on finding the Dolphin Inn.

It wasn't hard. The village consisted of half a dozen streets, a couple of shops, a square of green on which the war memorial stood, the church, the vicarage and the pub.

I'd hoped for a country hostelry, basic but cosy. Instead the Dolphin reared before me like a great landlocked ship, an edifice of chipped white concrete with ugly picture windows and vast tarmac parking area. This space was completely empty, and I drew the BMW as close as I could to the front door, aware of a keen wind outside which whipped the bare hedges into grotesque shapes. I stepped out to be met by a blast of icy sea air that took my breath away. I pulled my scarlet wrap tight around me, wishing I'd retrieved the Ralph Lauren coat from the dry-cleaner's.

Inside, the Dolphin lived up to its exterior threat. A cavernous, dingy room with leatherette booths met my eye, one-armed bandit in the corner and dartboard at the far end. On the bar was a long plastic tube containing a stacked pile of two-pence pieces, and behind it, the inevitable calendar bearing a half-naked girl, Miss March Winds. The place was deserted.

I called loudly, determined not to be downhearted, and then when no one appeared, I took off my shoe and rapped smartly on the counter with the heel.

'Miss Carlisle?' enquired a voice behind me, as though I could conceivably have been anyone else, and I turned, shoe in hand, to greet Mine Host. 'I've been watching out for you,' he said, improbably.

He was small, plump and ruddy-faced, and as far as I could tell un-objectionable, although his manner was suspicious, as though I couldn't possibly be satisfied with the Dolphin Inn, whatever he might do.

He led me through corridors dark with crimson flock, up gloomy winding stairs, along more passages hung with drab seascapes. The attic room itself was large and light, but there was no bathroom.

'The toilet's doon there,' he said pointing into the distance, 'and you've got your own phone. Private facilities, like I said.'

'Do you serve dinner?' I asked politely, thinking that whatever the weekend might require of me, I would surely need to eat.

'Aye . . . The special's on tonight. Sausage and chips.'

I lay down on the double bed and sank into unfashionable softness, weary, depressed and confused. I had travelled the length of the country to witness the burial of a woman I'd hardly known. Could I really pretend I was here because of her? And if not, then what was I hoping for?

I'd scarcely thought of Eva throughout the long day, and now I un-
packed my bag and took out the vanity case where I'd put the silver
cross, back in the grubby envelope that Duval had handed to me.

I fastened the cross round my neck once more, feeling its unusual
heaviness. Maybe I would try to discover its history while I was here.
Perhaps I would begin with the vicar of St Cuthbert's. Perhaps if I
could keep our conversation light, focus on minor matters – Eva, the
silver cross, her life as a vicarage daughter – perhaps then my meeting
with Michael would pass in safe, meaningless pleasantries.

I picked up the bedside phone, thinking of all my sister had said.
*Michael's about to remarry . . . Do bring Jamie to see us soon . . . He's like
a breath of fresh air . . . You're so well suited . . .*

I dialled my home number and listened while it rang out, on the wall
above the freezer in our Smallbone kitchen, on the Italian marble table
in our ceramic tiled hall, on the oak bookcase by our inglenook fire, at
the side of our great big bed in the jade and olive boudoir . . . So how
was my Lord Hamlet tonight?

'Yes?' he demanded irritably, and I knew at once that he'd picked up
the bedside phone.

'Sorry,' I said. 'Have you got company?'

'I was asleep, Beth. Why the hell are you ringing up at this time?'

'I just called to say I love you,' I trilled into the phone.

'Fuck off, darling,' he said, and replaced the receiver.

Outside my attic window the wind sang like a baleful siren. I could
hear the far-off boom of the sea on the shore, heartless, uncaring,
pounding away into eternity, unceasing and unchanged. Bullets of rain
battered the tiles above my head, and I began to doubt that I would ever
sleep amid such din. But it seemed to me then that there was nowhere
else I truly belonged. I might as well be here in the Dolphin Inn as
anywhere else. There was no respite from the machinations and confusions of human relationship, not here, not in my own home, not anywhere. Indeed, wasn't this what I'd always known? Why I ran my life
the way I did?

'Whatever you say, my lord,' I murmured into the buzzing phone as
I lay back on the bed. 'Whatever you say.'

Chapter Nine

Quasi-religious in its intensity, True Love makes fools of us all. To deny its power is to be lost to the world of passion, the only world that we, saddled with our bankrupt ideologies and our failed visions, seem able to inhabit or to understand.

Moonlight and Roses: The Cult of Romance in Western Society by Beth Carlisle (published by Harridan Press to accompany the Metro Television series)

The storm raged above the little attic room all night, threatening roof tiles and loosening a door somewhere in the bowels of the Dolphin Inn. The glass in my window trembled and the grey cord carpet beneath my bed strained at its tacks. The wind bellowed like some wild creature avenging the slaughter of its young, and at one point I flew from my bed to the window in fright, convinced I'd heard a human scream. But there was nothing beyond except utter blackness, not a street-lamp, not the glow from a nearby cottage, not a sign that anything survived in the elemental world outside.

Yet next day the village looked as pretty as pie, neat streets stretching down from the Dolphin to calm harbour waters gleaming gun-metal silver in the morning sun. A small fishing boat was gliding away from the jetty out to the blue brightness beyond, heading for the distant islands. The sea was flat as coloured glass, and I stared out of the attic window in disbelief. It seemed wholly improbable that the night's fury should have given way to such serenity.

'Sleep all right?' enquired Mine Host wryly, setting before me a great plate of cholesterol and a pot of pungent coffee that wouldn't disgrace a Turk. 'Not too noisy for you?'

I smiled weakly, requesting orange juice and toast as balm for the headache produced by the night's violence.

'You here for the funeral?' he demanded as he whipped away the offending platter, apparently deciding that small talk concluded, it was time to learn my business. 'Is it going to be on the telly? We were told it was a private do.'

This was interesting and I said so, inviting more.

'That's what the vicar said. No fuss, and no press.'

'Makes you wonder what Miss Delamere had to hide,' I said idly, and as I spoke, realised with faint excitement that this was a possibility I hadn't considered before.

'Is there anyone left who remembers Eva Brannen?' I asked eagerly. 'Anyone who knew the vicar's family or fought in the war with the Brannen boys?'

The Dolphin's dining room, a small box of a space overlooking a drab back yard, was empty but for myself and Mine Host, and as though my arrival represented a precious opportunity, he poured himself a cup of the vile coffee and sat down at an adjoining table.

'There was one old geezer who came out of the war,' he confided, 'but he was just a private. Not in the same class, you see . . . And anyways, he's dead. Dropped down right here in the bar last June.'

'Was there anyone else? Someone who came from the same social background?'

The germ of an idea was sprouting, and I didn't intend to let it die. But Mine Host shrugged and shook his head. It was a long time ago. The village had changed since the Brannens' day. It might look much as it did, but apart from the fishermen, most folk had moved away. Now it was in-comers, weekenders and commuters, people who wanted the rural life without the isolation of the countryside.

'I suppose there was the Forsters,' he ruminated. 'They used to own the Retreat, and there's Miss Emily Forster who's come back to live in the village. But the ones who would've known the Brannens, they're all gone now . . .'

I nibbled my soggy toast and supped my tepid juice politely, convinced in that moment that some secret lay behind Eva's choice of burial spot. It wasn't enough, I decided, that ancient family ties should bring her back to this unlikely resting place. And in a process of deduction owing as much to my own emotional state as to any logical pattern of thought, I imagined a long-lost sweetheart, buried in St Cuthbert's churchyard, calling his old lover from beyond the grave. Eva's words came back to me: *I fell in love long before I met Will Sutton . . . Very romantic!* My fingers fumbled towards the silver cross at my neck, and I was seized by the desire to find out.

'Tell me about the Forsters,' I urged, 'and about the Retreat...'

From Mine Host I learned that the Forsters had been the only notable village family in Eva Brannen's day. But with Sir Ralph's death the big house above the bay had ceased to be a family home and the surviving heir, Aidan Forster, had made it over to the Anglican Church, a retreat for wearied lay Christians and burnt-out clergymen. At the moment it flourished under the spiritual tutelage of the vicar of St Cuthbert's.

'We wouldn't get a bloke like Mick if it wasn't for the Retreat,' said Mine Host proudly. 'He'd be down at St Paul's or at one of the universities.'

'Mick?' I repeated, fascinated, staring down into my orange juice.

'Mick the Vic. Now he's the man you want.'

'You think so?'

'Mick knows what's what. He'll soon set you straight.'

With this discomfiting thought I set out to explore the village, unwilling as yet to present myself at the vicarage. That could wait, I reckoned, until I got my bearings, and until I'd got my story straight. The rationale was forming slowly in my head. I would play up my interest in Eva, maybe even suggest I was going to write a book. I would declare my belief that something extraordinary lay behind her association with the village. Eva, and my desire to uncover the secrets of her past, were reason enough to be here. I wouldn't have anyone think I'd come to uproot a piece of my own history, certainly not Michael Cameron himself.

It was warm enough to walk without my scarlet wrap, but I took it anyway, draping its protective folds around my shoulders, aware but uncaring of the unlikely image I presented.

I walked briskly out of the inn yard and down towards the harbour, shading my eyes against the sun's glare, taking in the glories of the landscape around me.

The village sat on a vast plain of cream sand, bordered to the west by a range of bare hills, the highest of which, even on this mild March morning, was tipped with glittering white. Two spurs of wicked black rock marked the perimeters of the bay and beyond lay a cluster of minute islands, barren outcrops of land that jutted into the blue from the turmoil of frothing waters around their base. The largest island boasted some kind of ruined building, its tower leaning perilously towards the foam, the seabirds that dived from its crumbling stones looking from this distance no more than tiny black insects borne on the wind.

The harbour was jammed with boats – ragged fishing vessels, smart painted dinghies, a couple of cabin cruisers, a handful of tattered yachts. It was busy too, with old men examining nets, children skipping along the jetty, a group of young women talking animatedly and pointing towards one of the yachts. They looked up as I passed by in my vivid cloak, and I walked determinedly on.

I turned away from the church and the graveyard where Eva was to lie, walking in the direction of the Retreat, Sir Ralph Forster's old house, an ugly grey sprawl of a building which brooded above the bay from its vantage point. I determined to seek out the remaining Miss Forster just as soon as I could. There might be family papers, or she might have heard the Brannens mentioned by her relatives. Certainly, an interview would serve to establish my interest in Eva, and I could make this convenient Miss Forster the subject of my opening talk with Michael.

I walked past the village store and the post office, skirted the edge of the village green to stare across its muddy waste at the war memorial, and on past a row of smart white cottages outside which city cars were being washed. The only sign of last night's wildness, apart from the quagmire of the green, appeared to be a felled fence and a few battered daffodils.

I tried to think of Eva walking the village streets with her father and brothers, imagining her planning the escape to Paris, nurturing her hopes of a career in the movies, wondering what encouragement she'd met, or what dismay she had caused. But my thoughts were increasingly drawn back to Michael, to all that had been and what might yet be. I knew I could scarcely delay any longer, that prevarication was increasing my anxiety. And so I turned away from the bustling harbour and the empty beach, walking back past the smart white cottages and the village store where a couple of local women were debating a money-off poster, around the muddy village green and the war memorial, back past the post office, closed half-day on a Saturday, until I came at last to the grubby white face of the Dolphin Inn.

The bar was still empty, and wondering how the landlord managed to make himself a living, I sat down opposite the bare-breasted Miss March Winds and ordered a double gin. I drank it slowly, summoning all my courage and my wit for what lay ahead. The time had come to confront the vicar of St Cuthbert's with his shady past.

'Michael, please hurry. I'm scared.'

We were lying in his great oak bed on what had become a weekly quest for the vaginal orgasm. Would we make it before September when term began? Would we make it without being caught?

'Put this pillow here,' he commanded, spreading my legs, 'and then raise your knees. There . . . How does that feel?'

'Bloody uncomfortable,' I said, removing the pillow. 'How the hell do you sleep on this thing? It's like a chunk of granite.'

'Okay. Try this cushion.'

He leaned over the side of the bed, and I caught at his arm anxiously.

'Let's just do it,' I pleaded. 'I can't help it if I'm scared.'

'It's all right,' he soothed. 'Everyone's out. They always are.'

Saturday afternoons saw the Camerons dispatched upon their various leisure pursuits: Lady Cameron to the Tapestry Guild which met in the church hall, Jack Cameron out with his horses, Jonathan playing squash in Market Sudborough, and Michael making love to me.

I'd gone willingly at first to the silent Cameron house, enchanted by its elegance and its calm. I'd been conducted through the great mahogany-panelled hall, shown the gold-ceilinged ballroom and the library where Michael's father liked to sit behind a leather-topped Jacobean desk admiring his first editions. I'd marvelled at the servants' kitchen, still complete with copper jelly moulds ranged upon open shelves, the ancient blackened range, now adorned with Lady Cameron's dried flower arrangements, the quaint winding staircase that led up to the attic quarters. At the top lay Michael's room, a huge airy space with magnificent sash windows which overlooked the rose garden. It had its own bathroom and a full-sized snooker table, testimony to what seemed, at first, an unlikely passion. It also had the biggest bed I'd ever seen, the head and foot boards intricately worked with carved flowers and fruit. The bed was low to the floor, it was covered with creamy white cotton sheets, and the joy of falling naked into its voluptuous crispness was one I never quite forgot.

But I was scared, and as the weeks went by I climbed the winding stairs with increasing reluctance. No one had disturbed us, no one had even hinted that our activities might be guessed, though I couldn't help wondering which of Lady Cameron's indomitable band of cleaners stripped the bed and what, if anything, might have been said to Her Ladyship about the state of the sheets. And I always knew, with the dread knowingness of one who courts the inevitable, that come one unlucky Saturday afternoon, we would be discovered.

'There's a door banging,' I gasped as Michael entered me having finally decided, it seemed, that one of us deserved release through penetration. 'Someone's coming!'

He heaved and jerked, then groaned and rolled from me, sweat glistening on the nape of his neck.

'But not you,' he murmured regretfully, turning over to stroke my cheek. 'At least, not yet . . .'

The house went quiet again. I forgot the banging door, forgot the fear of discovery, forgot everything except the exquisite sensation between my legs. To hell with the vaginal orgasm, I thought dreamily as I drifted to heaven.

When the bedroom door opened we rose from the rumpled sheets in perfect unison, as though a hidden string had pulled us both upright in the same swift action.

There was a moment's pause and then there she was, Lady Cameron herself, the pale skin faintly flushed, but calm, perfectly calm. And certainly not surprised.

'Get up,' she ordered coolly, addressing her son. 'Your father wishes to speak to you.'

I stared at her guiltily, humiliated, cowed, unable to justify my presence in Michael's bed, even to myself.

'And you,' she said slowly, still in the same controlled, dispassionate tone, fixing me with a gaze so icy I visibly shivered; 'you, Miss Carlisle, had better go home to your mother. For that's obviously where you belong.'

She paused, as though she wished this statement to take effect, but I had no idea what she meant, and when she saw I wasn't about to respond, she picked up my jeans and blouse from the chair where they lay and deposited them gingerly on the edge of the bed, as if they might contaminate either the eiderdown or herself.

'I never want to see you in this room again,' she said carefully, words delivered at an even pace so that a dimwitted child might understand. 'You may leave through the servants' quarters.'

Then she turned and departed as quietly as she'd come, closing the door gently behind her, leaving us alone among the ruins and recriminations of the afternoon.

The Dolphin Inn had no ice, so I drank lukewarm gin and tonic, commiserating with Mine Host about the difficulties of getting your fridge fixed on a Saturday. I also gleaned a few more personal details about the vicar of St Cuthbert's.

His daughter, Catherine, went to school in Alnwick, along with the landlord's own granddaughter, Kayleigh-Jane. His widowed mother, Beatrice, occasionally came to visit and seemed a rather remote sort of person, disinclined to take a drink at the village pub, unlike her son who liked a pint with the locals. His housekeeper, Lucy Robson, also widowed, lived at the vicarage with three young sons.

'A housekeeper!' I said in astonishment. 'It sounds positively Victor-

ian. What does she do, starch his collars and get him up in time for
Matins?'

'There's no Matins any more,' Mine Host replied.

Lucy, I learned, was a true paragon, the most wonderful woman on
God's earth, an excellent mother, a devout Christian, one who had risen
above tragedy and by unstinting self-sacrifice had rebuilt her children's
lives after the untimely death of their father. She was, I concluded, an
eminently suitable second wife for the vicar of St Cuthbert's.

I listened with heavy heart, not because I resented the blissful domestic arrangement that Mrs Robson and the vicar appeared to enjoy, but
because I didn't want to see anything of it. And if they were truly about
to marry, as my sister had suggested, I couldn't help but wonder what
she'd been told about me. Was I, perhaps, a buried piece of Michael's
past, something that demanded no more than a rueful reference now
that I was due to reappear? Or had our torrid romance been fully confessed? I couldn't decide which was worse.

Mine Host, taking a cue from my rejection of breakfast, offered me a
prawn sandwich, which I ate gratefully despite my fears about shellfish
being stored in a dicky fridge. Then I downed another gin and set out
for the vicarage on foot.

The day was still fair and I began to regret the cashmere wrap. I'd
dithered about what to wear, deciding eventually on a cream silk shirt,
my coffee-coloured Benetton sweater, matching Next leggings and crocodile-skin boots. But once dressed I felt like nothing so much as the
principal boy, and I was also uncomfortably warm. I contemplated a
short diversion on to the beach, thinking the sea air might cool me
down. But I walked on, knowing I was simply seeking to postpone the
moment.

At the vast walled graveyard, however, I stopped. I wanted to see the
Brannen family plot, and I also wanted a quick look at any Forster
graves. In my theory about Eva's romantic past, the Forsters seemed
the most likely candidates. I walked quickly through the yew gate, unnerved at the prospect of coming upon Michael unexpectedly, yet
nevertheless excited and curious.

I'd almost reached the church door when it opened suddenly. I froze
in fright and without waiting to see who might emerge, fled back down
the path and out on to the road again.

My heart was pounding by the time I arrived at the vicarage door,
and although I'd told myself I wouldn't hesitate, that I would ring the
bell immediately, I paused to take breath.

St Cuthbert's vicarage was a handsome Victorian country house
whose exterior could hardly have changed since Eva Brannen's day. I
gazed upon the same gardens, the same cobbled drive that Eva must

have known, and stood by the same front door. I closed my eyes briefly, calling up the vision of her tranquil, aged face. I reminded myself that I was here because of her, and then, failing to find a doorbell, rapped loudly upon an ugly brass knocker, noting that the salt air had turned it bright green. Michael's housekeeper, for all her reputed virtues, had been skimping on the Duraglit.

'Beth Carlisle! I'm so happy to meet you! I'm Lucy Robson. Please, do come in.'

She wasn't what I'd anticipated, despite, or perhaps because of, the eulogies from the Dolphin Inn. I'd expected someone neat and calm, with a faintly sombre air gained from her harrowing life experience. Instead I was confronted by an untidy, plump female whom I guessed to be somewhat older than Michael and myself. Dark hair strayed around her neck from two imperfectly placed combs and the face was long and lively, like a gypsy dancer in some cheap framed print from Boots. She didn't look remotely sombre, and instead of the reserve I somehow felt I warranted, she welcomed me effusively.

'We've all been waiting for you,' she cried, leading me into an over-heated sitting room. 'We thought you'd be here this morning. Now everyone's gone out, I'm afraid.'

I forced a smile, struggling between relief and disappointment, trying to decide if I should apologise for having failed to show up when expected, wondering how the vicar of St Cuthbert's spent his Saturday afternoons these days.

'Michael's taken the boys on to the beach,' Lucy said, as if in response. 'It's such a lovely day. Now Beth, what will you have for lunch? We've got chicken soup or cheese and tomato pie or cold roast pork . . .'

She was staring at me closely, and at the mention of food I began to feel queasy. Was it the stress of the moment? Was it the heat of the room? Or was it the prawn sandwich? I requested a cup of tea, and sat down uncertainly.

'Forgive me staring,' Lucy said. 'I couldn't help thinking that television doesn't do you justice. You're much prettier in real life!'

I forced another smile, trying to weigh her up. She seemed an unlikely choice for Michael, and yet already I could sense what the landlord of the Dolphin saw, a good-hearted woman, a survivor. I warmed to her despite myself, but I wondered again what she knew about me, and wished I had the nerve to find out. Left alone while she made the tea, I looked carefully around the room. One wall was covered in floor-to-ceiling books and another was taken up with a huge white marble fire-place in which a pile of driftwood blazed, the source of the oppressive heat. On the mantelshelf stood a silver-framed picture of Jonathan Cameron with an unknown woman and three grinning schoolgirls. Next to it was a portrait of Michael's mother, still with her hair in its painful pleat. There was no photo of Clare, nor of Jack Cameron.

It was the window wall, however, that took my attention. A generous bay looked out over the garden to the churchyard beyond, and in the bay stood a large leather-topped desk. I recognised it at once, even though I hadn't seen it for fifteen years, not since the Saturday afternoon when I'd faced Jack Cameron across it in the great library of the Cameron house.

Now I walked quickly over to the desk and ran my fingers across its ancient red leather. I swallowed hard, disturbed that this tangible reminder should affect me so, fighting the memory.

There was nothing much on the desk: an inert computer, a jumble of newspapers and magazines, and a small pile of books with a bible on the top. Impulsively, I moved the bible and the books underneath spilled over – a heavy, glossy hardcover volume and a slender paperback: *Against the Tide: A Biography of David Klein* by Jon Makepeace, and *The Freedom of the Kingdom* by Michael Cameron.

I picked up the paperback, then glanced up into the garden beyond the desk, and what I saw there drove all other thoughts from my mind. A slight, golden-haired child, legs as slender as a newborn fawn, was leaping down the path, waving excitedly. My breath came quickly, and I leaned upon the desk for support. The child waved again and I waved back, my heart thundering against my ribcage, my chest tight. Then in a moment she stood before me, mouth pursed in a toothless grin, grey eyes smiling, hand outstretched, the imagined daughter I'd once glimpsed in my dreams.

'I've seen you on the television,' she said, shaking my hand in a grave, grown-up gesture. 'You're Beth Carlisle!'

She was bold and direct, and her acute resemblance to her father gave her an ageless quality, as though generations of Camerons, all with the same bright hair and grey eyes, had combined to produce an epitome of themselves, a perfect example of the dominant gene, beautiful, intelligent and utterly entrancing.

'That's me,' I said steadily, back in control. 'And you, of course, are Catherine Cameron . . .'

'Katie,' she corrected. 'Everyone calls me Katie.'

'Hallo, Katie.'

'Hallo, Beth.'

Then she turned as suddenly as she'd arrived and skipped to the door. 'I wonder where Daddy is?' she said gaily. 'He'll be so pleased you've come!'

*

Left by myself in Michael's lavish bedroom while he went down-stairs to face his father, I began to cry, bitter, hostile tears of anger and regret.

'It's all right,' he'd muttered. 'I'll explain everything,' and I'd yelled in fury: 'Explain what? That when everyone's out we sneak into bed? They already know that! You're so stupid sometimes!'

It was Michael who'd got me into this, he who was the cause of my humiliation. How dare they treat me this way, these Camerons? What was I, some loose-living wench out to corrupt the young master? A dispensable female from the lower classes, tolerated for her services of sexual initiation and then banned from the house when her work was done? And what was the high and mighty Lady Cameron implying about my mother?

I put on my clothes and dried my tears, scrubbing away the traces of mascara that stained my cheeks. I straightened the sheets on the great carved bed and took one last look. I knew I wouldn't be lying in its shameful luxury again. Then I walked out of the room and down the main staircase. I had no intention of leaving through the servants' quarters.

In the great panelled hall I paused uncertainly. The house was quiet. I'd expected raised voices, but there was no hint of a disturbance, only an uneasy kind of peace. On the wall above the library door the ruddy face of Great-Uncle Malcolm, St Augustine's disciple, beamed down benignly. I stared back at the lurid painting in its ostentatious gilt frame, and then, before I quite knew what I was doing, I opened the library door and marched in.

Jack Cameron was sitting behind the leather-topped desk gazing out across the geranium-studded terrace and the immaculate lawns beyond. He was alone.

'Ah, Beth,' he said awkwardly, looking up, 'there you are . . .'

I walked up to the desk and stood before him like a naughty school-girl facing the head.

'I want to make one thing clear,' I said smartly, holding on to the angry tears. 'I know how to take care of myself. I'm not going to ruin Michael's great career at Cambridge. I'm not going to get pregnant.'

He looked away again, apparently absorbed by the potted flowers outside, swivelling idly on a fat padded chair that perfectly matched the red leather of the desk. He fumbled in a drawer and produced a pack of cigarettes. He offered me one and I shook my head dumbly. He cleared his throat and drummed his fingers lightly on the desk top.

'Well, that's good news,' he said at last, and looked away again.

I had prepared myself for argument, for reproach, and I didn't know what to make of this mild response. I sat down suddenly on the windowseat by the desk and clasped my trembling hands in my lap.

'I'm sorry,' I whispered, my anger evaporating in a bout of self-pity. 'I know I shouldn't have come here.'

'It's not for you to apologise,' came the measured reply. 'Michael should have more sense.'

'Where is he?' I whispered, remembering he'd been ordered downstairs to see his father, looking around as if he might suddenly materialise from behind one of the lush velvet drapes.

'Mounting the big defence with his mother. You know Michael . . . Always ready to state his case. Heaven knows how the Christian Debating Society will fare when he goes off to Cambridge again.'

He lit a cigarette and the acrid fumes drifted across the desk, enveloping me in an evil blue haze. I felt sick and confused.

'Did you speak to him?' I asked timorously, unable to fathom this unlikely turn of events.

Jack Cameron turned to me and smiled.

'Not to any great effect,' he said slowly. 'But he spoke to me.'

'What did he say?'

'That he loves you. That he intends to marry you. That nothing and no one will prevent him . . .'

I stood up and leaned against the ancient desk, fingering the soft pitted leather, fighting novel and conflicting emotions.

'I don't remember Michael asking me to marry him,' I said at last, resentment winning over elation.

'Oh, he probably doesn't feel the need to ask. Marriages are made in heaven, after all. Michael's got the Lord God Almighty on his side. Why should he worry about anyone else?'

I laughed because I imagined it was expected, and I smiled gratefully at Jack Cameron, a new and unexpected ally.

'I love your son,' I mumbled self-consciously. 'I'd like nothing better than to be his wife one day.'

'Then I hope you won't be disappointed, Beth. But I'd say Michael has an awful lot of growing up to do before he makes anyone a half-reasonable husband.'

Outside in the hall a door opened, and he stood up quickly, taking my arm to lead me out on to the terrace.

'I think you ought to go,' he said. 'I'll get Michael to call you as soon as he's free.'

I looked up at him, a tall, impossibly handsome man with wide grey eyes and thick gold hair just like his sons, and with all the certainty of a divine vision, I saw Michael thirty years into the future – my hope, my husband, the father of my children . . .

'Just for the record,' Jack Cameron said quietly, squeezing my arm as he propelled me gently away from the house, 'I've no objection to you and Michael doing exactly what you want. But I strongly suggest that you don't do it here, and at the same time, I feel compelled to offer a word of advice . . .'

He paused and I waited confidently, convinced now that if he were on my side, then his wife could do me no real harm.

'Michael has many good qualities,' Jack Cameron said slowly. 'He's loyal, he's generous, he's honest . . .'

I smiled up at him, my spirits high, my woes magically banished, hardly hearing what was said.

'But he's also very hot-headed, and he is, if you'll pardon me saying, exactly what I once was myself – an arrogant young sod.'

Still I smiled, like a winsome girl in a cheap romance, blithely ignoring the harbingers of doom.

'He'll always make a drama, and you'll have a hard time convincing him he might be in the wrong.'

This time I laughed, recognising the truth of what was said and dismissing it in the same instant.

'Don't let him break your heart, Beth. That would be a terrible waste. Promise me, will you?'

I laughed again. 'I promise!' I said.

And then I turned and ran away from the terrace, across the sculpted lawns and over the prim borders, through the rose garden and into the copse. At the gates I turned to look back, and I waved at the distant figure, still standing on the terrace smoking his cigarette, quietly surveying his territory, watching me, motionless, as I ran.

Lucy's tea was hot and comforting, but I still felt queasy.

'I think it's the prawns I ate for lunch,' I said, setting aside my cup. 'There's something wrong with the fridge at the Dolphin.'

She surveyed me carefully, and I guessed then that she knew something about my long-ago relationship with the vicar of St Cuthbert's, if not every last juicy detail.

'Bugger the tea,' she said in an unlikely turn of phrase for a clergyman's housekeeper. 'You need a drink. And so do I. It's been one hell of a morning. The chairman of the Stewardship Committee resigned, the downstairs loo overflowed, and to top it all, the cat had kittens.'

'I've drunk two double gins already,' I said.

'Then another won't do you any harm.'

She left the room and reappeared with a quart bottle of spirit, a jug of orange squash and two crystal goblets. She poured us each an alarming measure and then clinked her glass on mine.

'The housekeeper's secret vice,' she twinkled.

I tried vainly to form a question about Eva Delamere and the Brannens, about Duval, whose arrival in the village must surely be imminent, about the remaining Miss Forster and her relationship to the original family. But instead I took a large gulp of the gin and abandoned every pretence, both to Lucy Robson and myself.

'What did Michael tell you about me?' I mumbled.

'He reveals very little,' she replied and topped up our glasses so generously that I began to doubt I'd make it back to the Dolphin on my own two feet.

'However,' she confided, 'Sarah and I do gossip a bit when the lads take off in the dinghy and we're left in peace . . . So I do know that you were once . . . quite close.'

It took a moment for this to register.

'Sarah comes here? To see Michael?' More uncomfortable revelations, more angst.

'Well, yes . . . They visit every summer. Have done for the past four years, ever since Michael came here.'

I nodded, making out that I'd simply forgotten, unwilling to discuss my sister and what she might have said about our unhappy history.

'And you,' I asked quickly. 'How long have you been here?'

'Oh, I've always been here. I've lived at the vicarage with my boys since their father died. I was housekeeper for the previous vicar . . . Michael and Katie inherited me.'

'How lucky for them.'

'Lucky for me and my boys too.'

She smiled, and I smiled too, and then I had a sudden powerful urge to be gone, away from this blissful, fortuitous domesticity in which diverse parents and children blended into one harmonious whole, and from which, by implication if not intent, I knew myself to be utterly and irrevocably excluded.

'Michael's obviously busy, so I think I'll get back to the Dolphin,' I said briskly, standing up. 'I've a few things to do . . . I really should ring home . . .'

'Ah yes,' said Lucy, producing one more surprise. 'Don't neglect Jamie.'

I stared at her blankly, unable to guess at what was coming next.

'Sorry,' she grinned. 'That sounds a bit nosy. It's just that we're fans, Michael and I. We've seen him on stage a couple of times. Orlando, Macbeth . . . We're really looking forward to Hamlet!'

'Yes,' I said, dazed. 'Aren't we all?'

'That was a lovely article about you both in *Mews and Mansions*.'

To my intense embarrassment she shot across the room and delved among the pile of newspapers on top of the desk, producing the offending magazine and waving it cheerily in my face: *At home: Jamie Mac-Lennon and Beth Carlisle, the celebrated actor and the television star . . .*

'What a gorgeous house you have! I just love this picture of your bedroom.'

I swallowed hard. 'Well, you know what they say,' I mumbled foolishly. 'All that glisters isn't gold . . .' But then from the back of the house I heard the sound of children's voices, excited and high. A moment later Katie Cameron bounded into the room.

'Daddy's coming,' she announced, beaming at me triumphantly but eliciting only a weak, panicky smile in response.

Lucy scooped up the gin bottle, threw the magazine back on to its pile and steered the child firmly towards the door.

'Come on, Katie, we've lots to do. There's the cake to ice for the Brownies' party and the jam tarts still to make . . .'

'But the kittens,' Katie protested. 'When will I show Beth my kittens?'

She turned towards me, face set in an urgent plea, and I nodded brightly, promising to see the kittens at the earliest opportunity, aware that I wanted this little girl's approval with a passion that matched her own.

Then I heard a door open into the hall.

'There's Michael,' said Lucy, quickly ushering the child from the room. 'I'll tell him you're here.'

BOOK IV: Eva

Chapter Ten

Sometimes I think reunions are more painful than farewells. In Paris I find a new, unfamiliar Anya whose way of life and opinions are proving very different from my own. Indeed, I see now that I have been living in another world entirely, one where the old moral standards and virtues still apply, at least so far as women are concerned! In Paris, it seems, 'modern' women do not care about such matters as chastity or the sanctity of marriage. They do as they please, although I find myself wondering if they aren't merely doing what most pleases the men . . .

The Journals of Eva Delamere, edited by Blanche Duval

———————

Paris was truly itself that morning, a place both grey and golden, full of tawdry history and grand visions, crumbling apartment blocks and ornate palaces. The boulevards blushed with gaudy blossoms and the great white globe of Sacré Coeur glittered brazenly in the brilliant light. The sky was a foolish blue, painted by some wizard out to fashion a make-believe perfection. High in the chestnut trees songbirds twittered wildly, and the Seine crawled like molten silver towards its distant dissolution.

As Eva drew her first breath of this new and fragrant life, it seemed to her that the spinning world itself had gasped for air and been rewarded with a blast of pure oxygen, a revival it wasn't quite ready to receive. The result was a heady blend of anaesthesia and euphoria, an unthinking lightness of heart.

She had stepped from the train at the Gare du Nord that opportune day, poised on the indeterminate moment that is later seen to divide one era from the next, a slight girl with soft pale hair framing angular cheeks and wide violet eyes.

She was still dressed in her mourning cloak, but a black felt cap pulled at an angle across the shining hair gave her a jaunty look, not so much the tragic heroine, more the wry comedienne.

It was a curious fact, and she had seen it for herself in the grimy mirror of the station's washroom, but she seemed to have shed the bearing and demeanour of the North Country English girl, the gauche, unworldly clergyman's daughter she had been only days before. An unknown woman had smiled back from the washroom mirror, one who'd glimpsed the cold, dark heart of human affairs, who had swallowed hard, shrugged, and then smiled once more. Now there was nothing but to begin again.

'Eva Delamere,' she whispered softly to the strange woman in the mirror. 'You are Eva Delamere.'

She picked up her gloves from the washstand, adjusted the jaunty hat, then made her way out of the station confines into the bustling street. She looked around eagerly for the face she sought.

'Excuse-me, miss . . .'

A young man, dragging an oversized trunk behind him, was waving a rolled-up newspaper in her direction. She'd noticed him already, of course, for who could ignore the open-faced American with the lock of bright glossy hair that fell across his forehead and the loud, persistent voice? He had boarded the train at Valenciennes, had found himself an English-speaking companion in Eva's carriage, and had then proceeded to offer an incessant commentary upon the speeding countryside outside their window. This battlefield, that cemetery, the relevance of this victory, that defeat . . . Eva had kept quiet, determined not to give herself away. Now he faced her with the English newspaper she had left inside the train.

'You forgot this,' he said gravely. 'I thought you might like to have it?'

She shook her head, the slightest movement that stopped short of outright rudeness, but nevertheless, she hoped, made her lack of interest clear. But in responding at all, she had merely confirmed what he wished to know. She was English, not French as he'd first assumed.

'Been to Paris before?' he enquired, undeterred by her reticence. 'Hell of a place, this. Okay if you know your way around, not so hot if you've no one to show you the ropes.'

He slumped down on the oversized trunk at his feet, and Eva picked up her modest valise, irritated. Where was Anya? Why wasn't she here at the time they'd arranged?

'You've come from London?' the young American persisted. 'Interesting journey, eh? Right through the war zone . . .'

An unhappy thought suddenly occurred to him. 'Hell,' he said, running his hand through the lock of bright hair, 'I hope all that talk on the train didn't upset you . . . About the war, I mean?'

Eva turned, and before she had quite decided on an appropriate response, heard herself answer in rapid, flawless French. The young American need not trouble himself. She was unconcerned about the war. She'd scarcely heard what he'd had to say on the train. And now, if he would kindly leave her alone . . .

'French!' he muttered, disappointed, and she would surely have been free of him then but for a new and extraordinary force that burst upon them in that moment, dressed in a scarlet velvet two-piece with a matching pillbox perched upon the wild dark curls, eyes bright with excitement, face flushed from hurry.

'Anya!' they cried in unison, and then turned to stare at each other in astonishment while Anya herself gazed from one to the other in uncomfortable disbelief.

'Eva, my darling,' she said at last, flinging her arms around her friend, and then less certainly: 'Toby . . . Toby Truman!'

'Anya!' he repeated. 'Hell! Imagine bumping into you my first day back in Paris.'

'Yes,' said Anya, recovering herself. 'Imagine!' and then she laughed, tossing the dark hair and the absurd little hat. 'And what have you been doing to my poor dear Eva?' she demanded. 'Boring her absolutely silly, I'd guess!'

Poor dear Eva frowned suddenly, and removed one of her gloves. 'How do you do, Mr Truman,' she said coolly, extending her hand to the perplexed American. 'I feel I know you already, but since official introductions are nevertheless desirable, we'd better get on with it. I'm Eva Delamere. Neither English nor French as you now see, but a mixture of both.'

She had rehearsed such an introduction for when it was needed, and it was, she reasoned, entirely true. She would always be Eva Brannen, the true daughter of her beloved father, but she was someone else, too. Eva, who came from the sea, child of a wretched, nameless woman who'd worn French lace petticoats and travelled on the boat train from France to England one dark and desperate night . . . Eva, who had survived against all reasonable possibility . . . Eva, who was alone in the world, and yet unafraid . . . This Eva, she knew, would serve her best in Paris.

Toby Truman was embarrassed and confused, and he did not catch the startled glance that Anya threw her young friend. Instead he bowed, an inappropriate, self-conscious gesture that seemed to be all he could muster in the face of this beautiful, enigmatic young woman.

But in a moment he was himself again. 'Hell,' he said, turning back to Anya. 'No hard feelings, eh? I need some rooms, Anya. How are things at the old café? You reckon you could fit me in?'

'Not a chance!' cried Anya gaily, waving her arm at a passing taxicab and bundling Eva's valise inside. 'We're the most popular place in town. People are simply fighting for our rooms! Sorry . . .'

And then they were gone, both laughing now, falling back on to the cab's ample seat, hugging and kissing, Anya waving imperiously at the unhappy Toby.

Through the glittering city streets they went, past the Louvre and the Tuileries, along the bank of the shining river, through the crowded thoroughfares of Montparnasse, past rows of café proprietors setting out their gingham tablecloths and baskets of baguettes, through windy alleys where old women sunned themselves in doorways and barefoot children screeched like parrots.

'You certainly surprised dear Toby,' said Anya at last when the giggling and exclaiming was done. 'You should have seen his face! He thought you were French, and then you suddenly announced yourself like grand old Lady Forster herself. English to your little finger! What a clever girl you are, Mademoiselle Delamere . . .'

She looked at Eva seriously.

'Is this who you want to be?' she enquired softly, thinking of all Eva had related in her long letter from England. 'Am I really to say that you're Eva Delamere, half English and half French?'

'But of course,' laughed Eva, looking out of the taxicab window, enthralled. 'I'm starting again, Anya. And I'm trying out Eva Delamere to see how she performs. Perhaps I won't like her. If not, I can be plain Eva Brannen again.'

'Oh, you'll like her!' cried Anya in delight. 'I know you will. And I will too. Most certainly!'

They smiled at each other in comfortable conspiracy, an echo of their schoolroom days in league against the tyrant Aidan Forster. But their mutual understanding was tested in the very next moment.

'Tell me more about this Toby Truman,' Eva demanded. 'Who is he? How do you know him?'

'Oh, he's a writer,' said Anya with a shrug. 'They're everywhere, the writers and the Americans. I slept with his best friend from Boston.'

Eva's eyes widened. 'You did what?'

'Toby's best friend, Bertie Levine. I think he's from Boston . . . Toby got very high and mighty about it all because he's married. Bertie, that is.'

Eva said nothing, simply stared at her friend in undisguised shock, and Anya, seeing that she'd revealed too much too soon, rushed into an ill-prepared defence.

'Well, Eva, you should have seen his wife! What a stupid little creature she was. She followed Bertie everywhere, even to the café. It was plain the poor man was simply dying to get away.'

Still Eva said nothing, her mind suddenly possessed by an old, forgotten image: Harold Brannen and Lizzie Howard beside the laurel
bush in St Cuthbert's churchyard, Lizzie unlacing her camisole and
Harold lifting her long skirts high above her waist . . .

'It wasn't my fault,' Anya said peevishly. 'Bertie just wouldn't leave
me alone. Then all of a sudden his wife went back to Boston, or wher-
ever it was, and Toby had the cheek to say I'd ruined her life. Well,
really! She ruined her own life. She should never have married Bertie
in the first place . . . should she?'

Eva, unconcerned to grapple with this logic, had been seized by a new
and alarming thought.

'But Anya, weren't you scared? I mean, didn't you worry that you
might be . . .'

Anya laughed, relieved.

'What a goose you are, Eva. This is Paris, not St Cuthbert's. Women
here know all about that sort of thing . . . I can see you've got a lot of
catching up to do. Ah, here we are.'

The taxicab pulled into a quiet and shabby square, gaunt, drab
buildings surrounding a patch of vibrant green dotted with gaudy daffodils and bordered by rows of puny almond trees whose feeble branches proffered a few pale blossoms towards the brilliant sky.

The Café des Arbres, gleaming pink and white like a sugar cake
perspiring in the morning sun, was oddly pristine among the faded
terraces, and even at this early hour was clearly open for business, with
jugs of sparkling water on its scrubbed tables and the pungent smell of
roasting coffee drifting from its windows.

'Aren't we going to your father's house?' asked Eva, surprised.

Anya picked up the valise from the pavement.

'My father's away on business until next week,' she said briskly,
'and there's simply no point in the two of us staying all by ourselves in that gloomy old house. Now, Eva, do come in and meet
everyone.'

She leaned forward, and whispered into her friend's ear. 'You may
meet someone very special,' she confided with a giggle. 'For I
haven't told you the best news, Eva. I'm in love! No, really! It's
true. Madly in love. Oh, I'm sure you'll love him too. Just wait and
see . . .'

The Café des Arbres was no more than one large sunny room which
opened on to a tiny stone-flagged terrace overlooking the square. The
terrace was crammed with tables, but the room inside was sparsely
furnished, leaving a central floor space in which, Anya informed Eva

with undisguised pride, there was often dancing in the evenings. A long, polished bar dominated one corner, and behind it stood the door to a tiny, cramped kitchen out of which Jacob Klein produced the Polish borsch and chicken stew for which his café was rightly renowned. There was one other door, this leading into a gloomy corridor which in turn revealed a flight of narrow stairs winding ever upwards to a dozen tiny cubicles, the rooms for rent.

'So this is your little friend!'

Jacob Klein, an effusive, rotund individual as unlike his brother, Emmanuel, as it seemed possible to be, emerged from the kitchen door, folded Eva against his generous belly and kissed her swiftly on both cheeks.

Anya led Eva to a table by the window, clearly reserved for the very purpose, looking anxiously around the café to see who was eating there on this propitious morning, nodding and smiling and fluttering a hand when she spied a welcome face.

They had arrived just as breakfast was drawing to its leisurely close, the very best moment, it seemed, to command attention. With the bread and coffee done, and a gap to fill before the midday drinking began, everyone wished to meet the new arrival.

'This is Eva Delamere,' announced Anya grandly, 'my oldest friend. Her mother was French but she was brought up in England . . . So don't imagine you can tittle-tattle behind her back! She understands every word you say.'

Eva was suddenly nervous. She had prepared no family background, thought of no convenient fiction to explain herself. But she needn't have worried. The set at the Café des Arbres were only interested in explaining themselves.

That day she met Leonard Schultz, a magazine reporter from Arizona, and his wife, Arlene, a poetess . . . Randy Makepeace, a writer, from Connecticut and Arnold Steinem, a painter from Minnesota . . . Mr Peter Chessington, an English piano player, and Karl Schwartz, a composer from Berlin . . . Miss Jennifer Singleton, sometime from England, but now a Citizen of the World and engaged to Mr Makepeace . . . Tom Calvert from San Francisco, Bobbie Pascali from Brooklyn, Hart Dixon from Philadelphia . . . As the morning advanced towards lunch and the café began to fill with a bewildering array of young people, Eva became quite giddy from the introductions.

Anya whirled in the midst of it all, the scarlet velvet suit replaced by a full black skirt and white lace blouse, the long loose hair floating like strands of dark curled seaweed on her shoulders. She smiled, she laughed, she reached for new bottles behind the bar, she juggled plates of steaming food and bowls of coffee, and yet she managed to convey a sense of effortless enjoyment, as though this was the life to which she had truly been called.

'Eva, darling,' she said merrily in her friend's ear as she passed by, 'here's someone you simply must meet. But be careful with him. He has a tender heart . . . Before you know it, he'll be declaring he's in love!'

Anya produced her cousin Victor Martineau with a flourish, sliding her arm through his and tossing the dark curls in such an alluring manner that, for a moment, Eva wondered if this might be the one she meant to have.

'Victor works with my father,' Anya announced. 'He runs the business side of things and keeps everyone straight. He's my very favourite man!'

But Victor merely smiled archly and disengaged his arm. 'Don't believe it, Eva,' he said, sitting down at her table. 'I'm not her favourite at all.'

He was tall and serious-looking with a shock of rich, dark curly hair, a little older and quieter than everyone else. He took no time to sum up Eva's situation.

'You're tired from your journey,' he said, eyeing her carefully. 'Anya should have waited to bring you here. Why don't I escort you home so you can unpack and settle in?'

'But we're staying here,' Eva explained. 'Mr Klein is away . . .'

Victor looked keenly around the room, clearly intent on attracting Anya's attention, but failing to catch her eye.

'My uncle was most upset to miss your arrival,' he said at last, turning back, 'but your room is ready at the house. There's a maid to wait upon you, and a cook to prepare your meals. It's not necessary, and I may say, not altogether desirable, that you should stay at the café . . .'

Eva was startled, but before she could think of an appropriate response, Anya appeared suddenly at the table and in one deft, determined movement, swung Eva's valise from beside her chair and put an arm around her friend's shoulder, raising her to her feet.

'I'll show you upstairs, Eva,' she said briskly, flashing Victor a piercing glance. 'I'm sure you'd like to make yourself at home.'

It was later the same day that she met David Klein.

Unsettled by Victor's remarks about the café, Eva nevertheless followed Anya up the narrow stairs to a bare, bright room overlooking the square. She took her best dress and her night things from her valise and laid them carefully upon a chair, closed the shutters against the silver glare of the afternoon sky, and lay down on the stout iron bed which stood in one corner of the room.

When she woke, the strip of light beneath the shutter had turned from silver to purple and she could hear laughter from the square below, persistent and loud. She opened her window and peered down.

He was sitting alone at the edge of the terrace, a cigarette wasting in the ashtray beside him, a glass of beer at his elbow, apparently untouched. He was absorbed in a book, unperturbed at the raucous laughter which emanated from the café.

She knew at once that it was he, for the olive skin and wild dark curls of the Kleins betrayed him, and there was something about his self-imposed isolation, the way he sat with his book, oblivious to the frivolity around him, that reminded her of Emmanuel Klein. How often had she seen him thus, dark head bent over some learned text, while she and Anya had chattered in the little parlour at the Forsters' lodge cottage?

As she watched, unobserved, the laughter grew increasingly boisterous, but still he didn't lift his eyes, until suddenly two men tottered into view, one supporting the other, making for the steps that led down from the terrace into the square. At David Klein's table they paused, and as the more sober of the two turned to look back into the café, Eva recognised the young American, Toby Truman. His companion lurched towards David Klein, and banged his fist down upon the table.

'Come on, Bertie,' Eva heard Toby Truman say. 'Leave it alone,' and then they were gone, swallowed up into the darkening bustle of the streets beyond the square.

Eva closed the shutter once more. Something about the scene she had witnessed vaguely disturbed her, and to her confusion she was seized by a pressing and unexpected desire. Perhaps it was merely the residue of sleep, sour in her mouth and throbbing at her temples. Or perhaps, looking down upon this foreign courtyard, it was the sudden intimation that the past was truly gone, and that the Café des Arbres, for all Victor Martineau's veiled prohibition, represented the future. Or perhaps it was the bowed head of David Klein, the untouched glass at his side, prompting memories of all that had once been.

Whatever it was, Eva knew what she must do.

Outside it was spring, a season which recalled so much. She had mourned Harold Brannen in the bitter spring of 1915, long ago now, and Blanche Brannen too, even longer ago, had died in the merciless spring . . . And then her own beloved father, laid in the frosty spring soil of St Cuthbert's churchyard not four weeks ago . . .

Eva picked up her mourning cloak, wrapped it around her shoulders, and feeling unsure of herself and faintly foolish, crept down the narrow stairs towards the hubbub below.

Matthew Brannen, Harold, Edward, Richard . . . She had vowed to leave them all behind, and yet suddenly she longed to bring them to her in an act of remembrance, to regenerate their love and their protection, to incorporate history into the moment.

At the door into the café she hesitated, searching the crowded room for Anya. But Anya was nowhere to be seen, and as she scanned the unfamiliar faces anxiously, David Klein looked up from his book.

He was beside her in a moment.

'You're Eva, of course? Hallo!'

He introduced himself with the easy informality she already recognised as belonging to the Americans alone. Davy, not David, and she would join him for a drink, of course? Without waiting for her assent, he took her arm and steered her firmly through the tables towards the terrace.

'We seem to have lost Anya,' he said mildly, 'but it doesn't matter. I'm under strict instructions to fulfil your every desire.'

He smiled, and the grave blue eyes were suddenly enlivened, transforming a sombre expression into something wry and faintly mischievous.

'Is that so?' She was amused, but she was not to be deflected from her aim.

'Then there's something you can do for me. I'd like to go to church . . . to light a candle for my father . . . Can you direct me?'

'I'll do better than that,' he said, picking up his book from the table. 'I'll take you.'

Eva was momentarily nonplussed, and stared, confused, at the poetry book he clutched. *The Waste Land* she read. But Davy Klein, it seemed, was ruffled by nothing. If a guest in this most Jewish of households wished to attend church, then he, cheerfully assuming the role of host, would certainly oblige.

They walked out of the square to find Paris preening itself, the air heavily scented with blossom, the night sky dark as violets. The streets bustled with twilight revellers, chattering, laughing, waving to each other across the alleys. A youth darted from a shabby apartment block, weaving between the promenading couples, a loaf of bread tucked beneath his arm. After him toddled a stout madame, brandishing a carving knife. A wounded serviceman stood on a pavement corner, face turned blindly to the glittering stars above, extending a tin for alms. Eva's francs clattered on to the cheap metal, a thin, harsh sound in the rich babble round them. Then a pair of lovers stopped to kiss, so suddenly

and unexpectedly that Eva and Davy almost stumbled into them. She
looked up at him, and he laughed, encouraging her own merriment.

She was enchanted and excited. She was uplifted and refreshed. And
he seemed to catch her mood, for they talked easily and happily, as
though they'd always known each other, which in part, through Anya,
they had.

She talked of St Cuthbert's and the Brannens, of the Church High
School and Miss Lamont's lessons in dramatic art, of the Alnwick
Players and her own modest successes on the amateur stage, of Lizzie
Howard and young Harriet. She even, to her surprise, found herself
talking of Dr Orde and the extraordinary tale he'd told, and how, as a
result, she had transformed herself into Eva Delamere. Perhaps it was
because Davy Klein, as Anya's cousin, seemed no random stranger. She
felt no need to dissemble, nor to deny the past.

He looked down at her keenly as she spoke, trying to assess the
impact on her character of this unexpected history.

'The accidents of birth are irrelevant,' he said at last, rather gravely.
'It's what happens afterwards that counts.'

For his part, he talked of his father, Emmanuel's elder brother, who'd
emigrated from Germany with his childhood friend.

'They were only eighteen, and they had nothing between them, Saul
Bernstein and Isaac Klein . . . But they both did very well, in their
respective ways . . .'

He also talked of his mother, sent from her own home in Germany
to be his father's bride, of her early death and his father's ailing health,
and of the family business, building houses, first for humble immigrants
like themselves, then for up-and-coming Jewish tradesmen, and now for
the wealthy movie-makers who'd gone west for the weather. This was
the business he would pursue on his return.

'So what are you doing in Paris?' she asked.

'I'm supposed to be studying architecture,' he replied with a faint
grimace, 'but the truth, I guess, is that I'm just having a good time.'

They came at last to the church, a squat, unprepossessing pile of
blackened stones set on an ugly paved forecourt in a dingy sidestreet.

Eva had thought to find it empty, had imagined he would wait outside while she slipped in to light her candles, but as they approached,
the elegiac strains of a sung psalm wafted out on to the evening air, and
Davy made purposefully for the entrance.

'Seems to be a Mass,' he observed. 'Must be a Saint's day.' Then to
Eva's astonishment he swung open the heavy oak door and walked in,
beckoning her on.

Inside, the pews were crammed with huddled forms, old women in
black lace headpieces, young mothers with babies on their knees, dour-

looking men in shiny suits. They sat in awed silence awaiting the entrance of the priest while a sad-faced choir intoned the words of the twenty-second psalm.

'Maundy Thursday,' Eva breathed, wondering how she could possibly have forgotten, still perplexed by her companion's presence at her side.

He led her to a rear pew and they perched upon the end, uncomfortably close. He shuffled nearer to the enraptured old woman who sat beside him, allowing Eva and her mourning cloak the maximum room, and yet still their bodies touched, knee jammed against knee, hands nowhere to lie except precariously close to each other's. Eva's heart seemed to clamour against her chest and her breath came quickly. She closed her eyes and the plaintive singing rose to a crescendo around her while the air grew heavy with the sickly scent of incense. She felt her senses quicken beneath the terrible beauty of it all, the dark mystery at the heart of the Christian faith, and then she felt a touch at her elbow. Davy was urging her out of her seat so that the people beyond might move towards the communion rail.

Eva stood up, and to her shock, felt herself propelled forward, Davy close behind her. He was pushing her gently towards the altar, seemingly oblivious to the impropriety of such a step. Her heart began to pound faster; her hands were sticky and wet. She did not wish to draw attention to her dilemma, and she reached for his hand, hoping to convey by an urgent squeeze that now was the time for them to leave.

But he grasped her fingers tightly, almost seeming to caress them, and before she quite knew what had happened, he had steered her to the rail and was kneeling beside her.

The body of our Lord Jesus Christ, which was given for thee, preserve thy body and soul unto everlasting life . . .

She seemed to hear her father's voice repeating the age-old incantation, and in a dream she lifted her face to receive the bread, eyes closed for fear they might give her away.

It was over in a moment. No one had detected them. No one had guessed that here were two dissenters, one of them a Jew, the other a heretic against the Church of Rome. As she rose from the communion rail, she was aware of trembling hands, of weak, shaking legs. She had no thought now of her brothers or her father, and the candles she'd planned to light. She wanted only to be gone.

But Davy wasn't about to let her go.

'You can light your candles at the end of the service,' he whispered, pushing her gently back into their pew, and so she waited in mute agitation, fearing that at any moment they might be denounced.

But they weren't, and the candles were lit on the altar of the Holy
Vigil amid banks of perfumed lilies. One for Harold, one for Edward,
one for Richard . . . One for Blanche, one for Matthew Brannen,
and one for the unknown woman who lay in St Cuthbert's churchyard. Six candles for six extinguished lives, burning to their own ex-
tinction.

Outside the church again, Eva turned uncertainly to Davy.

'We had no right to take the holy bread,' she muttered.

'Whyever not? There were no thunderbolts. We haven't broken any
fundamental laws, Eva! We've merely bent a few man-made rules. If
there's a God up there –' he gesticulated towards the sparkling sky
above them – 'then I really can't believe he'd mind!'

He took her arm once more. 'Come on,' he said, 'I'll show you the
river and buy you a glass of wine to wash down your holy bread.'

She laughed, despite herself.

'You don't understand,' she reproached him gently. 'How could you?
You're not a Christian.'

He greeted this with evident hilarity.

'I'll let you into a little secret,' he whispered in her ear. 'Neither was
Jesus.'

If Eva were faintly shocked, then she was also curiously relieved by
his irreverence. Had she still been the devout clergyman's daughter, she
might have been offended. But she was no longer devout. Indeed, she
hardly knew whether to call herself a believer any more.

'I see you don't take religion at all seriously,' she said uncertainly,
rehearsing this daring idea for herself.

'On the contrary,' he said cheerfully, 'I take it very seriously indeed.
That's why I believe in challenging its myths and its misunderstandings. Maybe then we can defuse something of its terrible power.'

'Is it so terrible?' Eva asked, startled.

'What else keeps people from being themselves? Nothing so much,
I'd say, as the notion, mistaken though it may be, that somewhere
there's a God who watches everything you do and judges you accord-
ingly.'

The words were delivered without a hint of solemnity, and for a
moment Eva wondered if she were being teased. Was he mocking her
own supposed beliefs? She looked up at him quickly.

'But religion isn't just personal,' she objected, feeling herself called
to mount a defence. 'It's about people working and praying together,
building their own identity.' She hesitated. 'You, as a Jew, must see that
more than anyone.'

He laughed again, then took her hand, leading her across the
thronged pavements towards the bank of the glittering black river.

'Oh, I see it,' he said lightly. 'I see your identity, and I see my own. Let's just pray that our precious identity won't one day prove the death of us.'

'I can certainly pray for that,' she said.

'Then do,' he said, still laughing. 'Please do.'

If there is truly a moment when Destiny takes its protégés by the hand and gives a warning shake while inviting the fulfilment of its half-hidden hopes and unguessed desires, then perhaps this was it. Perhaps, in this one insignificant moment, the future stirred like a hibernating beast roused from its slumbers, sat up, took a look, and then sank back to await its proper awakening. Whatever, Eva, acutely aware of David Klein's touch upon her fingers, the cut of his shoulder on a level with her eye, the tone of his voice, at one time soft and faintly dry, the angle of his head, found herself seized by a powerful sense of the familiar. It was not that they had walked together before, nor spoken in just this wry manner, for indeed they had met only hours earlier. It was rather as though they always should, as though an every-day pattern had been glimpsed through the tantalising veil of tomorrow.

The intuition was gone as soon as felt, but she relinquished it reluctantly, looking up at him curiously, alert for his response.

'I guess we should get back,' he said uncertainly. 'But maybe we won't. Not just yet . . .'

They took a cab and cruised among the city's splendours, Davy pointing out each new vision as though the credit belonged to him alone. The Arc de Triomphe, the Champs-Elysées, the Place de la Concorde – Eva saw them all as she had never imagined, with a strange quickening in her heart, a sense of everything consumed mysteriously into Now, as though time itself had dissolved along with her old identity and there was only this moment and its infinite promise.

'You'll have to learn how to drink red wine,' he told her seriously as they loitered at a bar on the edge of the Jardin du Luxembourg. 'If you're to live in Paris, you'll find yourself downing a heck of a lot . . . Take it slowly, now! Don't throw it back like that. Sip, and then savour . . .'

Riding home to the Café des Arbres, her head lolling against his shoulder, it seemed as though the streets outside the taxi window had risen from the clay beneath to float upon the twilight breeze, unearthly strips of light twinkling on the rim of her vision, bearing her upward to magical new worlds. Ah yes, if it were only possible to ride for ever to the very edge of eternity . . .

'I'd like to stay here always,' she said dreamily. 'I hope I die in Paris.'

'Don't die yet,' he laughed. 'You just got here.'

'I mean in about a hundred years' time! I'll be buried in a quiet little cemetery on the edge of the city, and every evening at just this time, my spirit will rise up and wander among the crowds.'

He glanced at her swiftly, but she was staring out at the teeming streets, her pale face lit by an inner fire, the violet eyes wide.

'Hey, Eva . . . You feeling okay?'

She had stumbled from the taxi, and he'd caught her in his arms, clasping her tight so that, for a moment, they held each other's gaze. Her senses swayed, her lips trembled in the effort to voice an unformed thought, and he leaned towards her, about to speak. But then a vexed call from the café steps behind them put an end to all imaginings.

'Is that you?' demanded Anya, and they turned to confront her, momentarily perplexed.

'I've been showing Eva the sights,' Davy mumbled, releasing her from his grip. 'I guess she's feeling pretty tired.'

He left them abruptly, nodding curtly at Eva before bounding up the terrace steps into the bright café.

Anya stared after him then, quickly shaking off whatever irritation had possessed her, turned back to Eva. 'Well, what do you think of him?' she enquired merrily.

Eva said nothing, pulling her mourning cloak tightly around her shoulders, shivering slightly in the evening air.

'I knew you'd like him,' Anya said, linking her arm in her friend's. 'And I love him, Eva! No one's going to persuade me I don't. Not Victor, not my father, and not Davy's father either. My mind's quite made up!'

That night, when Eva had climbed the narrow stairs to her small, bare room above the café, eyes sore from the blue smoke that hung like a canopy over the room, throat dry and mind dulled, she could think only that her first day in Paris was over.

She had danced with Victor Martineau, and in watching him observe his cousins as they sat together at their table in the window, had suddenly understood the nature of his feelings for Anya and his reservations about her life at the café.

She had joked with Jacob Klein, and in receiving his good-natured teasing about the *mesdemoiselles* who so enlivened his café, had seen that he, too, was charmed by Anya, yet perhaps did not fully recognise the unfettered spirit she embodied.

She had sat with the young American writer, Toby Truman, who, it seemed, had secured a room at the café despite all competition, and in listening to his talk, had realised the full extent of Anya's power to enchant.

'You must meet Bertie,' Toby said. 'Bertie Levine. Bertie's old man is in the movies . . . He's a hot-shot agent. You know, back in America? Are you keen on the movies, Eva? Take it from me, it's the place to be.'

Eva, suddenly feeling alone in strange territory and grateful for his attentions, had nodded earnestly.

'I guess you could say I'm kinda . . . in charge of Bertie,' Toby said, eyeing her thoughtfully. 'He's in a pretty bad way right now. His marriage broke up.'

'I'm sorry to hear that,' Eva said carefully.

'Yeah . . . Well, it was always gonna happen. But that's not why he's in a bad way.'

They had both looked at Anya then, and Eva's face flushed, for she hadn't intended to reveal how much she knew.

'Maybe you could speak to Anya?' Toby asked suddenly, taking her by surprise. 'Maybe she doesn't realise just how upset old Bertie is. Truth to tell, she's none too keen to listen to me . . .'

But Eva did not imagine that Anya would listen to her either. And indeed, what could she say? How could she plead the case for Bertie Levine, or anyone else come to that, against David Klein?

Throughout the evening she had watched them in melancholy fascination, watched as Anya lit Davy's cigarettes, poured his Armagnac, fingered the button on his sleeve, nuzzled her nose into his neck. She had watched, and had seen that they were surely lovers, that Anya's passion for her cousin was no unrequited fancy, no passing caprice.

She had watched, and then she had related to Anya with careful informality everything – or nearly everything – that had been seen and done that evening: how kind and thoughtful her cousin had been to the newcomer, how he'd taken her to church and waited while she lit her candles, shown her the splendours of the city, tried to teach her how to drink red wine.

She had watched, and she had hidden the undeniable confusion she felt within, and she had seen – yes, she had clearly seen, she could not be mistaken – that for some indeterminate reason David Klein now seemed unwilling to meet her eye.

This unsettling observation accompanied her to bed, as indeed did all the events of that first portentous day in Paris, returning to possess her when she woke from sleep, not just the following morning, but on many, many mornings through the long months and years ahead.

Chapter Eleven

'One day, Eva, you'll experience passion. You'll believe that nothing could ever separate you from the one you love. But alas, there are many things that may go wrong . . .'

How long does it seem since my father said those words to me? A hundred years? Or was it only yesterday? One thing is certain. I may not have experienced passion, but I have seen what it can do. I have watched it enslave and consume, and I believe myself very fortunate in having the opportunity to observe how foolishly, and how wantonly, men and women can sometimes behave. I wish all this were not at my dearest friend's expense, but there's no denying that Anya's example provides my own protection . . .

The Journals of Eva Delamere, edited by Blanche Duval

The Divine Faith convalescent hospital was a building of startling beauty, shielded from the road by dense vegetation. Behind the dark evergreens and formidable cedars an immaculate lawn stretched to the house, its emerald brilliance shimmering before the honey-coloured mansion like a sheet of pure water.

During the war, Eva learned, the lawn had been ploughed to grow root vegetables and soft fruit. When peace returned, the restoration of the grass became a symbol of the new promise, its daily care a matter of pride and perfection. One of Eva's tasks, in the company of Sister Marguerite, the nurse tutor, was to water the primroses which bordered the lawn every evening at sundown.

Each day she walked the short journey from the dark, brooding terrace where Emmanuel Klein lived to the convent, content that the Sisters were in need of lay helpers and that her qualifications had secured her a means of support, and yet restless with her allotted duties, more menial, less satisfying, than her work at the Alnwick Memorial Hospital had once seemed.

'To nurse requires great humility,' Sister Marguerite informed her. 'But remember, Eva, no task is so humble that it cannot reflect the glory of God.'

Now, as Eva walked the long polished corridors of the convent in the shadow of some stately Sister, dispensing food and medicines, rousing an ancient patient from slumber to receive his soup or pressing a poultice to a limb, she wondered about the profession she had so readily entered. Certainly, to alleviate suffering was the duty, not only of a Christian as her father had taught her, but of every honourable citizen. But in the stillness of morning prayer at the convent chapel, or in a moment of sunny silence on the glittering grass outside the mansion, a small, dissenting voice would not be denied . . . Is this all? Is this to be my life?

She had settled happily enough into her new home, the immaculate house that Emmanuel Klein, ever busy with his building projects, seemed rarely to inhabit. But she well understood why Anya preferred the gaiety of the Café des Arbres. It was not simply that Davy lived there, though this was a powerful attraction. It was rather that the Klein household was run much as a business might be administered, with logs and ledgers for household duties, precise times for meals, strict schedules about the airing of linens and the changing of drapes, and devoted observance of Jewish conventions and customs.

This zeal was due in total to the Kleins' long-time housekeeper, and as the household spun to ceaseless demands for order and cleanliness, Eva began to understand how the lives of two motherless children, herself and Anya, had diverged across the years.

While both had been assured of the loving concern of their fathers, Emmanuel Klein had of necessity relied upon housekeepers, tutors and governesses to raise his daughter. Matthew Brannen, in contrast, had always set the tone of his household himself, allowing no one to override his wishes, nor indeed his foibles. It was a peculiar luxury afforded to a clergyman, whose home might be a province of the Heavenly Kingdom, for better or worse. For Eva, it had meant the security of knowing her father to be in charge.

Anya, meantime, obliged to accede to rules and regulations that were not of her making nor even her father's, had gone her own way as soon as the opportunity presented. Certainly, she remained the dutiful daughter, returning from the café when expected, observing mealtimes and customs with good grace whenever Emmanuel Klein was at home. But Emmanuel Klein was often away, and as soon as he was gone, Anya moved into the café.

The two friends spoke little of this arrangement, for Eva had found it impossible to approve Anya's love affair with her cousin. After all, both were guilty of deceiving the family. Only Victor knew the truth of it. Jacob Klein, it was clear, saw nothing but innocent affection between his nephew and niece, and while this, in Eva's view, rendered him guilty of naivety, it hardly excused the brazen exploitation of his good nature.

Anya's father, too, though he might occasionally ask about events or developments at the café, did not enquire too closely into his daughter's behaviour, seeming content to leave her to her own good sense. Eva could not fault this decision since she herself was subject to no guardianship, and indeed, Anya was of an age to order her own affairs. It was the mark of Emmanuel Klein's generosity and open-mindedness that he did not seek to control his daughter, but nevertheless, Eva wondered how he would feel if he knew the truth.

There was also the question of how David's own father might view the liaison with Anya, for Eva had learned that his family had always meant him to marry someone else.

Anya related this astonishing fact with unconcern.

'Of course, he doesn't love Rebecca Bernstein,' she'd explained. 'It's a business deal. The Kleins have connections, and the Bernsteins have cash.'

'But how will he get out of it?' Eva had asked, bewildered.

Anya merely shrugged.

'When a man's in love,' she replied knowingly, 'then he's not inclined to marry for any other reason.'

Eva was not so confident. She had divined that Anya's passion burned with alarming intensity, that all her hopes and desires were fixed upon Davy. She had also seen that, while he might admire his cousin and wish her happiness and security, he did not seem to understand that the fulfilment of both lay with him.

He was casual, almost careless, with Anya's affection, returning it easily and yet, it seemed to Eva, without promise. There was much laughing and playing the fool, much mimicking of grand romantic gestures, much wry debate and espousing of brave, unsentimental doctrine.

'Whether a man live one year or a thousand years,' he was fond of quoting from the Jewish prayer book, 'what does he gain? He will be as though he had never been . . .'

Eva was further discomfited to observe that Davy seemed unusually keen to encourage Anya's other suitors, always buying drinks or inviting them to dine at the table in the window. It was as though he half hoped Anya might switch her affections.

This largesse was not only offered to his cousin Victor, whose critical presence Davy seemed well able to tolerate, nor just to Karl Schwartz, the composer from Berlin, whose admiration for the mistress of the Café des Arbres was touching and faintly comic, but also included the

lovelorn Bertie Levine, who haunted the café like some inebriate shade
newly discharged, as Toby Truman, in a rare flash of irritation with his
old friend, once remarked, from the Hades Home for Incurable Alcoholics.

Eva had laughed uncertainly, pitying Bertie, and yet irritated herself
by his drunken melancholia.

'What will happen to him?' she'd asked Toby, not expecting a serious
answer.

'That rather depends on your friend Anya,' Toby had replied slowly.
'We'll have to see how she reacts when Klein sets sail for home and the
arms of Rebecca Bernstein . . .'

'You know about the Bernsteins?' Eva was startled that intimate
Klein business should be so openly discussed.

'Everyone knows about the Bernsteins. Remember, I told you Bertie's
old man was in the movies? Well, so are the Bernsteins. You ever heard
of Worldwide Pictures? Saul Bernstein owns the whole damn show.'

He had leaned across the table towards her, offering the cigarette she
always declined, wafting his own smoke away from her in a vain attempt
at gentlemanly protection.

'Tell me this, Eva,' he said quietly, nodding towards the floor where
Anya and Davy danced, their dark curls one indivisible glossy mass as
his head bent towards hers. 'How come the free spirits always end up
chaining themselves to the wrong guy?'

It was a question Eva did not care to pursue, for she understood only
too well the attraction of David Klein. He was physically compelling
with his clear olive skin and navy blue eyes, and easy company with his
lazy, wry manner. But it was more than this.

He was not like the others. He wasn't a dreamer, full of grand notions
about the future of mankind, but he wasn't a cynic either, maintaining
a lively interest in the political and moral debates which were the pulse
of the café. The future of Communism? The death of Religion? The
salvation that was Art? Among the would-be movie scriptwriters, the
poets and the magazine reporters, David Klein was a man with views,
but without the naked ambition which made so many of the orators, in
Eva's view anyway, rather suspect.

It was all very well to declare oneself for humanity, but to justify
cheating one's dimwitted concierge out of a month's rent on the
grounds of needing a new typewriter to complete one's masterpiece
seemed, so far as Eva were concerned, to undermine all credibility. Yet
Randy Makepeace had caused great amusement when he related this
tale, and everyone had applauded. Everyone except Eva herself, and
David Klein.

Davy didn't want to be a poet or a painter or a great composer like
Karl Schwartz. He even refused to call himself an architect, insisting

instead that he was merely a builder, and if Eva were inclined to dismiss this as affectation, then Davy was ready with an answer.

'It's a great calling,' he'd said mischievously. 'Just think about it, Eva. What could be more noble, more grand? We builders keep on toiling, brick upon brick, even though we know that time, the wind, war, or plain old entropy will turn everything into dust . . . That's real defiance. Real passion! These painters and writers, they imagine their art will live for ever. But no building will last for ever . . . We are the real artists. The artists of the Real.'

Eva had laughed despite herself, not knowing if she were meant to take him seriously at all, wary of revealing just how much she did.

'The Café des Arbres will probably crumble into dust before we do,' he said, looking round at the faded walls and pitted floors. 'I'd give it another twenty years at most. But there's the challenge, you see! When the café falls down, some modest, philanthropic builder will come along and hey presto, there'll be another café right here on the same spot . . .'

She'd laughed outright then, and he'd laughed too, but Toby, who'd been sitting at their table, was plainly unamused.

'Don't be fooled by this unassuming builder stuff,' he'd said to Eva later. 'David Klein thinks he's smarter than everyone else.'

Pondering it all, Eva thought this was probably true. Not simply that David Klein believed himself smarter than everyone else, but that maybe, in fact, he was. And if this were so, then the knowing display of superiority, however wittily expressed, however self-mocking or dry, constituted a flaw. But it didn't detract from his appeal.

Perhaps, Eva wondered, when she considered, as she often did, Toby's antipathy towards Davy, his appeal really was the appeal of 'the wrong guy'. Perhaps, she thought, there is something in each woman that yearns for the unattainable. Davy would never marry Anya, of this she felt certain. Perhaps Anya, although she might deny it and use all her charms to overcome it, knew this too. Perhaps this was why she wanted Davy so badly. And perhaps it explained why she, Eva, felt so powerfully drawn to her friend's lover.

For all that, she was determined to fight the feeling. There was nothing to be gained by falling in love with David Klein. He could not love her in return, although sometimes, when they found themselves alone at the table in the window, she fancied that some unvoiced thought hovered on the edge of their dialogue, a sub-text which each read silently with a vague, unsettling sense of regret.

They had never spoken of that first night in Paris, of that brief time, before Eva learned of the love affair with Anya, in which they had seemed poised upon some unspecified mutual understanding.

There was, Eva reasoned whenever she felt melancholy about this loss, nothing of any real nature to be mourned. Nothing momentous had happened, there had been no truly significant exchange. And yet, sometimes, when she settled down at night between the stiff, cold sheets in the lonely bedroom which, nominally, she shared with Anya in Emmanuel Klein's silent, cavernous house, she found herself reliving the odd sensation that had given its flavour to that strange, memorable night. That peculiar sense of the known dogged her still. The cut of his shoulder, the inclination of his head, the way he walked, smiled, linked his arm through hers, hailed a taxicab. She could not summon up that fleeting sensation of the utterly familiar once more, but she could not forget it either. Nor could she forget that Davy was Anya's lover and that both were flaunting the rules of right behaviour.

It remained, therefore, to dismiss all such fancy, to find other companions to divert her thoughts. And other companions, particularly young men, were not in short supply.

Arnie Steinem, the painter from Minnesota, made it his business to seek out Eva, and even asked her to sit for a portrait. But Eva didn't care for Arnie's paintings, and in truth, cared for Arnie rather less.

Pete Chessington, the English piano player, was also an admirer, and had once subjected Eva to an embarrassing serenade in a bar on the Boulevard St-Michel. Eva liked Pete, but he drank too much.

Bobbie Pascali was fun to be with, Hart Dixon wrote highly amusing doggerel about the Café des Arbres set, and Victor Martineau, whose unswerving devotion to Anya endeared him greatly to Eva, proved himself a worthy and reliable friend. Victor was always there, a courteous companion or protective escort, meeting Eva when hospital duty finished late, or arranging a taxicab when needed, providing an often necessary buffer between the uninitiated newcomer and the pack.

But it was Toby Truman who came closest to her heart.

'You and me, Eva,' he'd say, pouring her a glass of white wine and fixing an unabashed eye on the silver cross which always hung around her bare throat, 'we'd be a swell team. You're very pretty, you know that, don't you? You should be in the movies.'

'It's you who should be in the movies,' she laughed.

'We should both be in the movies,' he corrected himself. 'Why aren't we? What are we doing here? Why don't we set sail for New York tomorrow?'

As the months passed and the Divine Faith hospital seemed to consume more and more of her time, as her disapproval of David Klein and her attraction to him seemed to grow in curious tandem, and as the Café des Arbres appeared fixed in its languid ways for all eternity, Eva sometimes found herself wondering why not.

*

'There's a new admission on St-Thérèse ward, Eva. A Madame Martineau, discharged this morning from Pitié-Salpêtrière. She may have a little clear broth, and her dressing must be changed at twelve o'clock . . .'

Eva, who had been dusting the icons and re-laying the fire in the tiny whitewashed sitting room overlooking the lawn where Sister Marguerite liked to copy up her notes, glanced quickly at the nurse tutor.

'Madame Martineau?'

Eva had never met Victor's mother, though she'd heard a great deal from Anya about the truculent old aunt who liked to know everyone's business. The name was distinctive. Moreover, Victor had been out of Paris with his Uncle Emmanuel for some days. Had his mother been taken ill in his absence?

'She's a rather difficult old woman, I'm afraid. She doesn't think she should be here. On the one hand she's Jewish, and sees no reason to accept the good offices of Christians –' Sister Marguerite looked up briefly from her notes – 'and on the other, she says she has a son who's quite able to look after her himself. She could go home if she had someone to help. However, it seems there's no one at her address, not even a maidservant. So here she must stay.'

The Sister stood up and tucked her ledger into the fold of her voluminous sleeve.

'Be firm with her if necessary, Eva. We have a busy morning and the lawn is to be cut. Perhaps you will assist with gathering the clippings?'

Eva walked smartly to St-Thérèse ward, certain that however difficult Madame Martineau might prove, she could not possibly warrant less attention than a bag of grass clippings.

As soon as she opened the ward door, a tiny figure perched mutinously upon a great mound of starched pillows waved urgently across the room.

'Mademoiselle! If you please, can you find Eva Delamere, and tell her I am here? She is a friend of my son's.'

Eva sat down on the end of her bed.

'Madame, I am Eva Delamere. How can I help?'

The old lady struggled up from her pillows to grasp Eva's hand, and as she leaned forward, a glossy coil of dark grey hair tumbled from the top of her head and fell over her shoulder. She pushed it back impatiently.

'My dear, how fortunate! You see, I know all about you from Victor . . . He tells me everything! I was aware you worked here at the convent, and I was quite sure you would help me escape.'

'Escape?'

Eva pressed the thin hand in concern and gazed doubtfully at the heavily bandaged leg which lay crookedly on the bed, so large and unwieldy it seemed hardly to belong to its frail owner.

'Oh, tut! It's nothing. A small ulcer, that's all. But my dear, tonight Victor comes home! There's simply no need for me to be here. If you could find my clothes, and assist me to the street, I'd be able to get a taxicab.'

Eva smiled and nodded sympathetically.

'But Madame,' she murmured gently, 'if Victor comes back tonight, surely it would be sensible to wait until tomorrow morning. Is it really so terrible here?'

Madame Martineau looked briefly round at the bare room, the yellow distempered walls, the grey linen curtains, the rows of ancient women who languished in narrow iron beds, the solitary jar of primroses standing on a windowledge, their bright leaves yearning towards the life and light beyond.

'Well, my dear, it's not very jolly, is it? They may have told you I'm a frightful old woman who doesn't like nuns, and I may have said some such thing when I arrived. But the truth is that they have no sense of humour. I ask you, who'd wish to be ill in the midst of all this holy gloom? My dear, it's enough to finish you off!'

Eva laughed.

'I know what you mean,' she said quietly, vowing on a sudden whim that she would never end her own days in anywhere remotely like the Divine Faith convent hospital. 'It's certainly not at all jolly.'

Madame Martineau shook her tiny fist in the air.

'I won't spend a night in this place!' she declared. 'I mean to be home for Victor coming back. And of course, they can't make me stay! Not if I have someone to help me escape.'

'But the Sister says you don't even have a maid . . .'

'Oh, that last girl,' said Madame Martineau despairingly. 'She had no sense of humour either.'

At that moment the door of St-Thérèse ward swung open, and Sister Marguerite peered in, waving an imperious arm. 'The grass, Eva, if you will . . .'

Eva winked at Madame Martineau and followed the Sister out of the ward. 'I'll be back just as soon as I can,' she whispered.

Two hours later when the lawn had been shorn and all the cuttings bagged, Eva asked for a free afternoon.

'I know it's short notice, but I've checked with Sister Lorraine and she can do an extra duty. I'm happy to give up a half-day's pay.'

She was back in the whitewashed sitting room with Sister Marguerite, staring at the plaster figure on the crucifix above the fireplace, willing God or just the implacable Sister herself, to grant her request. For some reason she couldn't quite fathom, she passionately wished to help Madame Martineau.

'It's quite unorthodox, Eva. We must have reliability, you understand! May I ask why you suddenly need a free afternoon?'

'An errand of mercy, Sister, for a very dear friend,' replied Eva without so much as a blush or a blink.

'In that case,' said the Sister coolly, 'I can hardly refuse.'

Eva flew back to St-Thérèse ward, and then made her way out of the convent, across the sparkling grass to the street beyond where she hailed a cab for the Café des Arbres.

She'd hoped to persuade Anya to step in and help her aunt, but when she arrived she found the café all but empty. She stood on the terrace for a moment, nonplussed, but then turned at the sound of footsteps from the stairs.

It was David Klein.

'Where is everybody?' she cried.

'Gone to the movies. Special showing of René Clair's new film. *A Nous la liberté.*'

'Can you help, then? Your aunt is in trouble. Can you pretend to be Victor Martineau?'

'Good grief! I expect so . . . I look a bit like him. But whatever for?'

He listened doubtfully as she explained.

'My aunt doesn't altogether approve of me,' he said awkwardly. 'I suspect Victor has been telling tales.'

'She'll approve if you help her escape. I know that Sister Marguerite just won't let her go unless she thinks you're her son . . .'

The plan worked with a precision she had not dared to expect, and it was only when Davy had fooled the admissions Sister with an expert performance in flawless French, had enacted an exaggerated reunion with Madame Martineau, escorted both the patient and her accomplice back to Victor's home, and effortlessly carried the old lady up two flights of winding stairs to her sitting room, laying her gently on her favourite *chaise-longue* overlooking the bustling street below, that the truth of Madame's situation was revealed.

'Well, David,' she said somewhat grudgingly, directing Eva to a small bureau and a half-bottle of the finest brandy, 'I must thank you for your help, and now I must confess. I'm not absolutely certain that Victor will be back tomorrow. But it will only be a few days at the most, and I shall be perfectly all right.'

Eva was horrified, and the old lady had the grace to blush. But Davy merely chuckled, and raised his glass.

'Your very good health, Aunt Leah,' he said. 'I'm sure Eva will stay with you until Victor returns. And if she can't, then I can.'

There was, of course, no reason why Eva shouldn't stay, and once she'd forgiven Madame her deception, the three of them settled to an unexpectedly delightful evening.

Davy went shopping, and then cooked dinner. 'It runs in the family,' he laughed as Eva raised a surprised eyebrow at the skilful slicing and frying.

Madame, meanwhile, had instructed that two bottles of Beaujolais be opened and warmed.

'To you, my dears,' she declared, pouring out the wine. 'May you always be as happy as you are tonight!'

As the wine in the bottles fell, as the food was eaten and the fire fed, Madame began to tell Eva her story. She talked of her childhood in Poland and of Jacob Klein's emigration to France.

'Well, of course, my dear, we all came too. My mother, Emmanuel and I . . . And that is how I met Victor's father . . . My darling Philippe . . . But oh my dear, he was a Frenchman, not a Jew. Such an upset for my poor mother.'

Eva smiled and hoped she appeared sympathetic.

'Philippe's mother was a fine seamstress. She made French lace petticoats for Parisian ladies . . . She taught me how to sew. Eva, I must show you some of my lace.'

Here the tale halted while Madame refilled the glasses.

'But without your Uncle Emmanuel,' she said to Davy, 'we should never have prospered. He took care of us all. He lost his own dear wife, and then he set off to conquer the world, taking that slip of a girl with him . . .'

Madame shook her head at the mention of Anya, and glanced quickly at Davy, who simply stared into the fire, saying nothing.

'Yes, my dearest Emmanuel,' Madame said meditatively. 'He gave Philippe a job. He secured an apartment for my mother-in-law in the rue des Arènes . . . Even Philippe's poor dear sister, he tried to help . . .'

Madame had drunk a generous quantity of wine, and seemed to be dreaming.

'What happened to Philippe's sister?' Eva asked, but the question was never answered, for at that moment there came a great commotion from below, a violent hammering upon Madame Martineau's front door.

Madame looked out of her window.

'Why, it's Anya!' she cried. 'David, please, go down and let her in at once.'

Davy exclaimed beneath his breath, and without so much as a glance at Eva or a farewell to Madame Martineau, walked hurriedly from the room. They listened as he ran down the stairs, and when the door was opened, heard Anya's voice, excited and high. But then the door slammed, and there was silence.

Eva peeped over Madame's shoulder and they both stared down into the street below. The lovers were arguing, Anya's head thrown back in a gesture of dispute, Davy's shoulders hunched in resignation.

'Ah, she's come to reclaim him,' said Madame archly, 'and of course, he has to go . . . The poor boy doesn't have a chance!'

Her tone startled Eva.

'You're not fond of Anya?' she asked cautiously.

'I disapprove of her behaviour. My niece is accustomed to having her own way, Eva, and that is very bad for a young woman . . . However, she is Emmanuel's daughter. That gives her a special place in my heart. I'm only sorry that Victor loves her so dearly . . . It hurts to see her treat him like a fool.'

Eva looked away, not wanting to join in any criticism of Anya.

'Victor is not sensible when it comes to women,' Madame said sorrowfully. 'A sensible man would not be in love with Anya . . . A sensible man would be in love with you, Eva.'

Eva laughed, embarrassed.

'Nobody's in love with me,' she said.

Now Madame Martineau laughed.

'Oh, but you're wrong, my dear! I think I know someone who's very much in love with you . . . Don't you see it? Well, then, I fear it all goes to show, Eva, just how little you know about love . . .'

The Madame Martineau affair seemed to change everything. Eva no longer walked to the Divine Faith convent in a spirit of gratitude, nor performed her daily tasks with good grace. Carefully and resolutely, she began to plan her own escape from the hospital.

Victor, meantime, became reluctant to leave his mother by herself, and Toby slipped swiftly into the gap, making it his business to meet Eva from the hospital each time she worked late, to ensure she was never alone when a companion might be welcomed, to win not only her appreciation, which was hardly in doubt, but also her affection.

Then Anya finally moved out of her father's house into the Café des Arbres, a step Emmanuel Klein, absent for many weeks in Nice, was not able to question. And Bertie Levine was knocked down by an omnibus on the avenue du Maine.

This latter event owed much to Bertie's prodigious consumption of claret, and yet it, too, seemed inextricably linked to the night that Madame Martineau was prised from the care of the Divine Faith Sisters.

The truth was that, whatever had taken place between Anya and Davy that evening, and Anya told Eva nothing at all, it produced a marked reaction in Davy. He no longer joked or held court for Anya's many admirers. Indeed, he was rarely seen in the Café des Arbres any more, and Bertie, who now found himself with no certain route to Anya's company, became ever more sunk in morbidity and drink. He was, the café set agreed with evident concern but without taking any preventative action, a hazard to himself.

'Might knock some sense into him,' Toby declared to Eva when, with relief, they discovered Bertie's injuries to be minor. 'If it doesn't, then his old man will. I telegraphed this morning. He'll be on his way to Europe tomorrow.'

Eva, visiting Bertie in the hospital later that same day, could not help but feel sorry at his surly response to this news.

'Was it really necessary to send for Bertie's father?' she asked Toby when he came to meet her from the convent that evening. 'He seemed most awfully put out.'

'Hell, Eva, someone had to do something,' Toby said, kissing her swiftly and drawing her into his shoulder. 'It's no good just hoping everything will turn out okay. You have to make plans, you have to take steps.'

'I suppose so,' Eva replied doubtfully, finding herself wondering precisely what Toby's plans were, and just what part Bertie's father might play in them.

They arrived back at the café to discover Anya waiting anxiously, sitting alone at the table in the window, silver cigarette holder trailing from her lips, fingers nervously stroking the stem of her glass.

'Is he all right?' she asked Eva, ignoring Toby.

Eva sat down beside her friend.

'He's fine. A few bruises and a rather nasty cut on his forehead. Nothing that a couple of days in bed won't cure.'

'Not to mention a couple of days off the booze,' said Toby.

'It's not my fault he drinks!' Anya retorted.

'No. Well, maybe it's not a question of fault. More cause and effect, shall we say?'

'What cause?' Anya flashed back. 'I've given no cause!'

Toby gave a dry little laugh.

'Bertie came to Paris a regular married guy. He wasn't a saint, but he wasn't a drunk either. I don't know, maybe there's a whole heap of causes turned him into that. If so, then I reckon you're one of them.'

Eva looked up quickly. It was the one thing on which they always disagreed, this matter of Anya and Bertie.

'That's unfair,' she said sharply. 'A grown man must take responsibility for his own actions, particularly, I'd say, if he's married!'

Toby bent down, his face close to Eva's, making it clear that his words were for her and not Anya.

'Or about to be married, perhaps?' he asked icily.

Then he left them, striding briskly across the café to the stairs and disappearing from view without a backward glance. Anya laughed uncertainly.

'He doesn't like Davy,' she said, lighting another cigarette. 'He's made that quite plain. And Davy doesn't like him, either. They're natural enemies . . . And yet I can't think of a good reason. Not really. Somehow, I don't feel it's got all that much to do with Bertie. Do you?'

'I don't know,' muttered Eva, shaken by Toby's unexpected intensity. 'But I don't suppose it matters. Once they leave Paris, I imagine they'll never see each other again . . .'

The words were regretted as soon as uttered for Eva had no wish to raise the spectre of Davy's possible departure, but Anya seemed scarcely to hear. She leaned forward across the table and reached for the empty glass which stood next to her own.

'Have a drink with me, Eva. It doesn't look as though Davy's going to show up . . . He's been very busy. He's designing a new house for Paul and Helena Duval. Did he tell you that?'

'No! No, he didn't . . .' Eva had been missing Davy since the evening at Madame Martineau's, and she'd thought a great deal about that night. She'd thought rather less about St Cuthbert's and the life she'd left behind, but now mention of Helena brought a plague of memories reeling into her mind's eye like a line of drunken dancers out of time. Helena, opening the schoolroom door in the Forster house to find Aidan and Anya wrestling on the floor . . . Helena and Edward, swaying as they stepped from the *Island Star* on to the empty white beach . . . Paul Duval, his vacant sleeve swinging limply by his side as he sat in Matthew Brannen's sitting room . . .

'They have a big family,' Anya was saying. 'Four daughters, I believe. They need a larger house.'

Eva said nothing, momentarily shaken by the strength of her feeling on hearing Helena's name.

'The south is beautiful,' Anya said, staring down into her glass, 'so warm and gentle . . . I've wondered sometimes if I envied Helena. Do you envy her, Eva? Living there with her husband and children, presiding over a grand new house being built?'

Eva looked up in surprise, anxious now about what might be coming, feeling her chest grow tight and her breath quicken.

'Would you like to be married, Eva? To have a husband and children? I had always thought that I would, only now I'm not so sure . . .'

'I'm not sure either,' Eva replied, finding her voice. 'And I certainly wouldn't wish to be Helena at the moment. There's too much I want to do first.'

'Like what?'

Eva felt flustered, cornered, unsure of what she was saying. 'I want to travel,' she volunteered. 'To work in the theatre maybe . . .'

'Then you don't intend to marry Toby?'

'No! Whatever makes you ask?'

'Simple observation,' said Anya, reaching for her cigarettes once more. 'He's bound to propose, sooner or later. You'll have to decide what you're going to say.'

Eva considered this in mute discomfort. She was hardly unaware of Toby's feelings, and to be sure, she returned them. She returned them with warmth and with delight – with everything, indeed, except that strange, deep, unexplored welling within, that secret, hidden spring of emotion which, she knew from repute if not from experience, might properly be called desire.

'It's not like that,' Eva heard herself say.

'Like what? Like it is with Davy, you mean?'

Eva stared dumbly at her friend, turned away in confusion, picked up her glass and then laughed, an odd, scared little laugh, no more than a stifled emission of breath, so fleeting and insubstantial that Anya seemed unaware of any sound at all. Yes, that was it. There it was. An unwitting remark had revealed the truth. Why had she refused to acknowledge it before? Desire, the root of all her longing for David Klein . . . Desire, known at last by its absence in all she felt for Toby Truman.

'Yes,' she said, struggling to regain her composure. 'Exactly that. It's different with you and Davy.'

'Well, it's different now,' Anya said, looking away. 'Very different. You see, there's going to be a wedding, Eva . . . Fairly soon. It's just a matter of speaking to my father when he returns . . .'

Eva swallowed a choking sensation at the back of her throat which rose to stifle her words.

'I'm very happy for you,' she managed to whisper.

Anya smiled, a strange, melancholy ghost of a smile.

'There's something I should have told you before, Eva. I don't know why I didn't. Perhaps I thought you'd guess . . .'

And in that moment, of course, Eva did.

She smiled bravely back at Anya, she refilled the empty wine glasses, she tidied the strewn cigarettes, she prodded the last blackened stub from the discarded silver holder. Then she leaned across the table and grasped her friend by the hand.

'You're going to have a baby,' she said.

Chapter Twelve

I am very grateful that I maintain an innate sense of morality. Such a sense can only come from the teachings of one's childhood, and from a belief in the Spirit of True Religion, if not in God himself. Without the Spirit, we would be in danger of accepting everything done in the name of God as holy and proper. I hope I shall never fall into such danger, and I pray that my sense of rightful action will always preserve me . . .

The Journals of Eva Delamere, edited by Blanche Duval

A minor incident precipitated Eva's departure from the Divine Faith convent hospital.

She'd been on evening duty when she heard singing from the far end of St-Thérèse ward. Investigation revealed a sober birthday party in progress, three elderly ladies toasting a fourth, their chairs drawn up around her high metal bed, their glasses filled with weak tea.

It was Eva's idea to fetch a bottle of wine from the bureau in Sister Marguerite's sitting room. She had a key to the room, the patients had money to pay, and all were due for discharge that week. Bottles were regularly fetched from the sitting-room bureau for special luncheons or religious festivals. The Sisters were neither mean nor abstemious, and there seemed no reason not to approve the celebration.

Certainly, as Sister Marguerite was to remark later, it would have been both simple and sensible to mention the wine to Sister Lorraine, who was in charge that evening. But for some reason, Eva didn't.

'It is a question of discipline, you see,' Sister Marguerite said wearily, facing Eva from the settle in the whitewashed sitting room where she always sat. 'We must be able to rely on our nurses in matters of discipline. Nothing else is suitable.'

'Perhaps I shouldn't be working here,' Eva heard herself say, 'if you find me so unsuitable.'

'Perhaps not,' agreed Sister Marguerite surprisingly. 'But please be clear, Eva, that we are talking about discipline. We have no complaint about your work, and we will, of course, be happy to give you a reference . . .'

Eva stared in disbelief.

'You're dismissing me because of a bottle of wine?'

'I'm not dismissing you, Eva. I am suggesting that you may be unsuited to the Divine Faith hospital.'

'I see. So you are dismissing me? You really do find me unsuitable?'

'I think you should consider,' Sister Marguerite said softly, walking away for a moment to stare across the glittering emerald grass outside her window, 'that it is you who find us unsuitable, Eva, not the other way round.'

The rest of the day was spent in alternative moods of anxiety and elation. She didn't need the Divine Faith convent, of course! She could find another nursing post, perhaps at Pitié-Salpêtrière. She could wait on table at the Café des Arbres. She could keep accounts for Emmanuel Klein.

On the other hand, it was disconcerting to be dismissed, and Eva was in no doubt that she had been dismissed. What would her father have said? What might Mr Klein, who'd secured her job with the Sisters in the first place, think of her unplanned departure?

It was Toby who set the final mood.

'That's swell news,' he said when he met her that evening outside the convent door. 'This place is a waste of your talents, Eva. Now we can make real plans . . . But first, we celebrate!'

'All right,' said Eva, laughing. 'Where shall we go? To the café?'

In truth, she'd been avoiding the Café des Arbres in the days since Anya's revelation about her baby, unable to face David Klein in this new knowledge. She'd wanted to know how he'd responded to the news, what he intended to tell his family and Rebecca Bernstein, when the wedding might take place. But all her questions remained unasked, and Anya volunteered nothing more. Although Eva felt only sympathy and concern for Anya's plight, her earlier disapproval of the cousins' love affair had set a tone of reserve between the friends. It was plain that Anya did not wish to talk to Eva about Davy, and Eva, hardly daring to examine her own feelings on the subject, kept quiet.

But she missed Anya, and she missed Davy too. In the absence of his company, she'd taken to studying the book he'd lent her some weeks before, rereading the enigmatic lines of *The Waste Land* poem he so admired in the hope that they might offer some clue to her own inner restlessness. Alas, she'd been forced to conclude that the ache which pervaded her perception on waking each morning and settling to sleep each evening, was rooted in the person of David Klein himself and the fact that, try as she might, she could feel nothing but envy whenever she thought of the cousins and their future together.

Now, however, she felt anxious to see Anya again. She had urged her friend to move back into her father's house, to give up her work at the café and wait quietly for Emmanuel Klein's return. But Anya had refused, insisting that her Uncle Jacob needed help. How subdued, how melancholy she had seemed when Eva thought back. How unlike a bride-to-be.

'Not the café,' said Toby. 'We'll go over to Pete Chessington's place. There's someone I'd like you to meet.'

The bar on the Boulevard St-Michel where Pete Chessington played piano was dank, dingy and decrepit. It was also one of the most popular nightspots on the Left Bank. Tonight, however, it was deserted, except for Pete himself, a frayed *chanteuse* called Lucienne, Karl Schwartz, who was waving sheets of minutely scripted music under Pete's nose, and a handful of morose Americans who seemed to be arguing over a racing result.

'We're early,' Toby said, nodding at the Americans, 'but let's start as we mean to go on.'

He ordered a bottle of champagne, and Eva, as though driven to vindicate Sister Marguerite's opinions about unsuitability, drank her first two glasses at high speed.

'I don't know how I stuck it so long,' she declared. 'Imagine being sent there to die, surrounded by all those pious smiles! Do you think heaven's going to be like that? All discipline and no fun? You probably have to apply to St Peter for the corkscrew.'

'We'll be bored to death,' Toby agreed, his eye on the door into the street. 'Hey, look! Here comes Bertie and his old man.'

The bottle was done, so Toby called for another, and Bertie, who seemed in high spirits after his brush with the omnibus, soon ordered a third.

'Your very good health,' said Bertie's father drily, nodding at Toby and Eva rather as though he feared for the health of the entire assembly.

Eva tried to concentrate on the conversation, but found her attention wandering. She listened for a while to Pete's attempts at Karl's music, grimacing once when she met his eye, and then began to gaze round at the gloomy little bar, calculating that with a coat of distemper, some refurbished stools and a few contemporary pictures on the walls, it would all look a lot less depressing. Then business would improve, prices could be raised, profits would increase. Of course, business was pretty good anyway, which seemed to have a great deal to do with the talents of Pete Chessington. Maybe, thought Eva, if Pete were to play piano at the Café des Arbres, Jacob Klein would find his business improving. She wondered if there were room for a piano in the corner of the café . . .

'Writers,' said Bertie's father, 'are a dime a dozen. Nobody needs them. You wanna be a writer, you stick to what you're doing . . .'

'He's not doing much,' said Bertie, refilling the glasses.

The square footage of the inner room at the café was probably no more than forty. A grand piano would be out of the question.

'Same with pretty girls. You show me pretty girls who want to be actors, I'll show you a town full of broken dreams. Broken dreams and broken hearts. Nobody needs pretty girls.'

Of course, if you took the terrace into the reckoning, the square footage was a lot greater. Would it be possible to site a piano on the terrace?

'Someone must need new writers,' objected Toby. 'And someone must need pretty girls. What happens when the supply runs out?'

No doubt it would be necessary to obtain a licence before playing a piano in the open air. And there was the weather to consider, of course. All the same . . .

'The supply never runs out,' said Bertie's father. 'There's always some dumb fool writer ready to put his reputation on the line and ruin it in the process.'

'Toby's no fool,' said Bertie. 'And Eva's very pretty.'

'She can act too,' said Toby. 'She used to play Shakespeare back in England. Genuine Shakespeare. On the stage.'

At this point, Eva suspended her calculations and focused on her three companions, all of whom seemed suddenly to be staring at her intently.

'Nobody needs Shakespeare,' said Bertie's father, looking away. 'We got all the Shakespeare actors we can use.'

Toby stared down into his glass, contemplating the diminishing bubbles.

'Let's hear some Shakespeare, Eva,' said Bertie encouragingly. 'Give us a speech.'

Eva had drunk far more champagne than was usual, but she hadn't drunk so much she was about to leap to her feet and start quoting *Twelfth Night*. She laughed and shook her head.

'Hey, come on,' said Bertie, warming to the idea. 'We want Shakespeare, even if no one else does!'

Toby had begun to look uncomfortable, and as he caught her eye to motion her silently towards the door, Eva felt a sudden rush of pity and affection. His grand scheme had failed. He was disappointed, but now he was only concerned to spare her feelings.

She lifted her glass, took a long draught, and then leaned across the table towards Bertie.

'How about something a little more homely?' she enquired merrily. 'I can do cockney if you like!'

Toby laughed nervously, but Bertie rolled his eyes approvingly as Eva began to sing an old music hall refrain:

'Oh, you can't get many pimples on a pound of pickled pork . . . whether it comes from China, Japan or Carolina . . .'

Toby gazed at her, startled, and Bertie let out a whoop.

'Hey, what's that? Better than Shakespeare any day!' He turned to his father: 'You hear that, Pa?'

'Look, we don't need no cockneys,' his father said dourly, 'I'm telling you, cockney actors we do not need!'

'Worldwide Pictures needs cockneys!' Bertie declared triumphantly. 'Saul Bernstein just made *London Bridge*. Full of bloody cockneys!'

Bertie's father sighed.

'London Bridge is all done,' he said. 'And you take it from me, son, Saul Bernstein don't wanna know . . . I'm telling you now, Worldwide Pictures don't need nothing . . .'

Where this unpromising conversation might eventually have terminated none of them was destined to discover, for at that moment Victor Martineau walked briskly into the bar, his eyes anxiously scanning the now crowded tables. Eva knew at once that he was looking for her.

'What's wrong, Victor? What is it?'

'Thank God you're here. Can you come with me, Eva, please? Anya needs you.'

Eva didn't need to ask more, and with a hurried farewell to her startled companions, ran outside to Victor's waiting taxi. The cab lurched off through the teeming streets and neither of them spoke for several moments, until Victor, no longer able to conceal his agitation, suddenly grabbed Eva's hand.

'She wouldn't let me call a doctor,' he said. 'She wanted you. She was sure you'd be at Pete's place.'

'Try not to worry. We'll soon be there.'

Victor turned away, staring restlessly out of the taxi window, his fingers drumming against the glass. Then he turned back to Eva angrily: 'Where is David?' he demanded. 'Why isn't he at the café?'

She shook her head.

'I don't know,' she whispered, pressing her hand over his. 'I'm sure he'll turn up . . . I'm sure everything will be fine.'

But everything was not fine, a fact that was apparent the moment Eva entered Anya's room at the Café des Arbres.

'Let's have some light,' she said gently, snapping on the table lamp and opening the blinds. Then she looked down at her friend.

Anya lay on her bed, a tin pail at her side, a heavily stained sheet covering her legs. She was shivering silently into her pillow, shoulders heaving in rhythmic sobs, arms clutched to her breast.

Very carefully, Eva raised the soaked sheet, and Anya, grasping her hand in gratitude, suddenly sat up.

'Where's Davy?' she moaned to Victor, who lingered uneasily in the doorway. 'Isn't he here?'

'Not yet,' muttered Victor, 'but I'll find him,' and then he turned and clattered down the stairs into the café below.

'Help me, Eva,' Anya begged. 'Please help me . . .'

Eva fetched hot water, disinfectant and clean linen. She stroked Anya's hair and bathed her forehead, and whispered soothingly that she must try to rest. But she didn't think it the moment to tell Anya the truth: that there was nothing more she, nor anyone else, could do to help.

The dawn light was beginning to wake the café by the time it was over, and when Eva went downstairs, leaving Anya asleep, it was to find Toby sitting alone at the table in the window.

'Is she going to be all right?'

'I hope so,' Eva replied wearily. 'I just wish she'd given up working here. It mightn't have made any difference, but it would have been better for her.' She peered out on to the terrace. 'No sign of Victor?'

'He's been back a couple of times looking for Klein . . . But there's no sign of him either. He's a shrewd guy. Knows when to keep out of the way.'

'I'm sure he'll be here the minute he finds out. He's been working hard.'

'You're very quick to defend him, aren't you?'

Eva flushed. Was this true? Was this how it seemed?

'No, I'm not,' she faltered. 'I'm simply pointing out that he doesn't know what's happening.'

Toby shrugged.

'When Bertie's got trouble, it's Bertie's fault,' he said quietly, watching Eva's face as he spoke. 'He shouldn't have messed with Anya. Now Anya's got trouble, it's Anya's fault. She wasn't well. She shouldn't have gone on working. When does anything get laid at the door of your friend Klein?'

Eva turned to him angrily.

'I don't know what you mean,' she said.

'I think you do, but it doesn't matter . . .' He leaned towards her across the table, and unexpectedly took her hand.

'In a few weeks,' he said, 'David Klein will be out of here. He'll go home and marry Rebecca Bernstein, and Anya will never see him again. With luck, neither will you nor I . . .'

Eva was still angry, and she removed her hand.

'I'm leaving too,' said Toby, undeterred. 'I'm going to Hollywood, and I want you to come with me. I'm not promising it will work out, but I reckon we've as good a chance as most . . . Think about it, Eva. There's precious little to keep you here now you've lost your job. Pretty soon there won't even be David Klein's scintillating company.'

'There's Anya!' cried Eva hotly, ignoring this final comment. 'I'm not about to leave her!'

Toby reached for the jug of coffee on the table before him, seeming to consider his words.

'Anya was perfectly happy before you came,' he said at last, pouring the pungent black liquid into Eva's cup. 'I'd go as far as to say she was probably happier. She had Klein's attentions all to herself then. Whatever happens after tonight, she'll pick herself up and find someone new. There's always Karl Schwartz. She doesn't need you.'

Eva stared down into her cup. The acrid fumes of the coffee made her feel faintly sick. She was tired and she was distressed. She was also feeling the effects of an evening's drinking. She had been dismissed from her job and she had witnessed her dearest friend in severe pain. She was mortified by Toby's observations about David Klein, and she was deeply confused about her feelings for both men. The future looked uncertain, the past was irretrievable. The tears fell unchecked to her cheeks.

'Hell, Eva, don't cry. Please, honey, I didn't mean to make you cry . . .'

He stood up and raised her to her feet, folding her into his arms and kissing her hair. Then he led her out of the café and back up the stairs into his own room, where he pushed her gently on to his bed.

'You're dead beat, and so am I. We'll talk it over later when we both feel better . . .'

He lay down beside her and pulled her close, and Eva felt her body relax into his, lulled by his warmth, soothed by his strength.

'I'm sorry,' he whispered, 'I hate to hurt you, honey.'

And then, as Eva floated on to the plateau of dreams with the jumbled words of the *Waste Land* poem that David so admired beating through her brain, it seemed that she had inadvertently stumbled into a desert of feeble desires and derelict beliefs, a land in which thunder rumbled its unintelligible message, in which wind rattled the doors of ghostly ruined churches, rainclouds threatened the once blue horizon, and condemned prisoners wandered the arid plains for all eternity.

'I love you, Eva,' Toby said softly into her ear. 'You know that, don't you?'

But Eva, sleeping soundly, made no reply.

The next few weeks saw changes at the Café des Arbres. Anya moved out and back to her father's house while Eva moved in, taking over not only Anya's old room but also her job. Bertie Levine went back to America to visit his wife, Karl Schwartz left for Berlin, and Pete Chessington gave up his spot at the bar on the Boulevard St-Michel.

'I was wondering about a piano in the corner of the café,' Eva said tentatively to Jacob Klein. 'Just a small one, of course. Pete could play.'

It was done, and Pete duly arrived, bringing with him the ageing *chanteuse*, Lucienne. She in turn brought her admirers and patrons, and within a short space of time the café's clientele burgeoned so that, without anyone intending any displacement, the long-time regulars, Randy Makepeace, Arnie Steinem, Leonard and Arlene Schultz and the rest, began to seem less evident. There were new faces, French as well as American, customers with more money than the café was used to seeing, older couples who drank Pernod and champagne instead of red wine.

Eva, reckoning that Jacob could do with more help in the kitchen, found a girl to wait on the tables, and began to cook, devising new dishes from an old Jewish recipe book she found on the kitchen shelf. With Jacob's eager encouragement, she reorganised the tables in the café so that more customers could be accommodated. The table in the window no longer stood in isolation from the rest. Now there were three tables in the window, neatly packed together, and no favoured, secluded spot for lovers or solitary drinkers.

Eva was busy, far busier than she'd been before, and she saw little of either Toby or David Klein. Both were still living at the café, but Davy, Eva discovered, had rented an office in Montparnasse. Toby, meantime, while still writing the articles and stories that he constantly dispatched to a variety of newspapers and magazines, had taken clerical work at the American library to pay his passage home.

There'd been no more talk of his Hollywood plans, but Eva knew that the moment would come, just as she knew that Davy, too, would set sail for America some time in the coming weeks. The love affair between the cousins was over, and this, it seemed, without any of the elder Kleins knowing, or at least revealing that they had known.

Anya's father, certainly, gave no sign that he thought his daughter's indisposition anything other than a commonplace female complaint. Eva herself hadn't been told what happened on the morning after Anya miscarried, but when she'd woken that day, it was to learn that Davy had eventually returned to the café and had later conveyed Anya to her father's house.

Arriving at the Klein home that afternoon, however, Eva had found Victor, not Davy, in attendance on Anya, and her friend tight-lipped and withdrawn. Victor, too, had seemed reluctant to talk, and Eva had an unhappy sense of being excluded from Anya's confidence. Certainly, she'd been summoned in the crisis. But now the crisis was past, and there was nothing more she could offer.

In the days that followed, Anya came to seem curiously resigned to her changed situation. Indeed, she'd seemed as much concerned about her uncle's loss of a waitress as the cancellation of her wedding plans, and it was this anxiety that led Eva to offer her own services so quickly.

'Is the wedding really cancelled?' she'd asked Victor timorously, hardly believing that in the space of a few days so much of such magnitude could have been settled.

'There was never going to be a wedding,' Victor had replied curtly. 'Whatever Anya may have told you, that was never an option.'

Eva was left to consider this alone. Victor said nothing more. Anya, though keen to hear all about the changes at the café, never once asked about Davy nor whether Eva had seen him, and there was nothing Eva felt able to ask either of them herself. Even Toby kept off the subject, perhaps thinking he'd revealed enough already of his feelings towards David Klein.

Eva's own feelings were in turmoil. Only now that Davy had all but disappeared from the Café des Arbres did she realise how much she missed him. No one else's company seemed quite so entertaining, so stimulating. No one else could make her laugh in quite the same way, nor call forth her thoughts and beliefs in so precise or so passionate a manner. She had delighted in his irreverence and his charm. She knew there was no one else she would rather be with.

Analysing these emotions, Eva saw only too well that, as Toby had already pointed out, she had been ready to excuse David Klein many things. She had detached her understanding of him as Anya's lover from the heady experience of his attentions towards her.

He had always been attentive, ever since her first night in Paris when they had walked together by the Seine. Eva could not help but be aware of this special attention. She had seen it, Toby had seen it, and it had occurred to her to wonder, on more than one occasion, whether Anya had ever seen it.

Yet all such thoughts were now irrelevant. Davy was no longer attentive, indeed he no longer sought her company at all. And Eva was no longer inclined to forgive him. Anya's pregnancy and miscarriage had put an end to all indulgence. She had seen the truth: that the man who so entranced her had, at the same time, misused and abandoned her dearest friend.

She'd begun to think she might never see him again, that so ashamed must he be, he might leave without saying goodbye. But Emmanuel Klein put a sudden end to this idea.

Eva had called to visit Anya and found him sitting alone in his garden, reading a letter.

'Eva, my dear! You've missed Anya, I'm afraid. She's out walking with Victor . . . but I'm glad to have this opportunity of speaking with you . . .'

Emmanuel Klein, though often absent from Paris, had never failed to make Eva feel a valued member of his family. He had smiled indulgently at the news from the Divine Faith convent, he had encouraged her new role at his brother's café, he had thanked her for helping Anya in her trouble. Now he asked a favour.

'I have here a letter from Helena Duval. You know that my nephew has been designing her new house? He goes there next week to make the final preparations for the building. I'd be pleased, my dear, if you would accompany him. Helena asks specifically if you will. She's most anxious to see you again, and frankly, I feel it would do you good. You may also be of service in discussing the house plans. A woman's perspective, you understand . . .'

Eva gazed at him dumbly, and he hurried to brush away any possible objections.

'Now, don't worry, my brother can manage for a few days. The South is very lovely. David will drive you there, and you can see the countryside together.'

Eva found her voice at last.

'If you want me to go, then, of course . . .' Her assent tailed away, and she raised a hand to her burning face.

'I understand it may be hard to see Helena married to a man when it should have been your brother,' Emmanuel said gently. 'But Eva, if I may say, Helena is not like the rest of the Forsters . . . If she were, we should hardly have been given her commission. Go and see her, Eva. Go and meet her new family. I've already mentioned it to my nephew, and he's very happy to take you there.'

They left Paris early on a golden summer's morning, driving through

unstirring streets in a gleaming black open-topped convertible, Eva's
fine silvery hair streaming out behind her in the breeze, Davy's eyes
focused firmly on the empty road ahead.

Toby had been there to see them off, escorting Eva out of the Café
des Arbres and into the car, swinging her valise on to the back seat with
proprietorial ease, and kissing her firmly on the mouth before opening
the convertible's door and handing her in.

The two men barely exchanged a glance, and Eva, who'd been feeling
increasingly mutinous about the trip and was not inclined to pretend
cheerfulness, found herself deeply irritated. Whatever Toby and Davy
thought of each other, it was surely not beyond them to be civil in her
interest. She could hardly feel more uncomfortable about the visit to
Helena than she already did. Why shouldn't further discomfort be
spared?

She bade Toby a frosty farewell, and did not speak to Davy until
Paris had begun to fade behind them, greeting his comments on passing
landmarks and attractions to come with no more than the merest incline
of her head.

'You could have wished Toby goodbye,' she said at last. 'Would that
have been so difficult? I simply don't understand why you two are so
unfriendly.'

'Don't you?' he asked, his eyes never lifting from the road. 'Then
you're less perceptive than I thought.'

He seemed to regret the remark at once, and hastened to make light
of it.

'Toby's okay,' he said, glancing at her quickly, 'but he takes everything so seriously. What does he reckon will happen on this trip? That
I'll carry you off to my harem in Morocco?'

Eva ran a hand through her tangled hair.

'Perhaps he thinks I'll be as easily seduced as Anya,' she retorted,
intent on showing that her powers of perception were sharper than he
believed.

'Then I'm deeply flattered,' he replied brusquely, changing gear with
a roar that drowned the possibility of further conversation.

Now it was Eva's turn for regret, and for a moment she could scarcely
believe the words had been hers. She struggled for some remark that
would restore the hope of amity, but the tone had been set, and they
drove on into a yawning silence punctured only by polite inconsequen-
tialities and the briefest of essential stops.

The plains of Normandy passed by to the west; the lush green byways
of the Loire lay ahead. They were making for Orleans, and Eva thought
they might stop to view the cathedral, a possibility he'd suggested as
they left Paris. But if this had been his plan, it no longer suited his

purpose, and they skirted the city, heading out along the dusty open road to Tours.

Jacob Klein had provided a picnic basket, and now it sat on the car's back seat next to Eva's valise, a mocking reminder of what might have been, had they not begun so badly.

'Are you hungry?' she asked him at last, fearing he might never permit a rest, that they might arrive at the Duvals' in a state of famine.

'Not really,' he said, 'but you can open the picnic,' and for a moment she truly thought he meant her to eat as they drove along, all nicety abandoned in the urge to complete their journey as quickly as possible.

But he pulled the car off the road, carried the basket into a shady copse which lay above them, and pointed out a sprawling roadside café in the dip of the hill.

'We'll take an hour,' he said, and then laying the basket down beside her, set off for the café along the road without a backward glance.

Eva could have wept. Whatever her fears or her hopes for this trip, and she had stumbled between both before anxiety prevailed, her most tortured imaginings had not conjured up this sterile vision. Why, in heaven's name, had she made that remark about Anya? How petulant and mean-minded it now seemed. She opened Jacob's basket, and with mechanical deliberation began to eat from the little sandwiches and delicacies he'd provided.

It had all been prepared for their delight, careful packages of pâté and cheese-filled parcels of pastry, tiny sugar cakes and slices of almond brioche, even a bottle of white wine wrapped in a wet towel to keep cool. Eva opened the wine and poured herself a generous mug. If she had to dine alone, she might as well indulge herself.

It seemed much longer than an hour when she woke on the secluded patch of sunny grass where she'd eventually settled to find Davy sitting a little way off, drinking from a cup of wine himself and smoking a cigarette.

Her head felt light, her senses curiously clear, and only now, refreshed and restored, did she fully appreciate the splendours of the landscape around her. Valleys of bright green vines and pale gold meadows studded with lavender fell away at her feet. To her left, beyond the silver curl of the river, a distant tumble of ancient houses sprawled upon a rocky hill. From the village heart rose a glittering spire, its gilded point catching the afternoon sun in a flash of bronze. Behind her stretched the empty white road, shielded from immediate view by the dense copse of dark green poplars, and to her right stood a field of sentinel sunflowers, their furled orange buds as yet unyielding and tight. All was utterly still. No hint of breeze stirred the meadows, no insect moaned, no bird sang. The only sound came as Eva sat up, a faint rustling of the grass on which she lay, the smallest of sighs escaping her lips.

He turned, and she saw then that all his earlier hostility had gone. Now he smiled and offered her his hand.

'Better be moving,' he said. 'Time's getting on. Helena's place is off the beaten track. It may take some finding.'

'I'm sorry we quarrelled,' Eva said suddenly, her eyes bright with unshed tears. 'I'm sorry I said what I did.'

'I'm sorry too,' he said, looking down. 'Sorry that, right from the beginning, it went wrong for us.'

'What would have happened?' she whispered, knowing as she spoke that her words offered implicit compliance.

He paused for only a moment, staring deep into the brimming eyes, and then he moved towards her.

'This,' he said, and took her in his arms.

It seemed as though she stood outside herself and watched, just as she'd watched Harold with Lizzie Howard in St Cuthbert's churchyard all those years ago.

She saw him kiss her face and her hair, saw him slowly unbutton her blouse and take the silver cross between his fingers, saw him caress her shoulderblades, her throat, the nape of her neck, her breasts.

She saw his hand upon her calf, watched its inevitable progress to her knee, and gazed, fascinated, as it came to rest between her thighs. But then she closed her eyes, just as she'd done when she hid beneath the laurel bush in the churchyard, unwilling to witness anything more.

With her eyes closed, she could only feel, for there was nothing much to hear. He did not speak, and the heavy afternoon air was still mysteriously silent. She seemed to float in the quiet warmth of the day, alone except for the faint sound of her own breath as it rose with her awakening body.

His lovemaking was gentle and unhurried, and this, when she considered it afterwards, was what made it inexcusable. He had not fallen upon her in a fury of passion. She had not responded in unthinking abandon. Instead, he'd played the restrained lover, asking nothing she might not wish to give, offering only what she might wish to receive. And she'd played the eager initiate, dismissing all reservations, delighting in the ease of her arousal. His touch was precise, his rhythm sure, and she held nothing back, sensing that she was in command, that she could stop him whenever she chose.

But she didn't choose. She took him into herself, accepting his reassurances, trusting his control. She surrounded him, absorbed him, used his desire for herself. And when he at last withdrew, she clung to him tightly, digging her fingernails into the bare flesh beneath his shirt, pressing her face into his hair and pulling him down upon her once more.

'I've wanted you,' she heard herself say. 'Ever since that first night when we walked by the Seine . . . I've wanted you.'

'If you'd shown me that,' he replied, 'it would all have been different. But I was never sure. You always seemed so disapproving . . . And then there was Toby.'

'Not just Toby,' she said suddenly, sitting up. 'There was Anya, too. What about her?'

He sat up beside her, surveying the landscape which was rapidly losing its golden glow. The sky was tinged with ugly purple, and a bank of dark yellow cloud had settled above the spire of the distant church.

'It's going to rain,' he said. 'We'd better get the hood up on the car.'

Eva was not be diverted.

'What about Anya?' she repeated, clutching at his arm. 'How could we do this, and not think of her? We've betrayed her . . .'

He began to pack the picnic basket.

'No one has betrayed Anya,' he said shortly. 'Anya pleases herself, and if you fit into her scheme for a while, then that's fine. She cannot, I think, accuse me of betrayal.'

Eva stood up, deeply dismayed by this reply.

'But Anya was expecting your child!' she cried.

If he'd answered her then, had offered the consolation she sought or attempted to quell her rising anguish, then she might have listened, but he merely picked up the basket and glanced at the glowering sky.

'We must fix the hood,' he said urgently. 'It's going to pour.'

The first drops were already falling, cold needles pricking through their thin clothes, and the torrent began before they'd even reached the copse, a vicious unleashing of elemental power that quickly transformed the white road into a dirty running stream.

She stood by the car as he battled with the hood, her own inward struggle requiring all her energy.

'Help me, Eva,' he said impatiently. 'Fasten those studs.'

But still she stood, immobile, transfixed by her confusion. Desire, passion, betrayal . . . It all flooded upon her, drowning her spirits as surely as the deluge from the heavens soaked her clothes. She had surrendered to unworthy desire. She had sacrificed reason to passion.

She had betrayed not only Anya, who loved Davy, nor Toby, who loved her, but yet more damning, she had betrayed herself. Why had she fought so long against her feelings for Davy, if only to give way at the last? Hadn't she already seen his true nature, making love to his cousin while betrothed to another woman? How could she have encouraged his advances? She was seized by remorse and consumed with guilt.

'Get in the car, Eva! What on earth's the matter with you?'

She opened the door and slammed it behind her, all confusion suddenly banished, her mind made up.

'We had no right,' she told him. 'We were thinking only of ourselves. There was no concern for Anya. And none for your fiancée . . .'

He was delving in the back of the car, manoeuvring her valise on to the front seat, but now he stopped and and turned to face her.

'Who?' he enquired.

'Rebecca Bernstein. Aren't you supposed to be marrying her when you get home? Were you thinking of her when you were making love to me?'

'No,' he said, turning back to the valise, 'I was thinking of you. And now I'm thinking we should both get changed before we catch pneumonia.'

Eva was not interested in such practicalities.

'Drive me to Orleans,' she demanded. 'I'm taking the next train back to Paris.'

He caught his breath.

'Don't be ridiculous,' he said steadily. 'We must find a hotel and get out of these wet clothes. Helena Duval expects us tomorrow.'

'I'm not staying in any hotel with you. And as for Helena, I never want to see her, nor hear the name Duval, again!'

This response seemed irrational, even to Eva herself, and yet it summed up what she felt. She had never wanted to take this trip, she would not compound the mistake she had made, and she no longer cared what Helena nor anyone else might think. But nevertheless, she'd imagined Davy would try to explain himself, that he would seek to change her mind.

But instead he swung the car into the streaming road, turning it recklessly, heading back towards Orleans through the fog of flying water, peering closely through the windscreen in a supreme effort of concentration. The signposts they had passed in strained silence only hours before swam by amid a new and deeper silence, the intimacy they had shared seemed as remote as history.

'Have you nothing to say to me?' Eva asked in a small voice when finally they arrived at the station in Orleans.

'Nothing at all,' he replied with an odd little smile, opening the car door and handing out her valise. 'I can see you've got it all figured out. And it's clear you're the best judge of what's right and wrong. Goodbye, Eva . . . I hope everything works out the way you want.'

Book V: Beth

Chapter Thirteen

Like the Christian belief which spawned it, True Love demands suffering. Indeed, Victorian melodrama had its heroines literally fading away for want of the beloved. In reality consumptive, anaemic, or fainting from lack of air to their artificially constricted lungs, the mythology of True Love saw Victorian women dying because the very essence of life, the suitor's promise, had been cruelly withdrawn . . . And to this day romantic fiction revels in the plight of the forsaken one, the woman whose True Love is lost.

Moonlight and Roses: The Cult of Romance in Western Society, by Beth Carlisle (published by Harridan Press to accompany the Metro Television series)

Breathe deep, Beth. One, two, three, four . . . No need for anxiety, no need for shame. I am a mature, responsible person in charge of my own destiny. I live as I choose, I live as I choose . . .

And at this point in time I had chosen to travel the length of the land to attend the funeral of Eva Delamere, a woman I'd met only once. In so doing, I knew, I had finally, freely chosen to confront the pain of the past.

The parlour door swung open and there he stood at last: the Reverend Michael Cameron, vicar of St Cuthbert's, my past personified, the yesterday upon whom all tomorrows had once depended.

He smiled, he shook my hand, and he began with unbearable politeness.

'Hallo, Beth . . . You found us, then? How's the Dolphin? Not too bleak, I hope?'

He was precisely as I'd imagined. If he'd been fatter, or if the bright gold hair had thinned, if he'd lost the slow smile or the wide grey eyes had faded, then it might have been supportable.

But here he was, the matured embodiment of my adolescent longings, taller than I remembered, broader in the shoulders, face a little creased at the edges, fair hair unfashionably long and curling around the neat dog collar, familiar grey eyes that met mine with unmistakable reserve.

His gaze did not falter, and I saw at once how it was to be. There was nothing in the smile, the look, to suggest any acknowledgement of what once had been. Instead there was a cautious welcome, a show of pastoral concern for the visitor's well-being, and in these a practised wariness, the carefully maintained distance of one who does not wish to be mistaken.

'The Dolphin is fine,' I said stiffly, trying to match his self-possession with my own, 'though I'm glad I'm not staying a fortnight.'

There was no trace of intimacy as his hand briefly held mine, no hint of embarrassment or vulnerability at this visible reminder of his unholy past. We were as the most casual of old acquaintances, meeting without significant history. The vicar of St Cuthbert's, I guessed, was not a man easily dismayed.

'How long are you staying?' he enquired, motioning me on to the chesterfield in front of the blazing fire and taking up a neutral position on the edge of the old desk at the other side of the room. 'The funeral isn't until the day after tomorrow . . .'

I bristled, the hairs rising on skin that suddenly seemed precariously thin. He wondered why I'd arrived so early, why I wished to spend a moment longer than necessary in the Dolphin Inn.

'I plan to do a bit of research beforehand,' I said coolly. 'I may be writing a book, and I want to find someone who remembers Eva Brannen.'

'That may prove rather difficult,' he replied, unruffled. 'The village has changed a great deal since the Brannens' day . . . I haven't come across anyone myself.'

'Then perhaps I'll do better. It's my job to find things out.'

This remark was patently ludicrous. It might be my job to ask minor celebrities uncomfortable questions over the studio coffee table, but I was hardly the roving investigator.

'Well, I can only refer you once again to Daniel Duval. He'll be staying up at the Retreat. I'll let him know you're here.'

I shifted uneasily on the chesterfield.

'That won't be necessary,' I said, determining that I'd do my damnedest to prevent either Michael or Duval learning anything of my relationship with the other. 'I'll contact him myself.'

'Yes, of course.'

An uncomfortable silence fell upon the room, and I struggled to control a rising anguish, heartfelt and unexpected. The years rolled back like a dusty old tapestry suddenly exposed to the light, its colours still vivid and fresh. How could he fail to be moved? How was it possible to love another human being so totally, to share every cranny and nook of body and soul, to hope and scheme and believe and promise, and then be left with nothing to exchange but vacuous pleasantries?

I looked up at him, hoping to detect some small remnant of feeling, but he'd turned away, staring out over the top of his father's old desk into the garden beyond.

'Are you aware of any other connection that Eva had with this village?' I heard myself enquire, the voice as brittle as ice. 'What about the Forsters, for example, who used to own the Retreat? They must have known the Brannens?'

'Yes,' he said, turning back. 'Why do you ask?'

'Because I don't believe family sentiment alone brought Eva back here,' I said boldly. 'I think there's more to it, and I want to know what. She lived most of her life in Paris. Her husband will presumably be buried there. Why the hell should she want to lay her bones in this godforsaken place?'

He suddenly leaned forward and opened the drawer of the leather-topped desk, extracting a pack of cigarettes, fumbling around among his books for a box of matches. As he did so, the David Klein biography crashed to the floor, falling open at a faded portrait of the great movie-maker himself, and for a moment we both stared at it, startled. Then he bent to pick it up.

'Do you smoke?' he asked me.

'Of course not,' I said, irritated, wondering what it was about church or country life that drove a one-time anti-smoker to the weed. 'Nobody does these days.'

'You don't mind if I do?'

'How on earth could I mind? It's your bloody house.'

He nodded politely, then moved away from the desk to open a window in the bay, and I waited impatiently while he seemed to consider his next words.

'It's my understanding that family sentiment, as you term it, played a crucial part in Eva's decision to be buried at St Cuthbert's. She grew up here, she was happy here . . .'

He paused, and then in a decisive movement, stubbed out his cigarette in a saucer on the desk.

'And if you're asking about Mr Truman,' he went on, 'then I can tell you that when he dies, he wants his ashes scattered from the Golden Gate Bridge.'

'Do you get to perform that ceremony too?'

'Unfortunately not.'

'Never mind. Maybe you'll put on such a good show for Eva's send-off that he'll hire you there and then.'

This weak attempt at jollity was perceived as flippancy, and as his eyes hardened from measured politeness to evident dismissal, I longed to take it back. Oh please, Michael, don't bring out the worst in me. If the past has no tiny niche, no meagre scrap of meaning in the present, then at least attempt some modest pretence to spare my feelings. That can't be too much to ask, surely? Not from a God-fearing man of the cloth like yourself?

'I'm sorry I can't give you any further information as far as Eva is concerned,' he said slowly, turning away. 'There's nothing more I can say.'

'What about the remaining Miss Forster?' I persisted. 'Can she tell me anything about Eva's relationship with the family? Would she know if Eva had a secret lover?'

There was the briefest hesitation, and he raised an eyebrow in what I remembered at once as a gesture of disapproval.

'A secret lover,' he repeated slowly, 'from the Forster family? I can safely say you should forget that idea, although of course, you may speak to Emily if you wish. Her grandfather was Aidan Forster, the last owner of the big house.'

'Is he dead?'

'He was killed in the war.'

'Is his grave anywhere near Eva's?'

'No! No, it isn't . . . He was lost at sea along with the vicar of St Cuthbert's, Martin Orde . . . They volunteered together . . . Look, this is a crazy idea.'

'Then give me a better one,' I said smartly. 'You're interested in Eva yourself. Why else did you ring me up? Why else are you reading books about David Klein?'

We both looked down at the biography again, and David Klein smiled back, a poignant, enigmatic wisp of a smile frozen into history.

'There's very little about Eva in that book,' Michael said, looking away, 'and nothing that isn't generally known. Take it, if you like. Klein was a very interesting man . . .'

I stood up and flung my wrap around me, eager now for the solitude of the Dolphin Inn, certain that nothing good could come of prolonging this unprofitable interview, anxious to unpick my tangled emotions and patch up my bruised pride.

'I'm not interested in what's generally known,' I said. 'So I'll just root around in my own little way . . . Thank you for your help,' I added pointedly. 'I'm sure I won't need to trouble you further.'

But as I reached the sitting-room door, he seemed to think again.

'There's one other person who might talk to you,' he said quickly, 'although I'm not sure what he'll have to say.'

I turned round and faced him expectantly.

'Nick Howard . . . the novelist. He's here for the funeral. He's staying at the Black Swan in Alnwick.'

Now, for the first time, our eyes met in mutual recognition of the uncomfortable past; no more than a fleeting exchange of guarded remembrance, but nevertheless a step towards acknowledgement, for better or for worse.

'Nick Howard, the novelist,' I repeated slowly.

'Yes,' he said impassively. 'The same.'

'And what was he to Eva?'

'You'll have to ask him.'

It was the dismissive nature of this final remark that seemed to set the overriding tone of the whole interview. There was nothing more to be said, no further point in discourse, not on the subject of Eva, of Nick Howard, nor indeed, of anything else. I nodded curtly, I smiled, I muttered a terse goodbye, and then I walked out of the sitting room and closed the door smartly behind me, my legs trembling, my mouth dry.

Nick Howard, the novelist. I repeated the words to myself over and over again as I let myself out of the vicarage door, made my way past the towering, sea-stained edifice that was St Cuthbert's church, and then began the short walk back to the Dolphin Inn. Nick Howard, the novelist. Nick Howard, the novelist . . .

I didn't know whether to curse or to cry.

The weather had turned unseasonably cold and rainy. My mother's cottage grew dank and uncomfortable. The conservatory leaked, the sitting-room chimney smoked, the back boiler blew and there was no hot water.

I retreated to my bedroom with my books, intent now upon an essay that would astonish my year tutor. 'T. S. Eliot: The Poet Redeemed from *The Waste Land*.'

Outside my window, I watched the cottage garden fighting back. Leo Frankish was away at summer school in Exeter: The Death of the English Novel, Part Two. No one else cared much for gardening, and the regimented borders and potted shrubs rioted into mutinous profusion. The buttercups flourished again, and in the shade of the unruly hawthorn hedge, scores of wild poppies flung scraps of blood-red silk to the dark, wet earth beneath.

Michael had gone away. A two-week sailing trip with his brother and the Spencer girls, off the coast of Scotland. A yearly event, its timing long planned, there was nothing sinister about it, no suggestion that the Camerons were trying to keep us apart. Or so Michael insisted.

But in a fortnight I'd received no postcards, no phone calls.

'How's he supposed to phone?' Sarah asked wearily as I stamped around the cottage. 'He's in the middle of the sea.'

My mother was irritated and unsympathetic.

'Think about something else,' she advised me archly.

'I am,' I wailed, waving *The Waste Land* in the air. 'It doesn't help.'

I'd revealed nothing of the scene in Michael's bedroom when his mother had discovered us, nor confessed that I was no longer welcome in the Cameron house. I trembled to recall Beatrice Cameron's face as she threw open the door upon our energetic embraces, and I was mortified to think that I mightn't now be going to Jonathan's twenty-first birthday party. But still I said nothing to anyone. I was certain my mother knew anyway.

Jack Cameron had sent a bricklayer to rebuild our crumbling garden wall, and with a thoroughness that seemed beyond the call of neighbourly duty, had supervised the work himself. My mother donned an old mackintosh and rooted about in the stonework as the building proceeded. I watched them from my bedroom window, nodding and conferring, convinced their conversation centred on me.

'What did he say?' I demanded as my mother kicked off her Wellington boots in the hall. 'Please tell me!'

'He said he thinks the main drain could be damaged. That's why the conservatory's so damp.'

The call came early in the morning when my mother was out buying her newspaper and Sarah was still asleep.

'Beth? It's me. I'm in Edinburgh, but I can be in London by two-thirty. Will you meet me at King's Cross?'

'London?' I said, bewildered. 'I don't know . . . I mean, yes! Of course . . .'

I had no time to enquire where we might go when we met, how long we would stay, what he was doing in Edinburgh, or what I was supposed to say to my mother. I stared at the phone in my hand, perplexed. Why was everything so complicated? Why couldn't we simply be together?

The rain had lifted, the buttercups had opened their shiny hearts to the weak morning sun, and my mother sat reading in the conservatory, regardless of the main drain.

'I thought I'd go up to town today,' I said idly. 'There's a couple of books I need . . .'

'I'll drive you,' she replied without looking up. 'I need a few things in Leicester myself.'

'Er . . . Well, I'm after Frank Kermode's *Romantic Image*. They haven't got it in Leicester. I thought I'd try Foyle's.'

'You're going to London?' Now she did look up, and I stared back in guilty defiance.

'I need *Romantic Image*,' I said stubbornly. 'I have to go.'

As I boarded the train that would take me to St. Pancras, I tried to trace the reasons behind this subterfuge. What would she have said if I'd confessed to meeting Michael? Why did I feel the need to be so secretive? Somewhere at the back of my mind lurked the perception of a passion which frightened the grown-ups, and I smiled to myself, complacent in my naughtiness. Nothing, no one, could keep us lovers apart.

He was waiting when I arrived, and we fell upon each other with extravagant kisses and hugs, thwarted sweethearts forced to spend two whole weeks apart.

'Where are we going?' I laughed as he pulled me towards the taxi rank.

'To my parents' flat in Chelsea. We've got three hours before I have to get back.'

'You mean nobody knows you're here? But won't they miss you?'

'Not if I catch the five-thirty back.'

I was startled, and then immensely flattered, pulling him to me, gently biting the lobe of his ear, needing him to know how much I appreciated this extraordinary effort. The taxi driver stared stonily ahead and we sailed past Foyle's.

'Michael, wait! Let's stop for a moment. I told my mother I was buying a book . . .'

I was into the store before he quite knew what was happening, heading straight for the section cosily marked 'Lit. Crit.', intent on grabbing what I wanted and getting back to the taxi as soon as possible. But as I noisily rounded the appropriate corner, I found myself on the edge of a careful semicircle of chairs. Their silent occupants turned at my entrance and a tall, untidy middle-aged man looked up irritably from a central podium where he was holding court.

'Ssh!' said someone behind me. 'It's Nick Howard, the novelist.'

'We live and write in a post-Beckett world,' the Author declared, eyeing me sternly. 'The novel can never be the same again, and appeals to Dickens or Conrad, or even to Lawrence, must be seen for what they are. Revisionist attempts to impose meaning and structure on a universe which can't sustain them.'

A store assistant motioned me towards an empty chair and I sat down, grinning foolishly, urgently scanning the adjacent shelves for Frank Kermode.

'Beth, what on earth are you doing?' demanded Michael behind me, and a woman turned round to glare. I grimaced at Michael, mouthing a silent apology, and he sat down beside me with ill-concealed annoyance.

'It's Nick Howard, the novelist,' I whispered.

'But if art has no purpose,' trilled an anxious female voice from one of the chairs, 'may I ask, Mr Howard, why you write novels at all?'

'To illuminate the murky little corners of existence,' replied the Author wearily; 'to expose the vanities and the frailties of the species known as *Homo sapiens*. To divert, to pass the time, and, of course, to entertain . . .'

I suddenly spotted *Romantic Image* and reached up for it triumphantly, knocking over my chair.

'Do you have a point to make, young lady?' Nick Howard, the novelist, was now seriously cross.

'Well, no,' I heard myself say. 'I mean, what point could I possibly make? There isn't any point, is there? Surely this is the very point that you yourself were just making?'

A nervous titter ran round the circle of chairs, and Michael emitted a muffled guffaw. I grabbed his arm and together we ran to the cash desk, both of us laughing now.

As I paid we were encouraged to purchase *The Last Buffalo* by Nick Howard and invited to have our copy signed by the great man himself.

'I'll buy it,' said Michael, still laughing, 'as a souvenir. But thank you, no. We won't stay for the signing.'

And then the mad dash to the Chelsea flat, my delight at its peach and plum prettiness, the William Morris fabrics, the Chinese silk rugs, the Smallbone kitchen . . . And my refusal to make love in the sumptuous satin softness of the double bed.

'We can't do it in their bed,' I said squarely. 'Even you must see that.'

'It isn't their bed,' he objected, unbuttoning my blouse and slipping my bra straps from my shoulders. 'They never come here together. If you want the truth, they never sleep together.'

'What? Your parents don't make love?'

'No. Well, not to each other, anyway . . .'

His fingers found my nipples and I shivered in delight, but still I wouldn't lie down on the bed.

'Michael, that's awful. Why do they stay together? Why don't they get divorced?'

'Money, I imagine. That's why they married. But they seem reasonably happy. They don't throw things at each other or argue.'

'Not even about us?'

The question was ignored as he unzipped my jeans and thrust his hand into my knickers. I removed it at once.

'Not here!' I repeated firmly. 'I'm in quite enough trouble with your mother already.'

'On the sofa, then,' he said, resigned. 'But do hurry up. We haven't got long.'

And then all was given to the purpose at hand, flesh unto flesh, the collision of loins, the accommodation of orifice unto appendage, into me, out of me, up, up. Do it this way, Beth. Spread your legs. Put that knee there. Now you on top. Slowly . . . Is that right? Tell me, Beth, is that right . . . ?

'Yes,' I gasped, wishing, not for the first time, that he'd shut up and simply do it. 'Yes, that's right . . .'

Flesh unto flesh, atoms unto atoms, fusion, resolution, subsidence, and planted on that day somewhere deep inside me, a tiny seed of resistance, no more than the first pinprick of doubt, embryonic, unformed . . . What, I wondered vaguely, was the hallmark of true love? How might the bright gold of genuine devotion be distinguished from the dull base metal that is lust?

'Maybe this wasn't such a good idea,' I muttered as we searched the streets outside for a black cab, Michael anxiously consulting his watch. 'What if your mother finds out we've been here?'

'She won't,' he said, spying a taxi and dragging me into the raging traffic. 'As long as we're careful, we can come here any time. We can go to Paris too, if you like. My father has a flat there as well . . .'

'Paris?' I repeated, my objections to Cameron hospitality magically lifting. 'I've never been to Paris, but I'd love to go! My Grandfather Martineau lived there. In fact, he's buried in the cemetery at Montparnasse. My grandmother once told me he used to spend all his time at a seedy little café somewhere in the same district.'

We settled into the back of the cab and he took my hand, gently kissing the fingertips, one by one.

'I'll take you to Paris,' he murmured. 'I'll make love to you all day and all night, and if there's any time left, we'll visit your grandfather's grave and seek out his seedy little café . . .'

Then I was seized by an inexplicable sadness, fear for the unknown future, or regret for the unknown past, as though in that moment I hovered upon the empty shores of eternity, a piece of inconsequential matter without breath or form, a ghost among ghosts. Perhaps it was the sheer carnality of the previous hour, the planting of that tiny seed of doubt, the reduction of human intimacy to simple physical sensation, and the knowledge that all such sensation must one day cease. Or perhaps it was the thought of Grandfather Martineau, whom I'd never known and whose photograph I only dimly remembered, glimpsed once in my grand-mother's dressing-table drawer ... Whatever it was, I felt sudden hot tears behind my eyelids, and I buried my face in Michael's shoulder.

'I love you,' I whispered shakily. 'Promise you'll always love me.'

He lifted my face, concerned at the tears.

'I'll always love you,' he said softly. 'And one day you'll be my wife. Believe it, Beth. It's true.'

Then he pulled my body to his and I felt him rise hard against me, and I knew that if decency only allowed, he would have had me again, right there and then in the back of the taxicab. As it was, he discreetly lifted his hand to encircle one breast.

'Don't,' I mumbled, confused, pushing him away. 'Please don't.'

When I got home the conservatory had been emptied in preparation for a new anti-damp treatment and my mother and Sarah were prising up the floor tiles.

'We're getting to the bottom of it,' my mother sang, handing me a chisel. 'Jack's sending someone to check the drain tomorrow.'

There was no suggestion that I'd been gone suspiciously long, no interrogation about what books I'd bought or what else I'd done, but nevertheless I felt compelled to produce an alibi.

'There was a reading in Foyle's,' I said, hacking away at an obstinate tile. 'I stayed to listen for a while.'

'Who was it?' asked my mother. 'Anyone interesting?'

'Nick Howard, the novelist. What a pain! Seemed to think he was better than Dickens, Conrad and Lawrence all rolled into one ... You've read his stuff, haven't you?'

She paused, chisel in hand, and shot me a curious, questioning glance. Then the chocolate-coloured hair fell over her face and she bent to attack the floor once more.

'Yes,' she said. 'I've read his stuff ... Tell me, did you buy his latest novel?'

'Well, as a matter of fact we ... Er, yes. I mean, I did.'

I felt my cheeks begin to flush. What had happened to *The Last Buffalo*? Did Michael have it? Or had we left it in the flat? Who would find it? What might the repercussions be?

'I must have left it on the train,' I muttered with a panicky little laugh, 'Yes. That's it.'

My mother was intent upon the floor, hammering away with sudden and determined violence. It seemed a very long time until she spoke again.

'Well, I don't suppose you've missed much,' she said at last, sitting back upon her heels and staring at the weapon in her hand. 'Nick Howard is one of the smart boys, very learned, very accomplished. But in my humble literary opinion, none of it amounts to very much. He has no heart. Absolutely no heart at all . . .'

It was an odd little speech about a writer neither of us cared much for, delivered with a shrug and a throwaway laugh, trivial, inconsequential. And Nick Howard the novelist was never mentioned between us again.

But later, much later, when I was clearing out the conservatory after my mother's death, I discovered *The Last Buffalo* among her mountain of books. I often wondered whether she'd read it, or, if she had, whether she'd revised her opinion about Nick Howard's talents, and his lamentable lack of heart.

I swallowed my wrath, and instead of walking straight back to the Dolphin, veered off the main village road on to the beach. I didn't want to cross the churchyard in case I was still visible from the vicarage window, so I skirted the sea wall, dipping down into the grassy dunes. At once I found myself among the rock poppies, hundred upon hundred of canary-coloured blooms billowing across the edge of the shore, an incongruous, heart-stopping vision of extraordinary beauty that stilled my rage in a moment.

I picked my way carefully through the flowers, heading for the great expanse of silvery sand beyond. The sea glittered like mirrored glass, shading to emerald around the outcrops of the islands. The strange ruined stump on St Cuthbert's isle jutted to the heavens like an injured finger, and among the rocks at its base I could plainly see the fat, glistening bodies of the North Sea seals, lazing in the late afternoon sun.

I set off for the water's edge, inhaling the sharp salty air, berating myself for ever having imagined I could meet Michael with emotional impunity. It was always going to hurt like hell. This now seemed ridiculously obvious. It had been sheer madness, putting myself through that chilly interview. But I'd learned my lesson. Now I intended to stay out of his way, or at least ensure that I didn't find myself alone with him again.

I closed my eyes against the relentless magnificence of the sea and tried to think of Eva. How many times had she stood upon these windy shores staring out to the emerald horizon? What part had Nick Howard the novelist played in her life? I had no great desire to seek him out, nor could I believe, on past performance, that he'd prove very forthcoming. But my display in front of Michael seemed to commit me. I had made him believe I was determined to uncover Eva's secrets. I couldn't just give up and go home.

I opened my eyes again, and then became aware of someone sitting on the sand at the edge of the massed poppies. Lost in thought, I'd noticed nothing, but now as I neared the contemplative figure, I recognised Susannah Lamont. She was here for Eva's funeral, of course.

She leapt up at my approach.

'Beth!' She stared in surprise, unable, it seemed, to piece together any likely explanation for my appearance. 'What are you doing here?'

'Same as you, I imagine. I'm here for Eva's funeral.'

She seemed to think this over carefully, and then, in a sudden, unexpected movement she darted to my side and linked her arm through mine.

'Let's walk,' she said, and we set off along the empty beach together, as though we were old chums enjoying an accustomed stroll. Now it was my turn for confusion.

'I want to apologise for my behaviour in Paris,' she began, squeezing my arm, 'that day we met at *The Rose Garden* preview. You were perfectly polite to me, but I was very unfriendly . . .'

I looked down at my feet in the crocodile-skin boots, unable to think of a single sensible remark. I didn't give a damn about her being unfriendly. In fact, I rather preferred it. Certainly, I'd wondered if she'd been screwing Duval, but as he'd now dumped me, it hardly seemed to matter one way or the other.

However, something clearly mattered to Susannah. She took a long breath and squeezed my arm again.

'I admit I found it very difficult . . . You and Dan. He'd been so sweet to me . . . Giving me that part in *The Rose Garden* when really, I was in no fit state to play it . . . I didn't want to seem disapproving of your affair. But of course, I know his wife and children very well . . .'

I stared at her mutinously. This was infinitely worse than if she'd been bedding Duval, and I deeply resented this unnecessary reference to his family.

'Well, it's all over now,' I said haughtily. 'And no harm done.'

She stopped in her progress along the sparkling shore, taking both my hands in hers while high above us the seabirds screamed and jeered. I could scarcely think for the din, and I had no idea what to do in this confusing and unwonted situation. My face was stinging from the salt air, my hair felt like straw, and I'd begun to wonder if Susannah might be high, so strangely beatific and radiant did she seem.

'I want to say something to you, Beth – I hope you won't misunderstand me – I want to tell you to value your life . . . Not to waste your love . . . Jamie and Dan Duval, they're both very special men. They deserve the best, and so do you, of course . . .'

I received this garbled little speech with a sense of outrage, snatching my hands away from Susannah's and shoving them deep into my pockets.

'Is this a lecture or a sermon?' I began, but at that moment we were both alerted by a call. There, waving from the dunes above, stood a black-robed figure, quite plainly the vicar of St Cuthbert's. He advanced across the sand towards us, cassock floating behind him on the breeze, looking like nothing so much as St Cuthbert himself, the good shepherd diligently searching for recalcitrant sheep.

'Oh, there's Michael!' Susannah enthused. 'Have you met him yet? He's the most wonderful priest! He's been so very kind, so helpful to me.'

'Yet another special man,' I said drily as he approached, but the comment was lost upon Susannah.

He met my gaze briefly, then turned to my companion.

'The prayer group meets in ten minutes,' he said. 'I thought you might like to come.'

She nodded energetically, and then, to my acute embarrassment, suddenly leaned forward and kissed me on both cheeks. She linked her arm in Michael's, waved me goodbye, and left me, astonished and unsettled, to watch their halting progress across the dunes until they crossed into the churchyard and the sea wall hid them from my view.

I ran my hand through my lank hair and looked down at my boots. The wet sand had turned the leather chalky and stiff. Indeed, they looked well on the way to ruin. I knew how they felt, but like them, I was made of tough old stuff. A brush-up and polish would see us all fine, and I set off briskly back to the Dolphin.

Whatever Michael and Susannah were doing was no concern of mine, so to hell with them both. I would clean my boots, wash my hair, call up Nick Howard at the Black Swan in Alnwick, and order myself another large gin.

I went away to college, I read *The Last Buffalo* as part of my Modern Literature course, I complied with my mother's view of Nick Howard. I got drunk, I got high, I came top of my tutorial group, I met my best friend Vicky Henderson, and I came back. I couldn't wait to come back. I couldn't imagine the world without Michael to come back to. There was nothing if not the promise that however long we might be apart, however exciting or demanding our respective lives, we would always be together again.

'I thought you'd meet someone else,' my mother said testily. 'Someone you'd have a bit more in common with.'

There was nobody else. There was never anybody else. How could there be?

'We'll come back for our honeymoon,' he said the first time he took me to Paris, when we'd walked to the Cimitière de Montparnasse and put white lilies on my grandfather's grave, and done all the things that lovers do in the lovers' special city.

We walked and we talked and we laughed and we drank, but we never did track down the little café where Victor Martineau used to eat with his friends – mainly because I couldn't remember what it was called, and found, in any case, that I didn't much care. I had other things on my mind.

A honeymoon in Paris? Oh yes, Michael. Please. Let me die in Paris with you beside me. Always you, Michael. Only you. Always and only you.

Back at the Dolphin Inn, depression set in. My boots weren't responding to treatment, I had a thumping headache, and my meeting with Michael had induced a kind of creeping melancholia, rooted in the knowledge that our unlikely reunion had, if anything, compounded our estrangement. I was also seized by the unhappy intimation that from this point, things might get worse.

I lay down on the bed and closed my eyes, awakening an unknown length of time later to total darkness and a timorous, if persistent, knocking on my bedroom door.

'Someone called Nick Howard is asking for you in the bar,' said Mine Host, gazing with mild anxiety as I struggled to recognise both surroundings and situation.

I hadn't reckoned on this prompt response to the message I'd left at the Black Swan, and now I surveyed myself hurriedly in the tarnished mirror above my washbasin. I was fed up and hung over, but with a new layer of Estée Lauder on my eyelids, I didn't look so bad. Not sexy enough to intimidate the vicar of St Cuthbert's perhaps, but smart enough to impress an ageing novelist in decline.

Nick Howard was concealed in the darkest, dingiest corner of the Dolphin's bar, but even in daylight I wouldn't have recognised him. The fair hair was almost white, he had lost a great deal of weight, and he was dressed, incongruously, in a smart business suit and tie. He looked more like a marketing executive than an author, but I had no doubt that behind the restrained façade lay the same self-confident man of letters I'd glimpsed in the bookshop that distant day.

He stood up when I entered, smiling extravagantly.

'Beth Carlisle . . . This is an extraordinary pleasure. I had no idea you were coming to the funeral. I'm delighted to meet you.'

He offered his hand, letting it linger on mine a fraction longer than necessary, so that I glanced at him suspiciously and resolved at once to keep our encounter short. My intention was to lure him into a story, not into bed.

'As I explained in my message,' I said briskly, 'I met Eva Delamere the day she died. I'm very keen to learn more about her . . .'

I gave him an edited version of my meeting with Eva, omitting mention of the powerful effect she'd had upon me, or of the fact that, mysteriously, she had bequeathed me a piece of her jewellery.

'I may write a book if I feel she's sufficiently interesting,' I concluded smoothly, 'but so far nobody will talk to me. I thought you might.'

'Indeed I will, Beth – may I call you Beth? I feel I know you already, I've seen you so often on television. Please, let me buy you a drink.'

He was staring at me intently, and I heaved an inward sigh. The last thing I wanted was a macho literary ego requiring feminine massage, and although I didn't particularly relish running through my repertoire of assertion techniques, I could see he would have to be discouraged.

'Thank you, Mr Howard, but I only drink with friends. Never when I'm working.'

The effect of this mild put-down was surprisingly sure. He crumpled before my eyes, staring into the modest glass of whisky that stood on the grubby table before him, plainly embarrassed.

'I can't tell you much,' he mumbled. 'As a child, I knew Eva briefly. But after that I only met her twice . . .'

He fingered his glass of whisky, seeming to weigh up whether or not he should take a drink, finally deciding against.

'How did you meet Eva at all?' I prompted, sorry that he seemed so suddenly deflated, wondering whether I'd judged too hastily. He laughed awkwardly and picked up the whisky glass once more. 'A family connection,' he said slowly. 'My mother was Harriet Howard. Harold Brannen's bastard daughter, as she liked to declare . . .'

He took a careful sip of his whisky, and it was then that I recognised the mark of the reformed drinker, unable to give up but learning to treat the demon with respect, and I looked at him with new sympathy.

'I know Harold Brannen was killed at Mons,' I said gently. 'The war must have created a lot of bastard children.'

'Ah yes,' he answered. 'That's true. But Harriet believed she would have been a bastard anyway. Harold Brannen was a talented Cambridge scholar, you see. A scholar and a writer. He'd just taken a First in Classics when he went off to war . . . My grandmother, on the other hand, was an uneducated village girl, a landlord's daughter . . .'

He laughed again, and gestured at the grimy bar. 'You're looking at my ancestral home, Beth. My grandmother grew up in the Dolphin Inn.'

We both stared round at the flaking walls, the chipped tiled floor, the

tacky calendar picture behind the bar, and I considered Nick Howard's
sad little tale in silence, thinking as he spoke of Harold Brannen setting
off for war and his sweetheart Lizzie, alone and pregnant, of his baby
daughter Harriet, deprived of his influence on her life, and his young
sister Eva . . .

'What about Eva?' I asked him suddenly. 'You knew her as a child.
You said you met her twice after that.'

He picked up his whisky, swilling the minute measure of liquid round
in the bottom of the glass, and then setting it down on the table once
more without so much as taking a sniff.

'The first time was in the Sixties, in France,' he said. 'I was there on
a mission of mercy . . .'

'What mission?'

'My mother sent me to return a Brannen family heirloom, a little
filigree cross that belonged to Eva. She'd lost it years before, apparently.'

My hand flew instinctively to my throat, and I heard my breath
quicken.

'It was very valuable,' Nick Howard said reflectively, 'and it disappeared. I never found out how or why . . . Anyway, Eva was distraught
at its loss, and my mother got it back for her, years later.'

I stared at him in disbelief, then quickly detached the cross from
beneath my blouse and laid it on the table between us. 'Is this it?' I
demanded hoarsely.

He picked it up, clearly astonished, running the fine chain through
his fingers, stroking the worn gold.

'Yes . . . This is the Brannen cross . . . How extraordinary.'

'She left it to me. Why should she do that?' I beseeched.

He looked down.

'I wouldn't like to say,' he muttered.

'It seems that Eva had a lot of secrets,' I said brusquely, thinking in
that moment of Aidan Forster and wondering once more if this were
Eva's big secret. I decided to try it out on Nick Howard.

'What do you know about Aidan Forster?' I demanded. 'The son and
heir from the big house. He and Eva must have known each other . . .'

He threw me a questioning glance.

'Indeed they did,' he said slowly. He lifted the whisky glass, contemplated it briefly and then downed its remaining contents in one
gulp.

'I should tell you that Aidan Forster was my father,' he offered at last,
'but I know very little about him. My mother saw to that. He was killed
in the war, so I never met him . . .'

He looked at me carefully.

'What do you think about fathers, Beth?' he asked. 'Do you think they're unnecessary? Or do you think a good father is like a good wife? Beyond the price of rubies . . .'

I blinked in surprise, both at the unexpected revelation and the undoubtedly intimate nature of his question. Then I looked away. I was not about to recall my own experience of fathers for anyone, although to my chagrin, the face of Ray Carlisle suddenly rose before me, sallow and strained as it stared down into my mother's grave.

'Maybe we get the parents we deserve,' I said briskly, standing up and making to leave, not wanting to prolong our encounter. 'The law of karma. An individual's destiny prescribed by previous choices and mistakes . . . Isn't that what the Buddhists believe?'

'Is it?'

Nick Howard gave a dry little laugh and stared into his empty tumbler.

'Well, that would certainly explain things,' he said, raising the glass in mock salute as I walked out of the bar.

Chapter Fourteen

So what future now for our Romantic Heroine? She struggles, she weeps, she overcomes, but it is a brave, not to say broke, romantic novelist who tries to suggest that a woman's life may be whole and complete without her one True Love. Romantic heroines do not quit the chase to found all-female communes in the Orkneys or come out as lesbians. They meet a new man, or better still, after much heart-searching and pain, they get the old one back.

Moonlight and Roses: The Cult of Romance in Western Society, by Beth Carlisle (published by Harridan Press to accompany the Metro Television series)

Sunday morning, parish communion, St Cuthbert's church. Celebrant, the Reverend Michael Cameron. Preacher, the Reverend Joan Cunningham.

I'd hoped to hear the vicar of St Cuthbert's in full theological flow from the pulpit, to fix him with a sceptical eye as he rose to address his flock, to make my own judgement about the kind of priest he'd turned out to be. Instead I found myself in what I'd thought was an inconspicuous seat, fixed in turn, so it seemed, by the Reverend Joan Cunningham, a newly-fledged woman priest, I guessed, offering 'a few thoughts' on the nature of faith.

I had no taste for the Church and its esoteric ceremonies, but I told myself that it could only be instructive to meditate in the pews where Eva had sat as a dutiful, God-fearing child, absorbing, perhaps even questioning, the creed of Matthew Brannen, her father. I was mystified and disturbed by what I'd learned about the silver cross, and I intended to tackle Duval just as soon as he showed up for the funeral. I was also vaguely unsettled by my encounter with Nick Howard, but in truth neither Eva nor Howard, nor even Duval, was much in my thoughts as I made my way along the sea road from the Dolphin Inn to the church. I simply wanted to see something, anything, of Michael in his priestly role, to play out in morbid, secret fantasy how it might have been had I become a vicarage wife.

St Cuthbert's interior proved quite unlike the gloomy barn I'd imagined, pale sunlight shafting through two great coloured windows, one showing a sad-faced Madonna and Child, the other depicting St Cuthbert himself, white-haired and sober like a retired bank manager who'd suddenly seen the light.

The walls had been painted white, imbuing this northern outpost with an oddly Mediterranean air, and a glittering crucifix hung in a side chapel. The stations of the cross were posted on the church pillars, reinforcing the Roman imagery, and in a recess off the main aisle I glimpsed a small bank of devotional candles, a few flickering gamely in their dim hideaway. But everything else was solidly Victorian, from the stout polished pews and choir stalls to the huge mahogany pulpit which towered above the worshippers, and I was left with the impression of mild schizophrenia, a church divided between its robust English heritage and a melancholic longing for the soft Latin South.

I'd expected a meagre congregation, and was astonished to find the church half full when I arrived. There seemed few of the fishing and farming families I'd somehow thought would form the core of St Cuthbert's parish. Instead I was surrounded by immaculately suited middle-aged men, women in country casuals, and laughing teenagers in sweatshirts and jeans, clearly culled from a wide range of executive estates and commuter villages along the coast. But at the front, reassuringly, I could see the Church of England's stalwarts, the ancient ladies I remembered from my days at St Botolph's, still clad in violet silk and fox fur, their grey heads covered by garish turbans or scraps of black lace.

Everyone seemed to know everyone else, and I was soon swamped by attempts to put me, the stranger in their midst, at ease. Hallo, welcome, nice to meet you. And inevitably: 'Haven't we seen you on the television?' I normally responded to my public with regulation charm, but today I craved anonymity, and found it hard to summon the necessary grace. I smiled grimly and headed purposefully for the rear of the church.

Then the choir, the servers and the clergy marched in and I bowed my head, suddenly apprehensive, anxious not to be seen. I glimpsed the vicar of St Cuthbert's only from the corner of one eye, an unfamiliar figure in flowing white robes and green chasuble, and the lines of the hymnbook swam before me, a blur of incomprehensible jargon and cant.

'The Sacrifice of God is a broken spirit,' Michael began. 'A broken spirit and a contrite heart he will not despise.'

I tried to concentrate, but found it impossible. I was both bewitched and repelled, seduced by the elegiac music and Michael's low, dramatic delivery of the ancient texts, and yet appalled at the creaking apparatus by which all this was mediated, the Church ponderous with its councils and its committees, its wardens and its stewards, its Mothers' Union and its Young Wives, all of this conveyed by means of the parish news-sheet, pressed into my hand as I arrived. I read the minutiae of St Cuthbert's daily doings with fascination, and could think only of what might have been, of how the Young Wives might have taken to me as their vicar's lady, or me to them. I stole a covert glance at the women who pressed into the pews around me, marvelling at their denial of what the patriarchal Church had done to them and their sisters throughout the centuries. Did the elevation of the Reverend Joan Cunningham to the priesthood really make up for all that?

I gazed once more at the glowing Madonna, virgin and mother, un-touched by human hand and yet fecund and, seeming to catch some-thing of her mystery, hunched forward self-consciously in my seat, the words of a half-remembered incantation from St Botolph's floating through my mind: *O God, from whom all holy desires, all good counsels, and all just works do proceed; Give unto thy servants that peace which the world cannot give* . . .

'Faith is at the very heart of the good life,' declared the Reverend Joan Cunningham from the pulpit, snapping me out of my reverie, 'and I'm not just talking about faith in God. I'm talking about faith in our fellow human beings . . . Are we the kind of people who always believe the worst of others? Who imagine ulterior motives? Who harbour re-sentment based on a dim suspicion or preconception of what we reckon the other person is thinking?'

She paused to allow her words to sink in, and her audience waited dutifully.

'Or do we have the faith, the generosity of spirit, to see that other people can't always respond in the way we would wish? That, like us, other people make mistakes, say the wrong thing at the wrong moment, regret their action or inaction, and then fail to find a way to put things right . . .'

I barely heard a word she said, but spent my time watching Michael closely, alert for anything that might tell me something new, wondering if he'd seen me, if he cared whether I were there or not, if he might offer a gesture of reconciliation, and whether, if he did, I would accept it. But he seemed lost in his own reverie, a holier one, no doubt, than my own, and I divined nothing beyond total devotion to the duty at hand.

I stumbled through the Creed, received absolution for my sins, muttered a few more responses to a few more incomprehensible prayers, and then suddenly found myself on my feet, pressed on all sides by handshakes and beaming smiles, forced to grin back in excruciating embarrassment. *The peace of the Lord be always with you. And also with you . . .*

I felt a tap on my shoulder, and I turned to confront a smiling Susannah Lamont, who, unknown to me, had been sitting in the row behind, and who now leaned forward to peck me on each cheek.

'Peace be with you, Beth,' she murmured, enfolding me in her arms, and I drew back, startled, thinking she seemed to be making a habit of kissing me and wondering what on earth she was about.

I turned to face the altar again, but now I had no stomach for the rest, and when the congregation rose to file towards the communion rail and I saw Lucy emerge from a front pew, I slipped out of my seat and made my way into the churchyard. I didn't want to see Lucy, nor Susannah Lamont come to that, kneeling at Michael's feet receiving the bread and the wine, and I was anxious to be safely back in the Dolphin Inn, to be spared any further pleasantries.

But as I walked smartly out of the church porch, a small voice from behind confounded all plans.

'Beth! Where are you going? Surely you're coming to Sunday lunch with us?'

Katie Cameron, heart-breakingly beautiful in a pink cotton frock and matching straw hat, was gazing up at me beseechingly, looking for all the world as though my presence at lunch stood between her happiness and total despair.

'Everyone's coming,' she said anxiously. 'You must come too!'

I deduced that everyone would include the Reverend Joan Cunningham and very possibly Susannah Lamont, and that Lucy had deliberately omitted to invite me. I felt profoundly grateful to be spared, and tried hastily to muster a handful of convincing excuses.

'But you haven't seen my kittens,' Katie said sorrowfully. 'Surely you want to see them?'

'Well, yes I do, Katie. Very much.'

'That's settled then. If you can't come to lunch, you must come afterwards. And then you can stay for tea.'

I smiled vainly, muttering about important telephone calls and work that was waiting, yet I knew that I craved this little girl's company, and knew, too, that I'd do anything to win her affection.

'Okay,' I said at last, smiling bravely. 'Shall we say four o'clock?'

'I'll tell Daddy you're coming,' she cried as she skipped back into the church. 'He'll be so pleased!'

Then Michael's voice, low and portentous, echoed through the porch, relayed over the church intercom.

'Go in peace to love and serve the Lord,' he said, and I scuttled away across the churchyard, anxious that he might suddenly emerge and try to shake me by the hand, the liberal vicar humouring the antagonistic outsider, the pitying priest embracing the unrepentant sinner. I wasn't about to play sinners and priests with the vicar of St Cuthbert's . . . Nor would I let him gaze into my turbulent soul and find me wanting.

Michael Cameron, light of my life, lover, companion, friend, and evangelist.

'You genuinely believe this stuff, don't you?' I asked him curiously. 'God the Father. God the Son. You think it's all for real . . .'

We were lying on the mossy bank by the edge of the emerald copse above St Botolph's parish church, fresh from a skirmish at the Christian Debating Society. The Resurrection was a Ruse. A nervous, pimply youth called Giles had been cast as devil's advocate, a choice that seemed markedly unfair, given the eloquence of his adversary. I'd looked on in sympathy, bemused but oddly entertained.

It soon became clear that Giles was breaking the rules. In attempting to denounce the disciples as a bunch of country bumpkins who'd told a ridiculous lie about a walking corpse simply to save face, he'd effectively proved the case he'd been arguing against. Michael had only to press the message home.

'Which is more probable?' Michael had demanded of his docile audience. 'That a group of unsophisticated fishermen invented a ludicrous tale – a tale which, rather than bringing them prestige, power or fortune, eventually led them to their own executions . . . ?'

The rector of St Botolph's nodded approvingly and Giles gave every appearance of verging upon some ecstatic state.

'That these same fishermen,' Michael went on, 'practical, working folk that they were, immersed in the daily realities of life and death, suddenly persuaded themselves that all the hitherto accepted facts of physical existence had been contravened – that a dead man had come back to life?'

More nods. Smiles all round.

'Were they charlatans, these fishermen?' Michael enquired gravely. 'Were they con men? Or were they simply gullible fools?'

He paused dramatically, and we all waited in knowing anticipation.

'Or isn't it, on balance, more probable that Jesus of Nazareth, whose mission had ended in manifest failure, whom the fishermen had deserted as he hung on the Cross, and whom everyone believed dead and buried . . .'

Still we waited, breathless, unmoving, but not unmoved.

'That this Jesus overturned every expectation – that he did indeed walk from the tomb – that this, only this, and nothing less than this, could have transformed a traitorous group of terrified peasants into fearless apostles for the Church of Christ?'

Cheers. Applause. Motion defeated. Let's hear it for Jesus, and for Michael Cameron too . . . Hallelujah and goodnight.

Now he rolled over on the grassy bank and moved his hand from my bare knee where it had been resting.

'Of course I believe it,' he said seriously. 'And yes, I think it's for real. But that doesn't mean I take everything in the Bible literally.'

'Oh, you want it all ways,' I said, laughing. 'God the Father who raised Jesus from the dead, and God the Concept who'll be anything you decide.'

He sat up, staring down upon the squat grey hulk of St Botolph's beneath us, taking in the sweep of the tangled churchyard to the point where it met the borders of the Cameron estate, his face turned away towards the crimson sun which, just at that moment, seemed to perch in bloody profusion upon my mother's chimneypot.

'God the Father,' he said slowly, 'is just one way of saying that personal relationships lie at the heart of the universe. They're what count.'

For some reason, perhaps to do with my own paltry experience of fathers, this reply irritated me.

'That's shit,' I declared, standing up. 'Personal relationships? Tell that to the Pope. Tell that to thousands of women whose lives have been blighted by puritanical attitudes to sex . . .'

He stood up beside me and slipped his arm through mine, unperturbed, as he always seemed to be, by the knowledge that my faith didn't match his own.

'Well, yours hasn't been blighted, has it?'

He dangled the Bentley's keys in front of my nose, and I laughed despite myself.

But as we walked back to the church gate where the car was parked, I felt compelled to state my case, once and for all, just so there shouldn't be any mistake, now or in the future.

'Look, don't get me wrong . . . I think Jesus was a great guy. I'd be delighted if he rose from the dead. He sure as hell deserved it . . . But I can't see that it really matters, Michael, one way or the other. The world's still going to the devil. It hasn't made much difference, has it?'

'It's made all the difference to me,' he said quietly.

The Bentley sparked into life, and he swung away from the village, out towards the secluded, whispering green of the spinney.

'You don't mind making love to the ungodly?' I teased as we climbed into the back seat.

'I regard it as a mission,' he said, unbuttoning my shirt with a well-practised hand. 'And I've got a lifetime to convert you.'

'You'll never do it,' I laughed. 'I'm much too sceptical. I could never believe in life after death.'

'No?' He slipped the shirt from my shoulders and caressed both breasts, feather strokes from gentle fingers. 'But you believe in heaven, don't you, Beth . . .'

Onward, onward, lightly step. Laugh as you go, laugh as you come. To come is to die. Sex and death, inextricably entwined. The twin mysteries of the universe, the last enemies . . .

Afterwards, washed over by the melancholy aloneness that often follows sex, I returned to this unlikely theme.

'You don't really believe in the resurrection of the body, do you, Michael? I mean, you can't really think we're all going to end up clapping hands and singing songs around the glassy sea?'

'I believe in eternal life, Beth,' he said seriously, sitting up. 'And I believe it begins now. It's a matter of quality, not quantity, you see.'

A neat, smart answer. Clever, concise. A theological evasion of a peculiarly Anglican kind. No lies, no pretence. But no substance either.

It was the moment I realised he would surely be a priest one day.

I didn't want to be late for my tryst with Katie Cameron, but I didn't want to be early either, and so I found myself skulking in the outbuildings behind St Cuthbert's vicarage, waiting for the church clock to strike. There was little of interest in what I guessed had been the Brannen stables, just a few garden tools and a battered sea dinghy undergoing renovation. I gazed at it idly, wondering if Michael or Lucy's sons or some village handyman were engaged in the work. There was evidently a long way to go. Indeed, only the nameplate, *Island Star*, seemed to have received any attention so far. The letters were picked out in gold and scarlet paint, shiny and pristine against the dark stained wood of the dinghy's hull.

When St Cuthbert's clock announced the moment, I slunk out of the barn and made my way to the front door of the vicarage, wondering, as I knocked, what further emotional trials I might be required to endure.

'Daddy's out,' said Katie brightly, ushering me into the hall and quelling my immediate fears. 'Lucy's out too, but don't worry, Emily's here. And anyway, I can look after you.'

'Emily?'

'Emily Forster,' said a voice from behind me, 'How do you do?'

I turned to confront a slender young woman, neat and pretty, her shiny black hair cut into a stylish bob. She was leaning in the doorway of the sitting room, and she was watching me closely.

'I'm Michael's administrator,' she said with a guarded smile, 'up at the Retreat. And Aidan Forster was my grandfather . . . Michael said you wanted to talk about that?'

I shook my head, taking in her sensible country clothes, the navy denim jeans, the multi-coloured sweater and stout, strong boots, the kind that would never succumb to salt stains on the beach.

'Not any more,' I said.

She nodded, rather as though it were inconceivable, in any case, that anyone should wish to talk about her grandfather.

'You're staying for tea?' she enquired, smiling at Katie who was hopping about in front of us.

'Of course she is,' said Katie impatiently. 'Lucy's made a cake.'

'Then I'll do the sandwiches,' said Emily Forster, as if confirming her role in the household. 'Now off you go, Katie, and show Beth those kittens!'

I was seized with sudden intuition, and I stared back at Emily Forster unhappily. Of course, I had been wrong about Lucy Robson. She was not the object of my sister's high hopes for Michael's remarriage. How could I ever have imagined the vicar of St Cuthbert's in love with his sturdy housekeeper? Who had I been fooling or trying to reassure? Here, before me, stood the new woman in Michael's life. There could be no doubt about it.

With heavy heart I followed Katie up the long mahogany staircase to the next floor of the vicarage, trying to settle my thoughts upon Eva, to imagine her skipping up and down these steps, perhaps chased by Harold Brannen or one of her other brothers. But I could think only of Emily Forster and what she meant to Michael, and it was then I knew with sickening certainty that, however hard I tried, my feelings for the vicar of St Cuthbert's couldn't simply be consigned to the past.

'I moved the kittens into Daddy's bedroom,' Katie announced, snapping me out of my preoccupation. 'It's the sunniest room in the whole house.'

I stopped short in front of the door she had opened.

'I don't think we should go into your daddy's bedroom,' I faltered.

'Why not? He isn't in there.'

'I know that, Katie, but people's bedrooms are private. They don't want strangers tramping through.'

'You're not a stranger,' she said comfortingly. 'And anyway,' she added, 'he's not here so he won't know, will he?'

This was hard to dispute, and since I couldn't summon the presence of mind, or perhaps the strength of character, to desist, I followed her uncertainly into a huge, bright room whose magnificent bay window overlooked the shore and the bank of massed yellow poppies.

But it wasn't the view that took my attention, nor the basket of marmalade kittens that sat in the bay; it was the bed, the great carved bed with its intricate head and foot boards, low to the floor, just the way I remembered it from the Cameron house, covered now in a bright tapestry counterpane. I sat down upon it suddenly, fearing my knees were about to give way.

'Do you like cats?' asked Katie purposefully, depositing a handful of kittens on the bed in front of me. 'Would you like a cat of your own?'

'I've already got one,' I muttered distractedly, stroking a tiny scrap of fluff. 'She's called Thomasina . . .'

Then I remembered Thomasina's untimely end beneath the delivery truck, and wondered for a moment if I should take a kitten, for this had clearly been Katie's hope. But although, just days before, I'd been planning to replace Thomasina, something now held me back. For some reason, I no longer wanted another cat.

I glanced briefly around Michael's bedroom. There was nothing much to see: a bible on a chest, a black jacket draped around a chair, and my eye was drawn back to the bed. Had this Cameron heirloom been the marriage bed, the one in which Michael and Clare Spencer, the newly-weds, had conceived their daughter? Did Michael now make love to Emily Forster in it? Or didn't clergymen do such things? Why weren't they married already? Michael had been a widower long enough, and Emily Forster seemed very much at home in the vicarage. Was she wearing an engagement ring? I hadn't noticed.

'So you don't want a kitten?' Katie asked me, subdued.

'Not just at the moment,' I said guiltily, scooping the kittens off the bed and back into their basket. 'But maybe I can think of someone who does. My sister, perhaps. You've met Sarah, haven't you?'

I was prying now, and though I felt ashamed, I couldn't stop myself. The child nodded, and before I lost my nerve, I rushed on.

'Sarah told me your daddy might be getting married again,' I said brazenly. 'Should you like that?'

She gave it her consideration.

'I don't know. It depends who it was,' she said sensibly.

Then my gall deserted me. I had no idea how Katie Cameron had been affected by her mother's death, didn't know whether Michael might be trying to break his news gently, couldn't begin to guess at the relationship between her and Emily Forster. I had no right to question nor put notions into her head.

'Why don't we go for a walk?' I said quickly, keen now to be gone before I was discovered in the vicar's bedroom. 'We could find some ice-cream.'

'All right,' agreed Katie hesitantly, and I looked at her anxiously, afraid I'd gone too far.

'I've upset you,' I said in a small voice. 'I'm sorry.'

'It's all right,' she said bravely. 'I'm a bit upset, but it's all right . . . I really did think you might take a kitten . . . It's going to be an awful job finding them homes.'

I sensed my mother's growing disapproval of Michael whenever I came home from college, although nothing specific was said. It was more a matter of irritation at the mention of his name, of questions about exactly where I was going and when I would be back, of pointed comments about the amount of work I still had to do.

I was confused about the reasons for this disenchantment, for she'd seemed keen to encourage me at the start. It couldn't have anything to do with sex, as such. She was hardly in the dark about what we did on the back seat of the Bentley, and once she'd picked up my doctor's prescription without asking any questions.

Perhaps, I figured, she was worried I'd throw in my course and follow him to Cambridge.

It was certainly true that after our sojourn in Paris, my pleasure at the prospect of a new university year had dwindled. And as autumn approached, I could scarcely bear the thought of our parting. We had survived our first year, but how could I be absolutely sure he wouldn't meet a Girton girl, someone from his own background, someone his mother would approve? I was in no doubt that Michael's mother represented the greatest threat to our future. If anyone could drive us apart, it was she, although my own mother also seemed to be doing her bit.

Michael, however, was unconcerned. He appeared blessed with a divine sense of certainty, as though the future were truly pre-ordained. No opposition could thwart us. There was simply no question of either one of us meeting anyone else. We had only to endure the next few years, and then we would be together for ever.

'I've bought you something,' he announced, just two weeks before I left for college that second autumn, 'to help you remember me . . .'

We'd been walking in the spinney on a glowing September afternoon, stopping in Great-Great-Uncle Malcolm's folly to watch for the beam of sunlight through the stained-glass figure of St Augustine. But we'd arrived too late, or else the day was wrong, and though the mossy walls of the little chapel gleamed a bewitching golden green, no magical beam of light fell across the stone where we sat.

'What is it?' I asked moodily, unable to be consoled now that the farewell was almost upon us.

He'd deliberately played down the presentation of his gift, and now he produced it without ceremony or comment. I gaped in astonishment at the tiny black velvet box, and he laughed, suddenly self-conscious. I opened the box and stared down at a glittering solitaire diamond, large and undoubtedly expensive.

'If it doesn't fit,' he said, slipping it on my ring finger, 'it can be altered.'

But it did fit, perfectly, and I looked up at him with tears in my eyes.

'Oh Michael,' I whispered, 'I don't know what to say . . .'

'Say you love me, and that you'll marry me the moment you can.'

It didn't need to be said, and I kissed him passionately, wishing we had the car, wondering in faint alarm, for I'd become nervous about our lack of restraint, whether he'd want to make love to me then and there. For once, however, he merely pulled me close and hugged me.

'We must celebrate,' he said. 'It's a pity we have to do it alone, but there it is. I'll take you out to dinner tonight . . .'

I wasn't entirely sure why we had to celebrate our engagement alone. Certainly, I didn't expect Lady Cameron to open the champagne, but there was still Jack Cameron, who'd showed every sign of liking me, and Jonathan, Michael's brother, who'd always been amiable and courteous. And then, of course, there was my own family, my mother and Sarah. My sister, I was certain, would be pleased for me, and my mother, for all her covert disapproval, surely wouldn't begrudge my happiness?

But in that assumption, I was very wrong.

'Look,' I said dreamily, drifting back from our celebration dinner late that night on a cloud of romantic expectation. 'Look what Michael bought me . . .'

My mother blinked at the diamond ring as though immediate sensory perception could not be trusted. Then she looked up at my face, as if to confirm what was still only an awful suspicion. And then she went wild.

'Are you completely mad?' she shouted at me. 'Is there nothing in that stupid head of yours? Engaged! I never heard anything so ridiculous in all my bloody life. You're just nineteen, Beth! You're in the middle of university. You're going to be a journalist, remember?'

She began pacing round the conservatory, and I saw that she was shaking with rage.

'I'm still going to do all that,' I protested feebly. 'We won't get married until I graduate —'

'You foolish girl!' she yelled. 'What do you know about anything? You think you can marry Michael Cameron and have a life of your own? You think his mother will let him marry you anyway? Grow up, Beth. For God's sake get some sense!'

I sat down suddenly on the cane settee and burst into tears, unable to fathom this vehement response. My crying calmed her temporarily, and she sat down beside me, putting her arm around my shoulders.

'I only want the best for you, Beth,' she said tightly. 'You must know that. And I'm not having you going back to university with a bloody engagement ring on your finger.'

'But what's so wrong with Michael?' I beseeched her. 'I don't understand!'

'There's a lot wrong with Michael,' she said, making a visible effort at control. 'In the first place, he wants to be a priest. Think about it, Beth. You a vicar's wife? Making the bloody scones for the Young Wives' summer fair? You'll fit this in with your Fleet Street career, will you? Good grief, you're not even a bloody Christian!'

This seemed to set her off again, and she stood up from the cane settee and marched round the conservatory once more.

'In the second place, his mother just won't have it,' she said, battling to control her still evident fury. 'You're not in their class, Beth. You're not what she wants. And when it comes to it, Michael won't go against his mother. Has he gone home tonight and announced your engagement? Has he hell! It's your little secret, isn't it, Beth? To be celebrated on the quiet . . .'

I looked up at her, still crying, uncomfortably aware of how close to the truth this seemed.

'And finally,' she said, watching me closely, 'if Michael really loved you, he'd put your welfare first. But it has to be what he wants, doesn't it, Beth? What he decides is right?'

'I don't know what you mean,' I sobbed angrily, wondering as I spoke if I did.

'Then let me spell it out,' she said coldly, determined now, it seemed, to spare me nothing. 'You've acquired quite a reputation in this village, cavorting in the back of Jack Cameron's car with your clothes off. Everyone knows that Beatrice Cameron found you in Michael's bed and how angry she was . . . Does it never occur to you, Beth, that he's deliberately using you to challenge his mother?'

I stared in total shock, utterly perplexed by the extent of her wrath, unable to begin on any defence.

'I don't give a damn about your reputation,' my mother said calmly.

'As long as I know you're in charge of your own destiny, you can do as you choose, and to hell with them all. But I cannot accept that Michael, who says he loves you, who openly professes his high-minded Christian principles, shouldn't give a damn either . . .'

I wept bitterly then, accusing her of blatant double standards, inverted snobbery, hypocrisy and everything else that came into my head.

'I love him,' I cried, twisting the solitaire diamond ring round and round my finger, 'I don't care what you or anyone else thinks. I'm going to marry him one day.'

My mother bent down and put her face close to mine.

'Over my dead body,' she declared.

We bought ice-cream at the village store and then walked down on to the beach among the poppies. Katie had forgiven me for refusing a kitten, and now she talked animatedly about all kinds of subjects she thought would interest.

'See the ruined tower on that island?' she said, pointing out to sea. 'Well, somebody dived to his death from that tower, years ago. A storm knocked off a bit of the wall, and it was under the water, and he didn't realise. You can still see the bloodstains on the rocks!'

'Can you really? After all this time? How terrible! Who was he?'

'His name was Young Ralph Forster. I think that's what they called him . . . Then there was another storm, just a month later. A woman who was having a baby ran into the sea and drowned. But the baby was saved.'

'And I thought this was such a quiet place to live!'

'Oh no!' said Katie, rather put out by this suggestion. 'Haven't you heard about St Cuthbert?'

'Not the whole story. Tell me.'

It wasn't hard to listen. Katie Cameron absorbed me in a way no other child had done before, and her faithful resemblance to Michael made me feel that I knew her already, that I had only to make up for lost time and she would recognise me for the old friend I was.

'When the Vikings came,' she related, 'St Cuthbert's monks dug up his body. They carried it around for years, and then they built Durham Cathedral.'

'It sounds very gruesome. And very hard work.'

'Do you think they had the body covered up?'

'Yes,' I said, giving this due consideration, 'I'm sure they did.'

I found her enchanting, and I felt she liked me too. I longed to establish some bond between us, however tenuous, but short of changing my mind about the kitten, I could think of no way. I lay back on

the cool sand among the poppies, thinking it over, beginning, at last, to
relax. But the lull was short-lived.

'Oh look, there's Daddy and the boys in the boat!' Katie cried. 'Let's
see if they've caught any fish.'

She scrambled up from the poppies and skipped away across the
dunes, waving wildly and beckoning me on. I stood up and brushed the
sand from my pants, conscious of a grass stain at the knee, wondering
why I'd ever bought a cream trouser suit, looking down at the crocodile
skin boots, which had happily recovered overnight but which now
seemed ludicrously inappropriate on these rugged shores. I was acutely
aware of how improbable I looked in my smart city gear, and I followed
Katie uncertainly across the open beach.

They were pulling a small dinghy from the water, Michael and three
dark-haired, gangling boys, Lucy's sons, struggling on the wet sand
with a bag of flopping mackerel.

Out of clerical grab and in fraying jeans, feet bare and arms exposed
to the weak north sun, he seemed suddenly younger, closer to my memory, his hair the same bright gold, his hands, as I watched them pulling
nets and sandals from the bottom of the dinghy, deft and strong.

He looked up briefly.

'Fish for tea, Katie,' he said, looking away again and bundling the
assorted sandals together.

She knelt down on the sand to inspect the catch while I leaned self-
consciously on the side of the boat, mentally rehearsing a variety of
innocuous remarks.

'There's oil on the prow,' he said to me, still absorbed with the nets.
'Watch your clothes.'

Suddenly Katie stood up.

'Are you getting married again, Daddy?' she demanded.

He shot her a startled glance, and I felt my face begin to flush. I
turned away from them, staring out to sea, trusting that the breeze
would raise my colour and hide my guilt.

'Not this week,' I heard him say.

Katie laughed, and then the children were gone, bounding back
across the dunes towards the vicarage, calling, shrieking, chasing, and
we were left alone.

Slowly and carefully we picked our way through the dry heavy sand,
neither of us speaking. We were so close we might have touched, and
as I wobbled precariously on my heels, I wondered what would happen
if I suddenly plunged into a dip into the dunes. Would he stretch out
an arm to steady me, or would he let me fall?

The silence was unbearable, but he showed no sign of breaking it, so
in the end, I did.

'I met Nick Howard last night,' I said steadily. 'He told me a bit about Eva's family, but nothing really significant.'

There was a pause, and he seemed to be concentrating hard on the sand beneath his feet.

'No news of the secret lover, then?' he asked at last.

'Is that such a ridiculous idea?' I retorted, irritated by the belittling implication of this question. 'Don't lots of people conceive grand passions that they never get over? Long-ago affairs that continue to haunt them?'

The words were out of my mouth before I'd considered them, falling between us with embarrassing resonance. I could hardly believe what I'd said, and if he'd looked at me then, I would surely have offered a rueful and apologetic grimace. But he didn't. Instead he moved perceptibly away from me, glancing up towards the vicarage, as though calculating how far we had to go before we could reasonably separate.

'Daniel Duval has arrived at the Retreat,' he mumbled, looking down at the sand again. 'I think it would be a good idea to have a word with him . . .'

Now I felt less apologetic than infuriated, and I determined to snap him into some kind of direct response.

'Maybe you do,' I said crisply, 'but I know better. I've met Daniel Duval before, and I can confidently predict that I'll get fuck-all out of him. Exactly what I'm getting from you, in fact.'

This time he did look at me, a quick, uncomfortable glance that gave me some satisfaction, though he dropped his gaze again in the next instant.

'I can't tell you anything about Eva Delamere's life,' he said quietly. 'It's not my place to do that.'

Suddenly I didn't care what came next. I'd be damned, I decided, if I'd take tea at St Cuthbert's vicarage, watching while they fried their mackerel, eating Lucy's cake and Emily Forster's sandwiches, straining to be civil. I would state my case, and then I would be gone.

'If you won't tell me anything remotely interesting about Eva Delamere,' I said icily, 'then there's one thing, at least, which I think you must explain. You can tell me why the hell you rang me up in the first place.'

He said nothing, and I took pleasure in his visible discomfort.

'Well?' I demanded viciously.

'It would take some explaining,' he said at last.

'Try me. I've got all afternoon.'

But this pertinent point was never pursued, for at that moment we were interrupted by a shout, and looking up, saw a figure waving from the vicarage garden.

'There's Lucy,' Michael muttered. 'I'd better give her the fish. She's waiting to make tea . . . Mind you don't break your neck in those boots.'

And then he strode away across the last of the wiry dunes, hurrying towards the vicarage, never once looking back, the man of God, St Cuthbert's faithful disciple, spokesman for the Almighty, who had so very little to say to me.

I watched him for a moment, then turned swiftly on my boot heels and staggered away.

Chapter Fifteen

Where did it spring from, this all-pervasive, all-consuming belief in the power, the primacy of Romantic Love? Not from History, which gave us marriage as a social and economic contract, nor from Christianity, which stressed the duties and reponsibilities of fleshly union, and declared, quite unequivocally, that this was a lower state. From Art, perhaps? From painting, opera, poetry and novels? Certainly, artists throughout the ages have sought to stir the passions of others while giving vent to their own, but Art remains an esoteric activity for an elitist audience, and Romantic Love, with its mass appeal, must needs find succour in cruder soil. And what more crude, more blatant, more seductive, than the movie version of Love, dished up with sighs and kisses by those Hollywood moguls of the Thirties, men who in their dewy dreams begat a world of lovelorn picture-goers, women for whom life would ever after be viewed through a soft-focus lens . . .

Moonlight and Roses: The Cult of Romance in Western Society, by Beth Carlisle (published by Harridan Press to accompany the Metro Television series)

––––––––––

The day of the funeral dawned pitilessly bright, the waves on the North Sea glinting like strips of tinsel and young green life bursting forth from field and hedgerow, oblivious to death and loss, uncaring and unkind. Outside my attic window the seagulls whooped and wheeled, cruising into the endless blue, their dingy grey wings lit with silver from above. I followed their progress from the window as they swooped on to the foam-tipped waves and then headed out for the dark green waters beyond the islands. I watched the black bodies of the seals twisting and gleaming against the rocks, and idly traced the wash of a tiny scarlet-painted fishing boat as it made its way towards St Cuthbert's ruined tower. The world was about its business, and it would not stop to bury Eva Delamere.

I'd made a few decisions overnight. I did not intend to speak to Duval at the funeral, nor make any further enquiries about Eva's cross. Maybe I would have it valued on my return to London, or maybe I would simply accept Eva's gift as a tantalising little mystery that might never be solved.

I'd also given up on the idea of Eva's secret lover. After all, she'd been married to one man for over fifty years, and if she had ever loved anyone else, not Aidan Forster, it seemed, but maybe some other young blade who'd lived in the village, then her husband, Toby Truman, deserved to be left with his illusions and his secrets intact.

As for Michael, I planned a civilised farewell, making no mention of our skirmish the day before, nor indeed of anything personal. I would drive to the vicarage after breakfast, I'd take another look at Katie Cameron's kittens and promise to ask Sarah if she'd have one, and then I would say goodbye. Maybe I could keep in touch with Katie through Sarah, sending a birthday card, even a Christmas present. But maybe not. I had no claim on her affection, and I wouldn't try to make one. For the first time since I'd left Paris, I felt calm and in control. I was about to bury my strange encounter with Eva Delamere along with her bones. I meant to slip into the back of the church and leave for London the moment the service ended. The first episode of my TV series was due to be screened that night. I had interviews and appearances planned, as well as my book to promote. And I had to decide what I was going to do next.

I dressed carefully, taking the black Karl Lagerfeld suit from the wardrobe, sniffing it suspiciously. Every drawer and cupboard in my bedroom at the Dolphin seemed to stink of mothballs. I sniffed at the suit again. There seemed nothing a good squirt of Paloma Picasso couldn't hide.

I had a black velvet hat which I thought might impart a certain cachet at the funeral, and I tried it this way and that in the washstand mirror, pleased with the way I looked. Then I walked downstairs, consumed my warm orange juice and my cold toast, paid my bill, and took leave of Mine Host.

'You look very nice,' he mumbled as I left, not quite his usual effusive self that morning.

I cruised out of the great empty car park, glad to see the grimy edifice of the Dolphin Inn disappearing behind me, and pulled up outside the village store, planning to buy Katie some chocolates, my mind already skipping ahead to London. Maybe I could take Jamie a souvenir from

Northumberland, something truly dreadful, a plastic St Cuthbert or a pottery sheep. I was relieved, I realised, to be going home, and I was determined to forget Eva Delamere, Daniel Duval and, most of all, Michael Cameron, just as soon as I left.

But this new-found resilience was brutally, conclusively shattered the moment I walked into the village shop.

As I reached for a box of chocolates from the counter, there before me, spread out in brazen multi-colour, was the front page of the *Sun*.

I stared at the banner headline, transfixed. TWO'S COMPANY! THE RO-MANTIC WORLD OF BETH CARLISLE . . . Underneath was not one picture of me, but two, virtually the same, right down to the bottles of champagne on the table before me and the crystal wine glasses in my hand. The same, except that I was gazing lustily into the eyes of two different men.

'Can I help you, miss?'

I caught my breath. Goddamn Clive Fisher. The nerve of the man. But it was neat. It was clever. He'd tracked me down in Paris and snatched a picture as I drank with Duval. Then he'd persuaded me to pose with Jamie, and he'd shopped me on the very day my series was due to begin. The Romantic World of Beth Carlisle! It was the kind of stunt any hack would be proud of.

I paid for the chocolates, and not having the gall to pick up the newspaper, scuttled out of the shop and back into my car. I was trembling with shock. All I could think of in that moment was whether the *Sun* might be delivered to St Cuthbert's vicarage, and if Michael had read it.

Then other possible repercussions dawned. Suppose I came face to face with Duval at the funeral? How was Jamie going to react? What the hell would Sam Lutz and Metro TV have to say? I crashed the car into gear and began to drive, sailing past the vicarage, not knowing where I was going.

But by the time I'd reached the harbour road and glimpsed the golden blaze of rock poppies sweeping out into the bay, I'd begun to calm down. I was nothing if not resourceful. What was so incriminating about sharing a bottle of champagne? Dammit, I would brazen it out. I hadn't read all the details of his story, but even if Fisher knew where I'd been staying in Paris, I could still deny an affair. Daniel Duval was an old friend, wasn't he? No one was likely to say otherwise; not Jamie, and certainly not Duval himself. If we all kept cool, we might even be able to sue.

I drove back to the vicarage, summoning every ounce of composure. It was, I reasoned, highly unlikely that they took the *Sun* at St Cuthbert's. Only a couple of hours and I would be gone from the village for ever. Maybe I wouldn't have to face Michael in the knowledge that he'd read all the mucky details of my private life.

Lucy opened the front door.

'Sorry about tea yesterday . . . ' I began with a winning smile, but she gave me no chance to finish, ushering me hastily into the sitting room.

'Have you seen the *Sun*?'

'I thought you probably hadn't,' I muttered, deflated

'Sorry. We take all the papers. We like to keep up.'

I sat down on the chesterfield, fighting the urge to burst into tears. Breathe deep, Beth. Breathe deep. Repeat after me: I am a mature, responsible person in charge of my own destiny. I live as I choose, I live as I choose . . .

'I'll be frank,' Lucy said, sitting down beside me. 'Michael's a bit tetchy this morning. It's not just this stuff in the paper. My car won't start, and he wanted to borrow it. Also, Katie's gone into mourning because one of the kittens died . . .' She hesitated, then squeezed my hand, a kindly little gesture of solidarity that I received with gratitude.

'This is a big funeral, Beth. People coming from Paris, from America, all over the place. Funerals are always difficult. The families get upset, and there's a lot of pressure on the vicar to get it right.'

'You mean Michael wants me to stay away?'

'Good heavens, no! Anyone is free to go to a funeral . . . But he'd be reassured to think you were planning to sit at the back . . . That if Daniel Duval doesn't wish to see you, then he won't have to. He's one of the chief mourners, you see.'

She looked at me anxiously, keen to avoid offence. I said nothing, still struggling for control. In the window, on top of Jack Cameron's old desk, I could see an open copy of the *Sun*. It was clear Michael had read the whole story.

A door opened, and Lucy jumped to her feet.

'It still won't start,' I heard Michael mutter darkly from the hall.

'I'll call the garage,' Lucy said soothingly. 'You can use the Bentley, just for today.'

I didn't have time to consider the implications of this remark, for then he was in the room beside me, looking most unlike the vicar of St Cuthbert's in faded cords and a grease-stained T-shirt, weighing up my smart black suit and my velvet hat, making me feel at that moment as though I'd dressed for a fashion show, not a funeral. I felt a sudden surge of defiance.

'For your information,' I said coolly, 'I shall be sitting at the back of the church, and I will be leaving the moment the funeral is over.'

'Good,' he said abruptly, walking to the desk and extracting his cigarettes from underneath the newspaper.

Wounded by this brute response, I sailed on into my defence.

'May I suggest you don't automatically believe everything you read in the papers?' I said steadily. 'Daniel Duval is an old friend. It isn't a crime to drink champagne with a friend.'

He lit his cigarette, looked down briefly at the newspaper, and then turned to face me.

I stared back, bitterly aware in that moment of all he had once meant to me, of the hope and the pain we had shared, of just how badly our long-ago love had ended, of how barren this new beginning had turned out to be.

'I'm sorry,' he said with evident effort, 'I don't mean to be rude. I'm concerned about the funeral, that's all. It's no business of mine where you drink your champagne.'

'That page one story is shit!' I cried, propelled by this little barb into a foolish lie. 'There's nothing going on between me and Daniel Duval.'

'That's not what his wife says,' Michael replied slowly. 'But then, perhaps you haven't read page two?'

'Michael's gone to a funeral,' Jonathan told me solemnly, opening the kitchen door of the great Cameron house, the only entrance I ever felt brave enough to use after my spat with Michael's mother. 'He and Clare went together. They've been praying in church half the morning, and now they're off to weep at the graveside.'

'Who died?' I asked, surprised and alarmed. I'd been expecting Michael to take me shopping, and hadn't been informed of any family bereavement, either among the Camerons or the Spencers.

'Mrs Black from the village shop,' said Jonathan, raising one eyebrow, 'God rest her soul . . .'

Mrs Black, eighty-five if a day, inveterate gossip and peculiarly unpleasant old crone, had expired after taking a funny turn at the church fête, and while the village, and the Camerons in particular, had been suitably sympathetic to her remaining family, I hadn't considered that her death called for any in-depth mourning. I stared at Jonathan, perplexed.

'Michael wouldn't have gone by himself,' he said, 'but Clare persuaded him it was their Christian duty . . . So they went to pray for her soul. They've been there since eight o'clock.'

'Eight o'clock? You're joking!'

Jonathan raised the other eyebrow and shook his head. 'You think

Michael's got religion,' he said slowly, 'but Clare has something else entirely. Obsession, I'd say . . . '

While not begrudging the late and unlamented Mrs Black a respectful send-off, I was nevertheless piqued at missing my shopping trip and made my irritation plain. I needed shoes and books for college, and without Michael and the Bentley, I'd have to get the train.

'I'm not doing anything,' Jonathan said. 'I'll drive you,' and so it was that I sailed out of the Cameron estate in his classic MG, a roaring, rumbustious, exhilarating vehicle that you couldn't possibly make love in, I calculated, without severely dislocating your back. I found myself speculating about Jonathan's sex life, wondering if he ever sneaked any of his girlfriends into bed when his mother was out.

But I didn't enquire, not so much from respect for his privacy, as a keen desire to voice something else on my mind.

'I sometimes feel Clare tries to take Michael over when she and Fiona visit. They're always off to some church meeting together . . . I know she fancies him, and I know she doesn't like me.'

He glanced across at me.

'You don't have to worry about Clare,' he said. 'It's true she's set her sights on Michael, but he's not completely daft. Clare is heavy going. She's what you might politely call highly strung.'

'What would you call her?'

'I'd call her a pain in the bum,' he replied with a laugh. 'She and Michael only get on because they hardly see each other. If she lived nearby, they'd both get sick very soon. He's too liberal for her rampant evangelicalism . . . And she's too intense for his wry Anglicanism.'

'Michael can be pretty intense at times,' I said.

'I know. That's why he needs you to lighten him up.'

We spent an unexpectedly pleasant lunchtime shopping for my shoes and browsing in bookstores, stopping for a drink in a city pub, only returning to the subject of Clare Spencer as we pulled into the Cameron driveway once more.

'I hope Clare doesn't start on the resurrection of the dead over dinner. You should have heard her last year when her grandmother died. No, that's unfair!' he reprimanded himself. 'She was very close to her grandmother.'

'She should be so lucky,' I said irreverently. 'I was bloody glad to get rid of mine.'

He smiled uncertainly.

'What was it with your grandmother?'

'She was a total lunatic. She called herself the Lady of Shalott, and she used to live in a castle . . . One day she threw boiling oil on to a bailiff. It was just cooking fat, but it was bloody hot apparently, and she hurled a whole panful over her battlements!'

We both laughed uproariously at this unlikely image, Jonathan protesting that it couldn't possibly be true.

'I swear. You couldn't invent the tales about Rhoda. And they're all hilarious! Though, of course, it wasn't very funny for the bailiff . . .'

We were still laughing when we climbed out of the MG to be greeted by a stony-faced Michael who demanded to know at once where we'd been and what we'd been doing.

'Take it easy, little brother,' said Jonathan, slapping him on the back. 'I've brought her back to you safe and sound.'

Michael wasn't so easily placated, declaring frostily that if I'd waited only another half-hour, he would, of course, have been back to take me shopping himself.

'Never mind,' I said, linking my arm in his, 'I'm sure you had a lovely time at the funeral with Clare.'

It was a silly and faintly bitchy remark, unthinking and uncalled for, but it hardly warranted Michael's reaction. In a sudden spasm of fury, he smacked my arm away and strode off into the house, leaving Jonathan and me to our mutual embarrassment.

'I hate funerals,' I said to him with an uncertain little laugh. 'Seems to me they never do anyone any good.'

They began to gather outside St Cuthbert's church just before noon, nuns in neat blue habits from the Divine Faith convent, dark-suited men and women wearing black hats in large cars with Paris number-plates, curious villagers, and a small but significant number of Hollywood personnel. I recognised Lenny Levine, agent and entrepreneur, Jon Makepeace, biographer of David Klein, Robert Bernstein Junior, head of Worldwide Pictures, and his nephew Josh, director of the Bernstein Foundation. I also saw Duval, standing by the yew gate in a black leather lounge jacket, with Dr Blanche from the Divine Faith convent at his side.

I'd parked my car at the seaward end of the churchyard so that I could view the arrivals without being on display myself, and now I slid down into my seat and reached for my Ray-bans. I had no wish to embarrass Duval any further. His wife had already done it in style with an explicit, and no doubt lucrative, interview which detailed every last thrust of our tacky little affair. She knew exactly what we'd been doing, where and when. Their Love Nest in Paris. They Had Sex in Studio. Beth Bought Him Top Champagne. I'd been set up with single-minded intent, and could only marvel at Genny Duval's wrathful determination.

It contrasted sharply with the terse little line which read: 'Beth Carlisle's live-in lover, actor Jamie MacLennon, last night refused to comment.' I thanked God, and Jamie, for that. And whatever happened next, I knew I'd have no trouble fulfilling my pledge to keep out of Duval's way.

Then, as I peered over the dashboard, Michael emerged from the vicarage and walked across to the yew gate, transformed from the scruffy motor mechanic of only half an hour ago into the sombre black-robed vicar of Christ, shaman of the burial rites. He shook Duval by the hand, and I watched with a peculiar sense of the unreal as they nodded and conferred. Did either of them mention the pictures on page one and the story on page two? Or was their talk all of Eva Delamere?

Another long black car drew up at the yew gate, and there was a sudden buzz of activity outside the church. Duval stepped forward to open the car door, and a tall, stooping figure emerged, bare-headed, sober-suited, carrying a polished ebony walking cane. Toby Truman, I was certain. Dr Blanche hurried to kiss him, and Duval linked his arm in the old man's. It was obvious that Eva's husband was both intimately known and revered.

I'd begun to feel nervous about entering the church by myself, questioning what right I had to be here among Eva's family and friends, recalling our odd encounter in Paris and all that had happened since, wondering if I shouldn't simply say a silent prayer for her soul from my hidden vantage point in the BMW and then depart. I wished I had someone to sit with in church, and regretted not asking whether Lucy would be attending.

As if in answer to a prayer, there was a knock on the car window, and I looked up to see Nick Howard.

'Are you skulking?' he asked amiably as he slid into the passenger seat beside me. 'I must say I feel like skulking myself. Why don't we skulk together at the back of the church?'

I couldn't deduce from this whether he'd read Clive Fisher's story and was trying to console me, or whether he was still attempting to chat me up, but I was glad of his offer regardless, although still somewhat wary of his attentions. And I now had a commentator on the proceedings.

'Is that Toby Truman?' I asked as the old man walked into the church flanked by Duval and Dr Blanche.

'Yes, that's him. And that's Blanche Duval, Daniel's mother. And see him over there? The fellow with the black curly hair? That's Matthew Klein. He's a builder. Big business in Israel . . . And that's his wife, Rachael.'

I stared in astonishment as Dr Blanche disappeared into the church

with Toby Truman. This steely-faced woman, who'd witnessed my un-
seemly row with my lover when I'd turned up at the Divine Faith
convent unannounced, who'd steered me into bed when I'd tottered
drunkenly from Eva's sitting room, who'd accompanied me to the
chapel to view the body next morning, was Duval's mother? Her cool-
ness towards me that weekend was suddenly intelligible. She was
hardly unaware I'd been sleeping with her son. Was there no end to my
humiliation? I sank lower into the driving seat, mortified.

'Here comes the coffin,' Nick Howard announced, and a flat funereal
bell began to toll from St Cuthbert's, sending a chill into my heart and
the last few lingerers at the yew gate scurrying into the church.

A gleaming hearse drew up, and Eva's white coffin, the same coffin
I'd seen her lying in on that memorable morning, now laden with red
rosebuds, lilies, carnations and a little bundle of golden rock poppies
cut from the shore, was lifted effortlessly from the back of the limousine
by a forest of sturdy, professional hands. The pall-bearers stepped forward, among them Duval.

'Who are the rest?' I whispered, my throat dry.

'Well, that's Matthew Klein again, behind Daniel. And next to Daniel
at the front, that's Jesse, Matthew's son. Then comes Edouard Duval,
he's Daniel's father. And the other two are Trumans. Christopher and
Luke, Toby's grandsons.'

Nick Howard seemed to know it all, and to have no hesitation in
relaying it to me. But I couldn't begin to start working it out.

'Where do the Kleins fit in?' I asked, bemused. 'I thought Eva and
David Klein didn't get on? Everything I've read suggests they openly
disliked each other.'

But my informant wasn't listening. He was gazing in outright
astonishment at a white stretch limo, ostentatious and brutally incongruous, which now pulled up at the yew gate. Out stepped a tiny, bent
figure, wrapped in black fur, her face hidden by a large-brimmed hat
and black lace veil. Beside her in a moment were two burly young men
and a middle-aged woman carrying a pigskin vanity case.

'Good grief!' I exclaimed as the little party processed into the church
behind the coffin. 'Is that who I think it is?'

'It's Carlotta du Bois,' Nick Howard said quietly. 'I can hardly believe my eyes, but yes, it's her . . .'

Eva's coffin was swallowed up into the cavernous interior of St Cuthbert's and Nick opened my car door.

'Come on,' he muttered, his chatty mood suddenly transformed into
something much more subdued, 'let's go in.'

The church was filled with flowers and light, rainbow patterns from
the two great stained-glass windows reflecting on the polished grey slabs

of the floor, the lilies at the altar gleaming milky white like moonstones, the warm air heavy with the scent of roses.

As we slipped into a rear stall, half hidden behind a massive stone pillar, I saw Michael step forward from the altar to stand in front of the coffin.

'I am the resurrection and the life, saith the Lord,' he declared in his low, resonant tone. 'He that believeth in me, though he were dead, yet shall he live.' He was delivering the Prayer Book version of The Burial of the Dead, played to the pews with theatrical precision, no concession to modern taste or sensibility.

'Though after my skin worms destroy this body,' he told us gravely, 'yet in my flesh shall I see God.'

If much was expected of the vicar on this occasion, then Michael provided. His audience did not stir; no one coughed nor even wept.

'We brought nothing into this world, and it is certain we can carry nothing out. The Lord gave, and the Lord hath taken away; blessed be the name of the Lord.'

As I listened and watched, I understood for the first time just how powerful the appeal of a male priest in official role could be. No wonder the churches were full of women . . . What seductive vision of heavenly authority was this? How could any resist it?

'Behold I show you a mystery,' Michael read, facing us all from the pulpit, his bible resting upon a great carved eagle. 'We shall not all sleep, but we shall all be changed in a moment, in the twinkling of an eye . . .'

I looked down, unable any longer to fight the memory of another funeral, thirteen years before at St Botolph's church in the county of Rutland, a funeral far less beautiful, much more terrible than this one. Changed in the twinkling of an eye? I didn't believe it then, and I couldn't believe it now. Then the choir began to sing, a strange, haunting hymn that I'd never heard before. 'Now the Green Blade rises from the Buried Grain.' I stared down at my songsheet, trying to make sense of the words: 'Love will come again,' I read, 'like wheat that springeth green . . .'

It was when he came to give the address that Michael truly rose to the occasion.

'The thoughts I offer you, Eva's friends and family, today are not mine,' he began. 'I fear I couldn't have put them nearly so well . . . They were delivered from this pulpit by the Reverend Matthew Brannen, vicar of St Cuthbert's, more than seventy years ago. This is the sermon he preached after learning that his third and last son, Richard, had been killed in France. Eva was sitting in the front pew . . .'

The congregation hung upon Matthew Brannen's every word, and his successor at St Cuthbert's could hardly have conveyed his emotion better.

'Love is the life-beat of this cruel, unconscious universe,' Michael proclaimed, for all the world as though he were the Victorian clergyman reincarnated for the moment. 'Love, only Love, the name which all must speak . . .'

It was so passionate, so portentous, that I felt my flesh begin to prickle. When I looked down, I saw my fingers had clasped in an involuntary knot, and my knee seemed to be shaking. Beside me, Nick Howard sat in sober contemplation, staring at a hassock on the floor.

'There is nothing Love cannot achieve, so therefore, my friends, do not despise it . . .' Michael concluded. 'And never give way to Despair, my friends. Despair is the greatest, the most powerful, of the enemies of Love.'

There was some weeping then. I saw Duval hunch forward in his pew, and his mother, Blanche, put her hand on his shoulder. Matthew Klein bowed his head, and Susannah Lamont, whom I now noticed sitting with the Duvals, emitted an audible cry. Only Toby Truman sat erect, leaning on his ebony cane, gazing up at the beatific face of St Cuthbert shining high and clear above Michael's head.

Another hymn, the closing prayers, and then the pall-bearers moved to lift Eva's coffin, proceeding out of St Cuthbert's and into the churchyard. I cowered behind the pillar, desperate not to be seen.

'I'm not coming to the grave,' I muttered to Nick Howard, 'I'm leaving by the other door.'

I'd already worked out my escape. The side door would take me on to the secluded part of the churchyard which adjoined the vicarage. I could slip away, say my goodbyes to Katie Cameron, and so miss the graveside scenes and ceremonies. By the time I was ready to reclaim my car, it would all be over.

In the vicarage garden, however, I came upon another burial, the committal of one marmalade kitten to the dust. Katie had been crying, and Lucy, who was digging the hole, seemed faintly irritated.

'How did it go?' she asked me, looking up briefly.

'Michael was magnificent,' I said.

'He was? Then let's hope he comes home in a better mood than he went out . . . Was that really Carlotta du Bois arriving at the last minute?'

'Apparently so. Did anyone know she was coming?'

'Michael certainly didn't. He'd have had a fit. It's been quite a job keeping this whole thing quiet. The family wanted no publicity, but in a place like this, that's not easy. Still, there weren't going to be any really famous faces.' She laughed, and glanced at me quickly. 'Except for yours,' she added.

'Even I'm no match for Carlotta du Bois,' I said.

We walked back into the vicarage, Katie cheering up when I presented my chocolates, then went to view the remaining kittens, no longer housed in the vicar's bedroom but in her own, and I promised to press Sarah into offering a home.

'It's all right,' Katie said, making an effort to smile, 'I can ask her myself. They'll be here for the Easter holidays.'

'Will they? That's nice.'

For some reason I could hardly bear the thought of Sarah, Charles and their boys staying in Michael's house, going fishing in the dinghy, laughing and running along the beach, taking tea with Lucy and Katie.

'You could come as well, couldn't you?' Katie asked suddenly. 'What are you doing in the Easter holidays?'

'I don't usually have any Easter holidays.'

I felt perilously close to tears now, a mixture of the funeral experience, Genny Duval's onslaught, the prospect of facing Jamie, the knowledge that I was leaving St Cuthbert's for good, that I was never likely to see Katie again.

'Maybe you could come and see me in London,' I said briskly, knowing this was highly unlikely. 'I could show you round a television studio. Would you like that?'

She was less enthusiastic than I'd hoped, but nevertheless she smiled, offered me one of her chocolates and then, when I knew the time had come to go, took my hand and led me back down the mahogany staircase and into the sitting room. Lucy was standing by the window.

'Looks as though it's over,' she said, peering out. 'They're all going back to the Retreat. The Duvals are putting on a bit of a wake.'

I walked over to join her at the window, wanting to be sure I ran no risk of bumping into Duval or his mother, and it was then I saw the Bentley, Jack Cameron's old car, standing in the vicarage drive. My heart leapt into my throat.

'Ah, here's Michael,' Lucy said. 'I expect he wants to say goodbye.'

I walked out into the drive, meeting him just as we came abreast of the Bentley, and for a moment we stared at each other across the vast expanse of bonnet, just the way we'd done a hundred times before so long ago.

'It still looks in good shape,' I said directly.

'Yes,' he mumbled, looking away, 'it is . . . My father left it to me . . . To be truthful, it's a bit of a liability. Only does fifteen to the gallon.'

What, if anything, might have followed on this trite little exchange I wasn't destined to know, for at a shout from behind, we turned to see Nick Howard hurrying towards the vicarage.

'I was hoping you hadn't gone,' he called to me. 'Can you give me a lift to the airport please? I'd like to get away as soon as possible.'

He turned to Michael.

'That was quite a performance this afternoon,' he said, extending his hand. 'I'm sure Eva would have been very impressed. It was nice meeting you, Mr Cameron. Goodbye.'

'And it's goodbye from me too!' I snapped suddenly, quelling the urge to scream aloud and beat my fists upon the Bentley's gleaming chassis, furious with Nick Howard and even angrier with Michael, who seemed incapable of offering me anything other than meaningless pleasantries or sarcastic quips. I no longer cared about a civilised farewell, no longer held out hope of reconciliation, however insignificant or small.

'Remember me to my sister when you see her,' I said to him curtly, turning away. 'And don't give my private telephone number to anyone else, will you? I get quite enough nuisance calls as it is.'

Another farewell, another time, another reality. The interior of the Bentley, enveloped in the silent green gloom of the spinney, less than an hour to spare before my train left, and much of my crying still to be done.

'I can't bear to say goodbye,' I wept, 'I can't bear to go.'

'Then don't,' Michael said. 'Forget about college. Come back with me to Cambridge. We'll get married, find a flat, and you can work at McDonald's. That should just about pay the rent.'

I looked up at him through my tears, acutely aware of how little this would suit me, struggling with the uncomfortable paradox of wanting two mutually exclusive things at the same time.

'You're not serious,' I said anxiously.

'No, I'm not. But I wish I were . . .'

'Your mother would kill me. And you as well, probably.'

'On the contrary,' he said. 'My mother isn't the problem. I can handle her. But your mother is another matter altogether . . .'

This was unfortunately true. My mother had not relented in her opposition to Michael. She was barely civil to him when he called, would not comfort me in my depression at our parting, resolutely refused to discuss our engagement any further. So I no longer wore the diamond ring at home. The very sight of it provoked my mother's fury. Instead I bought a gold chain and hung it round my neck out of sight, remembering to slip it on to my left hand whenever I was meeting Michael. The fact that I'd forgotten once or twice, and that he hadn't commented, confirmed the covert nature of our betrothal, a conspiracy to which we both consented, it seemed, for undisclosed reasons of our own.

Now, however, the diamond ring was back on my finger and Michael stroked it meditatively.

'It will all work out,' he said softly. 'You'll get a great degree, you'll be a successful journalist . . . And you'll marry me. Wait and see.'

Although I desperately wanted all of this, I found it hard to fit the details together, and my mother's retort about baking scones for the Young Wives' summer fair had stayed with me. Would I ever make a vicar's wife? Was there any hope that Michael would keep God as a nice little hobby on the side, thus preserving me from this unwelcome fate?

'And what about you?' I asked tremulously. 'What will you do?'

'I'll be twenty-five before I'm doing anything,' he said.

Our eventual union seemed so distant at that moment, its pursuit so fraught and its achievement so unlikely, that I began to cry again, despising myself for my weakness, half wanting this painful farewell to be over so I could indulge my misery in full without embarrassing either of us any further.

'Don't,' he whispered, kissing my hair and pulling me to him, 'please don't,' and I knew from his tone that he meant to make love to me.

'There isn't time,' I wept, pulling away. 'I'll miss my train.'

'No, you won't. Take your clothes off. Everything. I want to look at you.'

'Michael, it's broad daylight,' I pleaded. 'Anyone could be walking by.'

'It's okay. Believe me. Nobody ever comes down here . . .'

In less than a minute I was naked on the back seat, receiving his detailed appraisal with some inhibition, feeling rather as though I were undergoing an intimate medical check, wondering, just a little peevishly, why he didn't take his own clothes off.

'Your hands are freezing,' I protested feebly, 'and I don't feel like it.'

'I'll soon change that,' he whispered, kneeling down on the floor of the Bentley and kissing the inside of my thighs, 'I know just how to do it.'

But I was worried about the train, and I couldn't relax, and after a few tense minutes, I faked it, surprised at just how easy it was, ashamed at myself for doing it, and annoyed with him because he couldn't tell the difference.

'See, you did feel like it.'

'Yes,' I said, trying to manoeuvre my wrist into view so I could see the time, 'Oh yes . . .'

'Swear to me, Beth,' he said as he pounded into me, 'swear you'll never do this with anyone else.'

'I swear,' I gasped, 'I swear . . .'

Afterwards, when he'd settled me on the train and we'd kissed good-bye a dozen times, promising to think of each other night and day, to phone every week, to focus all desires upon Christmas when we'd be together again at last, it occurred to me to extract my own promises.

'Tell me you'll never make love to anyone else,' I said suddenly, the tears beginning again now that the moment had arrived. 'You haven't sworn to me . . .'

He took my hand, squeezing it so hard that the solitaire diamond bit into my finger.

'I won't even be tempted,' he said.

Later, much later, I was forced to reconsider this bold remark, un-ravelling for my own enlightenment the inconsistency and hard-heartedness which so often seems to underpin moral righteousness. It was not, in so far as I understood the tenets of the Christian religion, a sin to be tempted. Indeed, it was a mark of the human nature which Jesus himself endured and overcame.

But Michael Cameron had set himself above reproach, beyond the mundane confusions which fail to distinguish lust from love, out of the reach, by virtue of intellect and spiritual insight, of ordinary sexual temptations . . . Except, of course, those to which he'd already suc-cumbed.

Nick Howard was withdrawn and uncommunicative, a fact for which I was grateful, and so we sped out of the village in silence, away from the flat green sea and into the mauve hills, heading south, winding through lanes overhung with blackthorn and fragrant with early blossom.

Neither of us spoke until we reached the airport road, when he seemed suddenly to recollect his manners.

'Thanks for the lift,' he said, sitting upright and peering out of the windscreen, 'I appreciate it.'

Then he turned to scrutinise me closely, and I felt the need to deflect his attention.

'So, tell me. Did Carlotta grant anyone an audience?' I asked quickly. 'I'd have loved the chance to speak to her.'

'She didn't say a word. Just walked from the church, got back in her limo, and drove off.'

He was still staring at me, and it was plain he meant to get personal.

'So, Beth . . .' he said slowly, 'where do you go from here?'

'Straight down the A1 and over Blackfriars Bridge,' I replied, deeply irritated by the evident intent behind this question. He sighed perceptibly.

'That's not what I meant.'

'Then I can't think what you meant, and frankly, I'd rather not know.'

He was hurt, but I didn't care. I had no intention of discussing my private life with Nick Howard, and if I could ward off the seemingly inevitable moment when he enquired if we might have dinner some time, then I would.

'I'm sorry,' he said. 'I couldn't help reading all that stuff in the paper this morning . . . But I don't mean to pry. I speak as one who's fucked up his own life, that's all. Many's the time I could have done with a sympathetic ear.'

He sounded so contrite, so woebegone, that for a moment I relented.

'What's so fucked up about you?' I asked curiously, remembering the careful way he'd handled his whisky that night in the Dolphin and wondering if drink were his only problem. 'You're very successful, aren't you?'

'I'm on my third divorce,' he replied. 'Some success.'

'Well, marriage isn't everything, is it? What about writing novels?'

'Funny you should ask,' he replied with a dry little laugh. 'I'm having trouble writing novels too. Can't seem to see the point any more.'

'To show up the murky little corners of our lives,' I suggested, unable to resist serving him up his own rationale. 'To expose the frailties of the species known as *Homo sapiens*. To divert, to pass the time, and, of course, to entertain . . .'

He glanced at me, surprised.

'Did I say that?'

'Something very like it. I heard you speak once, at a reading in London. It must be all of sixteen years ago . . .'

He considered this in silence, seemingly unable or unwilling to justify himself, either then or now.

'A lot has changed in sixteen years,' I said at last, seized now by the illogical urge to cheer him up. 'I seem to remember you were pretty gloomy about the point of writing even then. And it all looks much worse now. The triumph of market forces. The death of socialism. The defeat of liberalism. The failure of every good idea we ever had . . . What else can there be?'

He looked moodily out of the car window at the speeding northern suburbs, a grey, spare man with the gaunt features of the inveterate drinker, the writer dispossessed.

'Love is the life-beat of this cruel, unconscious universe,' he murmured at length, rather as though he were trying out this unlikely proposition on himself. 'That doesn't seem such a bad idea.'

I laughed. 'So now you're going to write a romance?'

He drew a deep breath.

'Isn't that what the readers really want?' he asked softly. 'Character, intrigue, a good old-fashioned plot . . . And then at the end, the triumph of love . . . Is that so very unacceptable, so utterly politically incorrect?'

He seemed genuinely to be asking, as though he had yet to make up his mind and I might truly be able to help.

'It's a falsification of experience,' I told him steadily, 'a lie we swallow at our peril. You should watch my TV show tonight.'

'All art is a falsification of experience,' Nick Howard said slowly, 'but that doesn't mean it's telling lies. I'm sorry I can't watch your show. I'll be on my way to New York.'

We had arrived at the airport, a tiny box of a building perched on a scrap of vacant land at the edge of the city, and I drew up as near the terminal as possible, anxious now to be on my way home.

He turned to me and smiled.

'Do you ever get to New York? Maybe we could have dinner some time?'

'I hate New York,' I said, looking him straight in the eye. 'And anyway, I'm on a diet.'

This time he laughed, a rueful kind of chuckle that seemed neither disappointed nor deterred.

'You misunderstand me,' he said, 'but it doesn't matter. Here's my card in case you change your mind some day.'

He was half-way out of the car door when I remembered something I'd wanted to ask him, something that had lain forgotten among the perils and partings of the day.

'Wait,' I said suddenly. 'You never told me about that second time you met Eva . . . What it was that took you to her funeral. Was it just because of old times? Please tell me. I'm still curious.'

He closed the car door again and sat for a moment, seeming to weigh up what he might say.

'I met Eva again just a few months before you did,' he announced at last, watching my face closely as he spoke. 'I went to see her because I'm in the process of digging up bones . . . Uncovering the past, shaking the bits to see which still rattle . . . Can you understand that, Beth?'

I nodded, fascinated and yet at some unknowing level, disturbed, unable to guess at what might come next.

'Now why were you there, Beth?' he asked, still watching me, his gaze never flickering. 'Did you imagine Eva might tell you what really happened the night Will Sutton died? I suspect you did . . . We all want that story, don't we?'

The light from the airport tower flashed across the windscreen, illuminating his face at intermittent intervals, making him seem like some ghostly, neon-lit narrator, an electronic Ancient Mariner, compelled to tell his tale.

'And did you get it?' I whispered. 'The story?'

'I got what you got, Beth. What everyone got from Eva. An invitation to confession . . .'

'And what did you confess?' I asked him, shivering in the sudden chill of the northern twilight, in my mind's eye transported once again to the whitewashed sitting room in the Divine Faith convent, staring up from Eva's wooden settle at the plaster Messiah on his gilded cross and the flow of sickening scarlet paint streaming from his side.

'Plenty,' said Nick Howard abruptly, his mood suddenly changing. 'That my second wife killed herself. That my sons no longer regard me as their father. That I haven't spoken to my mother in nearly twenty years . . .'

It took a moment for this last fact to register, and then I seized upon it eagerly.

'Your mother's still alive?' Somehow I had imagined Harold Brannen's daughter Harriet to be long dead.

'Oh, very much so,' Nick Howard said with a little laugh. 'My mother was at Eva's funeral this afternoon. She saw me, but she passed on by . . . I think that's the way it's always going to be.'

He gave a little shrug, a gesture of resignation that suddenly endeared him to me. I touched him, hesitatingly, upon the shoulder. It was a mistake, for then he turned to kiss me, a swift, chaste peck upon the cheek which, nonetheless, I met with embarrassment. But in the next moment he was gone, striding through the glass doors into the airport, embarrassed himself, I guessed, for he didn't give me a backward glance.

I watched him, bemused. I had wanted to ask about David Klein and his connection with the Kleins who'd been at the funeral. I'd wanted to know if he had any theories about who might have killed Will Sutton. Was it Carlotta du Bois? Was it David Klein? Or could it even have been Eva herself?

I looked down at the card Nick Howard had given me. Maybe I would call him in New York. But there again, maybe I would just forget the whole bloody thing.

Book VI: Eva

Chapter Sixteen

David Klein was a man who used opportunity without attracting the charge of opportunism.

Hired by Saul Bernstein, boss of Worldwide Pictures, in the summer of '32 to direct a low-budget movie starring an untried newcomer, Klein quickly turned Will Sutton into the studio's leading man.

'The Klein family business collapsed during the Depression. My daughter refused to marry him. David needed a break,' Bernstein was to say later.

Others told a different story. Certainly Klein was down on his luck and needed a job, but he was never likely to marry the dowdy Rebecca Bernstein, even though both families had once hoped for a wedding. In truth, Klein returned from Paris a disappointed man, and his passionate love affair with his cousin Anya would later be chronicled in colourful detail by those who were there at the time.

He was grateful, if cool, for the chance Saul Bernstein offered. 'I was never much interested in the movies,' he told a magazine reporter some time later, 'but I needed to work. I thought I'd give it a year until the building trade picked up.'

That year saw David Klein established as one of the most successful and influential picture-makers in the fermenting brew of talent, tenacity and hype that was Hollywood in the Thirties . . .

Against the Tide: A Biography of David Klein, by Jon Makepeace

———————

Eva woke early, swinging her bare legs carefully and quietly from the tangled bed on to the tiled floor, carefully for fear her toes might meet with a scuttling cockroach, quietly in case she woke her husband, who lay sprawled across the width of the mattress, arms clasped in passionate embrace around his pillow. He grunted as she moved, a strange half-strangled noise some way between a snore and a moan. It meant, she knew, that he'd been drinking last night.

She dressed quickly and effortlessly, sliding into her stockings and shift, eyes accustomed now to the morning gloom. Even as she stood, scanning the floor for insects, alert to the slightest movement between wardrobe and washstand, she saw the light change from mauve to rose, and then to pinky gold. The slats from the apartment shutters cast thin bars across the ruddy tiles of the floor and over the mottled cream walls, making the bedroom seem, as Toby had once remarked, like a goddamn prison. Eva shivered suddenly in the thin dawn air. Maybe they would soon be out of this crumbling apartment block, with its flaking plaster walls and mildewed banisters. Maybe, at last, things would start going their way.

She crept silently out into the hallway, past the living room where Harriet lay curled upon the sofa, past the box room where Nicky huddled in his blue-painted cot, into the kitchen where she heated last night's leftover coffee in a pan on the stove. She would breakfast later at Marco's when the first rush of customers was through.

Outside, she walked quickly between the straggling eucalyptus trees behind the block and across the sidewalk, increasing her pace until she reached the junction, anxiously scanning the empty road ahead. Once she had missed the early morning streetcar and had been forced to walk all the way down the boulevard to Marco's. The surly Italian had accepted her apologies and even offered her breakfast on the house. But he had docked her pay, and when she complained, had declared that his wife was demanding a new hat because she'd been obliged to wash the dishes herself. Eva had given way, but from that moment, she vowed to find a different job.

Today, the start of her last week at Marco's, she would not be late. Indeed, she was a little early. She leaned back against the strut of a billboard, waiting for the distant rumble which would herald the streetcar. '*Farewell Princess*,' read the billboard above her. 'Starring Will Sutton and Moira Sheen. Distributed by Worldwide Pictures. Produced by Saul Bernstein. Directed by David Klein.'

Eva didn't look up at the billboard. She knew only too well what it said. Instead she looked back across the canyon with its clutter of baroque mansions and mock-Tudor cottages, each of them perched upon its own little rocky outlet, a tiny world unto itself. The sky was eggshell blue, stretching in a vast shimmering arc across the canyon to the hills beyond. Already she could see the haze settling on the orange grove in the dip between the nearest hills. It was going to be a long hot day. But then, every day was long and hot, and seemed to bring its own inevitable dramas. Nothing in this town could happen without a show.

On Monday a hobo had died from dehydration in the vacant lot opposite Marco's, sliding with consummate grace from his seat on a splintered orange box as she'd watched from the restaurant window. She had run across to the little crowd gathered by the corpse, offering water and a cool towel and explaining she was a nurse, had felt for his pulse and raised one gnarled eyelid to peer into the unseeing blue beyond. But he was already dead, and Marco, rightly insisting that no more could be done, had ordered her back to work and called the downtown police.

Then, yesterday, a bar girl from the Calypso joint next door had found the body of a newborn baby boy wrapped in newspaper and hidden in a trash can. The scream could be heard three blocks away, but this time the police were on hand, screeching down the sandy road behind Marco's and then racing, like athletes released by a starting pistol, to the scene of the horror. When Eva peered out of the kitchen window on to the trash cans below, it was to see the bar girl weeping and declaiming, hands clutched to her bosom, delivering her performance to the audience.

Sometimes it seemed to Eva as though the whole town imagined itself part of some great production, reading from an unseen but well-rehearsed script. Even the tramp in the vacant lot had expired on cue, waiting until the restaurant was at its busiest.

Sometimes it felt as if she herself had been written into the plot. *Young Nurse and Reporter Husband come to Hollywood. She seeks Fame and Fortune as a Movie Star, but No Luck. He becomes a Scriptwriter for Kramer Brothers, but only produces Disastrous Scripts. They Quit, and Find Happiness as* . . . as what? Eva didn't know. The ending hadn't been written. But one thing she did know. She wasn't leaving the denouement up to Toby.

Since his contract with Kramer Brothers ended, Eva had learned quickly. She had learned that money, even a substantial amount of money, wasn't enough to keep you in style once you stopped earning. As well as money, you needed status. Status bought you credit. And if you didn't have status, then you needed nerve and confidence. Without those, no one else would have confidence.

She had also learned that the town of Happy Endings offered no guarantees, only an endless succession of hopes. Hope was a Christian virtue, that much she respected, but vain hope was a poison, polluting the soul and turning each sweet dream to bitterness. And Eva had seen vain hope. She had seen it on the faces of the street girls who patrolled the alley behind Marco's. She had seen it in the drunks who fell out of the Calypso bar each night. She had seen it in the endless stream of hobos and drifters who had no place to go and no prospect of work. She had even seen it in her husband. Eva herself was not without hope. But she understood how seductive, and ultimately how cruel, hope could sometimes prove.

The streetcar rolled into view, and she boarded it quickly, acknowledging neither her fellow passengers nor the conductor, choosing a seat at the back where no one was likely to join her or attempt conversation. This journey was her precious thinking time, the only half-hour in her hectic, mundane day when she might recollect, reconsider and dream. She thought of many things in this dream time: people and past events, imagined triumphs and real disasters, long-ago landscapes and much-loved friends. She thought of everything and everyone, indeed, except David Klein, who inhabited a luxurious hacienda less than a mile from her own humble apartment, yet might have been living on a different continent. Eva would not allow herself to think of David Klein, nor of Moira Sheen, Worldwide's leading female star, so often seen in his company. But sometimes she thought of Paris. She remembered her wedding to Toby, just three days before the boat sailed for New York, when Anya had cried and showered confetti into the bride's hair, kissing Toby tenderly on both cheeks and telling him to be happy.

Now Eva feared she might never see Paris again. When Emmanuel Klein had died she couldn't raise the fare, though she longed to be there for his funeral. Instead, she had written to Anya, a long rambling letter full of half-truths, inviting her to visit Hollywood, longing for her to come. And Anya had replied in her usual vivacious style. Bertie Levine was back in town! So was Karl Schwartz! The Café des Arbres was thriving! Her cousin Victor was getting married to a little English girl almost half his age . . . Uncle Jake was retiring and going home to Germany . . . Therefore, Anya was very sorry, she could not leave the café . . .

And that, it seemed, was the end of Paris.

Sometimes Eva thought of America and her first heady months in this strange new land, so beautiful, so big, opportunity thrusting from its core like lava bursting from the seams of its landscape in one great act of creation.

All had seemed possible then, yet if pressed, Eva could not have said what it was that she wanted. To be a great star like Moira Sheen? No, not that precisely . . . To see her husband hired as screenwriter on a million-dollar movie? That, of course, would be nice . . . To buy a ranch and farm the land? Perhaps. But now, six long years later, there was hardly enough cash to pay the rent on their two-bit apartment, the million-dollar movie had not come Toby's way, and Eva's own career had foundered, the result of bad luck, bad advice, and yes, she knew it only too well, bad grace.

'Hell, Eva, you got to care,' her agent had told her unhappily when yet another hope had crashed. 'You got to want this real bad, otherwise you ain't got a prayer . . .'

Not a prayer. How well that described her arid state of mind. Like the desert that nibbled at the edge of the city, her disappointment gnawed at her desires and her dreams.

And this, it seemed, was the end of America.

But sometimes, in a passing moment, Eva thought about St Cuthbert's, and then she found her spirits soothed. She remembered the great sweep of cream sand, smooth as gunpowder, the glittering string of islands that studded the emerald bay like bullets of jet, the high thin screams of the terns as they swooped for fish ends among the ragged boats in the bay, the gentle plash of the *Island Star*'s oars as it pulled through the milky water towards St Cuthbert's isle. And she remembered too the impassioned power of Matthew Brannen's voice, low and trembling yet ever resolute. 'Never give way to Despair, my Friends. Despair is the greatest, the most powerful, of the enemies of Love.'

These days, however, thoughts of St Cuthbert's invariably brought her back to a troubling dilemma. What was to be done about Harriet Howard and her young son Nicky? How long could they go on living in Eva and Toby's cramped apartment? What would happen to Nicky, who was, Eva feared, an encumbrance to his mother even now, if Harriet fulfilled her own desperate ambition and became a movie star?

Not that there seemed much prospect of this. In the long months since Harriet arrived on Eva's doorstep with Aidan Forster's child in her arms, there had been an endless succession of disappointments. Every day Harriet waited in line with countless other pretty young girls – actors, dancers and singers – every one of them with the talent to land the big part, if only they might be granted the prize of a screen test. Eva knew those queues. She'd stood in them herself, and in those early days, like all the rest, had waited for her moment, believing, trusting, that one day it would come. Only later did she see that success only came to those willing to trade body and soul for the chance.

But there had been happy times. Toby's Kramer contract had paid the rent on a sprawling house with a kidney-shaped swimming pool in the back yard, and together they had furnished and adorned it. Eva hadn't liked the house, although now she remembered it with fond regret. It had been ugly, vulgar and curiously cold, but looking back, it was infinitely preferable to the faded apartment block in front of the eucalyptus grove.

Yet she was not downhearted. She still had Toby, and he was still her admirer and her friend. And Toby still believed in the Big Break, which was, he maintained, just around the corner. And if Eva no longer believed in the Big Break herself, then she was content to bolster her husband's dreams while plotting a more practical future for them both. Her new job at Gracie's, the smartest restaurant on the block, a job she might never have found had it not been for Marco's meanness, would pay enough to get them out of the apartment. Not next week, nor even next month. But maybe by the end of the year.

'Marco's Diner,' intoned the conductor from the front of the street-car, and Eva rose from her seat. End of Dream Sequence, she said to herself. Enter Marco's. Lights. Noise. Coffee cups. Action.

Harriet was excited, but she was also cross.

'They're your friends!' she exclaimed, waving the letter in the air. 'And they're coming to stay with David Klein! Eva, can't you under-stand what this means?'

Harriet began pacing around the tiny living room, kicking aside Nicky's coloured bricks and the wooden fire engine Toby had bought him in a bankrupt sale. The child crawled after his mother, retrieving the scattered bricks.

'It means we might be invited to drinks at one of Rebecca Bernstein's famed soirées,' Eva said testily. 'It doesn't mean that David Klein will offer you a part.'

Harriet laughed, and ran a hand through her black bobbed hair. She looked extraordinary, this new Harriet, no longer Harold Brannen's blonde daughter, indeed, unrecognisable from the pretty, pale-faced girl she had been only a week ago. Now her lips were gashed with damson and her skin glowed an artificial bronze. Her temperament, however, had not changed with her appearance, though the two seemed to match rather better now.

'Give me half an hour with David Klein,' she declared, swinging the shining helmet of hair, 'and he's mine.'

Eva stood up and walked to the window, peering out of the shutters on to the dusty sidewalk, watching for Toby, needing him to counter Harriet, wondering how he would greet the news of the impending visit from Paris.

'Moira Sheen might have something to say about that,' she replied tartly, offering Hollywood's hottest rumour in a bid to deflect Harriet. Everyone was speculating that the lovely Moira was David Klein's girl.

'Who is this Victor Martineau?' demanded Harriet, careless of Moira Sheen's threat, plucking Nicky from the floor where he threatened her progress and dumping him on the sofa. 'Is he in the movie business too? How does he know David Klein?'

'We were all in Paris together,' Eva said warily, looking round from the window. 'Victor is David's cousin. He worked for Emmanuel Klein.

I don't suppose you remember Emmanuel? You were very young at the time. But you must remember Anya . . . That day when we all rowed out to St Cuthbert's Isle . . . The picnic?'

Harriet paused on her restless progress around the room, turning to Eva in evident amazement.

'What do you mean you were all together? You're telling me that you knew David Klein in Paris?'

Eva looked away again. 'Briefly,' she muttered.

Harriet sat down on the sofa and reached for her cigarette pack, extracting a long black Russian and twisting it viciously into her mother-of-pearl holder.

'You're a fool, Eva. I'm sorry to have to say it, but you are. Only a fool would work in a restaurant when she's an old friend of David Klein's.'

'He's not a friend,' Eva said carefully. 'I haven't set eyes on him in six years. In any case, he has the reputation of being a very shrewd man. Not the type to grant favours on the basis of some long-ago acquaint-ance . . .'

Harriet took a deep pull on the black Russian, and then slowly exhaled a perfect smoke ring into Nicky's face. The child coughed and spluttered, rubbing his eyes.

'I won't be asking for any favours,' she declared. 'I'm a professional actress who has appeared on the London stage. I'd be top of the bill now if it weren't for this little bastard . . .' She blew another smoke ring at Nicky. 'All I want is a test.'

'Then you'd better make up to Rebecca Bernstein,' Eva said unkind-ly, sweeping Nicky from the sofa and placing him back on the floor. 'She casts all the Worldwide movies.'

Harriet laughed.

'Don't rule anything out,' she said. 'I'm only Harold Brannen's bas-tard daughter. I've got nothing to lose . . .'

Eva refused to be shocked. Nothing that Harriet said or did shocked her now. If she had been shocked at the seduction of Aidan Forster, for so Harriet had described it, or the death of Lizzie Howard, related with not so much as a tear or a sorrowful sigh, then she quickly learned to disguise such emotion. And the tale of Harriet's extraction of several hundred pounds from the Forster estate – 'How else,' she had enquired of Eva, 'would I have raised the fare to Hollywood and equipped myself with the necessary wardrobe?' – was also allowed to pass. It wasn't possible to shame Harriet Howard, and in any case, Eva didn't mean to try. She had just enough guilt about her own upbringing as the fa-voured daughter of St Cuthbert's vicarage, and Harriet's banishment to a fisherman's cottage, to make silence seem the only option. So let

Harriet do as she pleased. She wouldn't get past Rebecca Bernstein, of this Eva felt quite certain.

'At last, the man of the house!' cried Harriet suddenly as a footfall sounded on the bare floorboards outside the living-room door, 'Toby, my sweet, just wait till you hear our news! We are all going to meet David Klein.'

Toby appeared tired and dishevelled, and Eva knew at once his day had been unsuccessful. Since he'd been fired from Kramer Brothers, he spent his days grubbing for newspaper stories he could sell. He looked older, she thought suddenly, his face showing tiny creases at the eyes, his fair hair, still with its wayward lock, lank and unkempt. Yes, the truth was plain. There was no work for hacks who'd been fired by Kramer Brothers, and at that moment Eva doubted there ever would be.

'Hi, honey,' he said, kissing her hair and slumping on to the sofa, 'Hi, kid!' He took Nicky on to his knee and then looked up at Harriet.

'What's this about David Klein?'

Harriet whirled around the room again, unable to control her glee.

'Well, now, your old friend Victor Martineau is coming to Hollywood with his bride. And of course, they'll be visiting here. But they're staying with David Klein! You know what this means, don't you, Toby? Eva can't see it, but you understand . . .'

Toby reached for the Russian cigarettes.

'Victor Martineau is married?' he enquired slowly, seeming to weigh it up and find the news incredible.

'A young English girl,' Eva muttered. 'They met when she was holidaying in Paris.'

'And he's coming here?'

'A honeymoon trip. Rhoda loves to travel. She longs to see America . . . Victor thinks he might do business over here. You can read the letter yourself.'

He took the letter from her and scanned its contents briefly, his face revealing nothing of his thoughts.

A sudden notion occurred to Harriet.

'You knew David Klein in Paris too!' she accused him, striding back to the sofa and standing above him. 'Hell, Toby, I thought better of you. You knew him, but you never tried to use him!'

'On the contrary,' Toby said coolly, tossing the letter aside, 'I've tried several times to see David Klein. I've sent him scripts, I've waited outside his office. I even tried to flag down his limo one time . . . He has never so much as acknowledged me, let alone considered hiring me.' He reached for another cigarette while Eva stared at him in undisguised shock.

'So,' he said, avoiding his wife's astonished gaze, 'Now we shall see.

We'll ask Victor to remind David Klein of his old friends. We'll let him
know we have someone we'd like him to meet, a professional actress
from the London stage . . . And then we shall see.'

Harriet emitted a shriek of pure joy and fell upon the sofa, throwing
her arms around Toby and covering his face with kisses while Eva stood
watching, dazed.

'Knock it off, Harriet,' Toby laughed, 'and get that goddamn hair
away from me.'

'OK,' said Harriet, laughing too. 'But one thing, Toby – and Eva, as
well! When we finally get to meet David Klein, please don't call me
Harriet . . .'

She got up from the sofa, pouting the damson lips and tossing the jet
hair in mock starlet pose.

'Just call me Carlotta,' she said. 'Call me Miss Carlotta du Bois.'

In the event, there was no need for embarrassing scheming. The invitation arrived only a few days later, a silver-embossed card in a stout
cream envelope, delivered by a uniformed chauffeur behind the wheel
of a great black Cadillac. *Miss Rebecca Bernstein is hosting a party at the
Klein Residence for Mr and Mrs Victor Martineau . . . The company of Mr
and Mrs Toby Truman is respectfully requested.*

'How am I going to get in?' Harriet demanded, staring at the card.

'You can go instead of me,' Eva said.

'Eva! Don't be so stupid . . .' Toby was irritated, and lately, his wife
had observed, didn't try too hard to conceal any wayward emotion.
'Victor is expecting to see you. And so, no doubt, is David Klein.'

Eva said nothing. There'd been no discussion of Toby's revelation
that he'd sought work at Worldwide Pictures. She'd tried to console
him, but he had not wanted her sympathy. The whole matter of David
Klein remained closed between them, as indeed it always had, ever since
that distant day when she'd returned to Paris declaring that she never
wanted to see him again.

How vengefully that wish had been granted! Davy hadn't come back
to Paris before her own departure, and in all the parties and premières
of Toby's Kramer days, she'd never once encountered him. David
Klein, it was said, didn't go to other people's parties. David Klein had
too much else to do.

Now Eva could only imagine Toby's humiliation, could only guess at
Davy's reasons for refusing him so much as the time of day.

But she'd given no hint of her distress, and lying awake in their
overheated bedroom with the slats of light from the sodium glare outside playing across the walls, she had truly felt herself to be imprisoned,

trapped in the unremitting landscape of regret and self-recrimination. Why had Toby felt unable to tell her the truth? What dark shadow had dogged their early, seemingly carefree years together? How might she remove its renewed threat? Her only chance, her only hope for what she now perceived to be her ailing marriage, seemed to be to stave off any meeting with David Klein.

'I'll call up Rebecca Bernstein,' Harriet said. 'I'll pretend to be Miss Delamere, and I'll say my niece is here on a visit from London . . . from the London stage, indeed.'

'No!' said Eva quickly. She would not have Harriet speaking on her behalf, wheedling in her name and revealing such blatant intent. 'I'll call up myself.'

She called that afternoon from Marco's, trembling as she dialled the Klein number, wondering how she would find her voice if he should answer himself, wishing the invitation had been in the form of a personal note or even a visit from Victor and his new wife.

Miss Rebecca Bernstein is hosting a party . . . Eva looked down at the glittering letters set on the parchment card. What was Rebecca Bernstein to David Klein, beyond his casting director and the daughter of his boss? She hadn't married him, so why did she host his parties? It was the question gossip writers loved to ask, but there was never any answer. And now there was a new and yet more tantalising question. What was Moira Sheen to David Klein? Had the lemon-haired siren of *Farewell Princess* fame captured the heart of Hollywood's Most Eligible Bachelor? Some said yes, and predicted a wedding. But some said no. Some said David Klein was far too busy for any kind of romance.

'Hallo? You've called David Klein's private number. How can I help?'

It wasn't him, of course, but a silken-voiced secretary who listened patiently to Eva's halting request.

'It's a bit of a cheek, I realise that, and it may not be possible, but I was wondering if . . . You see, my niece, Harriet Howard, who's visiting from London . . .'

Oh, dammit, that wasn't right. She shouldn't have said Harriet Howard. She should have said Carlotta de Vere, or whatever silly name it was that Harriet had dreamed up.

'I'll have to check with Miss Bernstein,' said the silky secretary. 'Hang on, please.'

And then, to her fascination and her faint dread, she heard the click of a second receiver and a low, distinctive female voice.

'Miss Delamere? This is Rebecca Bernstein. Yes, of course, your niece is very welcome. I'll inform Security . . . One minute, now. Someone here wishes to speak to you.'

Eva felt a pulse in her forehead begin to pound and for a moment the neon strip in Marco's kitchen seemed to dim.

'Hallo, Eva? Is that you?'

She was herself again at once.

'Victor! How wonderful to hear you.'

'I'm so sorry we haven't called to see you . . . Rhoda has been rather unwell . . . I have letters from Anya, and a small gift from my mother . . . We're so looking forward to the party! I can't wait for you both to meet Rhoda.'

His voice brought with it a rush of memories. The Café des Arbres on the day she'd first seen it, the scent of Jacob Klein's chicken stew simmering in the kitchen, the tattered heads of the gaudy daffodils in the square, the bank of glittering candles in the little church where Davy had taken her, and then their walk by the Seine and that curious sense of a future magically imposed upon the present, a future which, she reflected grimly, had now come to pass, bearing no slim resemblance to the vision she had glimpsed.

And though it pained her to recall, she could not help but remember that golden summer morning when she'd left Paris in David Klein's open-topped convertible, heading for Helena Duval's home in Toulouse, the journey she'd never completed. Would it all have been different if she'd managed to contain her moral indignation? If she'd been willing to listen and forgive? If it hadn't begun to rain at just that moment? If . . .

'Two ice-cream sodas,' Marco growled. 'Table Four.'

Eva picked up the frothing glasses, and in that moment made a brave decision.

She could not avoid meeting David Klein, that much seemed sure. But she would not be embarrassed. She would not dissemble nor cloak her desires, as the Prayer Book used to say. She would be honest. She would be bold. She would confess that times were hard, that life was a bit of a struggle. And then she would ask a favour of the man who never gave favours.

She would ask David Klein to give her husband a job.

Later, even years later, Eva found she could summon every detail of the party given for Victor and Rhoda Martineau.

She could feel again the warm wind that rose from the south as they left the apartment, whipping the dust of the sidewalk into her eyes, impaling Harriet's flimsy frock upon a cactus leaf, draping a stray eucalyptus branch across the bonnet of the yellow Chevrolet Toby had hired for the evening.

She could recall the exact shade of the bougainvillaea that hung around David Klein's estate, deep cerise petals cradled by paper-thin emerald leaves, the soft damp of the springy lawns as she tiptoed across them, the glittering midnight blue of the empty pool, and her first sight of the hacienda itself, gleaming white beneath a desert moon, its balcony lit with flickering electric candles.

She remembered the sharp, tingling taste of the pink champagne, the odour of the olives upon the canapés, the saltiness of the smoked salmon parcels, stinging her tongue as she tried to swallow. She heard again the gutsy rasp of the saxophone, the muted, elegiac wail of the trumpet. And she had only to close her eyes to see the faces once more, Moira Sheen, candyfloss hair and tight sugar-pink lips, Rebecca Bernstein, sallow skin and shrewd, solemn gaze, Will Sutton, tall and tanned like a young Greek god and already drunk, Christine Romaine, his wife, shoulders a mass of bright ginger curls and mouth set in a taut vermilion curve which threatened at any moment to erupt into a curse.

With cinematic precision, she remembered what everyone was wearing too . . . Her own magenta cocktail dress with its nipped and beaded bodice, Harriet's floating scarlet chiffon, Moira Sheen's oyster satin, slashed to the waist with only the tiniest of discs encircling her breasts, Rebecca Bernstein's plain black shift, Christine Romaine's rumpled cream blouse . . . And she could never forget how it had all begun.

They had parked the Chevrolet in a long line of limos stretching down to the gate, signed their names for the security guard in a great padded leather book, stepped on to the pristine cream carpet and taken their drinks from a maid with milky cocoa skin.

They walked into a salon hung with bright Impressionist paintings and furnished with curious but compelling pieces of sculpture. There was a discreet mahogany bar at one end, and behind it a wide staircase with gilt and alabaster banisters, the kind of staircase, Eva thought idly, that a movie star might glide down to make an entrance.

The room was already half full, a potent mix of the famous, once famous, soon-to-be famous, and a few nobodies, like themselves. There was no sign of David Klein.

Eva was nervous and yet resolute. She had no idea how she would greet him, how she would form her request, but she would not be intimidated. In any case, she hadn't come to see David Klein. She was there to meet Victor and his bride.

She scanned the room eagerly for her old friend, but he was nowhere to be seen. Then, as she searched the faces at the bar, a tall, dark, angular-cheeked woman detached herself from a laughing bunch of boys and advanced towards her.

'Eva Delamere! I'm Rebecca Bernstein . . . Glad you could come.
Now before we start to party, let's get a little piece of business behind
us. I'm looking for a French prostitute. How would you like to test for
Worldwide Pictures?'

Afterwards, returning to this moment, it was quite impossible to
imagine anything more unlikely. Toby's jaw drooped, Harriet's pink
champagne lurched on its stem, and Eva simply stared in disbelief.

'Think about it,' Rebecca said. 'It's a good part. You're not signed to
anyone at the moment, are you?'

Eva found her voice, although when she spoke a thin, high croak
sounded out, foolish and unrecognisable.

'As it happens, I'm starting a new job on Monday . . .'

She thought later that if Toby could have boxed her ears at that
moment, then nothing would have saved her. As it was he merely
grabbed her by the arm, digging his fingers into her bare flesh, demanding her compliance.

'She's not signed to anyone,' he said roughly. 'She'll be there Monday, or whatever day you say . . .'

Hope, in all its tantalising resplendence, had suddenly risen before
him, but Eva could think only that Monday was her first day at Gracie's
Restaurant. If she lost that job and failed to get the part, as she surely
would, then what price hope? She gazed at Rebecca Bernstein unhappily.

'Why me?' she faltered.

'I'm looking for someone authentic,' Rebecca said coolly, 'I don't
want some little Tennessee tart giving out with a French drawl . . . I
want the real thing. You're French, aren't you?'

Eva caught Toby's warning scowl and smiled uncertainly. Well, it
was almost true. She was half-French, wasn't she?

'It's a wonderful opportunity,' Harriet purred suddenly. 'What other
parts are you casting? I don't know if Eva told you, but I'm an actress
too . . . Not French, unfortunately, but very experienced . . . I could
send my details to your office?'

Rebecca Bernstein, who seemed not to have noticed Harriet until this
moment, now appraised her with professional eye.

'Who are you?' she enquired cautiously.

Harriet threw back the shiny black hair and prepared to make an
announcement, but Eva, ashamed of her earlier reticence, felt compelled
to redeem herself.

'This is Miss Carlotta de Vere,' she heard herself say, 'a veteran of
the London stage.'

Now Harriet looked set to kill her too, but she swallowed her wrath
and flashed Rebecca Bernstein a confident smile. 'It's Carlotta du Bois,'
she said grandly. 'And I would hardly describe myself as a veteran.

That is to say, I have considerable accomplishments behind me, but I'm only twenty-three . . .'

Rebecca Bernstein laughed.

'Well, Miss du Bois or de Vere,' she said slowly, 'come along with Eva on Monday and show me what you got.'

She nodded briefly, her attention taken by a group of boisterous new arrivals, but as she prepared to greet them, Eva, whose vocal chords seemed to have acquired an intent independent of her nerve, called after her.

'Are you hiring screenwriters for this new picture?'

'That's not my department. Mr Klein hires the writers.'

'Does he need anyone?'

'I really couldn't say . . .' Rebecca Bernstein glanced quickly at Toby, who now frowned down at his wife. 'You can ask him, of course . . . But I should tell you that Mr Klein only wants the best. He wouldn't hire a writer for sentimental reasons, for old times' sake.'

She smiled politely and left them.

'We already know that,' said Toby bitterly. 'For Chrissake, Eva! Have you never heard of pushing your luck?' He walked swiftly away towards the bar, almost knocking her drink from her hand as she tried to restrain him.

Eva blinked and gazed down into her champagne. Behind her, the swing band erupted into a mournful, mocking serenade. Out on the balcony the shimmering candles seemed suddenly to merge into one fiery mass. What had she done? She had meant to plead Toby's need to Davy himself, but in Rebecca Bernstein had fondly imagined that there might be an easier way. Now her plan had been mercilessly exposed and foiled.

'Eva, darling, cheer up! If we get parts in this picture, he won't need a bloody job, will he?'

Harriet, who'd quickly forgiven Eva for the de Vere slip, signalled imperiously to the cocoa-skinned maid, demanding more champagne.

'In any case, just leave David Klein to me. He may not be sentimental, but he's human, isn't he? He needs the things that all men need . . . Now, Eva, don't look so prissy! Sometimes it's hard to believe you've lived in Hollywood for the past six years. How do you think Moira Sheen got where she is today?'

They both gazed round the room. Moira Sheen was lying across David Klein's black velvet settee, eating peanuts and flicking the shells on to his carpet. A small crowd of courtiers loitered dutifully beside her, but she stared morosely past them, unwilling to be diverted.

'I'm glad I'm not where Moira is today,' Eva muttered.

'If it meant you had to sleep with David Klein? Heavens, Eva, you don't like him at all, do you? Well, I suggest you try very hard to forget whatever it is you've got against him. Anything else would be plain dumb.'

It seemed to Eva that the ghost of a confession hovered upon her lips, but whether she would ever have made it she didn't know, for it was then that she glimpsed Victor at last, standing anxiously at the bottom of the great staircase. She waved excitedly, and in a moment he was beside her, folding her into his arms and exclaiming in delight.

'Eva, my dearest, it's been so long . . . And I wasn't here to greet you! I'm afraid Rhoda has a headache, but she hopes to join us later. Eva! I must say you look wonderful . . .'

Victor looked good too. He seemed livelier, more jovial than she remembered, as though a young wife had awakened his zest for living. And it was also true, as Eva knew from Anya's letters, that Emmanuel Klein had left Victor a wealthy man. Years of hard work and devoted service to the Klein family business had paid off, and Eva was heartily glad to see him so happy and secure.

He smiled at Harriet. 'And who is this?'

'Carlotta du Bois,' she said, flashing a broad smile at Victor. 'I'm thrilled to meet you at last . . . But do tell us, because we're all very anxious to know – where is David Klein? Doesn't he even attend his own parties?'

And at that moment Eva saw him, leaning in the doorway to the salon, looking very little changed from the day she'd left him on the road to Paris, casually surveying his guests as though the party in his house had come as a faint surprise, and having reconciled himself to that, a matter of total indifference. Beside him stood a small, rotund man that she knew to be Saul Bernstein, and a little way behind them, the ageing, anxious figure of Bernstein's wife, Ruth.

Davy seemed to be looking for someone, and with a rush of warmth to her cheeks, Eva wondered for a second if it might be her. But then he saw her too, and as his gaze flickered over her face and he inclined his head in the briefest nod of recognition, she realised with shame that she was not the object of his search, and chided herself for permitting so rash a thought.

She saw as she watched him that he had changed after all. The wild dark curls had been tamed and the olive skin seemed paler, as though long hours spent in darkened rooms had sapped his colour. He seemed leaner too, and the wry smile she remembered had been replaced by something much more sombre, the ever-wary air of success.

Moira Sheen had also seen him, and now she slid from the sofa with as much grace as the oyster satin frock would allow. She walked swiftly to his side, slipped her arm through his and kissed him on the lips.

To Eva, still watching, it seemed plain that he had been looking for
Moira, but in a moment Rebecca Bernstein was between them, greeting
her father, leading her mother into the room and gently engineering
Moira aside.

'There he is!' exclaimed Victor suddenly, taking Harriet by the arm.
'Come on, Carlotta, I'll introduce you . . .'

Eva didn't follow them across the crowded floor. Instead she turned
swiftly to where Toby had elbowed a space at the bar, lodged between
the dashing Will Sutton, a gaggle of his shapely acolytes and, on the
edge of the circle, his baleful wife.

'That script was garbage,' Eva heard Will say to Toby as she approached. 'I could've written it better myself.'

Christine Romaine emitted a low, throaty laugh. 'You'd have to learn
to read first, honey,' she said to Will.

Toby glanced briefly at Eva, and then across to the doorway where
David Klein stood talking to Victor, ignoring Harriet, whose indefatig-
able resolution seemed, for once, to have deserted her. Now she stood
by the great director's side, silent and ill at ease.

'I suppose we'd better go and greet our host,' Toby said slowly,
meeting his wife's eye with evident challenge. She stared back dumbly,
knowing then that he had never forgiven her long-ago infatuation,
nor forgotten what had happened the day she left Paris with David
Klein.

'Hey, come on!' said Sutton, suddenly spying his mentor. 'What are
we waiting for?'

Slowly, nervously, Eva followed him across the great room towards
Davy, her flesh pimpling despite the heat of the night, her mouth
strangely dry.

'Eva . . . Toby . . . How are you?'

They stood in the doorway together, shaking hands with each other,
smiling guardedly. Behind her, Eva was aware of the brooding presence
of Saul Bernstein; no more than a whiff of cigar smoke, the grunt of
acknowledgement to some passing minion, and yet somehow unsettling.
He seemed to be listening closely to the talk, but he could hardly have
found it compelling.

No one mentioned Paris. No one remembered the Café des Arbres
nor brought up Anya's name. No one even mentioned Eva's
forthcoming test at Worldwide. With unspoken agreement, they dealt
only in evasions. Nice house. Lovely garden. Great staircase.

David Klein was reserved, dispassionate, and barely interested, it
seemed to Eva, in their polite remarks. Meanwhile Harriet looked on
anxiously, waiting with uncharacteristic patience for the conversation to
improve, and Victor consulted his watch.

Later, much later, Eva was to reflect on what happened next and wonder how the inexorable chain of events might have been reshaped on that night, if not altogether broken.

It seemed, looking back, as though the dance band's drummer must have sounded a roll at that moment, or perhaps that the entire band suddenly, and for some mysterious reason, ceased to play.

Whatever, the room fell silent and all eyes were drawn to the gilt and alabaster staircase. At the top stood a slender girl in a white silk ball-gown, utterly poised as though her entrance had been precisely timed, a great swath of chocolate-coloured hair floating to her waist, huge almond eyes framed by a perfect oval face.

She began her descent without a trace of hesitation, gliding from one stair to the next in perfect confidence as though she'd been rehearsing the steps all day. Down, down, she came, a goddess deigning to visit the mortals below, a beauty whose unadorned loveliness rendered all the little starlets before her no more than painted whores.

Down, down, she came, the white silk gown rustling as she moved, the chocolate hair swinging about her naked shoulders, the wide brown eyes fixed upon the distant doorway.

'Holy shit,' Eva heard Will Sutton mutter behind her. 'Who the hell is that?'

As he spoke, he slumped against Eva's arm, nearly falling to the floor. And as she turned to view his famous, idolised face, she caught upon it a look of naked desire, the drunkard glimpsing heaven and reaching out for his fill.

Later, Eva came to see that everything was then in place. When she recalled this evening in all its poignant clarity, the clothes, the colour of the bougainvillaea, Rebecca Bernstein's offer of a test, the moment she first glimpsed Davy standing in the doorway, the menacing moodiness of Saul Bernstein, she saw all of this to be nothing but mere detail. For on Will's face she had seen the shape of things to come, the anatomy of tragedy.

Yes, looking back, it was all too painfully clear.

Will Sutton was good as dead the night he set eyes on Rhoda Martineau.

Chapter Seventeen

The making of *Casey's War* is an episode in Hollywood history that leaves many questions unanswered. Why did David Klein, usually so cautious in his judgements, choose an unknown actress for the leading female role? Why was Moira Sheen originally offered the part of Sister Marie and then summarily replaced by Carlotta du Bois?

Toby Truman, scriptwriter on *Casey's War* and Eva Delamere's husband, reveals that the film marked the height of a covert struggle between Klein and Saul Bernstein.

'It was a classic tale,' he says. 'David was the guy with all the talent. But Bernstein had all the power.'

The true nature of that power only became apparent after Bernstein's death, but it seems likely that Klein suspected his boss's links with the Mob, and that he became increasingly concerned about Worldwide's growing debt to the Revenue. Certainly, he disapproved of Bernstein's unrestrained appetite for a succession of young starlets, and found his loyalty to his father's old friend severely strained.

'David wanted out of Worldwide Pictures,' Mr Truman confides, speaking from Paris where he still lives with Miss Delamere. 'He wanted his own studio, and he was trying to raise the cash in New York . . . But it didn't work out. Maybe he just didn't want it enough . . .'

Against the Tide: A Biography of David Klein, by Jon Makepeace

---

From the morning of the test, when Toby had driven her in the yellow Chevvy to the Worldwide lot and waited three hours to hear how it went, to the first day of the shoot, when she'd kissed Will Sutton a dozen times until her lip swelled blue and bitten, Eva could not believe she had the part.

'This car should go back to the hire company,' she'd snapped at Toby as he opened the passenger door on that first day. 'We can't afford it.'

'Sure we can,' he said easily, coaxing the Chevvy into gear and cruising past the studio gate, 'and I'm gonna find us a new house too. It will all be okay. Wait and see.'

He was right, but even after the confirming call from Rebecca Bernstein, Eva was still incredulous. Why would any producer, let alone the great David Klein, give an untried, unknown actress such a part?

For all that, she had acquitted herself well, despite a rather unpromising start. She'd been asked to produce a halting French accent for her test as the Parisian prostitute, and she had dared to question.

'Surely that isn't necessary? . . . I mean, the truth is, I'm not really French – that is to say, not one hundred per cent French . . .'

Rebecca Bernstein had initially been taken aback, and then forthright. 'You want this part, honey, you're French!'

So Eva marshalled all her fortitude and her gall, swallowed hard and thought of Miss Isabel Lamont, the Church High School, and those long-ago lessons in dramatic art. It mightn't be Shakespeare, but she could surely do it. Miss Lamont demanded no less!

The script was dull, the plot outrageously unlikely, and all Eva's instincts rebelled against the device of setting the soldier hero Casey between two extremes of womanhood, a street-walker and a nun. But she kept her doubts to herself, and heard the husky, broken English leave her lips with a certain astonishment.

Rebecca Bernstein laughed.

'*Très bien, Mademoiselle*,' she said approvingly. 'We'll tell the whole world you were born and bred in Paris.'

Harriet had also excelled, despite reservations about the role of the unworldly Sister Marie.

'I should be testing for Eva's part,' she'd moaned to Rebecca after the fourth take. 'I should be the prostitute. I'm not right for a bloody nun.'

'Not with that haircut, you're not,' Bernstein agreed.

This had been enough to make Harriet rethink her image, and now she was Harold Brannen's blonde daughter again, the hair having been cropped close to her scalp, highlighting her emerald green eyes and pale rose skin. The effect was striking. She looked like a novice preparing for first vows, and this convinced her that she did indeed want to play Sister Marie. But it wasn't to be. Instead, said Rebecca Bernstein, Mr Klein was considering another part in a new picture and a contract with Worldwide, the deal to be signed later.

'I love him!' Harriet said to Eva in jubilation. 'And I didn't even have to let my panties down! Not bad for Harold Brannen's bastard daughter, eh?'

For Eva there was a generous one-off deal to play against Will Sutton's Casey. Her eyes opened wide when she heard the sum.

'But I must tell you the truth,' Bernstein said harshly. 'You got this part because we needed someone French. So don't go thinking you'll be the next Greta Garbo. You won't.'

Eva, who wasn't at all sure she'd want to be the next Greta Garbo, received this judgement with good grace. Whoever had decided to give her the part, and whatever the reasons behind it, she knew she'd been unbelievably lucky. The rest was up to her.

'Who gets to play the nun?' she had enquired, and received an answer even more astonishing than her own unprecedented signing.

'Moira Sheen. She's a big name. We make big-name pictures, and although we've got Will, we have to remember that you're unknown . . . We need Sheen too.'

Harriet had screamed with laughter at this news.

'Moira Sheen? As a nun? Holy shit!'

This seemed to sum it up perfectly, and Toby, who'd opened a new bottle of bourbon which he now slopped into Harriet's glass, guffawed loudly. But Eva was deeply disturbed. Moira was wrong for the part of Sister Marie. They all knew it, and she couldn't believe Rebecca Bernstein, let alone David Klein, didn't know it too.

'I don't understand,' she said unhappily. 'Why would they cast Moira? It doesn't make any sense.'

'Maybe Miss Sheen wants to get serious,' Toby suggested, joining in the laughter.

Harriet stood up and wiggled her buttocks at Toby, both of them still cackling insanely.

'Or maybe it's a punishment,' Harriet said, winking coarsely at Eva. 'Maybe Moira wouldn't do what Mr Klein wanted? Maybe he was after something special, and Miss Sheen couldn't come up with the goods . . .'

Eva looked at them both in sudden distaste and walked swiftly across the room to the door.

'I'll check on Nicky,' she said tightly. 'All this row must be disturbing him.'

But the child was sleeping soundly in the sturdy wooden cot Toby had painted for him, his bright golden hair beaded with little drops of moisture, his tiny hand clasped into a fist. It was too hot for him in this wretched apartment, Eva thought miserably. Maybe Toby was right, and they should move out at once, even though her first paycheck was still some weeks away. Maybe some kindly real estate agent would take them on trust.

She leaned over and kissed Nicky gently on the forehead, aware as her lips brushed his soft, fair skin of a melancholy ache hovering on the edge of sorrow, not so much a yearning as a recognition of destiny. She would never have a child of her own. In six years of marriage, there had been no hint, no suspicion, of possible conception.

But then she admonished herself sharply. So be it! If she couldn't become a mother, then she would become something else . . . A French tart, *par excellence*, perhaps.

Back on the sofa, Toby and Harriet were still discussing David Klein.

'I wish I could talk to him,' Harriet said dreamily. 'I want to know what he's got in mind for me . . . Eva! When do you think he'll show? Why is he never on the lot?'

This was the question Eva also wanted to ask. She hadn't seen Davy since the night of the party. He had hired her for his picture, but he had done it through Rebecca. There had been no congratulations, no champagne signing, no gentle massaging of ego, the kind of things she might reasonably have expected. Instead, he seemed unconcerned about her encouragement or her instruction. David Klein's renowned attention to detail was mysteriously lacking when it came to *Casey's War*.

'He's got too much on,' Toby opined, waving the bourbon at Harriet and pouring them both a further hefty measure. 'There's Rebecca Bernstein and Moira Sheen to satisfy. And now he's probably screwing Rhoda as well.'

'Don't say that!' Eva stared at him in shock. 'Rhoda is Victor's wife!'

In truth, she'd found it hard to warm to the imperious Rhoda, finding a curious lack of interest beneath her apparent enthusiasm for Victor's old friends, as though she really were an exquisite vision without substance. But although Eva recalled Madame Martineau's doubts about her son's good sense when it came to women, she still credited Victor with some power to discriminate. And she would not countenance such a slander on Rhoda.

'Listen to me, honey,' said Toby smartly, showing all the impatience of a man irritated beyond endurance by his wife's innocence. 'Any guy would be screwing Rhoda, given half a chance.'

There was a brief pause while all three of them considered this proposition.

'Unless Will Sutton got there first,' said Harriet at last with another squeal of her raucous laughter. 'You wouldn't want to dive in after Will, now would you, Toby?'

The following week Toby announced he'd paid six months' rent on the chalet opposite Will and Christine's château, and moved them all out that same afternoon, pitching their few meagre possessions – a velvet stool, his desk and typewriter, Eva's dressing table, the coffee

percolator, Nicky's blue painted cot, the toy bricks and fire engine –
into the back of the Chevvy. Harriet insisted on a separate run for her
clothes, a chore that Toby, to Eva's surprise, undertook without complaint.

'You're gonna love it, girls,' he declared, his lately acquired moodiness
replaced by an enthusiasm which Eva recognised, and remembered with a
pang. 'And we've got Christine to thank. She put me on to the agent.'

The chalet was indeed very pretty, a timbered, Swiss-style cottage
with gingham curtains fluttering at its windows and bright red geraniums sprouting from terracotta pots on its terrace.

Eva didn't dare to ask about the rent, nor had she any idea where
Toby had found the money. She'd refused to ask David Klein for an
advance on her salary, a decision which had led to a vehement row.

'For God's sake, Eva! He owes us that much.'

'He owes us nothing,' she'd said grandly. 'And I won't beg.'

Then Toby, with the uncharacteristic violence born of extreme exas-
peration and too much drink, had flung his whisky glass across the
room, smashing it against the wall so that the liquid trailed down the
dingy cream distemper, an ugly reproach to them both.

'You won't do anything that might compromise your high and mighty
principles, will you, Eva?'

She had fled from the room then, furious with him for his lack of
understanding, angry with herself for her evident inability to act rationally in anything regarding David Klein. There was no good reason why
she shouldn't ask for an advance. Will had certainly done it, the ostentatious scarlet Bugatti which stood outside the Sutton château was evidence enough of that. But she could not bear to approach David Klein,
could not think how she would phrase her request, nor meet those dark
blue eyes in the remembrance of all that had gone before. And she knew
exactly why she could not ask. That most seductive, surreptitious of
sins, the kerb upon which so many a virtuous Christian soul had stumbled, was even now proving her greatest trial. Pride.

But pride, she told herself, could be honourable. And Toby ought
surely to understand this? Toby, who had once considered David Klein
his inferior, a man without moral scruple. Had so much changed that
Toby had lost all sense of pride?

She preferred to think not, and took comfort in the fact that the
advance was never mentioned again. But she couldn't imagine how he'd
raised the cash for the rent on the chalet. She didn't really believe that
some philanthropic landlord had taken him on trust. So perhaps Christine, blowsy, eccentric, foul-mouthed Christine, who seemed to have
taken a shine to both Toby and herself, had offered a loan . . .

But in the days that followed, when the newcomers became frequent guests at the Suttons' turreted château, which loomed like some Gothic set just across the road from the chalet, Christine gave no hint of any such generosity. Indeed, she confided to Eva that their own finances were none too rosy.

'See that toy,' she said, indicating the Bugatti which stood, resplendent and immobile, in the driveway. 'He can't even drive the fucking thing. Do you believe that, Eva? It cost a fucking fortune – and he can't even drive it!'

They were standing in Christine's boudoir, gazing down from its height like princesses marooned in some forbidden tower. Christine had been showing Eva her home – 'Dracula's fucking castle, I call it' – while below them Will, Toby and Harriet lounged upon the immaculate lawns.

'I might move out one day,' Christine declared, staring as Will rose from the lawn and slouched over to the Bugatti, rubbing the tip of its bonnet with his jacket sleeve and bending down to breathe upon the wing mirror. 'I might just leave the whole fucking pile to the Lady of Shalott . . .'

On the wall above Christine's bed hung a vivid tapestry depicting Tennyson's doomed heroine, spinning her web in muted browns and pinks while behind her the towered Camelot glimmered, gold and silver threads among the green embroidered forest.

'See her there? Isn't she lovely?' Christine asked softly. 'Almost as lovely as your friend Rhoda.'

It was undeniably true that the Lady of Shalott bore a remarkable resemblance to Rhoda, from the flowing chestnut tresses to the vast almond eyes and pale ivory skin. They even seemed to share the same expression, a dreaming unworldliness, the knowledge of infinite secrets never to be divulged.

Eva laughed uncertainly. She had no idea how Christine viewed her husband's infatuation with Rhoda, and no great wish to find out. But already tongues were whispering on the set. Who was the mysterious beauty who caused Will Sutton, the great star, the consummate pro, to fluff his lines whenever she appeared? Who sat silent and impassive in the wings, a personal friend of David Klein's, and ostensibly only an onlooker, and yet somehow, always the very centre of attention?

Eva had watched Will's desire grow by the hour, but she had tried to shake it off because Victor seemed so unconcerned.

'Oh, everyone loves Rhoda!' he'd said carelessly, eyeing his wife with an admiration hardly less than Will's own. 'You can't blame the poor chap for looking.'

So Eva had hidden her disquiet, but she had found herself wondering how it all might end, for Will Sutton, she knew, was not accustomed to mere looking.

'Rhoda's married to another man,' she told Will severely, but he had laughed at her, tweaking her long silver plait in the playful manner he adopted whenever he was in her company.

'Eva, you're one of life's innocents! Do you really expect the exquisite Rhoda Martineau to stay faithful to your old buddy Vic?'

'Yes, of course,' she'd said defensively. 'They've only been married a few months. Why would she do it if she didn't want to be his wife?'

'Because, my dear, darling, lovable Eva . . . Because Vic was the best guy going at the time. Picture the scene. Here's poor, beautiful Rhoda all alone in Paris, and here's nice, rich Victor. Very soon he's besotted, and nobody could blame him for that . . .'

'So?' demanded Eva unhappily.

'So, over the candles and the champagne he tells her all about himself. He's a builder. He used to work for the company Klein. Klein? Oh surely, Victor, you don't mean you know David Klein, the famous Hollywood director? Well, yes, Rhoda, actually, David Klein is my cousin – we could go visit him in Hollywood if you like!'

Will laughed again, and Eva had felt her spirits sink.

'So here she is,' he said. 'And now she can have the pick of the bunch.'

'Well, I hope she doesn't pick you,' Eva had said soberly, 'You're a married man yourself, Will. What about Christine?'

'Don't you worry about Christine,' he'd replied with a little smile. 'Christine understands.'

Now Eva surveyed Christine and the Lady of Shalott with growing unease, unsure what she should say, hearing her silence fall heavily in the stifling, scented air of the boudoir.

Christine sat down at her dressing table and began to brush her wild ginger curls. But her eyes remained fixed upon the unsmiling face of the Lady of Shalott, reflected in the mirror before her.

'It's a great disadvantage to be that beautiful,' she whispered to Eva. 'For if you can have any man, which man will you have? Will you choose wealth, or security, or love? Is one as good as another? Perhaps. But then to be sure, the one man you finally decide you must have will be the very one you can't have . . . the one in a million who remains impervious to your charms.'

Eva watched her nervously. What did she mean? Was she talking about Rhoda? Eva didn't care to ask. Christine's eccentricities were legendary. So was her temper. It was this, they said, that had ended her own contract with Worldwide Pictures. But it wasn't David Klein who'd thrown her out, it was Saul Bernstein himself. The full story had never been told, but while Will had become Worldwide's greatest male star, Christine had become gossip-column fodder, the pathetic, embarrassing wife on the sideline.

Now she flashed Eva a dark smile in the mirror.

'Women are so stupid,' she murmured, setting the brush back upon the dressing table. 'They only think about love and sex. They think men want these things, but men don't give a damn about love. And sex is just something to be grabbed along the way when the opportunity presents . . .'

She smiled again, the merest twitch of her bright scarlet lips, and picked up a powder sponge.

'Power. Money. Success,' she intoned. 'Those are the things men really want, whatever they might say when the lights go down.'

Eva laughed, a little more confidently this time. 'Maybe you're right,' she said.

'Take Saul Bernstein,' Christine invited. 'What do you see? A bastard if ever there was one. Does he like sex? Oh yes, and how . . . But in truth, he only wants those other things . . .'

Still Eva watched, fascinated, and faintly alarmed.

'Or take Will Sutton,' Christine murmured, picking up the hairbrush again. 'What do you see? A man who wants pretty women? Oh yes! But ask him to choose, and he'll have those other things . . .'

'What about David Klein?' Eva heard herself ask.

Christine laughed hoarsely and got up from the dressing table. She walked swiftly to the window and threw open the casement, infusing the heated room with a cooling breeze, breaking the spell.

'David? Oh, David's different. He's a romantic.'

She leaned out of the window, craning down towards the party below.

'Will Sutton!' she yelled. 'Get out of that fucking car before you kill yourself!'

Eva shivered, glimpsing suddenly a tangle of fractured emotions and lies: Rhoda, Victor, Will, and perhaps Christine herself. And she never got to ask if the Suttons had loaned Toby the money for the chalet.

The shooting of *Casey's War* called for a mock-up façade of a Parisian café to be built on the Worldwide lot, complete with Sacré Coeur, the Eiffel Tower and the Arc de Triomphe on the painted skyline behind it.

'You wouldn't see them all together like that,' Eva objected, only to receive a withering rebuke from Rebecca Bernstein.

'This is a motion picture, Eva, not a geography lesson.'

Once shooting got under way, Eva learned fast. She learned all the tricks of the trade: how to scale down emotion to the blink of an eye, how to kiss without bruising your lips or risking suffocation, how to exploit your best angle, how to make the camera love you.

All this she learned from Will Sutton, who, she quickly discovered, was good-natured enough when sober, and a raging bull as soon as a thimbleful of whisky hit his veins.

'Come on, honey, you can do it,' he'd whisper whenever she faltered on set, or, 'Hell, Eva, I know you've got more in your belly than this . . .'

Only when he was drunk did his gentlemanly concern for her inexperience slip.

'Goddam it, Eva, you're supposed to be a fucking hooker, for Pete's sake.'

Eva forgave every last thing Will Sutton said when the whisky was in him, simply because, without him, she was lost. Effectively, she had no director. Three weeks into the shoot, and David Klein still hadn't shown. Did he think *Casey's War* would produce itself by a process of immaculate conception? Or was he simply delegating? Eva didn't know.

'Are you directing this picture?' she'd asked Rebecca Bernstein one unproductive morning, and had received a stony reply.

'Women don't direct motion pictures. They just do the dirty work. So get on with it Eva, please. Let's see you act dirty . . .'

But the scene wouldn't happen.

'Makes you wonder how they ever won the goddamn war,' Will said, throwing aside the script.

Indeed, Eva thought. What with Casey and his whore, Vivi, not to mention the voluptuous Sister Marie, who had yet to make her appearance, the Great War appeared nothing so much as a heaven-sent opportunity for licentiousness.

The reality was very different. This was the war that had robbed Eva of her brothers. This was the war that had driven Matthew Brannen to the brink of despair.

At night, when she walked away from the plywood Paris, when she got back to the chalet and lay down in the bed she'd taken for her own, one image possessed her. She closed her eyes, and there before her hovered the taut and sorrowful face of Harold Brannen. She seemed to see him again on the day he'd left St Cuthbert's for ever, a tall, robust golden-haired hero. 'It will all be over by Christmas,' she seemed to hear him say, just as he'd declared to Lizzie Howard all those years ago.

'*Casey's War* is a joke,' she said bitterly to Toby. 'The script is terrible. Why does nobody make an honest war picture, one that tries to tell the truth?'

'Because an honest war picture wouldn't make any dough.'

'You think *Casey* will break the box-office records?'

'It doesn't matter, Eva. We're doing OK . . .'

Eva tried to discuss it with Harriet, but Harriet had no interest in the real war either, only in *Casey*'s version, or rather, the version she imagined David Klein was going to direct. Every day she accompanied Eva to the set, hoping to see him, and every day she was disappointed.

'Where is he?' she beseeched. 'When will he come?'

'He's in New York,' said Rebecca Bernstein, overhearing this, 'and you should be glad. He'd throw you off the set if he was here. He doesn't like onlookers.'

David Klein's prohibition didn't seem to apply to Rhoda, however. Not only was Rhoda passionately interested in everything to do with *Casey's War*, arriving at the same time as the actors, watching each scene intently, sometimes, Eva observed, scribbling notes on a little pad, but she was driven to the lot every day in her host's private limo.

'What is she doing here?' Harriet demanded. 'What's she writing in that book?' Eva had no idea, nor did she feel able to enquire.

Rebecca Bernstein was clearly irritated by Rhoda's presence, but nonetheless seemed incapable of dismissing her. And Eva suspected that Harriet was tolerated for just this reason. If Bernstein had barred Harriet from the set, which in Klein's absence she was surely entitled to do, then Rhoda's privilege would have been all the more evident.

As it was, the two of them, Miss Carlotta du Bois, the would-be starlet, and Madame Rhoda Martineau, the Lady of Shalott, sat behind the lighting rig in self-imposed silence and mutual suspicion.

The effect on Will, and therefore on the progress of the filming, was considerable. But worse, as far as Eva could see, was the fact that Rhoda's daily attendance gave him ground for hope. Why else, he reasoned, would a beautiful young woman haunt an unpromising film set, unless she were in love with its star?

'She has to do something,' Eva told him while trying to work this out for herself. 'Her host is in New York and her husband is very busy . . .'

'Sure he is,' replied Will with a laugh. 'And I mean to keep him that way.'

Eva had given up worrying about Victor. He seemed so confident in his choice of wife, so determined that his devotion should be repaid by her happiness, that Eva began to feel he must be right. In any case, there was nothing she could do. The Victor who had been in love with Anya, the Victor who'd escorted her home from the Divine Faith convent and bought her glasses of wine in the Café des Arbres, had been replaced by someone much more assured and daring. Victor had announced his intention to settle in America, declaring that as Rhoda

seemed so much at home, he might as well make the most of it. He had
begun to check out building sites in the Beverly Hills area, and believed
he could rekindle the Klein family business from the ashes of Depression. Will Sutton had very kindly loaned the scarlet Bugatti to assist in
his efforts.

'Quite a sacrifice,' mused Harriet as she and Eva, leaving the Worldwide lot early one afternoon, caught sight of Victor cruising past in the
Bugatti. 'Will must be hoping he'll drive it into a ravine. That would
be interesting, wouldn't it? The ravishing Rhoda Martineau, tragic
widow. Who would she ravish, do you think?'

Eva didn't know, nor was she concerned about Victor driving the
Bugatti into a ravine. Will's motives were plain enough, and they were
rather more prosaic. The further afield Victor went, the more Rhoda
was left to her own devices.

And the more Eva considered, the more devious those devices came
to seem. Rhoda was playing with Will, she was sure of it. She accepted
his admiration as though it were her due, and in return she offered
enigmatic smiles and smouldering glances. He'd invite her into his
dressing room, and Eva would hear them laughing together. But at the
end of the day, David Klein's limo always came to collect her, and
Rhoda was always driven home. Meantime, Will's frustration grew, but
Rhoda seemed unconcerned.

Rebecca Bernstein, however, was increasingly concerned, and Eva
watched her patience thinning by the day. Her temper with Will was
barely controlled, and her dislike of Rhoda blatantly obvious to
everyone except, it seemed, Rhoda herself.

Eva felt a certain sympathy for the prickly Rebecca, and hadn't forgotten her dry comment that 'women don't direct motion pictures'. It
was plain Miss Bernstein was abundantly capable, yet she was only the
casting director, subject always to the dictates of either David Klein or
her father.

Eva often found herself wondering about Rebecca's relationship with
Davy. Why had they never married as their families had intended?
Indeed, it was hard to imagine them as husband and wife, yet in many
respects Rebecca played the wife, hosting his parties, issuing his invita-
tions. How, Eva wondered, did Moira Sheen fit into this cosy little
scene?

A small incident served to throw some light on these speculations.

Moira swept on to the lot one morning, cocooned in sable, the candyfloss hair secured on top of her head by a large diamanté clip.

'Where's your father?' she demanded of Rebecca, and then receiving no satisfactory reply, 'So where's David? I must talk to one of
them . . .'

'Sorry,' said Rebecca icily. 'There's only me.'

They disappeared together into Davy's office and Eva watched them through the glass screen, Moira gesticulating and declaiming while Rebecca listened in apparent resignation. Then after a few moments, Moira walked out, slamming the glass door behind her, and Rebecca, striding back on to the set, caught Eva's eye.

'Sometimes,' she muttered, 'I get sick of pretty women.'

Instinctively they both looked at Rhoda, and then Rebecca laughed.

'God knows what she's writing in her little book. Let's hope it's enough to keep the great Mr Klein entertained . . .'

Eva didn't quite know what to make of this comment. She longed to know what Rhoda was writing, and as usual it was Harriet who provided the answer.

'I peeped into Rhoda's notebook this morning,' she confided after one disastrous day in which Eva's attempts at Vivi's seduction scene had ended with Rebecca Bernstein dismissing the entire crew and telling Eva to go home and get an early night.

'What did she write?' Eva asked unhappily.

'She wrote that you'd never make a hooker in a million years! That you couldn't sell your body for sex if you were starving!'

Harriet laughed.

'Now we know what Rhoda wants, don't we? She wants to be you! She's jealous!'

Eva, angry but close to tears, was silent. In that moment she cared nothing for Rhoda and her schemes, only for her own perceived failure. Will's careful tutoring had been to no avail. Never mind that she could kiss and cry and turn her cheek. It was painfully obvious that this picture was going to be one of the worst Worldwide had ever made, and her own performance a farce. The script was ludicrous, the characters incredible, the plot laughable. She'd be surprised if Saul Bernstein even put the studio name to it.

But why did it have to be so bad? Why couldn't there be a new script? A new and tougher vision of *Casey's War*?

One man had the answers, and Eva resolved to confront him the moment he returned from New York.

She knew David Klein was back in town the morning Rhoda failed to show up on the set.

She knew with a sickening understanding that she didn't care to examine too closely, and the knowledge was soon confirmed by Harriet, who always seemed to know everything, or if not, to have ways of finding out.

'He's back and he'll be here this afternoon,' she whispered to Eva between takes. 'He's going to view the rushes.'

Will, however, was so depressed by Rhoda's absence that he broke a Worldwide rule and took a drink on the set. And Rebecca Bernstein, in a fit of pique or perhaps of desperation, called a halt to the shooting, ordering everyone home. Eva wasn't going to confront David Klein on the Worldwide lot that afternoon.

But Harriet was.

'I'm not hanging around any longer. I'm going right in there. I'm going to knock on his office door, and I'm going to ask him straight what he's got in mind for me.'

'Good luck,' Eva said.

Left alone in the chalet, she could not settle. She wished she had Nicky to play with, but Harriet had hired a nanny for Nicky, and the nanny had taken him out walking.

She fixed herself a sandwich, she took a shower, she picked up a magazine. She reached for a pack of Harriet's black Russian cigarettes and observed herself in the ebony-edged mirror above the fireplace while she smoked one. Could she do it without making her eyes water? This was one trick Will hadn't managed to teach her.

She gazed out of the window at the Sutton château across the road. Was Christine home? Should she call up? Or should she try to find Toby?

The truth was she had no idea how to locate her husband. She didn't know where he spent his days, and increasingly, his evenings. Since the night of their row when he'd thrown his whisky at the wall, they'd had little to say to each other. And when she'd suggested moving into separate bedrooms, now that they had more space and needn't disturb each other, he had readily agreed.

The clock on the mantelpiece, a grotesque gilt thing supported by chuckling cherubs and disproportionate doves, an uninspired birthday gift from Toby, struck three, and then four. Eva stared at the clock in distaste. She was still staring half an hour later when the nanny came home with Nicky.

She bathed Nicky and cooked his supper, instructing the bewildered nanny to sit upon the settee and read her magazines. Then when the clock struck seven, and neither Harriet nor Toby had returned, she went upstairs to dress.

She chose a black velvet shift with a little jet-beaded jacket, her dark silk stockings and her highest-heeled shoes. Then she plaited her long silver hair and wound the plait into a coil at the nape of her neck. She shadowed her eyes with violet and applied the merest touch of honey-coloured lipstick. Then she checked the seams of her stockings, plucked a stray tuft from one eyebrow, dabbed perfume on her wrists, walked outside, got into the Chevvy and set off for David Klein's house.

The night air was heavy with heat, the sky above the canyon a startling, oppressive yellow-brown. She began to regret the velvet dress, yet although she was warm, she felt calm and cool within. This was the moment she had planned, and she meant to give it her best performance.

It didn't occur to her that he might still be at Worldwide, but as she turned the corner by the lot, she glimpsed his limo standing just inside the studio gate. She parked the Chevvy and after a brief exchange with the security guard she was on the lot, walking gingerly through the unaccustomed darkness towards the set of *Casey's War*.

She had no idea what she expected to find. Davy making love to Moira Sheen on the couch in his office? Arguing with Rebecca Bernstein about the terrible first rushes? Or signing up Miss Carlotta du Bois over a glass of champagne?

Whatever, she hadn't expected to come upon him sitting alone at the table in the mock-up café, a bottle of wine and two glasses at his side. He seemed lost in thought, staring at the painted Paris skyline with its ridiculous jumble of monuments. But for the expensive suit and the pale silk tie, he suddenly looked painfully like the tousle-haired apprentice builder she had first glimpsed at the Café des Arbres so long ago.

He stood up at the sound of her footfall.

'Becky? Is that you?'

'I'm afraid not,' she said, stepping into the light. 'It's me.'

He surveyed Eva for a moment, taking in the challenging angle of her chin, the evident determination in her eyes.

'Well then,' he said slowly, 'you'd better sit down and tell me why you're here.'

He poured her a glass of wine, but she didn't want to drink, she wanted to deliver her speech.

'I'm not here to tell you anything you don't already know,' she began smartly. '*Casey's War* is a lousy picture. It's a joke. The script is terrible, the story line is all wrong . . . What I want to know is why you're not directing it.'

He reached for his cigarettes and offered her one. She declined with a stiff little shake of her head.

'So it's a lousy picture,' he said at last. 'And we're paying you a lousy fortune to do it . . . That seems fair.'

'No,' she said calmly, 'it's not enough.'

'Not enough money?'

'I don't mean that. I mean there has to be something more. I don't want to be in a picture this bad.'

He seemed to think this over, his fingers tightening around the stem of his wine glass, his brow creased in a frown of concentration.

'You'll pardon me saying that in your position, a bad picture is better than no picture . . .'

'I won't pardon it,' she retorted, 'but I'll overlook it if you answer my question.'

This time he said nothing, simply raised his glass and gazed moodily into it. He was weighing his words carefully, she realised. He wasn't about to reveal anything he didn't wish her to know.

'If you don't want to do the picture, you're free to quit,' he snapped suddenly. 'I can switch the actors. Moira can play Vivi, and I'll find someone else for Sister Marie.'

Eva's heart began to hammer beneath the black velvet dress, and she heard herself utter a tiny gasp. This wasn't what she'd hoped for.

'I'll release you here and now,' he said, standing up. 'You can sign the papers in my office. Is that what you want?'

'No,' she whispered, and he had the grace to turn back at the tremor in her voice.

She picked up the glass of wine he had poured her, and trembling, took a drink. She had played it all wrong once more. Instead of trying to persuade, she'd set out to condemn. And who was she to do it? An unsuccesful actress who'd been given a break by one of Hollywood's best directors. No wonder he was angry.

'I'm sorry,' she said miserably. 'I have no right to question you. I just don't see why you can't make a decent war picture. One that shows what it did to ordinary people's lives . . . I know something about that. I watched all my brothers go off to that war, and I waited in vain for them all to come back.'

This was better. She had touched his conscience. He sat down beside her again and refilled his glass.

'This isn't a war picture, Eva. It's a story about a guy who gets involved with two scheming women. The war is in his conscience, in his desires. The real war just happens to be the background.'

'That shouldn't mean it doesn't matter. We ought to be able to show how the war changed them, Casey and Vivi and Sister Marie. How it made them bitter, and how they were able to take that bitterness and use it for something good. It could still have a happy ending . . . Happy endings sometimes happen in real life – don't they?'

She was departing from her script, but she was warming to her theme, and he was listening to her. He was listening in the way he used to listen, in the old days, when the set at the Café des Arbres talked of Culture and Art and Revolution and all those other things they half believed in.

'I know a picture has to make money,' she conceded, remembering what Toby had said to her, 'but surely it can still say something important? Only a cynic would say it can't ... You were never a cynic, were you, Davy?'

This was a gamble. She had evoked the memory of all they'd once known of each other, and it hurt her terribly to do it. She wondered if it hurt him too.

But there was no telling. He lit another cigarette. It was clear to her that he was still thinking hard.

'Money rules,' he said at last. 'You can't get away from it. I'm not being cynical when I say that. Just realistic.'

She picked up her glass and faced him squarely.

'That's what cynics always say,' she said.

He laughed then, and the tension between them was suddenly, magically broken. She smiled back, and felt her heart lift.

'Who's going to write this great screenplay?' he asked her carefully. 'The one where we show what the war did to Casey and all the rest, and how they turned their bitterness into something good?'

Eva shrugged. She didn't know.

'You? Or your husband, perhaps?'

She felt her cheeks begin to burn. This was unfair.

'Well, he couldn't produce anything worse than you've already got,' she muttered.

'I wonder,' said Davy slowly, still thinking hard.

He stood up then and faced the Paris backcloth, still turning it all over in his mind, loosening the pale silk tie, running a hand through the tamed dark curls, pulling on his cigarette. 'Okay,' he said, making his decision. 'Tell Toby to come and see me in the morning. Eight-thirty sharp. We'll talk it through.'

'Thank you!' she cried. 'Oh, thank you!'

She was astonished and deeply grateful, and she might have hugged him had she not feared that her embrace would be rejected. He was not about to restore anything of their former intimacy, and indeed, she ought hardly to be hoping for this herself. She was a married woman, after all.

She stood up to leave and he glanced quickly at his watch.

'Can I get my driver to take you home?'

'It's okay. I have my car.'

She hesitated. It was clear he wasn't leaving the lot himself. He was going to sit back down in the mock-up café with the half-full bottle of wine and the glasses, waiting for whoever he'd been expecting when she arrived.

'Are you waiting for Miss Bernstein?' she asked him timorously. 'Are you going to tell her you're rewriting the script?'

'I'm not waiting for Becky,' he said.

'Oh, I'm sorry. You're waiting for Moira, of course.'

'I'm not waiting for Moira,' he said.

'For Victor and Rhoda, then? Are you all going out?'

She heard her questions with alarm, aware that she had no licence to ask, surprised and shamed by her need to know.

But in contrast to his earlier irritation, he seemed unperturbed by her impertinence. He looked up at her, meeting her eye.

'I'm not waiting for Victor. He's away somewhere.'

'Oh yes. On one of his building sites . . .'

He was still looking up at her, willing her, it almost seemed, to make a judgement, to think the worst of him, the way she always had.

'I'm waiting for Rhoda,' he said softly. 'Just Rhoda.'

'Of course,' she said, smiling foolishly and turning away from the flimsy set. 'Rhoda. Yes. Of course.'

Only much later did she consider that, if she hadn't known better, she might just have thought he was trying to make her jealous.

The chalet was quiet when she got home, and she went straight upstairs, imagining everyone to be in bed. But while Nicky and the nanny were sleeping soundly, Harriet's room was empty and there was no sign of Toby. Perplexed, she went back downstairs to fix herself a coffee, and found him sitting on the sofa in the darkness, a bottle of bourbon by his side.

He was unimpressed with her news.

'David Klein never gave me a job before. You do something to make him change his mind?'

She might have smacked his face for this, but she didn't. Instead she went over the entire detail of the evening again, leaving nothing out.

'I told you he was screwing Rhoda,' Toby said.

'Well, that's his business,' Eva said, faltering at this thought, 'but his offer is genuine. I know it is. He wants you to rewrite *Casey's War*.'

Toby took another swig of his liquor.

'I wonder if that's what Saul Bernstein wants? He's the real boss at Worldwide. Maybe we'll find out when Harriet gets home.'

'Where is Harriet?' Eva asked uneasily, realising she knew nothing of what had happened to Miss Carlotta du Bois at Worldwide Pictures that afternoon.

'She called to say she's having dinner with Bernstein. Seems she didn't get to see Klein this afternoon, she saw the big guy instead. He's probably got her pants round her ankles right now.'

Eva jumped up from the sofa: 'Do you have to be so crude?' she barked.

'Oh, I'm sorry to offend your sensibilities, Eva! I know how refined they are . . . But it's time you learned the facts of life. Everyone's screwing someone in this town.'

She stared down at him with open disillusionment.

'I'm not,' she said.

That night as she lay down in her bed, willing sleep to come, it seemed to Eva that all the lessons of her life – her blissful childhood at St Cuthbert's, her love for Matthew Brannen, her bitter bereavements, her golden days in Paris – had proved no more than dust on the desert wind. She had learned nothing, achieved nothing, could see nothing fruitful in her future.

But then the spirit of hope, true hope, touched her heart with its silken wings, coaxing back to life all her resolution and her good intent. Yes, she could do it! She could play the French girl Vivi with conviction and fire. She could encourage Harriet to make her way without patronage or undeserved favour. She could even repair her crumbling marriage, given patience and determination. And if Toby turned down David Klein's offer, if he refused to write the script for *Casey's War*, why then, damn it, she would do it herself.

Chapter Eighteen

What really happened the night *Casey's War* was premièred?

The facts are these. Shortly after the performance ended, Will Sutton took Eva Delamere's Chevrolet, drove it into a ravine and drowned. No convincing explanation of why he'd been driving alone in the Los Angeles hills while his co-stars celebrated, nor why he hadn't been at the wheel of his own beloved Bugatti, was ever advanced.

Three days later, the Bugatti too was involved in a fatal accident, and a hapless car thief called Joe Lugisi met an untimely end. The car's brakes were found to have been tampered with, Christine Romaine was charged with Lugisi's murder, but before the courtroom drama could be played out, Romaine was also found dead, victim of the classic Hollywood suicide, empty pill bottle protruding from the pocket of her satin bathrobe.

Did Christine mean to kill her husband? Or did someone else want Will Sutton dead? Christine seemed to think so, and pointed the finger at Saul Bernstein, who stood to collect two million dollars on Sutton's death.

'The truth may never be known,' Toby Truman reflects. 'But I couldn't believe Christine would try to murder anyone. She was crazy. She was a drunk. But she was a great girl, and she sure as hell wasn't a killer.

'David knew all this,' Mr Truman adds. 'He went a little crazy himself after Will died. He vowed he'd get to the bottom of it . . .'

Alas, it was not to be. When the Nazis shot David Klein in Paris, they effectively ensured that the mystery of Will Sutton's death would never be solved.

Against the Tide: A Biography of David Klein, by Jon Makepeace

---

Toby rose to the challenge, as Eva had always believed he would. He sobered up, cut his hair, pressed his suit, and left for Worldwide Pictures, declaring he could write as good a script as the next guy.

He wasn't so sure when he got back.

'Hell, Eva, I don't know. Klein wants an anti-war picture, but no war scenes. No trenches, no shells, no ambulances, none of that stuff. It's all got to happen between Casey and the women . . . I can't see it. Really I can't.'

'I can,' Eva said.

They wrote it between them in less than two weeks, typing far into the nights, keeping awake on coffee and bourbon, arguing and debating, throwing out and retrieving, reworking again and again.

Every morning Toby went to Worldwide with their latest scenes. Every morning he came back with more changes, more demands.

'He likes all your lines, and throws out most of mine. It's as though he knew . . . Do you think he knows, Eva?'

'No, I don't,' she consoled him. 'And anyway, what does it matter?'

Privately, she thought Davy probably did know, simply because he understood her ideas and was likely to recognise them. He was also, it seemed certain, familiar with Toby's earlier work for Kramer Brothers, and Toby had never produced anything as good as the script for *Casey's War*. So why had he been invited to do it, if not because Davy imagined that she would work on it too? The bones of the story were there, and needed only her vision to inspire it. In the end it proved easy, and it was a pity, Eva thought with an uncharacteristic flash of resentment, that she hadn't discovered this unexpected talent earlier.

But she was an actress, not a screenwriter, and when the script was done she would have to return to the set and play her part. At least it was a more enticing prospect now.

'Moira Sheen is off the picture,' Toby reported on his return from Worldwide one morning. 'Seems she never wanted to do it in the first place.'

'So who plays Sister Marie?' Eva asked anxiously, knowing the answer before he spoke.

'Carlotta du Bois, of course.'

Of course. Harriet had decided that she wanted the part, and now she had Saul Bernstein's interest, she'd seen how to get it.

Eva couldn't explain precisely why this development filled her with foreboding, but it did. Harriet had moved out of the chalet with Nicky and into a penthouse suite on the strength of her encounter with Saul Bernstein. Since then, Eva had seen her only once, a meeting which hadn't gone well. She had tried to issue a kindly caution, to suggest that as David Klein had already offered a contract, Harriet didn't really need Bernstein.

'That shows how much you know,' Harriet had replied rudely. 'Klein only does what Saul tells him. Why mess around with the tea-boy when you can go straight to the boss?'

'Are you sleeping with Saul Bernstein?' Eva had asked unhappily, only to be greeted with one of Harriet's unnerving screeches of laughter.

'Don't be ridiculous, Eva! Of course I'm sleeping with him. What else do you expect me to do?'

'Rely on your talent?' Eva had suggested. 'Preserve your integrity?'

This rather high-minded response had invoked a suitably down-to-earth retort.

'Balls,' said Harriet. 'What's integrity ever done for you?'

Eva was forced to consider that Harriet's contempt was not entirely undeserved, but she pressed on nevertheless.

'He's married,' she said flatly. 'Don't you care about that?'

Harriet had laughed again, rather more soberly this time.

'You don't understand how the world works, do you, Eva? You're married yourself, but you don't know the first thing about marriage. Does it occur to you that Ruth Bernstein might be glad to have her husband's needs taken care of?'

'No!' Eva had said, astonished. 'No, it doesn't!'

'So what do you think happens when a man doesn't get what he needs in his own bed?'

Eva looked away.

'All marriages have their difficulties,' she said stiffly, 'but if you care about your wife, you don't go off and sleep with somebody else . . .'

Now Harriet looked away.

'Open your eyes, Eva,' she said at last. 'You're half asleep. And one day you're going to wake up with a terrible fright . . .'

Eva had been unable to shake off the portentous nature of this warning, for Harriet had seemed in that moment genuinely regretful, as though she glimpsed a reversal of fortunes, or even a catastrophe, dipping on the horizon of what appeared, at least in contrast with former times, a hopeful and well ordered world.

And now, as Eva considered the news that Moira Sheen was no longer to play Sister Marie, she remembered Harriet's warning with a nagging, unspecified alarm.

'What's going on?' she asked Toby urgently. 'Why is Moira off the picture?'

'There's trouble at Worldwide,' Toby said slowly. 'Trouble between Klein and Bernstein, and trouble with Moira Sheen. Take my advice, Eva. Don't ask questions, and keep your head down. That means steering clear of Harriet. Okay?'

Steer clear of Harriet? Eva gazed at her husband unhappily, deeply perturbed, unable to challenge this view.

'One other thing,' Toby said. 'Klein doesn't like the ending of *Casey's War*. Says it's too sentimental. Wants it rewritten.'

'No!' she cried, convinced this would be utterly wrong. 'Tell him the ending stays. Tell him from me!'

In the weeks that followed, even if she'd so wanted, Eva found it impossible to steer clear of Harriet.

Shooting began with the new script, and Harriet made it her business to visit the set each day, even when she wasn't filming.

No longer an onlooker, Miss Carlotta du Bois quickly took to centre stage, dominating *Casey's War* with the ease born of privilege, confident that whatever she said or did, no one would dare complain about Saul Bernstein's favourite.

Except, of course, David Klein. He alone made his feelings clear. Off the set he treated Harriet with icy disdain, and during filming he demanded endless re-takes, insisting that her intonation was wrong, that she had misunderstood a key line, that her expression in Sister Marie's prayer scene was 'more like a donkey in pain than a nun in holy rapture'.

'What the hell do you know about nuns?' Carlotta du Bois had screamed.

'Rather more than you, I suspect,' he had replied.

'I hate him,' Harriet told Eva, 'and I tell you this . . . He won't be around Worldwide much longer.'

He was equally demanding of Eva, but her he treated with patience and respect. Do it this way, Eva. Lift your chin. Stretch your neck. No, not like that. Like this . . .

'What do you know about harlots?' she had asked him cheekily in a rare moment when they found themselves alone.

'Nothing,' he said drily, meeting her eye, 'beyond what I observe in your little friend Miss du Bois . . .'

Eva wondered constantly about his feelings towards Moira Sheen and Rhoda, but there was never a chance to observe or weigh up, for neither was seen anywhere near the *Casey* set.

'Vic's getting jumpy,' Will Sutton told her with a confident little smile. 'He wants to keep Rhoda where he can see her. Well, wouldn't we all?'

Eva would not be drawn into any discussion of Victor, but Will now seemed so perky, so unlike the disappointed man who'd taken a drink when his beloved failed to show up on the set, that she began to think he must have been encouraged. What this meant for Victor Eva hardly liked to imagine, but if nothing else it surely meant that she had misunderstood Davy the night she'd gone to find him, the night he'd told her he was waiting for Rhoda.

This hope was rudely shattered one dark and windy evening when Eva sat alone in the chalet after filming, idly flipping through magazines and reflecting dismally on the lonely life of a movie star. She missed Nicky greatly, and it seemed Toby was never home these days. He'd bought his own car with his earnings from *Casey*, and now the yellow Chevrolet stood in the driveway awaiting her pleasure. But Eva had nowhere to go, and no one to go with.

There suddenly came a frenzied knocking and a voice she recognised as Christine Romaine's.

'Open the goddam door, Eva! I need your help.'

Christine was inappropriately clad in a blue sequined two-piece with a little feathered hat obliquely perched upon the unruly ginger curls, and she was clearly very drunk.

'It's Will, Eva. He got into a brawl at some downtown bar and the cops took him in. They're charging him with disorderly conduct . . . I gotta bail him out, but I'm too smashed to drive.'

Eva reached for her jacket and steered Christine towards the Chevvy.

'He was off the booze, Eva. Really he was. We both were . . .'

'What happened?' Eva asked, manoeuvring her into the passenger seat, half expecting a rambling diatribe concerning the Lady of Shalott.

Christine lit a cigarette, and Eva saw that her fingers were trembling.

'What do you know about Saul Bernstein, Eva? Who he's in with? What he's mixed up in?'

Eva shuddered in the damp night air and clicked on the car engine.

'I don't know anything about Saul Bernstein,' she muttered. Christine laughed shrilly.

'Well, you'll soon know plenty. You and everyone else. I've got evidence, Eva. Dates and times and witnesses. Shady deals, Mob money, even a murder . . . You'll see.'

Eva was unnerved, but she kept calm, driving steadily through the gusty night, eyes streaming in the acrid smoky air. She opened the driver's window, and closed it hurriedly when Christine yelped a protest.

'No one must see me,' she hissed.

'Okay,' Eva said gently. 'Try to relax. It won't take us long to get there . . .'

But as they drove through the canyon, past the great baroque mansions and the ornate brooding castles, Christine changed her mind.

'Take me to David's place,' she said suddenly. 'He'll know what to do. He'll get Will . . .'

Eva was deeply relieved. She had not relished the prospect of controlling a drunken Christine before the downtown cops, nor loading an equally drunken Will into the back of the Chevvy. She swung her car towards the Klein hacienda, wondering who she would find there. Not Rebecca Bernstein, she guessed. Rebecca hadn't been seen at Worldwide since the new version of *Casey* got under way. And not Moira Sheen, either. The more she thought about Moira with Davy, the more unlikely it seemed. Perhaps he would be alone, or dining with Victor and Rhoda.

The maid with the milky cocoa skin let them in, and then she was standing in the hall where she'd waited for her glass of champagne only a few short weeks ago, the night of the party. It seemed another lifetime, when she'd worked at Marco's and lived in the crumbling apartment block in front of the eucalyptus grove. And suddenly, in a flash of unhappy intuition, she saw just how much had changed since that night. The material reality of her life with Toby had become the promised land, but in that shadowy, interior terrain of emotions, beliefs and doubts, there had been a volcanic eruption. The map had been redrawn. Since the night of the party, she had lost her husband.

'Christine! What is it? What's happened?'

Davy was standing beside them, and Christine stumbled into his arms, weeping and pressing the wild ginger curls, still topped by the absurd feathered hat, against his chest. He glanced swiftly at Eva, inviting her to explain.

'Well, it's not the first time Will threw a punch,' he said quietly when she'd finished, his arms tightening around Christine. 'We'll go bail him out right away.'

If Eva had wondered why he kept them standing in the hall, why they were not taken into the salon nor invited to sit down, she got her answer when the door to the hallway suddenly swung open to reveal a vision Eva could only describe to herself as the Lady of Shalott. For a moment they all stared at each other while Rhoda stood utterly still, framed in the doorway, a picture of unblemished beauty in a crimson taffeta frock, the shining chestnut hair falling to her waist, the wide brown eyes curious and alert.

'It's all right,' Davy said quickly, ushering her back into the salon, 'I won't be long . . .'

He glanced awkwardly at Eva.

'I'll take Christine to the station. Can you get home okay?'

'Of course,' she said politely, trying to quell her rising dismay.

Outside in the Chevvy she waited until he left with Christine, watching while he handed her gently into his car, his arm still tight around her shoulders. She hadn't realised until this moment how much he cared for Will, nor indeed for the overblown, garrulous Christine, and now his concern for these two registered as a deep deprivation in her own life. She wished that if he mightn't want her as he once had, well then, that she might be the recipient of the same tenderness he felt for Christine. She wished for his arm around her shoulders. She wished for his reassurance in her ear.

Perhaps it was this that made her get out of the Chevvy and walk back into the house, although afterwards, when she thought it over, she could scarcely imagine what had possessed her, what rogue emotion had propelled her to reveal her feelings in such a manner. Perhaps, she told herself later, it was the realisation that Rhoda, for all her startling beauty and her poise, could not possibly be good enough for David Klein.

The maid let her in again.

'Mister Victor? Is he here?'

'No, ma'am. Just Missus Rhoda.'

It was exactly as she'd thought. She walked swiftly to the salon door and threw it open.

The french windows at the far end were ajar, and she could see Rhoda sitting at a dinner table on the balcony beyond. As she approached, she saw that the table was set for two. On the fine lace cloth sat a silver ice bucket, a display of pink rosebuds and a gilt candelabra. The candles were burning, and gave off a faint scent of lavender.

She walked smartly up to the french windows, her heels making no sound upon the thick cream carpet. Rhoda seemed to be dreaming, stroking the long golden stems of the candelabra, gazing out upon the lush purple bougainvillaea in the gardens beyond. Eva, not pausing for a moment to question her assumptions, stepped out on to the balcony.

'What do you think you're doing?' she demanded hotly. 'Where is Victor? Why aren't you with him tonight? What is all this?'

She gestured at the roses and the glowing candles while Rhoda, seeming barely surprised by this dramatic intrusion, stared back in mute unconcern.

'I must tell you, Rhoda, that I find your behaviour extraordinary,' Eva pursued, 'and I can only think that Victor doesn't know what's going on . . . If he did, he would surely take you back to Paris at once.'

She had no idea what response she might provoke – a haughty dismissal, an outburst, perhaps, or a flood of angry tears. Whatever, she could not have foreseen Rhoda's calm reply.

'I'm never going back to Paris,' she said serenely, tilting her lovely face so that a heavy strand of the chocolate-coloured hair fell across her cheek. 'My marriage to Victor is over. And one day I'm going to marry David.'

'No,' Eva whispered, and her instinctive denial hung on the air between them, naked and absurd.

'Yes,' Rhoda said softly. 'Wait and see . . .'

It didn't occur to Eva to question this confidence, nor to ask when the announcement might be made, for such was Rhoda's self-possession that her own grasp of events melted before it.

'What about Victor?' she asked desperately. 'Don't you care for him at all?'

Rhoda smiled and plucked a wilting rose petal from the table display.

'Of course,' she said. 'Victor is my friend.'

Eva gazed at her dumbly, unable to form a single sensible remark. She could think only that if Davy married Rhoda he would be lost to her for ever; lost, not simply as a lover which he surely was already, but lost as a confidant and a friend, roles she had fondly begun to imagine he might fulfil. She felt her eyes cloud with shaming tears.

'Poor Victor,' she whispered, hating the lie as she spoke, for the tears, she knew, were for herself.

'Yes, poor Victor,' said Rhoda meditatively, 'and poor Will Sutton too . . . It's a great shame, isn't it, Eva, that a woman can only marry one man at a time?'

Then she turned the wide almond eyes upon Eva, and Eva knew that she understood, and that in her understanding felt no sympathy nor pity, only triumph.

'I think you should go home now, Eva,' she said with an odd little laugh, throwing back the extraordinary hair. 'Go home to Toby. I'm sure you'll find him waiting for you . . . Just like a good husband should . . .'

After that, events seem to speed, like the jerky, mechanised moves of actors in a silent picture, and looking back, Eva found she could scarcely remember the content of conversations, nor the sequence of incidents.

There were costume fittings, make-overs, publicity shots and press calls. There were cuts and re-takes and arguments and debates. There was an interview with a cheeky gossip writer who asked outright if Will Sutton had fallen for Miss Delamere, or for Miss du Bois. There was speculation, rumour and back-biting. And between Eva and David Klein there was nothing but the most proper, the most professional of relationships.

She learned nothing of the intrigues at Worldwide, for Harriet had become tight-lipped, Rebecca Bernstein had disappeared, and Davy offered no confidences, no hint of anything that might be seen as intimate.

Then Rebecca made a rare appearance on the *Casey* set and took Davy aside. Eva watched them through the glass screen to his office, talking urgently, Rebecca pacing the room while he sat on the edge of his desk, shoulders hunched. But what was said, what was decided, Eva had no idea.

One morning, Saul Bernstein came to watch the shoot, exchanging not a single word with Davy; and when the meal break came he whisked Harriet away in his limo for lunch. As they left, Eva caught his eye, and matched his critical appraisal with her own. She did not like Saul Bernstein, and didn't care whether or not he liked her.

Later that day, Harriet took her to task.

'You ought to be polite to Saul,' she said coolly. 'If not out of courtesy, then out of simple self-interest.'

It was a welcome diversion when Will Sutton asked her to take him driving in the Chevvy, to teach him how to handle a car. Christine called up and begged Eva not to do it, but Christine was drunk and incoherent, and Will prevailed. After all, Eva told herself, she had nothing else to do when she left the lot, and teaching Will to drive would be an achievement. Christine would surely thank her in the end . . .

So each day, when the shoot was over, they drove out of the city and Will took the wheel. But Eva soon abandoned her lofty hopes.

'You're a terrible driver,' she told him unsympathetically after one particularly bone-shaking afternoon. 'Why don't you just give up? You could have somebody drive you around.'

'Nope. Don't ask me why, Eva, but I gotta learn to drive real good . . .'

Eva didn't know whether Will's ambition had anything to do with impressing Rhoda, and she had no intention of asking. Now she could not bear to hear Rhoda's name, nor think for a moment what might happen next. She'd avoided Victor since the night of Rhoda's revelation, no difficult feat since he was so often away, and seeing that Davy meant to offer no insight into his feelings, had begun on the unwelcome task of distancing herself from him. Now she would not meet his eye with a smile, nor look for the moments when they might be alone.

She also found herself increasingly distanced from Harriet, but this was not of her choosing. Harriet no longer offered any confidences, nor even opinions, and Eva saw only too clearly how this had happened. Although no one openly mentioned the tensions between Saul Bernstein and David Klein, everyone at Worldwide was perceived to be in one camp or the other. She, Eva, was for Klein. And Harriet was for Bernstein.

Once she asked Harriet if she might visit Nicky, and received a stony reply.

'Nicky has a wonderful nanny. He doesn't need anyone else.'

Eva didn't mention her own needs, nor suggest that a nanny, however wonderful, was no substitute for loving relatives. She saw that despite her best intentions, she'd been too quick to condemn Harriet, too ready to impose her own standards. Too late she saw that she had lost her last link with the Brannen family.

Indeed, when she cared to dwell upon it, she realised that she had lost virtually everyone who'd ever mattered to her. She had lost Davy, and Harriet and Nicky and Anya. And she had certainly lost Toby, though she clung to the desperate hope of all who see love fade before their eyes, the belief that by refusing to name or acknowledge the demon, it will somehow lose its power.

And so the days slipped by.

'What happens when *Casey* is over?' she asked Toby on a rare evening when she found him home.

'You tell me, honey,' he said carelessly, avoiding her eye. 'What do you want to happen?'

Eva didn't know. She wished Toby would stop fixing his ham and eggs and listen to her. But Toby didn't listen any more, and he didn't seem to have much to say for himself either.

'We can't stay in this house unless one of us gets another job,' she told him brusquely. 'Neither of us is contracted to do anything else at Worldwide.'

'That's true,' he agreed, sliding his eggs on to the plate.

'So what will we do?' she demanded testily, angry at his refusal to meet her fears and soothe them.

Now he looked up from his supper.

'I don't know what you'll do, Eva,' he said steadily, 'but speaking personally, I'm ready to quit.'

She stared at him, frightened by this reply, anxious not to probe it any further.

'But we worked so well on the script,' she objected. 'We could do that again. We could approach Davy with another idea . . .'

Toby pushed his plate away and got up from the table.

'Don't rely on David Klein for any more favours,' he said curtly. 'I don't think he'll be around Worldwide much longer.'

'But he's one of the best picture-makers,' she said, bewildered. 'Why would Bernstein let him go?'

'Because he's too clean, that's why. He won't go along with Bernstein's deals and schemes. David Klein doesn't know when he's well off, and he's about to pay the price . . .'

Toby glanced at his watch. 'I've got to go,' he said.

'Where?' she demanded suddenly, tired of the polite evasions and the loaded pauses. 'Where have you got to go? Why can't you stay here with me?'

He shrugged.

'I'm sorry, Eva,' he said quietly, 'I've just got to go . . .'

He was gone in a moment, leaving her alone once more.

And after that it seemed to Eva that the fast-action movie sped ever more rapidly to its unhappy finale, that there was nothing but the quick-fire succession of inexorable actions and unstoppable reflexes, too fleeting to catch, too cloaked to examine, too devious to question.

There was nothing, indeed, but the certain march towards death.

The night of the première fell hot and dark, the stars above the canyon dimmed by a thin purple veil of dust, the moon a misty half-globe, strung like an ineffective street-lamp in the black.

Eva dressed for the performance with heavy heart, fortified by two unusually stiff Martinis, knowing that whatever the public perception of *Casey's War*, her days at Worldwide were numbered.

Saul Bernstein didn't like her, that much seemed certain, and Davy hadn't been seen on the lot since the final cut. There were tales of midnight showdowns and rumours of studio defections. There were stories about Carlotta du Bois, her antipathy to David Klein and her friendship with Saul Bernstein, and there was much unkind gossip about Will and Christine. A fermenting brew of disaffection, treachery and spite seemed ready for the drinking, and there was no knowing who might take the first sip.

She had chosen an ivory satin gown trimmed with ostrich feathers at the bosom, its skirt slashed to the knee. Her silvery hair was piled high upon her head, making her resemble, she now considered, a rather sickly sugar cake. Her eyes were shadowed cornflower blue, her lips were painted a startling shade of plum, and she teetered on a pair of high-heeled gold sandals.

She stared at herself critically in her bedroom mirror. She felt giddy, and just a little sick. And the ivory dress was cut lower than she might have wished. Although the feathers covered most of her breasts, above them stretched a vast expanse of shoulderblade and neck. Indeed, she looked half dressed. She needed sapphires or pearls.

But she had no such thing. She arched her neck, turning this way and that to catch her reflection in the mirror. What did she have that she might wear?

A hesitant knock at her bedroom door interrupted these deliberations.

'Honey, you look amazing,' Toby said uncertainly, moving to stand behind her so that for a moment they comprised a striking tableau in the mirror: the beautiful movie star and her admiring husband. He fingered his bow-tie nervously and stepped back.

'I need something at my neck,' she complained, and as she spoke, knew at once what she should wear.

Her filigree cross, the Brannen cross, which she'd removed for fear of losing it to an eagle-eyed hobo as she left Marco's late at night, now lay in a little brown envelope concealed at the back of her dressing-table drawer. She opened the drawer and reached for it, relishing the vision of its delicate simplicity against her fine and fancy clothes.

'Hey, honey, I almost forgot,' Toby interjected suddenly, fumbling in the pocket of his evening jacket, 'I bought you this to wear tonight . . .'

He was handing her a black velvet pouch, urging her to open it, while she scrabbled frantically in her drawer.

'Here, I'll fasten it for you,' he said, extracting a glittering chain from the velvet pouch. At the end of the chain hung a single diamond suspended in a shell of gold.

'My cross,' she said desperately, 'I can't find my cross . . .'

Toby hung the diamond around her neck, his fingers fumbling clumsily against her skin.

'That looks good,' he said.

'Where is it?' she cried, turning to him. 'Where's my cross?' He sat down suddenly on her bed, extracting his cigarette case from his jacket, looking urgently round the room for a lighter.

'There's no easy way to tell you this,' he said brusquely, chewing nervously at his unlit cigarette, 'so I'll come right out with it. I pawned the cross. It was the only thing we'd got worth more than a couple of bucks . . . And I needed the dough for the rent on this place . . .'

She stared at him, appalled.

'But you redeemed it?' she whispered. 'You got it back?'

'I meant to, Eva, really I did. But I was late with the money, and they sold it. Made a heck of a profit on it too, I found out . . .'

He shook his head sadly and stood up from the bed.

'I'm sorry,' he said.

'Sorry!'

She spat the apology back in his face with a venom that startled them both, ripping his diamond from her neck and throwing it on the bedroom floor at his feet. Then she began to cry, not the gentle, crystalline tears befitting a movie star in full dress, but great racking sobs that started in her stomach and ended in her throat, threatening to bring her Martinis with them.

'For heaven's sake, Eva,' he said, alarmed. 'Don't take on so . . . I

know the cross belonged to your father, but it's not a tragedy, is it?
Nobody's dead . . .'

Still she sobbed, uncontrolled, inconsolable, as though the joy of all
the known world had vanished to be replaced by unmitigated despair.
The cornflower blue shadow rained down her cheeks and the plum
lipstick smeared across her chin.

'You're ruining your face,' he said desperately. 'Will and Christine
will be here any time. Eva! Listen to me! We have to go . . .'

She stood up and tore at the ivory satin, pulling at the zip until it
gave way between her fingers, and then as the dress fell to her feet,
kicking it across the floor. She faced him in her underwear. 'I'm not
going anywhere!' she screamed.

'You're crazy,' he shouted, his even temper suddenly gone. 'And if
you want the truth, you always were. You've blown all the chances you
ever had, Eva. And now you're lousing this up, just the same way.'

'What chances?' she shrieked, turning back to the mirror and clawing
at the ludicrous confection of hair. 'Tell me what chances!'

'You could have done a picture before now,' he yelled back, opening
the bedroom door. 'If you'd cared enough, you could have done it. You
could have called in David Klein's debt long before now.'

He slammed the door behind him, and Eva fell on to the bed, beating
the pillow with her fists as though it might be her husband's
head, flailing her legs in the air until the fury left her and she at last
lay still.

Only then did she consider that her outburst was hardly about the
filigree cross at all, that although its loss grieved her greatly, her anger
and her disappointment were directed at Toby himself, Toby and the
tottering façade that fronted her empty marriage like some grand movie
set with no substance, no weight, behind it.

She had no idea how long she'd lain there when, finally, there came
another cautious knocking at the bedroom door. It opened slowly and
she sat up, ready to apologise. But the face that peered nervously in did
not belong to Toby.

'Hi, sweetheart,' said Will gently. 'How you doing? You should know
that your public awaits you.'

He smiled, and despite herself, Eva smiled back. Then he took her
hand and lifted her purposefully from the bed.

'We gotta get you ready,' he whispered.

'I'll never be ready,' she said tearfully.

'Oh yes, you will,' he said. 'This is your night, Eva, and you're not
gonna miss it . . .'

'Toby,' she said tremulously, rubbing at her stained face. 'Where is
he?'

'He's escorting Christine,' Will said kindly. 'There's no one else to worry about, Eva. Just you and me . . .'

And afterwards, when she thought about Will Sutton and the night *Casey's War* was premièred, it was always the little things that she remembered . . . The way he combed out the tangles in her hair until it lay smooth and shining across her shoulders once more . . . The way he gathered up her dress from the floor and mended the zip with a tiny silver pin . . . The way he watched while she washed and repainted her face, advising her gravely about her colours and holding the lamp close to her cheek so that she might judge for herself . . . The way he bore her out on his arm and into the waiting limo as though she were a queen, worthy only of the greatest reverence and respect.

'I need something at my neck,' she said fretfully.

'No, you don't. You have beautiful shoulders. You're a sensation.'

She swept down the boulevard past Marco's diner in a daze, immured against further pain, and even against pleasure.

'We're going to be very late,' she said to him, not really caring whether they were or they weren't.

He laughed and raised her fingers to his lips.

'We're the stars, Eva,' he said. 'No one's gonna start without us.'

She saw it all through a glittering fog of disbelief . . . The massed smiles on the faces in the crowd . . . The scarlet carpet that engulfed her gold sandals . . . The salute of a uniformed footman . . . The deferential curtsy of the flower girl . . .

And then, embalmed for ever in her memory, came the moment when the curtain rose and she saw herself upon the screen, the movie star, the French-born actress Eva Delamere, lisping her way through the lines she had written herself.

'You're a genius, Eva,' Will whispered in her ear, and just for that moment, she imagined she was.

The illusion lasted until the curtain fell, until the applause faded and the bouquets heaped into her arms began to sweat, until the pop of photographers' bulbs flashed into silence, and the eager reporters pressing for her words went off with their notebooks . . . It lasted until, outside in the hot dark night, stepping into the limo once more, she caught sight of her reflection in the plate-glass window of the theatre foyer, and glimpsed a stranger, a pretender to herself, someone mimicking her manners, her actions, her speech, a painted impostor. And she saw then, saw in a blessed, freeing flash of self-knowledge, that her moment of fame was over. It was over because she would not pay the price.

Later, at the celebration party in Gracie's restaurant, she was aware of Davy grasping her hand.

'Congratulations, Eva,' he smiled.

And she registered Harriet's triumph, her jubilant generosity, as she threw an arm round Eva's waist and pulled her close. 'You made it, Eva!' she declared. 'You're on your way up!'

Then in the next moment, as though the devil himself had suddenly wagged a finger to underline the true direction she'd be taking, Eva found herself facing Toby across a table laden with lobster and salad potatoes.

'I'm not coming home, Eva,' he said. 'From tonight, you're on your own.'

'You've found someone else,' she heard herself say, and as she spoke, wondered why on earth this self-evident fact had never been voiced before. 'Who is she?'

'Nobody you know,' he replied, looking away. 'She's just an ordinary American girl. I'm going to marry her, Eva. I want a divorce . . .'

She felt the muscles of her stomach contract, the bile rise in her throat, but she had no time to plead, nor even to protest, for in the next instant Rebecca Bernstein was beside her, leading her away through the ranks of glittering guests, the starlets, the publicists and the writers, their lovers, their sisters, their long-lost cousins and their best friends . . . Everyone, it seemed, was there. And yet there was one beautiful face conspicuously absent.

'Where's Rhoda?' Eva asked Victor after the speeches. 'Why isn't she here?'

'One of her headaches,' he replied cheerfully. 'She's back at Davy's place. In bed.'

It took a while for Eva to register that Will was also missing. He had been at her side throughout the performance. He had taken her arm as they left the theatre. He had handed her into the limo and winked at her broadly.

'I'll make my own way,' he'd said. 'I'll borrow the Chevvy if that's okay . . .'

'Where's your handsome husband?' Eva asked Christine nervously at one point during that giddy, gaudy evening, to receive only a curse in reply, to watch Will's wife turn away towards Toby, and to see, with a sickening shock of understanding, that her own marital misdemeanours, her blithe unknowingness, her withdrawal from her husband's bed, the bitter row about the Brannen cross, had all been related to Christine, related and judged.

In the ladies' room mirror, Eva stared at the gaunt face rising above the ostrich feathers, and allowed herself to mourn.

'Oh, Toby,' she wept, 'I'm sorry . . . So sorry . . .'

And then, because movie stars don't cry in ladies' rooms, she dried her tears, repainted her face and went back to the party where, in a fleeting tableau among the moving revellers in their shimmering jackets and gowns, she glimpsed David taking Moira Sheen's hand to press it gently to his lips . . .

Now she could only look for her escape, and at last, when she'd drunk far more champagne than was sensible, when her head seemed set to float free from her shoulders, when she'd smiled until her face ached and, watching Toby kiss Christine goodbye before he left, had felt the tears begin again, she slipped away, Cinderella in her limo, waiting for the spell to end.

So it was that Eva never saw Will Sutton again, and knew nothing of his tragic fate until woken at dawn, alone and heavy-eyed, by the persistent ringing of her telephone.

'Dear God, no! It can't be true!'

'Oh, it's true all right, Eva. He sailed over the ravine like a bird in full flight. The Chevvy burst into flames, but he was thrown clear. The poor bastard was knocked out and drowned in a stream . . . The water was only six inches deep! How unlucky can you get?'

Eva, stunned, stared into the phone, unable to take it in.

'What a hoo-ha at the party when the cops turned up! Christine was screaming, Moira Sheen fainted, and your friend David Klein looked like he was having a heart attack . . . The big question, of course, is what Will was doing up in the hills . . . why he wasn't at the party. Maybe you know, Eva? The cops are going to ask. It was your car, after all . . .'

Eva was trembling, the walls of the chalet seeming to fall in upon her, a thick, sick lump in her chest threatening to rise and choke her.

'I don't know,' she whispered tearfully, 'I've no idea . . .'

'Well, he wasn't meeting the lovely Rhoda,' Harriet pronounced. 'She really was in bed with a headache! Though I wouldn't mind betting she was hoping for a much more interesting companion when the party ended . . . And I don't mean her husband!'

Eva was suddenly affronted by Harriet's flippant tone. Determined that such an appalling accident should command sorrow and respect, she snapped out a reprimand.

'Oh, for heaven's sake, Eva! I was fond of Will, but the man's dead. What does it matter what happens now? Look on the bright side, that's what I say . . . His life was insured for two million dollars. Worldwide's financial problems have been solved overnight!'

Eva slammed down the phone, horrified. How could Harriet say such a thing? Poor Will! Poor Christine . . .

She paced around the chalet, unable to think clearly. She knew she ought to visit Christine, but she retained a harrowing memory of estrangement, of Christine's disdainful stare when she'd spoken to her at the party. Would her condolences be wanted?

Then she saw that this was irrelevant. She had to offer her sympathy, regardless of the response it might meet. She reached for her jacket, thinking in her distraction that she could simply walk across the road to the Sutton château.

The reporters swooped the moment she opened her door.

'When did you last see Will Sutton, Miss Delamere?'

'Why was he driving your car?'

'Where was he going, Miss Delamere? Was he meeting someone in the hills?'

Eva, head down, said nothing, pushing her way through the forest of notebooks and pencils until at last she stood outside the château's ostentatious portico, pulling on the bellrope with more confidence than she felt, wondering who had been summoned to console Christine, knowing it had to be David.

To her discomfort, the door was opened by Toby.

'Ah, Eva . . .'

He looked at her awkwardly, no longer her husband, no longer her protector or friend, as strange to her in that moment as he had once seemed, long, long ago on a railway station in Paris.

'Is there anything I can do?' she asked, the polite, inconsequential offering of the outsider.

'Christine's upstairs,' he replied, beckoning her inside with an odd, unsettling authority. 'Klein is with her. The doctor has given her some pills.'

Eva lingered uneasily in the hallway, asking questions in a strained, halting staccato that seemed a semitone higher than her normal voice, ashamed of the need she felt to turn the conversation away from Will's tragedy to her own woes.

'He took the bend too fast,' Toby was saying. 'You know what a lousy driver he was . . .'

'But what was he doing up there? Where was he going?'

Toby shrugged. 'You know Will,' he said, looking away. 'I guess he was meeting a woman. Could be any one of a dozen.'

'I should never have lent him the Chevvy,' Eva quavered, but Toby shook his head.

'It wasn't anyone's fault.'

He hesitated.

'Christine's got it into her head that Saul Bernstein killed Will. And Klein is so cut up, I think he half believes it . . . It all sounds crazy to me. Okay, Will's life was insured. But all the studios insure their big stars. That doesn't mean they go round bumping them off to collect the dough.'

She stared at him, astonished that such a suggestion should find expression, thinking Christine must be truly deranged in her grief to imagine a murder, then remembering with an icy shock of suspicion the night Will had been arrested, the night Christine had begun to talk about Saul Bernstein . . .

'I'll call you,' Toby said, opening the door to let her out, 'I'll let you know what's going down.'

'When's the funeral?' she asked him unhappily.

'It's private. Christine doesn't want anyone there except family and close friends.'

Eva bit her lip. Hadn't she been a close friend? She looked up at her husband, tears burning behind her eyelids, a little pulse in her temple beginning to throb. Did he have no pity for her? Did he mean never to see her again, nor even to discuss their parting?

'Can't I put things right between us?' she whispered miserably. 'Is there no chance?'

He looked away.

'There was never any chance,' he said brutally. 'All our chances ended the day you left Paris with David Klein. I only wish I'd seen it at the time.'

The fast-action movie went into overdrive.

'Are you sitting down, Eva?'

Harriet's voice on the phone was brittle, excited, almost hysterical.

'Thank God I got you,' she said, 'I wanted to tell you before anyone else did. Now, Eva, you must stay put. Don't answer the phone, don't even go out until you've worked out what you'll say to the reporters . . .'

Eva, who'd spent three days utterly alone except for an uninformative visit from the Los Angeles police department, was absurdly pleased to hear from Harriet, no matter what fresh news she had to impart, but her effusive greeting was quickly cut short.

'Shut up, and listen to me! Christine has been charged with murder! She cut the brakes on Will's Bugatti, and some dumb fool went and stole it. He was killed outright!'

'Who?' Eva asked, bewildered. 'Who stole it?'

'Who? What the hell does that matter? Some bum called Joe Lugisi . . . Do you hear what I'm saying, Eva? You know what this means, don't you? Christine wanted to get rid of Will!'

Harriet could hardly form the words, and Eva, trying to make sense of it, could hardly believe what was being said. It was fantastic, incredible, unreal.

'If Christine wanted rid of Will,' Eva blurted out, 'she wouldn't touch the Bugatti. She knew he never drove it . . .'

Harriet seemed not to have considered this, and for a moment the line fell silent.

'Well, I don't know, Eva. That's what the cops are saying. Saul put up the bail, and they're letting her stay in the house till the preliminary hearing next week. But, she won't get away with it. Too much evidence against her . . .'

Eva stood up and walked to the window, staring out beyond the gaggle of reporters at her gate across to the Suttons' brooding château, her mind whirling, struggling to take it in.

'Christine loved Will,' she faltered, 'I know she did . . . Why would she want to kill him?'

'She thought he was cheating with Rhoda,' Harriet said flatly. 'It's the only explanation . . . The ridiculous thing is that Rhoda wasn't cheating at all. At least, not with Will. She didn't want him! She wanted David Klein.'

'Yes,' Eva said dully. 'I know.'

'A perfectly suited couple, if you ask me,' Harriet declared vehemently. 'I hope they'll be very happy together . . . You know, I suppose, that Rhoda has gone back to Paris?'

'No,' Eva whispered, 'I didn't know . . .'

'Oh yes. Victor got a telegram to say his mother's very ill. They left right after the accident. That was lucky, wasn't it? Rhoda's been spared any tricky questions about Will and the way she led him on . . . Now David Klein has left for Paris too! Gone to do battle with Victor for the lovely Lady of Shalott . . .'

Harriet let out a vicious chuckle.

'Rhoda and David – Beauty and the Beast. Let's hope they never show their faces in this town again!'

Faster, faster, reeling, spinning, turning, jerking, faster, faster . . .

Imprisoned in the chalet with her sorrows and regrets, wondering what on earth she might do next, where she should go, unwilling to brave the reporters and dodge the photographers, Eva heard the news of Christine's death over the wireless.

This time Harriet failed to call, and Toby, who'd either forgotten his promise to keep her informed or wilfully ignored it, didn't so much as send word to check on her welfare. Instead, he sent divorce papers for her to sign.

She wept for Christine, unwilling to believe she could plot a murder and then kill herself, yet unable to devise any other explanation.

She began to feel reason slipping away, as though the city of dreams had pitched her into a nightmare, departing from the script and rewriting the ending: misery, death, desertion, instead of romance.

Then the fast-action movie spooled to a halt, and the days began to jumble into one long, lonely stretch of time without form or foreseeable end. There were plenty of calls: from the publicity people at Worldwide, from the Bernsteins' minders and fixers, from the police, who, just as before, seemed to ask no pertinent questions at all . . . But there wasn't a single call from anyone who mattered.

She wondered constantly about David, imagining him walking along the banks of the Seine with Rhoda, and she longed for some word from Toby, if only a fond goodbye. There was nothing. Even Harriet seemed to have given her up.

Finally, when she thought she might never receive another visitor, the Worldwide security guard at her gate called to announce an arrival. Was Miss Delamere at home to a servant of Mr Klein's?

Eva opened the door of the chalet, and fell with unreserved delight upon this welcome emissary, the maid from the hacienda with the milky cocoa skin.

It was several moments before she realised that the woman hadn't been sent by David at all.

'Mister Victor asked me to come, ma'am . . . They went off in such a hurry, he didn't have time to call you up. He left a little gift from his mama in Paris. Says he forgot to give it you himself . . .'

The maid was handing Eva a tiny package wrapped in scarlet foil, and Eva, fighting foolish tears of disappointment, remembering Madame Martineau and the day she escaped from the Divine Faith convent, could only turn it over and over between her fingers, unable to open the gift for the emotion it might call forth.

'Mister David,' she asked the maid at last. 'Have you heard from him?'

'He's in Paris, ma'am . . . He went after Missus Rhoda and Mister Victor. We don't know when he's coming back.'

Eva hesitated, wondering what more she dare risk.

'Did the police speak to you? About Missus Rhoda?' she ventured at last.

This was the question Eva wanted answered, for in her own interviews with the Los Angeles police department, there had been no mention of Rhoda, no interrogation concerning Will Sutton's obsession with Mr Klein's beautiful house guest. And she, not knowing what to say, had said nothing, seeing that in the matter of Rhoda and Will, or indeed of Rhoda and David, she knew nothing. Nothing at all . . .

The maid clenched her fingers in her lap.

'They asked where everyone was, ma'am . . . The night Mister Will died. I told 'em Missus Rhoda was home in bed with a terrible headache . . . And she was, ma'am. I took her some hot milk myself.'

Eva summoned her courage for one final assault on the truth.

'Missus Rhoda – she once told me she didn't love Mister Victor any more. She said she was going to marry Mister David some day.'

The maid looked away, embarrassed, and Eva, deeply ashamed of this unorthodox enquiry into David's private affairs, mumbled out a tearful apology.

The maid stood up.

'It's right, ma'am,' she said reluctantly. 'Missus Rhoda, she wanted Mister David real bad . . . And when Missus Rhoda makes up her mind, I guess things usually work out that way.'

For a moment they stared at each other in mutual resignation, neither speaking nor moving to suggest anything more. Then the maid was gone, and Eva was left alone with a heaviness of heart that seemed set to sink her spirits for ever.

It was later that evening when she finally unwrapped the foil package, and froze in disbelief at what she saw. Inside was a tiny silk handkerchief, edged with French lace and decorated with daisy chains. In the corner was embroidered a single word: *Eva*.

Suddenly she was taken back to St Cuthbert's, to the great glittering spire of the church and the graveyard at the edge of the sea, to the gloomy vicarage parlour on the morning of Matthew Brannen's funeral, to the day she'd cleared his desk and found a tiny silk handkerchief, just like this one, concealed in a bottom drawer . . .

Her breath came quickly, and she thought she would surely faint. She seemed to see the glittering emerald horizon beyond the ruined tower on St Cuthbert's isle . . . to hear the mournful roar of the North Sea on the empty white sands of the bay . . . to drink in the musky fume of the rock poppies, those golden blooms planted for her brothers, as they shivered on the evening breeze borne in from the islands . . .

In a moment, all her confusion, her disquiet about the future, was gone. Of course. Why hadn't she seen it before? There was no other choice, nothing so obvious, so right.

At last she knew where she was going.

She was going home.

Book VII: Beth

Chapter Nineteen

If life has a purpose, or at least an aim, and if we believe in that purpose or aim, then we understand reality in a very specific way. But if we lose sight of our purpose, then we are bound, of necessity, to make our own reality. And so, often quite regardless of our deepest beliefs and highest hopes, we construct a mean-minded universe of confusion and despair. We do it in the way we interpret other people's reactions to us. We do it by brooding upon imagined hurts and perceived wrongs. We do it by compounding misunderstandings, by failing to make our true feelings clear, and by allowing pessimism its deadly rule. Thus we exist in a Hell of our own creation.

The Freedom of the Kingdom, by Michael Cameron

I dreamed that T. S. Eliot was directing Jamie in *Hamlet*.

'My dear boy,' he said, 'we must simply accept that here Shakespeare tackled a problem which proved too much for him.'

'Oh fuck off,' said Jamie, flashing his sword.

'No, really,' said Eliot. 'The intense feeling, ecstatic or terrible, without an object or exceeding its object, is something which every person of sensibility has known. However —'

'Don't tell me how I feel,' said Jamie. 'Go shove your objective correlative up your backside.'

Then the scene switched to *Casey's War*.

'Miss Carlisle,' said David Klein, 'I think you're admirably suited to the part of the prostitute. Miss Delamere, she can play the Virgin Mary . . .'

'No,' I said desperately, 'you're getting confused. Eva plays the Virgin Mary in *The Rose Garden* . . .'

'Never heard of it,' said David Klein.

I woke in a mild sweat, my bedroom strange and unwelcoming, a persistent knocking at my door . . . Dominic Lutz, my nine-year-old godson, bearing a cup of tea.

'Dad says you'd better get up if you want any breakfast because he's got to go to work.'

'I'll fix my own breakfast,' I said dopily.

'Oh no you won't,' shouted Sam from the stairs beyond. 'Get up now. I want to talk to you.'

I grimaced at Dominic and sat up. There was no escaping this latest moment of truth. I'd had one last night, and now I was about to get another.

I had driven home from Newcastle Airport at speed after I'd left Nick Howard, flying through flat, damp, motorway England, heart heavy, mind spinning. Would I be made to pay for my affair with Daniel Duval? What kind of retribution awaited me? How could I get out of it?

I'd shaken off all thoughts of Eva Delamere, and was deep in rehearsals for my contrition speech to Jamie when I stopped for petrol, and walking into the mini shopping gallery to pay, found myself facing a display of videos.

CLASSIC FILMS OF THE 1930S, announced the bottom shelf, and of course, there it was. *Casey's War* starring Will Sutton. Introducing Eva Delamere and Carlotta du Bois. Directed by David Klein. Distributed by Worldwide Pictures.

I picked it up uneasily, staring into Eva's misty, melancholy smile as she faced the camera, Will Sutton's arm clasped tight around her shoulder. I had seen her buried that very afternoon, and yet I couldn't escape her. Eva Delamere still wouldn't leave me alone. I paid for the video and stuffed it unhappily into my bag, knowing that even if I never watched it, I couldn't walk away and leave it on the shelf.

Then I'd driven on, my head full of Eva again, until, nearing midnight, I pulled up outside my home.

I'd been deeply relieved to find no reporters camped outside my door, and I'd begun to persuade myself that everything would be okay. The lights were still on. Jamie was still up. I turned my key in the lock, anxious to make my peace.

He was sitting on the sofa, reading from a sheaf of notes, and he didn't even look up as I entered.

'So you're back!' he said, enunciating his words with all the dramatic clarity required from one of England's premier Shakespearian actors. 'Well, darling, you can just fuck off again . . . Right now, if you don't mind.'

My home had never looked so warm and enticing as it did at this moment, blue and yellow flames flickering in the inglenook, lamps glowing softly on the tables.

I sat down beside him.

'I've been very careless,' I said soberly, reaching out to touch his arm. 'My only excuse is that I didn't know Duval was married to a prize bitch . . . I really am extremely sorry.'

He removed my hand with exaggerated disgust and placed it back in my lap.

'You're the prize bitch, darling,' he said, 'and that isn't simply a personal observation. The conclusion can be drawn by any casual onlooker.'

It was going to be harder than I'd thought.

'I'm sorry,' I said again, rather more tetchily this time. 'But let's not forget that you're hardly the conventional cuckold. Who's been sleeping in my bed, I wonder?'

'Nobody,' he said. 'I've been far too busy.'

'Well, I've said I'm sorry, for God's sake! What else do you expect me to do?'

'I expect you to read the writing on the wall, darling,' he replied slowly. 'You can do anything you like, you know – except make a fool out of me.'

Then, to my astonishment, he'd suddenly jumped up from the sofa, hauled me to my feet and manhandled me towards the front door, twisting my arm behind my back.

'What the hell are you doing?' I shrieked as I struggled ineffectively.

'I'm throwing you out, darling,' he'd said.

And he did.

Humiliated and furious, I'd kicked against the door, hammering on the glass until my knuckles were bruised.

'You can't do this!' I screamed. 'It's my house too! I'm going to call my lawyer.'

'Do it, darling,' he shouted through the door. 'Or why not call the police? That nice CID man should help you out if he's not too busy selling his story to the *Sun* . . .'

This brought me up short. It hadn't occurred to me that Clive Fisher might be in pursuit of my other ex-lovers. Why should he stop at Duval? Why not find every last no-hoper I'd ever been to bed with and offer them a few quid to spill the beans? I groaned, and laid my head against the doorpost.

'Please let me in, Jamie,' I whimpered. 'Where am I supposed to go at this time of night?'

'How about Paris?' he called back.

After that, I got practical. I could check into a hotel, of course, and if I had to, then I would. But there was just a chance that Vicky Lutz might not have left for Spain. She, and she alone, would take me in and dust me down without lecturing me on what a silly girl I'd been.

Alas, it was Sam who got up to answer the doorbell.

'I thought you'd moved out,' I said miserably.

'Well, I'm back,' he snapped. 'I'm looking after Dominic while Vicky's away.'

And with scarcely another word he'd ordered me to the spare room where, eventually, I fell into a fitful sleep.

Now he faced me across the breakfast table, grim-faced and uncompromising, my mentor and my sternest critic.

'*Moonlight and Roses* got some decent reviews,' he said, indicating a pile of newspapers spread out before him, 'though the tabloids couldn't resist mentioning Genny Duval. On the whole, however, they've been quite restrained . . . I'm inclined to think it's rather more than you deserve.'

'Rubbish,' I said hotly. 'That series is good television. My private life has nothing whatever to do with the programmes I make.'

'Yes, Beth,' he replied sharply, 'that's the problem. I think you'll find it's called hypocrisy.'

I stared down into my coffee, blinking back sudden tears. Was this true? Had I forfeited any right to comment on the vexed subject of romance because I'd been caught with another woman's husband? Perhaps. But if I owned up to being a hypocrite, where would that leave me? Would Genny Duval forgive me? Would Jamie take me back?

'Can you talk to Jamie?' I asked Sam anxiously. 'He's got to let me in the house. He might listen to you.'

'I've already talked to Jamie,' Sam said pointedly. 'I've warned him that the whole thing is going to blow up before long. The tabloids have got everything they need on you two. They're just waiting for the moment, and this is the first step . . . If you ask me, Beth, it's time to quit.'

'Quit Jamie? Don't be ridiculous.'

'It's ridiculous,' Sam said coldly, 'that nine years after you started living together, you're still playing to the gallery. Nobody believes any of this stuff, Beth. Will they get married, or won't they? Is this the great romance of all time? They're setting you up. And what's it all for, I ask myself? The two of you fight like cat and dog.'

I said nothing. Breathe deep, Beth, one, two, three . . . I am a mature, responsible person in charge of my own destiny . . .

'We don't fight all the time,' I said lamely. 'It's just these past few months that everything seems to have collapsed . . .'

'You can't stay in town,' Sam said, uninterested in any defence I might produce. 'And you can't go home to Jamie, even if he'd have you.

They're not going to leave you alone. It's too juicy a story. You'll have to lie low for a while.'

I stood up from the breakfast table and walked over to the kitchen window, staring out on the neat little patio garden that Vicky tended so carefully. Her prized ornamental cabbages were wilting, her rose bushes were rioting and her spring bulbs were sprouting amok. It was plain she hadn't been thinking much about gardening just lately.

'The garden's going to seed,' I said morosely.

'Don't change the subject,' Sam barked. 'We're talking about you.'

'So what about me?' I countered. 'Okay, my private life's a mess. That puts me on a par with just about everyone else I know . . . including you. What the fuck have you been doing in Camden Town?'

Now Sam stood up, clearing the cups from the table with scant regard for their safety and plunging them into the sink.

'I'm not front-page news,' he said, 'I'm just the fucking producer. It doesn't matter to anyone else what I do.'

A noise in the doorway alerted us to Dominic, who stood watching and listening, painfully neat in his school uniform, lunchbox in his hand.

'You all ready, son? Well, wait outside for your lift . . .'

I watched him go with heavy heart, hoping he hadn't caught the conversation, and then, because I always felt impotent when faced with Vicky's marital problems, sat down again at the kitchen table, glancing through the TV review columns that Sam had laid out.

Beth Carlisle's candy-box style, soft as milk chocolate on the outside, hard as a hazelnut within . . . Funny, but I would have put it the other way round . . . So you think you're an incurable romantic? A night with Beth Carlisle would soon change your mind . . . Funny, but I hadn't imagined it would take that long . . .

And then, perhaps because I felt sorry for myself and the unreasonable burden I seemed to bear as a public personality, I found myself fishing for any scrap of sympathy that Sam might have left.

'Do you remember Michael?' I asked him. 'Michael Cameron?'

He turned round from the sink at once.

'Michael? Yes, of course I remember . . . How could I possibly forget?'

'It's been thirteen years . . . But I met him again this weekend . . . At a funeral.'

The ploy had worked and Sam looked at me with sudden concern, sitting down beside me at the table. For a moment neither of us spoke.

'So,' he said at last, 'how was it?'

'Awful. He hasn't changed a bit. He's the same smug, superior, self-righteous bastard he always was.'

I laughed then, despite myself.

'I suppose he thought I hadn't changed much either,' I said.

Sam looked at me uneasily.

'I once told you to strike Michael Cameron from the record,' he muttered, 'pretend he never existed. That was good advice, Beth.'

'I remember it well,' I said, 'and I took it.'

Sam put his arm around my shoulder and dropped an awkward kiss on the top of my head, then seemed to make a decision, as though throughout our long and often fraught association, what might and might not be said had simmered just beneath the surface and only now came up to boil.

'It was the right advice at the time,' he said uncomfortably, 'but I've sometimes wondered whether it shouldn't have been reviewed after things settled down . . . You know, everyone was in shock – even me, and I hardly knew your mother. Nobody was behaving very rationally.'

I shook his arm from me angrily.

'You've got a nerve,' I said.

Sam had the grace to look shamefaced, but still he stumbled on.

'It may be best to face up to things, Beth,' he muttered. 'You know, confront the past. Decide you're not going to blot it out any longer. Tell Michael the truth, if that's what it takes . . . Go visit your mother's grave . . .'

I couldn't take in what I'd just heard, and for a moment I sat there, frozen in disbelief, furious at this unexpected assault on my carefully contrived defences. Then I stood up and reached for my coat.

'You save your fucking amateur psychology for yourself,' I advised him coldly. 'God knows, your marriage could do with it.'

And having thus set fire to this last little dinghy in my diminishing flotilla, I marched out into the grey London day.

Our second-year Eng. Lit. tutor was an odious, opinionated lecher, not totally unlike my mother's lover, the despised Leo Frankish.

'So, Miss Carlisle,' the tutor said gravely, attempting to look up my skirt while analysing my essay, 'The English Novel: Narrative in Decline . . .'

'There's no happy ending for the English novel,' I said, clamping my knees together. 'Only a never-ceasing succession of middle-class moans and literary dilemmas.'

He still had his eyes fixed on my crotch, and I shifted uncomfortably on the low settee, resolving to pick a hard-backed chair for the next seminar.

'It's a failure of nerve,' I said defiantly. 'We've lost the grand sweep novel with its universal human concerns. Now we can only write about writing . . .'

He seemed to recollect himself, and looked away.

'I see. And what would you say, Miss Henderson?'

Vicky, smirking at Sam, was caught off guard.

'Oh, I agree,' she said, blushing.

'Very sensible. Agreeing is always a lot less trouble than taking issue . . . And how about you, Mr Lutz?'

'I'd say stuff the English novel. It's nearly Christmas. Why don't we all go out and get drunk?'

The tutor stood up and smiled at me.

'Come on,' he said, 'I'll buy you a gin in the Common Room . . .'

I grimaced at Vicky and shot a pleading glance at Sam, who then draped a proprietorial arm around my shoulder.

'Face it, Beth,' he whispered as we all walked out together through the quad. 'One of us will have your knickers off before the end of term. Who's it going to be? Me or him?'

'Neither,' I said, laughing. 'I'm a one-man woman, and I'm going home to him next week.'

'Who is this guy?' asked Sam in mock despair. 'What's he got that I haven't?'

'Oh, you know, good looks, charm, breeding, that sort of thing . . .'

'Hmm. Sounds like the kind of guy your mother should warn you against,' he said with unintentional insight.

'She already did,' I'd muttered before I caught myself.

I bitterly regretted this little aside when my mother, arriving unexpectedly on the campus to drive me home for Christmas, took an instant shine to Sam, and he, perceiving his advantage, took pains to impress her with his deep regard for her daughter.

'He seems a nice boy,' my mother said in an unlikely, old-fashioned turn of phrase. 'I think it would be fun if the three of you found a flat together.'

'I could fancy your mother,' Sam announced, 'if I weren't already madly in love with you.'

'Control yourself, Sam,' Vicky said drily. 'She's engaged, remember?'

'Is she? Well, what happened to the ring, then? Seems she takes it off when her mama's around.'

He was teasing me, and I smiled uneasily, but already I could see the way things were going. My mother would push me into Sam's arms if she could, and Sam would aim to persuade me that a man my mother approved was a hundred times better than one she didn't.

At dinner in Hall they flirted with embarrassingly open intent.

'Now I know why Beth is so lovely,' Sam said, opening another bottle of sparkling wine. 'She takes after you.'

'You're very sweet,' she said. 'If I were twenty years younger, Beth wouldn't get a look in.'

I felt my irritation rise like bile.

'We're not remotely alike,' I said tersely to Sam. 'As you'd surely see if you laid off the wine . . .'

'Good heavens, Beth!' my mother said. 'Can't you accept a compliment? Although as a matter of fact, Sam, it's true – Beth doesn't look like the Martineau side of the family at all . . .'

'Martineau? That's a very romantic name.'

'My mother was a rather romantic figure,' she said, raising her glass and offering her best romantic smile; 'in her younger days, that is.'

I looked despairingly around the room for Vicky, also dining in difficult circumstances with her father and stepmother, and was relieved to catch her eye. We exchanged a sympathetic smile, and I felt better at once. Female solidarity was like the first glass of wine, soothing and invigorating at the same time.

'She was the real beauty,' I heard my mother say as I returned to the conversation. 'Her looks were legendary. Everyone fell in love with her, but it did her no good at all . . .'

I shifted unhappily in my seat and glanced at my watch. When was this agonising evening going to end?

'There's a photograph of her taken in America, standing on this amazing staircase in some hacienda place. She has long chestnut hair falling round her waist and she's wearing a white silk dress. She looks like something from the movies – you remember that picture, don't you, Beth?'

I wasn't inclined to remember my grandmother favourably at the best of times, and not at all now.

'Yes, she was like something from the movies,' I snapped. 'Lucretia Borgia, maybe, or one of the Brides of Dracula.'

Sam looked up in surprise, but my mother merely laughed.

'Beth and her grandmother didn't get on,' she said unnecessarily. 'Maybe they were just a bit too much alike . . .'

I was deeply offended by this throwaway remark and stood up from the dinner table at once, determined to interrupt their cosy mutual flattery and assert myself.

'Don't compare me with her,' I said steadily to my mother. 'It's a very serious insult.'

She was immediately contrite, knowing that however much we differed on other crucial matters, we were united in our view of Rhoda.

And later, in our shared hotel room, perhaps in penitence for this undeserved slight, she even ventured to apologise for her behaviour with Sam.

'I don't know what made me say that about Rhoda . . . Of course you're not like her at all. Nobody was ever like Rhoda. I was just trying to be friendly to Sam, you know. Sharing a few family secrets.'

I sat in front of the dressing-table mirror, morosely brushing my hair, saying nothing.

'I just thought it would be nice if you two got together,' my mother murmured regretfully, watching as I undressed and got into bed, 'but I don't suppose you'll ever forget Michael, will you? I don't suppose you can see that Sam's a better prospect altogether . . . He's such fun, Beth. I can't imagine him getting all moody and possessive, the way Michael does.'

I had retrieved the diamond solitaire from the chain around my neck and put it back on my ring finger, determined, after the evening's shameless attempt to divert my interest, that I would never let my mother browbeat me again.

'I like Sam,' I said firmly, 'but I'm in love with Michael. That's the way it is, and the way it will always be . . . I'm going to marry him, and I'm only sorry that you can't seem to accept it.'

She lay back on her bed, studying the ceiling rose with measured concentration, lost in some deep deliberation to which I wasn't party.

'I'm sure I don't know what's going on,' she said at last. 'The world's gone mad. Sarah told me yesterday she also wants to get engaged —'

'Oh no!' I said in disbelief. 'Not Charles!'

I'd been deeply unimpressed with the languid boyfriend my sister had produced from St Botolph's Christian drama group, considering him introverted and dull, the unlikeliest actor I'd ever encountered.

'Now then, Beth,' my mother chided. 'You can't declare your own autonomy in one breath and deny Sarah hers in the next.' She sat up on her bed and looked across at me.

'There's one respect in which you're both very like your grandmother,' she said slowly.

'Oh yes?' I muttered suspiciously. 'And what's that?'

My mother lay down again.

'Rhoda always got her man,' she said.

I slammed into my car and attempted to reverse out of my space.

'I've been waiting for you,' I heard a voice bellow from the pavement. 'You can't park here, you know. Permit-holders only!'

I flashed the window down, and smiled sweetly up into the bluff, aged visage of Sam's neighbour, a cartoon caricature of a man, handlebar moustache bristling, ruddy neck rising above lurid cravat.

'Fuck off, Brigadier,' I said.

His face turned an alarming shade of cerise.

'I could have called the clampers,' he boomed. 'I have the authority to do it, you know!'

I leaned out of the window.

'I suppose you won the fucking war as well?' I shouted. 'And all for the likes of me?'

He stepped back, astonished, and I roared off, my heart pounding, my fingers trembling on the wheel.

Unreal city. I was swallowed into a mass of slowly moving steel, thousands of commuters locked inside metal boxes, edging their way forward to unknown tasks at unknown desks. At least they had somewhere to go, if only they could get there. I had no idea where I was going, and as I crawled past King's Cross, staring fixedly at the road for fear of meeting the eye of a passing beggar or a whore, I considered that I had joined the multitude of the dispossessed. I might be cruising around in a BMW, but I was nevertheless out on Mean Street, effectively alone.

'You can't stay in the city,' Sam had said, without suggesting where I might go.

And then, perhaps because I found myself heading north on roads I'd travelled only a few days before, the answer occurred. I would swallow all pride and injured feeling. I would call on my sister again.

The decision made, I felt positively cheery. I could spend time with my nephews and make up to Sarah for my previous, somewhat fraught visit. I could even be nice to Charles if I put my mind to it. Perhaps I'd stop and buy some chocolates and some decent wine.

The once-familiar signs flashed by again. Peterborough, Stamford, Oakham . . . How often had I travelled this route and ignored the turn-off for my old home? How many times had I told myself I would never go back? What was it Sam had said that so enraged me? *Go visit your mother's grave* . . .

And before I quite knew what I was doing, I had swung the car from the motorway and on to the winding Rutland lanes I remembered so well from my youth.

Yes, here was the Night Owl country club where Michael used to waltz me, and here was the river where Jack Cameron moored his flashy cabin cruiser, and here, in the dip of a wooded hill, was the terrace of farm cottages that marked the rim of the Cameron estate. I felt my hands grow clammy on the wheel. Breathe deep, Beth, one, two, three four . . .

Then I was driving through the back streets of the village, my mouth dry, my pulse racing. What on earth was I going to do now I was here? Suppose I bumped into Jonathan Cameron, or even worse, his mother? I parked the car outside St Botolph's church, and sat for a moment, psyching myself to the deed.

There was no one about. The street that wound down to my mother's old cottage was empty, the churchyard silent. I got out of my car and walked through the creaking yew gate.

I wondered if I'd be able to locate the grave, but once among the headstones, it all returned with unwonted clarity. My mother's coffin had been carried from the church, past the monument to the village men lost in the Great War, and past the Cameron family tomb, over to the far wall of the graveyard. I remembered only too well that the wall dipped at this point, allowing a picture-postcard view of the Cameron mansion.

I walked straight to the plot, and with a strange numbness of heart, stared down at the weatherbeaten stone. ELEANOR JANE CARLISLE, BELOVED MOTHER OF ELIZABETH AND SARAH, TAKEN FROM US, AGED 42. GOD WILL WIPE AWAY ALL TEARS.

'Not mine,' I had vowed as her coffin disappeared from view that bright and terrible day. 'Never mine . . .'

But now I felt no tears, no shred of emotion beyond astonishment that I was actually standing upon the forbidden spot.

I saw that the stone was well scrubbed and the surrounding grass clipped, and also that the marble vase at the base of the headstone contained a dozen red rosebuds. I bent to examine them, but there was no card, and I was left to wonder if Sarah had splashed out for a special memory. But it wasn't my mother's birthday, nor the anniversary of her death. I stared at the flowers, puzzled. Had one of the Camerons placed them there?

Then I looked up towards the Cameron house, and saw that, while still handsome, it was wearing a little at its joints, just like the rest of us. I could see weeds sprouting between the stones on the terrace, and the frames to the long sash windows needed new varnish. While Jack Cameron was still alive, no doubt, the façade had been maintained. But his elder son, I guessed, had neither the means nor the inclination.

I turned and walked away from the grave on to the main street of the village. My mother's old cottage lay just out of view, beyond the bend at the bottom of the hill. I began to walk, my legs strangely weak, my breath coming in odd little gasps.

The first thing I saw was that the conservatory had gone. A paved patio stood on the site and the cottage leaned oddly over it, as though seeking a lost part of itself. The windows and front door had been replaced, our frosted-glass affair giving way to solid mock Tudor, and the roof had been tiled in garish Santa Claus red. It looked altogether foreign, but then, as I stopped and gazed at the gaping space where the conservatory had stood, I caught a vision of my mother sitting on the cane settee marking her students' essays, and the scene was transformed into the utterly familiar. How beautiful she'd been, with her long chocolate-coloured hair . . . How unsurprising that so many men had loved and wanted her . . . How tragic that her life had ended in such a way . . .

The door of the cottage swung open suddenly and a stout woman in green Barbour emerged, orange Labrador snapping at her heels. I scurried away in mild panic in case she guessed who I was, and arriving at the phone box outside the village store, the kiosk I'd sneaked to whenever I wanted to call Michael in private, I shot inside and turned my back on the street. There was nothing for me here. I didn't belong in the past. I needed the present. I wanted my life with Jamie back.

I picked up the receiver with trembling hands, dialled my home number and then listened while my own voice rang out: 'I suppose you think we've nothing better to do than talk to you? Okay, leave your number, and if we feel like it, we'll call you back . . .'

I slammed down the phone and dialled Metro TV.

'Sam? I just called to say sorry and to tell you where I am.'

He listened in silence while I rambled on about my sister and my nephews and then begged him to contact Jamie.

'I'm glad you're going to Sarah's,' he said at last. 'That seems a good idea . . . But Jamie should be left in peace. Think about it, Beth, for God's sake. This is the most important moment of his career.'

I swallowed hard, fighting the tears.

'I had a row with your neighbour,' I muttered, unable to grapple with this truth about Jamie and the knowledge of how insensitive I'd been. 'I parked in his space. He didn't have a heart attack or anything, did he? That would be a good follow-up for the *Sun*.'

'Frank Duffy? He's okay as far as I know. He's a decent old bloke, really. Lost his wife a couple of weeks ago . . .'

'It's not my fault,' I said, the tears perilously near. 'None of it's my fault . . .'

'Of course it's your fault,' Sam replied tartly. 'You just can't keep your knickers on.'

I walked swiftly out of the kiosk and back up the main street, averting my eyes from the adulterated cottage as I passed. Then I climbed into my car and took the road out of the village, up to the Cameron spinney. And when I reached the secluded, overhung lane that Michael had taken so many times in the Bentley, I swung the BMW down into the dank and silent green until it came to rest in just the spot where we'd always parked. Then I lowered my face to the steering wheel and wept.

'This is where I part company with the Puritans,' Michael said softly. 'Ours is an incarnational faith . . . We must celebrate the flesh. We must embrace the material life . . .'

We were standing in St Botolph's by the crib, shivering in the thin winter afternoon, waiting for the carol service to begin. Above us the three Advent candles glowed, behind us the lights on the Christmas tree winked, a nod towards paganism, a blatant concession to the secular.

'When were you ever in with the Puritans?' I whispered. 'Not since I've known you.'

He shot me a reproachful glance.

'Sometimes,' he muttered, 'I think you don't understand a word I say . . .'

'That's because you speak a load of theological claptrap,' I whispered back.

He smiled, unabashed, and reached for my icy hand which he plunged into his pocket, caressing the fingers and the solitaire ring.

'One day,' he said, 'I'll tell you all about the Incarnation.'

'I can't wait,' I murmured.

But in truth I wasn't so much in need of his superior understanding. Gazing on the crib and its pristine plaster figures, I felt I saw into the heart of the mystery, the god born out of blood and female pain, the king of the world lying amid the animal dung. And if this, and its relentless progress towards death and degradation at Calvary, could be transformed, made glorious, made good, then what else might defeat us? Nothing. Nothing at all. The whole world, redeemed, made sacred, rescued from irrelevance, had only to see itself as such . . . And then, having seen, to act. The word made deed. Faith and works, hand in hand.

'I won't be around much for the next week,' Michael said. 'I'm going on the soup run in the city centre.'

'Oh . . . okay. That sounds a good thing to be doing. Can I come too?'

'Well, not really, The fact is, we've got far more helpers than we need. It's a bit embarrassing. Half the volunteers have worse problems than the people we're trying to help.'

We walked out into the starry night and through the churchyard, our feet crunching upon frozen puddles, our breath hanging visible on the frosty air. It wouldn't be too comfortable on the soup run.

'Christmas, bloody Christmas,' I said. 'How sad.'

He hesitated.

'Yes,' he said at last. 'You sometimes wonder whether family life is better than no family life.'

I looked up at him, surprised, catching something in his voice I failed to recognise.

'Anything wrong?' I asked curiously.

'I just get sick of my family sometimes . . .'

'Why? What are they doing?'

'Oh well, you know,' he said quickly, unlocking the door of the Bentley and handing me in. 'The things families do . . . Now, where would you like to go?'

'Not to the spinney,' I said. 'It's too bloody cold. Maybe that's how the Puritans got their killjoy ideas . . . All those draughty mansions. No central heating. What do you think?'

'I think we'll go back to your place,' he said.

'To celebrate the flesh?' I teased.

'As long as your mother doesn't catch us and throw me out.'

Sex in the conservatory, sex in the hall, and sex in the kitchen, up against the wall . . .

Where was my mother that Christmas, leaving her daughters so much to their own devices and desires? Why was she never home, even late at night when Michael finished on the soup run? And where was Leo Frankish?

I didn't know, nor care too much, nor think to ask.

I stayed in the spinney some time, indulging a great surge of self-pity, the immediate source of which seemed unclear. Was I weeping for my mother, for the spent promise of my vanished youth, or for my fractured life with Jamie? Or was I, like Hamlet, simply weeping at the sight of the great unweeded garden?

I got out of the car and wandered down to the old ruined folly where I'd walked so many times with Michael, where he'd presented his diamond ring so many years ago, where once, looking up at the stained-glass window depicting St Augustine of Hippo, I had mused upon Sex and God and Socialism, all those things that seemed important then. What, I was forced to ask, seemed important to me now? Not God, and certainly no quaint, altruistic philosophy left lingering in the lost land of political ideas. Not sex, either. Sex was simply a given of the successful life, like good food and expensive clothes, there for the indulging. Which, of course, explained precisely what I'd been doing with Daniel Duval . . .

What, then? Work? *Moonlight and Roses: The Cult of Romance in Western Society?* My beautiful home on the banks of the Thames, now locked and barred against me?

In that moment there seemed precious little else, and for fear I might start howling again, I turned and strode smartly through the spinney, back to the BMW.

An hour later I was pulling into my sister's orderly cul-de-sac, feeling no less miserable and nervously anticipating the response I might meet. How would Sarah and Charles view my sudden notoriety? Would they be sympathetic or censorious? I had no idea.

The door was opened by a pretty, dark-haired girl of twenty or so, who knew me at once although I'd never set eyes on her before.

'Well, fancy that, it's Beth Carlisle! Nice to meet you at long last .. . Sarah's not here, I'm afraid. I'm keeping an eye on the boys.'

I assumed she must be a neighbour, or someone from church, and I walked moodily into the house, fearing I'd have to play the TV star until my sister got back.

'We watched you last night,' the girl began, sitting me down in Sarah's wretched kitchen with a mug of tea, 'and we thought you were pretty good.'

'Thanks,' I said grudgingly, looking round for my nephews who, like all children, always seemed to be there when you wished they weren't, and never around when you could do with them.

'I must say I agree with your views entirely. The propagation of romantic love is the last desperate ploy of patriarchy. The question, it seems to me, is what women do with this knowledge.'

'Yes,' I said gloomily, eyeing her with resignation, 'I guess so.'

'The choices are fairly stark. I mean, one wouldn't wish to use men simply for sex in the way they've always used us . . . So if you refuse to fall in love with them, what does that leave?'

'Celibates and lesbians,' I suggested, stirring my tea and glancing pointedly at my watch. 'When will Sarah be back, do you think?'

'That's all very well,' my pretty adversary declared, ignoring this question. 'But what if neither of those appeals to you personally? I mean, I can see the intellectual advantages of both, but what if you just happen to like fucking men?'

I groaned and ran my hand distractedly through my hair. Had this bright young thing been conjured up just to torment me? How could I get her to go away and leave me alone? Who the hell was she anyway?'

'This is all very interesting,' I said testily. 'Maybe you could watch part two of my series next week? Who did you say you were? I don't think I caught your name . . .'

She refilled my mug from the teapot, and looked me straight in the eye.

'My name is Emma,' she said steadily. 'Emma Carlisle.'

I said nothing, simply stared unhappily.

'Ray's daughter,' she went on. 'You knew he was married again, didn't you?' She grimaced. 'Divorced again, too,' she added.

'I had no idea you were in touch with Sarah,' I muttered.

'She's my half-sister,' Emma said with a little shrug. 'Why shouldn't we be in touch?'

At that moment I heard the front door open, and I looked up anxiously as Sarah walked into the room, her face pale and strained, her hair tied untidily behind her neck, her coat buttoned wrongly.

I jumped up at once, all questions about Emma Carlisle driven from my mind.

'What's wrong?' I demanded.

'How's Charles?' asked Emma in the same breath.

Sarah looked from one to the other of us, and then sat down at the kitchen table.

'He'll be all right,' she said to Emma. 'Are the boys upstairs in the playroom? Will you check on them please?'

Emma looked a trifle disappointed at this dismissal, but nevertheless complied with half-sisterly grace, leaving Sarah to tell me her tale, hesitatingly and with fortitude, while I listened in disbelief, and in shame.

'A year ago!' I cried in horror. 'He lost his job a year ago, and you never told me?'

'He didn't want you and Jamie to know. He felt such a failure. First he had to get out of teaching . . . And then this.'

'But thousands of people have lost their jobs under this bloody government! They've been sacrificed to the system . . . There's no blame attached.'

'I know that, Beth. But he was fired because he was too slow, and too old-fashioned. That's business, like it or not. And I suppose in some ways I understand. He was always a square peg in that job . . .'

I reached across the table and took her hand, mortified that she'd felt unable to confide in me, sobered that I'd read Charles so very wrongly.

'He's always suffered with depression, and this just tipped him over the top . . . I know you find him hard going, but the truth is he's very insecure, very vulnerable . . . He's always felt intimidated by you, Beth. Silly perhaps, but there it is.'

I stood up and walked to the kitchen window, staring out into the growing darkness, my heart heavy, my thoughts reeling. The brother-in-law I'd despised as a small-minded bore had been revealed as a walking casualty, a man without self-esteem or inner confidence, a fellow human being who'd cracked, a victim of unfortunate circumstance without the resources to overcome.

'They're very good on the ward,' Sarah was saying. 'He's been there before, and he's always much better afterwards . . . Maybe this time he'll agree to sell the house.'

I turned round from the window at once.

'You're short of money,' I said desperately. 'That's why you came to see me that weekend I was in Paris! You needed my help!'

She stood up, clearing the cups from the table and extracting tins from cardboard boxes, preparing to cook tea for her boys.

'It's okay now. The mortgage arrears have been paid, the phone's back on, and we're getting the kitchen fixed up . . . That will help when we come to sell.'

'Who paid?' I asked tearfully, hardly able to bear my own regret. 'Was it Ray Carlisle? I went to the grave this afternoon, Sarah – for the first time in all these years. There were a dozen red roses in her vase. Did he put them there? Why didn't you tell me you'd kept in touch with the Carlisles?'

She glanced at me nervously.

'It wasn't Ray,' she said defensively, and I saw then that history still hung too heavy upon us, that the ghosts of thirteen years ago, the wrath and recrimination surrounding my mother's death, the bitterness and the aching sense of betrayal, the hard words and the hatred, would not be exorcised in one afternoon.

The kitchen door opened, stalling any attempt at the task.

'Michael's on the phone,' Emma said to Sarah. 'He wants a word . . .'

I caught my sister's eye, and suddenly I knew who'd paid her mortgage and settled her phone bill, who was fixing up her kitchen and who'd given all the counsel and support that I should have been offering myself; who, even now, was usurping my rightful role as comforter . . . And the thought, instinctive, uncharitable, sprang to my lips.

'Blood money,' I muttered.

Then all the passion and the pain welled up inside me, and I wondered how I'd ever succeeded in facing Michael again without unleashing the fury and the hurt I knew I still felt. Thank God, I thought with uncharacteristic fervour, that I'd never have to see him again.

Now I was anxious only to make amends to my sister, to afford her any service, however small or insignificant, to let her know that I cared. I'd quite forgotten that I'd arrived needing her forbearance, that I had nowhere else to go, that if, for any reason, she didn't want me there, I'd be out on the road again. I was merely thankful that she seemed not to have read the *Sun*, that she didn't have my tawdry worries to add to her own substantial woes.

'Please, Sarah,' I begged as she came back into the room, 'there must be something I can do to help. If you don't need money, maybe I could –' I looked around urgently seeking inspiration – 'clean up the kitchen?' I finished lamely.

She flashed me a wan smile.

'Well, there is something you could do. I wouldn't dream of asking, except that I know you've already been there . . .'

'Anything,' I said grandly, rashly ignoring this vital clue. 'Ask me anything.'

'Would you take the boys up to Michael's place? He's having them over the Easter holidays. I feel they're a bit young to go on the train by themselves . . . It would be very helpful if you could.'

'Of course,' I said, smiling foolishly, seeing the grubby edifice of the Dolphin Inn rearing before me again. 'No problem.'

She hesitated.

'I'm so glad you've seen Michael again . . . that you could meet without too much bitterness or pain . . . It's more than I'd ever hoped for, Beth . . . Truly, it is.'

Chapter Twenty

Christians are notoriously accused of identifying sin with sex, thereby over-looking political, economic and social injustices which might properly be said to constitute 'sin' in the biblical sense, a turning away from God's will. It is certainly true that from St Paul onwards, the Church has failed to grapple with the mystery of human sexuality, jealous of its unlimited power for pleasure, threatened by certain forms of 'subversive' sexual beha-viour.

But if we say the Church has got it all wrong, that sexuality must be rescued at all cost from the dictates of conventional morality and ancient taboo, then we risk losing an important insight, one shared by feminism. Put simply, it is this: the world of political, economic and social relationships begins with me, in my home, in my bed. And so it matters very much what happens there.

The Freedom of the Kingdom, by Michael Cameron

No more than three days after I'd left St Cuthbert's never to return, I found myself cruising along the harbour road, past the bank of golden poppies and the white beach and into the cobbled driveway of the vicarage.

Katie Cameron was watching from the front-room window and ran out at once to greet Sarah's sons.

'You came for the Easter holidays after all!' she said, hugging me.

'Not really,' I said briskly, determined to control the mawkishness that Katie had previously called forth in my otherwise stoical soul. 'I'm afraid I can't stay very long.'

I'd already decided that I couldn't face the Dolphin Inn again, and planned to put up for a few days at the Black Swan in Alnwick once I'd settled my nephews. And once I'd told Michael Cameron what was on my mind.

'Where is he?' I demanded of Lucy, who, I soon divined, was less than delighted to see me again.

'He's doing a wedding interview. Young couple want to get married at St Cuthbert's.'

'Oh yes? What's he giving them? Sex education?'

She laughed nervously and shot me an awkward glance.

'Not exactly . . .' She grimaced. 'They're only nineteen . . . It's far too young, don't you think?'

'There's never a good age to get married,' I said curtly, settling myself on the chesterfield in front of the fire. 'And I'm inclined to think that if it weren't for the Church and its obsessive need to legitimise sex, the whole institution would be dead and buried by now.'

I was full of hell, and would not be denied.

'Oh yes,' said Lucy unhappily. 'We watched your programme the other night . . .'

'Would you tell Michael I'm here, please? I need to see him briefly, and then I'll be on my way.'

I had my speech carefully planned and my cheque book at the ready. I meant to pay him back for settling Sarah's mortgage arrears, in more ways than one . . .

Left alone, I got up and walked over to Jack Cameron's old desk in the window. Without a shred of conscience, I picked up the cigarettes which were lying on the desk top, nipped off the tips, and dropped them into the waste bin. Then I rifled through Michael's papers. An epistle from the Bishop about Lent sermons. A report from St Cuthbert's Stewardship Committee about the fall in planned giving. A letter from a grateful parishioner which began: 'My Dear Michael, I can hardly thank you enough for the care and compassion shown to my family at this difficult time . . .'

I considered ripping up all his correspondence as well, but in the end desisted, figuring this could only serve to reveal the depths of my antipathy. Better to save that . . .

The biography of David Klein was still lying on the desk, open at a chapter headed 'Death in Paris', and I flipped through it idly, brought back to thoughts of Eva once again.

I decided I would lift the book, and stuffed it into my handbag where it joined the video of *Casey's War*. I wasn't through with Eva Delamere just yet.

I heard a noise in the hall and moved away from the desk, stiffening myself for attack. Then the door to the room swung open and instead of confronting the vicar of St Cuthbert's as I'd intended, I found myself facing my erstwhile lover, Daniel Duval.

For a moment we stared in mutual embarrassment and faint shock.

'Beth . . .' he said at last, 'I'm so glad to see you . . . But what on earth are you doing here?'

'I came to see you,' I said quickly, encouraged by his conciliatory tone and unwilling to embark on any explanations involving my sister and her sons. 'I figured you'd still be here.'

He hesitated, and then held out his hand to me.

'I'm so very, very sorry,' he said. 'I saw you at Eva's funeral, and I wanted to tell you then, but you disappeared . . .'

'There's no call for you to apologise! I'm the one who ought to be sorry. I knew Clive Fisher was on to us, but I didn't tell you, and I did nothing about it myself. Then I let myself in for that stupid photo call with Jamie . . .'

'Ah yes,' he said. 'How are things with Jamie?'

Another sound from the hall send me into mild panic. I wanted to see the vicar of St Cuthbert's alone, on my own terms, and I caught at Duval's arm urgently.

'Let's get out of here!'

'I'm supposed to see Michael at three o'clock . . .'

'Oh fuck him,' I said recklessly. 'Where are you staying?' and we were out of the vicarage in a moment.

'I'm up at the Retreat,' he said as he climbed into my car and I prepared to roar away from the vicarage at speed. 'In the old lodge cottage . . . And I should tell you that I'm with my wife. She's not there at the moment, she's gone shopping. I mention it only because you may wish to avoid her.'

I glanced at him ruefully, surprised and yet relieved to hear they were still together.

'I imagine she'll want to avoid me,' I muttered, 'unless she's planning a right hook . . .'

'If you can bear it,' he said tentatively, 'I'd like to give her the chance to say sorry . . .'

The detail of other people's marriages is always mysterious, and I had no desire to hear on what grounds they were reconciled; I was merely grateful that whatever else was said about me, I wouldn't now get the marriage-breaker label hung around my neck.

'Genny met Clive Fisher at a party,' Duval was saying. 'He was already digging the dirt on you . . . The temptation was just too much for her, I'm afraid.'

'I hope it was worth it,' I said magnanimously.

'It was . . .'

He glanced at me anxiously, and I remembered just how much I'd liked him from the beginning, how funny and gentle and courteous he'd always been, how very unlike the average adulterer. Maybe that was what fooled me into thinking there wouldn't be a price to pay.

'This is very embarrassing, Beth,' he mumbled, 'and the morality of it is decidedly dubious, but I couldn't live with myself if I didn't confess . . . The truth is that Clive Fisher's story got Genny out of trouble. She's been able to settle a lot of her debts.'

'Good old Clive,' I said with as much sincerity as I could muster, wondering just for a moment if the Duvals had been in league against me. But no, I was the one who'd seduced him. As ever, I'd made all the running myself. Well, not any more. Goodbye to the sexual battlefield, at least for a while. I was due some compassionate leave.

We pulled in at the gateway to the old Forster mansion, now spruced and neatly institutionalised for the purposes of the C of E, and crawled through dense wooded paths, eventually arriving at a squat yellow-brick lodge cottage overhung with ivy and surrounded by early bluebells.

'It's beautiful,' I breathed. 'And what a wonderful place to lie low . . .'

'Eva played in this cottage as a little girl with her friend Anya . . . I feel close to her here,' he said, opening the door and leading me into a dark, panelled hall, and from there into a white-painted sitting room hung around with floral prints and jugs of bluebells.

'Will you ever tell me the truth about Eva?' I asked lightly as he sat me down on the sofa and fussed around me with biscuits and tea. 'How you met her? What she did after she left Hollywood? Who killed Will Sutton? I don't think you will . . .'

He smiled.

'Nobody killed Will Sutton,' he said softly. 'It was an accident. The night was dark, the road was treacherous, he was a hopeless driver, he took the bend too fast . . .'

I lay back on the sofa, relaxing in the warmth of the sunny room, wondering how long I'd got before Genevieve showed up and how I'd handle it when she did.

'Is that what Eva told you?'

'It's what she came to believe.'

'I'm disappointed,' I said, 'I can't help it.'

'Well, it's not quite that simple. There was a woman involved. Not Eva, not Carlotta du Bois, and not Christine Romaine . . . Someone else. Maybe I will tell you all about it one day. But it's too soon right now. We're still getting over Eva's death.'

'Okay,' I said, knowing now I couldn't push him. 'But if you won't talk about Eva, then answer me one other question – I'm sorry, but I must ask – what the hell were you doing having an affair with me?'

I didn't need to pry into his marriage, but this much I wanted to know.

He turned away from me.

'You won't like it,' he said.

'Tell me anyway.'

'I fell in love . . .'

I swallowed hard, fighting a sudden rush of tears at this unexpected offering, thinking back to our few indulgent months in Paris, suppers at the Café des Arbres, bottles of champagne, making love on the *chaise-longue* in his editing suite, long sexy phone calls from London to Paris . . . How little had I seen and understood?

'Hey, cheer up!' he said gently. 'This is supposed to be a happy ending, at least for me . . . But how about you, Beth? You still haven't told me what happened with Jamie.'

I scrabbled in my bag for a tissue.

'Jamie threw me out,' I sniffed. 'But it's only temporary. He'll have me back. He can't pay the mortgage without me.'

Duval sat down on the sofa beside me and I felt my spirits sink further, fearing that he would surely want answers to his own inevitable questions. What the hell was I doing with Jamie anyway? How come I seemed to be locked into what must look like a peculiarly masochistic form of mutual combat, strutting and straining and stabbing the air, but never once leaping out of the ring? I struggled to find the words, to explain that for nine years Jamie had been my best friend and protector, my still point in a wildly spinning world, but the rationale wouldn't come, perhaps, I recognised with an unwelcome flash of self-knowledge, because I steadfastly refused to examine the true reasons myself.

'I won't ask you about Jamie,' Duval murmured with enviable understanding. 'Maybe we all need a psychiatrist to explain us to ourselves . . . A psychiatrist, or a priest.'

'A priest?'

'Yes . . . It took Michael Cameron to help me work out why I'd fallen in love with you – and to make me see that if marriage is worth anything at all, then it demands perseverance and commitment, and above all, forgiveness.'

I looked at him critically, struggling for control, hoping to hang on to the last shreds of my objectivity, desperate not to reveal the turmoil that mere mention of Michael now seemed to produce in my troubled soul. Then I gave up.

'The sanctimonious sod,' I said.

*

'I'm very sorry, Michael,' I wept, twisting the diamond solitaire around my finger and willing him to look at me. 'Please tell me you forgive me!'

We were sitting in the front seat of the Bentley, deep in the heart of the whispering spinney, close enough to touch and a million miles between us.

'I really was very drunk. I didn't know what I was doing. And Sam was drunk too . . . We were celebrating.'

He said nothing, and still he wouldn't look at me, simply tightened his hands on the Bentley's leather steering wheel as though at any moment he might kick the car to life and plunge us down the wooded track into Uncle Malcolm's ruined chapel.

'I've done very well,' I said, 'I'm top of the final year group. I'm going to get a First . . . and Sam's got a job with the BBC . . . We had to celebrate.'

Now he did look at me.

'Do you usually celebrate in bed?' he asked.

I was very frightened, I felt weak and sick, and I could barely speak for crying.

'No! I swear I've never been to bed with anyone else . . .'

'Except Sam?'

'Yes. I mean, no! I didn't go to bed with Sam . . . That is, I didn't mean to go to bed with Sam. I just somehow ended up there.'

He'd gone silent on me again, sitting impassively while I pleaded and sobbed.

'We didn't do anything, I swear it. He didn't even touch me! And when I woke up I was still wearing my clothes.'

'Oh please, Beth,' he said, 'spare me the details.'

I was frantically trying to remember the details, but it wasn't easy. Did Sam touch me? Was I wearing my clothes? I hadn't the faintest idea. I only knew I'd been furious with him the following day, furious with myself for being so stupid, and quick to accept Sam's reassurances that he'd been far too drunk to perform. And if Vicky Henderson hadn't been plastered as well, I would have got away with it.

'That's the whole point!' I said desperately. 'There aren't any details. We got drunk. We fell into bed. We went to sleep.'

'The point,' said Michael very slowly, as though he were speaking to a half-wit, 'is not what you did or didn't do. It's more basic than that. The point is that if I hadn't phoned exactly when I did, and if Vicky hadn't been too drunk to lie, then I would never have known. You would never have told me . . .'

This was undeniably true. Only a fool would confess a drunken escapade to someone of Michael's moral stature, and though I might have behaved stupidly, I wasn't a fool. Even if Vicky had remembered what she'd said and given me prior warning, I would still have gambled on keeping mum. I would have rung him up, and I would have argued that, wanting Sam as she did and getting nowhere fast, Vicky had been imagining things.

But I'd been permitted no such easy escape. Michael had waited until I got home, he'd met me at the station in the Bentley, he'd driven me to the spinney, and he'd caught me completely off guard.

'I'm not making love to you,' he'd said as I began to take off my clothes. 'Not after Sam Lutz.'

Now I truly feared that it was all over, that he was about to demand the return of his ring, that all our passion and our plans had stalled upon a drunken fumble beneath the coverlet. I looked at him, searching urgently for something that would make it all right again. Please God, please help me . . .

'Forgive us our sins,' I mumbled through my tears, 'as we forgive those who sin against us . . .'

This proved to be very much the wrong remark.

'That's cheap,' he snapped.

'But isn't it what you're supposed to believe?' I asked, confused.

This was a genuine enquiry, but he must have perceived it as mocking, for suddenly and to my total shock, he leaned over from the driver's seat and hit me full in the face, not a restrained smack nor even a reprimanding slap, but a hefty clout that sent my head crashing back against the car window and my teeth into my cheek. I was too bewildered to fight back, and when he hauled me on to the back seat, too dazed to desist.

'Don't,' I cried ineffectually as he pulled down my pants. 'Please don't . . . I'm sorry.'

'Listen to me,' he said, unzipping his jeans. 'You're mine. You'll always be mine.'

I didn't struggle, partly because I felt it would be useless, partly because I feared he might really hurt me, but mostly because, with that peculiarly female logic born of perversity, I believed he was expressing his deepest feelings for me.

And afterwards, he was the one who cried, sobbing into my hair and kissing my face, begging my forgiveness, promising he would never hit me again.

'I love you so much . . . I can't bear to think of you with anyone else . . . I drive myself crazy wondering what you're doing . . . The whole world wants you, I know it. Not just Sam Lutz, everyone.'

I'd recovered my nerve by this time, and with it the power that comes from seeing tables satisfactorily turned.

'Oh shut up, Michael, for God's sake. I'm the one with the black eye.
You'll be lucky if I don't accuse you of rape.'

'Please don't say that . . .'

And of course, I didn't. But when I climbed into my bed that
night, sobered and reflective, I found myself pondering not only the
vexed issue of consent, but also the perils of Christian forgiveness.
How many times shall I forgive my brother? I knew the answer perfectly well and had no quarrel with it, but now I considered to what
extent the code of forgiveness might be used to legitimise sexual terr-
orism.

I knew Michael had frightened himself more than he had me, and for
my part I'd vowed that I would never again get drunk with any man
who'd declared his intention to get me into his bed.

But for the first time, a wider question nagged at my understanding, a doubt that I had always brushed aside. How would Michael
cope with the future I planned for myself, the career that would take
me away from his influence, the men I would meet and who might
want me? Was tonight's little scene no more than a painful aberration,
or had it revealed something dark and fundamental about our relationship?

I closed my eyes against this vision, but could not silence the refrain
that beat through my brain . . . How many times shall I forgive my
lover? Oh, again and again and again and again . . . And what shall I
forgive him? Oh everything, of course. Everything and anything, over
and over . . . Over and over again . . . Use me, abuse me, set me up,
knock me down . . . For ever and ever. Amen.

The spring sunshine infused the little lodge house with gold, touching
every corner and recess, filling the world with light and warmth, transforming my spirits. I couldn't believe how enchanting it was, and when
Duval took me into the garden, how utterly peaceful. Dense beech trees
surrounded a square of unruly grass, and through them a haphazard
path meandered, bringing us at last to the cliff and a view to stop the
angels in their tracks.

'It's heaven,' I said, gazing out across the wiry dunes and the silver
water of the bay. 'How did you come to be staying here?'

'My mother owns the cottage,' Duval replied to my surprise. 'The
Duvals and the Forsters are related. The big house was given to the
Church after the war, but the cottage remained with the family.'

'And where does Eva fit in?'

He smiled.

'You can't leave Eva alone, can you?'

I lifted the silver cross from where it lay beneath my blouse. 'It's Eva who won't leave me alone,' I said softly.

'What shall I tell you?' he muttered, almost to himself. 'It's a very complex web of relationships . . . I can't go into it all right now . . . But my father's mother was Helena Forster. Before she married my grand-father, Paul Duval, she was engaged to Edward Brannen, Eva's brother. He was killed in the First War.'

'So Eva and Helena, they were friends?'

'They were great friends.'

He glanced at his watch.

'I really must go. I have to see Michael Cameron.'

'More marriage counselling?' I enquired tartly, seating myself on a sheltered rustic bench carefully positioned to offer the best of the landscape. It was truly magnificent. The distant islands shone like polished stones in the silver, and the vast bank of rock poppies stretched in a golden platform down to the water's edge. I could see the church and the tumble of gravestones in the churchyard. I could see the vicarage, and standing behind the old stable buildings, a car that looked, even from this distance, very much like the old Bentley. Maybe Michael had parked it out of sight to spare my feelings. Or more likely, his.

'You really don't like him at all, do you? Women usually fall over themselves in the stampede.'

'Do they indeed? I thought he was going to marry the girl who runs the Retreat.'

He shot me a curious glance.

'My cousin Emily? Who told you that?'

It was Sarah who'd told me that, but I didn't want to say, so I rushed on with a list of questions about the Retreat in which I had scant interest.

'The Retreat is very much Michael's baby. It was nothing till he came here. Now it's a pastoral centre for the whole of the North-East. Spiritual care of the dying is mostly what they do . . . Dying and bereavement, that's where Michael sees his role at the moment.'

'Bereavement! What the hell does he know about that?'

My mother's death. Her broken body. The ebony coffin and its garish brass handles . . . Out of St Botolph's and past the Cameron family tomb . . . Breathe deep, Beth. One, two, three, four . . .

'Probably more than most of us,' Duval said, raising a questioning eyebrow. 'He lost his wife in an accident abroad. Their daughter was only two at the time. Pretty tough, wouldn't you say?'

I hadn't forgotten this traumatic piece of Cameron family history, but I had never allowed myself to dwell on Michael's marriage to Clare

Spencer, nor indeed her death, and now I felt mean-spirited and un-kind.

'Yes, of course,' I mumbled awkwardly. 'I'm sure the Retreat is doing a good job.'

'Michael is much admired, and Emily works very hard. She's a great girl, and they're clearly very fond of each other. But I doubt they'll get married.'

'Why not?' I asked grudgingly, unwilling to reveal the extent of my interest and still unsure what he might know, yet for all that, keen to discover the detail of Michael's private life.

'Various reasons, but not least that Michael's still grieving for his wife. I don't know the whole story, but he once told me he'd had a hard time, forgiving himself for her death . . . That's how he got into the bereavement work.'

I reflected upon this in silence. Forgiveness. How simple it sounded. Forgive us our sins as we forgive those . . . Yet how hard it was to achieve with the living, let alone the dead.

'Forgiving yourself for someone's death is the easy bit,' I said to Duval. 'It's forgiving the dead themselves that's so difficult.'

'That may very well be true. I'm tempted to say you should talk it over with Michael.'

'No thanks,' I said curtly.

He looked at me carefully, weighing his words.

'Beth, I do know that Michael is friendly with your sister . . . That you all knew each other years ago.'

So here it was, the scenario I'd dreaded all along, the knowledge that they had discussed me, the thought that Duval might have learned the whole truth about Michael and me . . .

'What did he tell you?' I interrupted. 'Please! I must know.'

He put his arm around my shoulder, gentle and concerned.

'Nothing more than that,' he reassured me. 'We've never talked about you, except in general terms of how affairs affect a marriage . . . He didn't even know it was you until he saw the story in the *Sun*.'

'That must have been a nice surprise,' I said, remembering the morning of Eva's funeral and how blunt and unsympathetic Michael had been.

'He was completely thrown. I think he was even more shocked than I was . . . That's when he told me he'd known your family years ago . . . I realised there must be rather more to it than that. But I wouldn't dream of asking, Beth. Not him, and not you.'

I smiled, inordinately grateful for this generosity, wondering if I could have been so forbearing in similar circumstances, or whether I might have insisted upon every tacky detail.

Duval looked at his watch again.

'I'm sorry, I do have to go. Eva left some money to St Cuthbert's. I need to sort out the details before we leave in the morning.'

'Yes, I must go too . . .'

I stood up from the bench and took one last breath of the salty air blowing in from the dunes. I was reluctant to leave, but I still hadn't fixed a place to stay.

He hesitated.

'You could always stay here,' he ventured. 'We're only around for another night. It will be empty from tomorrow, and like you said, it's a great place to lie low.'

'Stay here tonight with you and your wife? I don't think so . . . But thanks.'

'I'm sorry you won't meet Genny,' he said as we walked back to my car. 'Maybe you'll come and see us in Paris some time?'

I smiled at him, suddenly and foolishly sad.

'It seems unlikely,' I said, 'I was only there because of the filming. I never told you this, but the truth is – I've always hated Paris.'

I got off at the Gare du Nord, my face hot and sticky, my stomach heaving. I'd been sick twice, once on the boat from Folkestone and once on the train from Calais, and I wasn't sure how long it would be to the next time. I prayed Michael would be there to meet me.

He wasn't, and I paced up and down outside the station in the grimy rain, clapping my hand to my mouth when the fumes from a passing autobus threatened to overcome me, miserable, ill and annoyed. April in Paris. Chestnuts in blossom. Oh yeah.

It wasn't my first time in the city. There had been that one idyllic weekend nearly eighteen months before when we'd walked by the Seine, drunk champagne on the Champs-Elysées, and trawled the bars of Montparnasse in a fruitless, but captivating, bid to find the café once frequented by my Grandfather Martineau. I'd fallen in love with Paris at once, as everyone of any sensibility surely must. I longed to return, but somehow we'd never made it until this ill-starred weekend, only weeks away from my finals and less than a couple of months after our fracas in the Bentley. I'd looked forward to it eagerly, needing time alone with Michael to convince me that everything really was all right again.

'Sorry I'm late,' he said, kissing me perfunctorily on the cheek. 'What's the matter? You look terrible.'

'Thank you, dear,' I said stonily. 'You're so gallant. If you must know, I was sick on the train. Probably something I ate.'

'Not a hangover, is it?'

After this unpromising start I might have divined that things could only get worse, but still I believed in the magic of the lovers' city, as though Paris, even in the pouring rain with a stomach upset, couldn't fail to do its stuff. How wrong I was.

'I've got to lie down,' I said as soon as we got to the flat, 'I feel really rough.'

Jack Cameron's Paris apartment was a rambling, sunny string of rooms on the top floor of a shabby block just off the Jardin des Plantes. It was barely furnished, a few chairs and a sofa standing on polished wooden floors, and the first time I'd seen it, I thought it delightful. Today it looked spartan and depressing.

'I made you some tea,' Michael said, sitting down on the end of the bed. 'English tea-bags. None of your French rubbish.' He was trying hard, but he was unusually subdued, and I could hardly fail to catch his mood.

I sat up in bed.

'I feel a bit better now. Why don't you take off your clothes and get in beside me?'

He seemed to spend a long time considering it, as though what he normally did without a second thought now required a major decision, but at last he began to unbutton his shirt and I took a gulp of my tea, fervently hoping I could make it through without dashing for the bathroom. I needed him naked and close to me. With the flawed reasoning of one who intuits trouble and must assert her claim, I urgently needed to make love.

It wasn't a great success, and at one point I almost thought he wouldn't make it, but then he rallied for the final effort and exploded into me, collapsing in a sigh and then lying silent beside me. No kissing, no touching, no reassurance, and a decided reluctance to do what we always did.

'Have you gone off oral sex?'

'What? Oh, sorry, I was thinking about something else . . .' He caressed me absently between the legs, and I smacked his hand away.

'Don't force yourself,' I said.

He sat up.

'Beth, we have to talk. There's something I must say to you. This is very difficult for me, I don't know how to begin . . . I didn't want to tell you here in Paris, but I can't get through the whole weekend . . .'

I listened with growing anxiety, unable to concentrate for the turmoil in my gut, trying to follow a ramshackle argument about faith and right action and sex and spiritual needs. We had met too young. Spiritual awareness comes slowly, and requires much nurturing. We loved each other too much. Unrestrained passion is the enemy of the peaceful heart. We both had to think what we wanted from our lives.

God has a plan for each one of us . . . Then I ran to the bathroom and threw up.

'Are you all right?' he enquired anxiously when I returned.

My teeth were chattering and I thought I would surely faint.

'Do I look all right?' I gasped. 'What the hell is this about?'

'I have to let you go,' he said, biting his lip, 'I love you too much. It's not good for either of us . . . I've been told I have to let you go.'

It wasn't immediately clear whether this dictate had come from God, his mother, the Master of Trinity College or the Archbishop of Canterbury. But the finger of suspicion soon pointed heavenwards.

'You know I hope to be a priest – to have my vocation tested . . . And I'm sure you understand that I have to get my priorities right.'

'You mean I'm not number one any more?'

'I'll never love anyone else.'

'Except God, of course?'

'It's not a contest, Beth. Please don't say that.'

'Well, what then? What is all this? If it's not a contest, there's no problem. Priests get married, don't they? Or have you secretly gone over to Rome?'

I'd got back into bed, and was starting to feel a little stronger. I was also, now I'd gathered my wits, disinclined to take him too seriously. I was well used to his theological ramblings on the nature of moral choice and self-sacrifice. This was just more of the same, with an edge provided, I guessed, by what had happened on the back seat of the Bentley.

'Don't joke, Beth. This is very important. It's over between us. It has to be.'

'Michael, don't be ridiculous. You can't possibly mean you never want to see me again?'

He began to cry, and I began to panic.

'Don't tell me this has anything to do with Sam Lutz,' I begged, 'I can't bear it.'

'I wanted to kill you,' he wept. 'Really I did. But it's not about that. It's not even that I've finally recognised I can't hang on to you. We're travelling in different directions, Beth. You must see that.'

'But I love you,' I said, bewildered. 'Truly I do. I'll take your direction. Any time.'

'It's no good, Beth. I'm not saying I never want to see you again – I can hardly bear the thought of that. But we must have some time apart. Maybe in a few years' time, it will all come right —'

'A few years!'

I stared as though he'd gone truly mad, unable to believe he could possibly mean what I seemed to be hearing.

'Michael, people don't break up and then get back together in a few years! What the hell are we supposed to do in the meantime?'

I reached out for him, but he would not be consoled nor persuaded, and feeling queasy again as well as sick at heart, I prepared to give up, at least temporarily.

'Get back into bed,' I said, putting my arms around him. 'We'll talk it over in the morning.'

He flinched from me, and then stood up.

'I can't make love to you again,' he announced. 'I'll have to sleep on the sofa,' and still weeping, he walked out of the bedroom.

I watched him go, astonished. Then I was sick one more time, and staring at my wan and harassed face in the mirror above the washstand in the corner of the room, suddenly, implacably furious. All the way to Paris for this? Well, fuck him . . .

I got dressed and careered out into the teeming night, back to the Gare du Nord through dank and desperate streets, my feet and clothes soaked, my hair plastered to my cheeks. I couldn't find a cab, and I walked for what seemed like miles, no idea of direction, my stomach tight as a drum, my throat aching and sore. All the famous landmarks seemed to pass me by, looming out of the rainy gloom like picture postcards from hell, and somewhere by the Tuileries I lost a shoe. A drunk lurched out of an alley and grabbed at my bag, and a fat Frenchman propositioned me, waving a bundle of francs under my nose. I smelt his breath on my face, sour and hot, and I cried out in fright. I found myself by the river, alone on a dark and echoing walkway, and when I heard a footfall behind me, I began to sob wildly, running on my one shoe, panting and shaking, crazy and sick. Paris, I hate you . . . I'll always hate you . . .

But I made it back to the Gare du Nord, and I made it back to college, and once I settled to my work, things didn't seem so bad. Michael would get over it, I knew he would. I was still wearing his ring, after all. He hadn't asked for it back. And the best news: I'd landed a job with a radio station, selected from a hundred bright sparks who failed to impress the controller half as much as me. My career was beginning, the future unfolding, and Michael would be part of it.

This seemed so inevitable, so utterly right and obvious, that I didn't doubt it for a moment. There had been occasions in the previous three years when I'd wondered whether life might be simpler without someone of Michael's simmering intensity. When his passion and his spiritual questing seemed oppressive, and his sexual possessiveness a heavy burden. But such was the price of his devotion, and most times I could handle it, snapping him out of his seriousness with a wry put-down. Furthermore, I loved him deeply. He was the one for me. All the clever, posturing young men I'd met at university, including Sam Lutz, merely served to convince me.

So I threw myself into my finals, convinced it would all work out. Michael would think it over, and he would call me and apologise. There was nothing at all to worry about.

Only one small thing bothered me. For some inexplicable reason, my period was late.

To my dismay, the Black Swan was fully booked. What the hell were all these people doing in a godforsaken town like Alnwick on a freezing weekend in spring? The receptionist looked offended, and then looked again. I'd been recognised, and I strode out of the hotel in a mild paddy, wondering what I would do now. The Dolphin? Or should I take Duval up on his offer and go back to the lodge cottage?

I drove through the winding wooded lanes surrounding the Retreat once more, considering with some trepidation whether Genevieve Duval could possibly turn out to be as accommodating as her husband had suggested. I thought about the picture in the *Sun*, which had shown a petite, dark-haired woman whose mother hadn't proved to be second cousin to the Queen at all. That distinction, it seemed, belonged to her latest stepmother, and as revealed in her story, not only had she never met the Queen, she'd never met her father's fourth wife either.

I knocked on the cottage door, hoping I'd find Duval returned from his meeting with Michael, but instead there she was, much prettier than her picture in the *Sun*, long black hair hanging in an impressive pigtail down her back, wearing a cream wool designer jump suit. My first thought was whether she'd bought it with Clive Fisher's money, and my second to wonder why, when he had a woman like this at home, Daniel Duval should imagine himself in love with me.

'Beth . . . Dan told me you were here. I'm glad you came back. Come in, for God's sake. Have a drink.'

For a few moments we skirted the issue with talk of Alnwick, the Black Swan, and the virtues of red wine as opposed to white. Then she opened a classy Bordeaux and sat down on the sofa beside me.

'I hope I haven't screwed up your life. Dan says Jamie threw you out.'

'I have only myself to blame. It's a ludicrous idea that you should somehow apologise to me. Mine was the greater sin.'

She laughed and filled our glasses to the brim.

'Oh, let's not talk of sin,' she said. 'It's much too depressing.'

I was chary of saying or asking too much, and I listened in silence and growing discomfort while she related the tale of her meeting with Clive Fisher.

'Well, he was waving a lot of money, and I was very hard up,' she said gaily.

'Yes . . . I understand.'

'But I do have a few scruples, you know – although I usually manage to ignore them!'

She giggled, and I smiled uncertainly.

'And then, of course, I ended up in bed with him,' she laughed.

'With Clive Fisher?' I said, astonished. 'You're joking!'

'I wish I were! But so did you, didn't you, once upon a time? That's what he told me . . . Years ago, when you were on some radio station together. In fact, he still seemed to have a bit of a thing about you. I was worried at one point he was going to warn you off. And then I wouldn't have got the money!'

She laughed again, and I stared in acute embarrassment. Had I ever slept with Clive Fisher? Very probably, if he said so. My wild days on the radio station were no more than an alcoholic blur, and I couldn't be too sure what I'd done.

An alarming thought occurred to Genevieve.

'You won't mention that to Dan, will you? I didn't actually tell him about Clive . . . There didn't seem any point. And in any case, it was just a little lapse.'

'Only one?' I asked before I could stop myself.

She threw me a bemused glance, and I had the grace to blush. I was in no position to judge Genny Duval, and yet I was shocked by her confession, and immediately thrown into speculation about the state of her marriage.

'I have been wickedly unfaithful to my husband,' she announced, confirming all my suspicions. 'I have made him very miserable on a number of occasions. But then, he's made me very miserable too, in other ways . . . Now we're both making a big effort. I'm going to try very hard to be a good girl and he's going to wrestle with the revolutionary idea that there's more to life than making movies . . .'

I gazed at her uncomfortably, thinking I suddenly saw a marriage made in hell, remembering that Duval had never once criticised her to me, nor sought to explain or excuse himself, wondering how, when she'd set him up in such spectacular fashion, he'd ever found it in his heart to forgive.

Genevieve was drinking fast, faster than me, which generally took some doing, and I shook my head when she waved the bottle my way.

'Dan would like me to believe he's only been unfaithful once,' she confided merrily, 'and then he had the cheek to say that, technically speaking, since he'd already left me when he met you, it didn't count as adultery. The vicar of St Cuthbert's set him straight on that one. You know Michael Cameron, I suppose?'

'We've met,' I said dully, less concerned in that moment with Michael's role than with the sobering news that, all along, Duval had considered himself free to make love to me. Why had he never told me that? What difference might it have made if he had?

'Yes, the Reverend Mr Cameron is a real pain in the arse,' Genevieve was saying. 'I hope he watched your programme the other night because you really hit the nail on the head. The whole concept of romantic love is a male plot, designed to keep women drooling at the mouth. It's moralistic nonsense to insist that marriage is some kind of holy, inviolable state, and that we must all resign ourselves to having sex with just one person for the rest of our lives . . . Human nature isn't like that, is it?'

I couldn't begin to unpick this argument, nor to suggest that whatever I seemed to have said in *Moonlight and Roses*, I'd never sought to write off monogamous marriage as an honourable choice for those who believed in it.

'I wonder why you ever got married?' I asked her carefully.

She laughed and stood up to open a second bottle of wine. 'Because I was pregnant, of course!' she said, as though I'd not only lost all powers of deduction, but also common sense. 'Believe me, Beth, it changes everything. One day you've got the whole world at your feet, and the next your future has disappeared in a pile of dirty nappies . . . I should have had an abortion. I very nearly did. But no, he cried and he begged. He had to marry me, and in the end I gave in.'

My head was spinning, my spirits were plunging, and I'd begun to think longingly of the Dolphin Inn. I seemed to see Duval as he must have been fifteen years before, urging Genevieve to marry him, pleading with her not to have an abortion, and the vision was enough to break my heart.

I could have howled aloud, but instead I smiled weakly and accepted another glass of Bordeaux. I didn't want to discuss abortion or children or marriage or romantic love with Genevieve Duval. I wanted to go to bed and sob into my pillow, to weep in blissful isolation for all my mistakes and my lost opportunities, to begin to unravel all the tortuous emotional processes underlying this mortifying encounter with a woman I now disliked beyond all reasonable measure.

'Nice wine,' I muttered, seeking to divert her.

'Yes,' she said merrily, slurring the word ever so slightly and then raising her glass to clink it on mine. 'I know you like a little drink as well – Dan told me as much . . . In fact, we have a great deal in common, don't we, Beth?'

She emitted another of her irritating giggles.

'I've already made this point to my dear husband,' she confided, lurching across the sofa towards me. 'He fell in love with you because you reminded him of me! It's obvious, isn't it, Beth? You and me – we're two of a kind!'

Chapter Twenty-one

The Kingdom isn't always a comfortable place to be. There are no hard and fast rules by which we shall become loyal subjects, only the demand that we love one another. But how is it possible to live by love alone? How can we order our daily business in the light of such a demand? When we seem to be surrounded by those who would hurt or despise us, by those who harbour resentment against us, by those who would ridicule or deliberately misunderstand, then love not only seems a tall order, but a self-defeating one. And when we gaze on the horrors of the world, famine, war, genocide, plague, then love seems hopelessly inadequate. Surely what we need is not love, but political will and social action? A change of government? A revolution at the World Bank? An end to the arms trade? We may need all of these, but loyal subjects of the Kingdom are party to an extra understanding, and it is this: the significant battle for justice, for peace and for love, is the one that takes place in my own soul.

The Freedom of the Kingdom, by Michael Cameron

I slept surprisingly well, and awoke to furious rain on the window of my little room under the cottage eaves. I sat up in bed and fumbled for my watch. It was early, but not so early that folk with a plane to catch shouldn't be up and about.

I listened carefully, unsure how I would handle the goodbyes, wondering if the Duvals might have left without waking me. This was a comforting thought. I had no desire to set eyes on Genevieve again, and at the same time I had become rather wistful about Duval, a sentiment unlikely to do either of us any good.

I lay for another half-hour, and then, certain they must have gone, got up. It was immediately apparent that they hadn't left: suitcases standing in the hall, coats hanging on pegs. I dithered in the kitchen, wondering if I should take them tea, imagining myself knocking on their door and facing them over the tray as they lay in bed together. Perhaps not.

If the weather hadn't been so foul I would have walked to the cliff or explored the lanes around the Retreat, but there was no going out, and I sat on the sofa, idly flicking the TV between various breakfast show offerings, deeply thankful that my own era of rising at 3.30 a.m., five days a week, was over.

The breakfast fare was boring. Had it been that dull when I'd been dishing it up? Probably. I turned off the TV.

Then I remembered my video of *Casey's War*, and reckoning this might usefully provide something else to talk about as we all made our farewells, prepared to watch it.

A Worldwide Pictures Production, Starring Will Sutton. Introducing Eva Delamere and Carlotta du Bois. Directed by David Klein . . .

I was immediately immersed in my memories of Eva again. And although I'd seen the film before, I quickly realised that I'd never appreciated the control of the script, the tightness of the direction, nor indeed, the power of the performances. How melancholy and erotically restrained Eva had been as the French prostitute, Vivi. How poignantly she fell into Will Sutton's arms, and how prettily she turned her cheek as he bent to kiss her. How handsome and utterly American he had been. And how impressive a début Carlotta had made as the avenging Sister Marie.

'Oh God,' said a voice behind me. 'Not bloody *Casey's War*.'

Genevieve was not looking her best, nor feeling her best, it seemed, for she marched over to the TV and snapped it off at once, massaging her temples and glaring at me balefully.

'Sorry,' I said nervously. 'You've got a headache . . .'

'That bloody film always gives me a headache,' she said, clattering into the kitchen. 'Did you ever feel you were being haunted? I sometimes think there's no escaping bloody David Klein.'

Duval was standing in the doorway, and he smiled at me encouragingly, seemingly unbothered by his wife's ill-temper, enquiring how I'd slept, placidly accepting Genevieve's announcement that they couldn't depart until she'd washed her hair. He poured himself tea and sat down on the sofa beside me.

'Won't you miss your plane?' I asked unhappily as Genevieve drifted past us upstairs again. I was anxious for them to be gone, unable to bear the sight of them together.

'It doesn't matter. We'll catch the next one.'

He waited until she was out of earshot, and then switched on the video again.

'I haven't watched it for at least eighteen months,' he said with a little laugh.

We viewed in virtual silence, both of us hanging upon every line.

'David Klein was a very gifted director,' I said at last.

'Yes. Yes, he was.'

'I wonder what he would have made of *The Rose Garden*?' I said, half to myself.

'Unfortunately,' Duval replied, 'I know only too well. He would have said that the world changes, and art changes, but some things never change. That art, whether it's poetry, novels, cinema or music, requires coherence and beauty, and above all, vision, because these are the things that the human spirit craves.'

I stretched out my hand to his, an impulsive gesture I immediately regretted for the sudden physical contact seemed to shock us both, reminding us of all that had been.

'I thought *The Rose Garden* was very beautiful,' I muttered awkwardly. 'I wish I hadn't been tanked up on Clive Fisher's booze the day I saw it. Then I might have understood it rather better.'

He laughed and squeezed my hand before withdrawing his own.

'You probably wouldn't. Beauty it has, and vision too. But you need all three. Without coherence, you might as well be preaching the end of the world. That's what David Klein would have said.'

I looked at him curiously.

'You seem to know a lot about him.'

'I know all there is to know – the things you'll never find in any biography. One day I'll tell you the whole truth about David Klein . . . The next time you come to Paris.'

I blinked and swallowed hard, unable to imagine in what circumstance I might see him again without the dreadful Genevieve by his side, fighting a sickening longing to turn back the clock, filled with a sense of loss.

'When we were together in Paris,' I whispered, unable to stop myself, knowing the question to be foolish and unfair, 'why didn't you tell me that you'd left Genny?'

'Because you wouldn't have wanted to know,' he said briskly, standing up from the sofa and busying himself with saucers and cups. 'Now, shall I make some coffee? Don't miss this scene – it's the big one between Eva and Carlotta. They're both wonderful. Carlotta was much the better actress, of course, but Eva's performance has gained over the years. Now it looks like a triumph of dramatic restraint . . .'

He was dismissing all talk of intimate matters, and, chastened and subdued, I returned to *Casey's War*, watching as Eva and Will shaped up for the final love scene, gathering my own trammelled emotions as theirs rose to a shuddering crescendo.

'So, what do you think?' asked Duval as the credits rolled.

'I think it's a fine anti-war statement,' I said steadily, my wayward heart in check once more. 'All the more masterful because there's nothing of the war in it . . . But I confess I've always been dubious about the ending. Not only is it hopelessly romantic, but it's a bit too neat. Too coherent, you might say . . .'

He laughed.

'They used to argue about the ending,' he said.

'Did they? Eva and Toby?'

He looked at me carefully, as though wondering how much he might reveal, and then making his decision, surprised me.

'Not Eva and Toby,' he said. 'They were divorced right after Will Sutton died. I realise you must have thought they were still married – a lot of people did. But in fact, they only got together a few years ago, when they both found themselves alone again.'

I was taken aback by this news, having imagined Eva happily married to Toby Truman throughout her long life, and I wanted more detail at once, but a shout from above signalled an end to all our discussions.

'Please don't mention David Klein in front of Genny,' Duval said quickly. 'It doesn't go down well . . .'

They departed in a flurry of almost-forgotten clothes, hair slides and handbags, issuing warnings about the fridge and a window which wouldn't close once you opened it, urging me to stay as long as I wished, pressing me to visit them in Paris.

'Come and meet my children,' Genevieve invited in a loud stage whisper as he packed the car. 'Then you'll see how lucky you are not to have any.'

'I'm sure you don't mean that,' I said stiffly, glancing at Duval to see if he'd heard and recognising at once that, if he had, he didn't mean to react.

'Oh, but I do! Take a tip from me, Beth. If you're ever tempted to get pregnant, think again and cross your legs quick! Children are so terribly evident . . . They never go away.'

She kissed me on the cheek, declaring that she couldn't think of anyone she'd rather her husband went to bed with, and as I met Duval's eye for the last time, I caught the first intimation of his embarrassment. He had wanted his wife to apologise to me, but the price was my understanding of what she was.

I waved them goodbye with a mixture of intense relief and lingering regret, wondering if I would ever see Duval again, deeply, and I knew unjustifiably, resentful of Genevieve's role in his life. How could she say such a thing to me about his children, even if she meant it as a joke?

The rain had cleared, so I wandered along to the clifftop, and finding a path down, picked my way to the beach, inhaling the briny breeze from the sea, feeling my lungs expand and my cheeks burn. This was a good place to be. I was lucky to be here. I was a mature responsible person in charge of my own destiny. I wouldn't imagine myself belatedly in love with Daniel Duval, and I wouldn't think twice about Genevieve and her careless comments. What did she know? Nothing, nothing at all. I wouldn't think about her, nor her children, nor any children that I might have had myself. I would not contemplate what might have been.

And then, rounding a dip in the dunes, I suddenly came upon Katie Cameron, alone and absorbed in a sandcastle, looking so very like her father that it took my breath away.

The campus doctor was young and sympathetic, a pretty Asian woman, only a few years older than myself.

'I can't possibly be pregnant,' I told her with as much control as I could muster, hoping that if I sounded calm and authoritative I would in some way influence the outcome of events. 'I'm on the Pill.'

She looked down at her notes.

'I'm sorry, Miss Carlisle, the test was quite definitely positive. There can be no doubt. It now becomes a question of what you do next . . .'

She handed me a tissue from a box on her desk, and I wiped my eyes and blew my nose. Then I formed the tissue into a hard, even ball, twisting it relentlessly in the palm of my hand. This couldn't be happening. It couldn't be true. I'd been so careful. I'd promised my mother.

'But I took it at the same time every day!' I burst out accusingly, as though all the flawed promises of medical science were this one woman's responsibility and hers alone. 'I've never forgotten it. How can I be pregnant?'

She consulted the folder on her desk once more.

'You weren't taking any antibiotics, were you? No . . . Well, Miss Carlisle, the Pill is a very good contraceptive, but unfortunately it isn't one hundred per cent effective. Certain things can interfere with it. Perhaps you had a stomach upset? If you vomit a pill at your time of ovulation, then you may leave yourself unprotected. And if you have intercourse during that time . . .'

Paris, bloody Paris. Oh Paris, I hate you.

'There now,' said the doctor comfortingly, handing me more tissues and ordering a cup of tea over the intercom, 'it's not that bad. I see you're wearing an engagement ring . . . If you were intending to get married anyway, maybe you can just bring the wedding forward?'

A wedding? Me, walking down the aisle at St Botolph's in ivory silk with Sarah as bridesmaid and my mother and Lady Cameron standing together in the front pews? Toasting us with champagne? Both of them preparing to become grandmothers?

'There are a few difficulties,' I muttered, bitterly aware in that moment of the greatest difficulty, of the fact that I hadn't heard from Michael, nor succeeded in contacting him, since I'd left Paris. 'We had a row. We don't seem to be speaking at the moment.'

I heard the words through my tears, appalled and disbelieving, gazing distractedly at the shiny, antiseptic walls of the campus surgery and its threatening array of posters. WORRIED ABOUT SEXUALLY TRANSMITTED DISEASE? ARE YOU DRINKING TOO MUCH? GOT A PROBLEM YOU CAN'T SHARE?

'Oh dear,' said the doctor, 'I am sorry. Well, the important thing is not to make any hasty decisions. Give yourself time. I'm sure your fiancé won't let you down. Talk it over with him, and come back in a week.'

Outside the surgery on the windswept quad, I walked and wept and tried to think. Nothing had changed, I told myself. It was still my body, and everything in it belonged to me. I felt no different at all. I wasn't sick, I wasn't bloated, I wasn't any of the things you're supposed to be when you're pregnant. I could cope. I would survive. Nothing had changed.

But in truth, everything had changed. In a moment, my life had been irrevocably altered. Whatever happened, whatever I chose to do, I would never be quite the same again. Even if I had an abortion – and there was no shame, of course, in abortion for an intelligent, liberated young woman like myself – why, even then my history, medical and emotional, would for ever bear the mark.

I pressed a hand to my stomach, fumbling beneath my jacket and blouse, prodding, poking, stroking the flatness. Could it really be true? What would Michael say? What would he want to do? And what about my mother and my job on the radio station? I was eaten up with fear, with the threat of events beyond my control, and suddenly gripped by a burning resentment, an all-pervasive despair in the face of irrefutable womanhood. Yes, it was true. Gender was destiny. Freedom was illusory, a battle against biology requiring constant vigilance. You might cheat your fate for a while, but God knew, it would get you in the end.

Across the quad, Sam Lutz waved.

'Hi! Everything okay? You look a little peaky . . .'

'I'm okay, thanks. Just working hard.'

The men, they would never understand this merciless female destiny. Oh yes, they might feel trapped, pressured, intimidated, by a pregnant girlfriend. But they would never know what it meant to have something inside you, growing bigger day by day, feeding on your life, on all your dreams and your plans, casting its monstrous shadow across your future, sucking away at your autonomy, eating its path into your very soul.

'Fancy a drink?' asked Sam. 'I said I'd see Vicky in the Common Room. You look like you could use a couple of stiff gins.'

'I'll come and find you,' I said brightly. 'I have to make a quick phone call first.'

I'd already called Michael twice at his college, and left messages both times. I knew his exams were earlier than my own, and that it was now quite possible he'd gone home. With trembling fingers I dialled the number, praying he would answer, or if not him, then Jack Cameron or Jonathan.

'Hallo?' said Beatrice Cameron cooly. 'Oh, it's you, Beth. No, I'm sorry, Michael isn't here . . . He's gone abroad for the summer with Clare Spencer. They're working at a Christian youth camp in the South of France . . .'

I tried to keep calm, anxious to hang on to a semblance of normality, desperate not to give myself away.

'I really do need to speak to him,' I said, hearing my voice ring out, unnaturally cheery and casual. 'Can you give me the number?'

There was a long pause.

'Now listen, Beth,' Beatrice Cameron said carefully, 'Michael has told me everything. I understand it's very hard for you to accept, but he doesn't wish to see you again. There's nothing to be gained by ringing him up.'

Hysteria threatened, but still I tried to hang on.

'I must have the number,' I begged. 'Please give it to me.'

I could picture her standing by the leather-topped desk in the library at the Cameron house, the pale hair drawn back from her face in its alarming pleat, her mouth set in a tight seal of disapproval, and I saw her expression as she spoke, half-way between a sneer and a satisfied smile.

'I'm not giving you the number,' she said curtly. 'You must leave Michael alone.'

Then I cracked.

'You fucking cow,' I shrieked. 'I have every right to speak to him!'

She hung up at once and I stumbled out of the telephone kiosk, straight into Sam's arms.

'What is it?' he cried in alarm. 'Beth, what's wrong?'

'I'm having a baby,' I sobbed, clinging to his arm and burying my face in his jacket. 'I'm having Michael's baby. But he doesn't know, and I can't get hold of him. Oh God, whatever am I going to do?'

We looked at each other in surprise and mutual delight.

'Hi, Beth.'

'Hi, Katie. What are you doing on the beach all by yourself?'

I crouched down beside her and inspected the sandcastle, filling one of her little buckets and attempting to unmould it.

She watched critically, laughing when my efforts collapsed one after another.

'I was with the boys,' she said, glancing across to the churchyard, 'but they're playing a silly game. I didn't want to join in.'

I nodded in sympathy. Katie Cameron now had five boys for her holiday playmates, Lucy's three and Sarah's two. Little wonder she felt the need to sneak off.

'I think boys are pretty silly all round,' I said. 'Girls are much nicer.'

She looked at me seriously, as though weighing up whether this could possibly be true.

'Have you got any children?' she demanded.

'No, I haven't,' I said steadily. 'Just my nephews, Mark and Tom.'

'No girls?'

'Well, I do have a little god-daughter. She's called Chloe Lutz. But she's only three, so she doesn't really count. Not yet.'

This sob story seemed to put me in good stead, for Katie suddenly leaned over to one of her buckets, extracting a large pink shell and pressing it into my hand. I thanked her gravely, promising I'd always keep it on my dressing table, then remembering that at this peculiarly uncomfortable point in my life, I didn't actually have a dressing table.

I stood up, reminding myself of the need for self-control where Katie was concerned, fighting the desire, once more, to establish a bond which she might not want and which I didn't deserve. And yet, it was plain she liked me. It surely couldn't hurt, I told myself, to be genuinely friendly . . .

'Would you like to come to my house? I'm staying in the little cottage up by the Retreat. Have you ever seen it?'

'Oh yes, but I've never been inside,' she said enthusiastically. Then she hesitated. 'I'm not supposed to go off this bit of the beach. Daddy will be cross if I do. He's in charge of everyone today. Lucy's gone to Alnwick.'

I smiled with difficulty, my heart suddenly jealous at this vision of Michael, the dutiful father and exemplary parish priest, presiding over so many assorted children. Was it not my privilege, I thought with an

unexpected flash of avenging zeal, to relieve him of one of them, just
for the afternoon?

'There's no problem,' I said lightly to Katie. 'I'll ring up your daddy
when we get home and let him know where you are.'

We walked back up the cliff path to the cottage, and then we raided
the Duvals' freezer for a gourmet lunch of chicken in white wine sauce,
supplemented by fish fingers. We picked bluebells from the garden, we
found a Scrabble board in a cupboard, we watched children's TV and
we played I Spy, and then as darkness fell, she began to get anxious.

'When you phoned Daddy, did he say what time he'd pick me up?'

'No, he didn't,' I said, my conscience stirring at last. 'Shall I call him
now to find out?'

But before I made it to the phone, a squeal of car brakes on the road
outside the cottage announced the arrival of the Bentley, and the scene
which, since the moment when Michael had first rung me with news of
Eva's funeral, I'd always known would have to be played out.

'Ah, here's your daddy now,' I said to Katie, peering out of the
cottage window and wondering what process of deduction had finally
led the vicar of St Cuthbert's to my door. 'Oh dear – I'm afraid he looks
in rather a bad mood.'

I did what any girl in such a situation does and ran home to mother,
terrified of what she might say when she saw me. I'd already phoned
and blurted out my sorry tale, registering at once her resignation and
her disappointment, and now I urgently needed her love and her consolation. I prayed she wouldn't let me down.

She took me into the conservatory at once and sat beside me on the
cane settee, wrapping her arms around me while I sobbed and shook
and while Sarah, somewhat less sympathetic than expected, crashed
around in the kitchen, making tea.

'Don't cry, darling,' my mother said softly, stroking my hair. 'We can
work it out one way or another. You'll see.'

I was heartily glad to receive this reassurance, but I couldn't see how
on earth it would work out.

'Michael's away for the whole of the summer,' I wept, 'and they
won't tell me where he is. I'll be five months gone by the time he gets
back.'

My mother gesticulated impatiently at Sarah who was standing by the
conservatory door waving the teapot, looking rather as though, with a
little encouragement, she might bring it down upon my head. But she
left us alone, and my mother took my hand.

'Michael will be home very soon,' she told me gently. 'But before he gets here, you must decide what you want. It's no good leaving any decisions up to him.'

I stared in surprise through my tears. Michael coming home? How? Why?

'Jack's sent for him. And the tone of the communication is designed to get him back pretty fast.'

I considered this news unhappily, not at all sure I wanted any of the Camerons to know the truth before I'd told Michael myself. But then, I didn't know what I wanted, what was for the best. In the days since my visit to the doctor, I'd lurched between a desperate desire for a quick abortion to planning a life as the curate's wife, home-made scones for the church fête, and all.

'Did you have to tell Michael's father?' I asked grudgingly, subdued and confused.

'There was no other way. But don't worry, darling. He's very sympathetic, and very concerned about you. Michael won't get off lightly, take it from me.'

I could see that she certainly didn't mean to let him off lightly, and the prospect was somewhat unnerving. I couldn't imagine it would do any good to have Michael hauled home from France and taken to task, either by his father or my mother, or by a disapproving combination of both.

'It's not Michael's fault,' I said anxiously, keen now to defend him. 'And he can't be blamed for going away when he doesn't know what's happening . . .'

'It's not a question of fault,' my mother said severely. 'It's a question of responsibility. And anyway, it's Michael's fault that he dumped you in Paris, isn't it? Three years of sex whenever he feels like it, and then he decides that maybe this isn't such a good idea. Maybe God would like him to be rather more restrained. Contemplate his navel a bit more. Accentuate the spiritual. So . . . bye-bye Beth! Well, he has a nice surprise coming, doesn't he?'

I received this tart little speech with a mixture of shock and dismay, shocked because I hadn't distilled Michael's agonised ramblings into quite this bald analysis myself, and dismayed because I'd said nothing at all about Paris to anyone. Whatever my mother knew, it hadn't come from me.

'Who's Michael been talking to?' I asked querulously.

'His mother, of course, who related all to Jack with considerable glee. And while we're on the subject, Beth, it wasn't a good idea to call Beatrice Cameron a fucking cow on the phone . . . You must try to keep calm. We must all try to keep calm.'

I was trying very hard, but mention of Michael's mother set me off again. I knew she would do all in her power to keep Michael from me, and although, after the Paris débâcle, I'd managed to persuade myself he'd come round, I was suddenly, frighteningly, unsure of my claim.

'Now, come along,' my mother said briskly, standing up and leading me out of the conservatory. 'We're going to eat. You've got to keep up your strength!'

We sat down at the dinner table together, my mother bright and reassuringly cheerful, myself weepy and inert, my sister unusually ill-tempered and curt.

'What's the matter?' I asked her as we cleared the dishes into the kitchen and she snatched a pile of plates from my hand. 'Something's wrong.'

'You mean you've actually noticed that something else might be wrong? Oh, bravo, Beth!'

'What is it?' I asked, upset and hurt.

'It's Leo,' Sarah said morosely, 'Leo on the phone, night and day, Leo hanging round outside the door and hiding in the garden. Ask her about Leo, Beth. She needs to deal with Leo, but everything's on hold because of you and Michael . . .'

I stared at her blankly, unable to imagine how any dilemma involving one of my mother's lovers could possibly be influenced by me, but Sarah was not inclined to elaborate.

'It's not my place to tell you,' she snapped. 'Ask her.'

Back in the conservatory, my mother poured me a glass of wine and I sipped at it nervously, thinking that if I were going to have Michael's baby then I shouldn't be drinking. I couldn't help wondering just what the wine said about my mother's hopes. Did she want me to have an abortion? She hadn't even hinted as much, but I remembered only too well her earlier tirades against Michael and her fury at my engagement.

'What's this about Leo?' I asked, setting the wine aside and hoping she wouldn't notice. 'Is he causing trouble?'

'Leo was trouble right from the beginning,' she said reflectively. 'Silly really, the whole thing with Leo. Still, he did get me the job . . . But then he wanted exclusive rights in return.'

'You deserve better than Leo,' I said.

'Yes, Beth, I think I do. And, now that you ask, I must tell you that I have somebody new . . . Somebody very special. But I don't want to talk about him right now. I want to talk about you and Michael. I want to know what you hope he's going to say.'

So here it was, the moment to lay all my confusion and my doubts aside, and now that it had come, I found I didn't hesitate.

'I want him to take me in his arms,' I gulped, the tears beginning again, 'and tell me that he loves me, and that he'll marry me tomorrow . . .'

My mother stood up and walked over to the conservatory door, staring out into the gloomy garden beyond, testing the door to see if it were locked, snapping a window shut and pulling the curtain across.

'And what about your career?' she asked me carefully, turning round again. 'You did so well to get that radio job, Beth. I've always thought you had so much talent, so much sparkle . . . You could end up on TV, I'm sure of it. But not, I have to say, as a vicarage wife with a baby round your neck.'

'Michael could look after the baby,' I said foolishly. 'Priests work from home, don't they? I'm sure they can supervise a few children while they're at it . . .'

I was joking now, hoping my flippancy would conceal my very real misgivings, not so much about my thwarted career as about Michael's willingness to comply in this vision. And yet I couldn't believe he'd let me down, not after all we had been to each other.

'It isn't that easy, Beth. I speak from experience, remember. I was pregnant myself when I was just a bit older than you, and it wasn't a happy time . . .'

'I can imagine,' I said, feeling the depth of her sympathy and wanting to register my own. 'I bet Rhoda went mad.'

'She did. And she persuaded me to marry Ray, even though I knew it was the wrong thing to do. I didn't stand a chance against her.'

'Did you love Ray?' I asked her tentatively, remembering the time I'd gone to seek out my father and how he'd refused to see me. 'What was he like?'

We so rarely discussed the Carlisles and my mother's brief marriage that I hardly dared raise it all, but now she lay back on the cane settee and looked at me meditatively, as though she might finally share the secrets of her past.

'Ray was a bit like Michael in some ways,' she said at last. 'Very attractive, very passionate, and very jealous. If you want the truth, Beth, he hit me . . . more than once. But that wasn't the worst of it, really. He was obsessed with me, couldn't bear to have me out of his sight, wouldn't entertain the thought that I might complete my degree or have a career of my own. Not good husband material, I'm sure you'll agree.'

And in that moment I understood, for the first time, the root of all her opposition to Michael and felt its deep, if well-intentioned, injustice.

'Michael's not like that,' I said, trembling. 'Michael loves me.'

'Ah, yes. Of course. That's how they do it, how they keep getting what they want . . . Ray loved me too. Far, far too much . . .'

'That's very unfair!'

I was angry and bitterly hurt, unable to believe that she should make this brutal comparison, desperate to correct it. 'Michael isn't Ray,' I cried, 'Michael's different!'

She took a long draught of her wine, then set the glass down on the table before her and faced me squarely.

'So Michael never hit you?' she asked quietly.

I wept then, sobbing as though my heart would break, confounded by the logic that history always repeats itself, unable to voice my sincere belief that it didn't have to be so. And she was immediately contrite, taking me into her arms once more, stroking my hair and kissing the top of my head.

'I'm sorry,' she said, 'I know Michael isn't all bad . . . Let's not prejudge the issue, Beth. Let's wait and hear what he has to say.'

At that moment the telephone rang in the dining room and she ran to answer it, leaving me to dry my tears and reflect that in the end it really didn't matter what my mother said. It only mattered what Michael said, and that mattered more than anything had ever mattered before . . .

'That was Jack,' my mother announced when she returned after what seemed like an inordinately lengthy time. 'Michael's home, and he's been told the news. He's very taken aback, as you can imagine, but he wants to talk. You can see him any time you like.'

'Now,' I said eagerly, standing up, 'I want to see him now.'

'Not now, Beth,' my mother said, looking away. 'It's late, and he's been travelling most of the day. He's very tired, and he's going straight to bed. He'll see you tomorrow. Any time you like.'

And then I knew that however much I tried to convince myself, however much I clung to the promises made and the love we had shared, it wasn't going to work out the way I wanted. Michael wasn't going to take me in his arms and plead with me to marry him. Everything wasn't going to be all right.

But even then, I couldn't guess just how wrong it was going to be.

He was visibly shaken, and angrier than I'd ever seen him, except, perhaps, the night in the spinney when he'd accused me of cheating on him with Sam Lutz.

'Wait in the car, Katie,' he said tightly, 'I won't be long,' and then he turned to me, the grey eyes full of wrath and censure. 'What are you doing? Have you gone crazy?'

'There's no need to make a fuss,' I said smoothly. 'She's been here all afternoon with me. I did try to ring the vicarage, but I couldn't get through, and then I'm afraid I just forgot . . .'

'That's a lie!' he shouted. 'There's been someone at the vicarage all day. You didn't ring.'

'The line was busy,' I said, looking him straight in the eye and daring him to call me a liar again. 'I should have kept trying. I'm sorry.'

'Six hours! She's been gone six hours. I've looked everywhere for her . . . Do you have you any idea what I've been going through?'

I smiled sweetly, hoping to shock him, aiming for the kill. 'No,' I said. 'Not having children myself, I couldn't possibly. Could I?'

He turned away from me then, and I walked over to the dresser in the corner of the sitting room, grateful for Genevieve's extraordinary store of booze, everything from Tia Maria to Taboo, lined up upon the shelves. Then I poured myself a large gin and raised my glass.

'To parenthood,' I said, forcing him to face me again. 'Cheers!'

He was fighting to keep control, and I watched, malevolently encouraged by a series of gestures I remembered only too well from his youthful displays of emotion. He ran his fingers through his bright gold hair, swallowing rapidly, and then exhaled sharply, plunging his hands into his pockets. But then he did what he never used to do, and lit a cigarette.

'You're trying to punish me, Beth,' he said, trembling, 'and it may please you to know that this time you've succeeded very well.'

'You flatter yourself,' I said coldly. 'Why should I wish to punish you? I haven't given you a passing thought in thirteen years.'

'Then why did you do it? Why did you take her off the beach? You wanted to frighten me . . . How could you do that?'

'A spur of the moment thing,' I said. 'It was easy. Believe me.'

As I spoke, I could hardly believe myself, astonished at my willingness to inflict pain, at the depths of my bitterness and the alacrity with which it all came flooding to the surface, like crude oil in some tanker disaster at sea.

He sat down suddenly in a chair by the window, glancing quickly at Katie waiting in the car outside.

'I know it must be hard for you,' he said unsteadily, 'having to see me again after all this time. But it's hard for me too. Very hard. I can't believe that in addition to this, I deserve to have my daughter abducted.'

'Abducted? Don't be ridiculous.'

'Isn't that what I was supposed to think?'

I walked over to the sofa and slumped down upon it, kicking off my shoes and lying back on the cushions, from which vantage point I stared at him critically.

'You haven't changed a bit, have you?' I challenged. 'You always had to make a big scene about everything, didn't you? Well, your precious little girl is okay. And she's had a much nicer time, I might say, than if she'd spent the afternoon on the beach all by herself . . . I thought you were supposed to be looking after her? You're lucky it was only me who invited her out to lunch.'

He took a deep breath and pulled on his cigarette.

'I always wondered how it would be,' he said in a low voice. 'But I didn't expect for a moment you would be so very hostile.'

This remark only served to infuriate, for if nothing else I'd initially tried to be civil, succeeding, it seemed to me, rather better than he had.

'So what did you expect?' I demanded, my tone heavy with sarcasm. 'A cosy little chat about the people we used to be? A spot of reminiscing about the places we used to go? Or a quick fuck in the Bentley for old times' sake?'

He turned away from me, and for a moment I thought he intended to walk out of the cottage. But he didn't, and when he faced me again it was with priestly composure, the vicar confronting the stroppy parishioner, seeking to mollify.

'None of those,' he said carefully, eyeing me as I lay draped upon the Duvals' sofa. 'But I had hoped we might talk. I felt that might be good for us both.'

I laughed.

'And what should we talk about? Teenage sex? There's a good subject for a vicar. Or how about abortion? That's another good one.'

I'd taken the advantage again. The priestly composure collapsed, and he stared down at the floor.

'If you like,' he mumbled. 'If that's really what you want . . .' He hesitated: 'But it would probably do more good to talk about your mother's death.'

'Don't mention my mother. Don't even speak her name.'

'That's your real problem, Beth. Don't you see it?'

'Death is a fact of life. I have no problem with it, thank you, Reverend.'

'Then you're totally unique.'

He was gaining on me once more, and I hit back, a hasty, imprecise shot.

'Oh yes,' I said. 'The professional line from the bereavement counsellor . . . Don't bottle it up. Let it all come out. Confess and receive absolution. Hallelujah and goodnight!'

'Don't knock it, Beth. We're all in need of it.'

I was in real danger of losing my own composure now, and I threw back the gin in a futile bid to dilute my rage.

'You save your sermonising for the Duvals,' I said. 'They've obviously benefited greatly from it. A happier couple you couldn't wish to meet. But it won't work on me, I'm afraid.'

He considered this in silence, looking down at the floor once more, seeming to struggle with what he might say.

'I wonder what will work on you?' he enquired at length.

I stood up, angry beyond measure, aware that our roles had now been effectively reversed, that I was running out of control while he had put a rein on his emotion.

'What sort of question is that? How dare you suggest I stand in need of your help?'

'You need somebody's help,' he said quietly. 'That much is apparent.'

I couldn't trust myself to speak so I walked over to the dresser and poured a second gin, feeling his eyes upon me, furious that I'd somehow allowed him to triumph. I was going to cry, I knew it. A vast ocean of tears was about to engulf me, surging into every last fold of my tattered spirit, foaming, cascading, washing away the final remnants of my dignity. I glanced up, and saw him watching me closely, as though waiting for the storm. I took a long, deep breath. I had to hang on and get him out of the house before it happened.

'And what about you, Michael?' I demanded vehemently, rising to the final rally. 'What do you need? Nothing at all, it seems to me. You've got it all weighed up, the way you always had. Gift-wrapped in a nice little parcel marked Faith or God or Love or some such spurious thing . . . You're still full of shit, you know that? You're still a fucking hypocrite.'

He stood up and extinguished his cigarette, manifestly upset. I was back on top, the trophy about to be presented.

'It's not true I need nothing,' he muttered, walking towards the door and opening it. 'As a matter of fact, there's something I need very much indeed.'

'And what's that? I can't begin to imagine.'

'I need you to forgive me,' he said.

Book VIII: Eva

Chapter Twenty-two

In the summer of 1939, David Klein disappeared. The sprawling hacienda on the brow of the canyon was closed up. The staff, all but one security guard and one maid, were paid off. Enquirers were told only that Mr Klein had left for Paris, that no one knew when he might return.

In fact Klein, sickened by Will Sutton's death, the charges against Christine Romaine and his own suspicions about Saul Bernstein, had fled back to the arms of his cousin Anya, the only place he ever wanted to be. It was a fatal decision. His adored Anya was to prove the direct cause of his death.

Against the Tide: A Biography of David Klein, by Jon Makepeace

---

Eva alighted from the London train at Alnmouth, intending to take a taxicab straight to St Cuthbert's. But at the last moment her resolve deserted her, and she took a cab for Alnwick instead, scuttling into the Black Swan to order crumpets and a pot of tea for one.

It had taken a long time to get this far. She had dawdled through the heart of America, she had lingered in New York, she had booked a long and leisurely passage to Europe, and she had almost changed her mind about St Cuthbert's when the boat docked in Rotterdam, and she thought of Paris and Anya.

But she had made her decision. St Cuthbert's, land of her beloved father and her brothers, would claim her once more. She sailed on to Southampton.

Now that the moment had come, however, she hesitated to return to the village, fearing to appear as local girl made good who then, by a combination of tragedy, personal misfortune and something others might well view as sheer perversity, had once again been reduced to nobody. She understood herself, but would anyone else?

She sat in the bow window of the hotel's dining room, gazing out upon the rainy northern street, nervously avoiding the waitress's eye in case she might be recognised. She wanted no one to know who she was, for she was no longer Eva Delamere, movie star, and she had fashioned her long silver hair into a tight bun at the nape of her neck to make the point. Instead she was Mrs Eva Truman, divorcee, about to embark upon a new phase of her life, although at this point in time, she couldn't imagine what it might be.

In her last weeks at the lonely chalet in the canyon beneath the Hollywood hills, she'd written to the vicar of St Cuthbert's, and had received a most heartening reply.

My Dear Mrs Truman,
    I was delighted to receive your communication, and shall be equally delighted to welcome you back to St Cuthbert's. Your dear father, Matthew Brannen, is remembered with much fondness in the village, both for his care of parishioners, and for his profound preaching, on which latter note, I must tell you that I discovered a bundle of his sermons behind the old mantel in the kitchen. They are a source of much interest and inspiration, and you may wish to have them returned in order to preserve them for posterity . . .
    I look forward to your visit,
    Sincerely Yours, Martin Orde (Reverend)

Next, Eva had written to Miss Lamont, her old schoolmistress, who wrote back with unreserved joy.

My Dearest Eva,
    How wonderful to hear that you intend returning to St Cuthbert's! My little cottage is at your disposal for as long as you wish. I shall be so very thrilled to hear of your life in America, and also your news of Harriet Howard . . . You may be interested to know that my brother's son, Edgar, has enjoyed considerable success upon the London stage, and is about to play Hamlet! How splendid it would be if we could travel to the capital together to see him . . .
    With love, Isabel Lamont

And finally Eva had written to Anya, who replied as only Anya could.

My Darling Eva,
    How dare you think of going anywhere but Paris? The Café des Arbres is waiting for you, and so am I! Come at once. I shall set the table in the window with a bottle of fine red wine upon it . . .
    Best love, Anya

Eva had fretted over Anya's letter, trying desperately to read in what wasn't there. Anya had not mentioned Victor and Rhoda, nor David, and

now, as twilight descended upon the sodden streets outside the Black
Swan, Eva thought longingly of Paris and the Café des Arbres. Why on
earth hadn't she gone there instead? She knew only too well, but inevitably, she found herself wondering if she'd made the wrong decision.

She ordered a second pot of tea, and wiped the mist from the bow
window, looking out and seeing, not the Alnwick of her childhood nor
even of today, but the driveway beyond her chalet in Hollywood, and
across the dusty road, Will Sutton's brooding château . . . She was mus-
ing, mourning, remembering, still trying to work it all out. What
was the truth about Will's death? Was Saul Bernstein implicated,
as Christine had believed? Had Rhoda left Victor to be with David?
Were they together in Paris, wandering the fragrant boulevards
and planning their future? Ah, how she wished she might be there too
. . . But the events of her last days in Hollywood had argued keenly
against it.

She'd closed up the chalet and paid off the lease. The furniture she
arranged to be delivered to Toby's new address, and the odious gilt
clock with the cherubs and doves upon it, the birthday gift he'd once
bought her, she threw into the trash can. She wrote to him, telling him
she meant to return to St Cuthbert's, but she'd received no more than
a short note in reply, wishing her well and bidding a last goodbye. She
could scarcely believe that he never meant to see her again, nor indeed,
that their divorce had been finalised so promptly. As ever, it was Harriet, arriving at the chalet with Nicky to make her own farewells, who'd
set her right about the reason.

'He needed to be free in a hurry, Eva. Surely you guessed?'

But no, Eva, with a peculiar innocence that she was beginning to
regard as a heavy handicap, had not guessed, and the knowledge hit her
as a new blow. She was alone in the world, without direction or purpose, while Toby was to start afresh with a new wife and child. Too
late she understood Harriet's earlier warnings about being half asleep.
As predicted, she'd awoken with a terrible fright, and on waking, found
only her lofty ideals for company.

By sobering contrast, Harriet was doing rather well for herself, with
a new contract for six more films at Worldwide, and Bernstein even
promising that he'd leave his wife.

'He'll have to be told that's a bad idea,' she laughed, mercifully
quashing Eva's horrified vision of a wedding. 'That's the last thing I
want!'

But Harriet, who'd clearly been thinking things over, now knew there
was something she did want.

'I wish you wouldn't go, Eva,' she said passionately. 'You're all the family I've got . . . Let me speak to Saul – I'm sure there's a future for you at Worldwide.'

Eva bent down and folded Nicky into her arms, stroking his soft gold hair and kissing his ears, overcome by the terrible finality of it all, the swift succession of irrevocable events: Will and Christine dead, Victor and Rhoda departed, Toby divorced, Davy disappeared to Paris. How could she stay on, alone except for Harriet and Nicky whose future, she now saw, was inextricably linked to Saul Bernstein?

Eva could hardly bear to think of Harriet with the odious Bernstein, selling body and soul for a piece of Worldwide.

'I have to go,' she said in a muffled voice, as much to the child as to Harriet. 'I can't forget everything that's happened . . .'

'Eva, you're far too sentimental. Nobody can afford to live in the past! The world moves on, and if you don't go with it, one day you'll find yourself right back where you started. Imagine that! Back at St Cuthbert's!'

Eva stared at Harriet uncomfortably. She had not revealed her intention of returning to St Cuthbert's, knowing only too well what the response would be. Now, for a fleeting moment, she wondered if Harriet might be right. Perhaps you could never go back, except to disappointment and regret.

'Will nothing change your mind?' Harriet burst out. 'Will nothing persuade you to stay with Worldwide?'

Several things would have been required to change Eva's mind. If David Klein had come back to Hollywood, if he'd convinced her he thought Will Sutton's death really was an accident, if he'd patched up his differences with Bernstein, if he'd begged her to believe that he'd never once made love to Rhoda . . .

'Goodbye, Nicky,' Eva said, hugging the child with renewed ardour. 'Goodbye, Harriet.'

Harriet stood up.

'It's not Harriet,' she said curtly, 'it's Carlotta. You never understood that, did you Eva? You never understood at all.'

This seemed to be the last goodbye, but at the door to the chalet Harriet turned back, her green eyes bright with uncharacteristic emotion.

'I know that Toby lost your father's gold cross,' she said quietly, 'and I managed to find out who bought it. He's a collector of antiquities, and at the moment he won't sell. But one day, Eva, I'll get it back for you . . .'

Eva was astonished.

'Harriet! Who is he? Tell me at once!'

'It's no use. He won't part with it. But I won't lose sight of it. Don't worry. Harold Brannen's bastard daughter may be good for something yet!'

'I wish you wouldn't say that,' Eva muttered, feeling now that she should have tackled this implied slander on her brother long before. 'Harold loved your mother. I know he did.'

'Did he? Well, maybe he did, but that's a long way from saying he would have married her. Most men run a mile, you know, Eva, faced with that situation.'

Eva turned away, reluctant to say anything that might raise the spectre of Aidan Forster and little Nicky, fearing that any discussion upon this subject might reveal even deeper divisions between them.

They embraced briefly, and then Eva was left alone, wondering when she would ever see Miss Carlotta du Bois again. Had she judged too harshly? Perhaps. But there was no going back. She couldn't change her opinion of Saul Bernstein, whatever might yet be revealed about Will Sutton's death.

After that, there was nothing but to book her passage to Europe. She read Anya's brief letter over and over again, searching it for clues, imagining herself walking into the Café des Arbres to find David sitting there. And what would she say to him? Hallo, here I am, single again . . .

No, it would hardly do.

Then, on the last day before departure, there was one final, unexpected caller who served not only to validate this decision, but to answer some remaining, perplexing questions, further unsettling Eva's precariously bolstered calm.

Rebecca Bernstein arrived in her white Cadillac early that final morning, walking into the bare sitting room of the chalet and leaning against the mantelshelf. She lit a cheroot and regarded Eva with a critical eye.

'So, you're really going? You don't have to, you know. You could stay with Worldwide Pictures.'

'Don't tell me you need another little French girl?' Eva enquired, unable to keep the sarcasm from her voice.

Rebecca laughed drily.

'I don't want you as an actress, Eva. You played your part, and that was fine. But you know, and I know, this isn't for you. However, as a writer . . .'

For one unreal moment, Eva allowed herself to dwell on this prospect, but in the very next, saw what staying on would mean – a life without Toby, without David, a life in the city of dreams with her own dreams reduced to so much dust on the sidewalk . . .

'I don't think so,' she said steadily, turning away from Rebecca, 'I think it's time to move on.'

'Why? Because David's gone?'

Eva drew in her breath.

'No, of course not,' she faltered. 'What makes you say that?'

'Just a hunch,' Rebecca replied evenly. 'If it makes you feel any better, I can tell you it was quite a shock to me as well . . . I never imagined he'd go tearing off after Rhoda. Frankly, I thought better of him.'

Eva stared at her dumbly, wondering what Rebecca knew or had surmised, not wishing to give anything away.

'I don't know what he'll do now,' Rebecca was saying. 'He was trying to raise capital in New York. He wanted his own studio, but it didn't work out. I guess he'll just settle in Paris with Rhoda.'

Eva could not bear this prospect and she turned away from Rebecca, staring out from the chalet window to the Suttons' gloomy château, now shuttered and silent. She could see the casement to Christine's boudoir, and in her mind's eye could still see Christine sitting at her dressing table, combing the tangled orange curls and surveying the garish tapestry of the Lady of Shalott. She remembered all Christine had said; how she'd seemed to believe that Rhoda wanted Will. And she remembered too, the words of the maid who'd come to give her Madame Martineau's little gift: *Missus Rhoda, she wanted Mister David real bad . . . And when Missus Rhoda makes up her mind, I guess things usually work out that way . . .*

'Tell me the truth!' Eva suddenly demanded of Rebecca Bernstein, turning to face her. 'Tell me the truth about *Casey's War*, and why I was given the part. Tell me the truth about Davy and Rhoda, and about Moira Sheen . . .'

She startled herself by this little outburst, but Rebecca seemed unsurprised, pulling on her cheroot, uttering a little snort as she exhaled the thick, acrid smoke, still watching Eva closely.

'You were hired because there was no one else! No one who could sound like a genuine Parisienne, anyway . . . It was David's suggestion. He thought you could do it, and he was right.'

She hesitated.

'He also knew that you were broke. That you were working at Marco's dive . . . I guess he wanted to give you a chance.'

'I see,' Eva said dully, watching the pieces fall uncomfortably into place. 'He felt sorry for me.'

'He didn't want to embarrass you. That's why he didn't make you the offer himself. But you know, Eva, if you'd made a mess of the test, you wouldn't have got it. He didn't tell me I had to hire you. He left it all up to me . . . I was even going to direct. He said I could do it, as long as my father didn't find out.'

Rebecca stubbed out her cheroot on the mantelpiece, all the ashtrays long since having vanished into packing cases. Her mouth suddenly set in a thin, stubborn line.

'Then he changed his mind,' she said abruptly. 'He decided to take over the picture himself, rewrite the script, release Moira Sheen from a part she never wanted.'

Rebecca looked up at Eva.

'I don't know why . . . Maybe, after he failed to raise the dough in New York, he planned to quit altogether. But he figured he'd make one last picture – a good picture – a swan song before he walked out of Hollywood with Rhoda on his arm . . .'

Eva slumped down upon her one remaining chair, confused and sick at heart, trying to weigh it all up.

'Why was Moira cast as Sister Marie?' she demanded of Rebecca. 'Why did anyone ever think that was a good idea?'

Rebecca uttered a long, low laugh.

'Moira was my father's mistress,' she barked. 'She took over the job from Christine Romaine, and she was succeeded by your little friend Carlotta du Bois. Somewhere in between, she fell out with my father. *Casey's War* was to be her punishment. Sheen, the sex siren, playing a nun? Nice touch, eh? David released her when he took over the picture.'

She laughed again.

'But he had to give the part to Carlotta – my father insisted on that. What was a punishment to one of his whores was a prize to the other.'

Eva stared down at her fingernails, embarrassed and appalled. Now she understood something of Christine's antipathy to Saul Bernstein, and saw only too well how the boss of Worldwide Pictures was able to dispose of or discredit his former lovers. Christine, Moira, and in time, Harriet too . . . Where would it all end for her?

She didn't intend to seek Rebecca's opinion on this, and in any case a more immediate concern had taken hold. Her hands were trembling and her mouth was dry. She looked up at Rebecca.

'So there was nothing between Davy and Moira?'

'Nothing at all, although it amused them to pretend there was.'

'And you?' Eva pursued, gambling that as Rebecca seemed happy to answer any question, she might as well ask them all. 'Weren't you going to marry him once upon a time?'

Rebecca Bernstein looked away, past Eva's insistent gaze and into the rocky depths of the canyon beyond the window. She took a long time to answer, and when she finally spoke, her voice seemed distant and cool.

'Our families may have wished it,' she said, 'but it was always clear there was no obligation. David went off to Paris a free man. Unfortunately for him, and perhaps for me, when he returned he was anything but free . . .'

'You mean Anya?' Eva asked mutinously.

'Yes, of course I mean Anya,' Rebecca snapped. 'No one served to make David forget his cousin – until Rhoda came along, that is. So there's the truth about Rhoda. Lonely man, lovely woman. Bring on the violins. End of story.'

And then, in a flash of intuition, Eva saw what she had never seen before: the gifted, ambitious daughter of the boss, surrounded by vacuous beauties, nothing to offer except hard work and talent, those qualities curiously undervalued in a plain-faced woman. She looked at Rebecca with sympathy.

'You'd like David back?' she whispered.

'I'd like him back as director at Worldwide. If he'd managed to set up on his own, then I would've gone with him. As things are, I'll stay with my father. When he dies I'll take over the studio. And Miss Carlotta du Bois, or whoever, will be out on her arse.'

Eva nodded and smiled wanly, keen to end this painful interview, unable now to deduce its purpose or direction, anxious to be alone once more.

'Why did you come?' she asked Rebecca suddenly. 'Was it just to ask me to stay? I don't think so . . . You knew I wouldn't. There must have been something else?'

Rebecca hesitated.

'It occurred to me that you might be going to Paris, Eva . . . And that you might see David there . . . It was always clear to me that he liked you and respected your opinions. If anyone can persuade him to come back, make him change his mind about my father, then it's you.'

She turned away from Eva, looking out of the window across the canyon once more, her voice muffled, yet calm.

'Tell him from me that he'd be welcome back any time – and Rhoda, too, of course.'

Eva swallowed hard, then stood up and walked to the door, opening it for Rebecca.

'I'm sorry,' she said quietly, 'I'm going to England. I've no intention of visiting Paris, so I'm afraid I can't be your envoy. You'll have to find somebody else. I don't expect to see David Klein ever again.'

She booked into the Black Swan and next morning awoke to a golden summer's day, swallows cruising above the turrets of Alnwick Castle, the distant Cheviot hills festooned with yellow gorse. Her indecision of yesterday was gone, and she felt good. She had come home. She mightn't stay for ever, but for the moment, she was content.

She decided to leave her luggage at the Black Swan and take the omnibus to St Cuthbert's, and so set off for the station through the mellow stone streets she'd walked so many times as a young nurse cadet. Yes, here was the Alnwick Memorial Hospital where she'd gained her Nursing Certificate, and there was the little theatre where the Alnwick Players had presented *As You Like It* and *The Tempest*. How painfully long ago it all seemed. How much had changed, and yet in some respects, how little. She was still Eva Brannen, alone in the world as on the day she'd left St Cuthbert's for Paris, so many years ago . . .

The omnibus carried her through the landscapes of her childhood: the faded stone villages, the bright green fields with their ramshackle farmhouses, and then to the edge of the North Sea itself, cobalt blue on this radiant morning, and yet, Eva knew, cold as ice beneath its inviting beauty.

As they rounded the bay into the village, she felt her hands begin to tremble and her mouth grow dry. There was the harbour and the jetty, and the great sweep of white sand . . . And there were the dunes, still wiry and wild, and beneath them, awe-inspiring and heart-stopping, the great mass of billowing rock poppies, gleaming gold in the morning sun, the flowers she'd helped plant in memory of her brothers.

Just a moment more and the vicarage loomed into view, the great glittering spire of St Cuthbert's towering above it and the tangled churchyard stretching behind it, sloping down to the sea. Yes, there was the laurel bush where she had hidden on the day that Harold Brannen went off to war, and over by the seaward wall, the graves of Matthew and Blanche Brannen and the unknown woman who, heavy with child, had floundered into the sea one dark and desperate Easter's Eve . . .

'Are you getting off at the vicarage, miss?'

No, she told the conductor, fumbling for the extra penny he required, she was travelling to the far end of the village. Then she turned quickly to stare out of the window once more, anxious to conceal her emotion. She wasn't ready to walk into the vicarage parlour just yet, nor to greet the new vicar of St Cuthbert's.

Past the village green and the war memorial she went, craning to view the names carved into the granite. Yes, there they were, a little grimy but still plainly visible: BRANNEN, EDWARD; BRANNEN, HAROLD; BRANNEN, RICHARD . . .

On she went, past the Dolphin Inn, shabby and jaded in the full light of day, and up the winding road to the Forster mansion beyond which lay Miss Lamont's cottage. She peered through the dense trees of the estate to see if she might catch sight of the little lodge house where she'd laughed with Anya in another lifetime, and discussed the meaning of Marriage, Love, Constancy and other such momentous matters . . . But no, the thick dark foliage screened the cottage from the road.

'St Cuthbert's, North End,' announced the omnibus conductor, clearly believing he had a stranger on board who didn't know where she might be going.

She smiled at him uncertainly and alighted. Her legs felt weak and her throat seemed curiously constricted. She looked down at the address on the paper in her hand. Yes, there was Miss Lamont's house, the last in the row of fishermen's cottages, painted a pretty blue and cream, the front door open wide to let in the morning's warmth. Eva took a deep breath. She would be all right as soon as she got inside.

And of course, she was.

'Eva, my dear girl, you're here at last!'

Isabel Lamont folded Eva into her arms, clucking and exclaiming, announcing that a taxi would be sent at once to reclaim her luggage, showing her up to a little attic bedroom and then inviting her to sit by the kitchen window with its magical view of the bay, fussing around her with sandwiches and tea in a display of feeling which was most unlike the contained schoolmistress Eva had remembered.

'Now, in time you must tell me everything, my dear – but of course, not all at once, and not before you're good and ready.'

Eva began to relax. She smiled gratefully at Miss Lamont. She did not wish to talk of *Casey's War* and Harriet Howard, and those events, tragic and tawdry, which suddenly seemed a thousand miles away. She was no longer Eva Delamere, after all. She was Mrs Eva Truman, onetime Eva Brannen, with a failed marriage behind her and no great prospect before.

'It's good to be here,' she muttered. 'It's good to be back.'

They took dinner in the little kitchen overlooking the bay, and then later that evening, Isabel suggested she might visit the vicarage.

'The Reverend Orde is most keen to meet you, Eva. He's called several times, enquiring when you might be arriving . . . You'll like him, I promise.'

'Orde?' asked Eva. 'I've been wondering about that name.'

Indeed, ever since she had received Madame Martineau's mysterious gift, the embroidered handkerchief with its single name in the corner, she had been remembering old Dr Orde, Matthew Brannen's sceptical opponent, and the long-ago day when she had found the other handkerchief, so very like this new one, among her father's effects.

'Dr Orde died some years ago. This new vicar is his nephew,' Miss Lamont was saying. 'A man of vision, Eva. Vision and depth. Indeed, it seems to me that all the vicars of St Cuthbert's are gifted men . . . As though they've been drawn by the spirit of the place, and once here, find themselves mysteriously empowered to respond to its special challenge . . . The challenge of the new, Eva! Not to wrap up the Almighty in cloths of gold and serenade Him with pretty hymns, but to press on, beyond the restrictive boundaries of conventional belief.'

Miss Lamont, Eva concluded, hadn't changed so very much after all, and she dutifully listened to a little lecture on the modern face of the Christian faith, nodding at appropriate intervals, and then finally allowing herself to be ushered to the front door and pointed towards the vicarage. Miss Lamont meant her to visit the Reverend Orde, and it would not do to prevaricate.

She took the sea road until she reached the dunes, and then walked swiftly on to the sands, inhaling the salty evening air, stretching out her arms to the great rolling ocean beyond the bay, straining her eyes in the dying light for sight of St Cuthbert's isle and the old ruined tower. How much more of it had crashed into the foamy waters below since she was last here? She could see plainly enough. The tower was still standing, and on the rocks beneath, a cluster of shiny black seals lay preening themselves in the evening sunshine.

Eva laughed aloud, an expression of pure pleasure, and in a sudden, unthinking gesture, pulled the pins from the tight bun at the nape of her neck and shook her hair free. Then she began to run, as fast as she had ever run before, flying through the loose sand, jumping over the tufts of springy grass, for all the world as though she were six years old again with Richard Brannen at her heels . . .

Through the dunes she dashed, skirting the great bank of poppies, then along by the churchyard wall, skipping and dancing and gasping for breath, until she came at last to the church itself, silent and still in the gathering gloom, its vast oak doors thrown open in welcome to any passing worshipper.

She slipped inside, her heart clamouring, in part the result of her exertions upon the beach, but mostly in response to the poignant sensation of standing again where she had last stood for her father's funeral, and where, so many times before, she had listened to his words of wisdom and of praise.

Love is the life-beat of this cruel, unconscious universe . . . Love, only Love, the name which all must speak . . . Yes, here it all was, just as she remembered it: the great stained-glass window showing St Cuthbert with a white tern feeding from his hand . . . the solid mahogany lectern with the eagle perched upon it . . . the ornate, carved pulpit from which Matthew Brannen had surveyed his congregation and herself, sitting in the front pew . . .

Love, only Love, the name which all must speak . . .

Slowly, involuntarily, Eva sank to her knees. 'Father in Heaven,' she heard herself whisper, 'forgive my sins . . . Forgive my pride, and my self-righteousness, and all my foolish mistakes . . . Turn my life around, Father in Heaven . . . Give me courage, and give me hope . . . Show me your way.'

She had not prayed in years, and now she found her face wet with tears. But her spirit was quiet, and her heart uplifted. She remained kneeling for a few more moments, then stood up and walked out of the church, through the yew gate and across the road to the cobbled driveway of the vicarage, up to the front door with its familiar brass knocker. She did not hesitate, but rapped on the door at once.

She was answered by a neatly coiffured middle-aged woman who introduced herself as the vicar's housekeeper and exclaimed at Eva's dishevelled state, enquiring if she were feeling quite well.

Eva, standing in the hallway of her old home, looking towards the great mahogany staircase and the door of the parlour, firmly closed, remembering her father and her brothers with a curious, calming sense of joy, smiled back at the vicar's housekeeper.

'I'm very well, thank you,' she laughed. 'It's a little fresh on the beach, that's all.'

Then the parlour door flew open, and she was confronted by a beaming, shock-haired young man, the vicar of St Cuthbert's, the Reverend Martin Orde.

'Mrs Truman!' he cried, grabbing her energetically by the hand and pumping her arm up and down. 'At last! Now, come into the parlour at once. There is someone here who wishes to see you, who has been waiting most patiently for your arrival.'

Eva stared in surprise, unable to imagine what he might mean.

'Oh go in, go in, do go in . . .' he urged, pushing her into the room.

And there, on the sofa in front of the fire with a glass of ruby port in his hand, just like his Uncle Emmanuel before him, sat David Klein.

He looked up at her.

'Welcome home, Eva,' he said. 'What kept you?'

And receiving no reply to this most reasonable of questions, and no doubt considering that quite enough time had already been spent in the waiting, he proceeded to make himself clear.

'I hope you're not going to ask me what I'm doing here,' he said, taking a draught of the ruby port and surveying her wryly. 'I think I might find that extremely exasperating . . .'

Still she said nothing, unable to take it in, standing foolishly by the fireplace, her tangled hair falling around her face, her cheeks flushed and stained with salt from the sea wind.

'Just so there's no mistake,' he said sternly, seeming now as though he might already be a trifle exasperated, 'let me explain that I am, of course, looking for you . . . I've been waiting in Paris for weeks, expecting you every day, sitting in the window at the Café des Arbres.'

'I'm sorry,' she whispered, not knowing what she should say, hardly daring to think that this inadequate apology might suffice.

'And so you should be!' he said with a little laugh, reaching out for her hand and drawing her down on to the sofa beside him.

There followed a summer idyll which even the looming threat of war could not sully, a golden interlude in which, when Eva came to look back, it seemed the north wind never blew and the grey sea mist, which so often enveloped St Cuthbert's, never once descended.

'I love you,' he said. 'I've always loved you. I've never loved anyone else . . .'

And she, fearing to break the spell, launched no interrogation, content to wait for him to tell.

'I love you too,' she said humbly, scarcely believing that she deserved such happiness.

They walked each day on the empty white beach, they hired a car and drove into the hills, they patched up the old *Island Star*, which Martin Orde found languishing in the stables behind the vicarage, and rowed it out to St Cuthbert's isle.

One weekend they took the London train with Miss Lamont to see her nephew Edgar play Hamlet at the Queen's, a brooding, malevolent performance which somehow seemed to mirror the terrible events in Europe.

Another time they went to watch the Alnwick Players in *Twelfth Night*, with a new young graduate from the Church High School playing Viola.

And each night, when the moon rose silver over the bay and the seals settled down to sleep on the wet rocks, they sneaked back to the little lodge cottage where Davy was staying as Aidan Forster's guest – although Eva, with a scrupulous regard for propriety, always insisted that she be driven back to Miss Lamont's afterwards.

They talked endlessly of Will and Christine, of Harriet and Saul Bernstein, of all that Rebecca had revealed to Eva about the making of *Casey's War*, and of the fateful night Will Sutton died.

'Do you really think Bernstein wanted him murdered?' Eva asked tentatively; 'that he cut the brakes on both cars?'

David turned away from her.

'No,' he said at last, 'I don't. But he was perfectly capable of it. In the end, that's almost as bad . . . It's Christine I think of now . . . I should never have left her – but I had my reasons for going . . .'

He hesitated, regarding Eva unhappily.

'I find it very hard to believe Christine killed herself – or that she wanted to murder Will. It's just not possible . . .'

He looked down, unable, or unwilling, to continue.

'Was she really Bernstein's mistress?' Eva asked.

'Once upon a time. She soon realised her mistake, but by then it was too late. You don't walk out on a guy like Bernstein. Her career was over after that . . .'

'And Moira Sheen?'

He lay back on the warm sand then, and looked up at her. 'I haven't lived like a monk, Eva,' he said slowly. 'I must tell you the truth about Moira . . . We were lovers all the time she was Bernstein's mistress. He liked us to play up in public so his wife wouldn't know the real story – but we fooled everyone, a ridiculous double bluff, pretending there was something going on when all the time there was . . .'

Eva smiled uncertainly.

'But you didn't love her?'

'I loved her as much as she loved me – just enough to make a difference in the dead of night when things look bad and you wake up wondering if you're going to spend the rest of your life alone.'

After Hollywood they talked of Paris, of Anya and how she hadn't changed one jot, of all the Klein cousins had once meant to each other, and all they had not.

'You were very quick to judge, Eva. You never gave either of us a chance to explain.'

'She loved you,' Eva said.

'She may once have imagined she did. That's not the same thing at all.'

And they talked, too, of Eva's divorce.

'I knew you'd parted,' he said, 'but I didn't want to come rushing in. I was certain you knew how I felt . . . that you'd follow me to Paris. I was sure you'd have it all figured out . . .'

'I'm not much good at figuring things out,' Eva said sorrowfully, although she did wonder, privately, what she was supposed to have figured out concerning Rhoda. Whatever the truth, it seemed that, as usual, she'd got it all wrong, a view he appeared to confirm when at last she ventured to probe his feelings.

'Rhoda is Victor's wife,' he said curtly, as though this settled the matter for good, and she was left to reflect upon all her unanswered questions.

Instead, they returned to the subject of Toby.

'He told me once he tried to see you,' she said, wanting him to justify himself. 'He sent you scripts and waited outside your office. He even tried to flag down your car one day.'

'Did he? Well, he was one of many.'

'He was a friend,' she said reproachfully, 'and he needed a break.'

'Allow me some ordinary human feeling, Eva,' he replied drily. 'Toby got the girl. I got the money and the job. Don't blame me for pointing out the difference on a couple of occasions . . . Toby did all right in the end.'

And then, when the subject could no longer be avoided, they talked again of Victor and Rhoda, although, for Eva, the crucial things still remained unsaid.

'Did you see them in Paris?' she wanted to know.

'I visited my Aunt Leah, naturally. She's been very ill, I'm afraid. A stroke . . .'

Eva received this news unhappily, sorry to think of Madame Martineau suffering, wondering how well Rhoda might be expected to cope with an invalid mother-in-law.

'And Victor?' she enquired cautiously. 'Is he happy?'

David looked away.

'He seems so. Rhoda is expecting a child.'

'How lovely for them both,' Eva said, eyeing him searchingly.

They had walked that day to the edge of the cliff overlooking the bay, and were sitting upon a newly installed rustic bench, positioned to offer the most spectacular view of the beach and the islands. Now he suddenly leapt up and began to stride energetically down the cliff path on to the sand, Eva stumbling behind him in the effort to keep up.

'You don't want to talk about Rhoda,' she accused him when, finally, she stood breathless on the shore beside him.

He turned and took her in his arms, pressing his face into her hair.

'I don't even want to hear her name,' he said.

There was much discussion about all that had happened at Worldwide Pictures, and about David's disappointed hopes for a studio of his own.

'Corruption,' he said. 'Vanity . . . Excess . . . It's the way things always seem to go. You can't swim against the tide.'

And there was much talk about what they might do next.

'Paris?' she suggested, wanting to be there, despite Rhoda.

'To do what?' he asked.

'London, then,' she mused.

'The British picture industry?' he enquired dismissively.

They argued, and they debated. The decision, whatever it was to be,

waited upon the refurbishment of the Forster mansion, which Aidan
had commissioned Davy to undertake in preparation for a bequest to
the Church.

'We should go back,' Eva said without too much conviction.

'Back to Worldwide Pictures? I don't think so.'

'It doesn't have to be Worldwide. Anyone would hire David
Klein.'

'Yes. But I don't want to be hired by anyone – not by another studio
anyway. I don't mind being hired by Aidan Forster.'

Eva had been unsurprised by the ease with which David Klein,
movie-maker, became architect to the Forsters once more, for she
understood his need to be about some business or other. But Aidan
Forster himself had proved a total surprise.

She remembered a plump, self-opinionated child who had fought
with Anya on the schoolroom floor, and she brought to their reunion
an unhappy recollection of all that Harriet had told her. Whatever the
truth of the affair, Eva reasoned, Harriet had been left alone with a
young child, and Aidan could hardly escape censure for that.

But once again her preconceptions confounded her. She found a
handsome, mature, well-mannered man whose young wife, newly pregnant, seemed to have tamed him, who begged her to excuse his childhood excesses, and who wasted no time in taking her aside to press for
news of Harriet and Nicky.

'Greta knows all about it,' he said, 'and she understands. She'd even
take on Nicky and bring him up as her own . . . But I don't suppose
Harriet would want that?'

'I don't suppose so,' Eva said.

'I've asked David about Harriet, of course,' Aidan said with some
embarrassment, 'but I didn't get much of a reply.'

Eva could well imagine what might have been said, for on the matter
of Miss Carlotta du Bois, David had proved unrelenting. She trusted
that he'd tempered his opinion for Aidan.

'They're both doing well,' she declared with more confidence than
she felt. 'Nicky is a lovely little boy, and of course, Harriet is a very
fine actress. We haven't heard the last of her by any means . . .'

'I have,' Aidan replied soberly. 'She made it very clear what she
wanted from me – the money to go to America. Nothing more, nothing
less.'

He gazed at Eva unhappily.

'I don't seek to excuse myself,' he said at last. 'She was very young,
and I should have known better. But she was also very beautiful, and
very sure of herself.'

He hesitated.

'She used to declare that she was only Harold Brannen's bastard daughter . . . It was a kind of talisman for her, as though what it implied somehow justified anything she might do with her life.'

'It's a great pity,' he added sadly, 'when the accidents of birth and upbringing are allowed to set the tone for everything that follows. My own family life was none too happy, you know, Eva. My mother never recovered from my brother's death, and my father was a hard, cruel man. He cheated Emmanuel Klein out of a great deal of money. I only found out after he died, but by that time Emmanuel was dead too and there wasn't much left of the Forster estate.'

He smiled then and nodded towards the conservatory where Davy sat contemplating his designs.

'I have always wished to recompense the Kleins,' he said. 'I wrote to Anya suggesting she might like to have the lodge cottage, but I got a very sharp response.'

Eva laughed.

'I can imagine,' she said, knowing that Anya would find nothing to bring her back to St Cuthbert's.

'So I've offered it to David,' Aidan went on. 'You both seem very happy there. You may like to come back some day . . .'

Eva looked down, touched. There was nothing she would like better, and she prayed that it might be.

So the days were squandered. While David worked, she picked bluebells in the cottage garden or cooked fish from the harbour on an open fire or sometimes walked to the churchyard to lay fresh flowers on the graves. And when work was done, they wandered the clifftop paths together, or rowed across the bay in the *Island Star*. Then in the evenings, they strolled along the beach to say Compline at St Cuthbert's with Martin Orde, and later to debate in the vicarage parlour over a glass of port.

It amused Eva to hear them talk, as Matthew Brannen and Emmanuel Klein had talked so many years ago. The difference now was that she didn't feel constrained to keep quiet. Indeed, as the weeks had passed and she went regularly to pray at St Cuthbert's, a new confidence had possessed her, the growing strength of one who, not seeing all things clearly, nor believing that the human mind might ever unravel the mysteries of God, nevertheless feels intuitively that a final glorious vision awaits the unfolding.

Perhaps that was why, on the sultry September afternoon when all were gathered anxiously around the wireless in Aidan Forster's sitting room, the news did not affect her as gravely as the others.

'You should go back to America,' Aidan said at once. 'This isn't your war.'

'It's everyone's war,' David said quietly. 'If we don't see that now, then the day will surely dawn when we do.'

'It's true,' Greta said, close to tears. 'This war will change the world . . .'

'Let's not be too gloomy,' Martin Orde said bravely. 'It may all be over by Christmas . . .'

Eva said nothing, thinking in that moment of her beloved brother Harold, and a day long, long ago, when she had hidden beneath the laurel bush in St Cuthbert's churchyard.

Afterwards she and Davy walked back to the cottage in silence.

'I'm thinking of Anya,' he said at last, his voice choked with emotion, 'I'm thinking of my Uncle Jake, and my mother's sisters and all my cousins still in Germany . . .'

'Yes,' she said, 'I know . . . Why don't we go to Paris and see what we can do? At very least, we could persuade Anya to leave.'

He looked at her, surprised and uncertain, trying to work it out, wondering if it were possible.

'We're American citizens,' she said boldly. 'Residents of a neutral country. No one can touch us. We can go where we please.'

'How?' he asked her, his customary grasp on events deserting him. 'How can we do that when England is at war?'

Eva was inventing, theorising without foundation, but she was filled with a sense of the possible, of nothing ventured, nothing won.

'We could take a boat for Portugal or Spain . . .' she said, thinking aloud, 'Lisbon . . . Yes, that would be best. And from Lisbon, the trans-European express to Paris, through the Pyrenees.'

He opened the door of the lodge cottage, and at once they were enveloped in its sunny calm, the little white-painted sitting room, decked with dog roses, drawing them into its homely peace. He looked around it longingly, as though he were already making his goodbyes, and then he turned to her, drawing her into his arms.

'Marry me, Eva,' he said, 'and we'll take our honeymoon in Paris.'

'All right,' she laughed. 'When? Where?'

'As soon as possible. At the Register Office in Morpeth, I guess . . . and then afterwards at St Cuthbert's. Martin Orde will give us a special blessing.'

'Will he indeed? That's very revolutionary, blessing the wedding of a divorcee and an unconverted Jew . . .'

'Yes, well, the vicars of St Cuthbert's are a revolutionary lot. They go their own way.'

That night Eva didn't ask to be taken home to Miss Lamont's. Instead she lay quietly in bed while he slept, reading from a devotional booklet that Martin Orde had lent her, the revelations of a little-known female mystic, Julian of Norwich.

'Because of our good Lord's tender love to all those who shall be saved,' she read, 'He quickly comforts them, saying, "The cause of all this pain is sin. But all shall be well, and all shall be well, and all manner of thing shall be well." '

Eva closed her eyes. She did not know what trials and deprivations might yet lie ahead, could not imagine the terror and tragedy that another war would bring. But for the first time, she felt assured of one thing. The God of Martin Orde and Matthew Brannen, the God of all the vicars of St Cuthbert's, past and future, held her safe in his eternal keeping.

Chapter Twenty-three

The ease with which Klein entered Germany in the autumn of 1939, succeeded in convincing Nazi officials that he would collaborate on a film about the war effort, and thereby contrived to arrange exit visas for members of his family and certain Jewish friends, seems now to defy belief.

The explanation probably lies in a particular combination of favourable circumstances, from Hitler's desire to appease the Americans, to the peculiar arrogance and stupidity of certain high-ranking Nazi officers, only too willing to believe that a renowned Hollywood film director might be co-opted into the propaganda war, to a significant personal contact in the ranks of the SS, Captain Karl Schwartz, an old friend from his Paris days.

The daughter of a minor official at the American Embassy in Geneva, Georgina Lewis, remembers the refugees arriving and Klein arranging for the sale of his house in Hollywood to fund them.

'There weren't many of them, maybe only twenty in all, including his mother's younger sister, Judith, and a couple of cousins. The rest were people he met during his months in Germany, Jews who would undoubtedly have ended their days in the camps if it hadn't been for him.'

Against the Tide: A Biography of David Klein, by Jon Makepeace

---

They were married and gone from St Cuthbert's sooner than Eva could have imagined possible, Aidan and Greta Forster, Isabel Lamont and Martin Orde waving them off on the London train at Alnmouth, handkerchiefs fluttering ineffectually in the still autumn afternoon, confident exchanges and exhortations lingering on the calm air like so many fallen leaves on the railway platform.

Eva felt curiously unwell, a sick feeling just beneath her ribcage which she attributed to a mixture of excitement and fear. They were setting out on a perilous adventure, the outcome of which could only be guessed. Emboldened by the audacity of the whole enterprise, David had already made plans to travel on from Paris to Berlin. Eva would stay behind with Anya while he, the freewheeling, invulnerable American citizen, would endeavour to find Jacob Klein, his mother's two sisters and as many of the clan as might be persuaded, cajoled or smuggled back to Paris.

'And from Paris, home to America,' he said, all indecision gone, all doubts about the return to Hollywood subsumed. 'We've been away long enough.'

Eva, formerly so daring and optimistic, couldn't see how he would bring it off, and couldn't bear to contemplate the moment when they would have to part. But she kept silent, gazing upon the vanishing Northumberland countryside outside the carriage window, wondering when she might ever see it again, trying to focus all thoughts upon Paris and Anya, and yes, she could not deny it, meditating upon Rhoda too. Would they see her in Paris? How would she, Eva, cope with such a meeting?

She knew from Anya's letters that Victor and Rhoda were still living in Paris, and that Rhoda's pregnancy was progressing.

'A more unlikely mother-to-be I can't imagine,' Anya had written, 'except, perhaps, when I think back to myself seven years ago. What a lucky escape that was! But poor old Rhoda has to go through it. Of course, it couldn't happen to a nicer girl . . .'

Eva was ashamed of Anya's mockery, and of her own dislike. Yet she could not deny the strength of her feeling. Whatever the truth about Davy and Rhoda, and Eva still had no clear idea of what had passed between them, there was always Victor to consider. And Victor, she was increasingly certain, had been duped.

But, of course, she should not be thinking of Rhoda, nor of Victor, nor even of poor Will and Christine. The trials of individual lives were as nothing beside the full-scale tragedy of war. So Eva told herself. And yet, the image of Rhoda, standing on the staircase at the hacienda, dressed in white silk with the long chocolate-coloured hair flowing to her waist, still possessed her. The Lady of Shalott. How inappropriate Christine's epithet now seemed. Far from suffering an undeserved fate like Tennyson's ill-used heroine, Rhoda had escaped all the likely consequences of her actions.

'You're very quiet . . .' Davy took her hand, gently twisting the new wedding ring around her finger. 'Don't lose heart,' he whispered. 'We'll make it.'

On the boat to Lisbon, however, foreseen as the safest and least arduous part of their journey, Eva began to doubt that she would make it. The sea was like frosted glass, its smoothness broken only by spots of crystal. There was no wind, and even Biscay could not shake the ordered, elemental calm. But Eva was sick from the moment she stepped on board, unable to eat, unable to sleep in the warm and luxurious first-class cabin he had reserved.

Alone on deck, in the middle of the third night, she finally faced an alarming reality. It was no longer possible to excuse her sickness: not to him, and certainly not to herself. She could no longer avoid the truth. She was carrying a child.

She had considered the evidence earlier, and had quickly dismissed it. She was tired, she was fearful, she was excited. And in any case, she was unable to conceive. She had told him as much before they married, and had imagined that he seemed relieved. Certainly he had been quick to reassure her, insisting that this was one worry he could do without.

She leaned upon the deck rail, staring down into the blackness, unable to make sense of it. Why should such a thing happen now, at the most inconvenient moment, when it had never happened before? How could she give birth in the middle of a war that might not end? What kind of future awaited the unformed life inside her which, even now, was beating, pulsating, towards its inevitable being?

She shivered in the cool night air, pulling her wrap close around her shoulders, inhaling the salt spray from the waves beneath her, thinking in that moment of another boat, another pregnant woman, her own mother, lurching towards her watery death on the sands of St Cuthbert's, alone in the world, and unloved.

She, Eva, by contrast, was cherished and adored. She was not alone and unloved. But even if she were, the life within would still demand its own violent expression. It would claw its way into the world, just as she, a newborn infant given up for dead, had fought and clamoured for her life.

She looked up at the glittering sky above her, a billion particles of dust and debris sparkling with the energy of radiation, the matter of the universe spread out for her delight. She looked down at the teeming sea below, perpetual motion, an endless, restless charge of elemental power, the waters of life, nourishing the earth.

And then, in a fleeting, magical moment, the essence of which she would try to recapture on many a future night, it seemed to Eva as though the sky and the sea were as one with her own flesh, as though the heart which pumped beneath her goosepimpled skin, the stomach which churned and heaved and threatened to curtail all her lofty meditations, the fragile cluster of cells which clung to the wall of her womb, were formed of the same base stuff, the very material of creation.

She turned around from the deck rail and flung back her head, lifting her face to the dazzling heavens. War on earth might be the present reality. It was not the final truth. She would survive, and so would her child. The future awaited them both, for what was the future but a subtle, ever-more sophisticated rearrangement of those base particles of the past? Nothing could be lost, and ultimately, nothing sacrificed.

'All shall be well,' she said aloud to the listening stars, smiling as she spoke. 'All manner of thing shall be well.'

In Lisbon they found a city at peace with itself, and locating a grand colonial-style hotel on the edge of the medieval quarter, might almost have imagined themselves on holiday. With three days to spare before they could book berths on the Paris train, they wandered the quaint streets, ate grilled sardines in the open air and visited the Explorers' Museum. Eva felt hopeful and relaxed. On dry land once more, she had begun to feel stronger and was now looking for the moment to announce her news. But she was anxious not to worry Davy, for he was much concerned with tickets and timetables and maps and the practicalities of crossing the border between Switzerland and Germany. She was also half afraid he might send her back to England.

Should she wait until they reached Paris? Would he be angry if she did? She couldn't decide.

On their last evening, the moment seemed to have come. They were dining by moonlight on the hotel terrace, drinking rosé wine and listening to the mournful song of a mandolin, played with melancholy resignation by a young musician dressed entirely in black.

'He looks like Hamlet,' Eva said, amused. 'As though all the cares of the world had suddenly settled upon him and him alone . . .'

Davy smiled and reached for her hand.

'Maybe something terrible happened. Maybe his uncle killed his father. Something like that.'

'Or maybe,' Eva said, 'he's thinking about the war. Like Edgar Lamont's Hamlet . . . Lamenting the lost peace. War in the world, and war in the soul. There's no difference really.'

He smiled again and caressed her cheek.

'I might ask Edgar Lamont to Hollywood,' he said slowly. 'Set him up in the movies. What do you think?'

'I think I love you,' she said.

'Only think? After all this time?'

'I love you,' she said, hearing her voice heavy with emotion. She was about to speak when suddenly his mood seemed to change. He called for coffee and lit a cigarette, regarding her gravely across the table, considering his words. Was he thinking of Germany and what might lie ahead?

'There's something I must tell you before we reach Paris,' he said at last. 'Something I should have told you before.'

Eva felt her pulse begin to pound.

'About Rhoda?' she whispered, knowing it could hardly be anything else.

He stared out beyond the terrace into the hotel gardens, seeming hardly to see the mass of violet and scarlet orchids, the bougainvillaea and the lemon trees, now touched by silvery light. But Eva was gazing too, remembering only too well the lush gardens of the Hollywood hacienda and the night she'd found Rhoda dreaming on the balcony, dreaming of David and plotting to leave Victor . . . What was he about to confess? She hardly dared to think.

'Rhoda cut the brakes on Will's Bugatti,' he said brusquely. 'She meant to kill Victor, but it didn't work out the way she planned. Instead she killed that poor guy, Joe Lugisi . . . and Christine got the blame.'

Eva was astonished, unable to take it in or respond. It couldn't be true!

He leaned across the table towards her, waving his cigarette under her nose.

'And who is this Joe Lugisi?' he demanded. 'He's nobody, is he? Just a minor character in the sub-plot . . . a small-time thief who deserved all he got.'

Eva shook her head, stupefied.

'He had a wife and kids, Eva. He rented a trailer downtown. He had a life . . .'

She said nothing, simply stared in disbelief.

'I sent his widow ten thousand bucks,' David said at last. 'It seemed the least I could do.'

'You did what?'

'Ten thousand bucks,' he said dismissively. 'What's that for a life? Nothing. Nothing at all . . .'

Eva gazed at him in shock.

'Wait!' she said, trying to work it out. 'Are you telling me this is why you followed Rhoda to Paris?'

'It sounds crazy,' he said, as though in response to her reasonable doubt. 'That's why I didn't tell you before. And of course, she denies the whole thing! But I can assure you it's true. I'm telling you now so you'll understand why I won't be seeing Victor in Paris.'

Eva buried her face in her hands, and then looked up at him, still unconvinced.

'How do you know it's true?' she enquired gently.

He looked away.

'I knew Christine didn't do it,' he said quietly. 'I just knew. So, if not Christine, then who? It didn't take a lot of working out . . .'

Eva took a long draught of her wine, weighing it up. Rhoda had wanted David, this much she knew. But to plot a murder?

'Why would Rhoda want to kill Victor?' she asked unhappily. Behind them the mandolin burst into elegiac melody once more, and the young Hamlet moved towards their table, his face set in plaintive repose. David lit a second cigarette.

'She wanted to kill Victor because he stood in her way. When they met in Paris, he seemed like a good bet. But when she got to Hollywood, Victor didn't look so hot. Rhoda thought she could do better.'

Eva understood this. Indeed, Will had once said something very similar. But would Rhoda really turn killer?

'It's like something from the movies,' she muttered.

'Exactly. That explains it all . . . Rhoda always wanted a part to play. That's why she went to the set every day and made all those silly notes, pretending she was reporting back to me.' He shook his head, as though in the retelling it seemed yet more fantastic. 'Well, she got what she wanted,' he said sourly. 'She wrote herself a starring role.'

Eva, remembering Rhoda scribbling in her little notebook on the set, laughing with Will in his dressing room, plotting and scheming for ends that never seemed quite clear, was still unable to work it out.

'What was Rhoda doing with Will?' she demanded. 'Why did she lead him on like that, when all the time she wanted you?'

He looked away from her, his face contorted, lips set in a pained grimace.

'At the start,' he said with difficulty, 'I think either one of us would have done. Me or Will. But she soon saw that Will wouldn't do . . . Apart from anything else, he would never have left Christine.'

'And you?' Eva pursued, knowing she must now hear the truth 'Did you think yourself in love with Rhoda? Is that what you told her?'

He hesitated, searching her face intently, trying to determine her thoughts.

'I thought you were lost to me for ever,' he said, taking her hand in his. 'And yes, I admit I romanced Rhoda over bottles of wine and suppers on the balcony, and told her how lovely she was . . . But she was my cousin's wife. There could never have been anything between us – unless, that is, Victor was no longer around.'

He bit his lip.

'I can't believe I said that to her,' he faltered, 'but I did . . . I said it in the certain knowledge that Victor would always be around.'

He laughed bitterly.

'Rhoda was so very clever,' he said. 'She had it all planned. After the première, she was supposed to meet Will at some place he'd rented up in the hills. She'd been promising him for weeks – that's why he wanted to drive, you see. And he really thought this was going to be his big night . . .'

Eva listened with heavy heart, thinking of Will in the Chevvy, and Victor in the Bugatti, both of them intent upon satisfying Rhoda.

'And Vic was meant to follow Will that night,' David said slowly, 'in the Bugatti, you understand . . . She left this letter saying where they'd be. Except that she didn't mean to be there. Better to be safely home in bed if some poor fool is going over the canyon . . .'

Eva was still trying to fit the details together.

'What happened to the letter?' she asked tentatively.

'I found it first and tore it up. I wasn't going to have them slugging it out over Rhoda . . . I guess I saved Victor's life, but he's not thanking me for it. He doesn't believe a word, and of course, there's no proof. He told me straight to stay away from Rhoda. I'm only too glad – except that I can't bear for her to get away with it . . .'

Eva took a sip of her coffee and eyed him anxiously, seeing now why he'd kept silent before, knowing that he must have wondered how she would react, what she would think of his part in it all, whether she would believe him. She did believe him, but there was still one question she wanted answered.

'Did you ever make love to Rhoda?' she whispered.

There was a long pause in which the notes of the mandolin reached a shuddering crescendo and then died into a loaded silence.

'Oh Eva,' he said miserably. 'Remember the night you came to the lot to tell me *Casey's War* was a lousy picture? And I said I was waiting for Rhoda, just to see if I could make you jealous? It seemed that you didn't care for me at all . . . And then, right after you'd gone, Rhoda arrived . . .'

He looked down, and Eva was suddenly deeply sorry that he should find himself forced into this tawdry confession, that he should feel insufficiently assured of her loyalty and her love to know that the past was a closed book, its mistakes and its misunderstandings confined to the chapter notes.

She put her hand over his.

'Let's go to bed,' she said softly. 'I'm very tired, and this is our last night at peace. Tomorrow we go to war . . .'

They walked through the hotel's elegantly faded lounge, beneath the crystal chandeliers and up the rosewood staircase into their pink and gold suite, her arm through his, murder in their past, war in their future, but in the present, nothing more nor less than their all-consuming passion for each other.

'It only happened once,' he told her as they lay together in their vast four-poster bed, cocooned by mosquito gauze, enveloped in shamelessly luxurious silk sheets. 'But once was enough to betray Victor and entangle me in Joe Lugisi's death – to condemn me to eternal regret . . .'

'Hush,' she said gently, placing her finger against his lips and kissing his cheek. 'There's nothing more to say . . .'

'Corruption,' he whispered. 'Vanity . . . Excess. I saw it all in myself . . . I saw myself poised for the fall.'

'Hush,' she said again, pulling him close.

'How easy it is, Eva . . . The descent into total self-indulgence.'

'David,' she admonished. 'Be quiet. You've told me quite enough . . . And now, if you'll shut up for five minutes, I've got something I want to tell you . . .'

Paris was just as she'd dreamed it would be, bustling and golden, basking in the autumn sunshine, preening itself in one last luxurious burst of warmth before winter set in.

The streets were full of soldiers, the parks were crowded with pretty girls, and the Café des Arbres was busier than ever before, with a new clientele of working men and gaudily dressed young women.

Eva and Anya fell into each other's arms with tearful smiles, exclaiming and reassuring, insisting that neither had changed in the least. In truth, the years had been kinder to Eva than to Anya, although she'd lost none of her sparkle and verve.

'I'm like a glass of champagne,' she said laughing at this comment, linking her arm in Eva's and drawing her to the window table. 'So watch I don't get up your nose!'

There was much ground to cover, all the trials of the Hollywood years, the making of *Casey's War*, the fate of Harriet Howard, Eva's divorce and her new marriage. But at the Café des Arbres, still the centre of Anya's life, very little seemed to have changed, except for the departure of Jacob Klein, and the death of Emmanuel.

The condolences given, Eva pressed Anya for other news. Where were the Americans? Where was Pete Chessington? Whatever happened to Karl Schwartz?

'The Americans all went home! Even Bertie Levine finally went home . . . but Pete is still here. He still plays piano, Eva. You'll see him later tonight. And as for Karl, he joined the German army.'

David, looking round as though he'd found himself back in the Café des Arbres rather sooner than he might have wished, glanced up quickly at this remark.

'Do you know where he's stationed?'

'Karl? Well, yes I do. He wrote to me, just before the start of this silly war. Said I'd better watch out when the Germans came marching into Paris . . .'

He offered her a cigarette, and lit it for her. Eva watched with unsettling nostalgia as their dark heads bent together over the flame, reflecting upon how much simpler the world had seemed once upon a time, and how she, nevertheless, had still failed to sum it up.

'Can you find the letter for me?' Davy asked. 'I think I might look up our old friend Karl . . .'

They argued long and late about the possibilities and pitfalls of his plan, and it became clear that Anya did not approve in the least, insisting that she'd tried earlier to persuade her Uncle Jake back to Paris, only to be told he wouldn't be kicked out of his home.

'I don't blame him,' she said smartly. 'I wouldn't be kicked out myself.'

Entering Germany, she insisted, was a pointless, hazardous exercise, bound to fail, and hardly something to be undertaken by a man with a newly pregnant wife.

'Good God,' she said to Eva with characteristic forthrightness. 'He'll make you a widow before you're even a mother.'

'Is she right?' Eva asked him tremulously as they retired to their room above the café that night. 'Is there no chance of success?'

'I won't go if I think that's the case,' he said, sitting down on the end of the bed. 'And I won't go at all if you tell me you don't want me to.'

She knew then that, tempting though it was, she must not lose her nerve and beg him to stay, for what was true love but the gift of freedom, the assurance that a lover's power will never be used to coerce or to constrain?

'Of course you must go,' she said bravely. 'I should hate you to think of me.'

'Whatever I do, I'll be thinking of you,' he replied with an odd little smile. 'It's second nature to me.'

Next morning he went straight to the American Embassy while Anya and Eva, left alone to say all that couldn't be said the night before, took coffee together on the terrace.

There was an initial reserve between them, as though the shadow of the German expedition or Anya's dire prediction had changed the tenor of the reunion, and with unspoken agreement, neither of them mentioned the war.

Eva sipped at her bitter coffee nervously, unsure about the physical reaction it might produce, gazing around her in search of some innocuous conversation topic.

She could see that the café was run with care and precision, seeming to allow Anya the role of languid hostess while others rushed around doing the cooking and serving. But all the time she talked and laughed with her friends, Anya watched the café's business with an eagle eye, alert for a customer who had waited too long, who needed another drink, who wanted to settle his bill, who needed company or consolation. The reward was one of the liveliest cafés in Montparnasse, a place where old and young alike seemed keen to part with their money.

'You're doing well,' Eva said, indicating the crowded tables, but Anya did not want to talk about the café, nor even the handsome French waiter, ten years younger or more than herself, who nodded and smiled and gave Eva to understand that a very special relationship existed between himself and *la patronne*. Anya, deciding to abandon all reserve, had something else on her mind.

'Well, Eva, thank God you married him at last!' she declared, inspecting the coffee in her glass and raising an eyebrow. 'I was beginning to think I'd ruined your life – and I was quite certain Toby would never let you go. It was madness to marry him instead of David in the first place . . . You know that, don't you?'

Eva blinked unhappily, unsure she could even begin to explain that while she was happier now than she'd ever hoped to be, she hadn't been unhappy before, that although she loved David more than she could have imagined, she had loved Toby too, and missed him. And it was true, after all, that in the first place, David had never asked her to marry him . . .

'Toby was my best friend,' she muttered, looking away.

'Maybe he was, but you should never marry your best friend. Heavens above, that's why I never married Victor.'

Eva faltered at the mention of Victor and Anya looked at her keenly.

'What happened between Davy and Vic?' she asked curiously. 'Did they quarrel over Rhoda?'

'Rhoda just seems to make trouble,' Eva said uncomfortably, anxious to reveal no more than David would wish. 'She likes to have her own way.'

'Don't we all!' Anya laughed. 'That was our problem right from the beginning . . . Oh, Eva, what a mess it was! But you were so prissy and prim – you wanted everything to be scrupulously correct. It seemed impossible to tell you the truth.'

'What was the truth?' Eva asked uncertainly.

Anya looked away.

'He still hasn't told you, has he?' she said at last, laughing nervously
and stirring her coffee with vigour. 'You see, he's just the same as you,
Eva. Quite ridiculously moral and fair. He won't have you thinking
badly of me, even after all this time.'

Eva said nothing, simply waited.

'It wasn't his child,' Anya said at last, still laughing, although now
she seemed less nervous than embarrassed. 'I knew all along! But he was
terribly noble about the whole thing, just as you'd expect. He seemed
to take the view that even if it wasn't, then it might have been, so what
the hell . . .'

Still Eva said nothing, thinking only that the affairs of the human
heart were incomprehensible, that no matter what kind of revolution, or
evolution, overtook the planet Earth, there would surely always be confusion and pain and misunderstanding between women and men.

'I suppose you're wondering who?' Anya said, a trifle snappily. 'Well,
it could have been Bertie, or it could have been Karl – I couldn't say
for sure. There! I've really shocked you this time, haven't I, Eva?'

Now Eva laughed, despite herself.

'I'm surprised,' she admitted, 'I thought you were in love . . .'

'Well, so I was at the start! Who wouldn't be in love with David? He
was everything I thought I wanted. The poor boy didn't stand a chance
. . . And I'm sure he wanted me too, or believed he did – until he met
you, that is.'

Eva, remembering in that moment all their childhood debates about
marriage and love, found herself wondering just what it was that Anya
truly wanted.

'Well, I don't want to be a good Jewish wife,' she declared briskly.
'Or any kind of wife, come to that. It's a terrible trap, Eva . . . You
might just get away with it, married to David. But most women
don't. They shrivel and contract until they've got nothing left of themselves.'

She smiled and leaned across the table.

'And you know the worst thing? These poor deluded women succeed
in convincing themselves it's all for their own good . . . They're protected and loved. Venerated, even. Just like exhibits in some ruddy
museum . . . Well, no thank you! I'll take my chances on my own.'

The young French waiter appeared at their side again, bending his
lithe body to whisper in Anya's ear, and she rose to her feet at once,
called upon to intervene in some kitchen dispute, leaving Eva alone with
her thoughts.

Was marriage truly a terrible trap for a woman? Certainly, she had
once felt it to be so, left alone in her chalet at the foot of the Hollywood

hills . . . But she had contrived at her own enslavement, and this seemed to her the heart of it.

No one, woman or man, could ever be entirely free, and yet each was surely called to grasp whatever measure of freedom circumstance allowed, and use it for the best. And this was surely true for everything, from the privacy of the marriage bed to the public arena of war. She understood it in an instant. Freedom and responsibility, hand in hand, in life, and in death.

She stood up and walked out through the café, past the crowded tables where, even at this early hour, heavily painted girls were making friends with soldiers, and up into her room.

She lay down upon her bed, stretching her hand across her swelling abdomen, contemplating the mystery of human biology and its fraught historical union with the social institution of marriage, pondering upon Anya's frightening assertion that she might be a widow before she was a mother, trying to imagine the likely properties of the life inside her, its smile, its voice, its destiny.

A daughter? Yes, almost certainly, a daughter.

They would have to choose a name. And they would have to do it at once, before Davy left for Germany.

She closed her eyes. They would have to do it at once, she knew, in case he didn't come back.

'What was your mother's name?' she asked him.

'Deborah,' he said absently, gazing long and hard at the letter Karl Schwartz had written to Anya, turning it over in his hands as though it might reveal some unwritten promise.

'Oh,' said Eva, not at all sure this would do. 'Then what about your mother's sisters . . . your aunts?'

'What about them?' he muttered, pacing the floor in front of their bedroom window, still disappointed at the cautious response he'd received from the American Embassy, so determined to press ahead anyway that he seemed unable to rest for a moment. 'I don't even know if I can find them.'

'No,' she persisted, 'I mean their first names . . . What are they called?'

'Judith and Zia,' he said, uncomprehending. 'They lived next door to each other. I can remember my mother taking me there when I was just a child . . . I can still see the street. But they've probably moved a dozen times since then. I lost touch with them all after my father died. Too busy making movies.'

'Zia,' said Eva, considering. 'That's nice.'

He said nothing, simply picked up the Karl Schwartz letter once more and read it through for the hundredth time.

'He sounds friendly enough, don't you think? I mean, apart from this bit about the Germans marching into Paris, which he surely intends as a joke . . .'

'Zia Klein,' said Eva, trying it out.

'Well, of course, she's not a Klein . . . That's the real difficulty. I can't remember her husband's name. Was it Goldberg or Goldblum? Or was it Bergman? Hell, there must be hundreds of families with those names.'

'Then the Germans will have them all neatly logged,' said Eva, temporarily giving up, 'and Karl will know how to find out. He was very methodical.'

'Was he? I can hardly remember a thing about him.'

'He wrote very strange music. It was all terribly neat and precise. It was also unplayable, as I recall. Pete Chessington had a stab at it one night at that place on the Boulevard Saint-Michel.'

'Music,' said Davy slowly. 'What kind of music? Film music, would you say?'

'Maybe. I've no idea what he ever intended doing with it.'

He began to stride around the room again, evidently thinking hard, and Eva made one last attempt to settle the issue on her mind.

'Perhaps we should name the baby after my mother?' she ventured.

He turned from the window then and moved towards the bed where she lay, sitting down beside her and taking her hand in his.

'This baby's a girl, is it?' he enquired with a smile.

'I think so. I really do . . .'

'Then we'll name her when she's born,' he said firmly, stroking her cheek so that she shouldn't mistake his determination for impatience. 'We'll be together again by then. Believe it, Eva, please. I need you to believe it.'

'I believe it,' she whispered, her eyes bright with tears.

'Good,' he said briskly. 'Because I've decided I may as well go tomorrow. No sense in hanging about.'

She nodded, unable to trust herself to speak.

'One thing I must ask,' he went on in just the same insistent tone. 'I want you to move out of the café . . . I don't want you living here when I'm gone.'

'Whyever not?'

'Because the place is full of hookers. That's why not.'

'Do you think I'm in moral danger?' she teased him. 'I spent most of my evenings with hookers when I worked at Marco's diner.'

'It's not moral danger I'm worried about,' he said seriously. 'It's the ordinary sort. If by any grim chance the Germans do come marching into Paris, then this is just the kind of place they'll make for . . . I've told Anya as much.'

Eva could well imagine how Anya would receive such an assertion, and yet she knew he was right.

'Where am I to go?' she asked unhappily, imagining a lonely hotel room or an empty apartment.

'To the Divine Faith convent,' he replied. 'It's the obvious place. You'll be safe there – and you won't be alone.'

He hesitated.

'Victor's mother is being cared for by the nuns again. I guess Victor has other things on his mind right now . . .'

Eva considered this in silence. She was happy at the thought of encountering the irrepressible Madame Martineau once more, and indeed, she had questions she wished to ask about the embroidered handkerchief which still lay in her suitcase beside its mysterious pair from so long ago. But who else might she meet visiting Victor's mother at the Divine Faith convent?

'If you should run into Rhoda,' David said slowly, turning away from her, 'just keep quiet. Don't mention Will or Christine. Let it all go by. She got away with it . . . There's nothing we can do.'

She reached out for him then, taking him into her arms one last time, anxious not to let Rhoda overshadow their final night together, determined to live each day, each moment they were apart, in the belief that all would be well.

'So then, what was your mother called?' he asked her when they'd made love, very gently, and at last lay quiet, side by side on their tangled bed in the gloomy little room above the café.

'Eva,' she murmured, still thinking of the little lace handkerchief. 'My mother was called Eva . . .'

'No,' he said softly, his voice falling away as he pressed his face into her hair. 'That's not what I mean. I mean the mother who brought you up – Matthew Brannen's wife . . .'

But Eva, drifting off to sleep, was too tired to answer.

Sister Marguerite greeted Eva as though she were a prodigal daughter returned, summoning the rest of the Sisters to a joyous reception in the little whitewashed sitting room overlooking the lawn, toasting the expected infant with sparkling wine and urging nutritious tit-bits upon the mother-to-be.

'This is to be your very own room,' Eva was told, to her surprise.

'No, no! We insist. You need privacy and peace until your baby arrives.'

Eva was deeply grateful, and also chastened. Not only did the convent seem a much livelier, more cheerful place than she remembered, but the Sisters themselves seemed no longer the pious, unbending figures she had once considered them. Now she saw their rules as the necessary framework for a life of devotion, their singlemindedness as the vital underlying force of their vision. How uncharitable she had once been in her opinions; how lacking in perception.

Not least among reasons for Eva's new view were the three young Jewish girls employed in the convent as chambermaids, German refugees without proper papers or legal status in France.

'Oh, we can get them papers if need be,' said Sister Marguerite, smiling broadly in answer to Eva's questions, 'but for the moment they're safe here with us.'

It was, she informed Eva, only the smallest act of reparation. 'For centuries the Jewish people have suffered a terrible slander at the hands of we Christians,' she declared, plumping up the cushions on the wooden settle and instructing her new charge to lie down upon it. 'They have been cruelly persecuted for killing Our Lord when, of course, it wasn't them at all! Read your history books, Eva. Read the modern critics of the Bible. It was the Romans who killed Our Lord! And isn't that a bitter irony?'

Eva was both surprised and impressed. She could never have imagined that the woman who'd once sacked her for misappropriating a bottle of wine would harbour such unorthodox views.

'Oh come, Eva,' Sister Marguerite laughed. 'It wasn't about the wine at all . . . You were terribly bored here with us. You needed to be doing something else.'

Now Eva laughed too, unable to resist pointing out that if she'd grown older and wiser in the meantime, then the convent too seemed a little smarter than previously.

'Well, we've made a few changes,' Sister Marguerite agreed, still laughing. 'Some of the wards really were very dreary . . . But we still insist upon the lawn being trimmed to our satisfaction! Beauty, you see, Eva – it's a reflection of God, and essential to life. We must have beautiful gardens for our patients to gaze upon . . .'

Even Madame Martineau, so far as one could tell, seemed to have mellowed in her view of the Divine Faith convent.

Eva found her sitting in a sunny bay overlooking the lawn, eyes closed against the glittering light, frail hands folded upon a walking cane.

She had already been warned that her old friend had lost the power of speech, but was relieved to find her spirit undimmed. Madame Martineau had a familiar sparkle in her eye, and was happy to communicate by means of scribbled notes.

'You look fine,' she wrote, and Eva, needing to avoid the matter of Victor and Rhoda, gossiped about safe subjects: the convent and the café, St Cuthbert's and her marriage to David. Only when she thanked Madame Martineau for the gift of the embroidered handkerchief and produced its curious counterpart did the old lady become agitated.

She stared at the two handkerchiefs, both with the name *Eva* worked into the right corner, one decorated with daisy chains, the other, earlier article showing faded violets.

Then she picked up the old handkerchief and traced the letters of the name, her face drawn in a puzzled frown. Suddenly she signalled for her notepad.

Eva, she wrote, her fingers trembling with effort, *Eva* . . . And then when Eva looked on blankly, she took up her pencil and wrote again: *Martineau* . . .

Eva could make nothing of it, and saw at once that she should not pursue the matter for Madame Martineau was gesticulating wildly at her notepad, emitting strange, strangled gasps of distress.

'It's all right,' Eva said anxiously, patting her hand. 'Please don't upset yourself.'

Madame jabbed at the notepad, and then again at the faded handkerchief, but now Eva was concerned only to calm her down.

'It's nothing,' she said firmly, taking back the handkerchief. 'Believe me, it's of no account . . .'

And indeed, it wasn't, for what significance could a piece of long-ago history assume beside the momentous events of the present – the child growing inside her, the war raging on the frontier, the Jews hounded from their homes, her own husband departed to an uncertain fate?

Eva bent down and kissed Madame Martineau on the cheek, smiling reassuringly. She stayed until the old lady seemed soothed, then she walked swiftly back to her little sitting room, drawing the curtains against the darkening afternoon and settling herself in front of the fire. Finally she fell asleep, dreaming of a far-distant utopian day when the world would be at peace once more, and all the lost and dispossessed of every nation gathered in.

Chapter Twenty-four

David Klein was shot dead in the bar at the Café des Arbres on the day the first German troops meandered into Paris, only hours after his safe return from Geneva.

He was not the sole casualty of an ugly exchange between German soldiers and local prostitutes that night, a fracas in which Anya Klein tried to intervene. The café's English pianist, Pete Chessington, was also slain, and Anya herself was to die two days later from gunshot wounds.

Witnesses later reported that Klein had attempted to protect his cousin after she slapped a soldier in the face, almost certainly taking the bullet that was meant for her.

But whatever the intention of the man who fired, the killing of Klein was viewed as an unfortunate mistake, and the following day the Nazi commandant in charge of the Montparnasse district issued a formal apology to the American Ambassador.

Klein's body was swiftly buried in the Cimitière de Montparnasse, a simple headstone recording only his name, dates of birth and death. The fact of his Jewishness seems to have been conveniently overlooked, and a French priest was summoned to read the burial rites.

There were only two mourners at the funeral, an Embassy official and a waitress from the Café des Arbres, representing Anya Klein.

Sadly, the headstone marking Klein's grave disappeared some time after the end of the war, and the site of his final resting place is no longer known. Anya's grave remains, however, still tended by unknown friends who place flowers each year on the anniversary of her death.

Against the Tide: A Biography of David Klein, by Jon Makepeace

---

As the weeks passed and slipped into months, Eva found herself absorbed by a daily routine at the convent in which she assumed some of her old duties and took over new ones, comforting depressed patients, supervising the young Jewish girls in their cleaning of the wards, overseeing the trimming of the lawn.

Each morning she went to the chapel to pray for David's safe return, and each evening she joined the nuns for Benediction. Most of the time she felt calm and strong, uplifted and encouraged by the peaceful atmosphere of the convent, determined to keep her hopes high and her anxiety at bay for the sake of her coming child, who, she was quite certain, shared all her emotions. Sometimes, however, fear laid its icy fingers on her heart and she would huddle on her makeshift bed before the fire in the little sitting room, unable to sleep for wondering where he was, what he was doing, whether he might be dead or alive.

'Please God,' she wept, unable to contain or modify the desperate prayer which sprang to her lips. 'Please God, bring him back . . .'

She went often to the gloomy little church only a few streets from the Café des Arbres where David had taken her on the evening she first arrived in Paris, comforted by the memory, and as she sat alone in the semi-darkness, recalling the curious intimation of the future she had received that distant day. It had been, she now believed, a mysterious revelation of things to come, a glimpse into the ideal which, she now saw, she had been challenged to bring about. But was that vision to be cruelly curtailed? She could not say, and she struggled with her unbelief.

At first she went regularly to the Café des Arbres too, sitting at the window table with a glass of wine and gossiping with Anya, thankful for the distraction of music and laughter. But as her pregnancy advanced, the bustle and noise of the café seemed oppressive, and her visits became fewer. Then Anya would come to the convent and the two of them would take afternoon tea in the sitting room, dreaming upon the settle, reading the newspapers and the reports from the Front, planning a brave new future after the war. The war, after all, didn't seem so very terrible. There was nothing much happening, and they dared to speculate that it might be over soon.

Christmas came and went, and Eva celebrated Hanukkah with the young Jewish girls, lighting the candles in her sitting room and inviting a bemused Anya to attend.

'Good heavens, Eva, you'll end up more Jewish than the rest of us! David isn't bothered about all this stuff, you know . . . He feels like me. It's ancient history – no relevance to life today.'

'I intend to raise my child as a Christian and a Jew,' Eva said defensively, 'honouring both traditions . . .'

'Poor thing,' Anya replied tartly.

Victor also came regularly to the convent to visit his mother, but Rhoda was never with him, and slowly Eva found herself relaxing into his company as she'd done so many years before in Paris, and had hoped to do again when he'd visited America with his new bride.

Although they didn't speak directly of that time, and although David's name was rarely mentioned between them, they seemed often to hover upon some kind of declaration.

'I made a serious mistake,' Victor confided one time. 'I left Rhoda alone too much. She was very young, Eva . . . She was easy prey for a rogue like Will Sutton.'

On this occasion, Eva said nothing, remembering with a sudden stab of sorrow just how fond she'd been of Will. Certainly he'd been a rogue, and a drunkard too, yet somehow this failed to sum him up. There had been more, and maybe time would have allowed it to flower.

'I'm hoping for a daughter,' Victor told her on another occasion. 'A little girl just like Rhoda . . .'

Eva was able to respond to talk of babies.

'Yes, I'd like a daughter too,' she said. 'What shall you call her if the baby's a girl?'

'Eleanor Jane,' he replied, and then as though there might be room for doubt, added swiftly: 'Eleanor Jane Martineau . . .'

'That's very pretty,' Eva said, wondering in that moment what kind of a mother Rhoda would make and what fate might await little Eleanor Jane, 'and she'll be a pretty child if she takes after her mother . . .'

'I hope she will take after her mother,' Victor said, looking away. 'I hope that very much indeed . . .'

Eva was both embarrassed and sympathetic, not knowing quite what Victor meant, and yet sensing within him a deep regret. Could he be telling her he wasn't the father of Rhoda's child? What else did he know about what his young wife had done in those wild Hollywood days? Eva didn't ask, nor even hint that there was any question over Rhoda's behaviour. She didn't ask because part of her still doubted what she had been told, and because she had no wish to hear Davy decried for his suspicions.

But she could not avoid the subject of her husband altogether. As the days slid by and the pale white light of winter on the lawn outside the sitting-room window gave way to the pink of spring, she ventured less and less frequently into the world beyond the convent, and Victor became concerned.

'You shouldn't be here all by yourself,' he said shortly, one rainy afternoon when her spirits were low and her back aching. 'David shouldn't have left you.'

'I couldn't go with him,' she replied, 'and yet he had to go.'

'I confess I completely fail to understand my cousin,' Victor said slowly, 'I've never understood him. I couldn't see why he didn't marry Anya all those years ago, and I can't see why, having married you, he should abandon you here in the middle of a war . . . And of course, I can't forget that he was unspeakably unkind to Rhoda. He made the most ridiculous accusations . . .'

He seemed to interpret Eva's silence as compliance in this view, for he said no more, and then suddenly jumped up from the settle on which they had been talking and marched purposefully towards the sitting-room door.

'We shouldn't be fooled by this war, Eva,' he said harshly. 'It may not end quickly, and we may not see the Germans put to rout . . . You shouldn't wait for David. You should get out while there's still time.'

'Get out?' she repeated unhappily.

'Yes. Rhoda has decided she wants to return to England. Rather late in the day, I know, but I feel it's the right thing to do. I can't go with her, of course. I can't leave my mother behind . . . but you could go with her, Eva. The two of you together, on the train back to Lisbon . . . And then home to England.'

'No!' she exclaimed, astonished that he should imagine she might leave without Davy, wondering why, if the war were going to escalate, England should seem any safer than France, but he was gone before she had a chance to ask.

It was true that many people were leaving. Expatriate English and Americans, Parisians who had relatives abroad, even the young Jewish girls had departed, offered a safe passage, to Eva's intense relief, on a private boat sailing from Marseilles. But she would not leave – no matter what Victor said.

The next day he was back with a young official from the British Embassy, a tall, fair-skinned man who bowed when he was introduced and spoke in the clipped, dispassionate tones of the English upper class, managing to alienate Eva in a matter of seconds.

'This is Rupert Connaught,' Victor said gently, taking Eva's hand. 'He has advised me to send Rhoda home to her family, and he has very kindly offered to escort her to London . . . He will do the same for you.'

'I'll do as I please,' Eva said belligerently, snatching her hand from Victor's and turning away. 'I'm an American citizen.'

'With respect,' she heard Rupert Connaught say, 'that is hardly the point. You are entitled to return to England. In view of your condition, it would be foolish to do anything else . . .'

'Then I'm a fool,' Eva answered hotly, angry that Victor should put her in this position before a stranger. 'I'm staying here.'

Victor threw her a despairing glance.

'I shall speak to Sister Marguerite,' he muttered, walking towards the door. 'Perhaps she will be able to convince you . . .'

Left alone in the sitting room with Rupert Connaught, Eva felt intimidated and uncomfortable, cast in the role of the irrational woman while he looked on with ill-disguised scorn.

'I'm staying here,' she repeated firmly, just in case he might imagine her open to persuasion.

Rupert Connaught gave another little bow.

'Then I hope you don't regret your decision,' he said coolly. 'And I hope your child doesn't suffer as a consequence of it . . .'

Eva smiled stonily. She had taken a hearty dislike to the elegant Mr Connaught, even though he might only wish her the best, and she would not concede to his manifest knowingness.

'My child will be no worse off than many French children born at the same time,' she replied hotly. 'They will all have to take their chances . . .'

Suddenly he moved towards her, his expression changing in a moment from icy reserve to passionate concern.

'You might think of Rhoda,' he implored her, catching at her arm. 'She's so young, so very vulnerable . . . And her time is near. She needs someone to look after her. Another woman . . . a friend.'

Eva stared in astonishment, and then, as understanding dawned, she shook her arm free from his grasp, stepping back so she might survey him more clearly, seeking confirmation of her intuition. But Rupert Connaught had recovered himself.

'I am naturally concerned for her,' he said stiffly.

Eva laughed.

'Rhoda will be just fine,' she said softly. 'Take it from me, Mr Connaught. Rhoda knows how to look after herself.'

Madame Martineau died peacefully on the day the Nazis marched through the Ardennes, displacing this calamitous news and anaesthetising its immediate effect.

Eva, Anya and Victor had gathered at the old lady's bedside, and when the moment came, it was Anya who burst into loud sobs and wails, leaving Eva to comfort Victor.

'There's only my Uncle Jacob left,' Anya wept. 'He's the last of the Kleins. Isaac, Emmanuel and Leah – they're all gone now.'

'But their children are still alive,' Eva pointed out gently. 'You and Victor – and David. The Kleins live on . . .'

'Yes,' Anya said bravely, drying her tears and seeming suddenly to consider that Eva might be in need of comfort herself. 'I suppose that's true. We're all still here . . .'

There had been no word of David, and it was now nearly six months since Eva had kissed him goodbye at the Gare de l'Est on the first stage of his journey.

Their child would be born within a matter of weeks, the first of a new generation, excepting Rhoda's daughter, of course, born in London three months before.

Would David return for the birth of Eva's child as he had promised? She was now sure that he would, and as the child leapt and struggled inside her in the last weeks of its hidden life, a curious calm overcame her, a sense of all things falling gradually into place.

'Victor, there's something I always meant to ask,' she said when they sat quietly that evening; 'something concerning the gift your mother sent to America for me – the lace handkerchief. Do you remember?'

He was deep in thought, staring out of the window on to the shining grass, trimmed only that morning by Sister Marguerite.

Eva laid out the two lace handkerchiefs on the table in front of the fire.

'Your mother got rather upset when I showed her this one. She seemed to be telling me something. She wrote down my name, Eva, and then she wrote down your name, Martineau . . .'

Victor, still gazing out of the window, did not even turn round.

'Eva Martineau?' he enquired dully. 'She was my father's younger sister – an actress in the Paris Revue. She's been dead many years.'

Eva felt a pulse in her temple begin to pound.

'Could this be her handkerchief?' she whispered.

Now Victor turned from the window to inspect the two handkerchiefs, turning them over in his hands just as Madame Martineau herself had done.

'My mother sewed lace handkerchiefs and petticoats,' he said absently. 'This one with the daisies on, she sewed for you. This other seems very old, and it looks like her work . . . I suppose it may have belonged to Eva Martineau, but then, it could have belonged to any other young lady called Eva. My mother sewed hundreds of handkerchiefs over the past fifty years . . . Indeed, at one point we'd all have starved if it hadn't been for her sewing. She was a wonderful woman, Eva. She was a truly wonderful woman . . .'

Victor bent his head, turning away towards the window again, and Eva picked up the handkerchiefs, folding them with trembling hands, seeing that now was not the moment for further questions, yet knowing without doubt that the past and its mysteries were close to unravelling.

'Listen, Eva,' Victor burst out suddenly. 'There is something I must say to you.'

She looked up at him expectantly, hoping for something more concerning Eva Martineau, daring to believe that he might be about to reveal what had become of the young actress from the Paris Revue . . .

He knelt down beside her in front of the settle, taking her hands in his and stroking them gently.

'I believe you must face the fact that David may be dead,' he said gravely. 'He's not coming back to Paris, I'm convinced of it . . . But the Germans are coming, Eva. They could be here inside a month . . . We should leave. All of us. You, me and Anya.'

She squeezed his hand, not wanting to rebuff his obvious concern although she could think of nothing that would not seem a rejection of his care.

'I'm staying,' she said at last. 'I couldn't possibly leave now. David will come back. I know he will . . .'

And so she continued to insist throughout the alarming days that followed, refusing to accept what everyone else – Anya, Victor, and even Sister Marguerite – now believed to be inevitable. David would not come, but the Germans would . . .

Anya tried to make her leave, but wouldn't consider the idea of leaving herself, and Victor, torn between his need to follow Rhoda and his desire to see Eva and his beloved cousin protected, dithered and fretted and pleaded.

Outside the convent the roads and pavements teemed with people fleeing the city, but inside Eva's little sitting room all was peaceful and calm. There was no sense in worrying, she told herself firmly, and there was nothing for it but to wait and to pray.

David would come back, and he would come before the baby was born. He had promised, and he had asked her to believe it. What else could she do?

Her first pains coincided with the news that there were German troops on the streets, and she sat bolt upright on the wooden settle, clutching her swollen stomach and fighting for breath.

'There seems to be no resistance at all,' said Sister Marguerite, pressing her hand on the unborn child while staring hard at her silver fob watch, and for a moment Eva was unsure what was meant, the muscles of her womb or the citizens of Paris.

'Well, it won't be yet,' the Sister said confidently, lowering her ear to Eva's abdomen. 'In fact, I'd say that was probably a false alarm . . . There's a good few hours to go.'

A few hours, Eva thought desperately, only a few hours to birth and to surrender . . . Only a few more hours of freedom.

'Rest!' commanded Sister Marguerite, shaking out her thermometer and smoothing the bedclothes. 'Sleep while you can. If Victor comes I shall tell him you're not to be disturbed.'

Eva could not have imagined she would sleep, and yet as predicted, the pains subsided and she fell into a fitful doze, dreaming that she was back in the cottage at St Cuthbert's, drowsing on a golden summer's afternoon while David worked on the plans to turn Aidan Forster's home into a Centre for Spiritual Retreat . . . She almost fancied she could hear him call her name, feel his hand on her hair and his lips brushing her cheek . . .

Then she opened her eyes, and he was there.

'I'm back,' he announced, plainly seeing that she doubted the evidence of her own senses. 'Sorry I cut it so fine . . .'

Eva, overwhelmed, buried her face in his jacket, weeping and clinging to his shoulder, sobbing out his name over and over again. He held her close for a moment, then pushed her from him.

'Listen to me, Eva,' he said sharply. 'This may be a reunion straight out of the movies, but we don't have time for it. Get up now, and get dressed. I've got a car waiting outside. We're heading for the Spanish border.'

But at that moment she was seized by another spasm, crying aloud and sinking back on to the settle, doubling forward in the pain.

'We'll never make it to the border,' she gasped.

'Sure we will,' he said calmly, taking her hand. 'There may be one more of us when we get there, that's all.'

She smiled then through her tears, catching something of his confidence, willing herself to match his determination. He looked thinner than when she'd seen him last, more lean and fit, as though he had survived on his wits alone. His restless energy was undimmed and the dark blue eyes were fierce and bright. He would not be denied.

'What happened?' she asked him suddenly. 'Did you find them? Your Uncle Jake and your mother's sisters?'

'Some,' he said, 'but I can't tell you now. Hurry, Eva, please. There isn't much time.'

'Where did you get the car?' she asked him, rising cautiously and reaching for her clothes. She knew there wasn't a vehicle in Paris for sale or hire, and couldn't imagine how he'd done it.

'I stole it,' he said. 'And someone else will steal it back unless we move pretty quickly.'

Sister Marguerite, however, had foreseen this possibility and now she breezed in with an announcement, casting a critical eye upon what Eva

suddenly perceived to be David's dishevelled state, his muddy clothes
and his wild hair. What had he done, she wondered, in his determination to find transport for her?

'We've driven the car into the back garden,' Sister Marguerite
declared. 'It will be quite safe there . . . Now David, I strongly suggest that you don't depart at once. The streets are full of soldiers,
and we hear that the Luftwaffe have been firing on the fleeing refugees. Wait until dark. Then you can leave by the rear gate and find
your way through the sidestreets . . . You can drive the car across the
lawn.'

'Across the lawn!' cried Eva foolishly. 'He can't do that!'

'No,' David agreed, moving to the sitting-room window and looking
out, 'I don't think I can. The gate isn't wide enough.'

'Yes, it is,' said Sister Marguerite briskly. 'We've measured it. It's
close, but you'll do it if you're careful . . .'

She bustled about the room, helping Eva into her clothes, detailing
their escape route, an intricate system of back roads which would lead
them out of the city to the east, insisting that David take a bath and a
meal to set him up for the task.

'But what about Eva?' he demanded suddenly. 'We should leave at
once for her sake!'

Eva looked up at him then and saw the first sign of his uncertainty,
the knowledge that he faced an alarming challenge, the doubt that he
could do it. Sister Marguerite had seen it too.

'Some babies come quickly, and some take their time,' she said comfortingly. 'This one doesn't seem in too great a hurry. You can afford
to wait.'

When he'd been ushered from the room by a solicitous young
nun, however, Sister Marguerite wasted no time in giving Eva the
truth.

'I don't know how long it will be, though I doubt you'll make it to
the border. But if you start at once, you won't make it to the end of the
street . . .'

She hesitated.

'It would be better to convince him that all will be well,' she said
gently. 'In my experience, men aren't at their best in these matters.
They may do many brave and dangerous things, but faced with a baby
about to be born, they just collapse. You, however, must be prepared
for anything – to have your baby in a field if need be!'

Eva uttered a sharp involuntary denial, and then sank back once more
as another contraction overcame her.

'Courage, Eva!' said Sister Marguerite. 'You're a trained nurse. You
know what to do, and when the time comes you must instruct him . . .

I've prepared a package for you, everything you'll need, including scissors to cut the cord.'

Eva blanched, and then as Sister Marguerite grasped her hand in sympathy, felt herself relax.

'May God protect you,' the Sister whispered, and Eva truly believed in that moment that he would. She smiled bravely and sat down by the window overlooking the lawn, resting her head against the cool glass, breathing deeply, counting the time between contractions, as she had once been taught to do. The birth was not yet imminent, this much she knew, and she dared to believe they might make it to safety.

She must have slept for some time in this unconventional position, for when she woke, the light had gone from the lawn and the first stars were winking in the grey above the gardens.

She gazed into the darkened room, for a moment seeing only the glowing coals of the fire and the illuminated plaster crucifix which hung above the mantel. Then she saw David sitting on the wooden settle, his head in his hands.

'What's the matter?' she demanded, knowing at once that something had happened. 'Is it dark enough yet? When are we going?'

He looked up at her, and even in the gloom she could see that he was deeply troubled.

'I must be crazy,' he muttered as she snapped on the light and moved to his side. 'I can't believe what I've done . . .'

'What?' she asked him, frightened. 'What have you done?'

'I gave Victor my passport so he could go to the café and tell Anya I was back . . . I wasn't about to go myself and leave you alone again, and anyway, I knew it wouldn't make any difference. Anya will never leave Paris. What a stupid thing to do! God knows what's happened to Victor . . .'

'Your passport? But why?' Her heart was hammering inside her chest and she felt she would surely faint.

He sank his head into his hands again.

'Victor thought it would protect him and allow him to get Anya away . . . He reckoned he could pass himself off as me – David Klein, American citizen, Hollywood director, Nazi collaborator – it seemed a reasonable idea. We look alike, and the Germans think I'm a great guy . . .'

'Do they?' she whispered, unable to take it in yet seeing all too clearly that the chances of crossing the border without an American passport were severely diminished.

'For the moment they do. That may change when they discover several dozen ruined rolls of film in my hotel room . . .'

She wasn't following him, and now she could concentrate on nothing except a violent stabbing sensation, deep inside her. Her face contorted and he gazed at her in open alarm.

'Oh God, Eva,' he said, 'I don't know what to do. Victor left me his passport. Should we just take off with that? Or should we wait?'

It was Sister Marguerite who provided the answers, insisting that they couldn't delay any longer, declaring that not only would Victor's passport do as well as any other, but that Eva should have her own French passport too, extra insurance if they needed to pose as a local couple.

'I told you we had ways of providing papers. They all belonged to people who have died in the convent . . . Sister Lorraine takes some photographs and makes a few adjustments to the details . . . Now don't worry at all! Just concentrate on getting yourselves away.'

Within minutes Eva was staring at a genuine French passport containing a copy of her picture and, dazed, she opened it to see the name inside, carefully and unknowingly printed by Sister Lorraine. *Eva Martineau*, it read.

Now David was in action again, throwing Eva's cloak around her shoulders, grabbing her suitcases and parcels, hustling her out of the sitting room and into the garden.

'Goodbye, my dearest Eva!' called Sister Marguerite, and a chorus of nuns called after them: 'Goodbye, goodbye, God go with you . . .'

The car was a long, shiny black limo, a British-built Bentley, a beast of a thing which would surely never get through the garden gate.

Eva leaned on its side, breathing deeply, bracing herself against the coming pain. Then she got into the passenger seat, stared at the gate, and crossed her fingers.

'Mind the lawn!' she heard herself say as the car set off across the pristine green, its tyres sticking in the soft ground, a fountain of mud and grass shooting into the air behind them.

'To hell with the bloody lawn,' he said savagely, careering towards the gate.

'Mind the gate!' was her involuntary reply, and a moment later he hit it, crunching the wing of the car into the post with a sickening bang and throwing Eva on to the dashboard.

He swore, the only time she'd ever heard such a curse on his lips, and instead of asking whether she were all right, he leaned out of the window to inspect the wing and then jerked the car into reverse.

'You're going to hit it again,' she advised, 'on this side.'

He said nothing, simply edged the car forward with consummate precision until they were safely out of the gate and into the silent lane.

'It did look tight,' she said contritely.

'Shut up,' he snapped, his customary control giving way beneath the tension. 'Just sit there and shut up . . .'

And so they drove out of Paris on a brilliant cloudless night, just as they had done once before on a golden summer's morning, in total silence, each consumed by private thoughts and anxieties, neither wishing to voice the worst possibility, nor even to speculate on the best outcome, until, without sighting so much as an armoured car or a single soldier, nor even hearing a solitary shot, they came at last to the edge of the stricken city and the blessed vista of the open road beyond.

'We're running out of gas,' he said. 'We'll have to find another car.'

They had been travelling for three hours on roads that teemed with an extraordinary variety of vehicles, heading across open fields when they found columns of refugees hindering their progress, stopping frequently to allow Eva to unbend from the restrictions of the front seat, skirting towns and villages in a complex plan of David's own devising, weaving along farm tracks and country lanes in a tortuous, circuitous route south. And still, he calculated, they were some four hundred kilometres from the border.

Eva, who'd been giving all her concentration to her strengthening contractions, had not considered the need for fuel.

'Another car?' she quavered. 'You mean you'd steal another car?'

'That would make it four altogether. One just after I crossed the Swiss border, then an old farm wagon, and then this one. I could have a thriving career as a car thief if I never make it back to Hollywood.'

'Like Joe Lugisi,' she said unthinkingly.

He gave no reply, pulling the car from the road at a convenient verge and consulting his map by the light of a pocket torch.

'We're following the same route,' he said. 'The road we took that day we set off to Helena Duval's place . . .'

He glanced at her nervously

'If you can't make it to the border,' he said, taking her hand, 'we can always head for Helena's. I know how to get there.'

'So where are we now?'

'In the middle of nowhere. We'll have to make for the next village . . . It's only fifteen kilometres. We'll pick up a truck or a van.'

Eva glimpsed the figure at the window before he did, saw the steel of the farm rifle and the rough hand which cocked the trigger before he'd so much as turned his head, heard the guttural command to get out of the car, and then watched in frozen disbelief as David leapt from the driver's seat, the map still in his hand, to face the rifle's barrel.

She heard him arguing in rapid French.

'My wife is about to have a baby . . . We're heading for the border . . . And anyway, the car is almost out of gas.'

She watched in horror as the gun was pressed into his chest, and then a moment later, he opened the passenger door.

'Get out, Eva,' he said coolly. 'We're being hijacked . . .'

There were six of them, a family of husband, wife, three teenage girls and an elderly grandmother, and confronted by Eva, clutching her suitcase and Sister Marguerite's precious parcel, they suddenly seemed more sheepish than threatening.

'*Pardon*,' said the man with the rifle, shrugging his shoulders, and then as the old woman began to desist, pointing at Eva and wringing her hands, he jumped into the car, shouting for the others to follow. In less than a minute the rear lights had disappeared into the black and the two of them were left standing alone at the side of the road.

'Take it easy,' David muttered, as much to himself as to Eva. 'Take it easy, and think hard . . .'

He put his arm around her shoulders and led her purposefully away from the road, up a gentle bank and through a copse into a sloping field.

'I've got the map,' he said, still seeming to speak to himself. 'All I need is a car . . .'

Eva sank down on to the soft grass fearing this was surely the field in which, as Sister Marguerite had warned, she would give birth. How long would it be? Two hours or another ten? Her contractions seemed to have subsided again. She had no idea when the moment might come.

'I should have stayed in the car,' he said suddenly, his voice threatening to break, 'I should have driven off. That guy would never have fired . . . We would have been okay.'

'You couldn't have known that,' she soothed him, laying her hand upon his cheek. 'And anyway, we're still okay, aren't we? We're alive, and we're together . . . What more do you want?'

This was brave talk, much braver than she felt, for she knew he would have to go in search of another car. Fifteen kilometres to the nearest village – it would be hours before he got back. She lay down on the grass, breathing steadily and deep, willing herself not to panic, praying to God in heaven for their deliverance, becoming calmer and more composed, turning her mind to the practicalities ahead. And then, when her eyes had become accustomed to the gloom, she began to take in the moonlit landscape around her.

A valley of vines fell away before them, and to the left she could plainly see a river . . . And then to the right, a distant village perched upon a rocky hill, a cluster of muted lights winking beneath the sky . . .

'David,' she said suddenly, 'do you know where we are?'

'I told you . . . we're in the middle of nowhere. It's fifteen kilometres to the nearest village . . . That village there, right up that goddamn hill.'

She sat up with effort, and gestured at the valley before them.

'That day we were driving to meet the Duvals . . . When we stopped and made love for the first time . . . When I was so mad at you, and then it started to rain . . . This is it! The very same place!'

'Oh, highly romantic, Eva,' he said heavily, barely looking up, 'but hardly relevant right now.'

Eva could scarcely believe her ears.

'Romantic!' she shrieked in a burst of spontaneous rage. 'I'm about to have your baby in the middle of a field, and you think I'm being romantic! Listen, you dope. There was a café in the dip of the road. You went marching off and left me on my own . . . It can't be a hundred yards from here.'

He leapt to his feet at once.

'Dear God, I think you're right. Let's go – can you make it down the hill?'

'Of course I can,' she said testily, still angry with him, and now desperately afraid that the café might no longer be there, or if there, then silent and deserted.

And so it seemed as they approached the dilapidated building, no light showing and no visible billboard or sign to entice passing trade. But there were curtains at the windows, and tubs of flowers outside the door, and in a hidden courtyard at the back, well away from the road, a small delivery van,

'Get in,' he whispered, opening the bonnet and fiddling beneath it, 'and hold on tight. It may be a bumpy exit.'

The engine suddenly roared into life and he jumped into the driver's seat, breathing hard, swinging the little van out of the courtyard and on to the road, speeding away from a burst of lights and shouts in the café behind them.

'A full tank!' he yelled, elated, examining the dials and pressing his foot to the floor. 'Enough to get us to the border! We're going to make it, Eva. I do believe we're going to make it . . .'

Eva, finding the mass of her belly jammed against the van's metal dashboard and conscious of a novel stinging sensation between her legs, said nothing.

'Are you okay?' he asked her anxiously, bending over to adjust the passenger seat and free her stomach. 'Is everything all right?'

And when she still made no reply, he reached for her hand and lifted it to his lips.

'This will be a tale to tell our baby, won't it?' he said softly. 'How we crept out of Paris, and lost our car, and then stole another one, and finally made it to the border . . .'

She smiled then, feeling herself begin to relax once more, wanting to believe in his vision, willing that it might be so. 'Oh yes,' she said

wryly, catching his eye, 'it will be quite a tale to tell . . . Highly romantic, I'm sure.'

They drove through what remained of the night, and he told her of his
time in Germany, an astonishing and darkly comic account of a film that
never was, set to the incomprehensible music of Karl Schwartz, featur-
ing endless columns of marching Germans and shining tanks, and personally validated by Herr Goebbels himself.

'I don't know what they thought I was doing, but I tell you this, Eva.
One thing I learned – evil isn't impressive, nor even particularly frightening. Evil is utterly banal. It has to be possible to defeat the banal.'

He was not inclined to overstate his success, deeply sorry that he'd
been unable to find his Uncle Jacob, full of foreboding about what
might have happened to him, and to the family of his mother's youngest
sister, Zia.

'Karl tried to find out, but there were so many people being moved
about. Enforced labour, I guess, getting them to work the land for free,
although that isn't the way Karl put it . . . He said they were being
resettled in Poland, in a safer zone.'

Unable to help Zia, or Jake, he had nevertheless found Judith, her
husband and two children, and then turned his efforts to helping their
friends, a doctor and his wife, a tailor's family, three teenage classmates
of Judith's eldest son and an elderly couple, relatives of Judith's husband.

'Karl arranged all their exit papers. That was the ridiculous thing. He
wanted to help me. He knew I was Jewish – he knew all of them were
Jewish – but because he saw us as individuals, he believed we were
exceptions. We weren't like all the rest. We were worth helping.'

'What will happen to Karl?' Eva asked him.

'I don't know . . . The day I left I exposed all the film I'd taken,
pulled it out of the cans and piled it in the bath. The film was very
much Karl's project. He'll probably be shot . . .'

Eva shifted uneasily in her seat, stiff and sore and sick at heart. The
mission had surely been a success. All of the refugees had made it to
Geneva, and then on to Marseilles. They were now on their way to
America . . . Even one life redeemed was a triumph, but what about all
the rest? What about Karl Schwartz, who surely didn't deserve to be
shot? What about Victor and Anya?

'What do you think happened to Victor?' she whispered, turning to
him. 'Do you think he's okay?'

'I don't know, Eva . . . Maybe he got arrested in the café. Victor
doesn't always think straight. He rushes in . . . Well, I guess we all do

that sometimes . . . I hope he was arrested. I hope it isn't worse than that.'

'If he was killed,' she heard herself say, 'they'll think it was you . . .'

He reached over for her hand, unwilling to give her false hope, and yet anxious to console.

'It may be a long time before we find out,' he said, 'but somehow, I can't help feeling that whatever happens, Anya will be okay. She has an instinct for survival . . .'

Eva, whose own instinct for survival had kept her calm throughout the night, working with her body as it heaved and struggled towards the shedding of its load, controlling her breathing and relaxing into her pain, took this to heart. Yes, it was surely true that Anya would survive. Anya, so full of life, would find a way to keep it, just as they themselves had battled against the odds and overcome.

'Hell,' he said suddenly. 'This doesn't look so good . . .'

Dawn was rising over the remote and mysterious heartland of France, but a mere half a mile away, where the track they'd been following joined the main road, they could plainly see a long line of traffic snaking slowly towards the south.

Eva heard the engines above them in the moment that he spoke, the portentous roar drowning out his next words, then saw the aeroplanes swoop down to the line of traffic, watching, stunned, while the frantic cars and wagons swerved and spun. 'They're killing those people!' she cried in disbelief, but the stricken scene suddenly lurched from her view, and she stared ahead across a ploughed field into a dense thicket of conifers. David had swung the van from the road, racing and jerking towards cover, landing with a terrifying bump at the ditch before the wood.

Then, opening the driver's door, he dragged her across the front seat and into the trees, pushing her to the ground and covering her head with his arms while above them a solitary Messerschmitt dived for the kill.

They seemed to lie for minutes or more, deafened by the cascade of bullets upon the thick metal roof of the van, but it could only have been a matter of seconds before the pilot, convinced his work was done, soared into the pink sky above the wood.

'We're all right,' she whispered shakily, feeling his body move against hers. 'They missed us!'

He sat up cautiously and stared at the van.

'But they didn't miss the goddam tyres,' he said furiously.

He fetched a water bottle from the van, allowing her only the smallest swallow to preserve their supply, and then, lifting her gently to her feet, led her into the whispering shade of the thicket, pushing aside the briars that threatened her face, swinging her effortlessly, despite her extra weight, across muddy paths and puddles, pulling her to him when she cried out in her growing pain, repeatedly consulting his map.

'I can't go on,' she wept for the third time.

'Sure you can,' he said easily. 'Look, we're almost out of the wood. Don't worry. I know where we're going. Helena's place is close, I'm certain of it . . .'

And then they were standing in the early morning sunshine, feeling its first fingers warm the open ground before them, gazing upon lush emerald valleys and flower-studded hills, a scene of wondrous natural beauty which contained, so far as they could see, not so much as a solitary cottage nor farmhouse, not a church nor a herdsman's shack, not a single hint of human habitation.

'I thought there'd be a village,' he faltered, running his hand through his hair and looking at the map. 'Oh, God . . . Maybe we shouldn't have come through the wood. Maybe we should have gone back to the road.'

All through the night, since the moment they'd hit the gate at the Divine Faith convent, they had veered between jubilation and despair, each encouraging the other when spirits failed, consoling and supporting, chiding and comforting. But now she had nothing left to give him, and she sank to the grass without a word, panting and sobbing, feeling her baby's head press down into the birth canal, realising with a sudden flash of panic that she had left Sister Marguerite's vital parcel in the van.

'I'm going to walk to the brow of that hill,' he said. 'I'm sure we're in the right place . . . I think there's a road behind that hill . . .'

'No,' she begged, 'Don't leave me.'

'I'll only be a minute . . .'

'Please. Stay here with me. Pray with me.'

'You pray. I'm just going to that hill . . .'

'Bloody men,' she screamed after him. 'You never finish what you start!'

He set off for the hill, ignoring this undeserved slur, turning to give her a cheery little wave. 'Hang on!' he called.

Hang on? What did he know about biology, for heaven's sake?

And then, inexplicably, she found herself laughing through her tears, at first in sheer hysteria, but then, to her surprise, in genuine mirth at the simple inevitability of it all, the knowledge that whatever the affairs of countries and armies, whatever the dealings, devious or delightful, between women and men, whatever the time, the place, the conjunction of the planets or the stars, the processes of ordinary birth and death could never be denied.

With courage and with resignation, she hauled herself into a kneeling position. Her baby would be born in a field. So be it.

'Dear God,' she prayed aloud, a sentimental, melodramatic prayer springing unbidden to her lips, 'I would like to have my baby in a beautiful big bed with soft sheets upon it. But the Saviour of the world was born in a humble stable, and what was good enough for Mary is good enough for me . . .'

Then suddenly she heard him shout, and turned to see him running towards her from the hill, and behind him, another figure, an older man moving more slowly.

He was breathless when he reached her.

'Eva, I don't know who you're praying to – your God or mine – but whoever he is, he just came up trumps . . . I told you we were close . . .'

She gazed in confusion as he gabbled, allowing him to raise her to her feet, take one arm and hurry her across the field towards that other stumbling figure who, as he drew nearer, began to assume solid form, a tall, middle-aged man with dark hair, whose empty right sleeve was tucked into his pocket.

'Eva, my dearest girl,' the man cried as he approached. 'We must get you to the house at once! It's only a minute away . . . You know who I am, don't you? Harold Brannen's old friend.'

'Paul,' she whispered faintly, 'Paul Duval.'

'I've sent word to Helena,' he said gently, taking her other arm. 'My little boy, Edouard, has run to tell her . . . She'll get everything ready. Now don't you worry about a thing . . . All will be well.'

She lay in a beautiful big bed on the softest of sheets, her child wrapped in a pale pink shawl and nestled into the crook of her arm, her husband sleeping silently beside her, his tousled head resting against her shoulder.

The windows of the bedroom were thrown open to the evening sky, and on the terrace outside, a cricket sang. A faint breeze stirred the muslin of the curtain, and behind it a pungent honeysuckle trailed long, enveloping tendrils over the lintel. All was calm, all was still.

David stirred, and she realised then that he wasn't sleeping, but staring out, like her, into the lilac night beyond.

'What are you thinking?' she asked him.

'Right then I was thinking about *Casey's War*,' he murmured. 'About the ending. It was all wrong. We never should have had them going off into the sunset . . .'

She considered this carefully.

'What do you think they did after the story ended?' she enquired at length.

'Well, I don't know . . . The war was still on. Maybe they were killed. Maybe they fell out and got divorced, or maybe they survived and were simply worn out by the business of living . . .'

'Or maybe,' she said, 'they did what most people do. They got on with it, bringing up their children, making a home, trying to do a little bit of good in the world.'

The child stirred in its swaddling shawl, and she moved to cradle it, exposing one tiny fist to the balmy air. He sat up and took the tiny fingers in his hand.

'So you think Casey and Vivi had a whole bunch of kids and lived happily ever after?'

She laughed and turned to kiss his cheek.

'I'm certain of it. Maybe they did fall out sometimes, and maybe things got tough or a bit mundane . . . But maybe they had the love, and the will, and the guts to see it through together . . . Maybe that's what happy ever after really means . . .'

She put the child to her breast and they listened in silence to its little gurgling noises until at last it lay content once more.

'Maybe,' he agreed, lying down beside her again.

Book IX: Beth

Chapter Twenty-five

To partake of the psychological and emotional pain of Jesus through imaginative identification is to go some way towards transforming personal grief
and embracing the suffering of the world . . .

The Freedom of the Kingdom, by Michael Cameron

I became absorbed in David Klein's biography, greatly impressed by his
artistic achievements, immeasurably moved by the tale of his daring
escapade in Germany, deeply affected by a long interview with the aged
and regretful Moira Sheen who claimed him as the sweetest lover she'd
ever had, a man among men.

I must have fallen asleep over the book, for suddenly I was lying on
a high metal bed, my feet suspended in plastic stirrups, my eyes blinking in a mean neon glare from above, my body heaving to a merciless
rhythm all of its own. And I was screaming my head off.

'Now then, Elizabeth, don't make such a fuss. Women have babies in
all kinds of terrible situations. Out in the bush, and in the middle of
wars . . . while here you are in a nice safe hospital.'

The Sister was an ogre from hell, brandishing her stethoscope as
though it were a pitchfork, sticking her fingers inside me without so
much as a warning, let alone a request.

'Only three centimetres dilated,' she announced to the gathered assembly. 'There's a long way to go yet . . . Now then, Elizabeth, I hope
you're going to be a brave girl. You're disturbing the other ladies with
all this noise.'

'I want my mother,' I wept, 'I just want my mother . . .'

There was a muted exchange among the onlookers, and then Sister
Beelzebub moved back to the bedside.

'Your boyfriend's in the waiting room,' she said briskly. 'What's his name? Sam, isn't it? We'll send him in.'

'No!' I said in panic, struggling against the stirrups, trying to sit up and assert myself. 'I don't want him here!'

'You are in a tizz, aren't you? Very well, whatever you say. The customer's always right.'

She bustled out of the room, and a young midwife came forward to grasp my hand.

'Breathe deep, Beth,' she said kindly. 'One, two, three, four . . .'

In the background I could hear a persistent knocking, a sharp and repeated rap on the door to the labour ward.

'That's my mother,' I said urgently. 'She wants to be with me . . . She's trying to get in . . .'

Then, in the next moment, I woke in sudden alarm on the settee at the Duvals' cottage, my head thumping, my legs shaking, David Klein's weighty biography bearing down on my stomach, and a half-empty bottle of Genevieve's gin on the floor at my side. Someone was banging on the front door.

'Sorry to disturb you,' Emily Forster said, surveying my dishevelled state with obvious embarrassment. 'I was asked to check and see you were all right.'

Despite my confusion, I bristled at once, angry that this bright-eyed emissary should catch me at such a moment, irrationally put out by the exchange of her former countryside gear for a stylish grey suit.

'Were you?' I snapped, seeing no reason to conceal my irritation at her mission nor my antipathy towards Michael. 'Well, as you see, I'm perfectly all right. So just go tell him to fuck off.'

She stared at me for a moment, and then shrugged.

'Okay,' she said. 'If that's what you want.'

She began to walk down the path towards the lane, but then as I leaned in the doorway, breathing in the damp morning air and banishing the befuddling remnants of sleep, she turned back. 'He thought you might need the central heating on,' she called. 'I've got the instructions for the boiler if you want them . . .'

Then I realised it was Duval, not Michael, checking up on me; Duval, who'd hardly left my thoughts since the moment he disappeared over the horizon with his wife; Duval, whom, with all the elegiac longing of a Moira Sheen, I was beginning to recognise as the sweetest lover I'd ever had . . .

I summoned Emily Forster back with a shout and ushered her inside, feeling foolish and ungrateful, excessively anxious that no uncharitable message should find its way back to Duval, watching as she fiddled with the central heating boiler, offering trite and transparent comments about the weather and delving into cupboards so I might make coffee and amends.

'Blue Mountain,' I said unhappily, wondering if I had licence to open a new packet. 'Crikey!'

'Only the best for Genevieve,' Emily Forster said lightly. 'Just use it. She won't mind. She'll bring another dozen packs next time she comes.'

I said nothing, encouraged by this implied criticism of my adversary but unwilling to enter into any judgements myself, wondering what on earth Emily Forster must make of my rude welcome and sudden about-turn. Had she been told that I'd kidnapped Katie Cameron from the beach? Had she been told all about my long-ago romance with her boyfriend?

The boiler gurgled into life and I urged her to sit down on the sofa, sliding the gin bottle from view, caught between a marked reluctance to entertain any confidante of Michael's and a strong desire to befriend Duval's cousin. More than anything, I realised, I wanted an inside view on our affair and its repercussions, some idea of how his mother, his children and the rest of his family regarded me. But I hadn't the nerve to ask her outright.

'I see you're reading the new David Klein book,' she said, sipping her coffee and seeming to search for safe subjects. 'Good, isn't it? Pity it had to stop half-way.'

'Half-way?' I enquired absently, wondering how I might casually bring the conversation round to Clive Fisher and the *Sun*. 'How do you mean?'

'Oh well, you know,' she muttered awkwardly, looking away. 'All the rest.'

'All the rest about David Klein?'

Now I was staring at her intently, and as I stared, intuition dawned for the very first time, a fragile hint of understanding about something fundamental I had missed.

'Oh hell,' she said, 'I thought you knew . . . I just assumed Dan would have told you.'

'Eva,' I whispered, hearing my voice tremble as I spoke, 'Eva and David Klein . . .'

Emily Forster finished her Blue Mountain and rose from the sofa, scooping up her coffee cup and marching purposefully into the kitchen as though she were the host and I the humble guest. I followed meekly behind her, confirming our roles.

'It doesn't have to be a secret any more,' she said firmly, as much to herself as to me. 'It was never a secret anyway . . . It was just that for years and years nobody gave a damn about them . . . then all of a sudden Davy was declared a hero, one of the best Hollywood directors of all time, and a lot of biographers started snooping around . . . Eva didn't take kindly to it. She didn't want to talk about Will Sutton, or any of that . . .'

I knew only too well that Eva hadn't wanted to talk, and yet she'd told me enough. What was it she'd said as she sat in her sitting room at the Divine Faith convent, dreaming among the icons and nodding before the fire? *I fell in love long before I met Will Sutton . . . Once and only once. Very romantic . . .*

'Please,' I begged Emily. 'Please tell me . . .'

Then I listened in astonishment at the tale she told.

'They got married at the beginning of the war,' she said hesitantly, having made her decision but still reluctant. 'Then they went to Paris. They got caught up in the Nazi invasion, and they tried to escape. But they never made it.'

I could scarcely credit what I was hearing, and yet it seemed to have its own inexorable logic.

'Their daughter was born at about the same time . . . and you know who she is, don't you? Yes, of course, you do . . . Their daughter is Blanche Duval.'

I sat down suddenly at the kitchen table, mortified that something so obvious had never occurred to me before, thinking back to my intrusion at the convent and Duval's attempts to keep me from Eva . . . Now it was beginning to make sense.

'I'm surprised you didn't work it out,' Emily said, uniting us both in a view of my stupidity; 'that you didn't notice the family resemblance. Just take a look at the pictures in that book . . . can't you see it? Dan's the very image of his grandfather . . .'

I said nothing, reflecting with shameful self-interest that if Daniel Duval were only half the man of David Klein, then I had surely lost the lover of a lifetime.

'I don't know why he didn't tell me,' I muttered, but of course, I did. He'd doubted he could trust me, and who would blame him for that?

I also considered in that moment that he could certainly have rung me himself, if he'd wished, about the central heating boiler, or anything else of a more intimate nature. But he hadn't and, I guessed, didn't intend to.

I smiled wanly at my visitor as I showed her to the door, foolishly close to tears, thinking of Eva giving birth in Paris as her husband was shot, wondering if I would ever see their grandson again.

'He has a difficult life,' Emily said hesitatingly, clearly seeking to console me, 'and three children who love him very much . . .'

'Not to mention a bitch of a wife who won't let him go,' I heard myself say.

Emily looked down.

'Well, nobody knows the whole truth about another person, do they? Genevieve had a very unhappy childhood . . . I know you can't go on blaming your parents for ever, but all the same, it explains some things. Michael seems to think she has serious problems . . .'

'Oh yes?'

I was on my guard again, bile rising at mere mention of Michael's name.

'He thinks she's addicted to sex . . .'

I stared at Emily Forster in open contempt at this facile deduction, our fragile rapport suddenly shattered, our careful exchanges revealed as no more than futile misunderstandings. Addicted to sex? What the hell was that supposed to mean?

'Well, he should bloody know,' I said, closing the door in her face.

My mother gave me a sedative, and I fretted over whether I should swallow it or flush it down the loo. Pregnant women weren't supposed to take drugs, were they? Could one pill harm my baby? I sensed that my mother mightn't be too sympathetic to these fears, and I could see the logic of getting a good night's sleep before I met Michael in the morning. But in the end I couldn't bring myself to take it, and so spent a restless few hours going over the whole situation time and again until finally, I hit oblivion.

When I woke, the cottage seemed unnaturally quiet, no sound of my mother running her morning bath, no radio coming from her bedroom, no breakfast dishes clattering in the kitchen below me. It was Saturday, so there were no tutorials or seminars. And I knew she meant to be on hand when Michael arrived. Where could she be?

Downstairs I found my sister hunched over the dining table, staring into space.

'She didn't come home last night,' Sarah muttered in response to my enquiries. 'I can't think what's happened.'

We exchanged a nervous glance, each willing the other to soothe fears that were only too rational. My mother was a flamboyant driver, and had once pitched her car into a ditch, fracturing a shoulder-blade.

'Maybe she's with her new man,' I suggested.

'No,' Sarah said quickly, 'definitely not. And anyway, she said she'd be back . . .'

'If there'd been an accident, we'd know by now,' I said comfortingly. 'But we can ring the hospitals to make sure.'

This seemed unnecessarily dramatic given the flimsy evidence before us, and so we fixed breakfast and made coffee, expecting at any moment to hear her car on the road outside. I was also expecting to hear the Bentley, for now that I'd considered it carefully, I'd become convinced everything could only work out for the best. Michael couldn't possibly have veered from undying love to indifference, all in the space of a few short weeks. It would be okay. It had to be.

'I'm going to ask Charles to look for her,' Sarah announced suddenly, getting up from the breakfast table. 'He can check out a couple of places in town. Maybe she stayed over with friends . . .'

We looked at each other again, knowing this to be unlikely, if not impossible.

'Maybe we should go with him,' I faltered.

'No, no . . . We're probably worrying about nothing. I've got things to do – I said I'd help out with the church jumble sale. And you're waiting for Michael . . .'

Indeed I was, and I waited with a growing sense of fear and doubt. On this, the day I had to face the father of my unborn child, I felt truly pregnant for the first time, my breasts tender and heavy, my stomach swelling gently, but perceptibly, beneath my nightdress, my breakfast threatening to revisit me at any moment. How would I seem to him? I decided to take a bath and wash my hair, determined to appear as pretty and untainted as I could.

An hour later I was sitting on the cane settee in the conservatory wearing my new denim dress and my cowboy boots, every shining hair in place, my face carefully and discreetly painted, my eyes shadowed with the merest touch of emerald, nothing too tarty or vulgar. I looked good, even if I didn't feel it, and if Michael would only show, I knew I'd feel a great deal better.

But of the prospective father there was no sign at all, and as morning drifted towards afternoon, I became increasingly desperate. There was no sign of my mother or Sarah either, and in my isolation, panic threatened to overwhelm me. I had to do something.

I got up and dialled the Camerons' number, then replaced the receiver in the moment that it rang, my heart hammering inside my chest, my mouth dry and my legs weak.

But then a curious kind of calm overcame me, a resolve to face the demon of doubt and defeat it. I reached for my jacket and marched out of the cottage, up the hill and past the silent church, through the graveyard and across the lane towards the Cameron house. My hands were clenched in my pockets, but I was breathing deeply and evenly, intent on confrontation. I didn't care if I met Michael's mother, Jack Cameron or Michael himself. Whoever, I meant to keep my dignity and demand to know why I was being ignored.

'Good heavens, Beth,' said Jonathan Cameron gently, opening the front door and surveying my taut expression with evident alarm. 'What are you doing here all by yourself? Where's Michael?'

'You tell me,' I whimpered, my careful pose collapsing in a moment, and sobbing, I fell into his arms, surprised and deeply grateful for his obvious concern.

He led me through the great hall, past the library and the ballroom, and into the kitchen, sitting me down in an easy chair by the range, making me tea and then kneeling on the floor beside me, taking my hand in his and gently squeezing the fingers. He was so very like Michael, the same dark gold hair and wide grey eyes, and yet he seemed in that moment immeasurably older and wiser.

'So where the fuck is my little brother?' he demanded of no one in particular, and I found myself immensely comforted by the obscenity, seeing at once that it united us in mutual condemnation.

'I don't know,' I wept, 'I've waited all morning . . .'

'But he left here hours ago! He was on his way to see you . . .'

I looked down at him through my tears, bewildered. Now I was missing not only my mother but my fiancé, and a vision rose before me of the Bentley and my mother's little Fiat, locked in a desperate duel on the highway, one forcing the other off the road until both plunged to a bloody end in some bottomless ravine.

'No doubt he'll turn up,' Jonathan said. 'And then he'll really be in trouble.'

'You mean with your father?'

I was trying to keep calm, fighting the fear, reminding myself there were no bottomless ravines in Rutland.

'Yes . . . Michael was supposed to see you first thing. His courage obviously failed him . . . My father will not be pleased.'

'How about your mother?' I whispered.

He stood up then and walked away from me to the kitchen window, peering out to the winding driveway, evidently thinking hard. Then he turned back.

'I don't need to tell you about my mother, do I, Beth? You know the score. She'd do anything to stop you marrying Michael. He's her darling little boy, and you're not what she wants for him . . . It's as simple as that.'

I began to cry again, certain now that I would never triumph over Beatrice Cameron, needing to know what Michael expected of me, begging Jonathan to enlighten me.

'There aren't many options, are there? I mean, either he marries me, or I have an abortion . . .'

I had said the word I didn't want to say, and I'd said it in the certain belief that he would reassure me at once. Whatever else Michael wanted, he surely wouldn't want me to get rid of his child.

Jonathan shifted uneasily on his perch at the windowsill.

'I think you'll find Michael has surprisingly liberal views on abortion,' he said uncomfortably. 'You'd expect him to go for the sanctity of life, wouldn't you? But in fact he believes in a woman's right to choose.'

Then I knew that the possibility of abortion had not only been discussed but theoretically approved, and I felt the first seeds of resistance stir into life. A woman's right to choose? Well, that worked both ways, and I'd be damned if I'd let anyone choose on my behalf.

But this flash of defiance soon flickered and died.

'We're still engaged,' I said, twisting the diamond solitaire on my finger as though it were a magic ring with powers to save me or transform my sorry fate. 'That must count for something?'

Jonathan moved back to the chair and put his arms around me.

'There isn't going to be a wedding, Beth. I think you have to face that . . . In Michael's defence, I can only say that he's under enormous pressure. A pressure you don't yet know about . . .'

I stared at him, unable to imagine what it might be, yet fixing with despairing female logic upon a new and blindingly obvious possibility.

'Clare Spencer,' I cried out. 'They went away to France together . . . That's it! He's been sleeping with Clare Spencer!'

'Don't be silly, Beth. Of course he hasn't. Clare and Michael? That would be a real recipe for disaster.'

I shook him from me and stood up.

'What then?' I asked unsteadily. 'What pressure? Tell me!'

'I'm sorry, I can't do that. It's not my place. In Michael's absence, I can only suggest you go home and talk to your mother.'

He looked away then, and I was suddenly seized by a terrible presentiment of doom, a sickening fullness in the pit of my stomach that rose to engulf me, a choking black fog which seemed to descend upon all my senses. I stared at Jonathan for a moment, then turned and ran from the house, sobbing and stumbling through the rose garden, unheeding of the briars that grasped at my legs, out of the gate and down the hill towards my mother's cottage.

I saw the police car parked outside the conservatory as soon as I rounded the bend, and I knew in that very moment that she was dead. But still I clung to the vainest of hopes – a treatable injury, vital surgery, a life support machine . . .

I flung open the front door and fell into the hall, received at once by a sturdy woman officer and two grave-faced constables.

'What's happened?' I burst out. 'Where's my mother?'

But I could hear nothing at all for the most terrible din emanating from the living room, a weird, unearthly racket like nothing I'd ever encountered before, a high-pitched wail that most resembled some small, if vocal, animal trapped in unremitting pain.

It took me a full minute to work out what it was.

It was my sister screaming.

An evil grey mist descended on St Cuthbert's, wrapping the bay in a dingy veil, blocking the sea from view, obscuring the church and the spire, pitching the lush grounds of the old Forster estate into colourless gloom.

I wandered the dripping lanes around the cottage in a similar murk, keeping well away from the Retreat, bereft of human contact, unable to figure out where I ought to be, what I should be doing next.

I couldn't see the ocean, but I could hear it constantly as I walked, pounding away at the shores beneath me, reducing the islands to sand, throwing up wreckage and debris and then claiming it all back, relentless and yet oddly soothing. For the first time I considered that potential suicides could do worse than walk into that enveloping energy, giving themselves up to the flow. This was surely better than high buildings or railway lines, and I found myself wondering how many desperate souls had taken such a course over the centuries, selecting this lonely strip of beach to immerse themselves in the blessed waters of death. Hadn't Katie Cameron once told me something about a pregnant woman walking into the sea from this point? Who was she? What was her story?

I asked my first visitor in days, Michael's housekeeper Lucy Robson, who arrived with cautious enquiries about my welfare and a parcel of fresh mackerel.

'You're not feeling that miserable, are you, Beth?'

'Of course not,' I said tartly. 'When I go it'll be with a magnum of champagne and a bottle of paracetamol. In fact, I probably won't need the pills . . . Alcoholic poisoning will get me first.'

She laughed, and I poured us both a large gin.

'So who was this wretched creature who threw herself into the sea?' I demanded. 'I seem to remember Katie told me that her baby was saved?'

'It was years ago, before the First War . . . She was French, apparently. An actress from the Paris Revue. Came over on the boat train. Michael knows the whole story. You should ask him.'

We'd arrived at Michael in a matter of minutes, and I threw Lucy an irritated frown. Surely she could have spared me the subject for half an hour?

'Okay,' I said. 'Let's get it out of the way . . . I know I shouldn't have taken Katie off the beach. I gave Michael a bad fright, but he deserved it. I'm sorry.'

She looked at me closely, and then took a long swig of her gin.

'Why did he deserve it?' she asked quietly.

She'd caught me out, and I heard myself floundering among inept justifications about children being properly supervised and the dangers of seven-year-olds getting swept out to sea, until at last I faltered into embarrassed silence, furious with her and with myself.

'I'm not putting you on the spot,' she said apologetically. 'It's just that Michael's been in a bit of a state . . .'

'Has he? Well, that's nothing new. Michael was always in a bit of a state about something. He should be used to it by now.'

She finished her gin and stood up, lifting the mackerel from her basket and transporting them into the kitchen where they lay upon the worktop, lifeless eyes reproaching us both.

'You're very hard on him, Beth. He's desperate for a friendly word, but you won't give it, will you?'

I stared at the mackerel, repulsed and feeling faintly sick. 'The Camerons destroyed my family,' I said shakily. 'I can't find a friendly word for any of them.'

She said nothing, and in the silence that followed I tried to backtrack, anxious not to give myself away, still unsure how much she knew, keen to keep it to a minimum.

'Except for Jonathan,' I said. 'I always liked him . . . How is he, anyway? Lord of the Manor now . . .'

She smiled and picked up her basket.

'Jonathan's okay,' she said, 'apart from the daily trial of having to live in the same house as his mother.'

I looked down at the mackerel, resolving to give them a decent burial in the garden the moment she left, muttering apologetically that I never cooked for myself, praying she'd go quickly before I gave way to a rising tide of anguish that threatened my calm as surely as the sea below chafed away at the rocks.

'Had you realised it's Good Friday?' she asked me as I opened the front door. 'We have the three-hour devotion at St Cuthbert's . . . It's very moving. You should come.'

'Three hours! No thanks.'

'Well, you don't have to stay that long – although you may hear the vicar suggest that if Jesus endured three hours on the cross, the congregation can surely survive three hours in the pews.'

She laughed and squeezed my hand, and as I smiled back, she evidently considered that she might fire a parting shot.

'It wasn't really the Camerons who destroyed your family, was it, Beth?' she said slowly, eyeing me carefully and challenging me to agree. 'It was a man called Leo Frankish, wasn't it?'

A homicidal maniac murdered my mother. A desperate lunatic put his deranged hands around her lovely throat and squeezed and squeezed . . . She fought and she struggled, and her fingernails were clogged with skin from his face. Great handfuls of her chocolate-brown hair fell out upon the floor, and she hit him with the heel of her shoe. But in the end, like all men in such situations, he won, and her vast abundance of life was extinguished . . .

Then, in the manner of many a thwarted lover from the dubious annals of literary tradition, he killed himself, a critically uninspiring death, not with hemlock like Romeo, nor a sword like Antony, but with a hosepipe in his garage, a dirty, disgusting little suicide, devoid of style or grace.

He even had the nerve to leave a note, a mawkish, sentimental epitaph straight from a second-rate novel: 'To the only woman I ever loved . . . I couldn't bear to lose you . . . Sorry Ellie, so very sorry . . .'

Okay class, deconstruct that.

'Let it all come out,' advised the sturdy WPC. 'Don't bottle it up.'

It was hard to hear her above the row my sister was making, and as I watched the ineffectual Charles attempting comfort and frequently breaking down in tears himself, it occurred to me that one of us had better try to bottle it up.

Not that I seemed to have a choice in the matter. A deadly emptiness had settled upon my heart, robbing me of all emotion, overriding the pain I had so recently felt at Michael's failings, making my previously perilous plight seem no more than a minor inconvenience, reducing my responses to quips.

'You've got an interesting job,' I said to the perplexed policewoman. 'I bet you see this sort of thing all the time . . .'

Unable to help me herself, she made a vain if well-meant attempt to drum up some concerned relatives.

'We haven't got any,' I told her apologetically. 'My grandmother died seven years ago and my mother was an only child. Sorry.'

'What about your father?'

'He's never had anything to do with us, and we certainly don't want him turning up now.'

My sister paused, mid-howl. 'Oh yes we do!' she shouted, sounding like a comic echo from some raucous production of *Mother Goose*. 'Why should he escape? Get him here!'

'I don't think that's a terribly good idea,' I began mildly, and then took a step back into the conservatory as she lunged at me, fists raised.

'You shut your fucking mouth!' she yelled. 'It's your fucking fault she's dead!'

'Now then, Sarah,' said Charles desperately, 'there's no call for that kind of language.'

My sister had fallen to keening again, sinking to the floor in a fury of flailing arms and legs, and there was no dealing with her.

'What does she mean?' I asked Charles coldly. 'How can it possibly be my fault?'

He blinked at me unhappily, a stooping, bespectacled youth who would never make a competent teacher in a million years, out of his depth with his distraught fiancée and her combative sister, let alone a class of disruptive twelve-year-olds. He cleared his throat, asked the policewoman to leave us alone, and then tried to tell me in faltering, muted tones what no one else had yet seen fit.

'Your mother was about to leave the village . . . Selling the cottage and moving back to London . . . She wanted to set up house with . . .'

He searched for the words, embarrassed and unsure.

'With her new lover?' I finished, putting him out of his misery. 'So what? I'd worked that out already . . . Obviously something sent Leo over the top . . .'

Sarah rose from the floor like a pantomime witch, full of curses and hell.

'You're so fucking stupid,' she shrieked. 'You can't see your fucking hand in front of your fucking face . . . If it weren't for you, she'd have gone a month ago when she first told Leo . . . If it weren't for you, she'd never have hung around waiting for him to kill her!'

She was raving, making no sense at all, and I stared at her in growing disdain, determined I would bear no responsibility for my mother's ignominious death.

'She could have left with this new guy whenever she chose,' I said coolly. 'Who is he, anyway? Strikes me it's his fault as much as anyone else's . . .'

She walked across the room and put her face close to mine, hissing at me between her teeth.

'You and Michael,' she said. 'You're so busy fucking each other you wouldn't know if someone put a bomb under that Bentley . . . and you haven't even got the fucking sense to stop yourselves getting pregnant!'

I was angry now, and I pushed her roughly away, sending her sprawling on to the cane settee.

'Don't speak to me like that, you little bitch. This has nothing to do with Michael and me.'

She let out a great roar of fury, and then seemed to gather herself for an announcement, breathing deeply, clenching and flexing her fists, eyes fixed upon me.

'I'm going to say this very slowly,' she said, enunciating every syllable with exaggerated precision, 'and I'm going to use very short words so you'll be sure to understand. Now listen carefully, Beth. Watch my lips so you won't miss it . . .'

I stared at her, fascinated and appalled by a sister I simply didn't know, unable to guess at what might be coming.

'My mother was in love,' Sarah said. 'She was in love for the very first time in her life. They wanted to get married after his divorce, and they intended to live together in the meantime. She knew Leo would make trouble, and she timed it very carefully. They were due to leave last month and she was going to tell you all about it . . . But guess what?'

'What?' I asked, genuinely bewildered.

She was losing control again, voice rising and body trembling, lips quivering and eyes streaming, but she rallied for one last effort.

'Beth is having Michael's baby, that's what,' she said brokenly. 'Stop the clock. Nothing matters but this. Put everyone else's life on hold . . .'

'I don't know what you're talking about,' I said icily, and I didn't.

Charles cleared his throat again and fiddled with his spectacles, glancing nervously at me, waiting for the signal to speak, taking his cue when I raised an impatient eyebrow and finally coming out with it.

'Jack Cameron,' he said obligingly. 'Your mother was having an affair with Jack Cameron.'

The rain lifted and I walked down the cliff path to the beach, feeling my gloom unfold beneath the watery sun, gazing out across the flat grey sea to the islands, visible for the first time in days, watching the seals as they dived from the wet rocks to forage in the churning foam below. There were no fishing boats, a concession to Good Friday I guessed, but on the horizon a great white ship seemed to lie suspended, a beautiful, mysterious vessel, moving so slowly as to seem from this distance utterly still.

Whenever I walked on the shore I felt myself close to Eva, imagining her skipping along the sand with her brothers or playing tag among the gravestones in the churchyard, but now I couldn't think of her apart from David Klein. How sad that she'd never been able to bring him to this lovely place, how tragic that their marriage had been so brief . . . and how tempting to think that their story was as yet untold.

I walked on towards the vicarage, knowing Michael would be out of the way, intending to call and say hallo to my nephews. I hadn't exactly played the dutiful auntie since my arrival at St Cuthbert's; indeed, I hadn't set eyes on my sister's sons since I'd dropped them off, an omission which only occurred to me when I'd called Sarah to check on Charles.

'He's doing well,' she'd told me, sounding much brighter than I'd dared to hope. 'How are you? And how are the boys?'

I faltered out an affirmative reply to both questions, wondering if she'd imagined me taking them to the cinema, or out to tea, all of us together perhaps, Michael, Emily Forster and Katie . . . I couldn't bear this prospect, but still I felt I ought to do something, if only provide some pocket money.

But there was no reply at the vicarage, and when I wandered round the back to see if the children might be in the garden, to my discomfort I came upon the Bentley parked outside the old stable buildings.

I stared at it, mesmerised by the shining chrome and gleaming paintwork, and before I quite knew what I was doing, I had tried the door, and finding it open, slipped into the passenger seat I had occupied so many times.

The sensation of familiarity, of remembered dials and switches, of the scent of ancient leather and polished wood, of time redeemed, was cruelly immediate. I caught my breath, then lowered my head to the dashboard, overwhelmed by the tangible presence of history. The past seemed within my grasp once more, and I could almost believe that when I opened my eyes Michael would be beside me, reaching out to touch my hair or tell me that he loved me.

I sat for a moment, reflecting on all that had happened since I'd first arrived at St Cuthbert's, remembering with sudden shame our quarrel over Katie. How cold and ruthless I must have appeared . . . He'd asked me to forgive him . . . But how very unforgiving I had been.

Then I knew I had to see him, and I sprang from the Bentley, hurrying around to the front of the vicarage and into the churchyard. All thoughts of seeing my nephews were gone. I wanted only to be in Michael's presence, to hear his voice . . .

The church was silent and bare, stripped of all ornaments, not a flower in sight, a place of mourning and gloom, the scattered congregation kneeling in contrition. Even St Cuthbert, high above me in glassy splendour, looked sober and subdued. A huge wooden cross had been placed on the chancel steps, and as I slipped into a pew near the back, for a moment I couldn't see Michael at all. But then he suddenly stood up from behind the cross and spoke to the assembled worshippers in his low, sonorous voice.

'If you've ever been touched by a violent death,' he began, 'then you will know the kind of shocked reactions that occur . . .'

I felt my skin begin to prickle and my chest grow tight. I seemed to struggle for breath, and when I pressed my palms together they were wet with sweat. I waited, trembling, and then listened as he began to speak again.

'Some people wail and scream, some swear and curse their loved ones, looking for someone, anyone, to blame,' he said, 'while others seem to switch off, as though all normal emotional channels have been bypassed . . .'

I bent my head, unable to believe what I was hearing.

'We may wonder what the disciples went through on that day . . . Disbelief, anger, despair — the sickening knowledge that all hopes, all dreams and plans for the future, had ended in blood and betrayal . . .'

He seemed to be speaking to me alone, and I stared at him, stupefied.

'We may wonder where the courage to face life again, to forgive, to go forward, to grow, can possibly come from . . . And we may ask, quite reasonably, what price forgiveness when all around us we see the world proceeding on its unforgiving way at no apparent cost . . .'

He paused.

'But if the cost of forgiveness is high, then the legacy of resentment is higher, and this, I suspect, was the first lesson they had to learn in those terrible, empty hours between Friday afternoon and Sunday morning.'

I felt the tears wet on my cheeks, and in the effort to collect myself, I missed most of what followed, surfacing only for his final words.

'History hangs heavy upon us,' he said. 'The history of the Cross, of the mistakes of the Church, of the desecration of the world, of the persecution of the Jews and many others . . . And to all of this we add our own personal history, the private griefs that may be known only to us and to God . . .' He bowed his head, and then looked up at the congregation once more.

'But there is no going back,' he said. 'Only forward. Forward in hope and in trust . . . forward in forgiveness, and in love . . .'

I got up and stumbled from my pew, thankful that others were rising around me to make their way from the church, and once outside, ran swiftly through the graveyard on to the beach, my feet sinking into the soft sand, until I came to the great bank of golden poppies, falling at last into the sheltered hollow of the dunes, sobbing and panting for breath. I could think only of my mother and the day I'd gone to identify her body . . . the purple marks around her neck . . . the bare scalp where her hair had been torn from its roots . . . My hatred for Leo, my guilt that I'd never seen him as a potential murderer . . .

I cried and cried, and finally lay still, gazing up into the pale washed sky, inhaling the faint sweet smell of the poppies, running the silvery sand of the dunes through my fingers. Then I sat up and looked out to the horizon. The great white ship I'd seen earlier had moved closer to the shore, and now seemed to be sailing against the wind. It was a car ferry, I realised, probably heading from Norway to the Tyne, and I watched its stately progress with a curious, quiet sense of elation, as though its steady journey to port was in some way my own.

It was in this mildly euphoric state that Emily Forster found me.

'I'll bugger off if you tell me to,' she said with a little smile. 'But I saw you leave church, and wondered if you were okay . . .'

I scrambled upright, embarrassed that my likely response to any kindly enquiry should be so readily deduced, anxious to appear grateful and calm.

'I'm fine . . . It was just the sermon – it was very moving.'

'Ah yes,' she said, laughing. 'You caught Michael in declamatory mode. He's very good at it, though he lays it on a bit thick at times . . .'

'He seemed to be talking directly to me,' I faltered, knowing how ludicrous this sounded. 'All morning I'd been thinking about a very violent death . . .'

'Well, you've heard the voice of God,' she said.

I looked at her, startled, and she laughed again.

'Come on,' she said, 'I'll buy you a drink in the Dolphin. I don't know about you, but I've had enough religion for one day.'

We walked back along the beach and then up to the ramshackle pub where I'd vowed I'd never set foot again, and where the landlord poured me a drink on the house as though I were his most valued and esteemed customer, which when I came to consider, I probably was.

'What did you mean,' I asked Emily as we settled into a discreet booth, 'about the voice of God?'

'When a sermon seems to have been written just for you . . . when every prayer or lesson is loaded with significance . . . when all the thoughts and doubts you'd just been having are suddenly crystallised by something someone says . . .'

I thought this over carefully, wondering if it could possibly be true.

'If you'd come in half an hour earlier,' she said, 'you'd have heard him ranting on about political will and the arms trade, and it wouldn't have meant a thing . . . It's all to do with timing, you see.'

I looked at her with interest, aware that I'd been all too quick to write her off as one of the dull and worthy churchwomen I seemed to remember from St Botolph's. I wondered again about her relationship with

Michael, and I sought for some way to let her know that my hostility had dissipated, that the brusque remarks were at an end. In the end I settled for a straightforward apology, a plea to forgive my earlier behaviour.

'Look, Beth, I think you've been very brave. You don't have to apologise to me, or to anyone else.'

I knew then that she surely knew everything there was to know, and to my surprise, the knowledge came as a relief, releasing me, and her too.

'Are you going to marry Michael?' I asked her, feeling free to put the question directly.

'That's a wishful rumour put about by your sister, I'm afraid . . . For some reason Sarah has this great desire to see everyone nicely married off.'

'Too right,' I agreed ruefully. 'She's always asking when I'm going to marry Jamie . . .'

I glanced across at her, wondering what else she might tell me, trying to control an ignoble need to know.

'So there's nothing between you and Michael?' I enquired tentatively when she offered no more.

'Oh, I didn't say that . . .'

She hesitated, eyeing me carefully, seeming to consider her next words at great length.

'I know you must be curious about us,' she said at last. 'I would be if I were you . . . You're wondering if we have sex.'

I shook my head, embarrassed, but then I caught her eye, and nodded, shamefaced. We both laughed.

'I don't know what to tell you,' she said, looking away. 'I'd like to tell you the truth, but I don't think I can . . .'

I didn't know what to make of this, and knew only too well I'd no business trying to make anything of it, as Emily herself seemed suddenly to recollect.

'It's not right to discuss him,' she declared briskly. 'I'll simply say that you'd probably be surprised, that's all. Michael is a wonderful priest, full of compassion and wisdom and fire.'

She lifted her wine glass and surveyed me ruefully.

'But when it comes to his personal life,' she said, 'he quite often contrives to make Woody Allen seem well balanced.'

I smiled uncertainly, thinking back to Michael's marvellous exposition of the meaning of the Cross, reflecting on the dichotomy between universal truth and private reality, considering that the two could hardly be expected to coincide at every point in an individual's experience. Life was a journey, faith was a pilgrimage. God didn't cease to be or do his work just because his followers occasionally screwed up. This seemed so obvious, so deeply reassuring, that I wondered why on earth I'd never seen it before.

Emily reached for her glass.

'Can I ask you a personal question now?' she enquired.

'Sure,' I said bravely, accepting that whatever she wanted to know about Michael and me, I would have to reveal.

'Are you in love with my cousin Dan?' she asked.

I picked up my glass and stared into it.

'Hopelessly,' I said at last, believing it to be true.

Chapter Twenty-six

Our life is the life of the resurrected Jesus, and our song the song of angels
. . . Alleluia, Alleluia . . .

The Freedom of the Kingdom, by Michael Cameron

Next day I drove to Alnwick in search of Easter eggs for all the vicarage
children, a frustrating and initially fruitless exercise in which I was
reminded by numerous shop girls that I always left things too late.

But then, in a sidestreet sweet shop, I found a remaindered cache of
extravagant eggs which everyone else had been far too sensible to buy,
great golden globes done up in blue and white ribbons and filled with
liqueur truffles. The kids would probably all be sick.

There were seven left so I took the lot and set off back to St Cuthbert's with a hundred quid's worth of chocolate in my boot, determined
that from this moment on I would never again buy last-minute gifts for
my nephews. I would think ahead. I would ask what they wanted. I
would get to know them, for God's sake.

I pulled into the vicarage with some trepidation, wondering how, as
I hadn't spoken to Michael since the fracas over Katie, I might begin
to appear more amicable, hoping that Lucy would somehow smooth the
way.

But it was Michael himself who opened the door, looking just as
nervous, I realised, as I felt myself.

'Easter eggs,' I said foolishly, proffering the vulgar pile of glittering
foil.

He took them from me, surveying them dubiously.

'The kids will probably all be sick,' he said.

I followed him into the sitting room and saw then that I'd disturbed

him at work, for Jack Cameron's old desk was littered with papers and
open books, the computer screen winking out lines of words, his sermon,
I guessed, for Easter Day.

'That was very powerful stuff on Good Friday,' I said hesitantly.

He'd sat down at the desk again, tapping away at the keyboard.

'I hadn't realised you were there,' he said.

'You didn't see me?' I still half believed that he'd purposely directed
his words at me.

'You don't see much from up there,' he answered. 'You only really
notice if the folk in the front two pews start to glaze over.'

I smiled uncertainly.

'And did they?'

'No, but one bloke accused me of delivering a party political broad-
cast, and someone else took me to task about the stations of the cross
. . . Far too Roman for this parish, vicar! A fairly average response, I
suppose you'd say.'

'How do you deal with all that?' I asked him curiously, recognising
that it could take us some time to broach matters personal again, and
reckoning that matters pastoral would have to do instead.

He'd turned his attention back to the screen, anxious, I was certain,
to avoid launching out on our traumatic history once more, denying me
the chance to begin on any apology.

'Well, I've always been pretty upfront about my politics,' he said over
his shoulder. 'It lands me in hot water sometimes, but I've got used to
that. The same with my catholicism. It doesn't suit everyone, but I try
to offend as few people as possible . . .'

I nodded, thinking this seemed a good enough rationale, suddenly
seeing how fine a line the parish priest must tread between compromise
and conviction, so many people after their own God, so many unwilling
to countenance anyone else's. I didn't envy him his task.

It was plain he wanted to get on with his writing, and once I'd
established that the children were out with Lucy, there was nothing I
could do but leave him to it.

'You seem to have a gift for preaching,' I said awkwardly as I opened
the sitting-room door, still seeking to establish my new reconciliatory
mood, hoping he would perceive and understand the change. 'A knack
of finding the right words when they're needed . . .'

He turned from his father's desk, looked up at me briefly, and then
went back to his computer.

'Maybe I learned a bit in the meantime,' he said.

They called later that evening, Jack Cameron and his younger son, knocking gently on my mother's cottage door, standing deferentially in the hall, anxious and unsure.

'Hurray,' I said. 'The cavalry's arrived with bold Sir Jack in the van! Come in, do . . . Welcome to the wake.'

Neither of them spoke, so the initiative was all mine.

'This turned into a nice little family affair, didn't it?' I said to Jack. 'How long had you been fucking my mother, I wonder?'

Michael's father looked pale and deeply distressed, his eyes red and his hair unkempt, and as soon as my sister saw him she ran to his side, falling into his arms while they both wept.

'This is a touching little scene,' I said to Michael, beckoning him into the conservatory. 'Why don't we leave them to it? It seems a pity to intrude.'

He looked very pale himself, following me uncertainly, saying nothing.

'Sit down,' I invited, motioning him towards the cane settee. 'Have a glass of wine. Let's drink to Judgement Day, shall we?'

I'd drunk two large glasses of wine myself, thinking I surely deserved it, reckoning my unborn child could only forgive me. I'd also sent word to Vicky and Sam, asking them to come. Suddenly I knew who my friends were, and I knew that before too long I might need them very much.

'So,' I said to Michael, raising my glass, 'what can I do for you?'

He was confused and evidently upset, and still he could find nothing to say.

'You've called on me,' I snapped. 'Presumably you had a reason. What could it be? You weren't going to ask me to marry you, I suppose?'

Still nothing, and in a sudden melodramatic gesture, I plucked the diamond ring from my finger and dropped it into his hand. 'I'm afraid I'll have to turn you down,' I said. 'This morning I'd have accepted like a shot. But the world's a different place now.'

I was wondering whether he meant to speak at all, when he suddenly ran his hand through his hair and opened his mouth. 'I don't know what to say,' he muttered distractedly. 'I'm so very sorry about your mother . . .'

There had never been a situation in which his theology failed him, where his religious rationale was seen to be lacking, and I found myself perversely pleased by his discomfort, triumphant that my own stoicism was proving itself so much the more adequate.

'Oh come, Michael, I'm sure you can think of something . . . Cheer up, God Loves You? How about that? Or, Never Mind, We'll All Meet Up In Heaven? Something along those lines, maybe? That should do it.'

I wanted to see him cry, driven to call forth the tears that often came so easily, but he sat dry-eyed and unflinching, plainly unable to deal with me.

'A bloody fine clergyman you'll turn out to be,' I told him. 'What's happened to your pastoral manner? You're supposed to comfort the bereaved, you know.'

He'd fallen quiet again and I was becoming increasingly irritated, propelled to further provocation in my bid to elicit an emotional response.

'If we can't discuss my mother's murder, how about your father's adultery? You knew all about that, of course?'

'No,' he protested. 'I knew he was having an affair. I didn't know till yesterday that it was her . . .'

'You Camerons are a saucy lot, aren't you?' I taunted. 'Fuck the mother, fuck the daughter – I don't suppose it matters which . . .'

He blanched, stunned into silence once more, looking down at the diamond ring he still held, fiddling with the gold hoop and then finally dropping it into his pocket. Quite clearly he didn't mean to offer it back.

My heart gave a sudden heave and I was forced to summon all my resolve, repeating to myself a little ditty that I'd often heard on my mother's lips . . . I am a mature responsible person in charge of my own destiny . . . I live as I choose, I live as I choose . . .

'Okay,' I said, back in control. 'Next question. What would you like me to do about your bastard child?'

He bit his lip and looked down.

'I don't know,' he whispered.

'Shall I have an abortion?'

'I don't know,' he repeated.

'But you don't have any moral objections to abortion? No fears that we might be destroying one of God's little children?'

He hesitated, and I saw him struggle for the words, unable to form them, his lips pressed tight together, his eyes lowered.

'Answer me!' I shouted.

'I don't have any moral objections,' he managed at last.

I laughed then, the bitter, mirthless laugh of one who has been utterly betrayed by all that once seemed true and dear, staring at that moment into the pit, thinking, with the critical detachment beloved of the well-trained Eng. Lit. student, that this was surely how Hamlet must have felt.

'How weary, stale, flat and unprofitable,' I pronounced, 'seem to me all the uses of this world . . .'

'What?'

'Hamlet, my dear Michael . . . Oh, fie! 'tis an unweeded garden that grows to seed; things rank and gross in nature possess it merely . . .'

He stood up and moved towards me, forcing me to back up against the window, for I was determined he shouldn't touch me, trembling, but still not crying.

'I can't help it, Beth,' he stuttered. 'I don't know what to do about my mother . . . It will kill her if I say I'm going to marry you.'

I laughed again, more easily this time.

'Well, that would give us a common bond, wouldn't it? Two dead mothers . . .'

How long this unprofitable exchange might have lasted, or whether it would eventually have produced any resolution I wasn't to know, for at that moment Jack Cameron walked in on us, taking one look at Michael and ordering him outside to the Bentley. I watched him go, still shaking, and knew with a peculiar, freeing kind of power, that if I ever saw him again, there would be no hint of reconciliation in the encounter, no remnant of our former intimacy. I heard the front door close, heard the door of the Bentley slam, and saw my future assume a new and unknown shape.

'Nothing I say will make you feel any better, Beth,' Jack Cameron began, but I held up my hand in a commanding pose he could hardly override.

'Then don't attempt it,' I said steadily, breathing deep and hard, summoning every last vestige of my inner strength. 'And please understand that I never want to set eyes on you or your son again.'

He blinked at me and rubbed his hand across his face.

'Give Michael a few days,' he said. 'He's behaved badly, I know, but it hasn't been easy for him . . . His mother, you realise . . .'

'Never ever again,' I repeated slowly, pausing over each syllable like the heroine in some bad amateur production. 'Have you got that? I really hope you have . . . Because if either of you shows up at my mother's funeral, then I promise you a scene this village will never forget.'

I heard my own words with a certain astonishment, unsure where they'd sprung from and yet not doubting them for a moment, feeling no pity at all for him in his loss, knowing I would never forgive: not him, not Michael, not Michael's mother, nor my own.

Then I walked out of the conservatory, ignoring my sister and her fiancé who sat huddled together on the living-room couch, up the staircase which once, such a long, long time ago, my mother had lovingly stripped while Leo buffed and polished, and into my bedroom.

I lay down, still breathing evenly and deep, pressing my hands gently over my womb.

'Listen, kid,' I said aloud, my voice sombre and hushed, still locked into heroic role, 'we're in this together, right? And we're on our own. Sorry about that, but there's nothing I can do . . . It's just you and me, Baby . . . Okay?'

*

My grand resolution to befriend my nephews was put to the test at once, for walking out of the vicarage and on to the beach in pursuit of sea breeze, I met Lucy and all six children, returning from a nature trail along the cliffs.

Sarah's boys responded eagerly to my offer of ice-cream at the village store, but Lucy's trio were ordered indoors to perform Saturday duties, tidying rooms and cleaning shoes after their walk. Lucy, I guessed, ran a tight ship at the vicarage, and knowing little of children myself, but well imagining the chaos so many could cause, I was full of admiration.

'What about me?' Katie enquired plaintively, looking up at Lucy, clearly unsure whether she had licence to disappear with her kidnapper once more.

'You go with Beth,' Lucy said decisively. 'But please be back in time for lunch!'

'I'll make sure,' I said meekly, hardly daring to meet Lucy's eye.

My sister's sons, so like their father in physical appearance, were considerably more boisterous in manner than the reticent Charles, and they set off through the village with unnerving whoops and yells, pushing each other into ditches, sloshing through puddles and swinging on garden gates while Katie and I followed on with impeccable reserve.

But as we all walked back towards the vicarage with a disgusting array of multi-coloured lollies, Katie became keen to participate.

'We'll play hide and seek,' she cried as the churchyard came into view. 'Tom and Mark, you count to twenty, and we'll hide . . .'

I followed her obligingly through the gravestones and round the rear of the church until she came to a sudden halt before a huge and ancient laurel bush, its glossy leaves radiating towards the long grass beneath, and pulling aside a gnarled bough, she beckoned me in.

I said a quick prayer for my Chanel suit, and crawled into a magical green cavern, a vast hollow created by a freakish configuration of branches, sitting down on the soft dry earth beside her.

'What a great place,' I enthused. 'They'll never find us here!'

'An old lady showed it to me,' Katie confided. 'She used to hide here from her brothers when she was just a little girl like me . . .'

We sat in silence listening to the boys as they marauded through the churchyard, stifling giggles when they seemed about to find us, and then, as their voices drifted away, wondering just how long we ought to stay concealed.

It was too dull in the bush for I-Spy, and when I'd told her a silly story I once made up for the Lutz children, and she'd recited a poem from school, there was nothing much to do.

'Shall we sneak out and see where they are?'

'Oh, that would spoil the game. Unless,' she added, 'we went along the beach and up the cliff to your house . . . They wouldn't find us there, would they?'

I gazed at her uncomfortably through the emerald gloom, wondering what had been said about her last visit to the cottage, unsure whether she knew anything of my row with Michael.

'I got into a lot of trouble for taking you to my house,' I said at last.

'I know . . . You forgot to ring Daddy.'

'Yes. I'm very sorry about that. He was very cross with me. I hope he wasn't cross with you?'

'He wasn't cross,' she said, confounding all my expectations and throwing me into confusion. 'He was crying in the car on the way home.'

Then suddenly we heard him shout, calling her name across the church-yard, coming nearer each moment until he was abreast of the laurel bush. She jumped out to surprise him, and I peered through the leaves to see him swing her into the air, both of them laughing.

'Where's Beth?' he asked.

I emerged from the bush somewhat sheepishly, pulling leaves from my hair and brushing twigs from the Chanel jacket, conscious of a large hole in my tights and a grass stain on my skirt.

'There's a message for you,' Michael said, 'from Sam Lutz.'

'Sam?' I said in disbelief. 'He rang the vicarage?'

'Yes . . . He wants you to call him back.'

I glanced at him, flustered, but already he was striding back with Katie towards the vicarage, clearly flustered himself.

I followed, marching into the vicarage sitting room in a rage and closing the door behind me, picking up the phone on Jack Cameron's old desk, dialling Sam's number and barking down the line.

'What the hell are you doing phoning me here?'

'I had to get hold of you . . . Listen, Beth, I've just had lunch with this guy from the BBC . . . can you get back to London right away?'

'No, I can't. It's Easter weekend, for God's sake. I'm on holiday. And you shouldn't be having lunch with any guy from the BBC on Easter weekend. You should be with your kids, and he should be with his.'

'He hasn't got any kids,' Sam said, 'but he does have this great idea . . . Okay, I'm sorry I rang Michael. Sarah seemed to think it would be all right.'

'Well, it's not all right,' I hissed into the phone. 'The last time you saw Michael you gave him a black eye . . . Don't you think it might be upsetting, suddenly hearing from you?'

There was a long pause on the other end of the phone.

'He didn't sound upset,' Sam said at last. 'In fact, he was quite friendly.'

Outside the vicarage window I could see my sister's sons, back from the beach and now tearing around the cobbled courtyard with a football, Michael in goal between the gateposts, Katie jumping up and down, waving her arms in excitement, all of them yelling and laughing. And as I watched, the scene filled me with a deep, melancholy longing, as though I suddenly glimpsed a long-imagined fantasy made flesh, the future I had denied myself, the Rose Garden into which I'd never stepped, and I felt hot hard tears at the back of my throat.

'Well, I'm upset,' I gulped into the phone, 'I'm upset for him.'

'Good grief,' Sam said. 'Things must be looking up.'

'I wish Vicky was here,' I said. 'Do you think she'll be back in time for the funeral?'

'I'm afraid not,' Sam said, sitting down on the cane settee in the conservatory and pulling me close. 'I got word to their hotel, but they're touring around . . . Gone off into the Camargue.'

In the absence of my sister's support, and with the Camerons banished from my mother's cottage for good, I'd waited anxiously for Vicky and Sam, the only real friends I felt I had, but I'd wanted them both, and the news that Vicky was abroad with her father and stepmother came as a blow, if only because it permitted Sam exclusive comforting rights.

'You were brilliant this afternoon,' he said softly, stroking my hair and tightening his arm on my shoulder. 'I don't know how you did it . . . You're a star, Beth Carlisle.'

The formal identification of my mother's body had been a gruesome business, made bearable only by the unreality of it all: the long distempered corridors of the police morgue, the metal tray, like a giant wardrobe drawer, the faintly grubby sheet covering her face, all of it seeming to belong in some American cop drama, and not in my life at all.

I stared at the battered form on the slab while my friend, the sturdy WPC, looked on and behind me, Sam retched.

'That's her,' I said calmly. 'She doesn't look so good, does she? She wouldn't like anyone to see her that way.'

'Don't worry,' said my friend. 'She'll be fixed up.'

I wasn't concerned about fixing up for I'd assumed my mother would be cremated as soon as possible, but Sarah, still in vengeful mode, declared otherwise.

'I decide,' she'd shouted when I voiced my uncontroversial opinion. 'She'll be buried at St Botolph's, and don't you dare go against me!'

Charles and Sam exchanged knowing glances, each moving towards his charge with proprietorial authority.

'I'm sure it can be sorted out,' Sam said smoothly, 'if we all keep calm.'

'You mind your own fucking business,' my sister shrieked. 'Who the hell are you, anyway? What do you think you're doing here?'

Sam and I retreated to the conservatory, closing the door on Sarah's ranting, leaving Charles to wring his hands and reach for the sedatives my sister steadfastly refused to take.

'She's in a terrible state,' Sam said, taken aback. 'She should see the doctor again.'

I shrugged, unable now to make any inroad into Sarah's grief, concerned only to maintain my own indomitable control, thinking that if she hated me so much, as she certainly seemed to, then I'd simply disappear once the funeral was over, leaving her and Charles to it.

Sam took my hand and led me over to the settee.

'I'm sorry to bring this up,' he said firmly, sitting me down, 'but you should see a doctor too. Time's getting on. You need a referral for abortion.'

'I'm not having an abortion,' I said, rehearsing this unlikely decision for the first time outside my own head. 'I'm going to have my baby. I'm going to bring it up by myself.'

Everyone, I now saw, had wanted, indeed expected, abortion. My mother, Michael's mother, Michael himself. So to hell with them all. I wouldn't do it.

'What? Oh come on, Beth, that's crazy . . . Think about it. Think about your career. Imagine rushing home from the radio station to wash the nappies . . .'

I'd not only thought about it, I'd taken the calculated step of writing to the station manager to ask for a six-month delay on my appointment, owning up to my condition and reassuring him of my total dedication to the job once I'd given birth. In return I'd received an unexpectedly sympathetic letter, advising me to take as long as I needed, assuring me of confidentiality, and wishing me luck.

I had no doubt I could do it, and already I could see us, myself and Michael's daughter, a grey-eyed golden-haired angel, living in a chic little flat in Highbury, her playing contentedly under the watchful eye of a Mary Poppins, me bringing home the bacon and reading the news. It would be hard, but it would be rewarding, and we would always be there for each other.

Sam leaned over and kissed me gently on the lips.

'We'll talk about it later,' he said, establishing beyond doubt his intended role in any decision-making. 'You can't think straight at the moment.'

That night, no doubt because I wasn't thinking straight, we went to bed.

Charles had taken Sarah out for a drive in my mother's car and the cottage was cruelly peaceful, the garden, still bearing the fruits of Leo's attentions, heartlessly colourful and calm.

We opened the conservatory door and sat on the step, gazing across the fields to the church, and I told him about the day we'd moved in, a golden June evening just like this one, when we'd heard a magical string quartet amplified on the scented air, sounding out from the Cameron house.

Sam shifted uneasily on the step.

'About Michael . . .' he said uncomfortably. 'I hope I didn't louse things up between you? That night we all got drunk and Vicky told him on the phone we'd gone to bed . . .'

'No,' I said dully. 'It was nothing to do with you. Michael loused things up all by himself.'

'I've got a terrible confession to make, Beth. I hope you'll see I only did it because I'm totally nuts about you . . . That night . . . you were drinking vodka, remember? I got you doubles all evening, and I hardly had a drop myself. You were plastered, and I was stone-cold sober, but I still didn't manage to make love to you.'

'Oh,' I said, unconcerned and not much interested. 'Why not?'

'Because you just wouldn't have it. You were practically comatose, but you still fought me off. In fact, you kneed me in the balls.'

'Sorry,' I said absently, still thinking about my mother and our first night in the cottage, the way Leo had put his hand upon her head, as though he owned every hair, predicting that we couldn't live in the village and hope to escape the Camerons . . . What was it about Leo? What set him apart from other men who, for all their anger and their damaged pride, would never be driven to kill? Upbringing, circumstance, temperament, fate? There was no answer, of course, and probably never would be.

'I was all charged up,' Sam was saying, 'and you kept insisting you'd never do it with anyone but Michael. I was pretty desperate, Beth. So desperate that I left you to it and went to bed with Vicky instead . . .'

This was something Vicky hadn't told me, and now I stared at Sam in sudden disgust.

'There's nothing between Vicky and me,' he said quickly, clapping his hand across his heart. 'It was just sex. She knows how I feel about you.'

I also knew how Sam felt about me, and I was quite clear what I felt about him. But it didn't seem to matter. Nothing seemed to matter any more.

'It must be all that inbreeding in the upper classes,' Sam was saying. 'Michael Cameron is a total idiot. He had you all to himself, but he couldn't see it. You'd never have been unfaithful in a million years . . . Undying love, and he threw it all away.'

'Oh well,' I said idly, 'it doesn't matter now.'

Sam moved closer to me, slipping his hand around my waist, sliding it cautiously upward until it encircled one swelling breast.

'When this is all over,' he whispered, 'it will be time for you and me . . .'

Then I saw that I could break the last emotional bond with Michael in one symbolic act, freeing myself from foolish and discredited beliefs about fidelity and the trite romantic notion of one woman, one man, changing the world from fairytale to reality in a moment.

'Why wait?' I said dispassionately to Sam. 'We can do it now if you want . . .'

A deadly coldness seemed to have settled upon me, the cool of the mortuary slab, the chill of blunted emotions, so that I heard my responses echoing through an icy veil of calm, a numbing frost which rendered all experience the same unremitting shade of hard, glittering white.

Sam could scarcely believe his luck and followed me eagerly upstairs to the bedroom I'd once shared with my sister, all mine since she'd decamped to my mother's old room, sleeping alone in the great double bed while Charles, with uncomplaining propriety, put up on the living-room sofa.

'Push the beds together and lock the door,' I said to Sam, sitting down in front of my dressing-table mirror and unbuttoning my blouse. 'We don't want the avenging angel charging in.'

He watched, mesmerised, as I stepped out of my underwear and lay down on my bed.

'You're so very lovely,' he murmured, lying down beside me and running his hands across my thighs. 'I'm crazy about you, Beth . . . I've loved you from the moment you first walked into the Common Room . . .'

'Don't say that,' I snapped, jerked out of my passionless state by a flash of pure repugnance. 'Just get on with it. I don't want any of that romantic stuff . . .'

And it was then I discovered what an artful and sensitive lover Michael had been during our three-year courtship, how giving, and how, for all his occasional lapses, essentially undemanding . . . and how mistaken we'd both been in imagining that what happened one night on the back seat of the Bentley constituted rape. What I was now undergoing was much nearer violation.

'Be careful, Sam,' I pleaded. 'Remember I'm pregnant,' but Sam was incapable of being careful, and as he bore into me with all the energy and finesse of a high-powered drill, I focused on the ceiling above, biting my lip and clenching my fists, praying for it to be over.

'Sorry,' he said afterwards, 'I got carried away.'

It must have been the selfsame transportation that provided his motivation the following morning, for as we lay half asleep in the early sunshine, we heard Sarah bellowing from below, and he leapt from the bed in sudden fury, struggling into his clothes at top speed.

'It's time someone told your sister to shut it,' he announced.

I heard Sarah ascending the stairs, and the sound of footsteps behind her. 'She's in bed with her latest lover,' my sister shouted. 'The fucking tart . . .'

'I must take after my mother!' I screamed back through the door, stung at last into retaliation, utterly bewildered by the course Sarah's grief was taking, determined to endure no more of it.

Then I heard Michael's voice, unsteady but polite amid the hullaba-loo, a respectful and deferential request.

'I only want to talk to her . . . Please . . . just for a few moments . . .'

I pulled the bedclothes over my head, wrapping my ears in a protective cocoon of eiderdown, unable, for all that, to drown out the ugly noise below: Sarah cursing, Sam shouting, a crash of china, and then the slamming of the front door.

A moment later Sam was back, visibly furious, his bottom lip swollen, his cheekbone gashed a vivid scarlet.

'What happened?' I quavered, sitting up from my heap of bedclothes.

'She attacked me, that's what happened. Just went for me with her fingernails. I tell you, Beth, if she goes on like this much longer, she'll have to be certified.'

I stared at him impatiently, throwing a box of tissues from the side of my bed.

'No! I mean, what happened with Michael?'

Sam dabbed at his bloody lip.

'I hit him, of course,' he replied. 'And I told him that if he ever tries to see you again, I'll fucking kill him.'

I got back to the lodge to find the central heating boiler in distress, emitting disturbing groans and gurgles, and every radiator in the place stone cold. I fiddled with the dials and thermostats, trying to remember what Emily had done, wondering if I should ring the Retreat and ask for her help.

And then, seizing on this most fragile of excuses, I picked up the phone and dialled Duval's Paris number, thinking that if Genevieve answered I'd hang up without speaking, realising with faint shock that I was reducing myself to the role of discarded mistress, desperate for contact with the loved one, reaching for crumbs from the family table.

When he answered himself I was thrown, remembering numerous other calls from London to Paris during our affair, when I'd talked dirty on the phone and we'd both ended up in a sweet agony of unfulfilled desire.

'It's me,' I apologised, and hearing his reserve, rushed on into tedious details about the boiler and listened while he replied with equally tedious instructions until, at last, all that could possibly be said about central heating had been well and truly aired.

'Why didn't you tell me Eva was your grandmother?' I asked him then. 'I couldn't believe it when Emily told me about her and David Klein . . .'

It was clear he'd been prepared for this question.

'You have to understand that at the end everyone became very anxious, particularly my mother. Eva and Toby had been plagued by this latest biographer, Jon Makepeace . . . My mother had to deal with him. That's why she was so frosty when you turned up . . . Well, that's partly why. I can't pretend it had nothing to do with me or my marriage . . .'

I closed my eyes, seeing again the whitewashed sitting room in the Divine Faith convent, the plaster Messiah on the wall above the mantel, Eva nodding by the fire, the silver cross which I still wore beneath my blouse resting on the collar of her pearly silk dress . . .

'I'm sorry,' I said to Duval, deeply affected by the remembrance, 'I should never have barged in like that. I can't bear to think I upset her with stupid questions . . .'

'You didn't,' he said. 'I was upset, and my mother was upset, but Eva was a good deal tougher than any of us. She wasn't at all upset. As a matter of fact, she was very pleased to meet you.'

'I wish I'd asked about David Klein,' I said. 'I wish I had the chance to tell their story . . .'

There was silence at the other end of the phone, and it was plain he was thinking it over.

'You could have that chance,' he said at last. 'Certainly someone should tell their story. But it's not up to me. I'd have to ask my mother . . . Let me talk it over, and then if she agrees, you can come to Paris and see her.'

I was tantalised by this prospect, exceedingly anxious that Blanche Duval should consider me suitable to write about her mother, foolishly reassured by the knowledge that in this event I would see her son again, perhaps on a regular basis, perhaps even waiting around for the moment when his marriage broke down once more, as it surely would . . .

'I have to go,' he said suddenly, 'I'm collecting my daughter from her ballet class,' and with unspecified promises to call me, he hung up, leaving me alone with the boiler and a longing which startled by its intensity. Why hadn't I seen how much I'd cared for him? Why was it that only now, confronted by Michael and reliving my painful past, the present had seemed to fall into place? The more I thought about it, the more confused I became, until my feelings for both of them seemed to mesh into one seamless desire, past and present interweaving in a

melancholy web of frustrated hopes and half-forgotten ideals. They
were the only two men I'd ever loved, and I'd lost both of them. There
was no going back, and I could see no way forward either. I would
simply have to endure, as I had once endured the loss of my mother
and the loss of my child.

It was in this state of mind that I set out for St Cuthbert's the following morning, idling along the beach on the warmest spring day since I'd
arrived in the village, tasting the salt on my lips and feeling the wind lift
my hair. Before me I could see the poppies, gleaming golden in the sun,
and I determined to gather a small bunch right after the Easter Day
service and lay them on Eva's grave. Perhaps, I told myself in an unlikely
flight of fancy, Eva, looking down from some unimaginable heaven,
would see this small act and bestow her blessing on my literary plans.

The church was transformed from its Good Friday gloom, filled with
daffodils and white lilies, candles glowing in every crevice, the altar
decked in snowy white, St Cuthbert gleaming down from above, his
rainbow colours dancing in the shafts of sun on the stone flags beneath
him. And the pews were packed. Unlike Friday, when I'd been able to
slip unobtrusively into a rear stall, I now found myself ushered down
the aisle by a beaming churchwarden and seated at the end of the front
row. Michael would certainly be able to see me this morning.

I glanced round nervously, feeling ill at ease and out of place, but
then I saw Emily Forster half a dozen rows behind me, and catching
my eye she suddenly got up and squeezed into the front pew beside me.

'Here,' she whispered, flicking through the service book for me. 'It's
easy to follow.'

I was immensely grateful for this small kindness, wondering what I'd
done to merit such consideration from Michael's girlfriend, anxious to
register my thanks. But then the organ began to play, the choir set out
upon its procession around the church, Michael appeared at the top of
the aisle dressed in flowing white, and I found myself caught up in the
mysterious, euphoric rites of Easter Day.

'On the first day of the week,' Michael pronounced, 'the disciples
went to the tomb and they found the stone rolled away . . . Alleluia!'

This time I found that nothing of the service registered with my
conscious mind, not the readings, nor the hymns, nor even the sermon,
delivered from only a few feet in front of me. Instead, I felt myself
raised on a wave of spontaneous joy that seemed to reach out to me
from the congregation, a heady affirmation of all that was good about
being alive in this moment, this world, this church.

'Peace be with you,' said Emily, kissing my cheek, and I remembered
with sudden astonishment my earlier visit to St Cuthbert's when Susannah Lamont, to my embarrassment and discomfort, had also wished

me peace. And in a fleeting, uplifting intuition I realised that since that day, I had taken one small step along the road to resurrection.

'Peace be with you, Beth . . .'

Michael, descending from the chancel, had taken my hand, meeting my eye for a fraction of a second before moving on. I looked up at him briefly and smiled, the first unguarded smile I'd offered since the day we'd met again.

I hadn't taken communion since the Easter before my mother's death, and couldn't bring myself to do it now, so I sat silent in the pews while the choir broke into the haunting hymn I remembered so well from Eva's funeral. 'Love will come again,' they sang, 'like wheat that springeth green . . .'

Then, before I knew it, I was moving out of the church amid a chorus of alleluias, separated from Emily and unable to approach Michael for the hordes of well-wishers around him, all of them laughing and offering greetings as though it were some great party or wedding. 'Happy Easter,' they called, and I found myself smiling back, though I knew no one except Lucy, who waved at me and told me not to run away, and the landlord of the Dolphin who gave me a broad wink and promptly departed to open up his bar.

Losing sight of Lucy, I wandered through the churchyard to the beach and down to the waving bank of golden poppies by the dunes, humming the refrain from Eva's hymn, bending to pluck a modest bunch of blooms and then skirting the sea wall to enter the far end of the churchyard where Eva's grave lay.

It was quiet here, and I knelt down on the warm ground beside the simple headstone, pulling the faded blooms from the last of the funeral bouquets and placing the poppies in the little vase before the stone. For the first time since I'd met Eva in Paris, my heart felt light and my mind clear. I had forgiven my mother, and in some small measure, I had even begun to forgive Leo . . . My life still looked a mess, and yet somehow I felt that I would find a way through, a resolution of all my tortured relationships, from Jamie, to Sarah and Charles, to Vicky and Sam, and to Michael and Duval. It might not be immediate, and there would surely be steps back as well as forward. But I was a mature responsible person in charge of my own destiny. And with a little help from my friends, I would make it, one way or another.

Then I looked up and saw Michael waving at me across the churchyard, out of his priestly robes and back in his clerical suit, plainly seeking me out.

'I've been sent to invite you to lunch,' he said.

I scrambled up from my knees, accepting the invitation at once, unable to resist speculating on whether, if he hadn't been sent, he would

still have come, rushing to congratulate him on the service, apologising
for not having listened to his sermon.

'Did you see me start to glaze over?' I asked as we walked back to the
vicarage.

'You were looking at your feet,' he replied with a little laugh. 'I
thought you must be concentrating.'

'Unfortunately not. I was miles away. And now I've missed learning
about the resurrection . . .'

'Don't worry,' he smiled, opening the vicarage door. 'You can't really
learn about the resurrection. You can only feel it.'

I stopped and caught at his arm, making him face me in the brief moment before we were engulfed by children with Easter eggs and kittens.

'I do feel it,' I said. 'And there's something I want to tell you . . .'

He looked down at me, and I was astonished at how utterly familiar
he suddenly seemed, how well remembered, how recognisable from all
he had once been, how known.

'I'm terribly sorry about Katie and the beach,' I muttered, momentarily taken aback by the power of the vision. 'It was very wrong of me.'

'I'm sorry too,' he murmured with evident difficulty. 'I wish I could
have found some way to tell you before . . .'

'Sorry for what?' I heard myself say, thinking that in the matter of
Katie he had surely behaved with commendable restraint. 'You don't
have to apologise.'

He swallowed hard and took a deep breath.

'Sorry for asking you to marry me and then backing down at the
crucial moment,' he said, meeting my eye and holding my gaze. 'Sorry
for getting you pregnant . . . Sorry for letting you think I favoured an
abortion . . . Sorry for abandoning you to cope with your mother's
death all alone . . . How's that for a start?'

The sitting-room door in front of us suddenly burst open and the
children spilled into the hall, waving their great golden eggs, giggling
and shrieking, Lucy and Emily close behind them, and for a moment
we both stared at them, perplexed, unable to readjust or shake off the
sobering nature of the moment.

'Well, what are we waiting for?' Lucy laughed, linking her arm in
mine and handing Michael a bottle. 'Open the champagne! Let's celebrate! It's Resurrection Day!'

Chapter Twenty-seven

The resurrected life isn't one in which no pains or trials occur. On the contrary, the yearning after righteousness which is the mark of this new life may produce its own peculiar pain, the pain of witnessing a world which seems hell-bent upon its own destruction. But the resurrected life is one from which all perspective is changed so that no personal misfortune, no sadness, seems insurmountable, and no social or political evil insoluble . . . And this, surely, is the greatest of all God's gifts, the freedom of the kingdom. Freedom from fear, from despair, from superstition and from the shadow of death . . .

The Freedom of the Kingdom, by Michael Cameron

I phoned Sam and made my peace, promising to meet his man from the BBC, I spoke to Vicky at her mother's place in Spain, commiserating on the state of her marriage in a long and emotional call, and I rang Sarah to enquire after Charles, offering to drive her sons home. Then I dialled my home number, longing to hear Jamie's voice, and when I got my own deeply irritating recorded answer, decided to send him a postcard from St Cuthbert's instead.

'Buffoonery is a form of emotional relief (T. S. Eliot on Hamlet). I'm sick of playing it for laughs, and I'd love to come home . . .'

Then I began to clean up the lodge cottage, preparing to depart, fighting an unexpected regret that I must soon leave St Cuthbert's for the last time, thinking that if Blanche Duval sanctioned a book on Eva, then I would surely have reason to come back. But why should I wish to come back? For the islands and the sea, for the shoreline and the sands, for the whispering green lanes and pathways around the Retreat . . . there could be no other reason.

I'd spent Sunday night in the Dolphin with Emily Forster, watching, in some disbelief, while Michael played darts with a boisterous crew of fishermen and farmers who all addressed him as Mick the Vic, finding myself the centre of much attention and fuss, which wasn't unusual, but which, due to the fact that some tabloid survey had just named me the woman male readers would most like to sleep with, seemed suddenly hard to handle.

'You must get sick of it,' Emily sympathised, and I realised for the first time how much I did.

She and Michael were so clearly at ease with each other, so relaxed and affectionate, that I began to think my sister hadn't been imagining things after all. Maybe Emily had been trying to spare my feelings in suggesting there was nothing truly serious between them.

But what were my feelings? I had been much moved by Michael's direct acknowledgement of the hurt he'd caused me, finding a great burden of concealed resentment slipping from my heart, opening up my life to new and hitherto dismissed possibilities. I might have lost Michael, and I might have lost Duval, but this wasn't to say I'd never fall in love again, never get married or become pregnant once more. The future didn't have to be shackled by the past. I could break free.

I also felt I should make my own declaration to Michael, the truth that Sam had advised me to tell, but there'd been no opportunity for us to talk in private, and I began to think that maybe it were better left, that we should make our final goodbyes without any further harrowing scenes, though I was coming to dread our parting, fearing I might dissolve into tears when the moment arrived.

In the event, the parting was postponed.

'I was wondering if you could do me a favour,' he asked tentatively as we all walked back to the vicarage from an outing on the beach. 'I'm taking Katie to stay with Jonathan for a few days . . . Would you give us a lift when you go back to Sarah's?'

I was floored by this request, imagining myself driving up to the Cameron house and depositing Katie in the arms of her grandmother, a response which registered at once.

'My mother won't be there,' Michael said hastily. 'She's on holiday . . . cruising down the Nile.'

'Pity it wasn't up the Amazon,' opined Emily who'd been listening. 'People disappear into those rain forests for years.'

They both laughed, but Michael wouldn't meet my eye, and I was left to speculate on this tantalising insight into Cameron family life.

We had reached the back garden of the vicarage with its old stable block, the Bentley still parked outside.

'Why can't we go in our car?' Katie, who'd also been listening, suddenly demanded. 'We never go anywhere in our car.'

'It costs too much,' her father replied. 'We might as well go by helicopter.'

Katie was not convinced, and immediately grabbed my hand, pulling me over to peer into the Bentley's plush interior, extolling its virtues: the soft leather, the cigarette lighter, the cubbyhole under the dashboard where you could keep a spare pair of shoes and all your swimming things.

'And you can lie down full length on the back seat,' she told me solemnly. 'Really you can! Can't you, Daddy?'

I burst out laughing, unable to contain my mirth at this delicious little irony, but though Emily seemed equally amused, making me wonder if she'd ever tried lying down on the back seat of the Bentley herself, Michael was acutely embarrassed, shoving his hands into his pockets, hunching his shoulders and striding away from us into the vicarage.

'It's the best car in the world,' Katie said, annoyed, and it was left for Emily and I to agree that yes, of course it was.

I had a few things to do before I left. I wanted to order a wreath for Eva's grave, I wanted to lay flowers at the war memorial beneath the Brannen brothers' names, and I wanted to be shown around the Retreat, a task which Emily undertook, leading me through the elegant corridors and vaulted halls of the old Forster house, explaining her own work and Michael's.

'The bereavement groups are just a small part, really. Important, though. Michael always takes them in here —' She led me into a high-domed conservatory set upon the edge of the cliff offering a sweeping view of the bay and the islands.

'He tells the story of my great-grandmother,' Emily said, moving to the window, 'who sat right here and watched her son Ralph dive to his death from the tower on St Cuthbert's isle . . . She knew he was drowning, and yet she could do nothing to save him.'

I considered this terrible tale in silence, thinking of my own experience of tragic death, seeing that there was surely a great need for professional help.

'My sister went crazy when my mother was killed,' I told Emily. 'She completely turned against me, swearing and shouting all the time . . . I had no idea how to cope. Everything I said seemed to incense her. It soured our relationship. Things were never the same.'

'It's not uncommon,' Emily said. 'Remember Ophelia. She reacted in much the same way.'

I looked out to sea, thinking of poor Ralph Forster and his mother,

and then found myself wondering about Clare Spencer, about her
marriage to Michael and her own untimely death by drowning, remembering Duval's suggestion that Michael was still grieving, aware
that I'd made no mention of her, nor offered so much as a hint of
condolence.

'Michael's wife,' I said awkwardly to Emily, 'I knew her, of course
. . . Not very well, because she didn't like me, but I'm thinking I should
really say something to him about her.'

Emily stared out towards the ruined island tower.

'I wouldn't,' she said at last. 'Clare is very much Michael's weak spot.
Wait for him to tell you.'

I couldn't imagine how she thought he might tell me, for in the last
few days we were always surrounded by children or if not, then in
company with Lucy and Emily herself, relaxed meals and trips into
Alnwick and the surrounding countryside, myself easily accepted into
the party as though I had always been a valued family friend. We even
watched the third part of *Moonlight and Roses* together and considered,
between us, that it was really rather good.

'I don't know how it ever got made,' I laughed privately to Emily. 'I
spent most of my time in Paris in bed with Dan Duval . . .'

Then the moment to depart was upon us and we were waving goodbye: Tom, Mark and Katie in the back of the BMW and Michael in the
passenger seat, an odd reversal of our old roles in the Bentley, cruising
out of the vicarage courtyard and into the winding village streets, past
the church and the war memorial, up the steep incline that led to the
Retreat, along the hilltop lane towards the main road, the bay and the
islands laid out beneath us in one final seductive vista.

'This is the most beautiful place,' I said to Michael, trying to hide
the pangs I felt. 'You're very lucky to live here.'

'It won't last for ever,' he replied, looking back at the long sweep of
cream sand and the navy blue sea. 'Another year or so and we'll be
moving on.'

I was irrationally put out at this prospect, having somehow imagined
that Katie would grow up at St Cuthbert's with her father the permanent incumbent, Lucy for ever in charge of the domestic detail.

'Where will you go?' I asked him.

'Back to Cambridge, probably. That's considered my forte. Writing
obscure theological books for the faithful . . .'

He laughed, and I remembered the paperback that had been lying on
Jack Cameron's old desk next to the Klein biography, *The Freedom of
the Kingdom* by Michael Cameron, and resolved to buy it when I got
back to London.

I was impressed and amused by the way he entertained the children on a long and boring journey, organising games and silly joke competitions, intervening in disputes between the boys, always with an eye on Katie and her needs, dealing expertly and efficiently with one who felt sick, one who seemed to need the toilet every twenty miles, and one whose fruit gums disappeared under the seat, requesting far more stops than I'd made on the way up, allowing them time on the video machines in the motorway café where we had lunch. It was this that afforded our one moment of privacy.

'I want to thank you for the help you've given Sarah,' I said timorously, remembering how, when I'd arrived at St Cuthbert's this time I'd meant to tear into him on this very point. 'I feel terrible about the whole thing. I realise now that I don't know Charles at all . . . It didn't occur to me he might be depressed.'

'He was deeply affected by your mother's death,' Michael said quietly. 'He had nightmares for years afterwards. And of course, he had Sarah's grief to deal with. That wasn't easy. A lot of his problems date back to that time.'

And then I considered, with uncomfortable insight, that while Sarah had raved and I'd retreated into indifference, Charles had been left totally alone with his own distress. I hadn't given a damn about that; indeed, had hardly registered the fact that it was he, dispatched by Sarah to check up on my mother's whereabouts, who had discovered her mangled body and Leo's polluted corpse.

And it wasn't only Charles whose trauma I'd dismissed out of hand.

'Your father too,' I said unhappily. 'It must have been very hard for him . . .'

'My father recovered,' Michael replied. 'Things were bad for a while, but then he took hold of his life. I think losing your mother finally spurred him into action . . . He left home, went to live in Paris and made the house over to Jonathan. He was about to get married again when he died . . .'

He hesitated.

'My father was a good man,' he said with difficulty. 'A good father. I never blamed him for what happened . . .'

'I kept him from the funeral,' I faltered. 'I was so angry with all your family . . . even Jonathan. I knew he wanted to help. He wrote to me, but I tore it up. Then he phoned, and I told him to fuck off.'

Michael looked away.

'It was a terrible time,' he said.

I wanted to ask what he knew of his father's affair with my mother, whether as Sarah had insisted they'd truly intended to get married, but we had arrived at our most painful memories, courage suddenly seeming to fail us both, and then the children were back and we were

on the road again, speeding towards what would surely be our final
goodbye.

A great deal still remained unsaid, and yet I couldn't imagine under
what circumstances the rest might be aired, and so I comforted myself
that this limited reconciliation was far more than either of us might ever
have expected.

But there remained one further subject I felt I could broach, and as
we pulled up outside my sister's solid semi, freshly painted and
now bearing a FOR SALE sign in the garden, I turned to him swiftly,
waiting only until the children were out of the car and running up the
path.

'Sarah knows nothing about me and Daniel Duval. I'd really like to
keep it that way.'

'Of course.'

We were both embarrassed by the intimacy this conspiracy seemed to
provoke, as though mere mention of my ex-lover were enough to recall
just how much had changed between us, and yet he was plainly anxious
not to let it drop.

'I would like to apologise,' he began uncomfortably, looking away,
'for my behaviour the day I read that story in the *Sun* . . . I was very
rude to you. It was just such a shock.'

I grimaced, unwilling to remember.

'I guess I deserved it,' I said, 'the whole lot . . .'

He shook his head.

'No one deserves that. Poor Daniel was shattered. He tells me Genevieve is thoroughly ashamed of herself, but I have to say that if you
didn't know, you'd never think so . . .'

He looked across at me.

'I'm not a great fan of Genevieve,' he said wryly.

'I gather the feeling is mutual,' I replied, and we both laughed.

'Daniel and I have become good friends,' he said carefully, 'but I'd
like you to know that we've never discussed you . . . At least, that is to
say, not after I discovered his mysterious lover was you.'

Duval had told me as much himself, but I couldn't resist the urge to
probe further.

'So what did he say about me? While it was still a mystery?'

He glanced at me briefly, assessing my mood, and then looked
down.

'That it was a grand passion . . . and that he was utterly besotted.'

I received these tidings with gloomy resignation, wondering how in
the world I'd let Duval slip through my fingers and out of my life.

'So you told him to go back to his wife?' I said, unable to keep the
note of reproach from my voice.

'I told him what he already knew,' Michael replied quietly. 'That grand passions most usually end in disaster, and often make you feel pretty bad about yourself.'

And with this sobering, self-evident truth before me, I went in to greet my sister and my suffering brother-in-law.

We might have survived the inquest, Sarah and I, with our sisterly feelings severely rocked but retrievable. We might have survived the attentions of local newspapers, the whispering of appalled villagers, the heartbreaking attempt of Leo's ageing mother to apologise to us. We might even have survived Jack Cameron's discreet presence on the sidelines, keeping out of my way as I'd demanded, but always on call for Sarah, providing the only source of comfort that seemed to calm her at all.

We might have survived the funeral service, with all its aching beauty, the burial, so bitter, so bald, so utterly final, even the overwhelming sympathy of my mother's many friends, the shock of her students and the sorrow of her stunned colleagues.

But we could not survive the impact of Ray Carlisle.

He drove up to my mother's cottage in a dark green Jaguar, rapping on our door with undisguised authority, a tall, lean, handsome man whose picture I had seen among my mother's papers, who had once refused to meet me and sent his second wife to tell me so, and towards whom, I determined, I would muster no civil response at all.

But my morose silence paled beside Sarah's fury.

As Charles conducted him into the living room, announcing him uncertainly as 'Your father, Mr Carlisle', she launched herself at him, screaming and cursing, beating her fists upon his chest, crying out that he'd deserted her mother and thereby caused her death, leaving her alone in the world, victim of the likes of Leo.

'She needs psychiatric help,' Ray said coldly. 'We must call the local hospital. Elizabeth . . . get the telephone directory!'

'Don't call me Elizabeth,' I said. 'That's not my name.'

'We'll argue about the details later. What's your doctor's number?'

We were missing Sam, whom I'd dispatched to the funeral parlour to sort out the wreaths, and it was plain that Charles, staring despairingly at his weeping fiancée, would do nothing to avert her being carted off by the men in white coats. I would have to pacify Ray Carlisle myself.

'I'll find the number,' I told him nervously as he began to rummage beneath the telephone table, 'but let me make you a coffee . . . You've had a long journey.'

I led him into the conservatory, cast suddenly in the role of appeaser, guessing that whatever he took into his head to do would surely be carried through, an intuition rapidly validated by his quickfire questions about solicitors, insurance, estate agents and my mother's will, all of this preceded by the most cursory of condolences.

'We can handle it ourselves,' I said, deeply aggrieved by this assumption of responsibility. 'There's no need for you to trouble yourself.'

'Oh yes?' he said sharply. 'And what have you done so far?'

In truth very little had been done, because Sarah was in no fit state to make decisions and I felt no great concern about the outcome. My mother's money, I assumed, would be equally divided between us and we would go our separate ways. There was no need of solicitors at the moment.

'I hope you're on good terms with your sister,' Ray was saying, 'because she's the sole beneficiary of the life insurance. That's the way I set it up, although naturally I'd expect her to give some of the money to you . . . I've told her that.'

I stared at him, perplexed. Sarah had never mentioned any previous dealings with my father, and indeed, if she'd ever set out to track him down, I couldn't imagine she'd have met with any greater enthusiasm than I had myself.

'She came to see me,' Ray said helpfully, 'as you yourself once did. Of course, I told Sarah the whole situation. I felt I owed it to her. But it wasn't my place to explain it all to you . . . that was your mother's job.'

'What situation?' I asked uneasily, seeing a great chasm of uncertainty suddenly open at my feet. 'I've no idea what you're talking about.'

'Ah,' said Ray Carlisle knowingly. 'She didn't tell you . . . Well, Elizabeth, that's your mother for you, I'm afraid. Her courage failed her at crucial moments. A pity, you may think, that she wasn't more like your grandmother . . . Rhoda never failed nor faltered. Rhoda always saw things through.'

'Leave Rhoda out of this,' I muttered.

'Oh, it's quite impossible to leave out Rhoda,' he replied with a little sneer. 'Like it or not, your mother was Rhoda's daughter. Certainly, she attracted men in just the same way . . . I consider myself to have had a lucky escape. I suppose you know your grandmother poisoned her husband when she got tired of him?'

I looked at the man as though he were totally mad, as indeed he seemed to be, sitting on my mother's cane settee, sipping his coffee, exhibiting no shred of shame at confronting the daughters he had sired and then abandoned so many years ago, no hint of emotion at the terrible fate of the wife he once, presumably, had loved.

I summoned my wits to withstand his careless confidence, launching out on what I would once have considered an impossible task, the defence of Rhoda.

'My grandmother was a very difficult woman,' I said with dignity. 'She could be extremely unpleasant and she was often cruel. She was not, however, a murderer.'

Ray Carlisle shot me a long, penetrating stare.

'You talk to the younger Miss Connaught,' he advised me. 'She'll tell you what happened to her brother. She'll tell you how poor old Sir Rupert just got weaker and weaker while Rhoda played the grieving wife at his bedside and finished him off . . .'

I might have laughed aloud at this ludicrous tale, or even ordered him out of the house for such a slander upon my grandmother, but at this moment Sarah and Charles joined us in the conservatory, my sister pale and unusually dry-eyed, evidently considering that it might be prudent to make peace with her father.

He listened to her halting apology while I watched him in growing disgust, confounded by his insensitivity, astonished that my mother could ever have married him, remembering how she'd told me he'd beaten her, wondering about Rhoda and her part in their doomed union, thinking that if we could only get rid of him, my sister and I might make some belated move towards solidarity.

Alas, it was not to be.

'I'm sorry, Sarah, that neither you nor your mother saw fit to tell Elizabeth the truth about her parentage,' chided the man I'd always believed to be my father. 'I can't help feeling that was very remiss of you both . . .'

Then suddenly I seemed to see the floor of the conservatory float loose from its base, rising up to meet me while the windows fluttered and darkened, my chest tightening and my stomach lurching.

'He was someone your mother met at Cambridge,' I heard Ray Carlisle say as my knees buckled. 'She never would tell me his name . . .'

I felt Charles catch me as I reeled; kindly, brotherly arms handing me down on to the cane settee.

'She's okay,' I heard him reassure Ray. 'She's pregnant, that's all . . .'

I whirled in a grey tunnel of visions, seeming to see Rhoda and my mother arguing, imagining for a moment that Michael was beside me, registering Ray's disdain and glimpsing Charles's concerned frown as I drifted into unknowingness, the spinning world and all its trials sinking from me, a blessed blackness descending.

When I came round, Ray Carlisle was on the phone to his insurance company, Charles was waving a glass of water under my nose and Sarah was kneeling on the floor beside me, her face frozen in shock.

I sat up to survey a country in which everything seemed utterly and irrevocably changed, all familiar landmarks blasted from their place, all order and continuity shattered, all solid ground suddenly turned to shifting sand.

'Well, this has sorted things out,' I said calmly to Sarah, sipping at my glass of water and taking stock. 'We don't have to pretend to each other any more. We don't have to be friendly or concerned . . . or even speak to each other again if we don't feel like it. We're not sisters, after all.'

I was unaccountably nervous about seeing Sarah and Charles in company with Michael, but the only discomfort was mine, and they were all so easy with each other, Michael taking Sarah into his arms and kissing her, joking with Charles about the state of the garden and making an immediate, admiring inspection of the kitchen, that I soon began to relax.

My brother-in-law seemed cheerful and calm, but when I presented him with the remaining gold Easter egg from Alnwick, I found myself overwhelmed with effusive, almost tearful, thanks. This little difficulty was smoothly overcome by Michael, however, who insisted that the egg be opened and consumed there and then, all four of us downing sickly liqueur chocolates by the handful as though it were Christmas.

'Jamie called,' Sarah told me. 'He got your postcard. He seemed a bit anxious about you . . . I told him you'd be home tonight.'

I smiled, my heart lifting. Things were falling into place.

But I still needed to make my confession, and I watched anxiously for the moment, fearing we might have to depart before I had the chance to speak to Sarah alone, but Michael even took care of this, ushering Charles out into the garden for a private chat, leaving us to say what had never been said in all the years since my mother's death.

I didn't waste a moment, begging her to forgive my disappearance after the funeral, the years when I didn't contact her at all nor respond to her letters, the reserve I'd shown when Jamie at last took the initiative by inviting her to London and presiding over our frosty reunion, my failure to see what was happening to Charles.

'I can't forget I once said that we weren't sisters,' I wept, taking her hand. 'What a terribly wrong thing to say . . . Of course, we're sisters! We grew up together, we shared a wonderful mother . . .'

She wept too, falling into my arms and holding me close, anxious to unfold what had never been properly explained to me before.

'She really was a wonderful mother, Beth . . . And she felt so guilty about Jack, about not telling you what was going on. But she didn't want to muck things up with Michael. She wanted the two of you to come to your own decision, regardless of the fact that they'd fallen in love.'

'Beatrice Cameron put paid to that idea,' I said, remembering the sequence of events.

'Yes. She used the whole situation quite shamelessly. I don't think she cared about losing Jack at all . . . But Michael was a different matter. She just wasn't going to let him marry you, and she grabbed her chance to prevent it. And then of course, in the end she lost him too . . .'

There were other things Sarah wished to explain: her intermittent relationship with Ray Carlisle, her friendship with his daughter Emma, and the fate of the life insurance money, lost through a failed business venture, another futile attempt by Charles to find himself a niche.

Now the tears fell fast.

'You walked out of your home with nothing, Beth. Sam drove you away with no more than a suitcase . . . I didn't know if I'd ever see you again . . . I'd hate you to think Emma was some kind of substitute sister. She could never be that.'

'Don't worry about it,' I said, blowing my nose, 'and don't think another thing about the money. Financial problems are just about the only ones I've never had.'

She hesitated, smiling at me anxiously through her tears, still holding something back.

'But you were all alone, and you were pregnant . . . I know you had Sam, but I couldn't help thinking he was more trouble than help. He just took you over . . . It must have been very hard.'

I reached into my handbag for a fresh supply of tissues, handing us both a hefty pile, psyching myself for the final confession, the last hurdle. Breathe deep, Beth. One, two, three, four . . .

'Yes, it was hard, but that was largely my own fault. I let everyone think I was having an abortion, and maybe that would have been the sensible thing to do . . . But I didn't, Sarah. I had a baby boy. He weighed eight pounds four, he looked exactly like Michael, and he was adopted. I don't know who they were, but I'm sure they were good people, desperate for a child . . .'

I was sobbing now, unable to take in that I'd finally revealed what no one else knew, no one save Jamie and Vicky and Sam, and a demon Sister on a maternity ward.

Then I calmed down, and suddenly aware that Sarah was saying nothing, looked across at her with sickening intuition, seeing that my tortured confession hadn't proved a surprise at all.

'You knew! How could you have known? Not Sam, he wouldn't have told you . . . Jamie? It must have been Jamie!'

'No,' she said quickly, 'not Jamie. He's always protected you. He would never say anything he thought might cause you harm . . .'

She put her hand up to my face, wiping away my tears, preparing me as gently as she could for the next shock.

'Beth,' she asked quietly. 'What did you expect Michael to do? Did you really think a punch in the mouth from Sam would scare him off? That he wouldn't very quickly come to his senses and see what a terrible mess he'd made? And then try to put it right?'

I stared at her in anguish, silenced by this unimagined suggestion, hardly daring to think what might come next.

'He was distraught . . . He had a furious row with his mother and told her he was going to marry you. It was only his father who kept the lid on it all. He managed to calm Michael down and persuaded him to wait. Jack was sure you'd come round. Nobody thought you'd just vanish into the blue . . .'

I closed my eyes, trembling with new grief, seeing how my mother's death had blighted all rational and considered responses, locking each one of us into programmed patterns of behaviour, either dulled disbelief or excessive emotion.

'Michael tried every way to track you down,' Sarah was saying, 'and eventually he found Vicky. She wouldn't tell him where you were, but she did agree to keep him informed, to let him know you were all right . . .'

I was suddenly acutely aware that Michael was outside in the garden, that very shortly I'd have to climb back into the BMW and set off for the Cameron house, that soon I'd be facing Jonathan who, I could only guess, knew the whole story too, that all the defences of the past thirteen years were slowly falling, one by one.

'Did Vicky tell him everything?' I whispered.

'Everything. She was put in a terrible position. It was no easy task, coping with Michael. He kept ringing her up, crying down the phone and begging her to give you a message. Then Jack tried to persuade her . . . I even spoke to her myself. But she wouldn't do it, and it was clear why not. She was scared of upsetting Sam.'

Sarah hesitated.

'Vicky really seemed to think you and Sam would stay together. That's what she told Michael. It was very hard for him to accept . . .'

I stood up and walked to the window, staring out upon Sarah's tangled lawn, watching as Michael attacked the weeds and Charles advised, Katie and the boys tearing round between them, an unexceptional yet suddenly heartbreaking scene. Then Michael saw me watching and waved, indicating the car with a questioning nod. He wanted to be going. Somehow I would have to face it.

'Don't be angry with Vicky,' Sarah said anxiously. 'She was very upset and confused at the time, and I don't suppose her feelings for Sam made it any easier. She must often have wondered if she did the right thing . . .'

I smiled bravely at my sister and squeezed her hand, thinking of Vicky and the sad state of her marriage, knowing I would gladly spare her any further woe.

'It's okay,' I said to my sister, picking up my handbag. 'I'm not angry. I can see how difficult it must have been . . . And no message from Michael would have made any difference. I won't even mention it to Vicky. She did the right thing.'

'He's beautiful, Beth,' Vicky breathed, peering into the crib. 'Are you absolutely sure you're doing the right thing?'

'Of course she is,' Sam said impatiently. 'We've talked it through a hundred times. Are you ready, Beth? I'm parked on a double yellow . . .'

I was surveying myself in the washstand mirror, my new contours cruelly illuminated by a strip of merciless neon, my face ashen and grey, the colours of grief. I would have to get back into shape. I would have to cheer up.

'I want to hear her say it,' Vicky persisted, facing Sam in open challenge across the bed from which I'd so recently risen. 'I want to know she's making her own decision.'

'It's okay, Vicky,' I said quietly. 'I know what I'm doing.'

She was trying to catch my eye in the mirror, but I wouldn't meet her gaze, concerned only to shore up my precarious barricades before they all came tumbling down, anxious now to be gone.

Sam, seeming suddenly to recollect the need for a show of sensitivity, strode over to the mirror and stood behind me, resting his hands on my shoulders, a purposeful gesture of consolation.

'You'll have other babies,' he murmured in my ear. 'My babies . . .' and I smiled, pressing my hand over his. I would never have Sam's babies, nor indeed, would I have Sam himself, but now was not the moment to declare it.

'Surely Michael has a right to know?' Vicky said hesitantly. 'I mean, shouldn't he at least have the chance to —'

'Michael has been struck from the record,' Sam snapped smartly. 'He no longer exists. Isn't that right, Beth?'

'That's right,' I said steadily.

I did meet her eye then, and saw to my concern that she was close to tears. And they seemed in that moment to be my tears, the tears I could not, would not, shed.

'Leave us, Sam,' I said quickly, 'before you get a ticket.'

The door closed behind him and she fell into my arms, weeping and apologising in one breath.

'It's all right,' I soothed. 'Truly, it is . . . He'll get a much better mother than I'd ever make. I'm not ready for it, and anyway, I've got other things in mind . . .'

I heard these bold words with a curious sense of unfamiliarity, as though I stood outside myself and saw a new being of my own creation, unsentimental, invulnerable, refusing the fate of the wounded who must ever display their battle scars, determined to face forward, and never, never, to look back.

'I can't help thinking about Michael,' Vicky mumbled, but this time I cut her short.

'I will never forgive him,' I said stonily. 'Don't mention his name ever again.'

This seemed to convince her, and she dried her eyes, still apologising and smiling at me ruefully in the mirror.

'Give me one moment alone,' I said, pushing her towards the door. 'And if Sam's got a ticket, for God's sake try to calm him down.'

Then I walked across to the crib.

'This is goodbye,' I jerked out, taking the baby's tiny fingers in mine and brushing a bright golden lock from his forehead. 'I'm not going to give you any crap about this being all for the best . . . Of course, it's not – it's just the best under the circumstances.'

At the door I turned back, struggling for something more, but the words, whatever they were, would not find expression, and so I walked away along the dim hospital corridor, away from my child and out into the blinding light of the waiting world beyond.

We drove away from Sarah's home and into the country we'd travelled so often in the Bentley, so very, very long ago. Past the country club and the river we went, past the edge of the spinney and the Black Boar pub, up into the village and past the post office . . . Along the road to St Botolph's and past my mother's old cottage, up to the gates of the Cameron estate and into the long driveway that meandered around the house.

We'd hardly exchanged a word, listening instead to a tape cassette which Mark had lent Katie, a strange and rather grim story about two lost children, and when we pulled up outside the flight of stone steps and the familiar portico of the great mansion, he turned to me, concerned.

'Are you all right?'

'Yes,' I said calmly, 'I'm all right,' and I was.

Then the front door opened and Jonathan Cameron, older, heavier, looking unnervingly like his father, smiled down at us, three bright-haired girls with wide grey eyes spilling on to the steps behind him, calling for cousin Katie and their Uncle Michael, rushing to pull them both from the car.

'Beth . . . How amazing, and how absolutely wonderful to see you . . . after all this time! I can scarcely believe it!'

Jonathan put his arms around me and kissed me on the cheek, a welcome I'd hardly been expecting but, when it came, utterly natural and unforced.

'My wife, Frances,' he said, introducing a pretty red-haired woman whom I recognised from the photograph on the vicarage mantelpiece. 'She's a great fan of yours!'

I followed them into the house, wondering for one anxious moment if Beatrice Cameron had returned unexpectedly from her trip down the Nile, a worry that was soothed at once by Frances.

'Have no fear. She's away for another week at least. We're pinning our hopes on the crocodiles!'

I was startled by this frank and apparently universal view of her mother-in-law, but then I was overwhelmed by the memories that the great mansion evoked: the ballroom, the library with its portrait of Uncle Malcolm hanging over the doorway, before which I paused with a pang, the staircase that led up to Michael's old bedroom, the kitchen where Jonathan had tried to comfort me the very last time that I'd gone to the house . . .

'We'll have tea on the terrace,' Frances said. 'This is the first day it's been warm enough.'

Michael had brought presents for his nieces, paper flying machines which now whirled above the rose garden in front of the terrace while he and the four girls chased along the pathways.

'It's bliss when Michael comes to stay,' said Frances, watching and laughing. 'He keeps the kids amused for hours on end.'

Then she disappeared to make the tea, leaving me alone with Jonathan on the terrace where once I'd faced Jack Cameron and imagined, with a curious sense of recognition, the shock of future vision, that I would one day marry his younger son.

'I hope this isn't too hard for you, Beth, being here . . .' Jonathan said carefully. 'I was astonished when I heard you were going to St Cuthbert's. I couldn't imagine how Michael would handle it. I was worried it might prove too much for you both.'

'We've done all right,' I said briskly. 'A few skirmishes and one major fight. But after that, a gradual laying down of arms . . .'

'Did he talk about my mother?'

'No . . . No, he didn't.'

'Oh, that's a pity . . . He's very eloquent on the dubious privilege of being the favourite son.'

Jonathan raised one eyebrow and looked at me wryly.

'I'd like to tell you that my mother has mellowed,' he said quietly; 'that she saw the error of her ways and did something about it. But unfortunately, that isn't the case. Some people never change.'

And in that moment I thought suddenly of Rhoda, her constant dissatisfaction, her extraordinary insensitivity, her failure to recognise or return anything that looked remotely like love. The mysteries of human personality were surely unfathomable, and at least as mysterious as Rhoda's intransigence was my own mother's triumph above her example. How concerned and loving my mother had been . . . How very fortunate I was to have the memory of her devotion.

I swallowed hard, and tried to concentrate on Jonathan.

'So . . . Did Michael talk to you about Clare?'

'No,' I said uncomfortably, 'he didn't.'

Jonathan looked away for a moment, seeming to consider his words and then to reach a decision.

'I probably shouldn't tell you this,' he said slowly, 'but I'm going to anyway . . .'

I caught my breath, seeing I had finally to confront the fact that Clare Spencer, always on the sidelines of Michael's life, always so cool and so distant with me, waiting for her moment, had won the day and taken my place as his bride.

'They were very unhappily married, Beth,' Jonathan said soberly. 'Neither one any more to blame than the other . . . but both of them desperately miserable. Even now, it seems incredible that Michael actually did it. The only possible explanation is that Clare caught him at a low point, when he needed someone very badly. But once she'd got him, she very soon discovered that she didn't want him . . .'

I gazed at Jonathan in total astonishment, unable to imagine what might have persuaded Michael's wife she'd made a mistake, not knowing what response this unlikely revelation was meant to provoke.

'I'm very sorry to hear it,' I muttered at last, realising with a flash of guilty insight that I wasn't at all, fumbling around for something that might sound sincere, saved, mercifully, by the arrival of Frances with the tray.

We all took tea together, Katie visibly relaxing in the unaccustomed company of her own sex, the children giggling among themselves, the grown-ups talking of television, the Church, Charles's health and the likelihood of my sister selling her house easily.

'I hope Charles will be okay,' I said anxiously. 'I'm sure he would be if he could find something to do.'

'He may yet,' Michael said unexpectedly. 'I'm proposing him for administrator up at the Retreat . . . Emily's leaving,' he added. 'She's got a new job.'

I stared in surprise, mumbling that she would surely be missed, a sentiment with which, avoiding my eye, he avidly concurred.

Then there was nothing but to make my goodbyes, skirting awkward moments in which Katie clung to me, asking when I'd be going back to St Cuthbert's, and Jonathan's eldest daughter shook me solemnly by the hand, enquiring whether she might visit me at Metro TV, until alone with Michael at last, I walked out to my car.

Neither of us spoke until I was half-way in the driver's door, and then I saw I couldn't leave without embracing the final heartache.

'Why didn't you tell me you knew about the baby?' I asked him steadily. 'It was quite a shock when Sarah revealed you'd come looking for me . . .'

I'd caught him off guard, and he turned away from me suddenly, gazing across the formal gardens and the fields of the Cameron estate, into the churchyard where my mother and his father lay in their graves, up to the spire of St Botolph's, gleaming silver in the afternoon sun.

'I didn't think it right,' he stumbled. 'It seemed an imposition to burden you with all that. The last thing I wanted was to upset you . . .'

I wondered which of us would have been more upset, and reckoning it was roughly even, decided against offering any further rationale, fumbling around on the dashboard for my gloves, searching for some innocuous farewell.

But now that the truth lay before us at last, he didn't mean to let me off so lightly.

'When our child was born,' he asked tremulously, 'did you never think of contacting me?'

'Michael, I didn't . . . I wanted to cut all ties with the past. I can't tell you how hard it was. I was grieving for my mother, I was missing my home, my life was a mess. It was only Sam who kept me together . . . There was a time when I thought I'd keep the baby, but he persuaded me adoption was the right thing to do. Not that I'm blaming Sam . . . I wanted it too. I wanted my freedom. I wanted my future.'

He swallowed hard, fighting evident emotion.

'It would have worked out,' he said haltingly. 'I know I gave you a lot of heavy stuff in Paris, but it didn't take me long to regret it . . . And it was only my mother who made me hesitate. She was utterly ruthless with me. She exploited every last claim on my loyalty. That's no excuse, but even so, I can't help feeling I deserved a second chance.'

Now we were unable to face each other, and I got into the BMW, my heart lodged at the back of my throat, desperate to be gone, longing for the right parting words to spring to mind, unable to imagine what they could possibly be.

I pressed the window switch, and instead of offering a simple conciliatory goodbye, leaned out and blundered on with hapless disregard to compound our mutual agony.

'Well, I guess it's just one of those things,' I said inanely. 'And I'm sure our son is perfectly all right ... I called him Malcolm, after your uncle, because he reminded me of that daft picture above the library door. I expect they changed that. He's probably Darren or Jason, or some such bloody name by now.'

Still he wouldn't look at me, and he was saying nothing.

'Things haven't worked out too badly,' I heard myself gabble like some demented parrot. 'I mean, you have a lovely little daughter ... I know you lost Clare, and that's terrible ...' I faltered at this point, remembering all Jonathan had told me, but then rallied for a further inanity. 'However, you do have Emily,' I burbled. 'You'll still see her, I'm sure, even if she has got a new job ...'

I rambled on in deep embarrassment, producing ever-more-desperate pleasantries, until at last he rescued me.

'Yes,' he said, 'I'll still see Emily.'

'That's good,' I said eagerly. 'I like Emily ... She's great.'

'Yes,' he said. 'And how about you, Beth? How have things worked out for you?'

I kicked the BMW into life, and looked up at him.

'I'm okay. I'm fine. I've got Jamie, and if Daniel Duval would leave his bloody wife again, all my prayers would be answered ...'

For a moment I thought he might question the arrangement whereby I'd got Jamie and yet also lusted openly after Daniel Duval, but he didn't. Instead he smiled, a weak and distant smile.

'Well,' he said, 'you never know. Prayers are always answered, one way or another.'

I slipped the car into gear, hearing its tyres strain on the gravel, feeling the pull of the wheels.

'That's it, then,' I said foolishly, offering him a little wave. 'Goodbye, Michael.'

'Goodbye, Beth,' he said, and then stood back to watch my erratic progress down the driveway of the great Cameron house, on to the road and back to the life I'd left behind me.

*

'There, there, darling . . . I'm sorry I threw you out, but that stupid pic in the *Sun* was taking things a bit far. Even your old chum Clive Fisher seemed to think so! See what he sent you . . .'

Jamie was handing me a huge box of Belgian chocolates, done up in green and silver, a fortune's worth of calories from Harrods.

'Candice Carter brought them round. Seems they're bosom buddies, her and Clive . . . A rather intriguing combination, wouldn't you say, Tabloid Trash and Broadsheet Bunkum.'

I stared at the gaudy casket in disgust.

'He ruins my life, and then he buys me chocolates!'

'Now, now, darling . . . Your life's not ruined at all. I'm not too sure about your face though. Have you been eating properly? You're looking terribly scraggy around the old chops . . .'

'Thanks very much,' I sniffed, accepting the large gin I was offered and lying back on the sofa in my elegant sitting room before the inglenook fire, desperately glad to be home, anxious to make amends to Jamie, but none too keen to be insulted into the bargain. 'Why do I put up with you?'

'That's a very good question, darling. Why do we put up with each other? Maybe we should talk it through. Review the ground rules, as it were . . .'

He led me into the kitchen and sat me down at the counter, making me observe while he chopped slivers of chicken breast and salad vegetables, darting around me with spices and jars of mustard, waving his olive oil in the air with all the flamboyance of a TV chef.

'How's Hamlet?' I asked him, wanting to know. 'Still prevaricating?'

'Hamlet,' he said seriously, 'has proved a very heavy number . . . Life and death, you know, darling. And all the time, poor old Alex Chapman fighting HIV. It was quite a trauma when he took the final step. To be, or not to be . . .'

'Oh Jamie,' I said, hanging my head, 'I can't bear it. Why didn't you tell me what you were going through?'

'You were never here, darling . . . It's not the kind of thing you slip into conversation over the odd gin and tonic. And not only were you never here, you went away and fell in love! That's breaking ground rule number one, remember? We're supposed to tell each other if we fall in love.'

'Did I fall in love?'

He stopped, mid-chop, and surveyed me severely.

'Do you know how much time you've spent in Paris this past six months?'

'I was filming . . .'

'You were in bed with Daniel Duval. And when you weren't in bed, you were on the phone. You know, you can get arrested for making phone calls like that . . .'

I laughed and pinched a piece of cucumber, causing him to rap me on the knuckles with his pepper mill.

'I liked him. And it was the best sex I've had in years.'

'I'm delighted to hear it, darling. Nobody wants to spoil your fun. But it was imprudent, to say the least. Did your mother never warn you about married men? Especially ones with crazy wives?'

I looked away, unable to produce any light-hearted comment about my mother and married men, thinking about Duval and wondering when I might see him again, a point that clearly concerned Jamie.

'And now what, darling?' he demanded. 'Is he going to leave his wife? I don't think so. And if he isn't, that puts you right back where you started . . . Odious policemen and other assorted no-good fellows.'

'There's a chronic shortage of decent guys,' I protested.

'Tell me about it. I have the same problem myself.'

I looked at him then, feeling my eyes fill with sudden tears, remembering all we'd been to each other in the past nine years, and all we had not, seeing how sad and how crazy and how impossible it was, the desperate, doomed attempt to find one individual in the whole wide universe to love with all your body, mind and soul, although once upon a time, when the world was young, I truly believed I'd done it.

'You know what I think, darling?' He took my hand, sobered by the tears. 'I think it's high time you got married. Settled down and had a couple of kids . . .'

'Got anyone in mind?' I whispered.

'Not right at the moment. Unless someone persuades Daniel Duval that he's missed the chance of a lifetime . . .'

I stood up and walked over to the stove, prodding the steaming vegetables, sipping my gin, remembering that just a week ago, on Easter Sunday, I had seemed to feel my life falling into place, wondering how the rest of the process might possibly be achieved.

'That's not going to happen,' I said to Jamie, thinking it over. 'Next time I see Duval, it will be strictly business . . . I'm going back to Paris soon. I'm going to write a book about an old Hollywood actress – Eva Delamere.'

He looked across at me in evident surprise.

'Eva Delamere? What do you know about her?'

'Plenty. More than most, perhaps.'

Then I looked up at him.

'Why?' I faltered, 'What do you know about her?'

'Well, darling,' he said to my utter confusion, 'I know she was pals with your old granny. I didn't mention it at the time because I know exactly how you feel about your granny . . . but I had the privilege of a personal audience with Eva Delamere! I met her in Paris not six months ago.'

Book X: Eva

Chapter Twenty-eight

The blessing of a contented old age is not wisdom, nor peace, nor even humility, although, with diligence and prayer, all these may come. The blessing of old age is a profound sense of gratitude to God, a looking back in wonder to the pattern only now glimpsed, a confidence in the continuation of that selfsame thread of Providence . . .

The Journals of Eva Delamere, edited by Blanche Duval

Eva, dreaming and nodding by the fireside on an autumn afternoon, imagined herself answering the questions that Mr Jon Makepeace, biographer of the great David Klein, might put if he were in possession of the facts.

'Yes indeed, Mr Makepeace . . . a wonderful story. The escape from Paris, the triumph of love over adversity. But do you really want to hear the rest of it? So much that is unexceptional, so very far removed from Hollywood? Is that what your readers want? No, I don't think so . . . Why not end your story where it is?'

The words were on her lips when she woke on the wooden settle in her sitting room, and saw, for one fleeting moment, David sitting beside her, David as he was on the day they'd fled Paris together so many years ago, still with his mass of dark tousled curls and his bright blue eyes . . .

But of course, it wasn't David at all. It was Daniel.

'Grandmama, I'm sorry, I startled you. I thought you were fast asleep. Now please keep very quiet. I'm hiding.'

'Hiding?' Eva laughed. 'Who from? From Mr Makepeace?'

'No, of course not. Toby has taken Mr Makepeace into the garden. He's telling him who really killed Will Sutton . . . The FBI, wasn't it? Or was it the CIA? I'm sure Toby will think of something.'

Eva laughed again.

'Who are you hiding from?' she repeated.

'From Mama, of course! She wants me at a meeting of the hospital trustees. But I'm afraid I've got a more pressing engagement.'

'And what might that be?' Eva asked him wryly.

'This is something I could only tell my grandmother,' he replied solemnly, catching her eye. 'I'm meeting my girlfriend from the London plane. By the time the trustees get their tea and biscuits, I shall be in bed.'

Eva tried to assume a reproving frown, but failed in the attempt, and began laughing again.

'Now then, Daniel, don't take liberties with me. I don't want to hear a thing about it. What I don't know, I can't pass on to your mama . . .'

They both laughed then, and he looked at his watch.

'I must go . . . But tomorrow I start cutting the picture. Would you like to come and view the rushes? See how you look on the screen after all these years? Take tea at the Café des Arbres when we're through?'

'No, I wouldn't,' Eva said firmly. 'In my day the actresses never went near the editing rooms. You show your girlfriend the rushes and take her to tea at the Café des Arbres.'

'Oh I will,' he replied. 'Except that she requires bottles of champagne, not tea.'

Then he was gone, and Eva, moving to the window to see if she might spy Toby and Mr Jon Makepeace in conference, gazing out on the glittering grass, every bit as verdant and pristine as in the time of Sister Marguerite, began to wonder about her grandson's girlfriend. Whoever she was, she'd have to be smart to prove a match for Daniel's wife.

'Ah, good. You're awake. I thought you might come and take tea with the trustees? They do so like to see you . . . They've always got in mind that it's your money. Now, where's Daniel? He was here not half an hour ago, sitting on the lawn with Susannah Lamont . . .'

Blanche, always making time for business as well as patients and imagining that everyone else considered her meetings equally important, linked her arm in Eva's.

Eva smiled guiltily back.

'Daniel had to leave,' she said quickly, 'but I shall certainly come to the meeting . . . And how is Susannah today?'

She was anxious to know, yet also keen to deflect her daughter's questions on Daniel's whereabouts.

'None too happy today,' said Blanche slowly. 'I feel that she shouldn't be here. This is a hospice, and though I'm constantly telling people that they come here to live, not to die, I'm afraid Susannah doesn't see it that way . . . It's time she was getting back to the everyday world.'

They walked through the long corridors of the convent together, Eva leaning heavily upon Blanche's arm, talking of nothing much, everything indeed, except Daniel and Genevieve, planning a weekend at the big house in the South when Edouard returned from his latest business trip, laughing about the earnest Mr Makepeace and his persistent questions.

'I do believe,' said Blanche, 'that he'll start digging in the Cimitière de Montparnasse if someone doesn't stop him. Somehow he's going to find David Klein's grave! Don't you think we should tell him the truth, Mama?'

Eva had asked herself this many times since Mr Makepeace arrived at the Divine Faith convent, and while there could really be no reason to desist, something held her back, a hint of arrogance about his approach, perhaps, the plain belief that in dealing with herself and Toby he was merely touching the incidentals of David Klein's life. The real story, he had no doubt, lay with Moira Sheen and Carlotta du Bois, with Rebecca Bernstein and all those, like his grandfather, Mr Randy Makepeace, willing to recall the heady days of Paris in the Twenties and the love affair with Anya Klein . . .

'Oh, I don't know,' Eva said to Blanche. 'He's writing a very romantic story. Why should we spoil it?'

'Just occasionally,' said Blanche somewhat severely, 'I feel like pointing out that true romance endures. It goes on and on, and it's always faithful and kind. How many people do you know who were happily married for fifty years? That's the most romantic story . . .'

'Well then, you tell it,' Eva replied firmly. 'After I'm dead.'

It was two days later that Nick Howard arrived at the Divine Faith convent, requesting, most politely and deferentially, a meeting with Eva.

'I haven't seen Nicky in more than thirty years,' said Eva, puzzled. 'Not since he came to visit us at Toulouse . . . Toby! You remember Nicky Howard, don't you?'

'I remember him,' said Toby grumpily. 'Crowding us out of our apartment. We were okay in that place until Nicky and Harriet moved in.'

'Toby, my dearest, you're getting positively senile,' said Eva mildly. 'We were never okay in that apartment. You said it was like a prison, remember?'

'Did I? Well then, it was. An overcrowded prison.'

Blanche frowned.

'Now, now, no squabbling,' she said. 'Where do you want to receive Mr Howard, Mama? In here, or out in the garden? At the moment he's sitting on the lawn. It's a lovely day.'

'Oh dear,' said Daniel, peering out of the sitting-room window. 'I do believe he's been commandeered by our good friend Mr Makepeace . . . Well, that should be interesting. How old was Nicky Howard at the crucial time?'

'He was two,' Eva said, remembering.

'A toddler's-eye view of *Casey's War*,' said Daniel. 'Fascinating!'

They all laughed, though Eva wondered privately what Nicky Howard might say about his mother if suitably encouraged by the enthusiastic Mr Makepeace.

Daniel escorted her into the garden among the late summer blooms, the roses and the peonies bordering the turf, the clumps of coriander from the kitchen courtyard scenting the air, the fragrant honeysuckle over the old gate lifting on the breeze.

'See where they're sitting?' Daniel said to Eva. 'Right by the old gate! We should really tell the story of the night the Nazis walked into Paris and Grandaddy chauffeured you across the lawn – Mr Makepeace would faint away in sheer delight!'

'Chauffeured across the lawn!' Eva repeated with a little laugh. 'Now there you have it! History rewritten as romance. Your grandaddy hit that gate after he careered across the lawn, and swore most profusely, as I remember. Then he had the cheek to tell me to shut up. We didn't speak for the next two hours . . .'

'But you see, Grandmama,' Daniel said, 'these are the delightful little details that make it all the more romantic!'

They had been proceeding slowly across the lawn, as yet unnoticed, towards the bench where Nick Howard sat with Mr Makepeace, and now Eva considered that she would very much like to avoid any further interviews with David Klein's biographer. All that might be said about *Casey's War* and Will Sutton's death had been said many times, and she was heartily sick of it.

'Can you get rid of Mr Makepeace?' she asked her grandson. 'Take him back to the café or escort him round the cemetery? Anything to keep him happy and make him think he's getting somewhere.'

Daniel glanced at his watch, as he so often did these days, and Eva saw at once that this would prove an imposition.

'Oh, I'm sorry . . . Your girlfriend is waiting for you.'

'She's back at my apartment with a hangover,' he said. 'I've got to get her on her feet, otherwise she'll be in trouble.'

'Trouble?' asked Eva with a little sigh, accepting that she would ine-

vitably be drawn into Daniel's affair just as she'd always been drawn
into his marriage. 'What kind of trouble? She's not married, I hope.'

'Trouble from her boss. She's supposed to be working while she's
here in Paris, but she's not getting a great deal done . . .' He hesitated, and glanced at Eva. 'She's not married,' he said, 'but she does
have a boyfriend of sorts. He's gay. She says they have an amicable
arrangement, although to hear them talking on the phone you wouldn't
think so.'

Eva looked up at him despairingly, thinking there was no man alive
that she loved quite as much – except perhaps, her dear son Matthew.
It was Daniel's resemblance to David, of course. That, and the fact that
his life had often seemed so very miserable . . .

'Are you in love?' she asked him unhappily as they approached the
bench where Nick and Mr Makepeace sat.

'I'm utterly besotted,' he replied, 'but I'm not under any illusions.
She doesn't love me, and it will all end when she decides . . .'

Nicky Howard and his companion rose to their feet, Jon Makepeace
rushing forward to greet them, taking Eva's arm and leading her over
to the bench, still hoping for crumbs to feed his magnificent obsession.

Eva sat down and looked up at Nicky, thinking she would have
known him at once though he looked old and somewhat faded for his
years, pale and rather sad. She held out her hand to him, and dismissed
Mr Makepeace in the same instant, waving him off across the lawn with
Daniel, bound for the cemetery or the Café des Arbres, or a little box
room in a Montparnasse back street where David Klein, apprentice
builder, had once worked on his plans for Paul and Helena Duval's
country house.

'So, Nicky,' she said, gazing directly at him, 'how can I help?'

He seemed confused, and momentarily taken aback, as though he
hadn't bargained for this straightforward invitation, and then, needing
only the slightest encouragement, proceeded to offer, with much emotion and evident pain, the turmoil of his private life, a halting, harrowing story of three broken marriages and a suicide.

Eva listened with sorrow and with sympathy, interjecting to cheer
him and console, questioning him gently about his mother and his sons,
and finally, when he seemed dangerously close to tears, putting her
hand over his and stroking it gently, a silent gesture of support.

'You have not condemned me,' he said at last. 'I thank you for that
. . . But now, Eva, I come to the true purpose of my visit. I have
something to show you.'

He fumbled in his wallet and produced a carefully folded piece of
paper, a photograph cut from a magazine. He handed it to Eva.

'Does she remind you of anyone?' he asked.

Eva looked down at a pretty young woman with bright blonde hair cut to her neckline and wide emerald eyes, dressed in a stylish black two-piece, staring somewhat haughtily at the camera.

'She's very lovely,' Eva said, imagining that Nicky must be about to embark on a fourth marriage, and with a girl young enough to be his daughter. 'Who is she?'

'Her name is Beth Carlisle. She's English. A TV presenter, very talented and very successful. Quite famous, too. Have you heard of her?'

'I'm sorry,' said Eva, mystified, 'I'm afraid I haven't.'

He gestured at the photograph again, insisting that she look more closely.

'Doesn't she remind you of my mother?' he asked eventually. 'Harold Brannen's bastard daughter, Harriet Howard as she was when she arrived on your doorstep in the Hollywood hills all those years ago?'

Eva looked at the picture again, remembering, trying to work it out, seeing that Nicky needed her reassurance and her understanding, wondering what it was that he wanted her to know.

And then something about the expression of the young woman in the photograph – a certain self-possession, a hint of defiance, perhaps, a wilful refusal to embrace unhappy fate – hit a sudden chord. Indeed, she did resemble Harriet Howard, and yes, in the tilt of her head and her challenging smile, there was something of Harold Brannen, too . . .

Eva, understanding, handed the magazine cutting back to Nicky. 'Carlisle,' she said steadily. 'Yes, of course. Now I remember that name. Eleanor Carlisle, formerly Martineau . . .'

'Did you know she was murdered? Killed by a jealous lover?'

'Yes, I did . . . A friend of hers wrote to tell me. It was terribly tragic.'

Nicky took the photograph from her, staring at it intently.

'This is Ellie's elder daughter,' he said at last. 'Her daughter . . . and mine . . . But you guessed that at the time, didn't you, Eva? Or did Ellie tell you the truth herself? Please answer me. I need to know . . .'

She closed her eyes and seemed to see the past restored. A summer's eve at home, the magnificent home she had shared for so many years with David, built with his own hands, not a mile from Paul and Helena's house where they'd so fortuitously come to rest after their flight from Paris . . . The home where Matthew, her son, had been raised after the war, the home from which David had relaunched the Klein family firm, the home from which Blanche and Edouard Duval were married . . . Deep in the heart of the Toulouse countryside, stars like fairy lights

in the midnight blue that evening, crickets warbling on the terrace, lilac
hanging heavy on the air . . .

And from the bedroom above the sitting room, a baby screaming.

'What on earth is Blanche doing with that child?' enquired Helena,
who'd come to visit her newborn grandson and received a somewhat
testy welcome from her daughter-in-law. 'Should we go and see? I think
we should . . .'

Eva, concerned for Blanche and her new baby but doubting the wisdom of two doting grandmothers rushing upstairs with advice, shook
her head.

'He's hungry, that's all. Listen, he's stopped! She must be feeding him.'

But Blanche was not feeding, and a moment later she stormed into
the sitting room, the infant wakeful but mercifully quiet in her arms,
demanding to know where her husband might be.

'He's out,' Eva said apologetically. 'They've all gone down to the café
in the village. Edouard and Matthew, Nicky and Ellie . . .'

'Right!' cried Blanche in a rage. 'I'm going to find Edouard at once!
This is his baby too!'

Eva and Helena exchanged a wary glance, Eva reflecting unhappily
that since Nicky Howard had arrived from Cambridge with Rhoda's
daughter on his arm, life seemed to have been irretrievably jolted from
its normal placid course.

'Nicky's a bad influence,' Helena said, voicing Eva's thoughts as
Blanche flung out of the room. 'He reminds me of my little brother
Aidan . . . Aidan as a child. Do you remember how awful he was? How
he fought on the schoolroom floor with Anya?'

'I remember,' said Eva, laughing.

'But he grew up,' Helena said. 'And apart from his little lapse with
Harriet, he turned out very well. If he'd been spared, he'd have taken
Nicky in hand. I know he would.'

Privately Eva doubted that Harriet would ever have sanctioned any
such thing, or that Nicky Howard, reared in the best boarding-schools
England could offer and now the toast of its premier university for a
brilliant first novel, could be taken in hand at all, though Ellie Martineau was clearly doing her best.

'Still,' said Helena, 'Nicky did bring your beautiful gold cross . . .
That was very kind of Harriet, wasn't it? To keep track of it all these
years, and buy it back for you? She can't be all bad.'

Eva fingered the Brannen cross, scarcely able to believe that it was
back in her possession after so long, deeply grateful to Harriet, and to
Toby too, who'd written to say how happy he was that the necklet had
finally been returned. No, Harriet was far from being all bad, and perhaps Nicky would prove himself in time.

But his arrival with Ellie Martineau had been a considerable shock, the two of them spilling from an old jalopy into the driveway of the country house, an impossibly glamorous couple, Cambridge students with the world at their feet, smart as paint and knowing it.

He'd introduced her as Lady Rhoda Connaught's daughter, plainly aware of Rhoda's history, or at least some of it, declaring that his mother had told him she'd known Rhoda in Hollywood, though Ellie herself seemed mystified by this.

'There's some mistake,' she laughed to Eva. 'My mother's never been to Hollywood. I asked her, and she categorically denied it . . .'

Eva kept counsel about Rhoda, although she did enquire after Rupert Connaught, remembering his impassioned plea to her in those last, desperate days before the fall of Paris.

'My stepfather is dead,' Ellie replied somewhat tersely. 'He died from food poisoning. Life has been very difficult for my mother since then . . .'

On the matter of her own father, however, Ellie was more forth-coming.

'We found his grave in the Cimitière de Montparnasse . . . I put red roses on it . . . And we also found the bar where he used to drink with his friends. What was that place called, Nicky?'

'The Café des Arbres,' he replied.

'Did you know my father well?' Ellie asked Eva when they were alone together, and Eva did not hesitate in her reply.

'Victor Martineau was a fine man,' she told Ellie, 'and he would have been very proud of you . . .'

David had not been pleased at this unexpected reincarnation of Rhoda in his own home, and could hardly bear to be in the same room.

'Of all the students at Cambridge University,' he'd said acidly, 'your friend Mr Howard has to pick this one.'

'She's not Rhoda,' Eva replied firmly. 'And she's not to blame for anything Rhoda may have done.'

'She looks very much like her,' he retorted.

'Yes . . . and does she look like anyone else, do you think? Victor, perhaps? Rhoda obviously told her he was her father . . .'

David said nothing, simply gathered his plans and his ledgers and retreated to his office in the old barn.

It was perhaps fortunate that the visit coincided with one of his frequent trips to Israel, a trip Eva would normally have made too, but which, in deference to Blanche and baby Daniel, she decided against. Within a day of Ellie's arrival, David was gone and Nicky Howard took over as king of the castle, drinking late into the night with Edouard, captivating the impressionable teenage Matthew, romancing Ellie and infuriating Blanche.

And now, on this balmy starlit night, it seemed that matters had come to a head.

Eva, left alone after Helena's departure, had waited for them all to return, and hearing a car, rushed out anxiously into the drive, hoping to see Blanche and Edouard hand in hand, their baby sleeping peacefully between them.

But instead it was Ellie, all alone in Nicky's old jalopy. She was crying.

'I'm leaving,' she wept, 'I'm leaving first thing in the morning. I don't ever want to see him again . . .'

'My dear girl,' Eva soothed, 'whatever is the matter?'

Ellie, her face red and swollen, her dark chocolate-coloured hair, Rhoda's hair, hanging limply around her shoulders, seemed suddenly much less like her beautiful, cold-hearted mother, more human, much more vulnerable, and as Eva waited for the story, guessing the truth of it before Ellie had so much as begun, she was washed with a great wave of pity for Rhoda's child, divining that Rhoda would prove no help at all.

'I'm not even going to tell Nicky,' Ellie declared through her tears. 'I won't suffer the indignity of seeing him walk away from me . . . You promise you won't tell him?' she added anxiously.

'If that's what you want,' Eva said uncertainly. 'Though I'm inclined to say that a man should take responsibility for his child . . .'

Ellie Martineau stood up, smoothing down the extravagant hair and rubbing her face.

'Nicky will never take responsibility,' she said shakily. 'I saw that tonight for the very first time. I saw it when I looked at Blanche and Edouard with Daniel . . . I saw how different it was for them.'

Eva, only too aware of the recent rows between her daughter and son-in-law, tried gently to suggest that parenthood was seldom without some problems. But Ellie was writing her own script.

'I am a mature responsible person in charge of my own destiny,' she announced to Eva's consternation. 'I live as I choose . . . I live as I choose . . .'

And with that, she disappeared upstairs to her room.

Eva, wondering whether to go after her, was suddenly deflected by the return of Blanche and Edouard, their baby asleep as hoped, she looking triumphant, and he somewhat shamefaced.

'Mama,' implored Blanche, 'will you have Daniel with you tonight? We really do need some time by ourselves . . .'

And in the morning, busy with the baby, his bath, his diapers, the

cradle cap on his little head, all the things Blanche should really have
been doing herself, Eva missed the dawn departure of Ellie Martineau
... And, for a few hours at least, was spared the idle unconcern of
Nicky Howard who'd been seized overnight with the bones of a new
novel, and was already plotting better things to do.

'Grandmama,' said Daniel softly in Eva's ear, 'you have a very special visitor ... I didn't tell you he was coming – I wanted to surprise
you.'

Eva opened her eyes in the sunny sitting room and focused upon her
grandson standing next to a tall, fair-faced young man with wide grey
eyes, hair the colour of corn, and a slow, open smile.

'The vicar of St Cuthbert's!' Daniel declared with evident satisfaction. 'Michael Cameron ... who has very kindly agreed to bury you in
his churchyard! However, I've persuaded him to wait until you're dead,
and I've told him it may be a very long time ...'

'Not so long, I hope,' said Eva laughing. 'But my dear Mr Cameron,
I trust you haven't been summoned to Paris from St Cuthbert's just to
see me! I should be very cross with Daniel if I thought that were the
case.'

'He's here on holiday,' Daniel said, aggrieved. 'I should not imagine,
Grandmama, that your burial rites warranted dragging him away from
the Parochial Church Council or the Mothers' Union.'

Eva, considering this light-hearted remark to be extremely impolite,
glared at Daniel and flashed an apologetic smile at the vicar of St Cuthbert's who fortunately seemed unperturbed by the mockery, and indeed,
somewhat amused.

He'd brought a plan of the churchyard for her to see, pointing out
the plots occupied by Blanche and Matthew Brannen, suggesting that
Eva could be near them if she wished.

'There's another grave,' Eva said, looking carefully at the map he'd
laid out before her, 'over by the sea wall. We had a new headstone
erected there after the war.'

'You mean Eva Martineau?'

'Yes ... Did my grandson tell you the story?'

'Of course I told him, Grandmama,' Daniel said. 'This is one of the
few bits of our fascinating family history that you allow us to publish!
The poor man probably won't feel the same way about his bedroom now
he knows there was an impromptu Caesarean section right where he lays
his head each night ...'

This time it was Michael Cameron who appeared discomfited, glancing quickly at Eva to assess whether this comment were as indelicate as

it sounded, relaxing only when he saw her to be well used to her grandson's levity.

'Martineau . . .' he said. 'That's an unusual name. I knew someone of that name . . . At least, that was her maiden name.'

'They were a large family,' Daniel informed him. 'Philippe Martineau had seven brothers and six sisters. Eva was the youngest . . . There are still Martineaus all over Paris. Do we know any of them, Grandmama?'

'No,' said Eva, thinking in that moment of Victor and the grave in the Cimitière de Montparnasse, the headstone bearing the name of David Klein which Davy himself had removed after the war, and the replacement stone which recorded Victor's death. 'It's all so very long ago now . . .'

'Unfortunately, there's a shortage of space by the sea wall,' Michael Cameron said, pointing out the site on his plan, 'though we have been thinking of tidying it up a bit . . . Maybe cutting down the laurel bush . . .'

'The old laurel bush? Is it still there? Oh no, it shouldn't be cut down. It must be over a hundred years old.'

'Nearly as old as you, Grandmama!'

An interesting discussion then ensued about churchyards and their place in the ecology of the English countryside, a discussion which came to an end with Daniel's abrupt departure.

'Must go,' he announced suddenly, jumping to his feet and kissing Eva on the cheek. 'Call on me tomorrow, Michael, if you're free . . . I'll be on my own then,' he added.

Eva, divining the significance of this at once, waved him goodbye and then turned to the vicar of St Cuthbert's.

'So,' she said. 'Have you met Daniel's girlfriend?'

'Almost,' he replied, catching her eye, assessing her question and judging that he might speak freely. 'I'm afraid I embarrassed him by turning up at his apartment unannounced. But I didn't meet his girlfriend. She was still in bed.'

'I don't suppose, Mr Cameron, that you preach any sermons about adultery these days?'

He smiled.

'I would never condone adultery,' he said slowly. 'It causes too much pain . . . However, I'm also very mindful of another sin, the sin of moral self-righteousness – a sin, I must confess, that I've been guilty of myself. I fear a sermon on adultery from an unmarried clergyman would attract the selfsame charge . . .'

'You're a bachelor, Mr Cameron?'

She had imagined him to be married, seeing in him that easiness and warmth with women which a happy marriage calls forth, but she was mistaken.

'I'm a widower,' he said, looking away from her and out across the lawn where Mr Jon Makepeace sat in earnest conversation with Toby.

Eva looked out at the lawn too, wondering what Toby was saying now he'd agreed to be quoted in Mr Makepeace's book, thinking back, in a sudden, unexpected flash of sorrow, to their wedding in Paris so many years ago, how happy and hopeful he'd been, and how empty her own heart in the belief that she'd lost David for ever.

'Moral self-righteousness was my sin,' she heard herself say to Michael Cameron. 'It prevented me marrying the right person, at least in the beginning . . . And it also led me to marry someone who should only ever have been a friend . . .'

He looked back at her then.

'Me too,' he said quietly.

For his birthday, Toby insisted upon lunch at the Café des Arbres, sitting Eva down on the terrace in the noonday sunshine and ordering two glasses of champagne.

'Here's to being alive!' he said, lifting his glass to hers. 'I've decided I rather enjoy it. How about you?'

'Oh, yes!' she smiled. 'Although I don't want to be around too much longer . . . I don't want to be the last apple on the tree.'

He ordered *tarte l'oignon* and little bowls of radicchio lettuce, encouraging her to eat and entertaining her with tales of his grandson, who'd set out to bicycle from Alaska to Tierra del Fuego, but alas, had fallen in love on the banks of the Panama Canal.

'Now, Eva, I have a confession to make,' he said when they'd arrived at the coffee and were preparing to leave. 'Our friend the biographer, Mr Makepeace . . . He thinks we're still married, and I haven't disillusioned him. I hope you don't mind.'

'I don't mind,' she said. 'It seems simpler than the truth,' and indeed it did, for the process by which she and Toby, widowed within a month of each other five years ago, had come together for this final blessed *rapprochement* seemed imbued with a magical, almost divinely inspired symmetry, as though the great puppet-maker were indeed pulling the strings, or perhaps simply responding to a heartfelt, lonely prayer.

Toby hesitated.

'I'm starting to feel rather sorry for Mr Makepeace,' he said at last. 'He does seem to have it all so very wrong . . . We should tell him about Rhoda, you know. How she cut the brakes on Will's Bugatti . . . The truth about David . . .'

'Oh, I don't know,' said Eva. 'It's hard to see the point.'

'You're just jealous,' he said, teasing. 'All that stuff from Moira Sheen about him being the world's greatest lover . . .'

'No,' she said, laughing. 'No, I'm not.'

'Randy Makepeace, then . . . You're remembering what an old miser he was, how he sat in that seat right over there and told us all he'd cheated his concierge out of a month's rent.'

'No, no,' Eva protested. 'The poor man can't be blamed for his grandfather's shortcomings.'

'That's not all he can't be blamed for . . .'

Toby finished his coffee and stood up.

'There's something else I should tell you about Mr Makepeace,' he said, helping Eva to her feet and guiding her down the terrace steps. 'Unfortunately, a very predictable fate has befallen him . . . Here he is, a handsome young American all alone in Paris, needing a friend and a confidante, not to say a bedmate . . .'

Eva stopped in her stately progress out of the Café des Arbres and grabbed Toby's arm, looking up at him unhappily, sensing what was to come next.

'I'm afraid so, Eva. It seems Mr Makepeace is a pretty gullible kind of guy all round . . . Not only has he completely failed to uncover the truth about David Klein . . . He's fallen hook, line and sinker for your grandson's wife.'

Eva rapidly became very fond of the vicar of St Cuthbert's, finding in him an unhurried attentiveness, a calm, unobtrusive concern for all who crossed his path and might benefit from his care, a lively, imaginative grasp of theology and a willingness to be challenged on the more intractable tenets of the Christian faith.

'Do you believe in the resurrection of the dead?' she asked him squarely as they walked together in the convent garden. Blanche had spent the morning escorting him around the hospice, explaining her work, introducing him to some of her patients, asking him to spend a little time with Susannah Lamont, hoping he might draw on a tenuous connection, the fact that Susannah's great-great-aunt was buried in St Cuthbert's churchyard.

'I'm inclined to agree with Blanche,' he now said to Eva. 'It's the resurrection of the living that counts.'

'Oh come, Michael, I shan't let you off that lightly . . . You're right, of course, and yet the dead are always with us. They speak to us in dreams, they reach out for our understanding. We long to hold them in our arms once more. Or is it only the elderly who feel this way? And is it all an illusion?'

She was testing him, pushing him gently towards a declaration about his own tragedy, calling forth a confidence, a response to her friendship which he'd seemed about to offer earlier, but which since seemed to have failed him.

'I believe in the resurrection of Jesus,' he said slowly, 'because it seems to me illogical to believe otherwise . . . There would have been no Church without the resurrection, and if we fudge this central fact, then I have to agree with St Paul – our gospel is null and void.'

They sat down together on the bench by the old gate, looking back at the elegant sandstone mansion, no longer a convent as such since the number of Sisters had dropped so dramatically, but now a much-lauded institution caring for the victims of AIDS, launched by the esteemed Dr Blanche Duval and endowed with her father's money.

'This is such a beautiful place,' Michael said. 'All these years I've been coming to Paris and I never knew it was here . . .'

'Do you always take your holidays in Paris?' she asked him.

'My father had an apartment here and he left it to me in his will . . . I like to visit when I can.'

'And what does a bachelor clergyman do all by himself in Paris?' Eva heard herself enquire, a question that was just a little impertinent, and which caught him off guard.

'You sound like my mother,' he said archly.

'Do I?' said Eva apologetically, seeing at once that the comparison wasn't flattering. 'I'm sorry. I merely wondered if you had friends here?'

In truth she wondered if he had a girlfriend, but if he had, he didn't mean to tell her just yet.

'Sometimes I bring my daughter and my nieces,' he said. 'We go to Euro-Disney.'

'That must be fun,' Eva said doubtfully.

Then they were joined by Blanche, who wished to show Michael a folder of her patients' paintings and poems, and as they sat together discussing the work, Mr Jon Makepeace, the dogged biographer, strolled on to the lawn with a pretty companion who gazed up at him admiringly, tossing her long dark pigtail over her shoulder.

'Ah,' said Blanche, staring at them hard, 'Mr Makepeace and Genevieve . . . Have you met my son's wife, Michael?'

'Yes . . . I have. She's quite a character,' he said carefully.

'She's certainly that. Did she tell you how happy she is that her husband finally left her, and what a wonderful time she's having without him?'

He glanced at her and smiled uneasily.

'I assumed she must be joking,' he said.

'Only half joking,' Blanche replied. 'She has his house and his bank account, and he's on call for her children. And now she's free to do as she pleases, although as far as I can see, she always did that anyway . . . A happy ending, you may think, Michael – two people who should never have married in the first place are finally calling it a day. Isn't that so, Mama?'

'Now then, Blanche,' said Eva uncomfortably, 'don't appeal to me. They must be left to sort it out for themselves. We can't interfere . . .'

They all looked across at Genevieve, who had linked arms with Mr Makepeace and seemed to be much amused by some comment he had made, but he suddenly saw them watching and disentangled himself, offering an awkward wave.

Blanche stood up.

'Personally, I think a little interference is overdue,' she muttered. 'If Genny finds out her husband has another woman, then we'll all know about it . . . She may not want him herself, but she certainly won't let anyone else have him. Those who have Daniel's confidence should be pointing this out.'

She left them then, striding back across the lawn and into the house, breezing past her daughter-in-law and the intrepid biographer without so much as a glance, leaving Eva to stare after her unhappily.

'I think she means us,' Michael said.

'Then it will have to be you,' Eva replied quietly. 'I have tried to advise my grandson in the past, but this time I intend to keep my own counsel. It's become quite clear to me that these two are inextricably entwined. They will never set each other free. It's Daniel's girlfriend we should really be worrying about.'

'He doesn't seem to think so,' Michael said slowly. 'He describes her as unassailable. Impossible to hurt.'

'Good heavens!' said Eva, startled by such an unlikely idea. 'Then she must be a very unhappy girl. Who is she? Has he told you?'

Michael shook his head.

'He's playing his cards very close. I suspect she may be quite well known – an actress, perhaps. She seems to spend a lot of time at his editing suite.'

'And can you imagine that she won't be upset when Daniel decides to return to his wife, as he undoubtedly will?'

'I really couldn't say . . . But I suspect it's only this belief that makes the whole thing possible for Dan. He wouldn't be with her if he thought he might muck up her life. As it is, he reckons she's tougher than any of them.'

'Let's hope he's right,' Eva muttered.

And then, because there seemed nothing more to be said about the vexed situation between Genevieve, Daniel and his unknown girlfriend, they fell once more to matters theological.

'Will the dead live again?' she asked him.

'If we partake of the life and death of Jesus, then yes, it necessarily follows that we shall rise with him . . .'

'At the Omega moment,' she asked him, 'when the universe falls in upon itself and we discover that we are the very stuff of stars?'

He looked down at her in some surprise, not expecting this. 'You're a scientist, Eva,' he smiled, 'a scientist and a theologian.'

'No,' she laughed. 'Just an old woman with an enquiring mind.'

'The very stuff of stars,' he repeated slowly. 'I've had that intuition myself, walking along the shoreline late at night, the North Sea whipping against the spur and the heavens ablaze with light . . .'

Eva drew in her breath, for as he spoke she saw again the great sweep of white sand and the glistening rocks in St Cuthbert's Bay, the bank of golden poppies, the glittering church spire, the sturdy stone walls of the vicarage and the tangled graveyard where her loved ones lay . . . How dear, how familiar it all seemed, and how distant . . .

'I want to go back, Michael,' she said to him suddenly, 'I want to go back to St Cuthbert's one last time before I die.'

'Then I'll be very happy to escort you,' he replied at once. 'We can leave whenever you wish.'

Chapter Twenty-nine

Prayer is the means by which the Lord's work is done. We may not know how it is achieved, nor even, sometimes, the way in which it has been answered. But right prayer, the prayer that hopes to know the will of God, the prayer that seeks reconciliation and mercy, can never be denied. It will always flower and bear fruit.

The Journals of Eva Delamere, edited by Blanche Duval

They stood on the tip of the spur overlooking the bay, she leaning heavily upon him, and it was all as it had ever been, as she remembered it now with a strange sense of present and past merging into one infinite moment, on the day of Matthew Brannen's funeral.

The light from the east was palest pink, the faint rosy hue of hyacinths, the colour of eggshells, and the sky stretched in a vast silver dome across the steely water, the distant islands seeming to float in the foam, as though they'd finally broken free of the deep sea bed, the white roll of the dunes, tipped with the fading green of the poppies, shimmering in the autumn sun.

'The rock poppies are done,' she murmured. 'You need to be here in summer or spring to see them at their best . . .'

'They were beautiful this year,' he told her. 'They always are. Amazing that flowers should bloom so profusely in such dry sandy soil.'

She turned on his arm to gaze back towards the vicarage and the church, almost believing that if she were to close her eyes and open them again, she might see the young Harold Brannen saddling the old black mare and trotting round to the cobbled courtyard, about some parish mission for his father or off to pay court to Lizzie Howard at the Dolphin Inn.

'I once said I'd never come back,' she whispered, wondering now at the folly of this youthful vow. 'But then, after many years, I felt called to return . . . And it was here, beneath the loving eye of St Cuthbert, that my life was turned around. A resurrection, Michael.'

He smiled, and nodded.

'And you came back again after the war? To the lodge cottage . . . with David?'

'Yes . . . but not as often as we would have liked. We were always so busy. He spent much of his time in Israel . . . making the wilderness flower. I used to think he must be building Tel Aviv all by himself.'

Michael laughed.

'And nobody ever realised who he was?'

'Nobody was remotely interested,' she said. 'There was a minor fuss at the beginning of the war, when it was thought he had been shot. And some of the people he'd helped in Germany spoke up about what he'd done . . . But after the war he was quickly forgotten. It's only in the last few years, and oddly enough, since his death, that he's become a hero.'

A sudden breeze from the sea rustled the grass at their feet and she shivered, an involuntary tremor which he registered at once, urging her back to his car so that he might drive her the final half-mile to the vicarage.

'This is a most extravagant vehicle for a country parson,' she teased him, settling into the soft, leather-scented interior of his unlikely limousine. 'I hardly imagined that I should return to St Cuthbert's in such style.'

'Another legacy from my father . . . You're right, of course,' he smiled, 'it's embarrassing. I should sell it, but somehow I just can't. I have a sentimental attachment to this car.'

She glanced at him, thinking that for all their easy intimacy, a friendship rooted in mutual vision and belief, he still had not talked about his family background, his wife nor, indeed, his sentimental attachments.

She was about to pursue the matter when all such thoughts were suddenly driven from her mind by a vision unfolding through the car's windscreen.

Down on the shore among the dinghies and the beached yachts, a small fair-haired girl of seven or so ran laughing from a gaggle of boisterous boys, three wiry lads in cut-off jeans who chased her among the boats and away into the dunes, leaping over lobster pots, tripping and rolling in the sand. Herself. The ghost of her childhood skipping with her brothers in an everlasting dance of joy . . .

'Those children . . .' she said in a cracked whisper, wondering if her eyes deceived her. 'Can you see them?'

He looked out of the window.

'My daughter, Katie,' he said, 'and my housekeeper's sons. Little blighters. I'm always telling them to stay away from those lobster pots.'

She laughed then, relieved that the spirits had taken solid form, amused at the coincidence offered by one little girl and three growing boys, consoled by what had seemed, for one brief moment out of time, a glimpse, a blessed foreshadowing, of eternity.

He insisted that she stay at the vicarage to be attended by his house-keeper, and that she take his own bedroom, the room where she'd been born on a wild Easter's Eve in 1908, the room where she had nursed the dying Matthew Brannen and poured out her heart to her journal . . .

And so she lay down to sleep in a luxurious antique bed, yet another gift, she was told, from Michael's late father, and awoke the next morning to the view of the islands and St Cuthbert's ruined tower, still standing, indeed no more battered than when she'd last seen it five years ago, on the bleak spring day she'd grasped Blanche's hand and watched Daniel thrust David's funeral ashes on to the restless winds of the bay.

A cautious knock at the bedroom door interrupted these meditations.

'Daddy asks if you'd like coffee or tea?'

Katie Cameron was remarkably like her father, a golden-haired seven-year-old with wide grey eyes and a slow, serious smile, keen to befriend, quick to assess, and they walked down to breakfast as companions, drawing on that intuitive understanding which so often unites the very young and the very old, exchanging confidences and planning their day.

'I should like you to show me all your special places,' Eva said. 'And then I'll show you where I used to play when I was a little girl . . .'

So it was that after Eva had visited all the graves, Matthew and Blanche Brannen, Eva Martineau and Isabel Lamont, they came to the old laurel bush behind the church where she had hidden on the day her beloved brother Harold left for France.

'Now see,' she said to Katie. 'If you lift these branches here, you'll find a big green cave.'

The child disappeared inside, delighted with this discovery, exclaiming in excitement, and when Eva saw Michael approaching across the churchyard, she counselled immediate silence so that Katie might jump out and surprise him.

This was a great success, all of them laughing, Katie dancing around the laurel bush and making her father promise he'd tell no one else its secret.

'I shall only bring my very best friends here,' she declared. 'People I like very much . . .'

Then suddenly she was gone, spying the boys down upon the beach, racing through the churchyard, leaping over the tilting crosses and skirting the weatherbeaten angels, calling for her friends.

'She's lovely,' Eva said sincerely. 'A special child.'

'Yes,' he replied. 'My joy. My salvation.'

Eva waited, but he offered no expansion on this and so they walked slowly through the churchyard towards the sea wall, sitting down upon it to watch the children dodging the waves at the water's edge.

'It's not easy,' Eva said, 'for a man to bring up a young daughter alone. Although, I must say, my own father made an excellent job of it.'

'I'm lucky,' Michael said. 'I've got Lucy, who's an excellent surrogate mother. Then there's Frances, my brother's wife, and Fiona, my wife's sister, and Sarah, a very good friend . . . And Emily, of course.'

She glanced at him quickly. In the fleeting visit Emily had made to the vicarage after Eva's arrival, she had divined a close friendship between the vicar of St Cuthbert's and Aidan Forster's granddaughter. A close friendship which, nevertheless, didn't seem quite close enough.

'How old was Katie when your wife died?' she asked him now.

'Just two.'

'And how did it happen?'

'We were on holiday in Greece. My wife drowned in the hotel pool in the middle of the night . . .'

'That must have been terribly hard.'

'Young children are so resilient. Katie recovered amazingly quickly. A few weeks of sleepless nights, then she just seemed to get over it.'

'No, Michael . . . I meant hard for you . . .'

He stood up from the sea wall, waving at the scurrying children who were now heading for the lobster pots again, inviting Eva to take his arm and walk along the firm sand, asking if she were warm, or in need of her shawl.

Then at last he began to tell her what she always knew he would.

'It was very hard for me,' he said slowly as they walked. 'Much harder than most people realised . . . My wife was about to leave me when she died. She meant to go home to her parents and take Katie with her. The holiday was a final desperate attempt to save our marriage, doomed from the night we arrived . . .'

He hesitated.

'The terrible truth is that her death released me. I would have been a divorced priest with my child taken from me . . . As it is, I'm the brave widower, nobly raising his daughter alone.'

Eva considered this unhappy tale in silence, seeing that such a death dealt a double blow – not only the shock of the tragedy, but also the guilt that in a scrupulous heart accompanies any hint of hypocrisy, confusing, compounding the grief.

'Michael, this is very sad,' she said at last; 'a heavy burden to bear . . . But you can't punish yourself for ever. As a Christian you must believe that whatever the rights and wrongs of your marriage, you have been forgiven.'

They had reached the water's edge and he began to pick pebbles from the shore, skimming them across the glittering water, making them dip and bounce between the waves.

'I know I'm forgiven,' he said steadily. 'That's never been my problem. My marriage was a complete disaster from the wedding night onwards, but it wasn't all my fault. Some, but not all . . . I take a rational view of what happened. We were hopelessly wrong for each other. It never stood a chance.'

He was throwing his pebbles ever more energetically across the waves, arcing them into the sun so that they glinted as they fell, rough diamonds returning to their watery mine.

'The night she died,' he said flatly, 'we had a terrible row. She stormed out of our hotel room, and I went to bed – I should have gone after her, of course, except that I couldn't leave Katie . . . Next thing I knew, the manager was banging on the bedroom door. There was some evidence that she hit her head when she dived into the pool, and also a suggestion that she'd been drinking, although she wasn't drunk . . . But nobody saw what happened, so I've never really known . . . I spent a long time thinking it was my fault. But of course, it wasn't. It was just an accident. I accept that now.'

Eva listened in sorrowful silence, seeing that this tragic event had surely clipped and constrained his emotional life, blighting his hopes and undermining his confidence. But still she sensed this wasn't all.

'Well then, Michael,' she said at last, thinking they might as well get to the heart of the matter, 'if you don't blame yourself for the failure of your marriage, and you don't blame yourself for your wife's death, then what exactly is your problem?'

He threw one final pebble, an overweight, misshapen stone which hit the waves with an inelegant splash. Then he stuck his hands into his pockets and stared out to sea.

'My problem,' he said quietly, 'is that I've always loved somebody else.'

Next day Emily Forster took Eva to the Retreat, sitting her down with tea in the vast conservatory overlooking the bay, and then on to the lodge cottage, stuffy and unused these past few years, yet still charming and serene.

'I wish I could have seen the bluebells,' Eva said, thinking of that golden time before the war, the weeks she had spent here with David, the summer idyll which later assumed all the magic of a honeymoon, even though they were not then married. 'I'm here at the wrong time of year,' she said to Emily, 'I should have waited until spring . . .'

And then, in an odd, becalming, intuitive vision, Eva suddenly saw that she would indeed be back at St Cuthbert's in the spring, lying in the sheltered lea of the churchyard's seaward wall . . .

But this wasn't an insight she felt she could share, and so, as Emily wrestled with the central heating boiler, trying to warm the cold bones of the cottage, they talked of other matters: Emily's grandmother, Greta, still alive and living with her son in the South, Emily's role at the Retreat, the job she'd left behind in London in order to rediscover her Northumbrian roots, the next stage of her career, which would surely take her back to the city.

'Michael will miss you,' Eva said.

'I'll miss him too . . . but it's time to move on.'

She hesitated.

'He talked to you yesterday, didn't he? About his wife? And his grand obsession with another woman?'

'His grand obsession?' Eva repeated dubiously. 'Is that what it is?'

Emily administered a vicious kick to the boiler, goading it into life, pulling determinedly at knobs and switches, intent on response.

'That's what it is,' she said crisply. 'He hasn't seen her in thirteen years, not once since the day they broke up, but he can't let her go. He's a wonderful, warm and very wise parish priest . . . He's there for anyone who needs him. But his own emotional life is frozen. He will never love anyone else.'

They sat in silence for a moment, considering this dramatic prospect, listening to the boiler's vociferous complaints, watching a seagull swoop on to the cottage lawn and forage among the grass.

'This sounds very serious,' Eva said at last.

'Yes. And it's not getting any better. She's a TV star. Very successful, very glamorous. Her face is everywhere. He couldn't forget her if he wanted to, and of course, he doesn't . . . So he watches every programme she makes, as well as all the bloody repeats, and he buys every newspaper, every magazine, that carries some small item about her . . .'

Emily stood up and began to pace around the kitchen, clearly agitated.

'Other men keep *Playboy* in the bottom drawer,' she said furiously, 'but he has *Radio Times* and bloody *Woman's Own!*'

They both laughed then, the tension lifting, and Emily reached out for Eva's hand.

'Sorry to go on,' she said, 'but it gets a bit frustrating.'

'I can imagine,' Eva replied solemnly, considerably surprised at these revelations and reflecting that the ways of the human heart were infinitely astonishing. 'But I can't believe a man like Michael lacks the ability to recover from a failed teenage romance . . .'

'There's rather more to it than that,' Emily said, sitting down again. 'They were engaged, and she became pregnant. Effectively, he ditched her. There were mitigating circumstances – you'd have to meet his bloody mother to see just how mitigating – but even so, the fact remains. He ditched her. He's never forgiven himself, and now, all this time later, he still can't quite believe he lost her.'

'This,' said Eva unhappily, 'is a very sad tale.'

'It's a terrible tale. And it gets worse. In the middle of it all her mother was murdered. Her sister went barmy, her father turned up and told her he wasn't her father after all, and she had no one . . .'

Emily looked down, her anger gone and in its place a genuine sorrow.

'She went away and had the baby all by herself. Then she arranged an adoption . . . I look at her now on the TV screen, I think of what she went through, and I'm full of respect. She's a survivor. In grand style.'

Eva nodded, thinking suddenly of Daniel and Genevieve and another unplanned pregnancy, the baby that had become her beloved great-granddaughter, of betrayals and broken promises, of thwarted love, blighted passion and regret.

And it seemed to her in that moment, sitting in the little lodge cottage where her own blessed and faithful marriage had begun so long ago, that for all her mistakes and early foolish pride, a benevolent destiny had somehow brought her through, a destiny which took hold of her life only on the day when, arriving at Miss Lamont's house after the return from Hollywood, she had bounded along the beach to the vicarage, and falling into the church, had begun to pray . . . *Father in Heaven, forgive me . . . Turn my life around . . . Give me courage, and give me hope . . . Show me your way.*

'Well now,' she said to Emily. 'Something must be done.'

'About Michael? It's hard to see what. He's had several attempts to beat it, including some heavy-duty spiritual counselling. Now he's resigned to it. It's just something he has to live with . . . something which will keep him single for ever.'

Emily suddenly scrabbled in her bag for a handkerchief, dabbing her eyes and blowing her nose vigorously. Then she smiled at Eva.

'Don't think badly of him,' she said. 'He has never misled me, nor given me cause to hope . . . But, of course, like any woman in love, I thought I'd be the one to make the difference.'

Eva took her hand and squeezed it hard, sorry for them all, for Emily and Michael, for Daniel and Genevieve, for the unknown TV star . . .

'He needs to see her again,' Eva said. 'If only to ask her forgiveness.'

'That won't happen. He still visits her sister, but in all this time he's never even come close to meeting up with her . . . To be honest, I don't know if he could handle it. He'd probably burst into tears. And anyway, why should she agree to see him? If I were her I'd tell him to . . . Well, let's just say I wouldn't be very polite.'

'Nevertheless,' said Eva, 'he needs to see her again. Some way must be found . . . We must pray for them both. Pray for a way . . .'

She patted Emily's hand.

'Enough about Michael,' she said softly. 'What about you, Emily? Can you leave St Cuthbert's without too much regret and begin again?'

Emily sniffed into her handkerchief.

'Yes,' she said firmly, 'I can. I must. I've already spent far too long living in the shadow of Beth Carlisle.'

She found herself looking back, a summer holiday in the little lodge cottage, just herself, David and young Daniel, the two of them messing about with cine-cameras, producing an amateur movie on the life of St Cuthbert, recruiting a handful of bemused fisher lads to maraud across the shoreline.

'Eleanor Carlisle,' said David, waving a letter at Eva across the breakfast table, 'wishes to see me. That's Carlisle, formerly Martineau . . . You'll have to deal with it. I'm far too busy with Daniel's film.'

'Grandmama, will you play an Anglo-Saxon maiden?' her grandson implored. 'We've got enough Vikings, but we haven't got any victims . . .'

'No, I won't,' said Eva, laughing. 'I'm far too old to play an Anglo-Saxon maiden . . . David – I really do think you should see Ellie Martineau. It must have something to do with Rhoda.'

'Yes,' her husband replied firmly, making his position clear, 'it must. Now, Daniel, don't worry about victims. We can suggest the victims . . . We don't need to show them.'

The boy was spreading out his script for his grandfather's inspection, shuffling the papers around the breakfast table, rearranging his scenes and knocking over the marmalade jar.

'Vision, beauty and coherence,' David declared, frowning over the script. 'These are the things the human spirit craves, the things that all true art must seek to show . . .'

'A tall order,' Eva suggested lightly, 'for a home movie.'

But no gentle sarcasm was going to deflect the one-time Hollywood director, nor persuade him that instead of marching along the sands with his grandson, cameras aimed towards the islands and the milky sea, he ought to be entertaining Rhoda's daughter.

And so it was that three days later, when Ellie arrived at St Cuthbert's in a smart little Fiat, announcing Rhoda's recent death and offering a sealed envelope addressed to David, Eva was obliged to welcome her alone.

In the fifteen years since they'd last met, Ellie had grown from a pretty girl into a striking woman, the dark chocolate hair, so very like Rhoda's, cut to her shoulders, swinging around her face as she stepped from the car.

Eva decided to make her confession at once, the truth if not the whole truth.

'I'm sorry my husband isn't here. The fact is that he quarrelled with your mother many years ago . . . He's not inclined to forget it, and he doesn't want to know anything about her now.'

Ellie, far from being put out, appeared to understand and accept this immediately, waving aside Eva's apologies and declaring that she was happy to be visiting such a beautiful place, quite regardless of the outcome of her mission.

'My mother was a very difficult woman,' she said. 'I can well appreciate that he mightn't wish to be reminded. In delivering this letter, I'm performing my final service as a daughter, that's all. I don't mind if he never opens it, and I'm not offended that he doesn't want to see me.'

There were two other items that Ellie had found with the letter, poignant reminders of the long-ago past which hit Eva with an unexpected jolt, plunging her back into events never quite exorcised. One was a photograph of Rhoda dressed in her white silk ballgown standing at the top of the gilt and alabaster staircase in David's Hollywood mansion, Rhoda as she had been on the night Eva first met her, the evening of the party hosted by Rebecca Bernstein.

The other was a pressed flower, a piece of purple bougainvillaea cut from the lush gardens of the hacienda and carefully preserved throughout the years in a piece of gold foil.

Eva fingered the flower, wondering again about the truth of Rhoda's guilt, stemming a sudden rush of tears, remembering all who had been dear to her then – Will Sutton and Christine, Victor and Toby, Harriet and little Nicky Howard . . .

She looked up quickly at Ellie Martineau.

'Your child,' she said suddenly, 'Nicky's child . . .'

'She's fourteen now,' Ellie smiled, 'and she's a great girl! She survived Rhoda's cruel and callous disregard. She's a winner.'

Eva, remembering her fears for Ellie all those years ago, her intuition that Rhoda would hardly prove the loving mother and grandmother-to-be, saw then that in a blessed turn of fortune, or perhaps of Providence, the sins of the fathers, or indeed the mothers, were not inevitably visited unto the next generation . . .

'I have another daughter,' Ellie was saying, 'who's just turned twelve. She was Rhoda's favourite. Sarah could never do anything wrong, whereas Beth was quite often locked in the cupboard under the stairs. Imagine it! A five-year-old locked in the dark for hours at a time. It went on for months and months when I was out at work – I only found out when I was called to see Beth's teacher. She'd been taken into a photographic dark-room at school, and she screamed and screamed . . . I moved my girls away from Rhoda after that . . .'

She hesitated, smiling at Eva, seeming to weigh up what she might say without seeming presumptuous.

'That summer in Toulouse,' she murmured, 'when we arrived just after your grandson was born . . . I thought you were such a wonderful, happy family, all of you living together like that. Everything was so different for Blanche because she had you . . . I was wondering, did she ever go on to qualify as a doctor?'

'She did,' Eva replied. 'Though she never had any more children. Daniel was enough for her, and I must say, he's a bit of a handful. He's here at the moment, in disgrace with his parents for having ducked out of school to go to the cinema . . . He was caught watching a highly unsuitable film.'

Ellie laughed.

'It's not easy, bringing up children. I pride myself on the fact that mine seem to be turning out rather well. They're great friends, and that's very important to me. I can't forget that in truth they're only half-sisters. I would hate them ever to find out . . .'

She looked away from Eva, out into the cottage garden on to the rioting bluebells, away towards the overhung lanes which wound towards the Retreat.

'That's really why I left Sarah's father,' she said at last. 'There were other reasons – good reasons. But at the heart of it was the fact that Ray just couldn't treat them the same.'

'And yet he married you knowing the truth?' Eva enquired carefully.

'He married me after Beth was born . . . I was that shameful thing, an unwed mother. In the early Sixties, that was no joke. You can't imagine

how terrible Rhoda made me feel. It was like a curse! It sounds ridiculous, but I can't bring myself to tell Beth the truth, even now. I told
her I was pregnant when I married Ray, and I've let her believe he's
her father . . . Do you think that's terribly wrong?'

Eva, hardly prepared to be appealed to in such a manner, gave this
careful consideration, seeing suddenly how fortunate she had been in
avoiding any such dilemmas with her own children, Blanche and Matthew, both of them happily and faithfully married for many years,
neither of them having presented anything like the problem that Ellie
had given Rhoda, or the problem Ellie herself would surely face as her
daughter grew up and asked about her father.

'I don't know,' she said honestly. 'But if it's any comfort to you, I
myself spent many years without knowing who my parents were. And
in the end I came to see that it didn't matter in the slightest . . . I was
loved and cherished as a child by a man I believed to be my father.
Through his love he truly became my father . . . Love is the only thing
that counts, and if you love your daughters, then both of them will
flourish no matter what . . .'

This little speech seemed to affect Ellie deeply, for she suddenly
stood up and announced her departure, thanking Eva for her time,
insisting that she would be quite happy to put up at the Black Swan in
Alnwick, enquiring, as though she'd only just thought of it, whether
Eva had ever seen Nicky Howard again, waving aside Eva's repeated
apologies for David's absence.

'Good luck,' said Eva, kissing her goodbye. 'Say hallo to your lovely
daughters from me . . .'

'Oh, I haven't told them anything about this,' Ellie replied. 'Now that
Rhoda's dead and buried, we'd all do best to forget her . . .'

Later that night as they sat by the fireside, when the day's filming
had been dissected and discussed, St Cuthbert's story rewritten, and
Daniel finally persuaded to bed, Eva presented Rhoda's mementoes to
David.

'Who took that photograph?' she asked him, looking again at the
vision of loveliness, the chestnut-haired Lady of Shalott, standing on
the gilt staircase.

'I did,' he said, and tossed the picture into the flames.

He fingered the sealed letter, pausing for a moment before he threw
that, too, into the burning coals.

'It won't tell us anything new,' he said.

Eva, who considered that she knew her husband almost as well as he
knew himself, was nevertheless surprised and deeply perturbed by this
gesture, feeling that Rhoda had been denied any forgiveness, any last
absolution.

'It's not for me to forgive,' he replied when she chided him. 'And that's my final word on Rhoda.'

But it wasn't quite. As they lay in bed that night, Eva could not help but go over all that Ellie had told her, and as she tried to sleep she found herself possessed by one image: Rhoda locking her five-year-old granddaughter in a darkened cupboard under the stairs. And although she knew he wished to hear no more of Rhoda, Eva could not but share this appalling tale.

'What a terrible thing to do to a child! Just think of her, little Beth, her mother at work and her grandmother shutting her away . . .'

There was silence from the other side of the bed, and then at last he spoke.

'Little Beth,' he said, 'should think herself lucky. Rhoda might well have strangled her.'

After church one morning as they walked back through the vicarage garden, Michael opened the old stable where he kept his extravagant motor car, and Eva glimpsed something which quite took her breath away.

Matthew Brannen's old boat, the *Island Star*, lay mouldering in a corner behind the Bentley, a gaping hole in its stern, the lettering all but illegible. Yet it was certainly the *Star*, and Eva could only imagine that it had lain untouched in the stable block all these years.

'I was thinking of renovating it,' Michael said as they inspected the boat. 'And now I certainly shall . . .'

Eva fingered the faded wood of the prow and closed her eyes, taken back to a day when the Great War still raged across the Channel, when Edward Brannen and his sweetheart Helena Forster were guests of honour at a picnic party on St Cuthbert's isle, when she and Anya and baby Harriet Howard had idled their fingers in the cloudy sea while Matthew Brannen pulled at the oars of the *Island Star*.

How odd it seemed to think of Helena as she had been then, the daughter of the great Forster house, remote and so very refined, and to remember Helena, Paul Duval's wife, who had delivered Eva's child on a warm summer's day after the flight from Paris, who had become her friend and her constant companion for so many years in the French countryside . . . Helena who had finally helped to unravel the mystery of Eva's origins. Yes, had it not been for Helena, she would never have learned the truth about her parentage . . . How twisting and tortuous were the byways and the back roads of destiny.

'Can I visit St Cuthbert's isle?' she asked Michael suddenly. 'I would love to go one last time . . .'

'Yes, of course! We'll ask Lucy for a picnic.'

So it was that Eva was handed very gently into a new and pristine dinghy, Michael at the oars, Katie in the stern, the child trailing her hands in the chilly water, grabbing at passing clumps of seaweed and receiving an anxious ticking-off from her father.

And as he rowed, Eva began to entertain Katie with a strange story of embroidered handkerchiefs, all of them hand-made in Paris, and each of them worked with a name in the corner . . .

'Helena Forster, who lived in the big house which became the Retreat, she had one, and her mother too . . . They were brought back from Paris as a special gift by Helena's older brother . . .'

Katie listened with great interest, taking it all in, staring in excitement as one of the handkerchiefs, bearing Eva's own name, was produced for her to see.

'It was only because of the handkerchiefs,' Eva said, 'that the full story finally became known . . .'

Michael had already been given Daniel's version of the story, so now Eva told it just for Katie.

'One night,' she began, 'a pretty lady, an actress called Eva Martineau, went out to dine with her brother Philippe, and his wife Leah . . .

'They went to the Paris house of Leah's brother, Mr Emmanuel Klein . . . And in that house Eva met a young Englishman, the son of Mr Klein's business friend . . .

'He was very charming and very handsome,' Eva told Katie, 'and she fell immediately in love. The young man's name was Ralph Forster.'

By this time they had arrived at the island, and Michael beached the boat, lifting Katie and then Eva herself on to the shore, helping them up on to the causeway, guiding Eva towards the ruined tower as Katie danced at her feet and demanded the rest of the story.

'When Young Ralph returned to England, Eva Martineau found that she was going to have a baby . . . She wrote to him, and he promised to return and marry her. But then, on the morning of his twenty-third birthday, Ralph took a boat out to St Cuthbert's isle and dived from this very tower, not knowing that a freak storm had broken some of the stonework and thrown it down beneath the waves . . .'

Katie, much impressed by this dramatic tale, rushed to the platform at the bottom of the tower and stared into the sea. 'There's bloodstains on the rocks!' she shouted, turning back to Eva. 'You can still see them!'

'That's not blood,' Michael said, laughing but embarrassed. 'That's oil.'

'Well, maybe it's blood,' Eva agreed with Katie. 'You never know.'

'And then what happened?' Katie cried.

'Well that, I'm afraid, was the end of poor Ralph . . . And it was the end of poor Eva Martineau as well. When she heard of his death, she took the boat train from Paris and the Newcastle train to Alnmouth, and then she walked all the way to St Cuthbert's Bay. It was a terrible night – the sand was flying and the waves were high as housetops. She threw herself into the sea, not wanting to live any longer without her dear Ralph . . .'

Michael began to unpack the picnic, glancing from time to time at his two charges, eighty years between them and yet utterly familiar and natural with each other, listener and teller absorbed in the same experience.

'Now here's the nice bit of the story,' Eva said to Katie. 'A little boy who lived in your vicarage saw poor Eva Martineau on the shore, and shouted for a rescue party. She was brought inside the house, and although she died, her baby was saved . . .'

Eva produced the lace handkerchief again, allowing Katie to hold it.

'This was tucked into her petticoats, so everyone knew she was called Eva. And when her baby was born, a little girl, they called her Eva too . . .'

Katie looked at the handkerchief, then looked at Eva, and suddenly uncertain of the story's conclusion, laughed and skipped away to an enticing rock pool, rooting in the clear water for elusive pink shells, displacing large handfuls of sodden sand and depositing them uncomfortably near the picnic.

'That's quite a story,' Michael said to Eva, rescuing the sandwiches and admonishing his daughter.

'I'll never forget the day Helena told me! Of course, she didn't hear the story herself until years afterwards when her father was dying . . . But that's all it is, really. A story. It has no relevance to my life – no bearing on any of the things that subsequently happened to me. I believe, Michael, that we're not the prisoners of history at all. No matter what terrible things have happened in the past, we all have the chance to be free . . .'

He looked away, back towards the glittering shoreline and the distant sweeping dunes, the tiny hump of the vicarage and the needle that was the church spire, suddenly subdued, running his hand through his bright gold hair.

'I know you've been talking to Emily,' he said at last.

'She needed someone to talk to,' Eva replied.

'Yes, I see that . . . But please understand, it's not something anyone can do anything about. And whatever Emily may have led you to believe, my history doesn't blight my life. I function perfectly well. I do my job, I bring up my daughter. It's enough.'

She had upset him, and now she was sorry, but she doubted there was any other way to approach it.

'What would you do,' she asked him gently, 'if someone told you Beth Carlisle was going to walk into the vicarage sitting room?'

The name seemed to stun him for a moment, and he drew his breath in sharply, plainly unsettled.

'I'd probably start smoking again,' he offered, hoping to deflect her, turning round to the picnic basket and beginning to pack away the remains of their tea.

'That won't do,' she reproached him. 'I want a proper answer.'

'She's not going to walk into the vicarage sitting room,' he said curtly. 'That won't happen in a million years! It's unlikely I'll ever see her again, and part of me thinks that's probably for the best. What would she do, anyway? She'd hardly fall into my arms. I let her down very badly, and I can never forget that . . . Neither, I imagine, can she. It would only prove extremely painful.'

'Maybe it would,' Eva agreed. 'But hardly more painful than the situation you find yourself in at the moment.'

He appeared to think this over.

'There was a time,' he muttered, 'when I thought I might ring her up – I even went through her sister's address book, looking for her private number. But the number wasn't there. Sarah hadn't written it down. I took that as a sign . . .'

'Or an excuse?' Eva suggested.

He stood up then and shouted for Katie, making her drop a handful of shells back into the pool, scolding her when she tried to pick them out again, chucking the picnic basket into the boat and pulling the prow away from the rocks, chivvying Eva into her seat, and then striking out in silence for the shore.

Katie, blithely unaware of the changed mood, volunteered to sing Eva a selection of Geordie songs, one of them rather rude for a seven-year-old and yet eliciting no notice, let alone reprimand, from her father.

Eva, unable to stop laughing at Katie's efforts yet feeling very guilty at the intrusion she'd made into Michael's private emotions, found herself, for once, at a loss.

But when they reached the shore at last and he'd pulled the boat up beyond the watermark, Katie dashing away before them to show off her shells at the vicarage, he took Eva's arm and tucked it through his own, guiding her across the shifting sand with his customary concern.

'Sorry,' he said, looking down at her. 'As you see, it still hurts a great deal. I've had a very long time to reflect on it all, and even now I can

hardly bear to look back . . . I was so damnably sure of myself, so possessive, so certain of my right to every last bit of her . . . Then when I
thought she was slipping away from me, I told her it was over. I decided
that if I couldn't have everything, I'd have nothing. I even tried to dress
it up as some kind of noble sacrifice! Can you imagine anything more
arrogant, more perverse? No wonder her mother warned her against
me.'

He grimaced, tightening his grip on Eva's arm as they approached the
dunes.

'The worst thing,' he said quietly, 'has been the shame. After all these
years, I remain deeply ashamed. I loved her, she was having my child.
Yet I allowed myself to be persuaded that my duty lay elsewhere . . .'

He closed his eyes briefly.

'I can't tell you how terrible it was. She just disappeared with someone else. I couldn't reach her, I couldn't even find her . . . I prayed
night and day that somehow I would get her back . . . The prayer was
never answered, although another one was. I prayed she wouldn't have
an abortion, and she didn't. I'm immensely grateful for that consolation.
And very proud of her. She was so brave . . .'

Eva, feeling his distress, said nothing, but took his hand in hers and
held it tight.

'She should have been my wife,' he faltered. 'Every time she's on
TV . . . every time I see her face in a magazine I think it. She
should have been my wife. She should be living with me now – with
our son . . .'

Then, in a visible effort, he brightened.

'But contrary to appearances,' he said, 'I'm not without hope. As a
matter of fact, I do believe I'll see her again, but not until the day my
son comes looking for me . . . I've got no doubt that he will. Her child
won't be content to let his past remain a mystery. He'll find out all
about her – and about me too.'

Eva, thinking of her own past and its long-hidden mystery, wasn't so
sure.

'How do you know Beth will tell him the truth?' she asked gently.

He smiled.

'She put my name on the birth certificate,' he said, looking away
towards the darkening islands. 'I know because I went to St Catherine's
House and looked it up. It's the one thing that's kept me going all these
years . . .'

She lazed in the vicarage garden with Katie and Emily, she was escorted by Michael housekeeper's, Lucy Robson, into Alnwick and

taken to the Black Swan for tea, she visited the war memorial and laid flowers . . . and she went every day to church, sitting in her old pew at the front while Michael said the Mass, listening as he preached from the pulpit where Matthew Brannen had once roused his congregation of farmers and fisherfolk, reflecting that, as David had once said of the Reverend Martin Orde, the vicars of St Cuthbert's seemed to be a special breed.

'What's your favourite text?' she asked him. 'If you could pick only one verse from the whole Bible, which would it be?'

'Ecclesiastes, chapter eleven,' he replied after some thought, 'verse five. "As you do not know how the spirit comes to the bones in the womb of a woman with child, so you do not know the work of God who makes everything".'

'Yes,' she said softly, 'how true . . . We understand the biology of reproduction, and the history of evolution, and yet still we have no idea how the spirit infuses the flesh. Will we ever know, do you think?'

'I think we may,' he replied. 'And when we do, we shall find that science and theology have been talking about the same things all along . . .'

One morning, after Mass, she showed him the Brannen cross, detaching it from her neck and laying it across his palm, a battered but still beautiful artefact, the gift from her father so many years ago.

'It was said to belong to one of St Cuthbert's monks. I doubt that, but nevertheless it's very ancient. And very valuable. Toby was able to pawn it for six months' rent on a very smart piece of real estate in Hollywood!'

She smiled at the memory.

'I made a terrible fuss,' she told him. 'I kicked and screamed and tore off my dress when I found out. Only later did I remember what my father had told me – that it was just a piece of jewellery. It didn't have any magical powers.'

He looked at the cross, turning it over between his fingers, impressed.

'Not magical, perhaps,' he said. 'But it has great power as a symbol, uniting your family across the centuries . . .'

'I've no idea who I'll leave it to,' she laughed, fastening the cross around her neck once more. 'My daughter, I suppose, or Daniel's daughter. My father told me that when the moment came to pass it on, I should know . . .'

And then on the second Sunday morning of her visit, he preached a sermon about Love . . . Love, the fount of all moral insight . . . Love, the empowering agent, transforming lives . . . Love, the mystical source of all that is good and unselfish and true . . .

He read from a poem that she recognised at once.

'All shall be well and
All manner of thing shall be well . . . '

The congregation sat in mute awe, carried on the tide of his persuasion, and Eva, recognising the mark of the exceptional preacher, listened with respect and a peculiar sense of the perfectly known, the utterly familiar, as though Michael Cameron and Matthew Brannen had become one with each other in the pulpit, one with all the vicars of St Cuthbert's, and indeed, the whole Communion of Saints which seemed in that moment to hover in the aisles of the church like playful angels.

After the service, they walked along the beach in companionable silence, her arm in his as was usual, he kicking the stones and the seaweed from her path.

'T. S. Eliot,' she said at last. 'All shall be well . . . He took that line from Julian of Norwich . . . "Little Gidding", isn't it? My husband was an admirer of Eliot . . . despite his peculiar feelings about the Jews.'

And then she was seized by the potent, almost tangible memory of David Klein as she had first seen him, sitting at the table beneath the window at the Café des Arbres, his dark tousled head bent over his poetry book . . . And thinking of this first time, she could not but recall the last, when Daniel had cast the funeral ashes on to the tumultuous waters of St Cuthbert's Bay, and they had wept, Blanche and Edouard and Matthew and his wife, Daniel and all the rest – everyone except Eva herself. She, who'd felt so much grief, so much pain, on these wild northern shores, had not needed to weep at this, the hardest goodbye, for it had seemed to her then that the surging waves and the ashes of his bones and the silvery sky were one integrated element, all of it thrusting towards one glorious resolution, nothing wasted, nothing lost.

And afterwards, Daniel had read in Hebrew from the prayers for the dead, and Matthew had written in the sand: '*We Miss You . . . We Love You . . .*'

'I'm reminded of a sermon my father once preached,' she said pensively to Michael. 'Love is the life-beat of this cruel, unconscious universe . . . Love, only Love, the name which all must speak . . .'

He smiled down at her.

'That's it!' he said. 'Sounds so simple, doesn't it? Makes you wonder why the whole world can't see it . . .'

Chapter Thirty

We shall not be slaves to the pattern, for we are the pattern-makers, free to make and unmake, to laugh or to cry, to live and to die, to rest in peace until the Omega moment dawns . . . And on that day all will be loving, all will be joy . . .

The Journals of Eva Delamere, edited by Blanche Duval

Michael insisted on escorting Eva home to Paris, brushing aside all assurances that she would be well attended on the aeroplane, ignoring her suggestion that as Daniel spent so much time at Orly waiting for his girlfriend, he could surely contrive to pick up his grandmother too.

'I'm coming back to see Susannah,' Michael declared. 'I'm going to invite her to stay at the Retreat . . . It has nothing at all to do with you!'

And of course, Eva was very glad to have him, glad not only to have him manage her luggage and procure her a window seat, but glad to postpone what both of them sensed could only prove the final parting.

'I doubt that Susannah will leave Paris,' Eva told him. 'She seems to need Blanche on hand to soothe her fears.'

Michael nodded.

'Your daughter is a very gifted doctor,' he said.

'I believe she is. She works extremely hard, and though she deals each day with the most distressing deaths, she's never downhearted or depressed.'

Eva smiled.

'Faith, you see, Michael . . . I brought up my children in the Jewish faith and the Christian faith, and I persuaded them there was no

contradiction in being both Christian and Jew . . . It has given them
strength and breadth of vision.'

Alas, when they arrived back at the Divine Faith convent, it was to
discover Blanche's breadth of vision reduced to the spectacle of her
son's ailing marriage, and Eva, meeting her daughter as she slammed
into her office to telephone Daniel's apartment, was forced to a rueful
reminder that pride invariably precedes a fall.

'There's been a heck of a racket,' Toby told her, delighted to see her
back, welcoming her with a kiss and a small glass of cognac. 'Blanche
suddenly decided she'd had enough. She tore into Genevieve and ordered poor old Jon Makepeace off the premises . . . Now, I'm afraid, it's
your grandson for the high jump.'

Eva determined to stay out of it, urging Michael away to find Susannah Lamont and then hurrying back to the little sitting room where
Toby had prepared tea, locking the door behind her.

'If Daniel comes,' she told Toby, 'tell him I'm asleep.'

But it wasn't Daniel who eventually came hammering upon the sitting-
room door, weeping and trembling and asking to speak with Eva, begging her intervention and pleading for comfort. It was Genevieve.

Toby let her in, and Eva immediately abandoned all impartiality,
taking her into her arms and stroking her hair, waving Toby out of the
door, clucking and soothing, anxious only to console.

At last Genevieve dried her tears.

'How dare Blanche speak to me like that?' she demanded shakily.

'Well, dear, Blanche is trying to run a hospital. I expect she can do
without all these little diversions . . . People who shouldn't really be
in the convent at all. Not you, of course, but certainly Mr Makepeace.'

'I'm here,' Genevieve said tremulously, ignoring this careful reference to David Klein's biographer, 'because it's the only place I'm likely
to bump into my husband. Oh yes, he comes to see the children. But
he barely speaks to me. And I'm not allowed to go to his apartment.
It seems I'm not even allowed at the editing suite now! I went the
other day, and the door was locked. I knew he was there, but I couldn't
get in.'

Eva, wondering uneasily what Daniel might be doing behind the
locked doors of his editing suite, rushed on to reassure as best she
could, suggesting gently that if Genevieve were to stay faithful to her
husband, there might be some hope of reconciliation.

'He doesn't care,' she said, the tears beginning again. 'I could
sleep with the Pope, and he wouldn't care. He only cares about making
films . . .'

Eva nodded unhappily. She didn't accept that her grandson cared only for making films, but nevertheless she understood the basis of the charge.

'Perhaps if you were to take a little more interest?' she began tentatively, but this mild suggestion only served to send Genevieve into a rage, provoking a furious onslaught against David, whose legacy had provided the means for Daniel's esoteric film career.

'He doesn't want my interest! He never listens to my opinions . . . Yes, it's true I'm critical! But I'm not the only one. The fact is that if Dan didn't have his grandfather's money, he'd have to make films that people actually wanted to see . . . The bloody *Rose Garden*! What the hell is that supposed to be about?'

Eva sighed, seeing only too well the justification of this complaint yet knowing that Genevieve had sealed her own fate on the sidelines of her husband's career, pursuing an ever-more-frivolous life of shopping and parties and casual affairs while he retreated into work, the two of them chasing elusive goals along paths destined never to meet.

She found herself wondering if, as Blanche seemed to hope, this marriage might at last be ending, to the benefit of all concerned. Even the children, Eva thought, might gain from parents who lived apart in a careful truce . . .

'I want him back, Grandmama!' Genevieve suddenly burst out, quashing this fond vision in a moment. 'You've got to get him back for me . . . He listens to you. I'll try to be good, really I will! Speak to him for me . . . please . . .'

Eva, deeply unhappy with this commission and deducing that Genevieve knew nothing of Daniel's girlfriend, a revelation which would surely change everything for the worse, had no confidence in her ability to influence her grandson this time. Nor, indeed, did she know whether such a course would be wise. And when Genevieve had finally departed, she related all to Toby, seeking his consolation and his advice.

'She's right about his movies,' Toby said, coming at once to the point. 'They're garbage. He showed me a few rushes of *The Rose Garden* the other day – couldn't understand it at all. You were very good, of course . . .'

'Oh well,' said Eva, laughing, 'he's wanted me in one of his films for years. I thought this one seemed a good idea. T. S. Eliot, you know . . .'

'No,' said Toby, scratching his head, 'I'm afraid I don't. And I tend to agree with Genevieve. David endowed a lot of fine projects with his money. Daniel's career wasn't one of them.'

Privately, Eva inclined to the same view, but she felt obliged to defend her grandson.

'It's not like our day,' she reproached Toby. 'Novels, films, plays . . .

they don't have plots any more. They reflect life. Life isn't a plot . . .
It isn't a romance . . .'

'Oh no? Then what is it? What should it be?'

'You mean life?'

'I mean the attempt to make sense of it! Art, I suppose you'd call it,
and I tell you this, Eva – much of what passes for art these days is just
plain . . . garbage.'

'Oh, you're just a grumpy old man,' Eva replied crossly.

This spirited little exchange was cut short by the return of Michael,
much pleased by his meeting with Susannah who'd agreed to visit St
Cuthbert's and the Retreat, but quickly on guard at Toby's forthright
suggestion that he might be the one to tackle Daniel.

'I only offer advice if it's requested,' he said carefully.

'Then I'm surprised the folk at your church behave themselves at all,'
Toby answered smartly. 'A pastor should show the way!'

Michael laughed and glanced at Eva.

'Daniel isn't one of my parishioners,' he said, as much for her benefit,
she saw, as Toby's. 'And even if he were, I wouldn't see it as my duty,
or my right, to intervene in his personal life – unless somebody else
directly involved, his wife or his girlfriend, were to ask for my help, of
course . . .'

'That's it!' said Eva, suddenly seeing a way. 'You must talk to Genevieve!'

'Make sure you keep the door open,' Toby advised him darkly, 'so
you can shout for help . . .'

'Toby!' Eva interjected furiously. 'What's that supposed to mean?'

She glowered at her former husband, thinking that perhaps his lunch
had upset him, so garrulous and unsympathetic did he suddenly seem.

'Genevieve,' Toby retorted, taking no notice at all of Eva's reproving
glare, 'is addicted to sex! She can't stop doing it . . . I've seen it before
in other women. Rhoda was the same.'

'Nonsense!' cried Eva, infuriated by this undeserved comparison
between her grandson's wife and Rhoda. 'I never heard of such a thing
. . . Michael, please! Tell him it's not possible to be addicted to sex!'

Michael, plainly disconcerted to find himself the referee in such an
unlikely dispute between two octogenarians, gazed from one to the
other, choosing his words with caution.

'I think it's possible to be addicted to the sense of security that sex
brings,' he said at last. 'But of course, it's very brief . . . and when
there's no love or commitment between the people involved, then it's
also illusory.'

They each considered this solemn statement in silence, though
Eva was rather less concerned with its relevance than with wonder-

ing what Toby, never one to leave a matter unresolved, would offer next.

'They got married too young,' he finally ventured, seeing he'd upset Eva and seeking to make amends. 'That's the truth of it. Ridiculous, getting wed at twenty with a baby on the way. Of course, Daniel did the noble thing – but it seems to me they'd both have been better off if he'd ducked out. She could have had the baby adopted . . . What do you say, Michael?'

But the vicar of St Cuthbert's, usually so willing to face the thorny issue, to voice his careful opinions and do justice to all views, seemed suddenly reduced to confusion, muttering that he'd promised to meet Daniel for dinner at the Café des Arbres and would have to be leaving . . . and that while he couldn't guarantee any results, he would speak to Genevieve if they so wished.

And then he was gone.

'What the heck's the matter with him?' demanded Toby in surprise as the sitting-room door closed. 'Did I say something wrong?'

'No, dear,' said Eva soberly, patting his hand in a peace-making gesture. 'There are just some situations where it's impossible to say anything right.'

A few days later a very special visitor was announced as Toby and Eva lingered over breakfast.

'You're not going to believe this,' smiled Blanche, much calmed by the arrival of Edouard and cheered by the prospect of a week at home in Toulouse. 'Ladies and gentlemen, I give you – Miss Carlotta du Bois!'

She breezed into the sitting room, a diminutive figure wrapped in mink and black crêpe, still a vibrantly pretty woman with clear, spark-ling green eyes and carefully coloured hair.

'Well now,' she laughed, sitting down at the table with Eva and Toby. 'Isn't this just like old times?'

'Carlotta!' cried Toby in genuine delight. 'How wonderful to see you!'

'Enough of this Carlotta rubbish!' she beamed. 'I'm Harriet Howard, remember? Harold Brannen's bastard daughter . . .'

Eva, who hadn't seen Harriet in ten years, was equally delighted, and the two fell upon each other with kisses and hugs, Harriet declaring that she'd come to Paris specially to see Eva and couldn't think why she hadn't done it before, Eva remembering with regret that David and Harriet's mutual antipathy had always made it difficult for them to keep in touch.

'We only need Nicky here,' Harriet said, 'and then we'd have a full house – just like it used to be in that god-awful apartment! Do you remember it, Eva? Those shaky banisters? I used to be terrified Nicky would plunge down the stairs . . .'

'I remember,' Eva said.

They laughed and reminisced all morning, walking out on to the lawn in the late autumn sunshine, and then when lunchtime arrived, Blanche produced a bottle of Edouard's best claret.

'I don't want you all getting squiffy,' she warned them, 'but I think you deserve a little celebration.'

In truth, it didn't require a great deal to get Toby squiffy, and a glass later he was snoring gently on the wooden settle, leaving Eva and Harriet to the rest of the bottle.

'Are you really here just to see me?' Eva asked her then.

'Yes, I am – although I confess there's something else too. I know that Nicky came here to see you, Eva. I wanted to ask you about that . . .'

Harriet, seeming somewhat affected by the wine herself, suddenly reached into her vanity case for a handkerchief, sniffing into it and then dabbing at her eyes, an uncharacteristic show of emotion which moved Eva to immediate concern.

'Sorry,' Harriet muttered as Eva grasped her hand. 'It's very hard, you know . . . My only child, and he hasn't spoken to me in twenty years . . .'

Eva listened in silent sympathy to the story she'd already heard from Nicky, a tale of blighted family relationships, of pride, vanity and blind disregard, of sorrow, regret and the belated attempt to make amends.

'I've been a terrible mother,' Harriet said, drying her eyes at last. 'I hardly saw him when he was a baby, and then I packed him off to school in England . . . But he's paid me back, Eva. I've had to stand by and watch him ruin the lives of three women – you know that his second wife killed herself?'

'Yes,' said Eva unhappily, 'I know.'

'Her children – my grandsons – they disowned their father, and although they're very polite and send me birthday cards, they're not loving or close . . . It's not like having a family. It's not like your family, Eva.'

Eva could think only in that moment of Blanche and Edouard, so solicitous and concerned for her comfort, of Matthew and his wife in Israel, always writing and telephoning and urging her to visit, of Daniel, who considered her his confidante and friend, of her other grandchildren, Matthew's sons, and her great-grandchildren, all eight of them, their little gifts and tokens, their school reports and holiday snaps . . .

'I think Nicky is reviewing his life,' she said gently to Harriet. 'I think he wishes he'd done things differently.'

'Yes,' said Harriet sorrowfully. 'He wishes he'd married Eleanor Martineau, so now he goes to her grave and puts red roses on it, and he wonders if he should try to see her daughter – his daughter. The TV personality . . . Beth Carlisle.'

'How do you know all this?' Eva asked in genuine surprise. 'I thought the two of you had no contact?'

'I've had a private detective following him for the past fifteen years,' Harriet replied to Eva's astonishment. 'I know everything! Well, Eva, what else could I do? I had no other way of keeping in touch.'

'But couldn't you go to him? Tell him you were sorry, and ask him to forgive?'

'No,' said Harriet firmly, showing a flash of her old defiance. 'It's for him to make the first move, Eva. He's the one who rejected me . . . I can only wait.'

Eva, thinking back to Nicky Howard at Toulouse, his dangerous charm and his cool dedication to his career, understood even if she couldn't agree, and she stared at Harriet in deep compassion and concern, not knowing what she might do to help.

'I want to ask you about Eleanor's daughter,' Harriet was saying. 'She's my granddaughter, Eva . . . I can't begin to tell you how that makes me feel. I long to meet her, to shake her by the hand and say hallo. I know that Nicky wants to do the same. He sent his latest novel to her office, hoping she might interview him . . . He asked his agent to try to get him on her late-night show . . . but nothing happened. She was probably completely unaware of all this.'

She probably was, Eva thought, reflecting upon the odd chain of coincidence by which Beth Carlisle, unknown to her and yet familiar in so many ways, had entered her life and her prayers, a young person in whom she'd once had passing interest, and who now, through Nicky and Harriet, but principally through Michael Cameron, seemed to be assuming a major role.

'Oh, I'm not foolish enough to imagine she'd be delighted at the prospect of acquiring a new grandmother,' Harriet was saying. 'After all, Rhoda was her grandmother – it would hardly be surprising if she had a jaundiced view!'

'No,' Eva agreed. 'Rhoda used to lock her in a dark cupboard when she was a little girl.'

Harriet greeted this disclosure with outrage and shock, and the next half-hour was spent in discussing Rhoda, her extraordinary behaviour, her strange lack of moral understanding, her apparent need to manipulate and control all the men who admired her.

'She was very young,' Eva said, remembering Rhoda in her white silk ballgown standing on the gilt and alabaster staircase in David's Hollywood house. 'I don't suppose she can be blamed for all the things she did . . .'

'I was very young,' Harriet retorted, 'and like Rhoda, I made a lot of mistakes. Saul Bernstein was the big one . . . But I never murdered anyone! Or locked any children in dark cupboards,' she added, as though this were equally reprehensible.

'I suppose there were unhappy things in Rhoda's own childhood,' Eva said, trying to make sense of it. 'Events and sorrows that none of us knows about.'

'Perhaps,' said Harriet unwillingly. 'But, Eva, enough of this. I want to talk about Beth Carlisle. What do you know about her? What did Nicky tell you? Please . . .'

Eva hesitated, seeing she could hardly reveal what she knew about Beth and Michael, yet feeling she had very little else to offer.

'I know she's very talented, and very successful – and I know she's had sadness in her life. Her mother's death, of course, and other things . . . As a matter of fact, Harriet, I've been praying for Beth. Praying that a way might be found to resolve whatever pain and confusion still remain for her . . .'

Harriet, not the slightest bit interested in prayer or its mysterious purposes, nodded politely and then rushed on with new revelations.

'She has a very smart house on the banks of the Thames, and she drives a white BMW convertible . . . She's very well off, and she always wears designer clothes . . . She lives with an actor – a classical actor. Jamie MacLennon. I saw him play Macbeth in London. He was magnificent!'

Eva, taken aback at the detail of this information, surveyed Harriet keenly, not at all sure that such interest was proper or wise.

'Good heavens, Harriet,' she said sternly, 'I hope you haven't had a private detective tailing Miss Carlisle as well.'

'No, of course not!' Harriet said defensively. 'I read magazines and newspapers, that's all. But listen to this, Eva – here's something you won't find in the newspapers. Jamie MacLennon is homosexual!'

Eva considered this in silence, something pricking at the back of her memory, as though this latest piece of news about Beth Carlisle had stitched another fragment of her life into place, a piece which Eva couldn't yet see clearly . . .

'If it isn't in the newspapers,' she said slowly to Harriet, 'then may I ask how you know something so sensitive and so personal about the life of a total stranger?'

Harriet looked away, momentarily abashed.

'Well, I must confess I have made a few discreet enquiries . . . I wanted to know about her, Eva! I wanted to know if she was happy. She's very special to me. She's my granddaughter . . .'

Eva took Harriet's hand, moved and saddened by her obvious need, keen to offer her hope and consolation, but also anxious to advocate caution.

'Harriet,' she said gently, 'I must tell you what I told Nicky . . . It would be quite wrong to enter this young woman's life and announce yourself as her relative . . . I know how I myself would have felt if someone had told me Sir Ralph Forster was my grandfather. I wouldn't have been at all pleased, and I'd have had to consider that he knew the truth all along.'

'But I didn't know the truth all along,' Harriet whispered, biting her lip. 'I've only recently found out about Beth Carlisle – and I have no one else, Eva. No one at all . . .'

But then, in a rapid change of mood which Eva recalled as typical, Harriet suddenly recovered her humour, laughing at herself and her solemnity, declaring that, of course, it would be quite a shock to discover that your grandmother was the notorious Carlotta du Bois . . .

'But I did think she might like to meet me – that I might appeal to her rather more than Nick Howard, the terribly serious novelist . . . What do you reckon, Eva? Would she like to talk to me about my life in Hollywood?'

Eva laughed.

'Maybe she would . . . But you know what she'd ask, don't you?'

'What? What would she ask?'

'She'd ask who really killed Will Sutton!'

'Oh dear,' said Harriet, giggling so uproariously that she woke Toby from his snooze. 'That would be quite a tale, wouldn't it?'

The following morning there seemed to be an extraordinary number of visitors to the little sitting room: a friend of Helena's from Toulouse, a colleague of Matthew's from Israel who'd also known David, a woman who'd been just a teenage girl when war broke out, and who'd served at table in the Café des Arbres . . .

So it was that Eva nearly missed the morning's most significant visitor.

'Mama,' said Blanche, 'I'm trying to find Michael. Do you know where he is? There's someone here I'd like him to meet. A friend of Susannah's from London – a Mr MacLennon.'

Eva gazed at her daughter in outright astonishment.

'You mean Jamie MacLennon?'

'That's him. An actor. Unfortunately Susannah refuses to see him, and at the moment he's in the day room with Genevieve . . . I can't leave the poor man there much longer. If Michael were here, he might smooth the way.'

Michael, thought Eva, nonplussed, would not be well placed to smooth the way, and it seemed a sudden blessing that the vicar of St Cuthbert's, jolted out of his regular, somewhat austere routine by two successive trips to Paris, had become so intimate with her grandson, the two of them spending much time at the Café des Arbres while Daniel's girlfriend was about her business. Undoubtedly they were there this morning, sparing Michael the discomfort of coming face to face with Beth Carlisle's companion.

'I'll see him,' Eva said to Blanche, brushing aside her daughter's innocent insistence that she had no need to trouble herself, that she must be tired after so many visitors, that Mr MacLennon was no responsibility of hers. 'Show him in.'

She faced a lithe, dark, impossibly beautiful man with a grave and courteous manner, who took her hand and kissed it without making the gesture seem theatrical or embarrassing, who refused her offer of cognac and apologised for the imposition his arrival presented, who then sat down on the wooden settle, and unlike every other actor Eva had ever met, proceeded to talk about her rather than himself.

'As soon as your daughter mentioned the name, I remembered at once. *Casey's War*. One of the best movies of the Thirties . . . I've always been a great admirer of David Klein.'

Eva smiled, and then found herself inexplicably drawn to talk about David in a way that she rarely did, and never to a stranger.

'Yes. He made some fine pictures. But his heart wasn't in it, you know. He couldn't stand the double-dealing and the deceit . . . All the parties and the posturing . . . His temperament was entirely wrong for Hollywood. He came to see that in the end . . .'

'Did he? Well, I can sympathise. It's hard work, swimming against the tide.'

'Is that what you do, Mr MacLennon? Swim against the tide?'

Outside the window on the shimmering lawn the patients were assembling for a performance, a string quartet hired by Blanche as part of her therapeutic programme, and together they watched as the Sisters manipulated a fleet of wheelchairs over the glittering grass, arranging the ailing audience in a ragged semicircle, offering them glasses of sparkling wine and silver platters of canapés, all of it overseen and blessed by Blanche.

'Yes, that's what I do,' Jamie MacLennon said slowly, surveying the spectacle through the window and raising one hand in appreciation as the quartet began to tune up. 'Life requires us all to play a part – and as an actress yourself, you'll understand the dilemmas of one who always feels forced into a role. It's as though the curtain never comes down.'

He peered on to the lawn, his attention caught by a solitary figure making its way across to the wheelchairs, head bowed, shoulders hunched.

'Is that Susannah?' he demanded suddenly. 'Good grief, it is! What on earth is she doing?'

'She's aligning herself with the victims of AIDS, Mr MacLennon. She's looking at them and reminding herself that as they are, so will she be . . .'

He turned away from the window and faced Eva, his expression sorrowful, his manner respectful.

'To be HIV positive is not to have AIDS,' he said carefully. 'And in truth, there's no such state as dying. There's only alive and dead. Susannah is very much alive. Somebody should tell her.'

'Many people have tried to tell her . . . My daughter, of course, and an Anglican priest who's currently counselling her. But perhaps yourself, a colleague and a friend, might succeed where we have failed.'

He shook his head and sat down again.

'Mine is an ill-advised mission,' he said quietly. 'I'm here because a good friend begged me to come – begged me to speak to Susannah on his behalf. I expect you know who I mean. Alex Chapman. Susannah's lover. Ex-lover I should say . . .'

Eva nodded.

'And what does Mr Chapman wish to say to Susannah?' she asked unhappily.

He shrugged.

'In a word,' he said. 'Sorry . . .'

'That's a very difficult message to convey. Tell me, your friend Mr Chapman – is he bisexual?'

'So he says,' Jamie MacLennon replied.

'And you, Mr MacLennon, are you also bisexual?'

The question was out before she quite realised she meant to ask it, and she was at once deeply apologetic, mortified that her covert interest in the young man who stood before her should manifest itself so blatantly, and with such insensitivity.

'No, no . . .' he said, anxious to quell her distress. 'It's a perfectly reasonable question under the circumstances. The answer is no. I'm not bisexual. I sometimes think life would be simpler if I were.'

'That seems a bit unlikely,' Eva said doubtfully, and then they both began to laugh, a blessed relief from the tragedy of the subject under discussion, a spontaneous release of mirth which seemed to underwrite all attempts to make sense of the search for love, uniting them in an unexpected understanding.

'I'm sure you're right,' he said at last. 'Though my life as it is seems ridiculously complicated . . . My gay friends would say I'm a coward, still hiding in the closet. My bisexual friends would say why not have the best of both worlds . . . And my straight friends would say that, as to all appearances I lead a straight life anyway, why not go the whole hog.'

'And what would you say?' Eva asked.

He glanced at her and smiled.

'If anyone asked me,' he murmured, 'I would say that like most other people I know, I'm looking for someone to love – someone to share the secrets of my soul – someone to take my hand and walk off with me into the setting sun . . .'

He smiled again.

'That's hard to find, of course. It's particularly hard when your sexuality is unconventional . . . And when your deepest instincts rebel against much of what passes for love in a world obsessed with sex . . .'

She looked at him then with compassion and with respect, seeing in him that yearning towards wholeness which was surely the yearning of all humankind, seeing too that the ways of the human heart and the impenetrable mystery of desire would not be constrained, and that love would always seek its own means and its own expression.

'I hope you find what you're looking for,' she whispered.

After that, their conversation turned to other matters: to Genevieve, who'd told him, with less than total accuracy, that her mother was related to the Queen, to Hamlet, which he hoped to play, and Macbeth, which he'd recently played, to the state of the British theatre and the country's floundering film industry, and then back to Hollywood.

They talked too of Blanche and her work at the convent, of Edouard and his vast vineyard in the South, of Matthew and Rachael in Israel, and of the building trade.

'Your husband was a builder?'

'Yes . . . His firm went back several generations and involved many branches of the family. He wasn't always a builder. There was a period when he did something else entirely. But after the war, when he discovered that so many of his family had died, he wanted to go to Israel – to build houses and factories and hotels – to make the wilderness flower . . .'

She was on the point of telling him the whole truth, so relaxed and at ease did she feel in his company, but before she could begin on what she knew would prove an extraordinary revelation, Blanche returned from the concert on the lawn, apologising for her inability to sway Susannah, promising to keep Mr MacLennon informed of any progress, urging him to lunch at the convent before his departure.

He declined politely and rose to leave, taking Eva's hand once more, persuading her of his genuine pleasure in having met her, writing down his private telephone number for Blanche, and then offering them both a final, courteous farewell.

Eva, who'd been waiting to raise the matter on her mind and, finding no appropriate opening, suddenly feared that her opportunity might be disappearing for good. She waved a surprised Blanche out of the door and begged him to sit down again. Then she hurriedly embarked upon an urgent and somewhat ill-prepared speech.

'Mr MacLennon, I hope you will forgive me. This is going to sound most impertinent. I wouldn't wish you to think I were prying into your personal life . . . but the fact is, I couldn't let you leave without asking. You see, I have an interest in your young companion . . . Miss Carlisle.'

He looked at her curiously, plainly surprised.

'What interest?' he enquired directly.

For a moment Eva floundered, thinking of Harriet, Nicky and Michael and knowing she could hardly mention any of them, but then, with only a moment's guilty hesitation, she hit upon a device.

'I knew her grandmother,' she said, 'many years ago.'

'The Lady of Shalott,' Jamie MacLennon said slowly. 'Raving Rhoda . . . How very interesting. So tell me, do – was she as crazy as her granddaughter maintains?'

'I think she was,' Eva said, seeing at once that this was the most obvious, and most accurate, summing up of Rhoda. 'And what I wish to know, Mr MacLennon, is this . . . To what extent has Miss Carlisle been affected by her grandmother's treatment, and her mother's terrible death? I know all about that too, you see . . . Has she managed to overcome these sad events? Or has her life been shadowed by tragedy?'

For several moments he said nothing, deep in contemplation, surveying her solemnly, clearly wondering about this unlikely turn in the conversation, weighing it up and at last deciding there could be nothing untoward about it.

'Beth has never recovered from her mother's death,' he said quietly, 'nor from certain other traumatic things that happened around the same time. But I wouldn't say her life has been shadowed. She's no victim. She has wit, style and courage – and a great measure of inner resilience. I don't think anything her grandmother did could touch her.

'A strong character . . .' Eva said.

'She can be quite formidable. A lot of men are scared of her, and a lot of women are in awe. She often behaves very badly, but she has a redeeming quality which always brings her through. I guess you'd call it heart . . .'

Eva looked at him, moved.

'You love her very much,' she said.

'She frequently drives me round the bend. But yes, I love her very much . . . Without her generosity, I wouldn't live the way I do. She buys my clothes, runs my car and pays our ridiculously high mortgage. I would hate to lose her, but nevertheless I pray that one day she'll fall in love. That she'll find someone who can give her what she needs — what she deserves . . .'

'And what is that?' Eva whispered.

He smiled.

'Just the ordinary things. A child. Marriage, perhaps. A happy home. Unconditional love . . .'

Eva smiled back.

'I pray so too,' she said.

At the sitting-room door, he turned to her one last time.

'I'm rather surprised you haven't bumped into her,' he said slowly. 'She's here in Paris at the moment . . . Filming a new TV series. *Moonlight and Roses*, all about romance.'

He hesitated, eyeing Eva carefully.

'I gather she knows your grandson. She's been borrowing his editing suite . . .'

And then Eva, dumbfounded, saw it all.

She was remembering the Café des Arbres on a magical spring day, a belated celebration for her birthday, the cherry blossom blowing on to the terrace like sugar-pink snowflakes, the daffodils waving in the square, and three tables pushed together by the café's jovial proprietor in order to accommodate everyone, David and herself, Blanche and Edouard, Matthew and Rachael, all the grandchildren, and one very important newcomer, her first great-grandchild, Daniel and Genevieve's baby daughter.

For many years, after the war, after the fate of Anya and Victor became known, Eva could not bear to visit the café. But then, as with all who suffer and who eventually process their grief, the happy memories began to override the bad, so that now, whenever she sat on the terrace or at the table in the window, she seemed to feel Anya's presence, a spirit of irreverent merriment pervading the very air around her.

And on this day, in the midst of a long, joyous and noisy family party which only broke up when the new baby decided she'd had enough, Eva seemed to feel Victor's presence too, Victor as he had been on the day she first arrived in Paris, long before he met Rhoda, the Victor she remembered as so gracious, so courteous and so kind. Odd, that she should be remembering Victor on this, the last occasion that she saw Eleanor Carlisle . . .

David had bought a diamond ring for Eva's birthday, a ring which didn't quite fit, and now, as everyone prepared to drift back to the Klein town house, he declared that he would have it altered at once at a jeweller's just round the corner from the café. And Eva, sleepy, warm and relaxed, declined to go with him, saying she would wait and have one more cup of coffee at the table in the window, savouring the prospect of a half-hour alone to dream and reflect.

This was not to be, for she recognised Rhoda's daughter the moment she walked into the café, missing David by a matter of seconds, and without hesitation Eva waved at the slender, elegantly dressed woman, her mass of chocolate-coloured hair cut to her shoulders in a stylish pageboy, her expression searching and keen. Clearly she was expecting to meet someone who had not yet arrived.

'Eva . . . Good heavens, it must be nearly seven years! I often wondered if I'd bump into you at the Café des Arbres . . . And now, here you are!'

Eva welcomed Ellie to the table in the window, calling for more coffee and two small glasses of cognac, enquiring after her daughters, answering her questions about Blanche and Edouard, carefully avoiding any mention of Nicky Howard, or indeed, of Rhoda.

'What are you doing in Paris?' Eva wanted to know.

'I've flown over a few times lately . . . A friend has an apartment here . . . We snatch the odd weekend, and we usually eat at the café. I'm waiting for him now . . .'

Eva, recognising that only vexed friendships involved snatching the odd weekend, asked no more, demanding instead to know all about Ellie's girls.

'They're both at university,' she said, looking down. 'Sarah's in her first year, and Beth's about to take her finals . . .'

Eva waited, and then watched in concern as Ellie's eyes began to water, a show of emotion which clearly embarrassed, sending her reaching for the cognac.

'My dear girl,' Eva said gently. 'What's wrong?'

'I can hardly believe this is happening,' Ellie said, taking a large gulp of the cognac. 'I keep telling myself it can't be true . . . The fact is, Eva, you and I have played this scene before – twenty-one years ago at Toulouse, if you remember . . . And now history repeats itself.'

'Oh dear,' said Eva, seeing the truth at once. 'One of your daughters is having a baby?'

'Beth . . . Oh Eva, I can't tell you how much it hurts. I wanted everything for her . . .'

Ellie suddenly slammed her glass down upon the table and clenched her fists.

'I could kill him,' she whispered vehemently.

Eva, who'd all too recently found herself guiding Blanche and Edouard through this selfsame situation, who'd negotiated between Daniel and his parents, spoken to Genevieve's mother and tried to soothe trammelled emotions all round, now attempted to offer Ellie her own family experience by way of consolation.

'It doesn't have to be a disaster,' she said kindly, squeezing Ellie's hand. 'I must say we were all a bit concerned about Genevieve to begin with . . . Her background is very unstable. Her mother has a drink problem, and her father has had four wives. But of course, that's not her fault. Anyway, they got married, and it all seems to be working out . . . They now have a beautiful little girl, just two months old.'

Ellie, unfortunately, was not at all consoled by this happy tale, declaring that she'd do everything in her power to prevent her daughter marrying, thanking God and the British government for a liberal abortion law, insisting there could be no comparison at all between Daniel's situation and Beth's, apologising in the same breath for her uncharacteristic show of emotion.

'I'm sorry, Eva . . . I get so wild when I think about it. She wasn't eighteen when she met him, and still a virgin . . . Bloody miraculous in itself, considering how lovely she is . . . And he just took her over, right from the moment he saw her! He's so jealous and possessive, she'd have no hope of a career if she married him. And apart from all that,' she added darkly, 'he's a religious maniac.'

'Good heavens!' said Eva, startled. 'That sounds very serious . . .'

But Ellie didn't go on to elaborate, for at that moment her long-awaited friend arrived, a tall, good-looking middle-aged man with dark gold hair and a broad smile, who took her into his arms and kissed her lovingly on the mouth.

'This is Jack,' Ellie said, waving for another glass as she made the introductions. 'And this is Eva – an old friend. I'm afraid, Jack, I've been telling her all about it . . . I just can't seem to think of anything else.'

He threw Ellie a despairing glance and poured himself a cognac.

'My apologies, Eva,' he said drily, 'I'm sure you don't want to hear all about our convoluted family dramas.'

Ellie suddenly stood up from the table.

'I must call Beth,' she said, reaching for her handbag. 'She's handing in her thesis today . . . I've got to know she's all right. Sorry, Jack. I won't be long.'

'For God's sake, Ellie . . .' He caught at her arm and when he saw she would not be deterred, released her reluctantly.

'If you must speak to her,' he pleaded, 'then, Ellie, I beg you – tell her the truth. If you do, we needn't go back. We could stay right here in Paris! You'd never have to see Leo Frankish again . . .'

Ellie shook her head, and turned to Eva for support.

'He wants me to leave my daughters!' she said with a little laugh, laying her arm around his shoulders and dropping a kiss on to his hair so that he mightn't mistake her refusal for disenchantment. 'He thinks I can just walk away from them! Sell my house, and say okay girls, if you want to see me you'll have to catch a plane for Paris . . .'

Jack ran his hand through his hair, plainly aggrieved.

'They're grown girls, Ellie. They don't need you in the way they used to . . . You have your own life to lead.'

Ellie was still appealing to Eva, spreading out her hands, demonstrating her dilemma.

'He thinks Beth doesn't need me! She's pregnant, she's about to sit her finals, and meantime the father of her child announces that he's given up sex for God . . . Wonderful!'

Eva laughed uncertainly.

'I'm sure it can't be quite that bad,' she ventured.

Jack took a hefty draught of his cognac.

'Of course it's not that bad! He's pretty mixed up, I agree, but he loves her very much . . . And as soon as he finds out she's pregnant, he'll be begging her to marry him.'

'Exactly!' said Ellie bitterly.

They watched her run across the terrace and out into the square towards a telephone booth, staring as she picked up the receiver and fumbled for coins, then saw her relax as she began to speak.

'Bloody kids,' Jack said to Eva, attempting to lighten the moment. 'You no sooner get them out of your hair and off to college than they're back in tears telling you they're pregnant . . .'

Eva smiled.

'It will all work out,' she said quietly, 'one way or another.'

'Yes,' he said slowly, looking down into his glass, 'it will. And then, I suppose, we shall see which was the great love story, and which was just the minor plot . . .'

Eva, having no idea what to make of this, was about to call for more coffee when David suddenly reappeared with her diamond ring, shaking Jack somewhat cursorily by the hand and urging his wife home before the afternoon turned chilly, snappily brushing aside her suggestion that they wait for Ellie's return.

As they walked across the square, Eva rapped upon the telephone box, waving at Ellie and mouthing a sympathetic goodbye, marvelling at her husband's continuing intransigence in any matter concerning Rhoda.

'That Eleanor Carlisle seems to pop up all over the place,' he remarked as they waited for a cab.

'Yes . . . Three times in twenty-one years. She's made quite a nuisance of herself, hasn't she? Another seven years, and I suppose she'll be popping up again . . .'

David said nothing, ignoring this mild jibe; he took her hand in his, fondling the new diamond, unconcerned by anything, it seemed, beyond the search for a taxicab.

Eleanor Carlisle, formerly Martineau, was never to pop up again, of course. Just a month later Eva received a short note from Jack, left in the care of the Café des Arbres, informing her, with deep regret, of Ellie's tragic death.

Michael left Paris on a cold and rainy afternoon, taking a rather sombre farewell of Eva, expressing the hope that they would meet again in the spring, confessing his failure to make any progress in the matter of Daniel and Genevieve.

'She told me to mind my own business, and he told me that he's falling in love – a grand passion, he called it. I'm afraid the future of this marriage is looking rather bleak . . .'

But Eva, on this occasion, was unconcerned about her grandson or his wife. She had something else on her mind.

'Michael . . . Are you aware of the saying "I pray and coincidences happen . . . I cease to pray, and they no longer do"?'

'Yes,' he said. 'William Temple, I believe.'

'And do you remember telling me that once, when you failed to find Beth Carlisle's private number, you took it as a sign you shouldn't contact her?'

He looked away, saying nothing, the raw nerve exposed once more.

'Well, here's another sign for you,' Eva said calmly, handing him a piece of paper: the London telephone number which Jamie MacLennon had written down for Blanche.

He took the slip and gazed at it, baffled.

'That is Beth Carlisle's private number,' Eva said. 'You may ring it any time you wish . . .'

'Is this really her number?' he stammered, still staring at the slip of paper. 'I can't believe it . . . But even so, I don't see how I could ring her up out of the blue – I mean, what would I say? What reason would I give?'

'Pray for a reason,' Eva said, 'and one will present itself.'

He looked across at her, the wide grey eyes unnaturally bright.

'How did you get this?' he whispered.

'Coincidence,' she replied.

Autumn drifted into winter and then spring was upon her again, and those last days were, in some mysterious way, the best days, for in that time it seemed that all the joys and pains of the past were weaving into one harmonious whole from which no single sorrow, not even the greatest sorrow, her parting from David, could be extracted. All was as it was, and was surely meant to be. The path of destiny, glimpsed from the finishing end, seemed now to have wandered with true purpose, and all the roads untrodden and untravelled revealed for the wrong turnings they would have been. She felt content.

Nevertheless, the present still groaned with all the confusion of living, and there was no easy answer to the dilemma that still troubled her – what to do about Daniel, Genevieve and Beth Carlisle. Perhaps, she told herself, there was nothing she could do. Yet increasingly, she longed to do something, and she wished for someone who might share her concern.

She woke late that last morning, feeling a curious lightness in her limbs and a fluttering in her ribcage, as though a tiny bird were beating against its bars, struggling to escape. But the sensation was gone as soon as registered, and she rapidly turned her attention to the matters of the day: breakfast with Toby, an unwelcome request from Mr Jon Makepeace for a further interview, a long telephone call from Matthew, a cheery letter from Harriet . . .

And then, an unusual drowsiness settling upon her, she sat down by the fire in her little sitting room and closed her eyes.

When she opened them again, Harold Brannen was standing by the window, immaculate in his smart soldier's uniform and black shiny boots, leaning upon the sill and surveying her with a broad and well-remembered smile.

'Hallo, Eva,' he said. 'At last, we meet again.'

Eva, in her delight, found that she wasn't at all surprised to see him, that his unprecedented appearance, looking exactly as he'd done on the day they'd said goodbye, jumping into the trap behind the old black mare outside St Cuthbert's vicarage and waving until lost to view behind the spur of the bay, was only to be expected.

'Harold!' she cried aloud in joy. 'My dearest Harold!'

He was reaching into the pocket of his breeches, extracting what appeared to be a pile of telegrams, old-fashioned papers no longer used in the era of modern communication, but which Eva had seen many times as a child.

'We haven't got too much time,' he said cheerily, 'so we'd better get on with it. There are lots of messages. Everyone is longing to see you. Everyone hopes you'll hurry up.'

He shuffled through the papers, arranging them, it seemed, in some order of priority.

'Here's one from Papa,' he said, 'who wishes you to know that he has a new boat to take you sailing in . . . And here's one from Richard, who simply sends his love, and another from Edward, who thanks you most sincerely for your friendship to Helena . . .'

Eva listened while Harold reeled off another batch of kindly greetings, and then laughed in open astonishment as he waved one of them in the air above his head.

'This is from Anya,' he said with a mischievous wink. 'She wants you to know that the very best seat in the window is reserved especially for you. Not to mention the very best bottle of red wine!'

'Anya!' cried Eva, enthralled. 'I can't believe it!'

'Whyever not?' Harold enquired innocently. 'Don't tell me you thought the Jews went somewhere else!'

He clearly found this prospect hilarious, and suddenly began to laugh uproariously, his shoulders shaking, the tears streaming down his cheeks.

'David will think that very funny,' he said. 'There's a message here from him too, of course! But it's very long and rather personal. Maybe I'll just leave that one to your imagination . . .'

He was still laughing, and Eva, catching his gaiety as she'd so often done as a child, began to giggle too, a response quickly curtailed by the next telegram.

'Here's one from Rhoda,' Harold said. 'This is very short. It just says . . . Sorry.'

'Sorry!' Eva could hardly believe her ears, and she gazed at Harold in reproach, thinking this was one message he might have spared her.

'Yes. Very sorry,' Harold said soberly. 'Rhoda cut the brakes on Will's Bugatti and killed poor Joe Lugisi . . . But that's not all. Remember Rupert Connaught? Food poisoning, indeed!'

Eva began to tremble, deeply affected.

And then she recalled Rhoda's letter, sent to David after her death, which he'd burned without reading. What else had she been wanting to confess?

'Rhoda's child,' she asked Harold uncertainly, posing the question that had lain unanswered all these years. 'Who was the father of Rhoda's child?'

'Oh, don't worry your head about that!' Harold replied. 'It was Victor. Rhoda, of course, would have liked David to think it was him . . . But he was too clever for her. He burned the letter.'

Eva considered this in silence, reflecting on Rhoda's deviousness, and how the truth would never now be told, but in the next moment, a new shock came upon her.

'Here's one from Saul Bernstein,' Harold said briskly, unfolding another of his telegrams. 'He's very sorry too . . . He killed Christine, you see. Fed her pills and whisky and made it look like suicide – all so she wouldn't tell what she knew . . .'

Eva pressed her hand to her heart, feeling it clamour to escape its prison, drawing breath and finding that it rattled strangely in her throat, gazing at Harold in stunned disbelief.

He leaned towards her from the windowsill.

'What do you imagine hell to be, Eva?' he enquired seriously. 'Lakes of fire and brimstone? Well, that's a colourful idea, but the truth is rather more terrible . . . Can you imagine a greater torment, Eva my dear, than to discover that love alone is the source of joy, and that you've wasted all love's chances? Every last one . . . You'd be pretty sorry, wouldn't you?'

Harold seemed much affected by this, producing a large red silk handkerchief which Eva distinctly remembered Blanche Brannen buying him one Christmas, and wiping his eyes, gazing at his sister in manifest sorrow while she considered the pains of love irretrievably lost . . .

'Harold,' she said suddenly, seeing her opportunity, 'what shall I do about my grandson's marriage? About Michael and Beth Carlisle?'

Harold blew his nose on the red handkerchief.

'You must tell Daniel to go back to Genevieve,' he said at last. 'She loves him. She needs him. And he needs her too. As for Beth . . . Why not leave her the Brannen cross? That would give her something to think about. It might even send her to St Cuthbert's for your funeral . . .'

The Brannen cross? Eva's hand flew to the white-gold ornament at her throat, feeling it heavy and solid against her fingers, remembering the moment Dr Orde had offered her the grubby brown envelope in which it had been kept so long, thinking of the time it was pawned to pay the rent on the chalet in the canyon, recalling Harriet's mission to get it back and the arrival of Nicky Howard and his girlfriend Ellie at Toulouse, bearing the necklet in a little velvet box . . .

'Leave Beth the Brannen cross?' Eva asked uncertainly.

'Well, why not? She's a Brannen, isn't she? My great-granddaughter, no less! She may not be the last of the Brannens, but I'd say she'd do very nicely . . .'

'I've never even met her!' Eva protested.

Harold smiled broadly, one of his old, provocative smiles.

'Well, there's still time, Eva,' he said merrily. 'You're not dead yet!'

Eva laughed. 'I've no idea what I'd say to her anyway,' she murmured pensively.

Harold smiled again. 'Tell her this,' he said quietly. 'Tell her that no parting is ever permanent, no infinitesimal measure of love ever lost from the universe.'

'Oh, thank you, Harold,' Eva whispered gratefully. 'Thank you.'

She woke to find Toby sitting on the settle beside her.

'I've seen a ghost,' she muttered to him.

'Have you really? Well, there's a funny thing! I saw one myself, just the other night . . .'

She struggled upright, surveying him anxiously.

'Did you? Who was it? What did it say?'

'You're not going to believe this, Eva . . . It was Will Sutton. Bold as brass, sitting on the end of my bed. He told me to wrap up warm because the weather's going to change. That's the trouble with ghosts. They never tell you anything that really matters.'

'Oh, I don't know,' Eva said, laughing. 'The forecast isn't good, and you have had a nasty cold . . .'

She reached for his hand and squeezed it, reassured. She wanted nothing of ghosts, knowing that such things were mere illusion, that the dead sleep soundly in their graves until the Omega moment dawns.

And yet . . . and yet . . . She fingered the Brannen cross at her throat, remembering in that moment her father's dying words: 'When the moment comes to pass it on, Eva, then you'll know . . .'

Whatever the truth of her extraordinary vision, she meant to act upon it in one vital respect and speak to Daniel later that day. She would do it, she decided, when he came to kiss her goodnight as he always did. She would persuade him that his future lay with Genevieve, that he must begin once more upon the tortuous process of forgiveness and repentance . . . But she surely couldn't leave the Brannen cross to Beth Carlisle! Not to a woman she'd had no chance to weigh up for herself . . .

Then the sitting-room door opened to reveal Daniel himself, offering Eva a little brown paper parcel.

'Your prayer cards, Grandmama,' he said. 'I picked them up from the printers on my way over.'

The telephone on the oak bureau rang out, and as he moved to answer it, Eva opened her parcel, extracting the little cards that she liked to distribute among Blanche's patients. *All shall be well*, they declared. *All manner of thing shall be well* . . .

Behind her, Daniel emitted a muffled curse into the phone and suddenly slammed out of the sitting room, crashing the door behind him. Then a moment later, Blanche was in the room, her face a mask of taut disapproval, part anger, part pain.

'Well now, Mama,' she said stiffly, 'here's an interesting development. You have a visitor. A very unexpected visitor. Someone Daniel is most anxious to keep from you . . . Can you guess who she is?'

Eva gazed at her daughter, bemused, and then sobered.

'Yes,' she said quietly, packing her prayer cards away, 'I do believe I can . . . Toby, dearest, perhaps you'll leave us alone? Now, don't be upset, Blanche. It will all work out, I promise . . . Please don't worry . . . Just show my visitor in.'

Eva closed her eyes. The tiny bird hammered against her chest, struggling to be free. No parting ever permanent . . . No measure of love ever lost . . . How good, how true, how challenging a thought, to offer Beth Carlisle.

She reached for her newspaper and her magnifying glass, then rang the bell to summon a Sister. The fire needed stoking, the cognac replenishing . . .

She smiled to herself, confident now about the coming encounter. 'All shall be well,' she whispered aloud, 'all manner of thing shall be well.'

Book XI: Beth

Chapter Thirty-one

In romantic novels, all comes right in the final chapter. Ancient family secrets are uncovered, long-lost children find their parents, lovers are reunited
in orgasmic rapture, never to part again. And perhaps this is the most cruel
of all True Romance myths, the notion of happy ending, the irrational belief
that all loose ends can, and should, be neatly tied up, the hope that Life will
mimic Fantasy . . .'

Moonlight and Roses: The Cult of Romance in Western Society by Beth Carlisle (published by Harridan Press to accompany the Metro Television
series)

I took a cab to the Jardin des Plantes, and wandered through the shady
walkways, just as I'd done on the day I'd gone to meet Eva Delamere.
And just as on that day, Paris seemed to uplift and succour me, absorbing me into its proud and elegant heart, reminding of everything that
is beautiful and civilised and true.

I was early for my appointment at the Divine Faith convent, so I
lazed on a bench beneath a rosy copper beech, watching as a few stray
leaves drifted dreamily to the ground, reflecting on all that had happened in the months since I was last in Paris, reading again the letter
Duval had written me, with its astonishing revelations about Eva's life
as David Klein's wife.

It would make a very powerful book, the story of their escape from
Paris, the war years spent in the remote French countryside, their time
in Israel, their subsequent life together in France again, his career as a
master builder, hers as the organising power behind his business. I
could still scarcely believe that Blanche Duval wanted me to write it,
and I guessed that only the most startling revelation of all, the fact that

my grandfather had died in David Klein's place, qualified me, in her view, for the task.

I was, however, very anxious about meeting her again, remembering with deep regret and shame how I'd marched into the convent demanding to see her mother, earnestly repenting my torrid and ill-advised affair with her son, much in awe as a result of everything I'd learned about her work with HIV patients and the terminally ill.

But I'd been assured of her good will, and indeed, she'd sent me a little book that she'd edited of Eva's writings, journals kept throughout her life, together with a collection of Matthew Brannen's sermons, a bundle of letters exchanged between Eva and Anya Klein throughout the Hollywood years, and a long list of people who'd agreed to talk to me.

Blanche had even, to my amazement, secured the co-operation of Carlotta du Bois, who'd invited me to her home in Beverly Hills to talk about the making of *Casey's War*. And at Carlotta's suggestion, I'd also contacted Nick Howard in New York, figuring I might as well see him on my way to Hollywood, though I wasn't sure what else he might have to offer. After that, I planned a trip to Israel to meet Eva's son, Matthew Klein. I was on my way, I knew, to something good.

Now I strolled out of the Jardin des Plantes on the route I had taken that fateful day, coming again at last to the beautiful sandstone château that was the Divine Faith convent, walking nervously along the path beside the immaculate lawn, announcing myself deferentially at the reception desk, following meekly as an old Sister led me along the corridors I'd last walked on the day that Eva died.

Blanche Duval was waiting for me in the whitewashed sitting room, and as she gestured me towards the wooden settle offering me coffee or tea, but no cognac, I recognised with quiet relief just how much had changed since the day I'd sat beneath the plaster Messiah above Eva's mantel and blurted out my strident views about romance.

'I feel Eva's presence in this room,' I said humbly to Blanche, hoping this wasn't presumptuous. 'I'm very grateful to have met her.'

She smiled.

'We miss her very much,' she said, 'and we're very glad that at last the story of her life will be told.'

'I've been thinking about where to begin,' I said slowly. 'I thought maybe I'd start with the escape from Paris . . . David's triumphant return from Germany, and Eva, pregnant, waiting patiently for his return . . .'

Blanche nodded.

'That's the most dramatic part of the tale. After the escape, they had a very quiet war. They hardly saw any Germans where they were . . . My father did fight with the Resistance, it's true – he and my father-in-law, Paul Duval – but I wouldn't wish to exaggerate their exploits.

They blew up a few railway lines. They didn't, to my knowledge, shoot any Nazis.'

There were many other things I wanted to know: whether David Klein had ever intended to return to Hollywood, whether, throughout his extensive travels in Israel, America and Europe he'd ever been recognised, why Eva had failed to reveal the truth after his death . . .

Blanche considered all my questions carefully, suggesting that in order to arrive at answers I'd have to talk to a great many people, concluding that circumstance, as much as design, had decreed the course of her parents' lives.

'After the war, they came back to Paris . . . Here, to the Divine Faith convent. I was only five at the time, but I still remember Sister Marguerite, my mother's old friend, swinging me up into her arms and finding me a ball to play with on the grass. The lawn was so beautiful I hardly dared step on it, and that's when I first heard the story of how my father had driven a stolen car across the turf and demolished the gatepost . . .'

I gazed out of the sitting-room window on to the lawn, imagining the moment of departure, the nuns waving farewell, the car creeping forward, the slam of the gatepost falling . . .

'My mother was pregnant again at the end of the war,' Blanche was saying, 'and just as before, he went off and left her. This time he went to Poland, looking for his uncle Jake and his mother's family . . . That search, inevitably, took him to Auschwitz. When he came back he had a newborn son, a mission to go to Israel, and like so many Jews, an irrational sense of guilt at having escaped the horror . . .'

We talked then about war, about choices made in extremity, about chances lost and situations sealed, about seemingly insignificant decisions made in a moment, and their unguessed, unwonted ramifications.

'During the war, like so many of his Resistance friends, my father became a Communist . . . He wasn't a very good one, as it happened. My mother used to say he viewed religion and politics in exactly the same way. They were all right as long as you didn't take them too seriously . . . Nevertheless, he was a Party member for some years. And this, in itself, would have made any return to Hollywood problematic.'

'Is that why he didn't go back?' I asked. 'Because of McCarthy?'

She smiled and shook her head.

'It wasn't that straightforward. For a long time I think he believed he'd eventually go back. Then one day, he realised he wasn't a Hollywood director any more, he was a builder – which was what he'd always considered himself anyway, what he'd always imagined he would be . . .'

'A very wealthy builder,' I said, thinking of the hospice and its work which I knew he'd endowed.

'He was a multi-millionaire when he died, but they always lived very simply,' Blanche said. 'There was our family home in the South, which he built for my mother, and they also had a town house here in Paris . . . But nothing more. No yachts or castles or big limousines. And in the end he gave all his money away. My mother was provided for, of course, although after his death she moved here, to the convent, and her needs were very few. But hers was the only personal legacy . . .'

She hesitated.

'Apart from the money he left for Daniel's career,' she said quietly. 'That was my father's weakness, his little foible . . . They were so very alike, and Daniel could do no wrong in his eyes.'

We'd arrived at the subject I'd hoped to avoid, and now I gazed at her unhappily, wondering if I had the courage to say my piece or whether, all of it considered, I'd do better to keep quiet.

But she seemed to be waiting, and so at last, downcast and hesitant, I managed to speak my mind.

'I am deeply ashamed of my affair with your son,' I mumbled. 'I very much regret any distress I caused, to you, to his family, or to Eva . . .'

She looked up at me in evident surprise.

'I don't think you should blame yourself too much,' she said gently. 'After all, Beth, it takes two . . .'

'Yes. I know. We were equally guilty, but even so, that doesn't excuse me . . . The explanation, I think, is that I met him at a very vulnerable moment. Indeed, we were both vulnerable. He'd just left his wife, and I . . .'

Here I faltered, unwilling to embark on what I was sure would sound a confused and unlikely rationale, albeit it one which I now saw to be true, the understanding that for many years I'd been hoping for a man to replace Michael, subconsciously seeking that blessed fusion of bodies and minds which is so damnably rare, emerging from a ludicrous dalliance with the CID officer who'd investigated my burglary, surely the lowest point in my entire romantic history, and catapulting into the arms of the only man who'd ever seemed to match the passion and the promise of the one I'd wanted to marry.

'I think we both imagined ourselves a little bit in love,' I said to Blanche. 'But fortunately, we both came to see that wasn't the case . . . Now I'm only sorry to think that Eva knew all about it. I hope she didn't judge us too harshly.'

Blanche shook her head.

'She wasn't one to judge . . . In her younger days, she had something of a moralistic streak – you'll see that from the *Journals* – but she came to understand that human affairs were nothing if not complex and individual. Everyone took their problems to her in the end . . .'

'Yes,' I said, remembering how Eva had coaxed from me the tale of my mother's death, the birth of my child and the loss of Michael, reassuring me with what now seemed like mystical insight, seeking to convince me that no small part of love was ever lost from the universe. 'She was extraordinary. Everything about her was truly extraordinary.'

Blanche laughed.

'My father used to say she could have done anything. Nothing was impossible for her, and yet she seemed to do it all without really trying . . . She was a qualified nurse and a Hollywood actress. She wrote the script for *Casey's War*. At one point she ran the Café des Arbres, and she managed a vast building concern virtually single-handed, all the accounts and the contracts, the orders and the tenders . . . On top of that she raised her own children, and then my son. If she hadn't taken on Daniel, my own career would never have flourished . . .'

We considered this last attribute in companionable silence, Blanche lost in her own contemplation, myself reflecting upon the advantages bestowed by an extended family in which all parts seem to work for the good of the whole, thinking of my own mother raising her daughters with nothing but criticism and callous disregard from Rhoda, speculating upon how different it might have been.

'Did you ever hear Eva talk of my grandmother?' I asked Blanche.

She looked out at the gleaming gardens beyond the sitting-room window, seeming to weigh her words.

'After the war, when my parents learned the truth about Victor and Anya, they contacted your grandmother in England . . . She was, at that time, already living with the man who became her second husband . . . I never heard a great deal about her after that. I rather got the impression that she wasn't to be mentioned.'

I smiled, hoping to reassure Blanche of my inability to be wounded by any revelation concerning Rhoda.

'That figures,' I said. 'You wouldn't want to mention Rhoda if you could avoid it.'

Blanche looked at me carefully.

'Toby would talk to you about your grandmother,' she said slowly. 'You'll meet him when you go to America . . . He's gone back there, to be near to Harriet.'

'Harriet?'

'I mean Carlotta . . . Carlotta du Bois.'

'I'm longing to meet Carlotta,' I said. 'I can still hardly believe she's going to see me. She hasn't given an interview in thirty years . . . Tell me, do you think she's ready to talk about the night Will Sutton died?'

'Yes,' said Blanche laughing, reaching across to take my hand in a sudden, unexpected gesture of comradeship. 'Yes, I'm sure she is.'

Duval arrived at the convent just as I was leaving, and we greeted each other with cautious courtesy, both of us casting an embarrassed eye at Blanche, who quickly bade me a brisk farewell, reminding her son that he was due at a meeting of the hospital trustees in half an hour, and then left us alone. We walked out into the gardens together, towards the old gate through which David Klein once edged his stolen car, chatting guardedly about impersonal matters, my impending switch from Metro TV to the BBC, his next film, which, he declared with a little laugh, was going to be an old-fashioned romantic comedy with a tight script and a happy ending.

'I see *The Rose Garden* won some kind of award,' I said, trying to remember the detail. 'I read about it in the *Sunday Chron . . .*'

He grinned at me ruefully.

'It was a very minor and exceedingly obscure festival,' he said, 'and you should have seen some of the other films . . .'

We both laughed.

'I guess it's not possible to be David Klein in this day and age,' I said comfortingly. 'The demands of the market have changed too much.'

'He didn't think that,' Duval replied. 'He was horrified by the violence of much modern cinema, and what he saw as its inherent nihilism. He believed there was still a place for romance . . .'

'I'm sure he was right,' I said quietly, knowing that he was.

We talked then of his grandfather's Hollywood career, Eva's own varied career and the tantalising prospect held out to me by Carlotta du Bois, touching at last on subjects a little nearer home.

'I see Jamie's Hamlet got rave reviews,' he said tentatively.

'It's brilliant,' I said. 'Hamlet of the tortured sexual psyche . . . in love with Laertes as much as Ophelia. Very moving. Very pertinent.'

He seemed about to make some comment on the tortured sexual psyche, and then to think better of it.

'I don't suppose you see too much of him at the moment?' he ventured at last.

'On the contrary,' I said directly, 'I'm seeing a great deal more of him. Since I moved out, we've hardly been apart. He keeps bringing me food parcels, and when he's not on stage, he takes me out to dinner . . . I've warned him we'll have to be careful. At this rate we'll get our picture in the papers . . .'

He looked at me in faint shock.

'You moved out of your beautiful house?'

'I'm renting a little flat in Knightsbridge . . . Just until we sell. He would have moved out and let me stay, but I didn't want to be there without him. We both knew it was time to do it. But we've made a solemn vow that if we're still alone by the time we hit sixty, we'll buy a castle in Spain and retire together . . .'

He said nothing, thinking it over carefully, wondering, I guessed, if there were other implications of this development.

'I haven't got anyone else,' I told him, answering the unvoiced question. 'Nor am I looking. I've discovered that I rather like being alone. Except for sex, of course. That's a bit of a miss . . . But I expect I'll get used to it. Thousands of other single women do.'

'I don't imagine you'll wait too long,' he said with a quiet smile.

'Next time,' I said unthinkingly, 'I'm going for quality,' and then, realising what I'd said, rushed on in deep embarrassment to explain that, of course, I wasn't deriding our own little *amour* nor suggesting that his sexual performance was in any way lacking.

'It's okay, Beth,' he laughed. 'Don't apologise. I'm not sensitive . . .'

This little gaffe seemed to have broken the ice between us, and now I felt able to enquire after his family and his wife, hoping as I spoke that Genevieve wasn't off on one of her affairs.

'She's taking violin lessons,' he said uncomfortably. 'And seems to be doing very well . . . She was a talented musician when she was a girl. Then she met me and gave it all up. That's what she says anyway – though I've never quite understood how being pregnant stopped you playing the piano . . .'

'Ah, that's unfair,' I said, feeling called upon to defend Genevieve. 'Having a baby is a very emotional and demanding experience, particularly when you're young . . . I'm not surprised the piano suffered. If I hadn't had my own child adopted, I'm sure my career wouldn't have flourished in the way that it has. I wouldn't have had the creative energy to give to it.'

I'd imagined, without thinking too much about it, that Duval would have been informed of this hitherto unmentionable item from my personal history, but now I saw that it came as a considerable surprise.

'I assumed Michael would have told you,' I said awkwardly, realising too late that the vicar of St Cuthbert's might wish to conceal this piece of personal history himself. 'Don't mention it to him, please . . . I wouldn't want to embarrass him.'

Duval was plainly astonished.

'You had Michael's child?' he asked incredulously.

'A very long time ago. We would have married, I'm sure, but events conspired against us . . . It was all very painful, and I spent many years trying to pretend none of it happened. Until Eva's funeral, I hadn't seen him once . . . But now things have fallen into place. I don't feel bad about it any more.'

He looked at me curiously.

'I can see there's something different about you,' he said at last. 'You're much more relaxed . . . You seem at ease with yourself. Has meeting Michael done that?'

I shook my head.

'Don't faint away with shock,' I said laughing. 'I've had a religious experience! In St Cuthbert's on Easter Sunday . . . No visions or angelic choirs I hasten to add, just a feeling that if you looked at the world from a different point of view, it might all seem okay. I thought it would probably fade, but it hasn't . . . I've even started going to church! Jamie comes with me – St Luke's in Chelsea. It's the sort of place where you can just drift in and out. They won't grab you by the scruff of the neck and ask you to run the jumble sale or stand for the PCC.'

He seemed to think I couldn't possibly be serious, for he stared at me suspiciously, wrinkling his brow and fixing me with his dark blue eyes, weighing it up. Then he smiled.

'Well,' he said quietly, 'Eva would be pleased . . .'

'So she should be. It's all her doing.'

'No credit to Michael?'

'Oh yes, some to him. He's a very fine preacher. Almost as good as Matthew Brannen.'

'Eva said the same thing herself . . .'

I looked up at him in surprise, not imagining that Eva would ever have heard Michael preach, and then listening in some astonishment as he revealed she'd made a visit to St Cuthbert's six months before her death.

'Michael didn't tell you,' Duval said, 'because he knew you'd ask all sorts of questions which we weren't ready to have answered . . .'

A call from the convent doorway interrupted this discussion, and we looked up to see Blanche waving, beckoning her son inside, gesturing at her watch.

Duval stood up and we began to walk across the lawn towards the house.

'Michael's on holiday in Paris at the moment,' he said slowly. 'You probably knew he had an apartment here . . . As a matter of fact, he's waiting for me right now at the Café des Arbres. But I forgot about the ruddy hospital trustees – I'll have to call him. Unless, of course, you'd like to go yourself and give my apologies.'

'Daniel,' I said severely, looking up at him, 'I hope you're not trying to pair me off with the vicar of St Cuthbert's? I can tell you now it

won't work. Something to do with water and bridges. Too much of the
wet stuff flowing under too many arches . . .'

'I wouldn't dream of such a thing,' he said, laughing.

'So why, may I ask, are you laughing like that?'

He took my hand then and raised it to his lips, pausing only to check
that his mother was no longer watching.

'I'm laughing,' he said wryly, 'because to my certain knowledge, despite all the times we've been to bed together and all the times you
ripped off my clothes in the editing suite, that's the first time you've
ever called me Daniel.'

Michael was sitting at the window table in the Café des Arbres in a grey
suit, clerical shirt and dog collar, hardly looking like a holidaymaker.
He was smoking a cigarette and reading a book and, when I appeared
at his elbow, looked somewhat discomfited to see me.

'Didn't you know I was in Paris?' I asked, sitting down and waving
for coffee, remembering with a curious sense of distance and space the
time I'd last been in the café, mildly drunk and really rather pleased
with myself until the moment Clive Fisher's shadow fell across my
table.

'Yes. Yes, I did,' he muttered. 'Daniel told me you were coming, but
I didn't expect to see you myself . . .'

The bright gold hair was in need of a trim and he hadn't shaved,
giving him a vaguely rumpled air which contrasted oddly with the smart
suit and which seemed, suddenly, very beguiling.

'So you do discuss me!' I teased. 'I knew you were both lying.'

This mild attempt at levity didn't even evoke a half-smile, and I
glanced at him covertly, seeing that he looked nervous and ill at ease.
In the six months since we'd last met, it seemed the ground made up
over Easter weekend had once more been lost.

'I'm disturbing you,' I said briskly, deciding we'd do better to retain
that memory than this one. 'Sorry. I only came to tell you Daniel
couldn't make it —'

'No, don't go,' he said hastily, catching at my arm as I stood up to
leave. 'I'm just surprised to see you, that's all . . . Here, let me buy you
a glass of wine.'

I sat down again.

'I'm cutting down on my drinking,' I told him. 'I'm almost a reformed
character. No booze and no sex. I'm taking to cocaine instead . . .'

He looked at me uncertainly.

'Only joking,' I said as he appeared to think I wasn't. 'I've seen too
many people with nasty things where their noses used to be.'

He ordered a glass of wine for himself and another coffee for me, making a visible effort to relax, asking about my plans for the Eva book and my move to the BBC which he seemed to know all about, telling me what I already knew: that Charles hadn't got the administrator's job at the Retreat.

'I'm on the lookout for something else,' he said. 'I'll get him fixed up one way or another.'

'And what about Emily?' I asked. 'How's her new job?'

'Okay, I think. I've spoken to her a few times, but I haven't seen her since she left.'

This was a surprise, and I looked at him quickly once more, thinking he seemed subdued, almost depressed, in comparison with the calm and reflective parish priest I'd seen at Easter. I wondered again about his relationship with Emily, remembering how discreet she'd been in talking to me and how little she'd revealed, hoping that their parting hadn't had anything to do with my arrival at St Cuthbert's.

Then I asked after Katie and Lucy, and got another surprise.

'Lucy's getting married. They're all moving out after Christmas.'

'Married?' I echoed aghast, thinking of Michael and Katie all alone in the cavernous expanse of the vicarage. 'What on earth will you do?'

'We'll be fine,' he replied a trifle testily. 'It's been on the cards for some time so we've got quite used to the idea . . . I haven't always had a housekeeper, you know. Lucy came with the job, that's all.'

This seemed to dismiss the matter of Lucy's marriage and life at the vicarage without her, and as he reached for his wine and stared moodily into the glass, I searched for some other less personal subject, something that might nurture the germ of budding friendship that I'd glimpsed at Easter, green and hopeful, emerging from the barren soil of our unhappy history.

'I read your book,' I said at last. '*The Freedom of the Kingdom* . . . Very impressive, though the plot's a bit hard to follow . . .'

He laughed, and I began to think we might be getting somewhere, so I hurried on to draw him out, anxious to establish a common concern that might lead us away from difficult territory.

'The significant battle for justice and peace,' I said, remembering a line from his book which had interested me, 'takes place in your own soul. Do you really believe that? I mean, I live in London and the streets are full of beggars . . . So what do you do? You can't invite them home, and giving them a couple of quid isn't much good – but it doesn't seem much use, either, driving around in your flash car thinking well, never mind, the significant battle for justice and peace has already been won . . .'

He said nothing, staring out of the café on to the terrace and the square beyond, then he looked across at me, and I caught something in the wide grey eyes that I recognised from long ago, a hint of reproach, the suspicion that I was setting him up.

'It's a serious question,' I said quickly. 'Honestly. One day I was in a traffic jam, and a West Indian kid started banging on my car door and shouting. I drove off in a panic, then later I discovered my coat was hanging out of the door . . . He'd been trying to tell me. I should really have stopped and said thank you. And given him a tenner – or would that have been insulting? I just don't know . . .'

Still he said nothing, and I began to wonder if I'd offended him, thinking in that moment he was no less touchy than he'd ever been, reckoning that, whatever his reservations about me, I surely deserved the benefit of the doubt.

'Excuse me, Reverend,' I said lightly, 'I'm in need of your wisdom! Try to look on me as you would any other lost sheep.'

I'd managed to make him laugh again, and when he turned to me this time, I was relieved to see him genuinely amused.

'You don't strike me as a lost sheep,' he said.

'Well, you don't know me, do you?'

'No,' he said with a faint, elegiac smile, 'I don't suppose I do . . .'

I wanted an answer to my question about justice and peace, and I wasn't going to let him off the hook, so I pursued it vigorously, dredging up other comments from *The Freedom of the Kingdom* which I'd retained, knowing that I'd be furious with anyone who tried to serve me up a similar treatment based on one of my own books.

'Okay,' he offered at last, 'I'll say this . . . When the fight for justice and peace has been won in your own soul, then right action follows. That would mean giving two quid to a beggar, or more if you can afford it, but it wouldn't necessarily mean opening your car door to someone who looked threatening. It would mean weighing each situation and coming to the most loving conclusion . . .'

I watched him as he talked, thinking how attractive and sexually appealing he still was, wondering why on earth Emily Forster hadn't snapped him up, reflecting on what Jonathan had told me about his marriage to Clare Spencer, considering whether I'd ever have the nerve to ask him about it.

'Most significant of all,' he was saying, 'justice and peace in your own soul would mean supporting the political party most likely to address the needs of the homeless . . . It would mean praying for an end to social inequality, and protesting about it whenever the opportunity presented . . . and it would mean leading the kind of life which reflected your deepest beliefs.'

'Sounds hard,' I said.

'It's not easy,' he replied quietly. 'Living by the spirit of the law instead of the letter. Too much room for manoeuvre, for opposing interpretations. But that, of course, is the challenge.'

Now I was the one reduced to silence, wishing I'd never started out on this, not because I didn't want to know nor indeed, because I disagreed with anything he'd said. But simply because, having steered the conversation away from personal matters, I suddenly longed to turn it back, and couldn't see how.

Then he did it for me.

'As you're here in Paris, there's something I'd like to mention . . .' he said hesitantly, giving the impression he'd been debating for some time and had only just reached a decision. 'In the apartment, after my father died, I found a number of letters . . . exchanged between him and your mother. There's also some jewellery, things he bought for her and which she obviously only wore when they were here together . . . I offered them to Sarah, but she felt you should really have them. I hung on to them in case I ever saw you again . . .'

I swallowed hard, fighting a sudden rush of emotion, unsure how I'd cope with reading my mother's love letters or being presented with the jewellery Jack Cameron had bought her.

'Thank you,' I muttered. 'But I don't know . . .'

'Well, think it over. I could bring them to your hotel if you decided. Or you could come to the apartment.'

I thought then of the Camerons' rambling flat, of the night I'd hurtled out of it into the teeming streets of a hostile city, of the crazy scene played out on the fateful day my baby was conceived . . . And then, in a blessed act of free will, I put it all from me, feeling the last remnants of regret fall away. I smiled at Michael.

'I'll come,' I said jovially. 'But I ought to warn you, it's a dangerous thing inviting me to your apartment . . . I can see the headline in the *Sun* already: Vicar in Paris Sex Romp With TV Girl . . .'

He laughed and reached for his matches, extracting a cigarette from the pack on the table in an odd and unfamiliar gesture, looking away from me, unwilling to meet my eye.

'I should be so lucky,' he said.

I spent the rest of the afternoon deciding what I should wear that evening, reprimanding myself at the same time for the vanity of imagining that it mattered in the slightest, trying to unravel my feelings for the vicar of St Cuthbert's, concluding in the end that it was totally beyond me.

The truth, surely, was that I didn't know Michael at all, nor he me.

Thirteen years was more than a third of our lifetime, and it was folly to imagine that any useful sentiment might remain after such a length of time apart. The best I could hope for was a continuation of what I'd felt during Easter at St Cuthbert's; the beginning of *rapprochement*, the seeds of friendship.

So why was I yanking everything out of my wardrobe and spreading it over the bed in a bid to select exactly the right outfit? Right for what, I demanded morosely of my reflection in the hotel mirror. Right for reading my mother's old love letters? The very idea was ludicrous.

Nevertheless, I took a long, scented bath and washed my hair, dawdled over my make-up, put on my best apricot satin underwear, and finally selected a black silk dress and jacket, discreetly dusted with specks of silver lamé, a snip at the *prêt-à-porter* show last spring. I painted my lashes cobalt blue, my eyelids sparkling lilac and my lips spicy bronze, and tucked a white orchid from the dressing-table display into my lapel.

Then I chucked away the orchid and took a cab to the Cameron apartment, realising that I'd never forgotten where it was, although I must have passed it a dozen times when I'd been filming in Paris without giving it a second thought.

'You're early,' he said, plainly flustered, opening the door and ushering me in with exaggerated politeness. 'I wasn't expecting you until eight . . .'

He'd shaved, but his hair was still untidy, giving him a boyish air which struck a poignant resonance, and I had the distinct impression that I'd caught him trying to decide what to wear, for his collar was undone and his shirt half-buttoned, and there were three ties on the hall table beneath the mirror. I glanced at him with sudden amusement, consoled by this unexpected little coincidence, but he wasn't looking at me; rapidly he fastened his shirt and reached for a tie, running his hand through his hair in the anxious gesture I remembered so well.

He led me into the sitting room, a plain, airy space with high ceiling and polished floor which I dimly remembered from our first Paris visit more than fifteen years ago. The last time I'd been in the Cameron apartment, I hadn't gone anywhere except the bedroom and the bathroom.

'So, are you drinking tonight?' he asked me nervously, producing a bottle of Fleurie and two glasses. 'I'm afraid I haven't got any cocaine . . .'

I wished for some way to put him at ease, and began to feel I was extravagantly dressed in my smart black silk, possibly intimidating him. I took off my jacket and sat down on the sofa, thinking of a hundred times when I'd faced uptight TV guests and never once been stuck for a reassuring word . . . Now, to my chagrin, I couldn't think of a single appropriate remark.

Neither, it seemed, could he, and for a long, uncomfortable moment, we stared at each other over our glasses.

'I'll get the jewellery,' he said at last, standing up, and then he was handing me a little black velvet box containing a pair of emerald earrings, a platinum brooch and a heavy gold bangle, all of it exquisite and obviously expensive. I stared at the items unhappily, not knowing how I felt.

'And here are the letters,' he said, handing me two hefty bundles of papers, one festooned with pink ribbon, the other with blue. I fingered them incredulously, feeling the tears hard at the back of my throat. I hadn't expected the ribbons.

'He must have tied them up like that,' Michael said awkwardly. 'That's how they were when I found them . . . I know Sarah gave him his own letters back when she was clearing out. I guess he wanted them kept together . . .'

I was wondering how my eye make-up might withstand a reading of the letters, and I blinked rapidly, knowing I wouldn't look so good with sparkling lilac coursing down my cheeks. Then I began to untie the pink ribbon.

'You don't have to read them now,' Michael said quickly. 'You can take them away . . .'

I looked up at him.

'Don't you want me to read them now?'

'Well, the fact is . . . there's a great deal about us in those letters. It runs like a refrain all the way through . . . How are they going to tell us, what will we feel, are they going to muck up our lives – it might prove embarrassing for you, that's all.'

I tossed the letters to one side, fighting warring emotions: the desire to spare myself pain and the need to hear him declare himself, to offer some small insight into the way he felt.

'Who's the most embarrassed?' I heard myself ask. 'Me or you?'

'I don't know . . . Me, probably. But I am trying to make it easy for you.'

'Well, you're not succeeding,' I snapped back. 'It would make it easier for me if we actually allowed ourselves to get a bit more embarrassing . . . What does all this mean to you? How did you feel when you read these letters?'

He looked away.

'I sat right here and cried my eyes out,' he said flatly. 'Is that embarrassing enough?'

I felt my heart give a sudden lurch, and I would have reached out to him then, except that I'd no idea if he would respond, and I knew I couldn't countenance rejection.

'I won't read them,' I said hastily, 'I won't even take them away. Maybe now's the time to get rid of them. Tear them up, or burn them. I don't want the jewellery either. You're right. It's all too personal.'

For a moment he said nothing, fingering the stem of his glass, staring down into the purple wine, then he looked up at me.

'No,' he said slowly. 'It's you who's right . . . We should be getting a bit more personal.'

I smiled warily, unsure whether this was a welcome development, or whether the peculiar constriction in my throat was likely to betray me if he didn't tell me what I was now becoming sure I hoped to hear.

'Okay,' I said bravely. 'You start. Ask me anything you like. I don't mind how personal it is . . .'

I had imagined he would ask about our son, whether I ever thought of him, whether I'd grieved on his birthdays or shed a tear when he started school, and I was prepared to explain that no, I hadn't, that only by letting it all go had any of it been supportable . . . Or if not that, I imagined that he'd ask about my feelings for my mother, whether I'd managed to forgive her, if I ever thought about Leo Frankish and the desperate act which had changed my life for ever . . . Or if not any of this, I was certain he would ask about Duval and whether I still believed myself in love, a matter on which I was more than willing to be quizzed.

Instead he took a hefty draught of his wine, reached for his cigarettes and fixed me steadily with his wide grey eyes.

'Why have you spent the last nine years living with a guy who's gay?' he enquired.

I stared at him in surprise, knowing there was only one possible source of this information, suddenly angry with both him and Duval for their blithe insistence that they'd never discussed me.

He saw the change in my mood at once.

'It's true that Daniel told me,' he said quickly, 'but he didn't tell me anything else, I promise – except that he knew you didn't love him because you only ever called him Duval . . . even in bed.'

I laughed, despite myself.

'Everyone calls him Duval,' I said crossly. 'He's the great cult movie director. That's what he calls himself, for heaven's sake . . .'

'You haven't answered the question,' Michael said.

So then, haltingly and with unaccustomed effort, I set out on the explanation I'd never given anyone else, not even myself, but which Jamie had always accepted and implicitly understood: that I needed a buffer against men who wanted me all for themselves, that while I appeared comfortably paired off I was less likely to attract unwelcome proposals, that as long as I had Jamie, I could spare myself the risk of loving anyone else . . .

'Did you never hope to get married?' he asked me, his voice unsteady, his face turned from me.

'No,' I said briskly. 'I went off the whole idea of marriage for some strange reason. In any case, living with Jamie was better than being married. He cooked for me, took my stuff to the dry cleaner's, fed the cat – did all those little things that working girls find so hard to do for themselves, and did it without making any emotional demands . . . I hope I did something for him in return, but I guess you'd have to ask him that.'

He looked at me with sudden respect, and I saw that if he didn't quite understand, then he didn't disapprove

'You should meet Jamie,' I said. 'You'd like him. I'll get you tickets for *Hamlet* if you want.'

'Yes,' he said, surprised. 'Thank you . . .'

I picked up my wine and emptied the glass, all resolutions about booze temporarily suspended.

'Enough of this,' I said smartly. 'It's my turn for a personal question now. What went wrong with your marriage, Michael? How, when you'd known each other since you were kids, did you and Clare manage to make each other so desperately unhappy?'

This time he was taken aback, asking how I could possibly know such a thing, accusing Emily, Lucy and Sarah in turn, and finally eliciting from me that his brother was the culprit.

'You haven't answered the question,' I said.

He reached for the bottle of Fleurie, refilling his own glass and pointedly ignoring mine, clearly ruffled.

'Sex,' he said at last. 'That's what was wrong. There were plenty of other things, like the fact that we were totally temperamentally unsuited, and that in every important respect we didn't know each other at all – but in the end, it came down to sex. I couldn't be the lover she wanted. I thought she wanted friendship and companionship, and that was very naive and stupid of me . . . In fact, perfectly reasonably, she wanted sex.'

I gazed at him, astonished by this unexpected revelation, wondering if he'd somehow envisaged a sexless marriage, remembering with uncomfortable clarity how, under this very roof, he'd declared that unrestrained passion was the enemy of the peaceful heart . . . Well, so it might be. But my sympathy was suddenly with Clare Spencer, imagining herself to have a husband and getting a theology tutor instead.

'Don't misunderstand,' he said shakily, intuiting this line of thought. 'We did manage to conceive a child. I wasn't unwilling to make love to her – but it wasn't what she wanted. It wasn't good enough.'

'What was she expecting?' I asked, mystified, thinking back to all the pleasure we had shared, unable to work out how two people who'd felt

sure enough of each other to marry could possibly fail in bed if they
were both willing and able.

He was having difficulty forming the words, scrabbling around on the
floor beside the sofa for his cigarettes, running his hand through his
hair, plainly distressed.

'Michael,' I said gently. 'Take it easy. Just tell me the truth.'

'The truth,' he muttered, looking away, 'is that Clare expected to replace
you, to become what you'd been to me . . . But nobody could do that. It
simply wasn't possible . . . I couldn't make love to my wife the way I did
to you, I just didn't have the same level of desire. She knew it, and she
never let me forget it. She wanted every last detail of what we'd done
together, where, how, and how often. She gave me no peace . . .'

I listened in silence, desperately sorry for him, but determined to hear
him out.

'Eventually it got so I couldn't manage it at all, and she became very
bitter . . . She said I didn't love her as much as I'd loved you, and that was
hard for me to dispute. I did love her. I wouldn't have married her otherwise . . . But it was a different kind of love. It wasn't the overwhelming
passion I felt for you – and in the end, she forced me to admit it.'

He closed his eyes briefly and reached for another cigarette.

'If she'd lived, we would have parted,' he said haltingly. 'But as it
was, I had to learn a very hard lesson about myself and sex . . . which
is why I've never attempted it with anyone else. Why I never went to
bed with Emily, despite some very spirited efforts to persuade me. I
couldn't risk hurting her the way I hurt Clare . . .'

He looked back at me then, calm now, his wide grey eyes holding my
gaze.

'It was entirely fitting,' he said quietly, 'that sex should prove my
undoing. It's hard to imagine a more precise judgement on the way I
used to be . . .'

I felt my throat constrict and a pulse in my temple begin to throb,
and I knew then that I wanted him urgently, all caution and restraint
abandoned, all the careful conclusions about sex and love that I'd arrived at in six celibate months suddenly seeming no more than needless
restrictions. It was true that we were virtually strangers. It was true that
maturity and common sense required us to proceed towards any new
understanding at a stately pace. It was true that we ought to be rumi-
nating upon the folly of our youth and reflecting on the implications of
any renewed passion. But it was also true, to my considerable confusion,
that I didn't give a damn.

'Let's do it,' I said, standing up and kicking off my shoes. 'Let's do
it now. Is the bedroom still where it used to be, or have you moved
things around?'

He was so startled he all but choked on his wine, and then when he'd recovered, surveyed me in open shock.

'I couldn't possibly!' he said.

'Of course you could. It's like riding a bike. You never forget.'

He laughed, but he didn't get up off the sofa.

'Please, Beth . . . You're scaring the hell out of me.'

I reached for his hand and pulled him to his feet, then put my arms around his neck and kissed him.

'Look on it as a service to sex-starved clergymen,' I murmured in his ear. 'You can give me five hundred francs if you like. I'm running a bit low on cash . . .'

He laughed again, eyeing me in frank disbelief.

'I haven't got five hundred francs,' he said.

I marched out of the sitting room and into the bedroom, knowing that if he didn't follow me not only would I look extremely silly, but any future possibilities would be effectively quashed, and it was with considerable relief that I heard him come in and close the door behind me.

'Unzip my dress,' I said, peering through the gloom at the spartan bedroom thinking that it hadn't changed a bit, not even the position of the bed or the washstand in the corner where I'd thrown up. 'And put the light on, will you? Did I never tell you I was scared of the dark? My grandmother used to lock me in a cupboard when I was a little girl . . .'

He snapped on a table lamp and sat down on the bed, still unhappy and obviously unsure of himself.

'You're not scared of the dark,' he muttered. 'You're not scared of anything . . .'

He wasn't going to unzip my dress, so I did it myself, and then sat before him in my classy apricot underwear, hoping desperately that I hadn't misjudged the situation, thinking of my earlier quip about Vicar in Sex Romp With TV Girl, praying that he wouldn't feel compromised.

He looked at me as though he couldn't quite believe his eyes, and I waited, trembling with anticipation, knowing I could only do so much, that unless I were to risk a humiliating refusal, far too alarming to contemplate, he'd have to make the next move.

But he didn't touch me, and I felt my heart begin to pound with distressing speed.

'I'm very flattered that you want to make love to me,' he said soberly, looking me straight in the eye. 'You're trying to make me feel better, and I thank you for that . . . But this isn't the way.'

'On the contrary,' I said lightly, still hoping to joke him into it, 'I'm trying to make myself feel better. I've decided it's a bad idea to give up sex – too frustrating by far – so maybe you could do me a small service instead? I'd make a generous donation to St Cuthbert's roof repair fund . . .'

I was desperate now for his arms around me, or for any small crumb of physical contact that might persuade me it wasn't over yet, and as though in answer to this unvoiced plea, he took my hand. But at the same time he moved away from me perceptibly, edging across the bed, and when he spoke, it was with evident effort.

'You can't begin to know what it's been like for me,' he said gravely. 'How hard it was when you walked into the vicarage that day . . . I know I appeared cool and calm, but that was just a trick of the trade, something all young curates learn to stop them breaking down at funerals. In fact, I was so nervous, I could hardly speak. I began to think we'd never broach the subject at all . . . Then, just when it seemed we were getting somewhere, you disappeared again. I had no expectation of seeing you any more. In some ways, that was even worse than before . . .'

I felt a great surge of relief infuse my spirit, lifting me up towards an integration of all my confused longings and unspecified hopes, sweeping me on to the shores of a new and unfamiliar country in which all seemed certain and calm, its landmarks distant but serene, its territory gentle and kind. I reached out and touched his face.

'I won't disappear again,' I said unsteadily. 'Not permanently, anyway . . . I mean, I've got to go to New York and Hollywood and Tel Aviv, and then one or two other places the Beeb has in mind – but I'll come back.'

He shook his head.

'I'm not trying to extract any promises, Beth. That would be foolish. I'm just trying to explain why this would be wrong for me . . .'

'Then what would make it right?' I whispered unhappily, seeing now that I'd run out of ideas.

He said nothing, simply stared at me in my extravagant underwear, his eyes sorrowful and bright.

And then, unexpectedly, he reached forward to touch the gold chain at my throat, exclaiming in surprise and fingering the ornament in evident astonishment.

'That's Eva's cross,' I said, realising that I'd never told him about this curious little legacy. 'She left it to me. But for that, I don't suppose I'd ever have gone to her funeral . . .'

He held the cross between his fingers, turning it over as though checking its credentials, his expression disbelieving, his eyes still unnaturally bright.

'Do you always wear it?' he asked me, his voice uncertain and faint.

'Yes . . . But you don't see it unless I take my clothes off . . .'

And then suddenly, as though Eva's little gift had in some magical, mysterious way overcome all his reservations, he took me in his arms,

folding me into himself, eager and hard against me, kissing my hair and
stroking my cheek, fumbling ineptly with the catch on my bra, and as
I obliged him by kicking off the apricot satin knickers, running his
hands down between my thighs and parting my legs in a move that was
oddly, blessedly familiar, burying his fingers deep inside me, sighing
and trembling while I helped him out of his clothes.

For a few moments, the world hung suspended, the last time and
every other time we'd ever made love fusing into one unbroken memory
. . . And I saw then, in a strange, visionary flash of understanding, that
there was truly no discernible pattern to the ceaseless flow of history,
no meaning to be deduced from chance meetings or from random events
such as murder or pregnancy – no meaning or pattern, that is, except
for those that we ourselves impose and then interpret, changing our
lives for better or worse in according to point of view . . .

Neither of us spoke. There was no talk of love, no extravagant claims
or pacts, no mention of the future, nor indeed the past, only the moment in which two people acknowledged their need, and tried to satisfy
themselves and each other.

Once he'd entered me, it was over in seconds.

'Oh hell,' he said. 'That had to happen . . . I'm sorry . . .'

'It doesn't matter. You're out of practice, that's all.'

'But not totally out of touch,' he muttered uneasily. 'I'm supposed to
use a condom, aren't I?'

'Yes. That's my fault . . . It won't matter this once. I've always been
extremely careful, and you obviously don't represent any risk to anyone.
We'll use one next time.'

'There's going to be a next time?'

'I hope so,' I said. 'I thought in about half an hour . . .'

He propped himself up on one elbow, looking down at me as though
he still doubted the evidence before him, tracing the curve of my breasts
with his fingers, following the line of a faint silver stretch mark over my
groin, the one, solitary legacy of childbirth.

'I've missed you,' he whispered, and then, as though this might be
too much too soon, he turned away from me, reaching for the cigarettes
that had somehow accompanied him into the bedroom.

'What made you change your mind?' I asked him.

'Coincidence,' he said, turning back. 'I saw Eva's cross, and it reminded me of something she said about coincidence . . .'

I meant to ask him all about his meeting with Eva, but it was plain
he had something to ask me first, and I guessed what it was.

'Don't worry,' I told him solemnly, 'I'm not pregnant. I'm on the
Pill.'

There was a long silence in which it seemed all the gratuitous suffering and self-imposed sorrow of our youth had been caught and finally contained, and then at last he spoke.

'For some reason,' he said wryly, 'I find that less than totally reassuring.'

Then we both began to laugh, gales of blessed merriment consuming us, tears pouring down our faces, each of us shaking in a paroxysm of irrepressible mirth, barely able to draw breath for the manifest hilarity of it all.

'Shut up, Michael,' I gasped at last. 'This is our big romantic scene! We're ruining it.'

But this only made him laugh even louder.

'Big romantic scene?' he hooted. 'You've got a nerve! I've read your book too, you know. *Moonlight and Roses* – you don't believe any of that stuff, remember?'

It was a few moments more before I was able to speak again, and then I wiped my eyes, blew my nose, sat up on the bed and turned to face him, still laughing.

'I'm suspending my disbelief,' I said.

Epilogue

_____

The Candice Carter Interview: Beth Carlisle

It is three years since we last met, and my first impression is that she hasn't changed one bit.

She's still queening it on our TV screens, she's still writing stroppy books, she's still wearing extravagant designer clothes, albeit maternity style at the moment, she still lives in an exquisite house, out of London now in the rural calm of Cambridgeshire, and she still displays that faintly brittle edge.

She is also, of course, still making the tabloid headlines, if not in her own right, then certainly by association with her husband and her old paramours.

'Let's get that out of the way first,' she says with admirable forthrightness, fixing me with the famous emerald eyes. 'If you want to ask about Jamie, then you ought to talk to my husband. It really has nothing to do with me.'

In truth, I would very much like to talk to her husband, but since he's at the railway station dispatching his mother after a weekend visit, this isn't immediately possible. And risking Carlisle's wrath, for strictly speaking I've come to interview her about her bestselling book on David Klein, I decide to seek her opinion on the Jamie MacLennon rumpus.

For those who've been visiting Outer Mongolia this past fortnight, let me recount that MacLennon and his boyfriend, interior designer Simon Lejeune, had their union blessed in a Cambridge church by Beth's husband, the Reverend Michael Cameron.

It was meant to be a private service for a few close friends, but in the event it was rather more spectacular, involving most of the cast of *Midnight Sonata*, MacLennon's latest West End play, assorted TV personalities, including Beth herself, and a sizeable contingent from the press who delighted in dubbing the occasion 'a mock wedding', and whipping up a storm of protest from conservative churchgoers, gay bashers, right-wing MPs and Disgusted of Tunbridge Wells.

Had the Reverend Mr Cameron misjudged the situation?

'He knew it was controversial,' Beth says carefully. 'He knew he was taking a risk. But it wasn't done without a great deal of thought and discussion, not to say prayer . . . Jamie and Simon are close friends. They frequently come here to stay with us. Michael knows them both very well.'

What about the charge that he had brought the Church into disrepute?

'There is one view,' she suggests, 'which says that the Church is already in disrepute. For failing to address fundamental questions about the nature of human sexuality, for ignoring the very real needs of gay and lesbian people who might wish to affirm Christian ideals of fidelity in their own lives.'

I imagine that Carlisle's own amorous history might make her wary of saying too much about Christian ideals of fidelity, but in this I am wrong.

'I've made mistakes,' she says. 'I've done things I very much regret. But it's never too late to turn your life around . . .'

For a moment I almost imagine she might tell me to Repent and Believe, and I fancy she looks faintly embarrassed, but for all that, she's not changing her mind.

'Why is it,' she asks, 'that all we good liberal folk are so afraid to speak up for marriage and faithfulness? Surely these are the very things that make for harmonious lives? That doesn't mean everyone has to get married – but it does mean we shouldn't be debunking marriage all the time. It means we ought to cherish monogamy – to come out and declare that it's perfectly possible to commit yourself exclusively to one person for the whole of your life, and to find your happiness, your freedom, increased by this bond, not diminished.'

So Beth Carlisle is a born-again Romantic?

She laughs, the brittle edge softening, and we are temporarily interrupted by the arrival of her ten-year-old stepdaughter bearing a fat ginger cat called Cuthbert who immediately leaps upon Beth's knee and settles himself on the hump of her unborn child. For a few moments we all discuss the foibles and fancies of cats, and then Cuthbert jumps from her knee and stalks away, confirming our mutual opinion, at least on this particular subject.

'I still believe we have to tackle romantic mythology,' Beth says seriously; 'I still believe that much of what purports to be love in popular culture is damaging and demeaning to both men and women – but yes, if you will, I'm a born-again Romantic . . . My book is a love story, plain and simple. However, I fail to see why Romance as a literary convention can't be used to say something interesting and important.'

She looks at me wryly. 'Remember my book?' she enquires.

I am suitably reprimanded, and when I mention David Klein, I am quickly reprimanded once again.

'The book isn't about David Klein,' she says. 'It's about Eva Delamere. Of course, he's a principal player, but he doesn't have the starring role. That belongs exclusively to Eva. Eva, and her vision of the world . . .'

The book, she says, has proved a voyage of personal discovery, and among its unexpected delights has been the founding of an intimate friendship with Hollywood *grande dame* Carlotta du Bois, a regular guest in Cambridgeshire and expected again at the end of the month for the birth of Beth's child.

'She's the main source of the Hollywood material,' Beth says, 'but a great deal of what she told me never appeared in the book . . . That would be a different book, not one I could write.'

This is intriguing, but she won't be drawn, laughing good-naturedly and insisting that there are plenty of revelations in the book as it stands without the need for any more.

Indeed there are, and as they've already been well documented, and as the Delamere book is already a runaway success, I suggest tentatively that we might turn to more personal matters.

How does she view impending motherhood? Will the birth of her first child slow down her hectic schedule? In the past few months she has made an inspiring film about the actress Susannah Lamont and her battle with HIV, hosted a weekly TV show called *Religion and the Real World*, and campaigned for the crusading pressure group PAD (People Against Destitution) which aims to keep homelessness in the headlines.

'I'm looking forward to motherhood,' she says carefully. 'After all, I've waited a very long time. But I'm not dewy-eyed. I know it's hard work.'

Then she laughs again, and I see that the notorious brittle edge is really no more than a temporary nervous retreat into old habits. She is relaxed, she can smile at herself.

'I'm very lucky,' she says. 'I have a finely tuned support system. My brother-in-law is verger at a church in Cambridge, and that means my sister is always on hand . . . I've also got my best friend, Vicky, who's just moved out of London and set up home near by . . . Then there's my husband, of course. He's a natural with kids. They all love him. And he doesn't seem to mind how horrible they are.'

'Except,' pipes up his daughter who's still in the room playing with Cuthbert, 'when he's just stopped smoking!'

They are both amused by this and giggle like conspirators, which, I would guess, they are.

I am still hopeful of meeting the controversial Mr Cameron, but alas, it is not to be. He rings up to say his car has broken down, he is stuck in a garage by the railway station, he won't be home for lunch.

Beth offers to pick him up in the ostentatious Bentley which languishes outside on the driveway, a monument, it seems, to some unlikely passion of the Reverend's, and there then ensues a minor domestic argument which she loses.

'He doesn't want me to drive,' she says ruefully, patting her swollen stomach. 'Oh well, if he wants to spend all afternoon in the garage . . . His loss.'

But I am left feeling that the loss is somehow mine, that in having missed Beth Carlisle's husband, I have also missed the key to her quiet confidence.

For the truth is that first impressions are often wrong, and she is not the proud and prickly professional she used to be. She is calmer, more open, more giving. She's still prepared to state her case, still ready to take on the world for what she thinks is right. But the old belligerence has gone. In its place is a new quality, less tangible, less striking, and yet no less significant. Those of a religious turn of mind might call it peace.